"PEOPLE OF THE FIRST QUALITY THREW THEMSELVES IN THE
WAY OF MY OBSERVATION,"

THE ADVENTURES OF GIL BLAS ❧ ❧ ❧

OF SANTILLANE ❧ ❧ ❧

A NEW EDITION, CAREFULLY REVISED.

TRANSLATED FROM THE FRENCH OF LE SAGE

By TOBIAS SMOLLETT

A. L. BURT COMPANY, ❧ ❧ ❧ ❧
❧ ❧ ❧ PUBLISHERS, NEW YORK

PREFATORY MEMOIR.

ALAIN RENÉ LE SAGE, the author of "Gil Blas," was born at Sarzeau, near Vannes (Morbihan), 1668. He was the son of a law-yer, who unfortunately died early, leaving his child to the tutelage of an uncle, who neglected the care both of the lad's education and fortune. Happily, however, Père Bochard, of the Order of the Jesu-its, Principal of the College of Vannes, became interested in the boy on account of the natural talents he displayed, and cultivated his taste for literature. In 1693, Le Sage, then twenty-five, went to Paris "to prosecute his philosophical studies," with what ulti-mate end in view we are not told. The youth possessed a very handsome person and great literary ability. He was therefore soon admitted into those brilliant circles where the writers of the day and the French noblesse mingled. Here he secured many friends especially the Abbé de Lyonne, who settled upon the young genius a pension of six hundred livres, and made him besides many valu-able presents. This patron of literature, to whom posterity, as well as Le Sage, is indebted, rendered him a still more valuable ser-vice by directing his attention to the study of Spanish literature, which—once so fashionable in France, when queens of the house of Austria shared the throne—was then entirely neglected. Le Sage soon made use of his acquaintance with the Spanish drama; he translated several plays; which were published but not acted till 1702, when "The Point of Honor," translated from the Spanish, was performed at the Theatre Français; but without success.

In 1707, "Don Cæsar Ursin," translated by Le Sage from Cal-deron, was acted and condemned, while an original farce called "Crispin, Rival de son Maître," produced by him the same day, was received with marked applause, which probably induced him to produce, shortly afterwards, a regular comedy called "Turca-ret." This drama was intended to expose the odious rapacity and immorality of the Farmers-general or financiers, who grew rich by the basest means and most cruel exactions. These men, under-standing what was the subject of the play, used all their interest at court, which was great, to prevent its representation, and succeeded in delaying its performance for a time. They are said to have of-fered Le Sage a hundred thousand francs to suppress the comedy, but he refused the bribe, and "Turcaret" was acted with the great-est possible success. An anecdote is related respecting this pro-duction which shows the honorable pride and self-respect of the

author. He had been entreated to read his manuscript (according
to the fashion of the day) at the Hôtel de Bouillon; and had consented to do so. The hour appointed for the reading was noon,
but the dramatist was detained till two o'clock attending the
decision of a lawsuit in which he was deeply interested. When he
at length appeared and endeavored to apologize, the Duchess de
Bouillon heard him with haughty coldness, observing that he had
made her guests lose two hours waiting for his arrival. "It is easy
to make up the loss, madame," replied Le Sage; "I will not read
my comedy, and thus you will regain the lost time." He left the
hotel, and could never be persuaded to go to the Duchess's house
again.

Before the production of this play, Le Sage had established his
reputation as an author by the publication of "Le Diable Boiteux,"
which appeared in 1707. The title and plan of this work were
taken from the Spanish of Luez Valez de Guevara, "El Diablo
Cojuelo;" but the fancy, lightness, wit, and satire of the "Diable
Boiteux" were entire Le Sage's. The popularity of this work was
unbounded from its first appearance. One proof of the estimation
in which it was held was, that two young nobles entering a bookseller's shop, in which there was only one copy of the book, contested its possession in a duel, the victor carrying off the volume
as his trophy. It is known in England under the title of its first
translation, "The Devil upon Two Sticks." Le Sage's connection
with the Théâtre Français was broken off soon after the appearance of "Turcaret;" the precise cause of the rupture is not known,
but it is probable that the dramatist was provoked and disgusted
at the airs of superiority assumed by the performers towards authors,
which he has so humorously, and yet bitterly, painted in 'Gil
Blas." He now (1713) transferred his pen to the subaltern theater
called "La Foire," which had arisen at the side of the legitimate
drama in 1705, and was long abandoned to Italian buffooneries and
the pleasure of the populace. The Théâtre Français was very
jealous of this humble rival, and persecuted it bitterly. The actors
of the "Foire" opposed to the power and influence of their enemies, address, patience, and wit. Dialogue was forbidden at the
"Foire"—they sang their pieces. Song was prohibited—they acted
in monologues and pantomime. Le Sage and Fuselier had recourse
to another device, and acted their dramas with puppets instead of
real actors.

The sort of pieces represented at the Foire (or Fair) Theater
took at length the name of "Comic Opera," of which Le Sage
became the soul. He composed (probably assisted by his friends
Dominique and Fuselier) more than a hundred farces, interludes,
and light pieces for this theater—the home of vaudeville—and made
from these slighter works the chief part of the income by which he
supported his family in comfortable independence. Meantime he
was working at the novel which has procured him immortality.

In 1715 the three first volumes of "Gil Blas," ending at the
hero's first retreat to Lirias, appeared; and its success was at once
assured. Its excessive popularity induced Le Sage to add, some

time afterwards, a fourth volume, which again involved "Gil Blas" in the perils of a court life; but there is a certain amount of repetition in this continuation, though it enables the hero to redeem his moral character, and metes out poetical justice on some of the chief rogues of the story. "A French writer has said that it was received by the public with the same kind of admiration as that accorded to a decaying beauty, whose features remain the same, though their freshness and brilliancy are abated by time." *

The originality of the great French novel was much disputed at one time. Voltaire, jealous, no doubt, of its immense success, endeavored to prove that Le Sage had purloined it from a Spanish writer, but this and many other like attempts have been completely defeated.

There certainly existed in Spanish literature (and Le Sage was no doubt familiar with it) a species of low, comic romance in which the hero was a *picaro* or adventurer. Of this kind were Juan de Luna's "Lazarillo de Tormes," and the "History of Paul the Sharper," by Quevedo. "Guzman d'Alfarache," one of the best known of these novels, had been translated into most European languages, and some slight incidents in it appear to have suggested similar ones to the French author. But in none of them are found the subtle and poignant satire, the profound knowledge of human nature, the wit, and grace of "Gil Blas." Le Sage's style is original and delightful; graceful, facile, simple, and rapid. No translation could ever give the charm of the original, though (since it does not owe its renown to mere style) the book is admirable in every tongue.

Le Sage gave the French a version of Guzman d'Alfarache in 1732, which is really superior to the original, of which it is rather an imitation than a translation. He had published in 1717–21, "Roland l'Amoureux," a very bad imitation of the "Orlando Inamorato;" and in 1735, he gave the public a wise and witty dialogue called "Une Journée des Parques."

The chief work of Le Sage's old age was the "Bachelier de Salamanque." But like his own Archbishop of Grenada, he had written too long! In this novel a multiplicity of adventures replace the brilliant observations and admirably-drawn characters of his great work, and announce the declining powers of the author—yet it has been said that Le Sage preferred this romance to his wonderful novel, thus confirming by his personal experience the keen observation of his prime, and the fidelity of the portraits he had drawn. After the "Bachelor of Salamanca," Le Sage produced in 1740 his last original work, "La Valise Trouvée." His literary labor thus ended as it had begun, with a collection of letters resembling those of Aristenetus which he had translated in 1695, and which were his first published work.

Le Sage's domestic life was a very happy one. In 1694 he had married Mademoiselle Huyard of Paris, a very beautiful young woman, and the union had proved all that he could desire. He

---

had three sons and a daughter, whose filial piety made her devote her whole life to attending on her gifted father. His circumstances, though moderate, were always easy, for he possessed prudence and moral character as well as genius. One circumstance alone embittered a few years of his life. His eldest son, gifted with many great qualities, had been educated for the bar, but insisted on going on the stage. Le Sage, who had painted the life of an actor in the most ridiculous and hateful aspect, was excessively pained by his son's choice of a profession, especially as the young man entered the company of the Theater Français, against which Le Sage had so long waged a satirical war. Probably out of deference to his father's feeling, young Le Sage took the name of Montménil, and by the singular worth of his private character and his social talents, gained admittance into the first society in Paris. A reconciliation between the father and son was, however, at last effected, and Le Sage became so devoted to Montménil, that he could scarcely bear him out of his sight.

The death of this gifted actor, which took place September 8th, 1743, from cold caught at a hunting party, proved such a severe blow to his father that he retired for ever from Paris and from the world. The youngest son of Le Sage had also become an actor under the name of Pittenec. It was in the home of his second son, the Abbé Le Sage, therefore, that the aged author and his wife found a home in their old age. He (the son) had been made a Canon of the Cathedral of Boulogne, through the patronage of the queen, and had had a pension bestowed upon him. He was, therefore, able as well as willing to receive his parents and sister, and to give them support and shelter for the remainder of their days.

The life of Le Sage was prolonged beyond fourscore years. He was, however, afflicted by deafness, and had to use an ear-trumpet; but his conversation was so delightful, that when he was in the world, and frequented his favorite coffee-house in the Rue St. Jacques, Paris, the guests would gather round him, and even climb on chairs and tables, to catch the words of wit and wisdom which fell from the lips of the famous novelist.

Le Sage died in the winter of 1746–47, retaining to the last a high character for honor and high-mindedness, as well as the enduring fame of a great writer.

THE AUTHOR'S DECLARATION.

THERE are some people in the world so mischievous as not to read a work without applying the vicious or ridiculous characters it may happen to contain to eminent or popular individuals. I protest publicly against the pretended discovery of any such likenesses. My purpose was to represent human life historically as it exists: God forbid I should hold myself out as a portrait-painter. Let not the reader then take to himself public property; for if he does, he may chance to throw an unlucky light on his own character: as Phædrus expresses it, *Stultè nudabit animi conscientiam.*

Certain physicians of Castille, as well as of France, are sometimes a little too fond of trying the bleeding and lowering system on their patients. Vices, their patrons, and their dupes, are of every day's occurrence. To be sure, I have not always adopted Spanish manners with scrupulous exactness; and in the instance of the players at Madrid, those who know their disorderly modes of living may reproach me with softening down their coarser traits: but this I have been induced to do from a sense of delicacy, and in conformity with the manners of my own country.

GIL BLAS TO THE READER.

READER! hark you, my friend! Do not begin the story of my life till I have told you a short tale.

Two students traveled together from Penafiel to Salamanca. Finding themselves tired and thirsty, they stopped by the side of a spring on the road. While they were resting there, after having quenched their thirst, by chance they espied on a stone near them, even with the ground, part of an inscription, in some degree effaced by time, and by the tread of flocks in the habit of watering at that spring. Having washed the stone, they were able to trace these words in the dialect of Castille: *Aqui está encerrada el alma del licenciado Pedro Garcias.* "Here lies interred the soul of the licentiate Peter Garcias."

Heyday! roars out the younger, a lively, heedless fellow, who could not get on with his deciphering for laughter: This is a good joke indeed: "Here lies interred the soul." . . . . A soul interred! . . . . I should like to know the whimsical author of this ludicrous epitaph. With this sneer he got up to go away. His companion, who had more sense, said within himself: Underneath this stone lies some mystery, I will stay, and see the end of it. Accordingly, he let his comrade depart, and without loss of time began digging round about the stone with his knife till he got it up. Under it he found a purse of leather, containing an hundred ducats with a card on which was written these words in Latin: "Whoever thou art who hast wit enough to discover the meaning of the inscription, I appoint thee my heir, in the hope thou wilt make a better use of my fortune than I have done!" The student, out of his wits at the discovery, replaced the stone in its former position, and set out again on the Salamanca road with the soul of the licentiate in his pocket.

Now, my good friend and reader, no matter who you are, you must be like one or the other of these two students. If you cast your eye over my adventures without fixing it on the moral concealed under them, you will derive very little benefit from the perusal: but if you read with attention you will find that mixture of the useful with the agreeable, so successfully prescribed by Horace.

ADVENTURES OF GIL BLAS

OF SANTILLANE.

BOOK THE FIRST.

CHAPTER I.

THE BIRTH AND EDUCATION OF GIL BLAS.

My father, Blas of Santillane, after having borne arms for a long time in the Spanish service, retired to his native place. There he married a chamber-maid who was not exactly in her teens, and I made my début on this stage ten months after marriage. They afterwards went to live at Oviedo, where my mother got into service, and my father obtained a situation equally adapted to his capacities as a squire. As their wages were their fortune, I might have got my education as I could, had it not been for an uncle of mine in the town, a canon, by name Gil Perez. He was my mother's eldest brother, and my god-father. Figure to yourself a little fellow, three feet and a half high, as fat as you can conceive, with a head sunk deep between his shoulders, and you have ny uncle to the life. For the rest of his qualities, he was an ecclesiastic, and of course thought of nothing but good living, I mean in the flesh as well as in the spirit, with the means of which good living his stall, no lean one, provided him.

He took me home to his own house from my infancy, and ran the risk of my bringing up. I struck him as so brisk a lad, that he resolved to cultivate my talents. He bought me a primer, and undertook my tuition as far as reading went: which was not amiss for himself as well as for me; since by teaching me my letters he brushed up his own learning, which had not been pursued in a very scholastic manner; and, by dint of application, he got at last to read his breviary out of hand, which he had never been able to do before. He would have been very glad to have taught me Latin, to save expense, but, alas! poor Gil Perez! he had never skimmed the first principles of it in the whole course of his life. I should not wonder if he was the most ignorant member of the chapter, though on a subject involving as many possibilities as there were canons, I presume not to pledge myself for anything like certainty. To be sure, I have heard it suggested, that he did not gain his preferment altogether by his learning: but that he owed it exclusively to the gratitude of some good nuns whose discreet factor he had

been, and who had credit enough to procure him the order of
priesthood without the troublesome ceremony of an examination.

He was obliged therefore to place me under the correction of a
master, so that I was sent to Doctor Godinez, who had the reputation of being the most accomplished pedant of Oviedo. I profited
so well under his instructions, that by the end of five or six years
I could read a Greek author or two, and had no very inadequate
conception of the Latin poets. Besides my classical studies, I applied to logic, which enabled me to become an expert arguer. I
now fell in love with discussions of all kinds to such an excess,
that I stopped his Majesty's subjects on the high road, acquaintance or strangers, no matter! and proposed some knotty point of
controversy. Sometimes I fell in with a clan of Irish, and an alter-
cation never comes amiss to them! That was your time, if you are
fond of a battle. Such gestures! such grimaces! such contortions! Our eyes sparkling, and our mouths foaming! Those who

✦ "I MOUNTED MY MULE, AND SAW THE OUTSIDE OF THE TOWN."

did not take us for what we affected to be, philosophers, must have
set us down for madmen.

But let that be as it will, I gained the reputation of no small
learning in the town. My uncle was delighted, because he prudently considered that I should so much the sooner cease to be
chargeable to him. Come here, Gil Blas, quoth he one day, you
are got to be a fine fellow. You are past seventeen, and a clever
lad; you must bestir yourself, and get forward in the world. I
think of sending you to the university of Salamanca: with your
wit you will easily get a good post. I will give you a few ducats
for your journey, and my mule, which will fetch ten or twelve pistoles at Salamanca, and with such a sum at setting out, you will be
enabled to hold up your head till you get a situation.

He could not have proposed to me anything more agreeable: for I was dying to see a little of life. At the same time, I was not such a fool as to betray my satisfaction; and when it came to the hour of parting, by the sensibility I discovered at taking leave of my dear uncle, to whom I was so much obliged, and by calling in the stage effect of grief, I so softened the good soul, that he put his hand deeper into his pocket than he would have done, could he have pried into all that was passing in the interior of my hypocritical little heart. Before my departure I took a last leave of my papa and mamma, who loaded me with an ample inheritance of good advice. They enjoined me to pray to God for my uncle, to go honestly through the world, not to engage in any ill, and above all, not to lay my hands on other people's property. After they had lectured me for a good while, they made me a present of their blessing, which was all my patrimony and all my expectation. As soon as I had received it, I mounted my mule, and saw the outside of the town.

CHAPTER II.

GIL BLAS' ALARM ON HIS ROAD TO PEGNAFLOR; HIS ADVENTURES ON HIS ARRIVAL IN THAT TOWN; AND THE CHARACTER OF THE MEN WITH WHOM HE SUPPED.

HERE I am, then, on the other side of Oviedo, on the road to Pegnaflor, with the world before me, as yet my own master, as well as master of a bad mule and forty good ducats, without reckoning on a little supplementary cash purloined from my much-honoured uncle. The first thing I did was to let my mule go as the beast liked, that is to say, very lazily. I dropped the rein, and taking out my ducats, began to count them backwards and forwards in my hat. I was out of my wits for joy, never having seen such a sum of money before, and could not help looking at it and sifting it through my fingers. I had counted it over about the twentieth time, when all at once my mule, with head raised, and ears pricked up, stood stock still in the middle of the high road. I thought, to be sure, something was the matter; looked about for a cause, and perceiving a hat upon the ground, with a rosary of large beads, at the same time heard a lugubrious voice pronounce these words: Pray, honoured master, have pity on a poor maimed soldier! Please to throw a few small pieces into this hat; you shall be rewarded for it in the other world. I looked immediately on the side whence the voice proceeded, and saw, just by a thicket, twenty or thirty paces from me, a sort of a soldier, who had mounted the barrel of a confounded long carbine on two cross sticks, and seemed to be taking aim at me. At a sight which made me tremble for the patrimony of the Church committed to my care, I stopped short, made sure of my ducats, and taking out a little small change, as I rode by the hat, placed to receive the charity of those quiet subjects who had not the courage to refuse it, dropped in my contribution in detail, to convince the soldier how nobly I dealt by him. He was satisfied with my liberality, and gave me a blessing for every kick I gave my mule in my impatience to get out of his way; but the infernal beast, without partaking in the slightest degree of my impatience, went at the old steady pace. A long custom of jogging on fair and softly under my uncle's weight had obliterated every idea of that motion called a gallop.

The prospect of my journey was not much improved by this adventure as a specimen. I considered within myself that I had yet some distance to Salamanca, and might, not improbably, meet with something worse. My uncle seemed to have been very imprudent not to have consigned me to the care of a muleteer. That, to be sure, was what he ought to have done; but his notion was, that by giving me his mule, my journey would be cheaper; and that entered more into his calculation than the dangers in which I might be involved on the road. To retrieve his error, therefore, I resolved, if I had the good luck to arrive safe at Pegnaflor, to offer my mule for sale, and take the opportunity of a muleteer going to Astorga, whence I might get to Salamanca by a similar conveyance. Though I had never been out of Oviedo I was acquainted with the names of the towns through which I was to pass; a species of information I took care to procure before my setting out.

I got safe and sound to Pegnaflor, and stopped at the door of a very decent-looking inn. My foot was scarcely out of the stirrup before the landlord was at my side, overwhelming me with public-house civility. He untied my cloak-bag with his own hands, swung it across his shoulders, and ushered my Honour into a room, while one of his men led my mule to the stable. This landlord, the most busy prattler of the Asturias, ready to bother you impertinently about his own concerns, and, at the same time, with a sufficient portion of curiosity to worm himself into the knowledge of yours, was not long in telling me that his name was Andrew Corcuelo; that he had seen some service as a sergeant in the army, which he had quitted fifteen months ago, and married a girl of Castropol, who, though a little tawny or so, knew how to make both ends meet as well as the best of them. He told me a thousand things besides which he might just as well have kept private. Thinking himself entitled, after this voluntary confidence, to an equal share of mine, he asked me in a breath, and without further preface, whence I came, whither I was going, and who I was. To all this I felt myself bound to answer, article by article, because, though rather abrupt in asking them, he accompanied each question with so apologetic a bow, beseeching me with so submissive a grimace not to be offended at his curiosity, that I was drawn in to gratify it whether I would or no. Thus by degrees did we get into a long conversation, in the course of which I took occasion to hint that I had some reasons for wishing to get rid of my mule, and travel under convoy of a muleteer. He seemed on the whole to approve of my plan, though he could not prevail with himself to tell me so briefly; for he introduced his remarks by descanting on all the possible and probable mischances to which travellers are liable on the road, not omitting an awkward story now and then. I thought the fellow would never have done. But the conclusion of the argument was, that if I wanted to sell my mule, he knew an honest jockey who would take it off my hands. I begged he would do me the favour to fetch him, which was no sooner said than done.

On his return he introduced the purchaser, with a high encomium on his integrity. We all three went into the yard, and the mule was brought out to show paces before the jockey, who set himself to examine the beast from head to foot. His report was bad enough. To be sure, it would not have been easy to make a good one; but if it had been the pope's mule, and this fellow was to cheapen the bargain, it would have been just the same: nay, to speak with all due reverence, if he had been asked to give an opinion of the pope's great toe, from that disparaging habit of his, he would have pronounced it no better than the toe of any ordinary man. He laid it down, therefore, as a principle, that the mule had all the defects a mule could have: appealing to the landlord for a confirmation of his judgment, who, doubtless, had reasons of his own for not controverting his friend's assertion. Well! says the jockey, with an air of indifference, What price have you the conscience to ask for this devil of an animal? After such a panegyric, and master Corcuelo's certificate, whom I was fool enough to take for a fair-dealing man and a good judge of horse-flesh, they might have had the mule for nothing. I therefore told the dealer that I threw myself on his mercy: he must fix his own sum, and I should expect no more. On this he began to affect the gentleman, and answered that I had found out his weak side when I left it to his honour. He was right enough in that! his honour was his weak side! for instead of bidding up to my uncle's estimate of ten or twelve pistoles, the rascal had the impudence to offer three ducats, which I accepted with as light a heart as if I had got the best of the bargain.

Having disencumbered myself of my mule in so tradesmanlike a manner, I went with my landlord to a carrier who was to set out early the next morning for Astorga, and engaged to call me up in time. When we had settled the hire of the mule, as well as the expenses on the road, I turned back towards the inn with Corcuelo, who, as we went along, got into the private history of this muleteer. When I had been pestered with all the tittle-tattle of the town about this fellow, the changes were just beginning to ring on some new subject; but, by good luck, a pretty-looking sort of a man very civilly interrupted my loquacious friend. I left them together, and sauntered on without the slightest suspicion of being at all concerned in their discourse.

I ordered supper as soon as I got to the inn. It was a fish day: but I thought eggs were better suited to my finances. While they were getting ready I joined in conversation with the landlady, whom

I had not seen before. She seemed a pretty piece of goods enough, and such a stirring body, that I should have concluded, if her husband had not told me so, her tavern must have plenty of custom. The moment the omelet was served up I sat down to table by myself, and had scarcely got the relish of it, when my landlord walked in, followed by the man who had stopped him in the street. This pleasant gentleman wore a long rapier, and might, perhaps, be about thirty years of age. He came up to me in a most friendly manner possible. Mr. Professor, says he, I have just now heard that you are the renowned Gil Blas of Santillane, that ornament of Oviedo and luminary of philosophy. And do my eyes behold that very greatest of all great scholars and wits, whose reputation has run hither so fast before him? Little do you think, continues he, directing his discourse to the landlord and landlady, little do you imagine, I say, what good luck has befallen you. Why, you have got hold of a treasure. In this young gentleman you behold the eighth wonder of the world. Then running up and throwing his arms about my neck, Excuse me, added he; but worlds would not bribe me to suppress the rapturous emotions your honoured presence has excited.

I could not answer him so glibly as I wished, not so much for want of words as of breath; for he hugged me so tight that I began to be alarmed for my windpipe. As soon, however, as I had got my head out of durance, I replied, Signor cavalier, I had not the least conception that my name was known at Pegnaflor. Known? resumed he in the same pompous style; we keep a register of all great persons within a circuit of twenty leagues round us. You have the character of a prodigy here; and I have not a shadow of doubt, but one day or other Spain will be as proud of numbering you among her rare productions, as Greece of having given birth to her seven wise men. This fine speech was followed as before; and I really began to think that with all my classical honours I should at last be doomed to share the fate of Antæus. If I had been master of ever so little experience, I should not have been the dupe of his rhodomontade. I must have discovered him by his outrageous compliments, to be one of those parasites who swarm in every town, and get into a stranger's company on his arrival, to appease the wolf in their stomachs at his expense; but my youth and vanity tempted me to draw a quite opposite conclusion. My admirer was very clever in my eyes, and I asked him to supper on the strength of it. Oh! most willingly, cried he: with all my heart and soul. My fortunate star predominates, now that I have the honour of being in company with the illustrious Gil Blas of Santillane, and I shall certainly make the most of my good fortune as long as it lasts. My appetite is rather delicate, but I will just sit down with you by way of being sociable, and if I can swallow a bit! only just not to look sulky; for we philosophers are careless of the body.

These words were no sooner out of his mouth, than my panegyrist took his seat opposite to me. A cover was laid for him in due form and order. First he fell on the omelet with as much perse-

"WITH THIS STING IN THE TAIL OF HIS FAREWELL SPEECH HE VERY COOLLY TOOK HIS LEAVE."

verance as if he had not tasted food for three whole days. By the complacency with which he eyed it I was morally certain the poor pancake was at death's door. I therefore ordered its heir-apparent to succeed; and the business was despatched with such speed, that the second made its appearance on the table, just as we;—no:—I beg pardon;—just as he had taken the last lick of its predecessor. He pressed forward the main business, however, with a diligence and activity proportioned to the importance of the object he had in view : so that he contrived to load me with panegyric on pane-gyric, without losing a single stroke in the progress of mastication. Now all this gave me no slender conceit of my pretty little self. When a man eats, he must drink. The first toast of course was my health. The second, in common civility, was my father and mother, whose happiness in having such an angel of a son, he could not sufficiently envy or admire. All this while he kept filling my glass, and challenging me to keep pace with him. It was impossible to be backward in doing justice to such excellent toasts and senti-ments : the compliments with which they were seasoned did not come amiss; so that I got into such a convivial mood, at observing our second omelet to disappear not insensibly, as just to ask the landlord if he could not find us a little bit of fish. Master Corcuelo, who to all appearance played booty with the parasite, told me he had an excellent trout; but those who eat him must pay for him. I am afraid he is meat for your masters. Meat for our masters ! exclaims my very humble servant in an angry tone of voice : that is more than you know, my friend. Are you yet to learn that the best of your larder is not too good for the renowned Gil Blas of Santillane? Go where he will, he is fit to table with princes.

I was very glad that he took up the landlord's last expression ; because if he had not, I should. I felt myself a little hurt at it, and said to Corcuelo with some degree of hauteur : Produce this trout of yours, and I will take the consequences. The landlord, who had got just what he wanted, set himself to work, and served it up in high order. At the first glance of this third course I saw such pleasure sparkling in the parasite's eyes, as proved him to be of a very complying temper; just as ready to do a kindness by the fish, as by those said eggs of which he had given so good an account. But at last he was obliged to lay down his arms for fear of acci-dents; as his magazine was crammed to the very throat. Having eat and drank his fill, he bethought him of putting a finishing hand to the farce. Master Gil Blas, said he, as he rose from the table, I am too well pleased with my princely entertainment to leave you without a word of advice, of which you seem to stand in much need. From this time forward be on your guard against extravagant praise. Do not trust men till you know them. You may meet with many another man, who, like me, may amuse himself at your ex-pense, and perhaps carry the joke a little further. But do not you be taken in a second time, to believe yourself, on the word of such fellows, the eighth wonder of the world. With this sting in the tail of his farewell speech he very coolly took his leave.

I was as much alive to so ridiculous a circumstance, as I have

ever been in after-life to the most severe mortifications. I did not
know how to reconcile myself to the idea of having been so egregiously taken in, or, in fact, to lowering of my pride. So, so! quoth
I, this rascal has been putting his tricks upon travellers, has he?
Then he only wanted to pump my landlord! or more likely they
were both in a story. Ah! my poor Gil Blas, thou hadst better
hide thy silly head! To have suffered such knaves as these to turn
thee into ridicule! A pretty story they will make of this! It is sure
to travel back to Oviedo; and will give our friends a hopeful prospect of thy success in life. The family will be quite delighted to
think what a blessed harvest all their pious advice has produced.
There was no occasion to preach up morals to thee; for verily thou
hast more of the dupe than the sharper in thy composition. Ready
to tear my eyes out or bite my fingers off from spite and vexation,
I locked myself up in my chamber and went to bed, but not to
sleep; of which I had not got a wink when the muleteer came to
tell me that he only waited for me to set out on his journey. I got
up as expeditiously as I could; and while I was dressing Corcuelo
put in his appearance, with a little bill in his hand;—a slight memorandum of the trout!—But paying through the nose was not the
worst of it; for I had the vexation to perceive, that while I was
counting over the cost, this hang-dog was chuckling at the recollection of the night before. Having been fleeced most shamefully
for a supper, which stuck in my stomach though I had scarcely
come in for a morsel of it, I joined the muleteer with my baggage,
giving to as many devils as there are saints in the calendar, the
parasite, the landlord, and the inn.

CHAPTER III.

THE MULETEER'S TEMPTATION ON THE ROAD; ITS CONSEQUENCES, AND THE SITUATION OF GIL BLAS BETWEEN SCYLLA AND CHARYBDIS.

I WAS not the only passenger. There were two young gentlemen
of Pegnaflor; a little chorister of Mondognedo, who was travelling
about the country, and a young tradesman of Astorga, returning
home from Verco with his new-married wife. We soon got acquainted, and exchanged the usual confidence of travellers, telling
one another whence we came and whither we were going. The
bride was young enough · but so dark-complexioned, with so little
of what a man likes to look at in a woman, that I did not think her
worth the trouble. But she had youth and a good crummy person
on her side, and the muleteer, being rather less nice in his taste,
was resolved to try if he could not get into her good graces. This
pretty project occupied his ingenuity during the whole day but he

deferred the execution till we should get to Cacabelos, the last place where we were to stop on the road. We alighted at an inn in the outskirts of the town, a quiet convenient place, with a landlord who never troubled himself about other people's concerns. We were ushered into a private room, and got our supper snugly: but just as the cloth was taken away in comes our carrier in a furious passion :—Death and the devil! I have been robbed. Here had I a hundred pistoles in my purse! But I will have them back again. I am going for a magistrate ;—and those gentry will not take a joke upon such serious subjects. You will all be put to the rack, unless you confess, and give back the money. The fellow played his part very naturally, and burst out of the room, leaving us in a terrible fright.

We had none of us the least suspicion of the trick, and being all strangers, were afraid of one another. I looked askance at the little chorister, and he, perhaps, had no better opinion of me. Besides, we were all a pack of greenhorns, and were quite unacquainted with the routine of business on these occasions. We were fools enough to believe that the torture would be the very first stage of our examination. With this dread upon our spirits, we all made for the door. Some effected their escape into the street, others into the garden: but the whole party preferred the discretion of running away to the valour of standing their ground. The young tradesman of Astorga had as great an objection to bone-twisting as the rest of us : so he did as Eneas, and many another good husband has done before him ;—ran away and left his wife behind. At that critical moment the muleteer, as I was told afterwards, who had not half so much sense of decency as his own mules, delighted at the success of his stratagem, began moving his motives to the citizen's wife : but this Lucrece of the Asturias, borrowing the chastity of a saint from the ugliness of the devil who tempted her, defended her sweet person tooth and nail ; and showed she was in earnest about it by the noise she made. The patrol, who happened to be passing by the inn at the time, and knew that the neighbourhood required a little looking after, took the liberty of just asking the cause of the disturbance. The landlord, who was trying if he could not sing in the kitchen louder than she could scream in the parlour, and swore he heard no music but his own, was at last obliged to introduce the myrmidons of the police to the distressed lady, just in time to rescue her from the necessity of a surrender at discretion. The head officer, a coarse fellow, without an atom of feeling for the tender passion, no sooner saw the game that was playing, than he gave the amorous muleteer five or six blows with the butt end of his halberd, representing to him the indecency of his conduct in terms quite as offensive to modesty as the naughty propensity which had called forth his virtuous indignation. Neither did he stop here ; but laid hold of the culprit, and carried plaintiff and defendant before the magistrate. The former, with her charms all heightened by the discomposure of her dress, went eagerly to try their effect in obtaining justice for the outrage they had sustained. His Worship heard at least one party ; and after solemn deliberation pronounced the offence to be of a most heinous nature. He ordered him to be stripped, and to receive a competent number of lashes in his presence. The conclusion of the sentence was, that if the Endymion of our Asturian Diana was not forthcoming the next day, a couple of guards should escort the disconsolate goddess to the town of Astorga, at the expense of this mule-driving Acteon.

For my part, being probably more terrified than the rest of the party, I got into the fields, scampering over hedge and ditch, through enclosures and across commons, till I found myself hard by a forest. I was just going for concealment to ensconce myself in the very heart of the thicket, when two men on horseback rode across me, crying, Who goes there? As my alarm prevented me from giving them an immediate answer, they came to close quarters, and holding each of them a pistol to my throat, required me to give an account of myself; who I was, whence I came, what business I had in that forest, and above all, not to tell a lie about it. Their rough interrogatives were, according to my notion, little better than the rack with which our friend the muleteer had offered to treat us. I represented myself however as a young man on my way from Oviedo to Salamanca; told the story of our late fright, and faithfully attributed my running away in such a hurry to the dread of a worse exercise under the torture. They burst into an immoderate fit of laughter at my simplicity; and one of them said: Take heart, my little friend; come along with us, and do not be afraid; we will put you in a place where the devil shall not find you. At these words, he took me up behind him, and we darted into the forest.

I did not know what to think of this odd meeting; yet on the whole I could not well be worse off than before. If these gentry, thought I to myself, had been thieves, they would have robbed, and perhaps murdered me. Depend on it, they are a couple of good honest country gentlemen in this neighbourhood, who, seeing me frightened, have taken compassion on me, and mean to carry me home with them and make me comfortable. But these visions did not last long. After turning and winding backward and forward in deep silence, we found ourselves at the foot of a hill, where we dismounted. This is our abode, said one of these sequestered gentlemen. I looked about in all directions, but the deuce a bit of either house or cottage : not a vestige of human habitation ! The two men in the mean time raised a great wooden trap, covered with earth and briars, to conceal the entrance of a long shelving passage under-ground, to which from habit the poor beasts took very kindly of their own accord. Their masters kept tight hold of me, and let the trap down after them. Thus was the worthy nephew of my uncle Perez caught, just for all the world as you would catch a rat.

CHAPTER IV.

DESCRIPTION OF THE SUBTERRANEOUS DWELLING AND ITS CONTENTS.

I NOW knew into what company I had fallen; and I leave it to any one to judge whether the discovery must not have rid me of my former fear. A dread more mighty and more just now seized my faculties. Money and life, all given up for lost! With the air of a victim on his passage to the altar did I walk, more dead than alive, between my two conductors, who finding that I trembled, frightened me so much the more by telling me not to be afraid. When we had gone two hundred paces, winding down a declivity all the way, we got into a stable lighted by two large iron lamps suspended from the vault above. There was a good store of straw, and several casks of hay and corn with room enough for twenty horses: but at that time there were only the two which came with us. An old negro, who seemed for his years in pretty good case, was tying them to the rack where they were to feed.

We went out of the stable. By the melancholy light of some other lamps, which only served to dress up horror in its native colours, we arrived at a kitchen where an old harridan was broiling some steaks on the coals, and getting supper ready. The kitchen furniture was better than might be expected, and the pantry provided in a very plentiful manner. The lady of the larder's picture is worth drawing. Considerably on the wrong side of sixty!—In her youth her hair had been of a fiery red; though she would have called it auburn. Time had indeed given it the fairer tint of grey; but a lock of more youthful hue, interspersed at intervals, produced all the variegated effect of the admired autumnal shades. To say nothing of an olive complexion, she had an enormous chin turning up, an immense nose turning down, with a mouth in the middle, modestly retiring inwards, to make room for its encroaching neighbours. Red eyes are no beauty in any animal but a ferret :—hers were purple.

Here, dame Leonarda, said one of the horsemen as he presented me to this angelic imp of darkness, we have brought you a young lad. Then looking round, and observing me to be miserably pale, Pluck up your spirits, my friend; you shall come to no harm. We want a scullion, and have met with you. You are a lucky dog! We had a boy who died about a fortnight ago: you shall succeed to the preferment. He was rather too delicate for his place. You seem a good stout fellow, and may live a week or two longer. We find you in bed and board, coal and candle; but as for day-light, you will never see that again. Your leisure hours will pass off very agreeably with Leonarda, who is really a very good creature, and tolerably tender-hearted; you will have all your little comforts about you. I flatter myself you have not got among beggars. At this moment the thief seized a flambeau; and as I feared, "with zeal to destroy;" for he ordered me to follow him.

He took me into a cellar, where I saw a great number of bottles and earthen pots full of excellent wine. He then made me cross several rooms. In some were pieces of cloth piled up; in others, stuffs and silks. As we passed through I could not help casting a sheep's eye at the gold and silver plate peeping out of the different cupboards. After that, I followed him into a great hall illuminated by three copper lustres, and serving as a gallery between the other rooms. Here he put fresh questions to me · asking my name;—why I left Oviedo;—and when I had satisfied his curiosity: Well, Gil Blas, said he, since your only motive for quitting your native place was to get into something snug and eligible, to be sure you must have been born to good luck, or you would not have fallen into our hands. I tell you once for all, you will live here on the fat of the land, and may souse over head and ears in ready money. Besides, you are in a place of perfect safety. The officers of the holy brotherhood might pass through the forest a hundred times without discovering our subterraneous abode. The entrance is only known to myself and my comrades. You may perhaps ask how it came to be contrived, without being perceived by the inhabitants in the neighbourhood. But you are to understand, my friend, that it was made long ago, and is no work of ours. After the Moors had made themselves masters of Granada, of Arragon, and nearly the whole of Spain, the Christians, rather than submit to the tyranny of infidels, betook themselves to flight, and lay concealed in this country, in Biscay, and in the Asturias, whither the brave Don Pelagio had withdrawn himself. They lived in a state of exile, on the mountains, or in the woods, dispersed in little knots. Some took up their residences in natural caves, others in artificial dwellings under-ground, like this we are in. In process of time, when by the blessing of Providence they had driven their enemies out of Spain, they returned to the towns. From that time forth their retreats have served as a rendezvous for the gentlemen of our profession. It is true that several of them have been discovered and destroyed by the holy brotherhood: but there are some yet remaining; and, by great good luck, I have tenanted this without paying any rent for it almost these fifteen years: Captain Rolando, at your service! I am the leader of the band; and the man you saw with me is one of my troopers.

CHAPTER V.

THE ARRIVAL OF THE BANDITTI IN THE SUBTERRANEOUS RE-
TREAT, WITH AN ACCOUNT OF THEIR PLEASANT CONVER-
SATION.

JUST as Captain Rolando had finished his speech six new faces
made their appearance in the hall; the lieutenant and five privates
returning home with their booty. They were hauling in two great
baskets full of sugar, cinnamon, pepper, figs, almonds, and raisins.
The lieutenant gave an account of their proceedings to the captain,
and told him they had taken these articles, as well as the sumpter-
mule, from a grocer of Benavento. An official report having thus
been made to the prime-minister, the grocer's contribution was
carried to account; and the next step was to regale after their la-
bours. A large table was set out in the hall. They sent me back to
the kitchen, where dame Leonarda told me what I had to do. I
made the best of a bad bargain, finding the luck ran against me;
and, swallowing my grievances, set myself to wait on my noble
masters.

I cleaned my plate, set out my sideboard, and brought up my
wine. As soon as I announced dinner to be on table, consisting of
two good black peppery ragouts for the first course, this high and
mighty company took their seats. They fell to most voraciously.
My place was to wait; and I handed about the glasses with so but-
ler-like an air, as to be not a little complimented on my dexterity.
The chief entertained them with a short sketch of my story, and
praised my parts. But I had recovered from my mania by this
time, and could listen to my own panegyric with the humility of an
anchorite or the contempt of a philosopher. They all seemed to
take a liking to me, and to think I had dropped from the clouds on
purpose to be their cup-bearer. My predecessor was a fool to me.
Since his death, the illustrious Leonarda had the honor of presenting nectar to these gods of the lower regions. But she was now
degraded, and I had the felicity of being installed in her office.
Thus, old Hebe being a little the worse for wear, young Ganymede
tripped up her heels.

A substantial joint of meat after the ragouts at length blunted
the edge of their appetites. Eating and drinking went together:
so that they soon got into a merry pin, and made a roaring noise.
Well done, my lads! All talkers and no listeners. One begins a
long story, another cuts a joke; here a fellow bawls, there a fellow
sings; and they all seem to be at cross purposes. At last Rolando,
tired of a concert in which he could hardly hear the sound of his
own voice, let them know that he was maestro di capella, and
brought them into better tune. Gentleman, said he, I have a question to put. Instead of stunning one another with this infernal din,
had we not better enjoy a little rational conversation? A thought

is just come into my head.   Since the happy day that united us we
have never had the curiosity to inquire into each other's pedigrees,
or by what chain of circumstances we were each of us led to embrace our present way of life.   There would be no harm in knowing
who and who are together.   Let us exchange confidence: we may
find some amusement in it.   The lieutenant and the rest, like true
heroes of romance, accepted the challenge with the utmost courtesy,
and the captain t¬ld the first story to the following effect :—

Gentlemen, you are to know that I am the only son of a rich
citizen in Madrid.   The day of my birth was celebrated in the family
by rejoicings without end.   My father, no chicken, thought it a
considerable feat to have got an heir, and my mother was kind
enough to suckle me herself.   My maternal grandfather was still
living : a good old man, who did not trouble himself about other
people's concerns, but said his prayers, and fought his campaigns
over and over again ; for he had been in the army.   Of course I was
idolized by these three persons ; never out of their arms.   My early
years were passed in the most childish amusements, for fear of
hurting my health by application.   It will not do, said my father,
to hammer much learning into children till time has ripened their
understanding.   While he waited for this ripening, the season went
by.   I could neither read nor write : but I made up for that in
other ways.   My father taught me a thousand different games.   I
became perfectly acquainted with cards, was no stranger to dice, and
my grandfather set me the example of drawing the long bow, while
he entertained me with his military exploits.   He sung the same
songs repeatedly one after another every day ; so that when, after
saying ten or twelve lines after him for three months together, I
got to boggle through them without missing, the whole family
were in raptures at my memory.   Neither was my wit thought to
be at all less extraordinary ; for I was suffered to talk at random,
and took care to put in my oar in the most impertinent manner
possible.   O the pretty little dear ! exclaimed my father, as if he
had been fascinated.   My mother made it up with kisses, and my
grandfather's old eyes overflowed.   I played all sorts of dirty and
indecent tricks before them with impunity ; everything was excusable in so fine a boy : an angel could not do wrong.   Going on in
this manner, I was already in my twelfth year without ever having
a master.   It was high time ; but then he was to teach me by fair
means : he might threaten, but must not flog me.   This arrangement did me but little good ; for sometimes I laughed when my
tutor scolded : at others, I ran with tears in my eyes to my mother
or my grandfather, and complained that he had used me ill.   The
poor devil got nothing by denying it.   My word was always taken
before his, and he came off with the character of a cruel rascal.
One day I scratched myself with my own nails, and set up a howl
as if I had been flogged.   My mother ran, and turned the master
out of doors, though he vowed and protested he had never lifted a
finger against me.

Thus did I get rid of all my tutors, till at last I met with one to
my mind.   He was a bachelor of Alcala.   This was the master for

a young man of fashion. Women, wine, and gaming, were his principal amusements. It was impossible to be in better hands. He hit the right nail on the head : for he let me do what I pleased, and thus got into the good graces of the family, who abandoned me to his conduct. They had no reason to repent. He perfected me betimes in the knowledge of the world. By dint of taking me about to all his haunts, he gave such a finish to my education, that barring literature and science, I became an universal scholar. As soon as he saw that I could go alone in the high road to ruin he went to qualify others for the same journey.

During my childhood I had lived at home just as I liked, and did not sufficiently consider, that now I was beginning to be responsible for my own actions. My father and mother were a standing jest. Yet they were themselves thrown into convulsions at my sallies; and the more ridiculous they were made by them, the more waggish they thought me. In the meantime I got into all manner of scrapes with some young fellows of my own kidney; and, as our relations kept us rather too short of cash for the exigencies of so loose a life, we each of us made free with whatever we could lay our hands on in our own families. Finding this would not raise the supplies, we began to pick pockets in the streets at night. As ill luck would have it, our exploits came to the knowledge of the police. A warrant was out against us; but some good-natured friend, thinking it a pity we should be nipped in the bud, gave us a caution. We took to our heels, and rose in our vocation to the rank of highwaymen. From that time forth, gentlemen, with a blessing on my endeavours, I have gone on till I am almost the father of the profession, in spite of the dangers to which it is exposed.

Here the captain ended, and it came to the turn of the lieutenant. Gentlemen, extremes are said to meet;—and so it will appear from a comparison of our commander's education and mine. My father was a butcher at Toledo. He passed, with reason, for the greatest brute in the town, and my mother's sweet disposition was not mended by the example. In my childhood, they whipped me in emulation of one another; I came in for a thousand lashes of a day! The slightest fault was followed up by the severest punishment. In vain did I beg for mercy with tears in my eyes, and protest that I was sorry for what I had done. They never excused me, and nine times out of ten flogged me for nothing. When I was under my father's lash, my mother, not thinking his arm stout enough, lent her assistance, instead of begging me off. The favors I received at their hands gave me such a disgust, that I quitted their house before I had completed my fourteenth year, took the Arragon road, and begged my way to Saragossa. There I associated with vagrants, who led a merry life enough. They taught me to counterfeit blindness and lameness, to dress up an artificial wound in each of my legs, and to adopt many other methods of imposing on the credulity of the charitable and humane. In the morning, like actors at rehearsal, we cast our characters, and settled the business of the comedy. We had each our exits and our entrances; till in the evening the curtain dropped, and we regaled at the expense of the dupes we had deluded in the day. Wearied, however, with the company of these wretches, and wishing to live in more worshipful society, I entered into partnership with a gang of sharpers. These fellows taught me some good tricks: but Saragossa soon became too hot to hold us, after we had fallen out with a limb of the law, who had hitherto taken us under his protection. We each of us provided for ourselves, and left the devil to take the hindmost. For my part, I enlisted in a brave and veteran regiment, which had seen abundance of service on the king's highway: and I found myself so comfortable in their quarters, that I had no desire to change my berth. So that you see, gentlemen, I was very much obliged to my relations for their bad behaviour; for if they had treated me a little more kindly, I might have been a blackguard butcher at this moment, instead of having the honour to be your lieutenant.

Gentlemen,—interrupted a hopeful young freebooter who sat between the captain and the lieutenant,—the stories we have just heard are neither so complicated nor so curious as mine. I peeped into existence by means of a countrywoman in the neighborhood of Seville. Three weeks after she had set me down in this system, a nurse child was offered her. You are to understand she was yet in her prime, comely in her person, and had a good breast of milk. The young suckling had noble blood in him, and was an only son. My mother accepted the proposal with all her heart, and went to fetch the child. It was entrusted to her care. She had no sooner brought it home, than, fancying a resemblance, she conceived the idea of substituting me for the brat of high birth, in the hope of drawing a handsome commission at some future time for this motherly office in behalf of her infant. My father, whose morals were on a level with those of clodhoppers in general, lent himself very willingly to the cheat: so that with only a change of clouts the son of Don Rodrigo de Herrera was packed off in my name to another nurse, and my mother suckled her own and her master's child at once in my little person.

They may say what they will of instinct and the force of blood! The little gentleman's parents were very easily taken in. They had not the slightest suspicion of the trick; and were eternally dandling me till I was seven years old. As it was their intention to make me a finished gentleman, they gave me masters of all kinds; but I had very little taste for their lessons, and above all, I detested the sciences. I had at any time rather play with the servants or the stable boys, and was a complete kitchen genius. But tossing up for heads or tails was not my ruling passion. Before seventeen I had an itch for getting drunk. I played the devil among the chamber-maids; but my prime favourite was a kitchen girl, who had infinite merit in my eyes. She was a great bloated horse-godmother, whose good case and easy morals suited me exactly. I boarded her with so little circumspection that Don Rodrigo took notice of it. He took me to task pretty sharply; twitted me with my low taste; and, for fear the presence of my charmer should counteract his sage counsels, showed the goddess of my devotions the outside of the door.

This proceeding was rather offensive; and I determined to be even with him. I stole his wife's jewels; and ravishing my Helen from a laundress of her acquaintance, went off with her in open day, that the transaction might lose nothing in point of notoriety. But this was not all. I carried her among her relations, where I married her according to the rites of the church, as much from the personal motive of mortifying Herrera, as from the patriotic enthusiasm of encouraging our young nobility to mend the breed. Three months after marriage, I heard that Don Rodrigo had gone the way of all flesh. The intelligence was not lost upon me. I was at Seville in a twinkling, to administer in due form and order to his effects; but the tables were turned. My mother had paid the debt of nature, and in her last agonies had been so much off her guard as to confess the whole affair to the curate of the village and other competent witnesses. Don Rodrigo's son had already taken my place, or rather his own, and his popularity was increased by the deficiency of mine; so that as the trumps were all out in that hand, and I had no particular wish for the present my wife was likely to make me, I joined issue with some desperate blades, with whom I began my trading ventures.

The young cut-purse having finished his story, another told us that he was the son of a merchant at Burgos; that, in his youth, prompted more by piety than wit, he had taken the religious habit and professed in a very strict order, and that a few years afterwards he had apostatized. In short, the eight robbers told their tale one after another, and when I had heard them all, I did not wonder that the destinies had brought them together. The conversation now took a different turn. They brought several schemes upon the carpet for the next campaign; and after having laid down their plan of operations, rose from table and went to bed. They lighted their night candles, and withdrew to their apartments. I attended Captain Rolando to his. While I was fiddling about him as he undressed: Well! Gil Blas, said he, you see how we live! We are always merry; hatred and envy have no footing here; we have not the least difference, but hang together just like monks. You are sure, my good lad, to lead a pleasant life here; for I do not think you are fool enough to make any bones about consorting with gentlemen of the road. In what does ours differ from many a more reputable trade? Depend on it, my friend, all men love two hands in their neighbour's purse, though only one in their own. Men's principles are all alike; the only difference lies in the mode of carrying them into effect. Conquerors, for instance, make free with the territories of their neighbours. People of fashion borrow and do not pay. Bankers, treasurers, brokers, clerks, and traders of all kinds, wholesale and retail, give ample liberty to their wants to overdraw on their consciences. I shall not mention the hangers-on of the law; we all know how it goes with them. At the same time it must be allowed that they have more humanity than we have; for as it is often our vocation to take away the life of the innocent for plunder, it is sometimes theirs for fee and reward to save the guilty.

CHAPTER VI.

AFTER the captain of the banditti had thus apologized for adopting such a line of life, he went to bed. For my part, I returned to the hall, where I cleared the table, and set everything to rights. Then I went to the kitchen, where Domingo, the old negro, and dame Leonarda had been expecting me at supper. Though entirely without appetite, I had the good manners to sit down with them. Not a morsel could I eat; and, as I scarcely felt more miserable than I looked, this pair so justly formed to meet by nature, undertook to give me a little comfort. Why do you take on so, my good lad? said the old dowager: you ought rather to bless your stars for your good luck. You are young, and seem a little soft; you would have a fine kettle of fish of it in the busy world. You might have fallen into bad hands, and then your morals would have been corrupted; whereas here your innocence is insured to its full value. Dame Leonarda is in the right, put in the old negro gravely, the world is but a troublesome place. Be thankful, my friend, for being so early relieved from the dangers, the difficulties, and the afflictions of this miserable life.

I bore this prosing very quietly, because I should have got no good by putting myself in a passion about it. At length Domingo, after playing a good knife and fork, and getting gloriously muddled, took himself off to the stable. Leonarda, by the glimmering of a lamp, showed me the way to a vault which served as a last home to those of the corps who died a natural death. Here I stumbled upon something more like a grave than a bed. This is your room, said she. Your predecessor lay here as long as he was among us, and here he lies to this day. He suffered himself to be hurried out of life in his prime: do not you be so foolish as to follow his example. With this kind advice, she left me with the lamp for my companion and returned to the kitchen. I threw myself on the little bed, not so much for rest as meditation. O heaven! exclaimed I, was there ever a fate so dreadful as mine? It is determined then I am to take my leave of daylight! Beside this, as if it were not enough to be buried alive at eighteen, my misery is to be aggravated by being in the service of a banditti; by passing the day with highwaymen, and the night in a charnel-house. These reflections, which seemed to me very dismal, and were indeed no better than they seemed, set me crying most bitterly. I could not conceive what cursed maggot my uncle had got in his head to send me to Salamanca; repented running away from Cacabelos, and would have compounded for the torture. But, considering how vain it was to shut the door when the steed was stolen, I determined, instead of lamenting the past, to hit upon some expedient for making my escape. What! thought I, is it impossible to get

"THIS IS YOUR ROOM."

off? The cut-throats are asleep; cooky and the black will be snoring ere long. Why cannot I, by the help of this lamp, find the passage by which I descended into these infernal regions? I am afraid, indeed, my strength is not equal to lifting the trap at the entrance. However, let us see. Faint heart never won fair lady. Despair will lend me new force, and who knows but I may succeed?

Thus was the train laid for a grand attempt. I got up as soon as Leonarda and Domingo were likely to be asleep. With the lamp in my hand, I stole out of the vault, putting up my prayers to all the spirits in paradise, and ten miles round. It was with no small difficulty that I threaded all the windings of this new labyrinth. At length I found myself at the stable door, and perceived the pas-sage which was the object of my search. Pushing on I made my way towards the trap with a light pair of heels and a beating heart: but, alas! in the middle of my career I ran against a cursed iron grate locked fast, with bars so close as not to admit a hand between them. I looked rather foolish at the occurrence of this new diffi-culty, which I had not been aware of at my entrance, because the grate was then open. However, I tried what I could do by fumbling at the bars. Then for a peep at the lock; or whether it could not be forced! When all at once my poor shoulders were saluted with five or six good strokes of a bull's pizzle. I set up such a shrill alarum, that the den of Cacus rang with it: when looking round, who should it be but the old negro in his shirt, holding a dark lan-thorn in one hand and the instrument of my punishment in the other. Oh, ho! quoth he, my merry little fellow, you will run away, will you? No, no! you must not think to set your wits against mine. I heard you all the while. You thought you should find the grate open, did not you? You may take it for granted, my friend, that henceforth it will always be shut. When we keep any one here against his will, he must be a cleverer fellow than you to make his escape.

In the mean time, at the howl I had set up two or three of the robbers waked suddenly; and not knowing but the holy brotherhood might be falling upon them, they got up and called their comrades. Without the loss of a moment all were on the alert. Swords and carabines were put in requisition, and the whole posse advanced forward almost in a state of nature to the place where I was par-leying with Domingo. But as soon as they learned the cause of the uproar, their alarm resolved itself into a peal of laughter. How now, Gil Blas, said the apostate son of the church, you have not been a good six hours with us, and are you tired of our company already? You must have a great objection to retirement. Why, what would you do if you were a Carthusian friar? Get along with you, and go to bed. This time you shall get off with Domingo's discipline; but if you are ever caught in a second attempt of the same kind, by Saint Bartholomew! we will flay you alive. With this hint he retired, and the rest of the party went back to their rooms. The old negro, taking credit to himself for his vigilance, re-turned to his stable; and I found my way back to my charnel-house, where I passed the remainder of the night in weeping and wailing.

CHAPTER VII.

GIL BLAS, NOT BEING ABLE TO DO WHAT HE LIKES, DOES WHAT HE CAN.

FOR the first few days I thought I should have given up the ghost for very spite and vexation. The lingering life I led was nearly akin to death itself; but in the end my good genius whispered me to play the hypocrite. I aimed at looking a little more cheerful; began to laugh and sing, though it was sometimes on the wrong side of my mouth; in a word, I put so good a face on the matter, that Leonarda and Domingo were completely taken in. They thought the bird was reconciled to his cage. The robbers entertained the same notion. I looked as brisk as the beverage I poured out, and put in my oar whenever I thought I could say a good thing. My freedom, far from offending, was taken in good part. Gil Blas, quoth the captain one evening, while I was playing the buffoon, you have done well, my friend, to banish melancholy. I am delighted with your wit and humour. Some people wear a mask at first acquaintance; I had no notion what a jovial fellow you were.

My praises now seemed to run from mouth to mouth. They were all so partial to me, that, not to miss my opportunity;—Gentlemen, quoth I, allow me to tell you a piece of my mind. Since I have been your guest, a new light breaks in upon me. I have bid adieu to vulgar prejudices, and caught a ray at the fountain of your illumination. I feel that I was born to be your knight companion. I languish to make one among you, and will stand my chance of a halter with the best. All the company cried Hear!—I was considered as a promising member of the senate. It was then determined unanimously to give me a trial in some inferior department; afterwards to bespeak me a good desperate encounter in which I might show my prowess; and if I answered expectation to give me a high and responsible employment in the commonwealth.

It was necessary therefore to go on exhibiting a copy of my countenance, and doing my best in my office of cup-bearer. I was impatient beyond measure; for I only aspired after the honours of the sitting, to obtain the liberty of going abroad with the rest; and I was in hopes that by running the risk of getting my neck into one noose I might get it out of another. This was my only chance. The time nevertheless seemed long to wait, and I kept my eye on Domingo, with the hope of outwitting him: but the thing was not feasible; he was always on the watch. Orpheus as leader of the band, with a complete orchestra of performers as good as himself, could not have soothed the savage breast of this Cerberus. The truth is, by the by, that for fear of exciting his suspicion, I did not set my wits against him so much as I might have done. He was on the look-out, and I was obliged to play the prude, or my virtue might have come into disgrace. I therefore stopped proceedings till the time of my probation should expire, to which I looked forward with impatience, just as if I was waiting for a place under government.

Heaven be praised, in about six months I gained my end. The commandant Rolando addressing his regiment, said: Comrades, we must stand upon honour with Gil Blas. I have no bad opinion of our young candidate; we shall make something of him. If you will take my advice, let him go and reap his first harvest with us to-morrow on the king's highway. We will lead him on in the path of honour. The robbers applauded the sentiments of the captain with a thunder of acclamation; and to show me how much I was considered as one of the gang, from that moment they dispensed with my attendance at the sideboard. Dame Leonarda was reinstated in the office from which she had been discharged to make room for me. They made me change my dress, which consisted in a plain short cassock a good deal the worse for wear, and tricked me out in the spoils of a gentleman lately robbed. After this inauguration, I made my arrangements for my first campaign.

CHAPTER VIII.

GIL BLAS GOES OUT WITH THE GANG, AND PERFORMS AN EXPLOIT ON THE HIGHWAY.

IT was past midnight in the month of September, when I issued from the subterraneous abode as one of the fraternity. I was armed, like them, with a carabine, two pistols, a sword, and a bayonet, and was mounted on a very good horse, the property of the gentleman in whose costume I appeared. I had lived so long like a mole under-ground, that the daybreak could not fail of dazzling me: but my eyes got reconciled to it by degrees.

We passed close by Pontferrada, and were determined to lie in ambush behind a small wood skirting the road to Leon. There we were waiting for whatever fortune might please to throw in our way, when we espied a Dominican friar, mounted, contrary to the rubric of those pious fathers, on a shabby mule. God be praised, exclaimed the captain with a sneer, this is a noble beginning for Gil Blas. Let him go and trounce that monk: we will bear witness to his qualifications. The connoisseurs were all of opinion that this commission suited my talents to a hair, and exhorted me to do my best. Gentlemen, quoth I, you shall have no reason to complain. I will strip this holy father to his birth-day suit, and give you complete right and title to his mule. No, no, said Rolando, the beast would not be worth its fodder: only bring us our reverend pastor's purse; that is all we require. Hereupon I issued from the wood and pushed up to the man of God, doing penance all the time in my own breast for the sin I was committing. I could have liked to have turned my back upon my fellows at that moment; but most of them had the advantage of better horses than mine; had they seen me making off, they would have been at my heels, and would soon have caught me, or perhaps would have fired a volley, for which I was not sufficiently case-hardened. I could not therefore venture on so perilous an alternative; so that claiming acquaintance with the reverend father, I asked to look at his purse, and just put out the end of a pistol. He stopped short to gaze upon me; and, without seeming much frightened, said, My child, you are very young; this is an early apprenticeship to a bad trade. Father, replied I, bad as it is, I wish I had begun it sooner. What! my son, rejoined the good friar, who did not understand the real meaning of what I said, how say you? What blindness! give me leave to place before your eyes the unhappy condition. Come, come, father! interrupted I, with impatience, a truce to your morality, if you please. My business on the high road is not to hear sermons. Money makes my mare to go. Money! said he, with a look of surprise; you have a poor opinion of Spanish charity, if you think that people of my stamp have any occasion for such trash upon their travels. Let me undeceive you. We are made welcome wherever we go, and pay for our board and lodgings by our prayers. In short, we carry no cash with us on the road; but draw drafts upon Providence. That is all very well, replied I; yet for fear your drafts should be dishonoured, you take care to keep about you a little supply for present need. But come, father, let us make an end: my comrades in the wood are in a hurry; so your money or your life. At these words, which I pronounced with a determined air, the friar began to think the business grew serious. Since needs must, said he, there is wherewithal to satisfy your craving. A word and a blow is the only rhetoric with you gentlemen. As he said this, he drew a large leathern purse from under his gown, and threw it on the ground. I then told him he might make the best of his way: and he did not wait for a second bidding, but stuck his heels into the mule, which, giving the lie to my opinion, for I thought it on a par with my uncle's, set off at a good round pace. While he was riding for his life, I dismounted. The purse was none of the lightest. I mounted again, and got back to the wood, where those nice observers were waiting with impatience to congratulate me on my success. I could hardly get my foot out of the stirrup, so eager were they to shake hands with me. Courage, Gil Blas, said Rolando; you have done wonders. I have had my eyes on you during your whole performance, and have watched your countenance. I have no hesitation in predicting that you will become in time a very accomplished highwayman. The lieutenant and the rest chimed in with the prophecy, and assured me that I could not fail of fulfilling it hereafter. I thanked them for the elevated idea they had formed of my talents, and promised to do all in my power not to discredit their penetration.

"I ASKED TO LOOK AT HIS PURSE, AND JUST PUT OUT THE END
OF A PISTOL."

After they had lavished praises, the effect rather of their candour than of my merit, they took it into their heads to examine the booty I had brought under my convoy. Let us see, said they, let us see how a friar's purse is lined. It should be fat and flourishing, continued one of them, for these good fathers do not mortify the flesh when they travel. The captain untied the purse, opened it, and took ont two or three handfuls of little copper coins, an Agnus-Dei here and there, and some scapularies. At sight of so novel a prize, all the privates burst into an immoderate fit of laughter. God be praised! cried the lieutenant, we are very much obliged to Gil Blas: his first attack has produced a supply, very seasonable to our fraternity. One joke brought on another. These rascals, especially the fellow who had retired from the church to our subterraneous hermitage, began to make themselves merry on the subject. They said a thousand good things, such as showed at once the sharpness of their wits and the profligacy of their morals. They were all on the broad grin except myself. It was impossible to be butt and marksman too. They each of them shot their bolt at me, and the captain said · Faith, Gil Blas, I would advise you as a friend not to set your wit a second time against the church: the biter may be bit; for you must live some time longer among us, before you are a match for them.

CHAPTER IX.

A MORE SERIOUS INCIDENT.

WE lounged about the wood for the greater part of the day, without lighting on any traveller to pay toll for the friar. At length we were beginning to wear our homeward way, as if confining the feats of the day to this laughable adventure, which furnished a plentiful fund of conversation, when we got intelligence of a carriage on the road drawn by four mules. They were coming at a hard gallop, with three outriders, who seemed to be well armed. Rolando ordered the troop to halt, and hold a council, the result of whose deliberations was to attack the enemy. We were regularly drawn up in battle-array, and marched to meet the caravan. In spite of the applause I had gained in the wood, I felt an oozing sort of tremour come over me, with a chill in my veins and a chattering in my teeth that seemed to bode me no good. As it never rains but it pours, I was in the front of the battle, hemmed in between the captain and the lieutenant, who had given me that post of honour, that I might lose no time in learning to stand fire. Rolando, observing the low ebb of my animal spirits, looked askew at me, and muttered in a tone more resolute than courtly: Hark ye! Gil Blas, look sharp about you! I give you fair notice, that if you play the recreant, I shall lodge a couple of bullets in your brain. I believed him as firmly as my catechism, and thought it high time not to neglect the hint, so that I was obliged to lay an embargo on the expression of my fears, and to think only of recommending my soul to God in silence.

While all this was going on, the carriage and horsemen drew near. They suspected what sort of gentry we were, and guessing our trade by our badge, stopped within gun-shot. They had carabines and pistols as well as ourselves. While they were preparing to give us a brisk reception, there jumped out of the coach a well-looking gentleman richly dressed. He mounted a led horse, and put himself at the head of his party. Though they were but four against nine, for the coachman kept his seat on the box, they advanced towards us with a confidence calculated to redouble my terror. Yet I did not forget, though trembling in every joint, to hold myself in readiness for a shot. but, to give a candid relation of the affair, I blinked and looked the other way in letting off my piece ; so that from the harmlessness of my fire, I was sure not to have murder to answer for in another world.

I shall not give the particulars of the engagement; though present, I was no eye-witness and my fear, while it laid hold of my imagination, drew a veil over the anticipated horror of the sight. All I know about the matter is, that after a grand discharge of musquetry, I heard my companions hallooing Victory ! Victory ! as if their lungs were made of leather. At this shout the terror which had made a forcible entry on my senses was ejected, and I beheld the four horsemen stretched lifeless on the field of battle. On our side, we had only one man killed. This was the renegade parson, who had now filled the measure of his apostasy, and paid for jesting with scapularies and such sacred things. The lieutenant received a slight wound in the arm ; but the bullet did little more than graze the skin.

Master Rolando was the first at the coach-door. Within was a lady of from four to five and twenty, beautiful as an angel in his eyes, in spite of her sad condition. She had fainted during the conflict, and her swoon still continued. While he was fixed like a statue on her charms, the rest of us were in profound meditation on the plunder. We began by securing the horses of the defunct ; for these animals, frightened at the report of our pieces, had got to a little distance, after the loss of their riders. For the mules, they had not wagged a hair, though the coachman had jumped from his box during the engagement to make his escape. We dismounted for the purpose of unharnessing and loading them with some trunks tied before and behind the carriage. This settled, the captain ordered the lady, who had not yet recovered her faculties, to be set on horseback before the best mounted of the robbers ; then, leaving the carriage and the uncased carcases by the road-side, we carried off with us the lady, the mules and the horses.

CHAPTER X.

THE LADY'S TREATMENT FROM THE ROBBERS. THE EVENT OF
THE GREAT DESIGN CONCEIVED BY GIL BLAS.

THE night had another hour to run when we arrived at our subterraneous mansion. The first thing we did was to lead our cavalry to the stable, where we were obliged to groom them ourselves, as the old negro had been confined to his bed for three days, with a violent fit of the gout, and an universal rheumatism. He had no member supple but his tongue ; and that he employed in testifying his indignation by the most horrible impieties. Leaving this wretch to curse and swear by himself, we went to the kitchen to look after the lady. So successful were our attentions, that we succeeded in recovering her from her fit. But when she had once more the use of her senses, and saw herself encompassed by strangers, she knew the extent of her misfortune, and shuddered at the thought. All that grief and despair together could present, of images the most distressing, appeared depicted in her eyes, which she lifted up to heaven, as if in reproach for the indignities she was threatened with. Then, giving way at once to these dreadful apprehensions, she fell again into a swoon, her eyelids closed once more, and the robbers thought that death was going to snatch from them their prey. The captain, therefore, judging it more to the purpose to leave her to herself than to torment her with any more of their assistance, ordered her to be laid on Leonarda's bed, and at all events to let nature take its course.

We went into the hall, where one of the robbers, who had been bred a surgeon, looked at the lieutenant's arm and put a plaister to it. After this scientific operation, it was thought expedient to examine the baggage. Some of the trunks were filled with laces and linen, others with various articles of wearing apparel : but the last contained some bags of coin ; a circumstance highly approved by the receivers-general of the estate. After this investigation, the cook set out the side-board, laid the cloth, and served up supper. Our conversation ran first on the great victory we had achieved. On this subject said Rolando, addressing himself to me, Confess the truth, Gil Blas ; you cannot deny that you were devilishly frightened. I candidly admitted the fact , but promised to fight like a crusader after my second or third campaign. Hereupon all the company took my part, alleging the sharpness of the action in my excuse, and that it was very well for a novice, not yet accustomed to the smell of powder.

We next talked of the mules and horses just added to our subterraneous stud. It was determined to set off the next morning before day-break, and sell them at Mansilla, before there was any chance of our expedition having got wind. This resolution taken, we finished our supper, and returned to the kitchen to pay our respects to the lady. We found her in the same condition. Nevertheless, though the dregs of life seemed almost exhausted, some of these poachers could not help casting a wicked leer at her, and giving visible signs of a motion within them, which would have broken out into overt act, had not Rolando put a spoke in their wheel by representing that they ought at least to wait till the lady had got rid of her terrors and squeamishness, and could come in for her share of the amusement. Their respect for the captain operated as a check to the incontinence of their passions. Nothing else could have saved the lady; nor would death itself probably have secured her from violation.

Again therefore did we leave this unhappy female to her melan-· choly fate. Rolando contented himself with charging Leonarda to take care of her, and we all separated for the night. For my part, when I went to bed, instead of courting sleep, my thoughts were wholly taken up with the lady's misfortunes. I had no doubt of her being a woman of quality, and thought her lot on that account so much the more piteous. I could not paint to myself, without shuddering, the horrors which awaited her; and felt myself as sensibly affected by them, as if united to her by the ties of blood or friendship. At length, after having sufficiently bewailed her destiny, I mused on the means of preserving her honour from its present danger, and myself from a longer abode in this dungeon. I considered that the old negro could not stir, and recollected that since his illness the cook had the key of the grate. That thought warmed my fancy, and gave birth to a project not to be hazarded lightly : the stages of its execution were the following.

I pretended to have the colic. A lad in the colic cannot help whining and groaning; but I went further, and cried out lustily, as loud as my lungs would let me. This roused my gentle friends, and brought them about me to know what the deuce was the matter. I informed them that I had a swinging fit of the gripes, and to humour the idea, gnashed my teeth, made all manner of wry faces till I looked like a bedlamite, and twisted my limbs as if I had been going to be delivered of a heathen oracle. Then I became calm all at once, as if my pains had abated. The next minute I flounced up and down upon my bed, and threw my arms about at random. In a word, I played my part so well that these more experienced performers, knowing as they were, suffered themselves to be thrown off their guard, and to believe that my malady was real. All at once did they busy themselves for my relief. One brought me a bottle of brandy, and forced me to gulp down half of it; another, in spite of my remonstrances, applied oil of sweet almonds in a very offensive manner : a third went and made a napkin burning hot, to be clapped upon my stomach In vain did I cry mercy; they attributed my noise to the violence of my disorder, and went on inflicting positive evil by way of remedy for that which was artificial. At last, able to bear it no longer, I was obliged to swear that I was better, and entreat them to give me quarter. They left off killing me with kindness, and I took care not to complain any more, for fear of experiencing their tender attentions a second time,

TRICHON.L

"IN I WENT, AND PUTTING A PISTOL TO HER BREAST."

This scene lasted nearly three hours. After which the robbers, calculating it to be near day-break, prepared for their journey to Mansilla. I was for getting up, as if I had set my heart on being of the party; but that they would not allow. No, no, Gil Blas, said Signor Rolando, stay here, my lad; your colic may return. You shall go with us another time; to-day you are not in travelling condition. I did not think it prudent to urge my attendance too much, for fear of being taken at my word; but only affected great disappointment with so natural an air, that they all went off without the slightest misgiving of my design. After their departure, for which I had prayed most fervently, I said to myself: Now is your time, Gil Blas, to be firm and resolved. Arm yourself with courage to go through with an enterprise so propitiously begun. Domingo is tied by the leg, and Leonarda may show her teeth, but she cannot bite. Pounce down upon opportunity while it offers; you may wait long enough for another. Thus did I spirit myself up in soliloquy. Having got out of bed, I laid hold of my sword and pistols; and away I went to the kitchen. But before I made my appearance I stopped to hear what Leonarda was talking about to the fair incognita, who was come to her senses, and, on a view of her misfortune in its extremity, took on most desperately. That is right, my girl, said the old hag, cry your eyes out, sob away plentifully, you know the good effect of woman's tears. The sudden shock was too much for you; but the danger is over now the engines can play. Your grief will abate by little and little, and you will get reconciled to living with our gentlemen, who are very good sort of people. You will be better off than a princess. You do not know how fond they will be of you. Not a day will pass without your being obliged to some of them. Many a woman would give one of her eyes to be in your place.

I did not allow Leonarda time to go on any longer with this babbling. In I went, and putting a pistol to her breast, insisted with a menacing air on her delivering up the key of the grate. She did not know what to make of my behavior; and, though almost in the last stage of life, had such a propensity to linger on the road as not to venture on a refusal. With the key in my hand I directed the following speech to the distressed object of my compassion: Madam, Heaven sends you a deliverer in me; follow, and I will see you safe whithersoever you wish to be conducted. The lady was not deaf to my proposal, which made such an impression on her grateful heart that she jumped up with all the strength she had left, threw herself at my feet, and conjured me to save her honor. I raised her from the ground, and assured her she might rely on me. I then took some ropes which were opportunely in the kitchen, and with her assistance tied Leonarda to the legs of a large table, protesting that I would kill her if she only breathed a murmur. After that, lighting a candle, I went with the incognita to the treasury, where I filled my pockets with pistoles, single and double, as full as they could hold. To encourage the lady not to be scrupulous, I begged she would think herself at home, and make free with her own. With our finances thus recruited, we went towards the stable, where I marched in with my pistols cocked. I was of opinion that the old blackamoor, for all his gout and rheumatism, would not let me saddle and bridle my horse peaceably, and my resolution was to put a finishing hand to all his ailments if he took it into his head to play the churl; but, by good luck, he was at that moment in such pain that I stole the steed without his perceiving that the door was open. The lady in the mean time was waiting for me. We were not long in threading the passage leading to the outlet; but reached the grate, opened it, and at last got to the trap. Much ado there was to lift it, which we could not have done, but for the new strength we borrowed from the hopes of our escape.

Day was beginning to dawn when we emerged from that abyss. Our first object was to get as far from it as possible. I jumped into the saddle: the lady got up behind me, and taking the first path that offered, we soon galloped out of the forest. Coming to some cross-roads, we took our chance. I trembled for fear of its leading to Mansilla, and our encountering Rolando and his comrades. Luckily my apprehensions were unfounded. We got to Astorga by two o'clock in the afternoon. The people looked at us as if they had never seen such a sight before as a woman riding behind a man. We alighted at the first inn. I immediately ordered a partridge and a young rabbit to the spit. While my orders were in a train of execution, the lady was shown to a room, where we began to scrape acquaintance with one another; which we had not done on the road, on account of the speed we made. She expressed a high sense of my services, and told me that after so gentlemanly a conduct, she could not allow herself to think me one of the gang from whom I had rescued her. I told her my story to confirm her good opinion. By these means I entitled myself to her confidence, and to the knowledge of her misfortunes, which she recounted to the following effect.

CHAPTER XI.

THE HISTORY OF DONNA MENCIA DE MOSQUERA.

I WAS born at Valladolid, and am called Donna Mencia de Mosquera. My father, Don Martin, after spending most of his family estate in the service, was killed in Portugal at the head of his regiment. He left me so little property that I was a bad match, though an only daughter. I was not, however, without my admirers, notwithstanding the mediocrity of my fortune. Several of the most considerable cavaliers in Spain sought me in marriage. My favorite was Don Alvar de Mello. It is true he had a prettier person than his rivals; but more solid qualities determined me in his favor. He had wit, discretion, valor, probity; and in addition to all these, an air of fashion. Was an entertainment to be given?

His taste was sure to be displayed. If he appeared in the lists, he always fixed the eyes of the beholders on his strength and dexterity. I singled him out from among all the rest, and married him.

A few days after our nuptials, he met Don Andrew de Baësa, who had been his rival, in a private place. They attacked one another sword in hand, and Don Andrew fell. As he was nephew to the corregidor of Valladolid, a turbulent man, violently incensed against the house of Mello, Don Alvar thought he could not soon enough make his escape. He returned home speedily, and told me what had happened while his horse was getting ready. My dear Mencia, said he at length, we must part. You know the corregidor: let us not flatter ourselves; he will hunt me even to death. You are unacquainted with his influence; this empire will be too hot to hold me. He was so penetrated by his own grief and mine as not to be able to articulate further. I made him take some cash and jewels; then he folded me in his arms, and we did nothing but mingle our sighs and tears for a quarter of an hour. In a short time the horse was at the door. He tore himself from me, and left me in a condition not easily to be expressed. It had been well if the excess of my affliction had destroyed me! How much pain and trouble might I have escaped by death! Some hours after Don Alvar was gone, the corregidor became acquainted with his flight. He set up a hue and cry after him, sparing no pains to get him into his power. My husband, however, eluded his pursuit, and got into safe quarters; so that the judge, finding himself reduced to confine his vengeance to the poor satisfaction of confiscating, where he meant to execute, labored to good purpose in his vocation. Don Alvar's little property all went to the hammer.

I remained in a very comfortless situation, with scarcely the means of subsistence. A retired life was best suited to my circumstances, with a single female servant. I passed my hours in lamenting, not an indigence, which I bore patiently, but the absence of a beloved husband, of whom I received no accounts. He had indeed pledged himself, in the melancholy moments of our parting, to be punctual in acquainting me with his destiny, to whatever part of the world his evil star might conduct him. And yet seven years rolled on without my hearing of him. My suspense respecting his fate afflicted me most deeply. At last I heard of his falling in battle, under the Portuguese banner, in the kingdom of Fez. A man newly returned from Africa brought me the account, with the assurance that he had been well acquainted with Don Alvar de Mello; had served with him in the army, and had seen him drop in the action. To this narrative of facts he added several collateral circumstances, which left me no room to doubt of my husband's premature death.

About this time Don Ambrosio Mesia Carillo, Marquis de la Guardia, arrived at Valladolid. He was one of those elderly noblemen who, with that good breeding acquired by long experience in courts, throw their years into the background, and retain the faculty of making themselves agreeable to our sex. One day he

happened by accident to hear the story of Don Alvar; and, from
the part I bore in it and the description of my person, there
arose a desire of being better acquainted. To satisfy his curiosity, he made interest with one of my relations to invite me to
her house. The gentleman was one of the party. This first interview made not the less impression on his heart for the traces
of sorrow which were too obvious on my countenance. He was
touched by its melancholy and languishing expression, which gave
him a favorable forecast of my constancy. Respect, rather than
any warmer sentiment, might perhaps be the inspirer of his wishes.
For he told me more than once what a miracle of good faith
he considered me, and my husband's fate as enviable in this respect, however lamentable in others. In a word, he was struck
with me at first sight, and did not wait for a review of my
pretensions, but at once took the resolution of making me his
wife.

The intervention of my kinswoman was adopted as the means of
inducing me to accept his proposal. She paid me a visit; and in the
course of conversation, pleaded, that as my husband had submitted
to the decree of Providence in the kingdom of Fez, according to
very credible accounts, it was no longer rational to coop up my
charms. I had shed tears enough over a man to whom I had been
united but for a few moments as it were, and I ought to avail myself of the present offer, and had nothing to do but to step into
happiness at once. In furtherance of these arguments, she set forth
the old marquis's pedigree, his wealth and high character: but in
vain did her eloquence expatiate on his endowments, for I was not
to be moved. Not that my mind misgave me respecting Don
Alvar's death; nor that the apprehension of his sudden and unwelcome appearance hereafter, checked my inclinations. My little liking, or rather my extreme repugnance, to a second marriage, after
the sad issue of the first, was the sole obstacle opposed to my relation's urgency. Neither was she disheartened: on the contrary, her
zeal for Don Ambrosio resorted to endless stratagems. All my
family were pressed into the old lord's service. So beneficial a
match was not to be trifled with! They were eternally besetting,
dunning, and tormenting me. In fact, my despondency, which increased from day to day, contributed not a little to my yielding.

As there was no getting rid of him, I gave way to their eager
suit, and was wedded to the Marquis de la Guardia. The day after
the nuptials, we went to a very fine castle of his near Burgos, between Grajal and Rodillas. He conceived a violent love for me:
the desire of pleasing was visible in all his actions: the anticipation
of my slenderest wishes was his earliest and his latest study. No
husband ever regarded his wife more tenderly, no lover could pour
forth more devotion to his mistress. Nor would it have been possible for me to steel my heart against a return of passion, though
our ages were so disproportioned, had not every soft sentiment
been buried in Don Alvar's grave. But the avenues of a constant
heart are barred against a second inmate. The memory of my first
husband threw a damp on all the kind efforts of the second. Mere

"MADAM, FOR HEAVEN'S SAKE, COMPOSE YOURSELF."

gratitude was a cold retribution for such tenderness ; but it was all I had to give.

Such was my temper of mind, when, taking the air one day at a window in my apartment, I perceived a peasant-looking man in the garden, viewing me with fixed attention. He appeared to be a common laborer. The circumstance soon passed out of my thoughts ; but the next day, having again taken my station at the window, I saw him on the self-same spot, and again found myself the object of his eager gaze. This seemed strange! I looked at him in my turn ; and, after an attentive scrutiny, thought I could trace the features of the unhappy Don Alvar. This seeming visit from the tombs roused all the dormant agony of my soul, and extorted from me a piercing scream. Happily, I was then alone with Inès, who of all my women engaged the largest share of my confidence. I told her what surmise had so agitated my spirits. She only laughed at the idea, and took it for granted that a slight resemblance had imposed on my fancy. Take courage, madam, said she, and do not be afraid of seeing your first husband. What likelihood is there of his being here in the disguise of a peasant ? Is it even within the reach of credibility that he is yet alive ? However, I will go down into the garden, and talk with this rustic. I will answer for finding out who he is, and will return in all possible haste with my intelligence. Inès ran on her errand like a lapwing ; but soon returned to my apartment with face of mingled astonishment and emotion. Madam, exclaimed she, your conjecture is but too well grounded ; it is indeed Don Alvar whom you have seen ; he made himself known at once, and pleads for a private interview.

As I had the means of admitting Don Alvar instantaneously, by the absence of the Marquis at Burgos, I commissioned my waiting-maid to introduce him into my closet by a private staircase. Well may you imagine the hurry and agitation of my spirits. How could I support the presence of a man, who was entitled to overwhelm me with reproaches ? I fainted at his very foot-fall as he entered. They were about me in a moment—he as well as Inès ; and when they had recovered me from my swoon, Don Alvar said—Madam, for heaven's sake, compose yourself. My presence shall never be the cause of pain to you ; nor would I for the world expose you to the slightest anxiety. I am no savage husband, come to account with you for a sacred pledge ; nor do I impute to criminal motives the second contract you have formed. I am well aware that it was owing to the importunity of your friends ; your persecutions from that quarter are not unknown to me. Besides, the report of my death was current in Valladolid ; and you had so much the more reason to give it credit, as no letter from me gave you any assurance to the contrary. In short, I am no stranger to your habits of life since our cruel separation ; and know that necessity, not lightness of heart, has thrown you into the arms.... Ah ! sir, interrupted I with sobs, why will you make excuses for your unworthy wife ? She is guilty, since you survive. Why am I not still in the forlorn state in which I languished before my marriage with Don Ambrosio ? Fatal nuptials!—alas ! but for these, I should at least have had the consolation in my wretchedness of seeing the object of my first vows again without a blush.

My dear Mencia, replied Don Alvar, with a look which marked how deeply he was penetrated by my contrition, I make no complaint of you ; and far from upbraiding you with your present prosperity, as heaven is my witness, I return it thanks for the favors it has showered on you. Since the sad day of my departure from Valladolid, my own fate has ever been adverse. My life has been but a tissue of misfortune ; and, as a surcharge of evil destiny, I had no means of letting you hear from me. Too secure in your affection, I could neither think nor dream but of the condition to which my fatal love might have reduced you. Donna Mencia in tears was the lovely, but killing spectre that haunted me ; of all my miseries, your dear idea was the most acute. Sometimes, I own, I felt remorse for the transporting crime of having pleased you. I wished you had lent an ear to the suit of some happier rival, since the preference with which you had honored me was to fall so cruelly on your own head. To cut short my melancholy tale—after seven years of suffering, more enamored than ever, I determined to see you once again. The impulse was not to be resisted ; and the expiration of a long slavery having furnished me with the power of giving way to it, I have been at Valladolid under this disguise at the hazard of a discovery. There, I learned the whole story. I then came to this castle, and found the means of admission into the gardener's service, who has engaged me as a laborer. Such was my stratagem to obtain this private interview. But do not suppose me capable of blasting, by my continuance here, the happiness of your future days. I love you better than my own life ; I have no consideration but for your repose ; and it is my purpose, after thus unburdening my heart, to finish in exile the sacrifice of an existence which has lost its value since no longer to be devoted to your service.

No, Don Alvar, no, exclaimed I at these words ; you shall never quit me a second time. I will be the companion of your wanderings ; and death only shall divide us from this hour. Take my advice, replied he, live with Don Ambrosio ; unite not yourself with my miseries, but leave me to stand under their undivided weight. These and other such entreaties he used ; but the more willing he seemed to sacrifice himself to my welfare, the less did I feel disposed to take advantage of his generosity. When he saw me resolute in my determination to follow him, he all at once changed his tone ; and assuming an aspect of more satisfaction, Madam, said he, since you still love Don Alvar well enough to prefer adversity with him before your present ease and affluence, let us then take up our abode at Bétancos, in the interior of Galicia. There I have a safe retreat. Though my misfortunes may have stripped me of all my effects, they have not alienated all my friends ; some are yet faithful, and have furnished me with the means of carrying you off. With their help I have hired a carriage at Zamora ; have bought mules and horses, and am accompanied by perhaps the three boldest of the Galicians. They are armed with carabines and pistols.

waiting my orders at the village of Rodillas. Let us avail ourselves of Don Ambrosio's absence. I will send the carriage to the castle gate, and we will set out without loss of time. I consented. Don Alvar flew towards Rodillas, and shortly returned with his escort. My women, from the midst of whom I was carried off, not knowing what to think of this violent proceeding, made their escape in great terror. Inès only was in the secret; but she would not link her fate with mine, on account of a love affair with Don Ambrosio's favorite man.

I got into the carriage, therefore, with Don Alvar, taking nothing with me but my clothes and some jewels of my own before my second marriage; for I could not think of appropriating any presents of the Marquis. We travelled in the direction of Galicia, without knowing if we should be lucky enough to reach it. We had reason to fear Don Ambrosio's pursuit on his return, and that we should be overtaken by superior numbers. We went forward for two days without any alarm, and in the hope of being equally fortunate the third, had got into a very quiet conversation. Don Alvar was relating the melancholy adventure which had occasioned the rumor of his death, and how he recovered his freedom, after five years of slavery, when yesterday we met upon the Leon road the banditti you were with. He it was whom they killed with all his attendants, and it is for him the tears flow, which you see me shedding at this moment.

CHAPTER XII.

A DISAGREEABLE INTERRUPTION.

DONNA MENCIA melted into tears as she finished this recital. I allowed her to give a free passage to her sighs; I even wept myself for company, so natural is it to be interested for the afflicted, and especially for a lovely female in distress. I was just going to ask her what she meant to do in the present conjuncture, and possibly she was going to consult me on the same subject if our conversation had not been interrupted; but we heard a great noise in the inn, which drew our attention whether we would or no. It was no less than the arrival of the corregidor, attended by two alguazils and their marshalmen. They came into the room where we were. A young gentleman in their train came first up to me, and began taking to pieces the different articles of my dress. He had no occasion to examine them long. By Saint James, exclaimed he, this is my identical doublet! It is the very thing, and as safely to be challenged as my horse. You may commit this spark on my recognizance; he is one of the gang who have an undiscovered retreat in this country.

At this discourse, which gave me to understand my accuser to be the gentleman robbed, whose spoils to my confusion were ex-

clusively my own, I was without a word to say for myself, looking
one way and the other, and not knowing where to fix my eyes.
The corregidor, whose office was suspicion, set me down for the
culprit ; and presuming on the lady for an accomplice, ordered us
into separate custody. This magistrate was none of your stern
gallows-preaching fellows, he had a jocular epigrammatic sort of
countenance. God knows if his heart lay in the right place for all
that ! As soon as I was committed, in came he with his pack.
They knew their trade, and began by searching me. What a forfeit to these lords of the manor ! At every handful of pistoles,
what little eyes did I see them make ! The corregidor was absolutely out of his wits ! It was the best stroke within the memory
of justice ! My pretty lad, said his Worship with a softened tone,
we only do our duty, but do not you tremble for your bones before the time : you will not be broken on the wheel if you do not
deserve it. These blood-suckers were emptying my pockets all the
time with the their cursed palaver, and took from me what their
betters of the shades below had the decency to leave—my uncle's
forty ducats. They stuck at nothing ! Their staunch fingers, with
slow but certain scent, routed me out from top to toe ; they whisked
me round and round, and stripped me even to the shame of modesty, for fear some sneaking portrait of the king should slink between my shirt and skin. When they could sift no further, the
corregidor thought it time to begin his examination. I told a plain
tale. My deposition was taken down ; and the sequel was, that he
carried in his train his bloodhounds, and my little property, leaving
me to toss without a rag upon a beggarly wisp of straw.

Oh the miseries of human life ! groaned I, when I found myself
in this merciless and solitary condition. Our adventures here are
whimsical, and cut of all time and tune. From my first outset from
Oviedo, I had got into a pleasant round of difficulties ; hardly had I
worked myself out of one danger, before I soused into another.
Coming into town here, how could I expect the honor of the corregidor's acquaintance ? While thus communing with my own
thoughts, I got once more into the cursed doublet and the rest of
the paraphernalia which had got me into such a scrape ; then plucking up a little courage, never mind, Gil Blas, thought I, do not be
chicken-hearted. What is a prison above-ground, after so brimstone a snuffle as thou hast had of the regions below ? But, alas !
I halloo before I am out of the wood ! I am in more experienced
hands than those of Leonarda and Domingo. My key will not open
this grate ! I might well say so, for a prisoner without money is
like a bird with its wings clipt ; one must be in full feather to flutter out of distance from these gaol-birds.

But we left a partridge and a young rabbit on the spit ! How
they got off I know not ; but my supper was a bit of sallow-com-
plexioned bread, with a pitcher of water to render it amenable to
mastication ! and thus was I destined to bite the bridle in my dungeon. A fortnight was pretty well without seeing a soul but my
keeper, who had orders that I should want for nothing in the bread
and water way ! Whenever he made his appearance I was inclined

to be sociable, and to parley a little to get rid of the blue devils; but this majestic minister was above reply, he was mum! he scarcely trusted his eyes but to see that I did not slip by him. On the sixteenth day, the corregidor strutted in to this tune—You are a lucky fellow! I have news for you The lady is packed off for Burgos. She came under my examination before her departure, and her answers went to your exculpation. You will be at large this very day if your carrier from Pegnaflor to Cacabelos agrees in the same tale. He is now in Astorga. I have sent for him, and ex-pect him here; if he confirms the story of the torture, you are your own master.

At these words I was ready to jump out of my skin for joy. The business was settled! I thanked the magistrate for the abridgment of justice with which he had deigned to favor me, and was getting to the fag end of my compliment, when the muleteer arrived, with an attendant before and behind. I knew the fellow's face; but he, hav-ing as a matter of course sold my cloak-bag with the contents, from a deep-rooted affection to the money which the sale had brought, swore lustily that he had no acquaintance with me, and had never seen me in the whole course of his life. Oh! you villain, exclaimed I, go down on your knees and own that you have sold my clothes. Prythee, have some regard to truth! Look in my face; am not I one of those shallow young fellows whom you had the wit to threaten with the rack in the corporate town of Cacabelos? The muleteer turned upon his toe, and protested he had not the honor of my acquaintance. As he persisted in his disavowal, I was re-committed for further examination. Patience once more! It was only reducing feasts and fasts to the level of bread and water, and regaling the only sense I had the means of using with the sight of my tongue-tied warden. But when I reflected how little innocence would avail to extricate me from the clutches of the law, the thought was death; I panted for my subterraneous paradise. Take it for all in all, said I, there were fewer grievances than in this dungeon. I was hail fellow well met with the banditti! I bandied about my jokes with the best of them, and lived on the sweet hope of an es-cape; whereas my innocence here will only be a passport to the galleys.

CHAPTER XIII.

THE LUCKY MEANS BY WHICH GIL BLAS ESCAPED FROM PRISON, AND HIS TRAVELS AFTERWARDS.

WHILE I passed the hours in tickling my fancy with my own gay thoughts, my adventures, word for word, as I had set my hand to them, were current about the town. The people wanted to make a show of me! One after another, there they came, peeping in at a

little window of my prison, not too capacious of daylight; and when
they had looked about them, off they went! This raree-show was a
novelty. Since my commitment, there had not been a living creature at that window, which looked into a court where silence and

"PEEPING IN AT A LITTLE WINDOW OF MY PRISON."

horror kept guard. This gave me to understand that I was become
the town-talk, and I knew not whether to divine good or evil from
the omen.

One of my first visitors was the little chorister of Mondognedo,
who had a fellow-feeling with me for the rack, and an equally light pair
of heels. I knew him at once, and he had no qualms about acknowledging me as an acquaintance. We exchanged a kind greeting, then
compared notes since our separation. I was obliged to relate my
adventures in due form and order. The chorister, on his part, told
me what had happened in the inn at Cacabelos, between the muleteer and the bride, after we had taken to our heels in a panic. Then
with a friendly assurance at parting, he promised to leave no stone
unturned for my release. His companions of mere curiosity testified their pity for my misfortune; assuring me that they would lend
a helping hand to the little chorister, and do their utmost to procure
my freedom.

They were no worse than their word. The corregidor was applied to in my favor, who, no longer doubtful of my innocence,
above all when he had heard the chorister's story, came three weeks
afterwards into my cell. Gil Blas, said he, I never stand shilly-
shally: begone, you are free; you may take yourself off whenever

you please. But, tell me, if you were carried to the forest, could you not discover the subterranean retreat? No, sir, replied I; as I only entered in the night, and made my escape before day-break, it would be impossible to fix upon the spot. Thereupon the magistrate withdrew, assuring me that the gaoler should be ordered to give me free egress. In fact, the very next moment the turnkey came into my dungeon, followed by one of his outriding establishment, with a bundle of clothes under his arm. They both of them stripped me with the utmost solemnity, and without uttering a single syllable, of my doublet and breeches, which had the honor to be made of a bettermost cloth almost new; then, having rigged me in an old frock, they shoved me out of their hospitable mansion by the shoulders.

The taking I was in to see myself so ill equipped, acted as a cooler to the usual transport of prisoners at recovering their liberty. I was tempted to escape from the town without delay, that I might withdraw from the gaze of the people, whose prying eyes I could not encounter but with pain. My gratitude, however, got the better of my diffidence. I went to thank the little chorister, to whom I was so much obliged. He could not help chuckling when he saw me. That is your trim, is it? said he. As far as I see, you cannot complain that your case has not been sifted to the bottom. I have nothing to say against the laws of my country, replied I; they are as just as need be. I only wish their officers would take after them! They might have spared me my suit of clothes; I have paid for them over and over again. I am quite of your mind, rejoined he; but they would tell you that these are little formalities of old standing, which cannot be dispensed with. What! you are foolish enough to suppose, for instance, that your horse has been restored to its right owner? Not a word of it, if you please: the beast is at this present in the stables of the register, where it has been impounded as a witness to be brought into court: if the poor gentleman comes off with the crupper, he will be so much in pocket. But let us change the subject. What is your plan? What do you mean to do with yourself? I have an inclination, said I, to take the road for Burgos. I may light on my rescued lady; she will give me a little ready cash; I shall then buy a new short cassock, and betake myself to Salamanca, where I shall see what I can make of my Latin. All my trouble is, how to get to Burgos; one must live on the road. I understand you, replied he. Take my purse: it is rather thinly lined, to be sure; but you know a chorister's dividends are not like a bishop's. At the same time he drew it from his pouch, and inserted it between my hands with so good a grace, that I could not do otherwise than accept it, for want of a better. I thanked him as though he had made me a present of a gold mine, and tendered him a thousand promises of recompense, to be duly honored and punctually paid at doom's-day. With this I left him, and skulked out of the town, not paying my respects to my other benefactors; but giving them a thousand blessings from my heart.

The little chorister had reason for speaking modestly of his purse, it was not orthodox. By good luck, I had been used for these two months to a very slender diet, and had still a little small change left when I reached Ponte de Mula, not far from Burgos. I halted there to inquire after Donna Mencia. The hostess of the inn I put up at was a little withered, spiteful, emaciated bit of mortality. I saw at a glance, by the mouths she made at me aside, that my frock did not hit her fancy; and I thought it a proof of her taste. So I sat myself down at a table; ate bread and cheese, and drank a few glasses of execrable wine, such as innkeepers technically call cassecoquin. During this meal, which was of a piece with the outward appearance of the guest, I did my utmost to come to closer quarters with my landlady. Did she know the Marquis de la Guardia? Was his castle far out of town? Above all, what was become of my lady marchioness? You ask many questions in a breath, replied she, bridling with disdain. But I got out of her, though by hard pumping, that Don Ambrosio's castle was but a short league from Ponte de Mula.

After I had done eating and drinking, as it was night, I thought it natural to go to bed, and asked for my room. A room for you! shrieked my landlady, darting at me a glance of contempt and pride; I have no rooms for fellows who make their supper on a bit of cheese. All my beds are bespoke. There are people of fashion expected, and our accommodations are all kept for them. But I will not be unchristian: you may lie in my barn: I suppose your soft skin will not be incommoded by the feel of straw. She spoke truth without knowing it. I took it all in silence, and slunk to my roosting-place, where I fell asleep like a man, the excess of whose labors are his ready passport to the blessings of repose.

CHAPTER XIV.

DONNA MENCIA'S RECEPTION OF HIM AT BURGOS.

I WAS no sluggard, but got up the next morning betimes. I paid my bill to the landlady, who was already stirring, and seemed a little less lofty and in better humor than the evening before; a circumstance I attributed to the endeavors of three kind guardsmen belonging to the holy brotherhood. These gentlemen had slept in the inn: they were evidently on a very intimate footing with the hostess: and doubtless it was for guests of such note that all the beds were bespoke.

I inquired in the town my way to the castle where I wanted to present myself. By accident I made up to a man not unlike my landlord at Pegnaflor. He was not satisfied with answering my question to the point; but informed me that Don Ambrosio had been dead three weeks, and the marchioness his lady had taken the resolution of retiring to a convent at Burgos, which he named.

I proceeded immediately towards that town, instead of taking the road to the castle, as I had first meant to do, and flew at once to the place of Donna Mencia's retreat. I besought the attendant at the turning-box to tell that lady that a young man just discharged from prison at Astorga wanted to speak with her. The nun went on the message immediately. On her return, she showed me into

DONNA MENCIA.

a parlor, where I did not wait long before Don Ambrosio's widow appeared at the grate in deep mourning.

You are welcome, said the lady. Four days ago I wrote to a person at Astorga, to pay you a visit as from me, and to tell you to come and see me the moment you were released from prison. I had no doubt of your being discharged shortly: what I told the corregidor in your exculpation was enough for that. An answer was brought that you had been set at liberty, but that no one knew what was become of you. I was afraid of not seeing you any more, and losing the pleasure of expressing my gratitude. Never mind, added she, observing my confusion at making my appearance in so

wretched a garb; your dress is of very little consequence. After
the important services you have rendered me, I should be the most
ungrateful of my sex, if I were to do nothing for you in return. I undertake, therefore, to better your condition: it is my duty, and the
means are in my power. My fortune is large enough to pay
my debt of obligation to you, without putting myself to inconvenience.

You know, continued she, my story up to the time when we
both were committed to prison. I will now tell you what has happened to me since. When the corregidor at Astorga had sent me
to Burgos, after having heard from my own lips a faithful recital
of my adventures, I presented myself at the castle of Ambrosio.
My return thither excited extreme surprise: but they told me that
it was too late; the marquis, as if he had been thunderstruck at my
flight, fell sick; and the physicians despaired of his recovery.
Here was a new incident in the melancholy tragedy of my fate.
Yet I ordered my arrival to be announced. The next moment I
ran into his chamber, and threw myself on my knees by his bedside, with a face running down with tears and a heart oppressed
with the most lively sorrow. Who sent for you hither? said he as
soon as he saw me; are you come to contemplate your own contrivance? Was it not enough to have deprived me of life? But was
it necessary to satisfy your heart's desire, to be an eye-witness of my
death? My lord, replied I, Inès must have told you that I fled
with my first husband; and, had it not been for the sad accident
which has taken him from me for ever, you never would have seen
me more. At the same time, I acquainted him that Don Alvar
had been killed by a banditti, whose captive I had consequently
been in a subterraneous dungeon. After relating the particulars
of my story to the end, Don Ambrosio held out to me his hand. It
is enough, said he affectionately, I will make no more complaints.
Alas! Have I in fact any right to reproach you? You were
thrown once more in the way of a beloved husband; and gave me
up to follow his fortunes: can I blame such an instance of your
affection? No, madam, it would have been vain to resist the will
of fate. For that reason I gave orders not to pursue you. In my
rival himself I could not but respect the sacred rights with which
he was invested, and even the impulse of your flight seemed to
have been communicated by some superior power. To close all
with an act of justice, and in the spirit of reconciliation, your return hither has re-established you completely in my affection
Yes, my dear Mencia, your presence fills me with joy: but alas! I
shall not long be sensible to it. I feel my last hour to be at hand.
No sooner are you restored to me, than I must bid you an eternal
farewell. At these touching expressions, my tears flowed in torrents. I felt and expressed as much affliction as the human heart
is capable of containing. I question whether Don Alvar's death,
doting on him as I did, had cost me more bitter lamentations.
Don Ambrosio had given way to no mistaken presage of his
death, which happened on the following day; and I remained mistress of a considerable jointure, settled on me at our marriage.

"I RAN INTO HIS CHAMBER, AND THREW MYSELF ON MY KNEES BY HIS BEDSIDE."

But I shall take care to make no unworthy use of it. The world shall not see me, young as I still am, wantoning in the arms of a third husband. Besides that such levity seems irreconcilable with the feelings of any but the profligate of our sex, I will frankly own the relish of life to be extinct in me; so that I mean to end my days in this convent, and to become a benefactress to it.

Such was Donna Mencia's discourse about her future plans. She then drew a purse from beneath her robe, and put it into my hands, with this address: Here are a hundred ducats simply to furnish out your wardrobe. That done, come and see me again. I mean not to confine my gratitude within such narrow bounds. I returned her a thousand thanks, and promised solemnly not to quit Burgos, without taking leave of her. Having given this pledge, which I had every inclination to redeem, I went to look out for some house of entertainment. Entering the first I met with, I asked for a room. To parry the ill opinion my frock might convey of my finances, I told the landlord that, however appearances might be against me, I could pay for my night's lodging as well as a better dressed gentleman. At this speech, the landlord, whose name was Majuelo, a great banterer in a coarse way, running over me with his eyes from top to toe, answered with a cool, sarcastic grin, that there was no need of any such assurance; it was evident I should pay my way liberally, for he discovered something of nobility through my disguise, and had no doubt but I was a gentleman in very easy circumstances. I saw plainly that the rascal was laughing at me; and to stop his humor before it became too convulsive, gave him a little insight into the state of my purse. I went so far as to count over my ducats on a table before him, and perceived my coin to have inclined him to a more respectful judgment. I begged the favor of him to send for a tailor. A broker would be better, said he; he will bring all sorts of apparel, and you will be dressed up out of hand. I approved of this advice, and determined to follow it; but, as the day was on the point of closing, I put off my purchase till the morrow, and thought only of getting a good supper, to make amends for the miserable fare I had taken up with since my escape from the forest.

CHAPTER XV.

GIL BLAS DRESSES HIMSELF TO MORE ADVANTAGE, AND RECEIVES
A SECOND PRESENT FROM THE LADY. HIS EQUIPAGE ON
SETTING OUT FROM BURGOS.

THEY served me up a plentiful fricassee of sheep's trotters, almost the whole of which I demolished. My drinking kept pace with my eating: and when I could stuff no longer, I went to bed. I lay comfortably enough, and was in hopes that a sound sleep would have the kindness without delay to commit a friendly invasion on my senses. But I could not close an eye for ruminating on the dress I should choose. What shall I do, thought I? Shall I follow my first plan? Shall I buy a short cassock, and go to Salamanca to set up for a tutor? Why should I adopt the costume of a licentiate? For the purpose of going into orders? Do I feel an inward call? No. If I have any call, it is quite the contrary way. I had rather wear a sword than an apron: and push my fortune in this world, before I think of the next.

I made up my mind to take on myself the appearance of a gentleman. Waiting for the day with the greatest impatience, its first dawn no sooner greeted my eyes, than I got up. I made such an uproar in the inn, as to wake the most inveterate sleeper, and called the servants out of bed, who returned my salute with a volley of curses. But they found themselves under a necessity of stirring, and I let them have no rest till they had sent for a broker. The gentleman soon made his appearance, followed by two lads, each lugging in a great bundle of green cloth. He accosted me very civilly, to the following effect: Honored sir, you are a happy man to have been recommended to me rather than any one else. I do not mean to give my brethren an ill word: God forbid I should offer the slightest injury to their reputation! They have none to spare. But, between ourselves, there is not one of them has any bowels; they are more extortionate than the Israelites. There is not a broker but myself that has any moral sense. I keep within the bounds of a reasonable profit. I am satisfied with a pound in the penny;—no, no!—that is wrong:—with a penny in the pound. Thanks to heaven, I get forward fair and softly in the world.

The broker, after this preface, which I, like a fool, took for chapter and verse, told his journeymen to undo their bundles. They showed me suits of every color in the rainbow and exposed to sale a great choice of plain cloths. These I threw aside with contempt, as thinking them too undrest; but they made me try on one which fitted me as well as if I had been measured for it, and just hit my fancy, though it was a little the worse for wear. It was a doublet with slashed sleeves, with breeches and a cloak, the whole of blue velvet with a gold embroidery. I felt a little hankering after this particular article, and attempted to beat down the price. The broker, who saw my inclination, told me I had a very correct taste. By all that is sacred! exclaimed he, it is plain you are no younker. Take this with you! That dress was made for one of the first nobility in the kingdom, and has not been on his back three times. Look at the velvet, feel it, nothing can be richer of of a better color and for the embroidery, come now! tell truth: did you ever see better workmanship? What is the price of it? said I. Only sixty ducats, replied he. I have refused the money, or else I am a liar. The alternative could not fail in one proposition or the other. I bid five and forty: two or three and twenty would have been nearer the mark. My worthy master, said the broker coolly I never ask too much. I have but one price. But here, added he, holding up the suits I had thrown aside take these: I can afford to sell them a better bargain. All this only inflamed my eagerness to buy what I was cheapening; and as I had no idea that he would have made any abatement, I paid him down sixty ducats. When he saw how easily a fool and his money were parted, I verily believe that in spite of the moral sense, he heartily repented not having taken a hint from the extortionate Israelite. But reconciling himself as well as he could to the small profit, to which he professed to confine himself, of a pound upon a penny, he retreated with his journeymen. I was not suffered to forget that they must have something for their trouble.

I had now a cloak, a doublet, and a very decent pair of breeches. The rest of my wardrobe was to be thought of: and this took up the whole morning. I bought some linen, a hat, silk stockings, shoes, and a sword; and concluded by putting on my purchases. What pleasure was it to see myself so well accoutred! My eyes were never cloyed, as it were, with the richness of my attire. Never did peacock look at his own plumage with less philosophy. On that very day, I paid a second visit to Donna Mencia, who received me with her usual affability. She thanked me over again for the service I had rendered her. On that subject, rapid was the interchange of compliments. Then, wishing every kind of success, she bade me farewell, and withdrew, without giving me any thing but a ring worth thirty pistoles, which she begged me to keep as a remembrance.

I looked very foolish with my ring! I had reckoned on a much more considerable present. Thus, little satisfied with the lady's bounty, I measured back my steps in a very musing attitude: but as I entered the inn door, a man overtook me, and throwing off his wrapping cloak, discovered a large bag under his arm. At the vision of the bag, apparently full of current coin, I stood gaping, as did most of the company present. The voice of angel or archangel could not have been sweeter, than when this messenger of earthly dross, laying the bag upon the table, said: Signor Gil Blas, the lady marchioness desires her compliments. I bowed the bearer out, with an accumulation of fine speeches; and, as soon as his back was turned, pounced upon the bag, like a hawk upon its quarry, and bore it between my talons to my chamber. I untied it without loss of time, and the contents were—a thousand ducats! The landlord, who had overheard the bearer, came in just as I had done counting them, to know what was in the bag. The sight of my riches displayed upon a table, struck him in a very forcible manner. What the devil! here is a sum of money! So, so! you are the man! pursued he with a waggish sort of leer, you know how to—tickle the—fancies of the ladies! Four and twenty hours only have you been in Burgos, and marchionesses, I warrant you, have surrendered at the first summons!

This discourse was not so much amiss. I was half inclined to leave Majuelo in his error; for it flattered my vanity. I do not wonder young fellows are fond of passing for men of gallantry. But as yet the purity of my morals was proof against the suggestions of my pride. I undeceived my landlord, by telling him Donna Men-

cia's story, to which he listened very attentively. Afterwards I let
him into the state of my affairs; and, as he seemed to take an interest in them, besought him to assist me with his advice. He ruminated for some time; then said with a serious air: Master Gil
Blas, I have taken a liking to you; and since you are candid enough
to open your heart to me, I will tell you sincerely what I think
would suit you best. You were evidently born for a court life: I
recommend you to go thither, and to get about the person of some
considerable nobleman, But make a point either of getting at his
secrets, or administering to his pleasures; unless you do that, it
will be all lost time in his family. I know the great: they reckon
nothing upon the zeal and attachment of a real friend; but only
care for pimping sycophants. You have, besides, another string to
your bow. You are young, with an attractive person: parts out of
the question, for they are not at all times necessary, it is hard if you
cannot turn the head of some rich widow, or handsome wife with a
broomstick for her husband. Love may ruin men of fortune; but
it makes amends by feathering the nests of those who have none.
My vote, therefore, is for Madrid: but you must not make your appearance there without an establishment. There, as elsewhere,
people judge by the outside; and you will only be respected according to the figure you make. I will find you a servant, a tried domestic, a prudent lad; in a word, a fellow of my own creation. Buy
a couple of mules; one for yourself, the other for him; and set off
as fast as you can.

This counsel was too palatable to be refused. On the day following I purchased two fine mules, and bargained with my new
servant. He was a young man of thirty, of a very simple and godly
appearance. He told me he was a native of Galicia, by name
Ambrose de Lamela. Other servants are selfish, and think they
never can have wages enough. This fellow assured me he was a
man of few wants, and should be contented with whatever I had
the goodness to give him. I bought a pair of boots, with a portmanteau to lock up my linen and my money. Having settled with
my landlord, I set out from Burgos the next morning before sunrise, on my way to Madrid.

CHAPTER XVI.

SHOWING THAT PROSPERITY WILL SLIP THROUGH A MAN'S
FINGERS.

WE slept at Duengnas the first night; and reached Valladolid on
the following day, about four o'clock in the afternoon. We alighted
at the inn of the most respectable appearance in the town. I left
the care of the mules to my fellow, and went up to a room whither
I ordered my portmanteau to be carried by a waiter. As I felt a

little weary, I threw myself on a couch in my boots, and fell asleep involuntarily. It was almost night when I awoke. I called for Ambrose. He was not to be found in the house; but made his appearance in a short time. I asked him where he had been: he answered in his godly way, that he was just come from church, whither he went for the purpose of thanksgiving, by reason that we had been graciously preserved from all perils and dangers between

"YOU ARE HE, NOBLE SIR, THE VERY MAN OF WHOM I WAS
IN QUEST."

Burgos and Valladolid. I commended his piety; and ordered a chicken to be roasted for supper.

At the moment when I was giving this order, my landlord came into my room with a light in his hand. That cursed candle served to introduce a lady, handsome, but not young, and very richly attired. She leant upon an usher, none of the youngest, and a little blackamoor was her train-bearer. I was under no small surprise when this fair incognita, with a profound obeisance, begged to know if my name might happen to be Signor Gil Blas of Santillane ? I had no sooner blundered out yes, than she released her sweet hand from the custody of the usher, and embraced me with a transport of joy, of which I knew less and less what to make.   Heaven be praised, cried she, for all its mercies.   You are he, noble sir, the very man of whom I was in quest.   By this introduction I was reminded of my friend the parasite at Pegnaflor, and was on the point of suspecting the lady to be no better than an honest woman should be : but her finale gave me a much higher opinion of her.   I am, continued she, first cousin to Donna Mencia de Mosquera, whom you have so greatly befriended.   It was but this morning I received a letter from her.   She writes me word that having learnt your intention of going to Madrid, she wished me to receive you hospitably on your journey, if you went this way.   For these two hours have I been parading the town.   From inn to inn have I gone to inform myself what strangers were in the house; and I gathered from the landlord's description that you were most likely to have been my cousin's deliverer.   Since then I have found you out, you shall know by experience my gratitude to the friends of my family, and especially to my dear cousin's hero.   You will take up your abode, if you please, at my house.   Your accommodation will be better.   I wished to excuse myself ; and told the lady that I could not be so troublesome : but her importunities were more than a match for my modesty.   A carriage was waiting at the door of the inn to convey us.   She saw my portmanteau taken care of with her own eyes, because, as she justly observed, there were a great many light-fingered gentry about Valladolid—to be sure there were a great many light-fingered gentry about Valladolid, as she justly observed !   In short, I got into the carriage with her and the old usher, and suffered myself to be carried off bodily from the inn, to the great annoyance of the landlord, who saw himself thus weaned from all the little perquisites he had reckoned on from my abode under his roof.

Our carriage, having rolled on some distance, stopped.   We alighted at the door of a handsome house, and went upstairs into a well-furnished apartment, illuminated by twenty or thirty wax candles.   Several servants were in waiting, of whom the lady inquired whether Don Raphael was come.   They answered, No. She then addressed herself to me : Signor Gil Blas, I am waiting for my brother's return from a country seat of ours, about two leagues distant.   What an agreeable surprise will it be to him to find a man under his roof to whom our family is so much indebted! At the very moment she had finished this pretty speech we heard a noise, and were informed at the same time that it was occasioned by the arrival of Don Raphael.   This spark soon made his appearance.   He was a young man of portly figure and genteel manners. I am in ecstasy to see you back again, brother, said the lady ; you will assist me in doing the honors to Signor Gil Blas of Santillane.   We can never do enough to show our sense of his kindness to our kinswoman, Donna Mencia.   Here, read this letter I have just received. Don Raphael opened the envelope, and read aloud as follows. "My dear Camilla, Signor Gil Blas of Santillane, the savior of my honor and my life, has just set out for court. He will of course pass through Valladolid. I conjure you by our family connection, and still more by our indissoluble friendship, to give him an hospitable reception. and to detain him for some time as your guest. I flatter myself that you will so far oblige me, and that my deliverer will receive every kind of polite attention from yourself, and my cousin, Don Raphael.

"Your affectionate cousin,

"*Burgos.*   Donna Mencia."

What! cried Don Raphael, casting his eyes again over the letter, is it to this gentleman my kinswoman owes her honor and her life? Then heaven be praised for this happy meeting. With this sort of language, he advanced towards me; and squeezing me tightly in his arms: What joy to me is it, added he, to have the honor of seeing Signor Gil Blas of Santillane! My cousin the marchioness had no need to press the hospitality. Had she only told us simply that you were passing through Valladolid, that would have been enough. My sister Camilla and I shall be at no loss how to conduct ourselves towards a young gentleman who has conferred an obligation. not to be repaid, on her of all our family most tenderly beloved by us I made the best answer I could to these speeches. which were followed by many others of the same kind, and interlarded with a thousand bows and scrapes. But Lord bless me, he has his boots on! The servants were ordered in, to take them off.

We next went into another room, where the cloth was laid. Down we sat at table, the brother, sister, and myself. They paid me a hundred compliments during supper. Not a word escaped me, but they magnified it into an admirable hit! It was impossible not to observe the assiduity with which they both helped me out of every dish. Don Raphael often pledged me to Donna Mencia's health. I could not refuse the challenge; and it looked a little as if Camilla, who was a very good companion, ogled at me with no questionable meaning I even thought I could perceive that she watched her opportunity as if she was afraid of being detected by her brother. An oracle could not have convinced me more firmly that the lady was caught; and I looked forward to a little delicate amusement from the discovery, during the short time I was to stay at Valladolid. That hope was my tempter to comply with the request they made me, of condescending to pass a few days with them. They thanked me kindly for indulging them with my company, and Camilla's restrained. but visible transport, confirmed me in the opinion that I was not altogether disagreeable in her eyes.

Don Raphael, finding I had made up my mind to be his guest for a few days, proposed to take me to his country house. The description of it was magnificent. and the round of amusements he meditated for me was not to be described. At one time, said he, we will take the diversion of the chase. at another that of fishing;

and whenever you have a mind for a saunter, we have charming
woods and gardens. In addition, we shall have agreeable society.
I flatter myself you will not find the time hang heavy on your
hands. I accepted the invitation, and it was agreed that we should
go to this fine country house the following day. We rose from the
table with this pleasant scheme in our mouths. Don Raphael
seemed in ecstasy. Signor Gil Blas, said he, embracing me, I leave
you with my sister. I am going presently to give the necessary
orders, and send invitations round to the families I wish to

CAMILLA.

be of the party. With these words he sallied forth from the
room where we were sitting. I went on chatting with the
lady, whose topics of discourse did not belie the glances of her
expressive eyes. She took me by the hand, and playing with
my ring, You have a mighty pretty brilliant there, said she, but it
is small. Are you a judge of jewelry? I answered, No! I am
sorry for that, resumed she, because I was in hopes you could have
told me what this is worth. As she uttered these words, she
showed me a large ruby on her finger; and, while I was looking at

It, said—An uncle of mine, who was governor of the Spanish settlements in the Philippine isles, gave me this ruby. The jewelers at Valladolid value it at three hundred pistoles. It cannot be worth less, said I, for it is evidently a very fine stone. Why, then, since you have taken a fancy to it, replied she an exchange is no robbery. In a twinkling she whisked off my ring, and placed her own on my little finger. After this exchange, a genteel way enough of making a present, Camilla pressed my hand and gazed at me with expressive tenderness; then, all at once breaking off the conversation, wished me good-night, and retired to hide her blushes, as if she had been ready to sink at the indiscreet avowal of her sentiments.

No one hitherto had trod less in the paths of gallantry than my-self! Yet I could not shut my eyes to the vista vision opened to me by this precipitate retreat. Under these circumstances, a country excursion might have its charms. Full of this flattering idea, and intoxicated with the prosperous condition of my affairs, I locked myself into my bed-room, after having told my servant to call me betimes in the morning. Instead of going to sleep, I gave myself up to the agreeable reflections which my portmanteau, snug upon the table, and my ruby excited in my breast. Heaven be praised, thought I, though misfortunes have been my lot, I am unfortunate no longer. A thousand ducats here, a ring of three hundred pistoles' value there! I am in cash for a considerable time. Indeed Majuelo was no flatterer, I see clearly. The ladies of Madrid will take fire like touchwood, since the green sticks of Valladolid are so inflammable. Then the kind regards of the generous Camilla arrayed themselves in all their charms, and I tasted by anticipation the amusements Don Raphael was preparing for me at his villa. In the mean while, amid so many images of pleasure, sleep was on the watch to strew his poppies on my couch. As soon as I felt myself drowsy, I undressed and went to bed.

The next morning, when I awoke, I found it rather late. It was odd enough that my servant did not make his appearance, after such particular orders. Ambrose, thought I to myself, my devout Ambrose is either at church, or abominably lazy this morning. But I soon let go this opinion of him to take up a worse; for getting out of bed, and seeing no portmanteau, I suspected him to have stolen it during the night. To clear up my suspicions, I opened my chamber door, and called the religious rascal over and over again. An old man answered, saying—What is your pleasure, sir? All your folks left my house before day-break. Your house! How now! exclaimed I; am I not under Don Raphael's roof? I do not know the gentleman, said he. You are in a ready-furnished lodging, and I am the landlord. Yesterday evening, an hour before your arrival, the lady who supped with you came hither, and engaged this suite of apartments for a nobleman of high rank, travelling *incognito*, as she called it. She paid me beforehand. I was now in the secret. It was plain enough what sort of people Camilla and Don Raphael were; and I conjectured that my servant, having wormed himself into a complete knowledge of my concerns, had betrayed me to these impostors. Instead of blaming myself for this sad accident, and considering that it could never have happened but for my indiscretion in so unnecessarily betraying my confidence to Majuelo, I gave bad language to the poor harmless dame fortune, and cursed my ill star in a hundred different formularies. The master of the ready-furnished lodging, to whom I related the adventure, which perhaps was as much his as mine, showed some little outward sensibility to my affliction. He lamented over me, and protested he was deeply mortified that such a play should have been acted in his house; but I verily believe, notwithstanding his fine words, that he had an equal share in the cheat with mine host at Burgos, to whom I have never denied the merit of so ingenious an invention.

CHAPTER XVII.

THE MEASURES GIL BLAS TOOK AFTER THE ADVENTURE OF THE READY-FURNISHED LODGING.

AFTER the first transports of my grief were over, I began to consider, that instead of giving way to remorse, I ought rather to bear up against my ill fate. I summoned back my resolution, and, by way of comfort, said to myself as I was dressing—I am still in luck that the knaves have not carried off my clothes and what little money I had in my pocket. I gave them some credit for being so considerate. They had even been generous enough to leave me my boots, which I parted with to the landlord for a third of their cost. At last I sallied out of the ready-furnished lodging, unencumbered, heaven be praised, with baggage or attendance. The first thing I did was to go and see if my mules were still at the inn where we alighted the evening before. It was not to be supposed that Ambrose would have neglected a due attention to them; and it would have been well for me if I had always taken such exact measure of his character. I learned that he had not waited for the morning, but had been careful to fetch them by over night. Under these circumstances, satisfied I should never see them again, any more than my portmanteau, I walked sulkily along the streets, musing on the future plans I should adopt. I was tempted to go back to Burgos, and once more have recourse to Donna Mencia; but, regarding this as an abuse of that lady's goodness, and being aware, moreover, what a fool I should look like, I thought it best to forego that idea. I made a vow too for the future to be on my guard against women. I could have sent the chaste Susanna to the house of correction. From time to time my ring caught my eye, it was a present from Camilla! and I was ready to burst with anguish. Alas! thought I, I am no judge of jewelry, but I shall be by experience of these hucksters who exchange without a robbery. I need not go to a jeweler to be told I am an ass! I can see my own face in my ruby.

Yet I did not neglect to know the truth respecting the value of my ring, and showed it to a lapidary, who rated it at three ducats. At such an estimate, though as much as I expected, I made a formal surrender to the devil, of the Philippine isles, the governor and his niece or rather, I only restored his own subjects to their lawful sovereign. As I was going out of the lapidary's shop a young fellow brushed by me, and on looking round, made a full stop. I could not recollect his name at first, though his features were perfectly familiar to me. How now, Gil Blas, said he, are you ashamed of an old acquaintance? or have two years so altered the son of Nunez the barber, that you do not know him? Do not you recollect Fabricio, your townsman and schoolfellow? How often have we kept, before Doctor Godinez, upon universals and metaphysics!

These words did not flow so fast as my recollection, and we embraced with mutual good-will. Well, my friend, resumed he, I am overjoyed to meet with you. Words fall short. . . . . But how is this? Why, you look like—as heaven is my judge, you are dressed like a grandee! A gentleman's sword, silk stockings, a velvet doublet and cloak, embroidered with silver! Plague take it! this is getting on in the world with a vengeance. I will lay a wager you are in with some old moneyed harridan. You reckon without a host, said I, my affairs are not so prosperous as you imagine. That will not do for me, replied he, I know better things; but you have a mind to be close. And that fine ruby on your finger, master Gil Blas, whence comes that, if I may be so bold? It comes, quoth I, from an infernal jade. Fabricio, my dear Fabricio, far from being point, quint, and quatorze with the ladies of Valladolid, you are to know, my friend, that I am their complete bubble.

I uttered these last words so ruefully, that Fabricio saw plainly that some trick had been played upon me. He was anxious to learn why I was out of humor with the lovely sex. I had no difficulty in satisfying his curiosity; but as the story was a long one, and besides we had no mind to part in a hurry, we went into a coffee-house to be a little more at ease. There I recounted to him, during breakfast, all that had happened to me since my departure from Oviedo. My adventures he thought whimsical enough; and testifying his sympathy in my present uneasy circumstances, added —We must make the best, my good lad, of all our misfortunes in this life. Is a man of parts in distress? he waits patiently for better luck. Such an one, as Cicero truly observes, never suffers himself to be humbled so low, as to forget that he is a man. For my own part, that is just my character; in or out of favor there is no sinking me; I always float on the surface of ill-luck. For example, I was in love with a girl of some family at Oviedo, and was beloved by her in return. I asked her of her father in marriage, he refused. Many a young fellow would have died of grief; but no ! mark my spirit, I carried off the little baggage. She was lively, heedless, and coquettish: pleasure consequently was always upper-most to the prejudice of duty. I took her with me for six months backwards and forwards about Galicia; thence, adopting my taste for travelling, she had a mind to go to Portugal, but in other com-pany—more food for despair. Yet I did not give in under the weight of this new affliction; but, improving on Menelaus, thought myself much obliged to the Paris who had whispered in the ear of my Helen, for ridding me of a bad bargain; I therefore determined to keep the peace. After that, not finding it convenient to return to the Asturias and balance accounts with justice, I went forward into the kingdom of Leon, spending between one town and another all the loose cash remaining from the rape of my Indian princess; for we had both of us birdlimed our fingers at our departure from Oviedo. I got to Palencia with a solitary ducat, out of which I was obliged to buy a pair of shoes. The remainder would not go far. My situation became rather perplexing. I began already to be re-duced to short allowance; something must be done. I resolved to go out to service. My first place was with a woolen-draper in a large way, whose son was a lad of wit and fashion; here was a com-plete antidote to fasting, but then there was a little awkwardness. The father ordered me to dog the son, the son begged my assist-ance in imposing on the father; it was necessary to take one side or other. Entreaties sound more musical than commands, and my taste for music got me turned out of doors. The next service I entered into was with an old painter, who undertook, as a matter of favor, to teach me the principles of his art; but he was so busy in feeding me with knowledge, that he forgot to give me any meat. This neglect of substance for shadow disgusted me with my abode at Palencia. I came to Valladolid, where, by the greatest good luck in the world, I was hired by a governor of the hospital; I am with him still, and delighted with my quarters. My master, Signor Manuel Ordonnez, is a man of profound piety. He always walks with his eyes cast downwards, and a large rosary in his hand. They say that from his early youth, having been a close inspector of the poor, he has interested himself in their affairs with un-wearied zeal. Charity draws down a blessing on the charitable, everything has prospered with him. What a favorite of heaven! The more he does for the poor, the richer he grows.

As Fabricio was going on in this manner, I interrupted him. It is well you are satisfied with your lot; but, between ourselves, surely you might play your part better in the world. Do not you believe it, Gil Blas, replied he; be assured that for a man of my temper a more agreeable situation could not possibly have been devised. The trade of a lackey is toilsome, to be sure, for a poor creature; but for a lad of spirit it is all enchantment. A superior genius, when he gets a service, does not go about it like a lumpish simpleton. He enters into a family as viceroy over the master, not as an inferior minister. He begins by measuring the length of his employer's foot; by lending himself to his weaknesses, he gains his confidence, and ends with leading him by the nose. Such has been my plan of operation at the governor's. I knew the pilgrim at once by his staff; his wish was for an earthly canonization. I pretended to believe him to be the saint he wished to be taken for, hypocrisy costs nothing. Nay, I went further, for I took pattern by him; and playing the same part before him which he played before others, I out-cozened the cozener, and by degrees got to be *major domo.* I am in hopes some day or other, under his wing, to have the fingering of the poor's-box. It may bring a blessing upon me as well as another; for I have caught the flame from him, and already feel deeply for the interests of charity.

These are fine hopes, my dear Fabricio, replied I; and I congratulate you upon them. For my part, I am determined on my first plan. I shall straightway convert my embroidered suit into a cassock, repair to Salamanca, and there, enlisting under the banner of the university, fulfill the sacred duties of a tutor. A fine scheme! exclaimed Fabricio, a pleasant conceit! What madness, at your age, to turn pedant! Are you aware, you stupid fellow, what you take upon yourself by that choice? As soon as you are settled, all the house will be upon the watch, your most trivial actions will be minutely sifted. You will lead a life of incessant constraint; you must set yourself off with a counterfeit outside and affect to entertain a double set of the cardinal virtues in your bosom. You will not have a moment to bestow on pleasure. The everlasting censor of your pupil, your days will pass in teaching grammar and administering saintly reprehension, when he shall say or do any thing against decorum. After so much labor and confinement, what will be your reward? If the little gentleman is a pickle, they will lay all the blame on your bad management; and you will be kicked out of the family, it may be without your stipend. Do not tell me then of a tutor's employment; it is worse than a cure of souls. But talk as much as you will about a lackey's occupation, that is a sinecure, and pledges you to nothing. Suppose one's master not to be immaculate? A servant of superior genius will flatter his vices, and not unfrequently turn them to account. A footman lives at his ease in a good family. After having ate and drank his fill, he goes to bed peaceably, without troubling himself who pays the bills.

I should never have done, my dear fellow, pursued he, were I to enumerate all the advantages of service. Trust me, Gil Blas, discard for ever your foolish wish of being a tutor, and follow my example. So be it: but, Fabricio, replied I, governors like yours are not to be met with every day; and if resolved to go to service, I should like at least to get a good situation. Oh! you are in the right, said he, and that shall be my concern. I will get you a comfortable place, if it were only to snatch a fine fellow from the jaws of the university.

The near approach of poverty with which I was threatened, and Fabricio's apparent good case, having more weight with me than his arguments, I determined to wear a livery. On which we sallied forth from the tavern, and my townsman said: I am going to introduce you to a man, to whom most of the servants resort when they are on the ramble; he has eaves droppers about him to pick up all that passes in families. He knows at once where the servants are going away, and keeps a correct register, not only of vacant places, but of vacant masters, with their good and bad properties. The fellow has been a friar in some convent or other. In short, he it was who got me my place.

While we were conversing about so singular an office of intelligence, the son of Nunez the barber took me into a street which had no thoroughfare. We went into a mean house, where we found a man about fifty writing at a table. We wished him good-day, with quite as much humility as became us: but, whether it was from natural pride, or that, from a habit of seeing none but lackeys and coachmen, he had got a trick of receiving his company with an easy freedom, without rising from his seat, he just gave a slight nod. He seemed surprised that a young man in embroidered velvet should want a place; he had rather expected me to have wanted a servant. However, he was not kept long in doubt, since Fabricio said at once: Signor Arias de Londona, give me leave to introduce one of my best friends. He is a youth of good connections, whom adverse circumstances have reduced to the necessity of going to service. Have the goodness to provide for him handsomely, and you may trust to his gratitude. Gentlemen, replied Arias coolly, this is the way with you all; before you are settled, you make the finest promises in the world: but afterwards, Lord help us! your memories are very short. The deuce! replied Fabricio, why you do not complain of me? Have not I done the thing genteelly? You ought to have done it much better, rejoined Arias: your place is better than a clerk in a public office, and you paid me as if I had quartered you upon a poor author. Here I interfered, and told Master Arias, that to convince him I was not a shabby fellow, I would make up my acknowledgments beforehand; at the same time taking out two ducats, with an assurance of not stopping there if he got me a good berth.

He seemed to like my mode of dealing. There are, said he, some very good places vacant. I will give you a list of them, and you shall take your choice. With these words, he put on his spectacles, opened a register on the table, turned over a few of the leaves, and began reading to this effect: Captain Torbellino wants a footman; a hasty, hare-brained, humorsome chap; scolds incessantly, swears, kicks his servants, and very often cripples them. Go on to the next, cried I, at this picture; such a captain will never do for me. My sprightliness made Arias smile, and he went on with his catalogue thus: Donna Menuela de Sandoval, a superannuated dowager, peevish and fantastical, is in want at this very time; she keeps but one, and him never for four-and-twenty hours. There has been a livery in the house for these ten years, which fits every new-comer, whether tall or short. They only just try it on; so that it is as good as new, though it has had two thousand owners. Doctor Alvar Fanez wants a journeyman; an eminent member of the faculty! He boards his family very handsomely, has everything comfortable about him, and gives very high wages: but he is a little too fond of experiments. When he gets a parcel of bad drugs, which happens very often, there is a pretty quick succession of new servants.

Oh! I do not in the least doubt it, interrupted Fabricio, with a horse-laugh. Upon my word, you give me a fine character of your customers. Patience, said Arias de Londona; we have not yet got to the end: there is variety enough. Thereupon, he continued to read on: Donna Alfonsa de Solis, an old devotee, who lives two-thirds of her time at church. and always keeps her servant at her apron string, has been in want for these three weeks. The Licentiate Sédillo, an old prebendary of the chapter here, turned away his servant yesterday evening. . . . . Halt there, Signor Arias de Londona, cried Fabricio at that passage; we will stick to the church. The Licentiate Sédillo is one of my master's friends, and I am very well acquainted with him. I know he has for his house-keeper an old hypocrite, called Dame Jacintha, who is complete mistress of the family. It is one of the best houses in Valladolid. A very idle life, and plenty of excellent meat and drink. Besides, his reverence is an old, gouty, infirm man, likely soon to make his will: there is a legacy to be looked after. That is a delightful prospect for one of our cloth! Gil Blas, added he, turning round to me, let us lose no time, my friend, but go immediately to the licentiate's house. I will introduce you myself, and give you a character. At these words, for fear of missing such an opportunity, we took a hasty leave of Signor Arias, who assured me, for my money, that if I failed here, he would do something as good for me elsewhere.

BOOK THE SECOND.

CHAPTER I.

FABRICIO INTRODUCES GIL BLAS TO THE LICENTIATE SÉDILLO, AND PROCURES HIM A RECEPTION. THE DOMESTIC ECONOMY OF THAT CLERGYMAN. PICTURE OF HIS HOUSEKEEPER.

WE were so dreadfully afraid of offending against the regular hours of the old licentiate, that we made but a hop, skip, and jump, from the street with one outlet, to the prebendal residence. The gates were barred: but we ventured to announce our arrival. A girl of ten years old, the housekeeper's professed niece, and slander could not gainsay the relationship, opened the door to us. As we asked to speak with his reverence, Dame Jacintha made her appearance. She was a lady of ripe person and parts, but by no means past her prime; and I was particularly attracted by the clearness of her complexion. She wore a long woolen gown of the most ordinary quality, with a large leathern girdle, whence hung suspended a bunch of keys on one side, and on the other a tremendous string of beads. As soon as we got a glimpse of her, we made our obeisances with all possible reverence. She returned our salutation with similar good breeding, but with an air of modesty, and eyes communing with the ground.

I have been told, said my fellow servant, that the reverend the Licentiate Sédillo wants an honest lad, and I have one at his service with whom he will be well satisfied. The superintendent of the household turned up her eyes at these words with a significant side glance at me, and, finding it difficult to reconcile my laced jacket with Fabricio's exordium, asked if it was this fine gentleman who was come after the place. Yes, said the son of Nunez, it is this interesting and engaging youth. Just as you see him, the ups and downs of this transitory life have compelled him to wear an epaulette; but fate will have made him ample amends, added he, with an affected languish, if he is so happy as to be an inmate here, and to profit by the society of the virtuous Jacintha. The patriarch of the Indies might have sighed for the virtuous Jacintha at the head of his establishment. At these words, this withered branch of piety withdrew her penetrating regards from me, to contemplate this courteous spokesman. Struck with certain lines which were not new to her, in his face, I have some floating idea of having seen you before, said she; but my memory wants a lift. Holy Jacintha, replied Fabricio, it is enough for me to have been blessed with your pious notice. Twice have I been under this venerable roof with my master, Signor Manuel Ordonnez, governor of the hospital. Ah! just so, answered the lady chamberlain, I recollect! You are an old acquaintance. Well-a-day now! Your very belonging to Signor Ordonnez is enough to prove you a youth of merit and strict propriety. A servant is known by his place, and this lad could not have had a better sponsor. Come along with me; I will introduce you to Signor Sédillo. I am sure he will be glad to engage a lad at your recommendation.

We followed Dame Jacintha. The canon lived in the lower part of the house, in a comfortable suite of wainscoted apartments. She begged us to wait a moment in the ante-chamber, while she went into the licentiate's room. After some private parley with him, merely that he might know what he was about, she came to tell us we might walk in. We kenned the old cripple, immersed in an elbow chair, with a pillow under his head, cushions under his arms, and his legs supported on a large stool, stuffed with down. We were no niggards of our bows as we advanced; and Fabricio, still taking the lead, not only repeated over again what he had said to the housekeeper, but set about extolling my merit, and expatiated in an especial manner on the honors I had gained in the schools under Doctor Godinez on all metaphysical questions: as if it was necessary for a prebendary's footman to be as learned as his master. However that might be, it served as a tub to the whale. Besides, Dame Jacintha did not look forbidding, and my surety received the following answer: Friend, I receive into my service the lad you recommend. I like him well enough, and as for his morals, they cannot be much amiss, since he presents himself under the wing of a domestic belonging to Signor Ordonnez.

As soon as Fabricio saw me safe landed, he made a low bow to the prebendary, a still lower to the lady, and withdrew in high good humor, whispering in my ear that we should meet again, and that I had only to make good my footing. As soon as he had left the room, the licentiate inquired my name, why I had left my native place; and drew me on by his questions to relate my adventures before Dame Jacintha. They were both highly amused, above all by my last rencounter. Camilla and Don Raphael gave such play to their risible muscles, that I thought old chalkstone would have burst: for, as he laughed with all his might, so violent a cough laid hold of him, as went very near to have carried him off. His will was not made. What an alarm for the housekeeper! Trembling, distracted, off she flew to the good man's succor, and just like a nurse with a puking child, paddled about his forehead and tapped him on the back. Luckily it was a false alarm; the old gentleman left off coughing, and the housekeeper tormenting him. When it was over, I was for going on with my narrative; but Dame Jacintha, in awe of a second fit, set herself against it. She therefore took me with her out of the room to a wardrobe, where, among several suits, was that of my predecessor. This I was to take, and leave my own in its room, which I was not sorry to see laid up safe, in the hope it might be of further use. After this, we went together to get dinner ready.

I knew what I was about in the art of dressing meat. Dame Leonarda, with whom I had served my time, might have passed for a very decent plain cook; but a mere turnspit to Dame Jacintha. The latter might almost have borne away the bell from the archbishop of Toledo's man. She was mistress of every thing; gravy soups of the most delicious texture and relish; and, for made dishes, she could season them up or soften them down to the most delicate or voluptuous palate. At dinner-time we returned to his reverence's apartment. While I was arranging the grand concern close by his arm-chair, the lady of all work crammed a napkin under the old boy's chin, and pinned it behind his back. Without losing a moment, in marched I with a stew, fit to be set before the first gourmand in Madrid, and two courses, to have tickled the gills of a viceroy, only that Dame Jacintha had touched the spice-box with discretion for fear of exasperating the gout. At the first glimpse of this goodly mess, my old master, whom I conceived to have lost the use of his limbs, made me to understand that his arms were exempted from the interdict. He availed himself of their assistance, to get clear of his pillow and cushions, and proceeded gayly to the attack. His hand shook, to be sure; but somehow or other it contrived to do its duty. He sent it backwards and forwards fast enough; though it brought but half its cargo to the landing-place at a lading: the table-cloth and napkin took toll. I carried off the soup when he had done, and brought in a partridge flanked by two roast quails, which Dame Jacintha cut up for him,

She took care to make him take a good draught of wine, a little lowered at proper intervals, out of a large, deep, silver cup, which she held to his mouth, as if he had been an infant. He winged the partridge, and came down slap-dash upon all the rest of the dishes. When he had done cramming, that saint of the saucepan unpinned his napkin, reinstated his pillow and cushions; then, leaving him composed in his arm-chair to the enjoyment of his usual nap after dinner, we took away, and demolished the remainder with appetites worthy of our master.

The dinner of to-day was the ordinary bill of fare. Our canon played the best knife and fork in the chapter. But the supper was a mere bauble; seldom more than a chicken and a little confectionery. I larded my inside in this house, and led a good easy life. There was but one awkward circumstance; and that was sitting up with my master, to save the expense of a nurse. Besides a strangury, which kept him on the fidget ten times in an hour, he was very much given to perspire; and in that event, I shifted him. Gil Blas, said he, on the second night, you are an active, clever fellow; I foresee that we shall jog on very well together. I only just give you a hint to keep in with Dame Jacintha; the girl has been about me for these fifteen years, and manages all my little matters; she comforts my outward man, and I cannot do too much for her. For that reason, you are to know, that she is more to me than all my family. There is my nephew, my own sister's son; why, I have turned him out of doors, only to please her. He had no regard for the poor lass: and so far from giving her credit for all her little assiduities, the saucy rascal swore she did not care a farthing for me! But nowadays, young people think virtue and gratitude all a farce. Heaven be praised, I am rid of the varlet. What claim has blood, in comparison with unquestionable attachment? I am influenced by a give-and-take principle in my connections. You are right, sir, replied I; gratitude ought to be the first thing, and natural affection the last. Ay! resumed he; and my will shall be a comment on that text. My housekeeper shall be residuary legatee; and you shall have a corner in a codicil, if you go on as well as you have begun. The footman I turned off yesterday has lost a good legacy, by not knowing where to hit the right nail on the head. If the blockhead had not obliged me, by his ill behavior, to send him packing, I would have made a man of him: but the beggar on horseback gave himself airs to Dame Jacintha! Then master lazybones did not like sitting up! I might pass the night as I could, provided he had no trouble with me. Oh! the unfeeling scoundrel! exclaimed I, in the true spirit of Fabricio, he was not a man to be about so good a master. The lad for your money should be a humble, but confidential friend; he should not make a toil of what ought to be a pleasure, but think nothing of going through fire and water for your ease.

These professions were not lost upon the licentiate. Neither were my assurances of due submission to Dame Jacintha's authority less acceptable. Puffing myself off for a servant, who was not afraid of work, I got through my business as cheerfully as I could. I never complained of my nursery. Though to be sure it was irksome enough; and if the legacy had not settled my stomach, I should have sickened at the nature of my employment. It is true I got some hours' rest during the day. The housekeeper, to do her justice, was kind enough to me; owing to the insinuating manner in which I wormed myself into her good graces. Suppose me at table, with her and her niece Inésilla! I changed their plates, filled their glasses, never thought of my own dinner before they had everything they wanted. This was the way to thrive in their esteem. One day when Dame Jacintha was gone to market, finding myself alone with Inésilla, I began to make myself agreeable. Were her father and mother alive? Oh! no, answered she; they have been dead this long, long time; for my good aunt says they have, and I have never seen them. I religiously believed the little innocent, though her answer was not of the clearest; and she got into such a humor of talking, as to tell me more than I wanted to know. She informed me, or rather I inferred it from her artless simplicity, that her good aunt had a good friend, who lived likewise with an old canon. The temporalities of the church were under his administration; and these lucky domestics reckoned upon entwining the spoils of their masters round the pillars of the hymeneal temple, into whose sanctuary they had penetrated by anticipation. Dame Jacintha, as I have said before, though a little stricken in years, had still some bloom. To be sure, she spared no pains to cherish it : besides daily evacuations, she took plentiful doses of all-powerful jelly. She got her sleep in the night too, while I sat up with my master. But what perhaps contributed most to the freshness of this everlasting flower, was an issue in each leg, of which I should never have known, but for that blab Inésilla.

CHAPTER II.

THE CANON'S ILLNESS; HIS TREATMENT; THE CONSEQUENCE · THE LEGACY TO GIL BLAS.

I STAID three months with the Licentiate Sédillo, without complaining of bad nights. At the end of that time he fell sick. The distemper was a fever; and it inflamed the gout. For the first time in his life, which had been long, he called in a physician. Doctor Sangrado was sent for; the Hippocrates of Valladolid. Dame Jacintha was for sending for the lawyer first, and touched that string; but the patient thought it was time enough, and had a little will of his own upon some points. Away I went therefore for Doctor Sangrado; and brought him with me. A tall, withered, wan executioner of the sisters three, who had done all their justice for at least these forty years! This learned forerunner of the undertaker had an aspect suited to his office : his words were weighed to a scruple; and his jargon sounded grand in the ears of the uninitiated. His arguments were mathematical demonstrations; and his opinions had the merit of originality.

After studying my master's symptoms, he began with medical solemnity: The question here is, to remedy an obstructed perspiration. Ordinary practitioners, in this case, would follow the old routine of salines, diuretics, volatile salts, sulphur and mercury; but purges and sudorifics are a deadly practice! Chemical preparations are edged tools in the hands of the ignorant. My methods are more simple, and more efficacious. What is your usual diet? I live pretty much upon soups, replied the canon, and eat my meat with a good deal of gravy. Soups and gravy! exclaimed the petrified doctor. Upon my word, it is no wonder you are ill. High living is a poisoned bait; a trap set by sensuality, to cut short the days of wretched man. We must have done with pampering our appetites: the more insipid, the more wholesome. The human blood is not a gravy! Why then you must give it such a nourishment as will assimilate with the particles of which it is composed. You drink wine, I warrant you? Yes, said the licentiate, but diluted. Oh! finely diluted, I dare say, rejoined the physician. This is licentiousness with a vengeance! A frightful course of feeding! Why, you ought to have died years ago. How old are you? I am in my sixty-ninth year, replied the canon. So I thought, quoth the practitioner, a premature old age is always the consequence of intemperance. If you had only drank clear water all your life, and had been contented with plain food, boiled apples for instance, you would not have been a martyr to the gout, and your limbs would have performed their functions with lubricity. But I do not despair of setting you on your legs again, provided you give yourself up to my management. The licentiate promised to be upon his good behavior.

Sangrado then sent me for a surgeon of his own choosing, and took from him six good porringers of blood, by way of a beginning, to remedy this obstinate obstruction. He then said to the surgeon; Master Martin Onez, you will take as much more three hours hence, and to-morrow you will repeat the operation. It is a mere vulgar error, that the blood is of any use in the system; the faster you draw it off the better. A patient has nothing to do but to keep himself quiet; with him, to live is merely not to die; he has no more occasion for blood than a man in a trance; in both cases, life consists exclusively in pulsation and respiration. When the doctor had ordered these frequent and copious bleedings, he added a drench of warm water at very short intervals, maintaining that water in sufficient quantities was the grand secret in the materia medica. He then took his leave, telling Dame Jacintha and me, with an air of confidence, that he would answer for the patient's life, if his system was fairly pursued. The housekeeper, though protesting secretly against this new practice, bowed to his superior authority. In fact, we set on the kettles in a hurry; and, as the physician had desired us above all things to give him enough, we began by pouring down two or three pints at as many gulps. An hour after we beset him again; then, returning to the attack time after time, we fairly poured a deluge into his poor stomach. The surgeon, on the other hand, taking out the blood as we put in the water, we reduced the old canon to death's door in less than two days.

This venerable ecclesiastic able to hold it out no longer, as I pledged him in a large glass of his new cordial, said to me in a faint voice—Hold, Gil Blas, do not give me any more, my friend. It is plain death will come when he will come, in spite of water; and, though I have hardly a drop of blood in my veins, I am no better for getting rid of the enemy. The ablest physician in the world can do nothing for us, when our time is expired. Fetch a notary I will make my will. At these last words, pleasing enough to my fancy, I affected to appear unhappy; and concealing my impatience to be gone: Sir, said I, you are not reduced so low, thank God, but you may yet recover. No, no, interrupted he, my good fellow, it is all over. I feel the gout shifting, and the hand of death is upon me. Make haste, and go where I told you. I saw, sure enough, that he changed every moment: and the case was so urgent, that I ran as fast as I could, leaving him in Dame Jacintha's care, who was more afraid than myself of his dying without a will, I laid hold of the first notary I could find; Sir, said I, the Licentiate Sédillo, my master, is drawing near his end; he wants to settle his affairs; there is not a moment to be lost. The notary was a dapper little fellow, who loved his joke; and inquired who was our physician. At the name of Doctor Sangrado, hurrying on his cloak and hat: For mercy's sake! cried he, let us set off with all possible speed; for this doctor dispatches business so fast, that our fraternity cannot keep pace with him. That fellow spoils half my jobs.

With this sarcasm, he set forward in good earnest, and, as we pushed on, to get the start of the grim tyrant, I said to him: Sir, you are aware that a dying testator's memory is sometimes a little short; should my master chance to forget me, be so good as to put in a word in my favor. That I will, my lad, replied the little proctor; you may rely on it. I will urge something handsome, if I have an opportunity. The licentiate, on our arrival, had still all his faculties about him. Dame Jacintha was by his bedside, laying in her tears by wholesale. She had played her game, and bespoken a handsome remembrance. We left the notary alone with my master, and went together into the ante-chamber, where we met the surgeon, sent by the physician for another and a last experiment. We laid hold of him. Stop, Master Martin, said the housekeeper, you cannot go into Signor Sédillo's room just now. He is giving his last orders; but you may bleed away when the will is made.

We were terribly afraid, this pious gentlewoman and I, lest the licentiate should go off with his will half finished; but by good luck, the important deed was executed. We saw the proctor come out, who, finding me on the watch, slapped me on the shoulder, and said with a simper: Gil Blas is not forgotten. At these words, I felt the most lively joy; and was so well pleased with my master for his kind notice, that I promised myself the pleasure of praying for his soul after death, which event happened anon; for the surgeon having bled him once more, the poor old man, quite exhausted, gave up the ghost under the lancet. Just as he was breathing his last. the physician made his appearance, and looked a little foolish, notwithstanding the universality of his death-bed experience. Yet far from imputing the accident to the new practice, he walked off, affirming with intrepidity, that it was owing to their having been too lenient with the lancet, and too chary of their warm water. The medical executioner, I mean the surgeon, seeing that his functions also were at an end, followed Doctor Sangrado.

As soon as we saw the breath out of our patron's body, Dame Jacintha, Inésilla, and myself, joined in a decent chorus of funeral lamentation, loud enough to produce a proper effect in the neighborhood. The emblem of a life to come, though she had more reason than any of us to rejoice, took the soprano part, and screamed out her afflictions in a most pathetic manner. The room in an instant was crowded with people, attracted less by compassion than curiosity. The relations of the deceased no sooner got wind of his departure than they pounced down upon the premises, and sealed up everything. From the housekeeper's distress, they thought there was no will; but they soon found their mistake, and that there was one without a flaw. When it was opened, and they learned the disposition of the testator's principal property, in favor of Dame Jacintha and the little girl, they pronounced his funeral oration in terms not a little disparaging to his memory. They gave a broad apostrophe at the same time to the godly legatee, and a few blessings to me in my turn. It must be owned I had earnèd them. The licentiate, heaven reward him for it, to secure my remembrances through life, expressed himself thus in a paragraph of his will—
Item, as Gil Blas has already some little smattering of literature, to encourage his studious habits, I give and bequeath to him my library, all my books and my manuscripts, without any drawback or exception.

I could not conceive where this said library might be; I had never seen any. I only knew of some papers, with five or six bound books, on two little deal shelves in my master's closet; and that was my legacy. The books too could be of no great use to me; the title of one was, The complete Man Cook; another, A Treatise on Indigestion, with the Methods of Cure; the rest were the four parts of the breviary, half eaten up by the worms. In the article of manuscripts, the most curious consisted of documents relating to a lawsuit in which the prebendary was once engaged for his stall. After having examined my legacy with more minuteness than it deserved, I made over my right and title to these invidious relations. I even renounced my livery, and took back my own suit, claiming my wages as my only reward. I then went to look out for another place. As for Dame Jacintha, besides her residue under the will, she had some snug little articles, which, by the help of her good friend, she had appropriated to her own use during the last illness of the licentiate.

CHAPTER III.

GIL BLAS ENTERS INTO DOCTOR SANGRADO'S SERVICE, AND BE-
COMES A FAMOUS PRACTITIONER.

I DETERMINED to throw myself in the way of Signor Arias de Londona, and to look out for a new berth in his register; but as I was on
my way to No Thoroughfare, who should come across me but Doctor
Sangrado, whom I had not seen since the day of my master's death.
I took the liberty of touching my hat. He kenned me in a twinkling, though I had changed my dress; and with as much warmth
as his temperament would allow him; Hey day! said he, the very
lad I wanted to see; you have never been out of my thought. I
have occasion for a clever fellow about me, and pitched upon you
as the very thing, if you can read and write. Sir, replied, I, if that
is all you require, I am your man. In that case, rejoined he, we
need look no further. Come home with me; it will be all comfort:
I shall behave to you like a brother. You will have no wages, but
everything will be found you. You shall eat and drink according
to the true faith, and be taught to cure all diseases. In a word, you
shall rather be my young Sangrado than my footman.

I closed in with the doctor's proposal, in the hope of becoming
an Esculapius under so inspired a master. He carried me home on
the spur of the occasion, to instal me in my honorable employment; which honorable employment consisted in writing down
the name and residence of the patients who sent for him in his
absence. There had indeed been a register for this purpose, kept
by an old domestic; but she had not the gift of spelling accurately,
and wrote a most perplexing hand. This account I was to keep. It
might truly be called a bill of mortality; for my members all went
from bad to worse during the short time they continued in this system. I was a sort of book-keeper for the other world, to take
places in the stage, and to see that the first come were the first
served. My pen was always in my hand, for Doctor Sangrado had
more practice than any physician of his time in Valladolid. He had
got into reputation with the public by a certain professional slang,
humored by a medical face, and some extraordinary cases, more
honored by implicit faith than scrupulous investigation.

He was in no want of patients, nor consequently of property.
He did not keep the best house in the world: we lived with some
little attention to economy. The usual bill of fare consisted of
peas, beans, boiled apples or cheese. He considered this food as
best suited to the human stomach, that is to say, as most amenable
to the grinders, whence it was to encounter the process of digestion. Nevertheless, easy as was their passage, he was not for stopping the way with too much of them: and, to be sure, he was in
the right. But though he cautioned the maid and me against repletion in respect of solids, it was made up by free permission to

drink as much water as we liked. Far from prescribing us any
limits there, he would tell us sometimes—Drink, my children;
health consists in the pliability and moisture of the parts. Drink
water by pailsful, it is a universal dissolvent; waters liquefies all
the salts. Is the course of the blood a little sluggish? this grand
principle sets it forward; too rapid? its career is checked. Our
doctor was so orthodox on this head, that he drank nothing him-·
self but water, though advanced in years. He defined old age to be
a natural consumption which dries us up and wastes us away: on

SANGRADO.

this principle, he deplored the ignorance of those who call wine old
men's milk. He maintained that wine wears them out and cor-
rodes them, and pleaded with all the force of eloquence against
that liquor, fatal in common both to the young and old, that friend
with a serpent in its bosom, that pleasure with a dagger under its
girdle.

In spite of these fine arguments, at the end of a week a looseness
ensued, with some twinges, which I was blasphemous enough to

saddle on the universal dissolvent, and the new-fashioned diet. I stated my symptoms to my master, in the hope he would relax the rigor of his regimen, and qualify my meals with a little wine, but his hostility to that liquor was inflexible. If you have not philosophy enough, said he, for pure water, there are innocent infusions to strengthen the stomach against the nausea of aqueous quaffings. Sage, for example, has a very pretty flavor: and if you wish to heighten it into a debauch, it is only mixing rosemary, wild poppy, and other simples, but no compounds.

In vain did he crack off his water, and teach me the secret of composing delicious messes. I was so abstemious, that remarking my moderation, he said—In good sooth, Gil Blas, I marvel not that you are no better than you are; you do not drink enough, my friend. Water taken in a small quantity serves only to separate the particles of bile and set them in action; but our practice is to drown them in a copious drench. Fear not, my good lad, lest a superabundance of liquid should either weaken or chill your stomach; far from thy better judgment be that silly fear of unadulterated drink. I will insure you against all consequences; and if my authority will not serve your turn, read Celsus. That oracle of the ancients makes an admirable panegyric on water; in short, he says in plain terms that those who plead an inconstant stomach in favor of wine, publish a libel on their own bowels, and make their organization a pretence for their sensuality.

As it would have been ungenteel in me to have run riot on my entrance into the career of practice, I affected thorough conviction; indeed, I thought there was something in it. I therefore went on drinking water on the authority of Celsus, or, to speak in scientific terms, I began to drown the bile in copious drenches of that unadulterated liquor; and though I felt myself more out of order from day to day, prejudice won the cause against experience. It is evident, therefore, that I was in the right road to the practice of physic. Yet I could not always be insensible to the qualms which increased in my frame, to that degree, as to determine me on quitting Doctor Sangrado. But he invested me with a new office which changed my tone. Hark you, my child, said he to me one day, I am not one of those hard and ungrateful masters, who leave their household to grow grey in service without a suitable reward. I am well pleased with you, I have a regard for you, and without waiting till you have served your time, I will make your fortune. Without more ado, I will initiate you in the healing art, of which I have for so many years been at the head. Other physicians make the science to consist of various unintelligible branches; but I will shorten the road for you, and dispense with the drudgery of studying natural philosophy, pharmacy, botany, and anatomy. Remember, my friend, that bleeding and drinking warm water are the two grand principles; the true secret of curing all the distempers incident to humanity. Yes, this marvellous secret which I reveal to you, and which nature, beyond the reach of my colleagues, has failed in rescuing from my pen, is comprehended in these two articles—namely, bleeding and drenching. Here you have the sum total of my philosophy; you are thoroughly bottomed in medicine, and may raise yourself to the summit of fame on the shoulders of my long experience. You may enter into partnership at once, by keeping the books in the morning, and going out to visit patients in the afternoon. While I dose the nobility and clergy, you shall labor in your vocation among the lower orders; and when you have felt your ground a little, I will get you admitted into our body. You are a philosopher, Gil Blas, though you have never graduated; the common herd of them, though they have graduated in due form and order, are likely to run out the length of their tether without knowing their right hand from their left.

I thanked the doctor for having so speedily enabled me to serve as his deputy; and, by way of acknowledging his goodness, promised to follow his system to the end of my career, with a magnanimous indifference about the aphorisms of Hippocrates. But that engagement was not to be taken to the letter. This tender attachment to water went against the grain, and I had a scheme for drinking wine every day snugly among the patients. I left off wearing my own suit a second time, to take up one of my master's, and look like an inveterate practitioner. After which I brought my medical theories into play, leaving them to look to the event whom it might concern. I began on an alguazil in a pleurisy; he was condemned to be bled with the utmost rigor of the law, at the same time that the system was to be replenished copiously with water. Next I made a lodgment in the veins of a gouty pastry-cook, who roared like a lion by reason of gouty spasms. I stood on no more ceremony with his blood than with that of the alguazil, and laid no restriction on his taste for simple liquids. My prescriptions brought me in twelve rials; an incident so auspicious in my professional career, that I only wished for the plagues of Egypt on all the hale subjects of Valladolid. I was coming out of the pastry-cook's whom should I meet but Fabricio, a total stranger since the death of the licentiate Sédillo! He looked at me with astonishment for some seconds; then set up a laugh with all his might, and held his sides. He had no reason to be grave, for I had a cloak trailing on the ground, with a doublet and breeches of four times my natural dimensions. I was certainly a complete original. I suffered him to make merry as long as he liked, and could scarcely help joining in the ridicule; but I kept a guard on my muscles to preserve a becoming dignity in public, and the better to enact the physician, whose part in society is not that of a buffoon. If the absurdity of my appearance excited Fabricio's merriment, my affected gravity added zest to it; and when he had nearly exhausted his lungs—By all the powers, Gil Blas, quoth he, thou art in complete masquerade. Who the devil has dressed you up in this manner? Fair and softly, my friend, replied I, fair and softly, be a little on your good behavior with a modern Hippocrates. Understand me to be the substitute of Doctor Sangrado, the most eminent physician in Valladolid. I have lived with him these three weeks. He has bottomed me thoroughly in medicine; and, as he cannot perform the obsequies of all the patients who send for him, I visit a part of them to take the burden off his conscience. He does execution in great families, I among the vulgar. Vastly well, replied Fabricio; that is to say, he grants you a lease on the blood of the commonalty, but keeps to himself the fee-simple of the fashionable world. I wish you joy of your lot; it is a pleasanter line of practice among the populace than among great folk. Long live a snug connection in the suburbs! a man's mistakes are easily buried, and his murders elude all but God's revenge. Yes, my brave boy, your destiny is truly enviable in the language of Alexander, were I not Fabricio, I could wish to be Gil Blas.

To show the son of Nunez, the barber, that he was not much out in his reckoning on my present happiness, I chinked the fees of the alguazil and the pastry-cook; and this was followed by an adjournment to a tavern, to drink to their perfect recovery. The wine was very fair, and my impatience for the well-known smack made me think it better than it was. I took some good long draughts, and without gainsaying the Latin oracle, in proportion as I poured it into its natural reservoir, I felt my accommodating entrails to owe me no grudge for the hard service into which I pressed them. As for Fabricio and myself, we sat some time in the tavern, making merry at the expense of our masters, as servants are too much accustomed to do. At last, seeing the night approach, we parted, after engaging to meet at the same place on the following day after dinner.

CHAPTER IV.

GIL BLAS GOES ON PRACTISING PHYSIC WITH EQUAL SUCCESS AND ABILITY. ADVENTURE OF THE RECOVERED RING.

I WAS no sooner at home than Doctor Sangrado came in. I talked to him about the patients I had seen, and paid into his hands eight remaining rials of the twelve I had received for my prescriptions. Eight rials! said he, as he counted them, mighty little for two visits! But we must take things as we find them. In the spirit of taking things as he found them, he laid violent hands on six, giving me the other two - Here, Gil Blas, continued he, see what a foundation to build upon. I make over to you the fourth of all you may bring me. You will soon feather your nest, my friend; for, by the blessing of Providence, there will be a great deal of ill health this year.

I had reason to be content with my dividend; since, having determined to keep back the third part of what I received in my rounds, and afterwards touching another fourth of the remainder, half of the whole, if arithmetic is anything more than a deception, would become my perquisite. This inspired me with new zeal for my profession. The next day, as soon as I had dined, I resumed my medical paraphernalia, and took the field once more. I visited several patients on the list, and treated their several complaints in one invariable routine. Hitherto things went on under the rose, and no individual, thank heaven, had risen up in rebellion against my prescriptions. But let a physician's cures be as extraordinary as they will, some quack or other is always ready to rip up his reputation. I was called in to a grocer's son in a dropsy. Whom should I find there before me but a little black-looking physician, by name Doctor Cuchillo, introduced by a relation of the family. I bowed round most profoundly, but dipped lowest to the personage whom I took to have been invited to a consultation with me. He returned my compliment with a distant air; then, having stared me in the face for a few seconds—Signor Doctor, said he, I beg pardon for being inquisitive, I thought I had been acquainted with all my brethren in Valladolid, but I confess your physiognomy is altogether new. You must have been settled but a short time in town. I avowed myself a young practitioner, acting as yet under the direction of Doctor Sangrado. I wish you joy, replied he politely, you are studying under a great man. You must doubtless have seen a vast deal of sound practice, young as you appear to be. He spoke this with so easy an assurance, that I was at a loss whether he meant it seriously, or was laughing at me. While I was conning over my reply, the grocer, seizing on the opportunity, said—Gentlemen, I am persuaded of your both being perfectly competent in your art; have the goodness without ado to take the case in hand, and devise some effectual means for the restoration of my son's health.

Thereupon the little pulse-counter set himself about reviewing the patient's situation; and after having dilated to me on all the symptoms, asked me what I thought the fittest method of treatment. I am of opinion, replied I, that he should be bled once a day, and drink as much warm water as he can swallow. At these words, our diminutive doctor said to me with a malicious simper—And so you think such a course will save the patient? Never doubt it, exclaimed I in a confident tone; it must produce that effect, because it is a certain method of cure for all distempers. Ask Signor Sangrado. At that rate, retorted he, Celsus is altogether in the wrong; for he contends that the readiest way to cure a dropsical subject is to let him almost die of hunger and thirst. Oh! as for Celsus, interrupted I, he is no oracle of mine, as fallible as the meanest of us, I often have occasion to bless myself for going contrary to his dogmas. I discover by your language, said Cuchillo, the safe and sure method of practice Doctor Sangrado instils into his pupils. Bleeding and drenching are the extent of his resources. No wonder so many worthy people are cut off under his direction. . . . . No defamation! interrupted I with some acrimony: a member of the faculty had better not begin throwing stones. Come, come, my learned doctor, patients can get to the other world without bleeding and warm water; and I question whether the most deadly of us has ever signed more passports than yourself. If you have any crow to pluck with Signor Sangrado, write against him, he will answer you, and we shall soon see who will have the best of the battle. By all the saints in the calendar! swore he, in a transport

of passion, you little know whom you are talking to. I have a
tongue and a fist, my friend; and am not afraid of Sangrado, who
with all his arrogance and affectation, is but a ninny. The size of
the little death-dealer made me hold his anger cheap. I gave him
a sharp retort he sent back as good as I brought, till at last we
came to cuffs. We had pulled a few handfuls of hair from each
other's heads before the grocer and his kinsman could part us.
When they had brought this about, they feed me for my atten-

"PULLED A FEW HANDFULS OF HAIR FROM EACH OTHER'S HEADS."

dance, and retained my antagonist, whom they thought the more
skilful of the two.

Another adventure succeeded close on the heels of this. I went
to see a huge chanter in a fever. As soon as he heard me talk of
warm water, he showed himself so averse to this specific, as to fall
into a fit of swearing. He abused me in all possible shapes, and
threatened to throw me out at window. I was in a greater hurry
to get out of his house than to get in. I did not choose to see any
more patients that day, and repaired to the inn where I had agreed

to meet Fabricio. He was there first. As we found ourselves in a tippling humor, we drank hard, and returned to our employers in a pretty pickle, that is to say, so-so in the upper story. Signor Sangrado was not aware of my being drunk, because he teok the lively gestures which accompanied the relation of my quarrel with the little doctor, for an effect of the agitation not yet subsided after the battle. Besides, he came in for his share in my report; and feeling himself nettled by Cuchillo—You have done well, Gil Blas said he, to defend the character of our practice against this little abortion of the faculty. So he takes upon him to set his face against watery drenches in dropsical cases? An ignorant fellow! I maintain, I do, in my own person, that the use of them may be reconciled to the best theories. Yes, water is a cure for all sorts of dropsies, just as it is good for rheumatisms and the green sickness. It is excellent, too, in those fevers where the effect is at once to parch and to chill, and even miraculous in those disorders ascribed to cold, thin, phlegmatic, and pituitous humors. This opinion may seem strange to young practitioners like Cuchillo; but it is right orthodox in the best and soundest systems : so that if persons of that description were capable of taking a philosophical view, instead of crying me down, they would become my most zealous advocates.

In his rage, he never suspected me of drinking : for, to exasperate him still more against the little doctor, I had thrown into my recital some circumstances of my own addition. Yet, engrossed as he was by what I had told him, he could not help taking notice that I drank more water than usual that evening.

In fact, the wine had made me very thirsty, Any one but Sangrado would have distrusted my being so very dry, as to swallow down glass after glass : but as for him, he took it for granted, in the simplicity of his heart, that I began to acquire a relish for aqueous potations. Apparently, Gil Blas, said he with a gracious smile, you have no longer such a dislike to water. As heaven is my judge! you quaff it off like nectar. It is no wonder, my friend, I was certain you would take a liking to that liquor. Sir, replied I, there is a tide in the affairs of men : with my present lights, I would give all the wine in Valladolid for a pint of water. This answer delighted the doctor, who would not lose so fine an opportunity of expatiating on the excellence of water. He undertook to ring the changes once more in its praise, not like a hireling pleader, but as an enthusiast in the cause. A thousand times, exclaimed he, a thousand and a thousand times of greater value, as being more innocent than our modern taverns, were those baths of ages past, whither the people went not shamefully to squander their fortunes and expose their lives, by swilling themselves with wine but assembled there for the decent and economical amusement of drinking warm water. It is difficult enough to admire the patriotic forecast of those ancient politicians, who established places of public resort, where water was dealt out gratis to all comers, and who confined wine to the shops of the apothecaries, that its use might be prohibited but under the direction of physicians. What a stroke of wisdom! It is doubtless to preserve the seeds of that antique frugality, emblematic of the golden age, that persons are found to this day, like you and me, who drink nothing but water, and are persuaded they possess a prevention or a cure for every ailment, provided our warm water has never boiled; for I have observed that water, when it has boiled, is heaviest, and sits less easily on the stomach.

While he was holding forth thus eloquently, I was in danger more than once of splitting my sides with laughing. But I con trived to keep my countenance: nay, more; to chime in with the doctor's theory. I found fault with the use of wine, and pitied mankind for having contracted an untoward relish to so pernicious a beverage. Then, finding my thirst not sufficiently allayed, I filled a large goblet with water, and after having swilled it like a horse: Come, sir, said I to my master, let us drink plentifully of this beneficial liquor. Let us make those early establishments of dilution you so much regret, to live again in your house. He clapped his hands in ecstacy at these words, and preached to me for a whole hour about suffering no liquid but water to pass my lips. To confirm the habit, I promised to drink a large quantity every evening; and, to keep my word with less violence to my private inclinations, I went to bed with a determined purpose of going to the tavern every day.

The trouble I had got into at the grocer's did not discourage me from phlebotomizing and prescribing warm water in the usual course. Coming out of a house where I had been visiting a poet in a phrenzy, I was accosted in the street by an old woman who came up and asked me if I was a physician. I said yes. As that is the case, replied she, I entreat you with all humility to go along with me. My niece has been ill since yesterday, and I cannot conceive what is the matter with her. I followed the old lady to her house, where I was shown into a very decent room, occupied by a female who kept her bed. I went near, to consider her case. Her features struck me from the first; and I discovered beyond the possibility of a mistake, after having looked at her some little time, the she-adventurer who had played the part of Camilla so adroitly. For her part, she did not seem to recollect me at all, whether from the oppression of her disorder, or from my dress as a physician rendering me not easy to be known again. I took her by the hand, to feel her pulse; and saw my ring upon her finger. I was all in a twitter at the discovery of a valuable, on which I had a claim both in law and equity. Great was my longing to make a snatch at it; but considering that these fair ones would set up a great scream, and that Don Raphael or some other defender of injured innocence might rush in to their rescue, I laid an embargo on my privateering. I thought it best to come by my own in an honest way, and to consult Fabricio about the means. To this last course I stuck. In the mean time the old woman urged me to inform her with what disease her niece was troubled. I was not fool enough to own my ignorance; on the contrary, I took upon myself as a man of science, and after my master's example, pronounced solemnly that the dis-

order accrued to the patient from the defect of natural perspiration; that consequently she must lose blood as soon as possible,
because if we could not open one pore, we always open another,
and I finished my prescription with warm water, to do the thing
methodically.

I shortened my visit as much as possible, and ran to the son of
Nunez, whom I met just as he was going out on an errand for his
master. I told him my new adventure, and asked his advice about
laying an information against Camilla. Pooh! Nonsense! replied
he, that would not be the way to get your ring again. Those
gentry think restitution double trouble. Call to mind your imprisonment at Astorga: your horse, your money, your very clothes, did not
they all centre in the hands of justice? We must rather set our wits
to work for the recovery of your diamond. I take on myself the
charge of inventing some stratagem for that purpose. I will delib-
erate on it in my way to the hospital, where I have to say but two
words from my master to the purveyor. Do you wait for me at
our house of call, and do not be on the fret: I will be with you
shortly

I had waited, however, more than three hours at the appointed
place, when he arrived. I did not know him again at first. Besides that he had changed his dress and plaited his hair, a pair of
false whiskers covered half his face. He wore an immense sword
with a hilt of at least three feet in circumference, and marched at
the head of five men of as swaggering an air as himself, with bushy
whiskers and long rapiers Good day to you, Signor Gil Blas, said
he by way of salutation behold an alguazil upon a new construction, and marshalmen of like materials in these brave fellows my
companions. We have only to be shown where the woman lodges
who purloined the diamond, and we will obtain restitution, take
my word for it. I hugged Fabricio at this discourse, which let me
into the plot and testified loudly my approval of the expedient. I
paid my respects also to the masquerading marshalmen. They
were three servants and two journeymen barbers of his acquaintance, whom he had engaged to act this farce. I ordered wine to
be served round to the detachment, and we all went together at
night-fall to Camilla's residence. The door was shut, and we
knocked The old woman taking my companions to be on the
scent of justice, and knowing they would not come into that neighborhood for nothing was terribly frightened. Cheer up again, good
mother said Fabricio we are only come here upon a little business which will be soon settled At these words we made our
entry, and found our way to the sick chamber, under the guidance
of the old dowager who walked before us, and by favor of a wax
taper which she carried in a silver candlestick. I took the light,
went to the bed-side, and making Camilla take particular notice of
my features, Traitress, said I, call to mind the too credulous Gil
Blas whom you have deceived Ah! thou wickedness personified,
at last I have caught thee. The corregidor has taken down my deposition, and ordered this alguazil to arrest you. Come, officer,
said I to Fabricio, do your duty. There is no need, replied he,

"THE OLD WOMAN, ON HER KNEES, ENDEAVORED TO MELT
THEIR STUBBORN HEARTS."

swelling his voice, to inflame my severity, The face of that wretch is not new to me; she has long been marked with red letters in my pocket-book. Get up, my princess, dress your royal person with all possible dispatch, I will be your squire, and lodge you in durance vile, if you have no objection.

At these words, Camilla, ill as she was, observing two marshalmen with large whiskers ready to drag her out of bed by main force, sat up of herself, clasped her hands in an attitude of supplication; and looking at me ruefully, said Signor Gil Blas, have compassion on me. I call as a witness to my entreaties the chaste mother whose virtues you inherit. Guilty as I am, my misfortunes are greater than my crimes. I will give you back your diamond, so do not be my ruin. Speaking to this effect, she drew my ring from her finger, and gave it me back. But I told her my diamond was not enough, and that she must refund the thousand ducats they had embezzled in the ready-furnished lodging. Oh! as for your ducats, replied she, ask me not about them. That falsehearted deceiver, Don Raphael, whom I have not seen from that time to this, carried them off the very same night. O ho! my little darling, said Fabricio in his turn, that will not do, you had a hand in the robbery, whether you went snacks in the profit or no. You will not come off so cheaply Your having been accessory to Don Raphael's manœuvres is enough to render you liable to an examination. Your past life is very equivocal; and you must have a good deal upon your conscience. You will have the goodness, if you please, just to step into the town jail, and there unburden yourself by a general confession. This good old lady shall keep you company; it is hard if she cannot tell a world of curious stories, such as Mr. Corregidor will be delighted to hear.

The two women, at these words, brought every engine of pity into play to soften us. They filled the air with cries, complaints, and lamentations. While the old woman on her knees, sometimes to the alguazil and sometimes to his attendants, endeavored to melt their stubborn hearts, Camilla implored me, in the most touching terms, to save her from the hands of justice. I pretended to relent. Officer, said I to the son of Nunez, since I have got my diamond, I do not much care about anything else. It would be no pleasure to me to be the means of pain to that poor woman; I want not the death of a sinner. Out upon you, answered he, you set up for humanity! you would make a bad tipstaff. I must do my errand. My positive orders are to arrest these virgins of the sun; his honor the corregidor means to make an example of them. Nay! for mercy's sake, replied I, pay some little deference to my wishes, and slacken a little of your severity, on the ground of the present these ladies are on the point of offering to your acceptance. Oh! that is another matter, rejoined he; that is what you may call a figure of rhetoric suited to all capacities and all occasions. Well, then, let us see, what have they to give me? I have a pearl necklace, said Camilla, and drop ear-rings of considerable value. Yes, but, interrupted he roughly, if these articles are the produce of the Philippine Isles, I will have none of them.

You may take them in perfect safety, replied she: I warrant them real. At the same time she made the old woman bring a little box, whence she took out the necklace and ear-rings, which she put within the grasp of this incorruptible minister. Though he was much such a judge of jewelry as myself, he had no doubt of the drops being real, as well as the pearls. These trinkets, said he, after having looked at them minutely, seem to be of good quality and fashion : and if the silver candlestick is thrown into the bargain, I would not answer for my own honesty. You had better not, said I in my turn to Camilla, for a trifle, reject so moderate and fair a composition. While uttering these words, I returned the taper to the old woman, and handed the candlestick over to Fabricio, who, stopping there because perhaps he espied nothing else that was portable in the room, said to the two women : Farewell, my dainty misses, set your hearts at rest, I will report you to his worship the corregidor, as purer than unsmutched snow. We can turn him round our finger; and never tell him the truth, but when we are not paid for our lies.

CHAPTER V.

SEQUEL OF THE FOREGOING ADVENTURE.   GIL BLAS RETIRES
    FROM PRACTICE, AND FROM THE NEIGHBORHOOD OF VAL-
    LADOLID.

AFTER having thus carried Fabricio's plan into effect, we took our leave of Camilla's lodging, hugging ourselves on a success beyond our expectation ; for we had only reckoned on the ring. We carried off without ceremony all we could get besides. Far from making it a point of conscience not to steal from a description of ladies whose names are commonly associated with rogues, we thought to cover some scores of other sins by so meritorious an action. Gentlemen, said Fabricio, when we were in the street, my counsel is for returning to our tavern, and devoting the night to a regale. To-morrow we will sell the candlestick, the necklace, the drop ear-rings, and then share the prize money like brother adventurers, after which every man shall tramp home again, and make the best excuse he can to his master. His worship the alguazil's idea seemed equally bright and judicious. We returned rank and file to the tavern, some in the pious hope of finding a plausible excuse for having slept abroad, others in a desperate indifference about being turned out of doors without a character.

We ordered a good supper to be got ready, and sat down to table with our physical and mental powers in full vigor. The relish was heightened by a thousand pleasant anecdotes. Fabricio, of all men in the world, having the happy knack of a chairman in a company of jovial spirits, kept the table in a roar. There escaped from him I know not how many charges of true Castilian wit, worth more either in the schools of philosophy or the exchange of commerce than the drug of Attic salt. While we were in a full pea' of laughter, we were made to laugh on the other side of our mouths by an unforeseen occurrence. There appeared at table a man of no contemptible prowess followed by two other as ill-looking dogs as ever existed. After this specimen we had three others, and reckoned up to a dozen, marching in by triplets. They were armed with carbines, swords, and bayonets. We could not mistake their office, and were at no loss to guess their business. At first we had a mind to be refractory; but they beset us in a instant, and kept us under, as much by their numbers as by their weapons. Gentlemen, said the captain commandant in a jeering strain, I have been informed by what ingenious artifice you have recovered a ring from the custody of a lady no better than she should be. Undoubtedly, the device was admirable, and well deserves a civic crown; the patriotism of our police will not be found wanting. Justice, with her lodgings to let for gentry of your description, will not be deficient in her acknowledgments for so brilliant a display of genius. The company to whom this introductory address was directed, looked a little sheepish on the occasion. Our countenances fell; and Camilla had her full revenge. Fabricio, however, though pale and puzzled, made an attempt at a defence. Sir, said he, we did it in the innocence of our hearts, and of course we shall be forgiven this not immoral fraud? What the devil, replied the commandant in a rage, do you call this a not immoral fraud? Moral or immoral, it may bring you to the gallows. Besides that the power of restitution is too sacred to be assumed by the individual, you have made away with a candlestick, a necklace, and a pair of drop ear-rings: and what is worse, you have committed your rascalities in the livery of the law. Scoundrels dressing themselves up like the pillars of morality to undermine its very foundation! I shall wish you much joy if you are condemned to nothing worse than mowing the salt marsh. When he had impressed it on our convictions that the affair was even more serious than our first fears, we threw ourselves on his mercy, and implored him to have pity on our tender years, but his stubborn heart was relentless. He rejected moreover the proposal of relinquishing the necklace, ear-rings, and candlestick; nay, he was deaf to the rhetoric of my ring: perhaps because I offered it before too many witnesses: in short, he was the most obdurate dog of his kennel. He ordered my companions to be handcuffed, and sent us in a body to the public prison. As we were on our way, one of the marshalmen acquainted me that Camilla's old vixen, suspecting us not to be licensed scouts of justice, had dogged us to the tavern; and having satisfied her doubts, in revenge informed against us to the patrole.

We were searched in the first instance. Away went the necklace, the ear-rings, and the candlestick. They picked my pocket of my ring, and my ruby of the Philippine Isles; without even sparing the few fees I had received in the forenoon for my prescriptions : so that it was plain trade was carried on by the same firm at Valladolid as at Astorga, and that all these reformers held the same creed. While they rifled me of my trinkets and money, the lord in waiting of the patrol made known our adventure to the interior agents of legal rapine. The trespass appeared so audacious that the majority voted it capital. A few kind souls were of opinion that we might come off with two hundred lashes a-piece, with a few years on board the galleys. Waiting his worship's sentence, we were locked up in a cell, where we lay upon straw, spread over our stable like a litter for horses. There might we have foddered for an age, and at last have been turned out to grass in the galleys, if on the morrow Signor Manuel Ordonnez had not got wind of our affair, and determined to release Fabricio ; which he could not do without making a general jail delivery. He was a man of the first credit in the town his interest was exerted for us, and partly by his own influence, and partly by that of his friends, he obtained our enlargement at the end of three days. But the period of delivery is always moulting time with jail birds ; the candlestick, the necklace, the ear-rings, my ring, and the ruby, all was left behind. One could not help repeating those excellent lines of Virgil, beginning with *Sic vos non vobis*.

As soon as we were at liberty we returned to our masters. Doctor Sangrado received me kindly ; My poor Gil Blas, said he, it was but this morning I was acquainted with thy misfortune. I was just setting about an active canvass for thee. We must derive comfort from adversity, my friend, and attach ourselves more than ever to the practice of physic. I affirmed that to be my intention ; and in truth I laid about me. Far from wanting employment, it happened by a kind providence, as my master had foretold, to be a very sickly season. The smallpox and a malignant fever took alternate possession of the town and the suburbs. All the physicians in Valladolid had their share of business, and we not the least. We saw eight or ten patients a day ; so that the kettle was kept on the simmer, and the blood in the action of transpiring. But things will happen cross ; they died to a man, either by our fault or their own. If their case was hopeless, we were not to blame ; and if it was not hopeless, they were. Three visits to a patient was the length of our tether. About the second, we sometimes ran foul of the undertaker ; or when we had been more fortunate than usual, the patient had got no further than the point of death. As I was but a young physician, not yet hardened to the trade of an assassin, I grieved over the melancholy issue of my own theory and practice. Sir, said I, one evening to Doctor Sangrado, I call heaven to witness on the spot that I have never strayed from your infallible method ; and yet I have never saved a patient : one would think they died out of spite, and were on the other side of the great medical question. This very day I came across two of them, going into the country to be buried. My good lad, replied he, my experience nearly comes to the same point. It is but seldom I have the pleasure of curing my kind and partial friends. If I had less con dence in my principles, I should think my prescriptions had set their faces against the work they were intended to perform If you will take a hint, sir, replied I, we had better vary our system. Let us give, by way of experiment, chemical preparations to our patients; the worst they can do is to tread in the steps of our pure dilutions and our phlebotomizing evacuations. I would willingly give it a trial, rejoined he, if it were a matter of indifference, but I have published on the practice of bleeding and the use of drenches; would you have me cut the throat of my own fame as an author! Oh! you are in the right, resumed I; our enemies must not gain this triumph over us; they would say that you were out of conceit with your own systems, and would ruin your reputation for consistency. Perish the people, perish rather our nobility and clergy! But let us go on in the old path. After all, our brethren of the faculty, with all their tenderness about bleeding, have no patent for longevity any more than ourselves; and we may set off their drugs against our specifics.

We went on working double tides, and did so much execution, that in less than six weeks we made as many widows and orphans as the siege of Troy. The plague must have got into Valladolid by the number of funerals. Day after day came some father or other to know what was become of his son, who was last seen in our hands; or else a stupid fellow of an uncle, who had a foolish hankering after a deceased nephew. With respect to the nephews and sons, on whose uncles and fathers we had equalized our system of destruction, they thought that least said was soonest mended. Husbands were altogether on their good behavior, they would not split a hair about the loss of a wife or two. The real sufferers to whose reproaches we were exposed, were sometimes quite savage in their grief; without being mealy-mouthed in their expressions, they called us blockheads and assassins. I was concerned at their bad language; but my master, who was up to every circumstance, listened to their abuse with the utmost indifference. Yet I might have grown as callous as himself to popular reproach, if heaven, interposing its shield between the invalids of Valladolid and one of their scourges, had not providentially raised up an incident to disgust me with medicine, which from the outset had been disgusted with me.

The idle fellows about town assembled every day in our neighborhood for a game at tennis. Among the number was one of those professed bullies who set up for great Dons, and are the complete cocks of the tennis-court. He was a Biscayan, and assumed the title of Don Roderic de Mondragon. His age might be about thirty. His size was somewhat above the common, but he was lean and bony. Besides two sparkling little eyes rolling about in his head, and throwing out defiance against all bystanders, a very broad nose came in between a pair of red whiskers, which turned up like a hook as high as the temples. His phraseology was so rough and uncouth that the very sound of his voice would throw a quiet man into an ague. This tyrant over both the rackets and the game was lord paramount in all disputes between the players; and there was no appeal from his decisions, but at the risk of receiving a challenge the next day. Precisely as I have drawn Signor Don Roderic, whom the Don in the foreground of his titles could never make a gentleman, Signor Don Roderic was sweet upon the mistress of the tennis-court. She was a woman of forty, in good circumstances, as charming as forty can well be, just entering on the second year of her widowhood. I know not how he made himself agreeable; certainly not by his exterior recommendations, but probably by that within which passeth show. However that might be, she took a fancy to him, and began to turn her thoughts towards the holy state of matrimony; but while that great event was in agitation, for the punishment of her sins she was taken with a malignant fever, and with me for a physician. Had the disorder been ever so slight, my practice would have made a serious job of it. At the expiration of four days there was not a dry eye in the tennis-court. The mistress joined the outward-bound colony of my patients, and her family administered to her effects. Don Roderic, distracted at the loss of his mistress, or rather disappointed of a good establishment, was not satisfied with fretting and fuming at me, but swore he would run me through the body, or even frown me into a nonentity. A good-natured neighbor apprised me of this vow, with a caution to keep at home, for fear of coming across this devil of a fellow. This warning, though taken in good part, was a source of anxiety and apprehension. I was eternally fancying the enraged Biscayan laying siege to the outworks of my citadel, There was no getting a moment's respite from alarm. This circumstance weaned me from the practice of medicine, and I thought of nothing but deliverance from my horrors. On went my embroidered suit once more. Taking leave of my master, who did all he could to detain me, I got out of town with the dawn, not heedless of that terrible Don Roderic, who might waylay me on the road.

CHAPTER VI.

HIS ROUTE FROM VALLADOLID, WITH A DESCRIPTION OF HIS FELLOW-TRAVELER.

I TRUDGED on at a great rate, and looked behind from time to time, to see if that dreadful Biscayan was not following me. My imagination was so engrossed by the fellow, that he haunted me in every tree and bush; my heart was in my mouth for fear of every foot-fall. But I took courage again at the distance of about a league, and went on more gently towards Madrid, whither I proposed directing my steps. I had no attachment to Valladolid. All my regret was at tearing myself from Fabricio, my dear Pylades, of whom I had not so much as taken my leave. It was no grievance to give up physic; on the contrary, I prayed heaven to forgive me for having tampered with it. Yet I did not count over the contents of my purse with less pleasure, because they were the wages of murder. In this I took after those ladies who retire with a fortune to lead pious lives, and think it hard if they may not fatten religiously on the hard earnings of their libertine profession. I had, in rials, somewhere about the value of five ducats, and this was the sum total of my property. With these I designed reparing to Madrid, where I had no doubt of finding a good service. Besides, I wished above all things to be in that magnificent city, the boasted epitome of the world and all its wonders.

While I was recollecting what I have heard of it, and enjoying beforehand the pleasures it affords, I heard the voice of a man coming after me, and singing till he had scraped his throat. He had a wallet on his back, a guitar suspended from his neck, and a long sword by his side. He got on at such a rate, as soon to overtake me. Who should it be but one of the two journeymen barbers with whom I had been in jail for the adventure of the ring. We knew one another at once, though we had shifted our dresses, and were in a thousand marvels at meeting so unexpectedly on the highway. If I testified my delight at having such a fellow-traveler, he seemed on his side to feel an excess of rapture at the renewal of our acquaintance. I told him why I had left Valladolid, and he trusted his own secret to me in return, by stating himself to have had a little brush with his master, on which they had taken an everlasting leave of one another. Has it been my pleasure, continued he, to have taken up my abode longer in Valladolid, ten shops would take me in for one that would have turned me out; since, vanity apart, I may safely say there is not a barber in all Spain better qualified to shave all sorts of beards, with the grain or against the grain, and to curl a pair of whiskers. But I could no longer fight against a hankering after my native place, whence I departed full ten years since. I wish to inhale a little of my own country air, and to learn the present situation of my family. I shall be among them the day after to-morrow, at a place called Olmédo, a populous village on this side of Segovia.

I resolved on accompanying this barber home, and going to Segovia for the chance of a cast to Madrid. We began entertaining one another with indifferent subjects as we went along. The young fellow was perfectly good-humored, with a ready wit. After an hour's conversation, he asked me if I was hungry. I referred him to the first house of call for my answer. To stop dilapidations till we get there, said he, we may renew our term by a little breakfast from my wallet. When I am on a journey I am always my own caterer. None of your woollen drapery, nor linen drapery, nor any of your frippery or trumpery. I hate ostentation. My wallet contains nothing but a little exercise for my grinders, my razors, and a wash-ball. I extolled his discretion, and agreed with all my heart to the bargain he proposed. My appetite was keen and sharp set for a comfortable meal; after what he had said, I could expect no less. We drew aside a little from the high road, and sat down upon the grass. There my little journeyman barber laid out his provisions, consisting of five or six onions, with some scraps of bread and cheese; but the best lot in the auction was a little leathern bottle, full, as he said, of choice, delicate wine. Though the solids were not very relishing, the calls of hunger did not allow either of us to be dainty; and we emptied the bottle too, containing about two pints of a wine one could not recommend without some remorse of conscience. We then rose from table and set out again on the tramp in high glee. The barber, who had heard some little snatches of my story from Fabricio, entreated me to furnish him with the whole from the best authority. It was impossible to refuse so munificent a host; I therefore gave him the satisfaction he required. In my turn I called on him, as an acknowledgment of my frankness, to communicate the leading circumstances of his terrestrial peregrinations. Oh! as for my adventures, exclaimed he, they are scarcely worth recording, a mere catalogue of common occurrences. Nevertheless, since we have nothing else to do, I will run over the narrative, such as it is. At the same time he entered on the recital nearly in the following terms.

CHAPTER VII.

THE JOURNEYMAN BARBER'S STORY.

I TAKE up my tale from the origin of things. My grandfather, Ferdinand Perez de la Fuenta, barber-general to the village of Olmédo for fifty years, died, leaving four sons. The eldest, Nicholas, succeeded to the shop, and lathered himself into the good graces of the customers. Bertrand, the next, having taken a fancy to trade, set up for a mercer; and Thomas, who was the third, turned schoolmaster. As for the fourth, by name Pedro, feeling within himself the high destinies of learning, he sold a dirty acre or two which fell to his share, and went to settle at Madrid, where he hoped one day to distinguish himself by his genius and erudition. The other three brothers would not part; they fixed their quarters at Olmédo, marrying peasants' daughters, who brought their husbands very little dowry, except an annual present of a chopping young rustic. They had a most public-spirited emulation in child-bearing. My mother, the barber's wife, favored the world with a contribution of six within the first five years of her marriage. I was among the number. My father initiated me betimes in the mysteries of shaving; and when he saw me grown up to the age of fifteen, laid this wallet across my shoulders, presented me with a long sword, and said—Go, Diego, you are now qualified to gain your own livelihood; go and travel about. You want a little acquaintance with the world to give you a polish, and improve you in your art. Off with you! and do not return to Olmédo till you have made the tour of Spain, nor let me hear of you till

"THERE MY LITTLE JOURNEYMAN BARBER LAID OUT HIS
PROVISIONS."

that is accomplished. Finishing with this injunction, he embraced me with fatherly affection, and shoved me out of doors by the shoulders.

Such were the parting benedictions of my sire. As for my mother, who had more the touch of nature in her manners, she seemed to feel somewhat at my departure. She dropped a few tears, and even slipped a ducat by stealth into my hand. Thus was I sent from Olmédo into the wide world, and took the road of Segovia. I did not go two hundred yards without stopping to examine my bag. I had a mind to view its contents, and to know the precise amount of my possessions. There I found a case with two razors, which must have traveled post over the chins of ten generations, by the evidence of their wear and tear, with a strap to set them, and a bit of soap. In addition to this, a coarse shirt quite new, a pair of my father's shoes quite old, and what rejoiced me more than all the rest, a rouleau of twenty rials in a linen bag. Behold the sum total of my personals. You may conclude master Nicholas, the barber, to have reckoned a good deal on my ingenuity, by his turning me adrift with so slender a provision. Yet a ducat and twenty rials, by way of fortune, was enough to turn the head of a young man unaccustomed to money concerns. I fancied my stock of cash inexhaustible; and pursued my journey in the sunshine of brilliant anticipation, looking from time to time at the hilt of my rapier, while the blade was striking against the calf of my leg at every step, or tripping up my heels.

In the evening I reached the village of Ataquinés with a very catholic stomach. I put up at the inn; and, as if I meant to spend freely, asked, in a lofty tone, what there was for supper. The landlord examined my pretensions with his eye, and finding according to what cloth my coat was cut, said with true publican's civility— Yes, yes, my worthy master, you shall have no reason to complain: we will treat you like a lord. With this assurance, he showed me into a little room, whither he brought me, a quarter of an hour afterwards, a ragout made of a great he cat, on which I feasted with as famous an appetite as if it had been hare or rabbit. This excellent dish was washed down by so choice a wine, that the king had no better in his cellars. I found out, however, that it was pricked; but that was no hindrance to my doing it as much honor as the he cat. The last article in this entertainment for a lord was a bed better adapted to drive sleep away than to invite it. Figure it to yourself about the width of a coffin, and so short that I could not stretch my legs, though none of the longest. Besides, there was neither mattress nor feather bed, but merely a little straw sewed up in a sheet folded double, which was laid down clean for every hundredth traveler, and served the other ninety-nine, one after another, without washing. Nevertheless, in such a bed, with a stomach distended to a surfeit by friscaseed cat, and then raked by sour wine, thanks to youth and a good constitution, I slept soundly, and passed the night without being disturbed.

On the following day when I had breakfasted, and paid the reckoning as I had been treated, like a lord, I made but one stage to Segovia. On my arrival, I had the good fortune to find a shop, where they took me in for my board and lodging; but I staid there only six months; a journeyman barber, with whom I got acquainted, was going to Madrid, and drew me in to set off with him. I had no difficulty in procuring a situation on the same footing as at Segovia. I got into a shop of the very best custom. It is true, it was near the church of the Holy Cross, and that the neighborhood of the Prince's Theatre brought a great deal of business. My master, two stirring fellows, and myself, could scarcely lather the chins of the people who came to be shaved. They were of all trades and conditions: among the rest, players and authors. One day, two persons of the last description happened to meet. They began conversing about the poets and pieces in vogue, when one of them mentioned my uncle's name: a circumstance which drew my attention more particularly to their discourse. Don Juan de Zavaleta, said one, will never do any good as an author. A man of a cold genius, without a spark of fancy! he has written himself down at a terrible rate by his last publication. And Louis Velez de Guevara, said the other, what has he done? A fine work to bring before the public! Was there ever anything so wretched? They mentioned I know not how many poets besides, whose names I have forgotten: I only recollect that they said no good of them. As for my uncle, they made a more honorable mention of him, agreeing that he was a personage of merit. Yes, said one, Don Pédro de la Fuenta is an excellent author; there is a sly humor in his compositions, blended with solid sense, which communicates an attic poignancy to their general effect. I am not surprised at his popularity both in court and city, nor at the pensions settled on him by the great. For many years past, said the other, he has enjoyed a very large income. He lives at the Duke de Medina Celi's table, and has an apartment in his house, so that he is at no expense: he must be very well in the world.

I lost not a syllable of what these poets were saying about my uncle. We had learnt in the family, that he made a noise in Madrid by his works; some travelers, passing through Olmédo, had told us so; but as he took no notice of us, and seemed to have weaned himself from all natural ties, we on our side lived in a state of perfect indifference about him. Yet nature will prevail: as soon as I had heard that he was in a fair way, and had learned where he lived, I was tempted to go and call upon him. One thing staggered me a little; the literati had styled him Don Pédro. This don was an awkward circumstance: I had my doubts whether he might not be some other poet of the name, and not my uncle. Yet that apprehension did not damp my ardor. I thought he might have been ennobled for his wit, and determined to pay him a visit. For this purpose, with my master's leave, I tricked myself out one morning as well as I could, and sallied from our shop, a little proud of being nephew to a man who had gained so high a character by his genius. Barbers are not the most diffident people in the world, I began to conceive no mean opinion of myself; and riding the high horse with all the arrogance of greatness, inquired my way to the Duke de Medina Celi's palace. I rang at the gate, and said, I wanted to speak with Signor Don Pédro de la Fuenta. The porter pointed with his finger to a narrow staircase at the fag end of the court, and answered—Go up there, then knock at the first door on your right. I did as he directed me ; and knocked at a door. It was opened by a young man, whom I asked if those were the apartments of Signor Don Pédro de la Fuenta. Yes, answered he, but you cannot speak to him at present. I should be very glad, said I, just to say, How are you ? I bring him news of his family. An you brought him news of the pope, replied he, I could not introduce you just now. He is writing, and while his wits are at work, he must not be disturbed. He will not be able to receive company till noon ; take a turn, and come back about that time.

I departed, and walked about town all the morning, incessantly meditating on the reception my uncle would give me. I think, said I within myself, he will be overjoyed to see me. I measured his feelings by my own, and prepared myself for a very affecting discovery. I returned punctually to the appointed hour. You are just in time, said the servant : my master was going out. Wait here a moment : I will announce you. With these words, he left me in the anti-chamber. He returned almost immediately, and showed me into his master's room. The face struck me all at once as a family likeness. To be sure he was the very image of my uncle Thomas : they might have been taken for twins. I bowed down to the ground, and introduced myself as the son of Master Nicholas de la Fuenta, the barber of Olmédo. I likewise informed him, that I had been working at my father's trade in Madrid, for these three weeks, as a journeyman, and intended making the tour of Spain to complete my education. While I was speaking, my uncle was evidently in a brown study. He seemed to doubt whether he should disown me at once, or get rid of me with some little sacrifice to decency. The latter course he adopted. Affecting the affable : Well, my good kinsman, how are your father and your uncles ? Do they get on in the world ? I began thereupon by laying before him the family knack at propagation. All the children, male and female, called over by their names, with their godfathers and godmothers included in the list ! He took no extravagant interest in the particulars of my tale ; but leading to his own purposes, Diego, replied he, I am quite of your mind. You should go from place to place, and see a variety of practice. I would not have you tarry longer at Madrid ; it is a very dangerous residence for youth ; you may get into bad habits, my sweet fellow. Other towns will suit you better; the state of society in the provinces is more patriarchal and philosophical. Determine on emigration ; and when your departure is fixed, come and take your leave. I will contribute a pistole to the tour of Spain. With this kind assurance, he handed me out of the room, and sent me packing.

I had not worldly wisdom enough to find out that he wanted to get quit of me. I went back to our shop, and gave my master an account of the visit I had paid. He looked no deeper than myself into Signor Don Pédro's motives, and observed : I cannot help differing from your worthy uncle, so far from advising you to travel the provinces, the real thing would be, in my opinion, to give you a comfortable settlement in this city. He is hand and glove with the first people ; it is an easy matter for him to establish you in a great family ; and that is a fortune at once. Struck with this lucky discovery, which seemed to settle the point without difficulty, I called on my uncle again two days afterwards, and made a modest proposal to him for a situation about some leading character at court. But the hint was not taken kindly. A proud man, living

"DETERMINE ON EMIGRATION."

at free quarters among the great, and dining with them in a family party, did not exactly wish that, while he was sitting at my lord's table, his nephew should be a guest in the servants' hall. Little Diego might bring a scandal on Signor Don Pédro. He had no hesitation, therefore, in fairly turning me out of doors, and that with a flea in my ear. What, you little rascal, said he in a fit of extravagance, do you mean to relinquish your calling? Begone, I consign you to the reptile whose pernicious counsels will be your ruin. Take your leave of these premises, and never set your foot on them again, or you shall have the reception you deserve! I was absolutely stunned at this language, and still more at the peremptory tone my uncle assumed. With tears in my eyes I withdrew, quite overcome by his severity. Yet, as I had always been lively and confident in my temper, I soon wiped away my tears. My grief was even turned into resentment, and I determined to take no further notice of this unnatural relative, whose kind offices I had hitherto been contented to want.

My attention was henceforth directed to the cultivation of my professional talent; I was quite a plodding fellow at my trade. I scraped away all day; and in the evening, by way of relief to my scraping, I twanged the guitar. My master on that instrument was an old *Senor Escudero* whom I shaved. He taught me music in return; and he was an adept. To be sure he had formerly been a chorister in a cathedral. His name was Marcos de Obregon. He was a man of the world, with good natural parts and acquired knowledge, which jointly induced him to fix on me as an adopted son. He was engaged as an attendant on a physician's lady, resident within thirty yards of our house. I went to him in the evening, when shop was shut, and we two, sitting on the threshold of the door, made up a little concert not displeasing to the neighborhood. It was not that our voices were very fine; but in thrumming on the catgut, we made a pretty regular accompaniment to our duet, and filled up the harmony sufficiently for the gratification of our hearers. Our music was particularly agreeable to Donna Mergelina, the physician's wife; she came into the passage to hear us, and sometimes encored us in her favorite airs. Her husband did not interfere with her amusement. Though a Spaniard and in years, he was not possessed with jealousy; besides, his profession took up all his time; and as he came home in the evening, worn out with his numerous visits, he went to bed at an early hour, without troubling himself about his wife or our concerts. Possibly, if he thought about them at all, he might consider them as little likely to produce dangerous consequences. He had an additional security in his wife. Mergelina was young and handsome with a witness; but of so fierce a modesty, that she started at the very shadow of a man. How could he take umbrage at an amusement of so harmless and decorous a nature? He gave us leave to sing our hearts out.

One evening, as I came to the physician's door, intending to take my usual recreation, I found the old squire waiting for me. He took me by the hand: saying that he wished to take a little walk with me before we struck up our little concert. At the same time he drew me aside into a by-street, where, finding an opportunity of opening his mind: Diego, my good lad, said he with a melancholy air, I want to give you a hint in private. I much fear, my good and amiable youth, that we shall both have reason to repent of beguiling our evenings with little musical parties at my master's door. Rely on my sincere friendship: I do not grudge your lessons in singing and on the guitar; but if I could have foreseen the storm now brewing, in the name of charity! I would have selected some other spot to communicate my instructions.   This address alarmed me.   I entreated the gentle squire to be more explicit, and to tell me what we had to fear ; for I was no Hector, and the tour of Spain was not yet finished.   I will relate to you, replied he, what it concerns you to know, that you may take proper measure of our present danger.

When I got into the service of the physician, about a year ago, he said one morning, after having introduced me to his wife : There, Marcos, you see your mistress : that is the lady you are to accompany in all her peregrinations.   I was smitten with Donna Mergelina : she was lovely in the extreme, a model for an artist, and her principal attraction was the pleasantness of her deportment.   Honored sir, replied I to the physician, it is too great a happiness to be in the train of so charming a lady.   My answer was taken amiss by Mergelina, who said rather crustily, A pleasant gentleman this !   He is perfectly free and easy.   Believe me !   His fine speeches may go a begging for me.   These words, dropped from such lovely lips, seemed rather inconsistent ; the manners and ideas of bumpkins and dairy-maids coupled with all the graces of the most lovely women in the world !   As for her husband, he was used to her ways ; and, hugging himself on the unrivaled character of his rib, Marcos, said he, my wife is a miracle of chastity.   Then, observing her put on her veil, and make herself ready to go to mass, he told me to attend on her at church.   We were no sooner in the street than we met, and it was no wonder, blades who, struck with Donna Mergelina's general carriage, told her a thousand flattering tales as they passed by.   She was not backward in her answer ; but silly and ill-timed, beyond what you can conceive.   They were all in amaze, and could not imagine how a woman should take it amiss to be complimented.   Why really ! madam, said I to her at first, you had better be silent, or shut your ears to their addresses, than reply with asperity.   No, no, replied she : I will teach these coxcombs that I am not a woman to put up with impertinence.   In short, her absurdity went so far, that I could not help telling her my mind, at the hazard of her displeasure,   I gave her to understand, yet with the greatest possible caution, that she was unjust to nature, whose handiwork she marred by her preposterous ferocity ; that a woman of mild and polished manners might inspire love without the aid of beauty ; whereas the loveliest of the sex, divested of female softness, was in danger of becoming the public scorn.   To this ratiocination, I added collateral arguments, always directed to the amendment of her manners.   After having moralized to no purpose, I was afraid my freedom might exasperate my mistress, and draw upon me some taunting repartee.   Nevertheless she did not mutiny against my advice ; but silently rendered it of no avail, and thus we went on from day to day.

I was weary of pointing out her errors to no purpose, and gave her up to the ferocious temperament of her nature.   Yet, could you think it ? the savage humor of that proud woman is entirely changed within these two months.   She has a kind word for all the world, and manners the most accommodating.   It is no longer the same Mergelina who gave such homely answers to the compliments of her swains: she is become assailable by flattery; loves to be told she is handsome, that a man cannot look at her without paying for it: her ears itch for fine speeches, and she is become a very woman. Such a change is almost inconceivable: and the best of the joke is, that you are the worker of this unparalleled miracle. Yes, my dear Diego, it is you who have transformed Donna Mergelina; you have softened down the tigress into a domestic animal; in a word, you have made her feel. I have observed it more than once; and never trust my knowledge of the sex, if she is not desperately in love with you. Such, my dear boy, is the melancholy news I have to communicate, the awkward predicament in which we stand.

I do not see, said I in my turn to the old man, that there is anything so melancholy in this accident, or any peculiar awkwardness in being the object of a pretty woman's partiality. Ah! Diego, replied he, you argue like a young man: you only see the bait, without guarding against the hook: pleasure is your lure; while my thoughts are directed to the unpleasant circumstances attending it. Murder will out. If you go on singing at our door, you will provoke Mergelina's passion; and she probably, losing all command over herself, will betray her weakness to her husband, Doctor Oloroso. That wretched husband, so complying now that he thinks there is no ground for jealousy, will run wild, take signal vengeance upon her, and perhaps play some dog's trick or other to you and me. Well, then! rejoined I, your reasons shall be conclusive with me, and your sage counsels my rule. Lay down the line of conduct I am to adopt for the prevention of any left-handed catastrophe. We will have no more concerts, was his peremptory decree. Do not show yourself any more to my mistress: when the sight of you does not inflame her, she will recover her composure. Stay within doors: I will call in upon you, and we will torture the guitar with impunity. With all my heart, said I, and I will never set my foot again in your premises. In good truth, I was determined to serenade no longer before the physician's door, but henceforth to keep within the precincts of my shop, since my attractions as a man were so formidable.

In the mean time good Squire Marcos, with all his prudence, experienced in the course of a few days that the plan he had devised to quench Donna Mergelina's flame produced a directly opposite effect. The lady on the second night not hearing me sing, asked why we had discontinued our concerts, and the reason of my absence. He told her I was so busy as not to have a moment to spare for relaxation. She seemed satisfied with that excuse, and for three days longer bore the disappointment of all her hopes like a heroine; but at the end of that period, my martyr to the tender passion lost all patience, and said to her conductor—You are playing false with me, Marcos; Diego has not discontinued his visits without a cause. This mystery must be unraveled. Speak, I command you; conceal nothing from me. Madam, answered he, making use of another subterfuge, since the truth must be told, it has often happened to him to find the cloth taken away at home after the concert; he cannot run the risk any longer of going to bed without his supper! What, without his supper! exclaimed she in an agony, why did not you tell me so sooner? Go to bed without his supper! Oh! the poor little sufferer! Go to him this instant, and let him come again this evening; he shall not go home starving any more, there shall always be a luncheon for him.

What do I hear? said the squire, affecting astonishment at this language; oh heaven, what a reverse! Is this you, madam, and are these your sentiments? Well-a-day! Since when are you so compassionate and tender-hearted? Since, replied she significantly, since you have lived in this house, or rather since you disapproved my disdainful manners, and have labored to soften the acrimony of my temper. But, alas! added she, in a melting mood, I have gone from one extreme to the other. Proud and insensible as I was, I am become too susceptible, too tender. I am enamored of your young friend Diego, and I cannot help myself; his absence, far from allaying my ardor, only adds fuel to the fire. Is it possible, resumed the old man, that a young fellow with neither face nor person should have inspired so strong a passion? I could make allowance for your feelings, if they had been set afloat by some nobleman of distinguished merit. . . . . Ah! Marcos, interrupted Mergelina, I am not like the rest of my sex; or rather, spite of your long experience, your penetration is but shallow if you fancy merit to have much share in our choice. Judging by myself, we all leap before we look. Love is a mental derangement, forcibly drawing all our views and attachments into one vortex; a species of hydrophobia. Have done then with your hints that Diego is not worthy of my tenderness; that he has it is enough to invest him with a thousand perfections too etherial for your gross sight, and perhaps too unsubstantial for any but a lover's perception. In vain you disparge his features or his stature; in my eyes he was created to undo, and encircled by the hand of nature with the glories of the opening day. Nay, more, there is a thrilling sweetness in his voice; his touch on the guitar has the taste of an amateur, and the execution of a professor. But, madam, subjoined Marcos, do you consider who Diego is? The meanness of his station. . . . . My own is very little better, interrupted she again; though were I of noble birth, it would make no difference in my sensations.

The result of that conference was that the squire, concluding he should make no impression on the mind of his mistress, gave over struggling with her obstinacy, as a skillful pilot runs before the storm though it carries him out to sea from his intended port. He did more: to satisfy his patroness he paid me a visit, took me aside, and after having related what had passed between them— You see, Diego, said he, that we cannot dispense with the performance of our concerts at Mergelina's door. Absolutely, my friend, that lady must see you again; otherwise she may commit some act of desperation fatal to her good name. I was not inexorable, but answered Marcos that I would attend with my guitar early in the evening; and despatched him to his mistress with the happy tidings. He executed his office, and the impassioned dame was out of her wits with joy, in the delicious prospect of hearing and seeing me in a few hours.

A most disagreeable circumstance, however, was very near disappointing her in that hope. I could not leave home before night, and for my sins, it was dark as pitch. I went groping along the street, and had got, may be, half way, when down from a window came upon my head the contents of a perfuming pan, which did not tickle my olfactory nerves very pleasantly. I may say that not a whiff was wasted, so exactly had the giver taken measure of the receiver. In this situation I was at a loss on what to resolve: to go back by the way I came, what an exhibition before my comrades! It was surrendering myself to all their nasty witticisms. Then again, go to Mergelina in such a glorious trim, that hurt my feelings on the other side. I determined, at length, to get on towards the physician's. The old usher was waiting for me at the door. He said that Doctor Oloroso was gone to bed, and we might amuse ourselves as we liked. I answered that the first thing was to purify my drapery, at the same time relating my misfortune. He seemed to feel for me, and showed me into a hall where his mistress was sitting. As soon as the lady got wind of my adventure, and had confirmed the testimony of her nose by the evidence of her eyes, she moaned over me as grievously as if my miseries had been mortal; then, apostrophizing the absent cause of my foul array, she uttered a thousand imprecations. Well, but madam! said Marcos, do moderate this ecstacy of grief; consider that such casualties will happen, there is no occasion to take on so bitterly. Why, exclaimed she with vehemence, why would you debar me from the privilege of weeping over the injuries of this tender lamb, this dove without gall, who does not so much as murmur at the affront he has sustained? Alas! why am I not a man at this moment to avenge him!

She uttered numberless soothing expressions besides, to mark distinctly the excess of her devotion, and her actions corresponded with her words; for while Marcos was employed in wiping me down with a towel, she ran into her chamber and brought out a box furnished with every variety of perfumes. She burned sweet-smelling drugs, and perfumed my clothes with them, after which she drenched me in a deluge of essences. The fumigation and aspersion ended, this bountiful lady went herself and fetched from the kitchen bread, wine, and some good slices of roast mutton, set by on purpose for me. She forced me to eat, and taking a pleasure in waiting on me, sometimes carved for me, and sometimes filled my glass, in spite of all that Marcos and myself could do to anticipate her condescension. When I had done supper, the gentlemen of the orchestra struck the key note, and tuned their sweet voices to the pitch of their guitars. We played and sung to the heart's delight of Mergelina. To be sure we took care to carol none but amorous ditties; and as we sung, I every now and then leered at her with such a roguish meaning, as to throw oil upon the fire, for the game began to be interesting. The concert, though the acts were long, was not tedious. As for the lady, to whom hours seemed to fly like seconds, she could have been content to exhaust the night in listening, if the old squire, with whom the seconds seemed to lag like hours, had not hinted how late it was. She gave him the trouble of inforcing his moral on the lapse of time by at least ten repetitions. But she was in the hands of a man not to be turned aside from his purpose, he let her have no rest till I was gone. Sensible and provident as he was, seeing his mistress given up to a mad passion, he dreaded lest our harmony should be resolved by some discord. His fears were ominous: the physician, whether his mind misgave him of foul play, or the spirit of jealousy, hitherto on its good behavior, had a mind to harass him gratuitously, bethought himself of quarreling with our concerts. He did more, he put a broad negative upon them; and, without assigning his reasons for acting in this violent way, declared that he would suffer no more strangers to come about his premises.

Marcos acquainted me with this mortifying declaration, particularly leveled against my rising hopes. I had begun bobbing at this dainty cherry, and did not like to lose my game. Nevertheless, to act the part of a faithful reporter and true historian, I must own my impatience did not affect my health or spirits. Not so with Mergelina, her feelings were more alive than ever. My dear Marcos, said she to her usher, it is only from you that I look for succor. Contrive, I beseech you, that I may see Diego in private. What do you require? asked the old man with a reproachful accent. I have been but too indulgent to you. I am not a person to crown your wanton wishes at the expense of my master's honor, your good fame, and my own eternal infamy; the infamy of a man whose past life has been one continued series of faithful service and exemplary conduct. I had rather leave the family than stay in it on such scandalous conditions. Alas! Marcos, interrupted the lady, frightened out of her wits at these last words, you wring my heart by talking in this manner. Obdurate man! Can you bear the thought of sacrificing her who lays all her present agony to your account? Give me back my former pride, and that savage soul you have taken from me. Why am I no longer happy in my very imperfections? I might now have been at peace, but your rash counsels have robbed me of the repose I then enjoyed. You, the corrector of my manners, have tampered with my morals. . . . . But why do I rave, unhappy wretch as I am? why upbraid you thus wrongfully? No, my guardian angel, you are not the fatal source of my miseries; my evil destiny had decreed these tortures to await me. Lay not to heart, I conjure you on my knees, these transports of a disordered imagination. Oh mercy! my passion drives me mad, have compassion on my weakness; you are my sole support and stay: if then my life is not indifferent to you, deny me not your aid.

At these words her tears flowed in fresh torrents, and stifled her lugubrious accents. She took out her handkerchief, and throwing it over her face, fell into a chair, like a person overcome by her affliction. Old Marcos, who was perhaps one of the most tractable go-betweens in the world, could no longer steel his heart against so touching a spectacle. Pierced to the quick, he even mingled his tears with those of his mistress, and spoke to her in a softened tone—Ah madam, why are you thus bewitching! I cannot hold out against your sorrowful complaints, my virtue yields under the pressure of my pity. I promise you all the relief in my power. No longer do I marvel at the oblivious influence of passion over duty, since mere sympathy can mislead my footsteps from its thorny paths. Thus did this pander, whose past life had been one continued series of faithful service and exemplary conduct, sell himself to the devil to feed Mergelina's illicit flame. One morning he came and talked over the whole business with me, saying at his departure, that he had a scheme in his head, to bring about a private interview between us. At the thought my hopes were all re-kindled, but they glimmered tremblingly in the socket at a piece of news I heard two hours afterwards. A journeyman apothecary in the neighborhood, one of our customers, came in to be shaved. While I was making ready to trim his bushy honors, he said—Master Diego, do you know anything about your friend, the old usher, Marcos de Obregon? Is he not going to leave Doctor Oloroso? I said, No. But he is though, replied he; he will get his dismission this very day. His master and mine were talking about it just now in my hearing, and their conversation was to the following effect:—Signor Apuntador, said the physician, I have a favor to beg of you. I am not easy about an old usher of mine, and should like to place my wife under the eye of a trusty, strict, and vigilant duenna. I understand you, interrupted my master. You want Dame Melancia, my wife's directress, and indeed mine for the last six weeks, since I have been a widower. Though she would be very useful to me in housewifery, I give her up to you, from a paramount regard to your honor. You may rely upon her for the security of your brow; she is the phœnix of the duenna tribe—a spring-gun and a man-trap set in the purlieus of female chastity. During twelve whole years that she was about my wife, whose youth and beauty, you know, were not without their attractions, I never saw the least semblance of manhood within my doors. No, no! by all the powers! That game was not so easily played. And yet I must let you know that the departed saint, heaven rest her soul! had in the outset a great hankering after the delights of the flesh; but Dame Melancia cast her in a new mold, and regenerated her to virtue and self-denial. In short, such a guardian of the weaker sex is a treasure, and you will never have done thanking me for my precious gift. Hereupon the doctor expressed his rapture at the issue of the conference; and they agreed, Signor Apuntador and he, on the duenna's succeeding the old usher on this very day.

This news, which I thought probable, and turned out to be true, disturbed the pleasurable ideas, just beginning to flow afresh, and renovate my soul. After dinner, Marcos completed the convulsion, by confirming the young drug-pounder's story: My dear

Diego, said the good squire, I am heartily glad that Doctor Oloroso has turned me off; it spares me a world of trouble. Besides that it hurt my feelings to be invested with the office of a spy, endless must have been the shifts and subterfuges to bring you and Mergelina together in private. We should have been rarely graveled! Thanks to heaven, I am set free from all such perplexing cares, to say nothing of their attendant danger. On your part, my dear boy, you ought to be comforted for the loss of a few soft moments, which must have been dogged at the heels by a thousand fears and vexations. I relished Marcos' sermon well enough, because my hopes were at an end, the game was lost. I was not, it must be confessed, among the number of those stubborn lovers who bear up against every impediment; but though I had been so, Dame Melancia would have made me let go my hold. The established character of that deunna would have daunted the adventurous spirit of a knight-errant. Yet, in whatever colors this phœnix of the duenna tribe might have been painted, I had reason to know, two or three days afterwards, that the physician's lady had unset the man-trap and spring-gun, and given a stop to this watchdog of lubricity. As I was going out to shave one of our neighbors, a civil old gentlewoman stopped me in the street, and asked if my name was Diego de la Fuenta. I said, Yes, That being the case, replied she, I have a little business with you. Place yourself this evening at Donna Mergelina's door; and when you are there, give a signal, and you shall be let in. Vastly well! said I, what must the signal be? I can take off a cat to the life: suppose I was to mew a certain number of times? The very thing, replied this Iris of intrigue; I will carry back your answer. Your most obedient, Signor Diego! Heaven protect the sweet youth! Ah! you are a pretty one! By St. Agnes, I wish I was but sweet fifteen, I would not go to market for other folks! With this hint, the old procuress waddled out of sight.

You may be sure this message put me in no small flutter. Where now was the morality of Marcos? I waited for night with impatience, and, calculating the time of Doctor Oloroso's going to bed, took my station at his door. There I set up my caterwauling, till you might hear me ever so far off, to the eternal honor of the master who instructed me in that imitative art. A moment after Mergelina opened the door softly with her own dear hands, and shut it again with me on the inside. We went into the hall, where our last concert had been performed. It was dimly lighted by a small lamp, which twinkled in the chimney. We sat down side by side, and began our tender parley, each of us overcome by our emotions, but with this difference; that hers were all inspired by pleasure, while mine were somewhat tainted by fear. In vain did the divinity of my adorations assure me that we had nothing to fear from her husband. I felt the access of an ague, which unmanned my vigor. Madam, said I, how have you eluded the vigilance of your directress? After what I have heard of Dame Melancia, I could not have conceived it possible for you to contrive the means of sending me any intelligence, much less of seeing me in private. Donna Mergelina smiled at this remark, and answered: You will no longer be surprised at our being together to-night, when I tell you what has passed between my duenna and me. As soon as she came to her place, my husband paid her a thousand compliments, and said to me: Mergelina, I consign you to the guidance of this wary lady, herself an abstract of all the virtues: in this glass you may look without a blush, and array yourself in habits of wisdom. This extraordinary personage has for these twelve years been a light to the ways of an apothecary's wife of my acquaintance; but how has she been a light to them? . . . . why, as ways never were enlightened before: she turned a very slippery piece of mortal flesh into a downright nun.

This panegyric, not belied by the austere mien of Dame Melancia, cost me a flood of tears, and reduced me to despair. I fancied the din of eternal lectures from morning till night, and daily rebukes too harsh to be endured. In short, I laid my account in a life of wretchedness, beyond the patience of a woman. Keeping no measures in the expectation of such cruel sufferings, I said bluntly to the duenna, the moment I was alone with her: You mean, no doubt, to exercise your tyranny most wantonly on my poor person; but I cannot bear much severity, I warn you beforehand. I give you, moreover, fair notice, that I shall be as savage as you can be. My heart cherishes a passion, which not all your remonstrances shall tear from it: so you may act accordingly. Watch me as closely as you please; it is hard if I cannot outwit such an old thing as you. At these taunting words, I thought this saracen in petticoats was going to give me a specimen of her discipline. But so far from it, she smoothed her brow, relaxed her surly features, and primming up her mouth into a smile, promulgated this comfortable doctrine: Your temper charms me, and your frankness calls for a return. We must have been made for one another. Ah! lovely Mergelina, little do you fathom my character, to be deceived by the fine compliments of your husband the Doctor, or by my Tartar contour! There never was a creature more fortified against moral prejudices! My inducement for getting into the service of jealous husbands is to lend myself to the enjoyments of their pretty wives. Long have I trodden the stage of life in masquerade; and I may call myself doubly happy, in the spiritual rewards of virtue, and the temporal indulgences of the opposite side. Between ourselves, mine is the system of all mankind in the long run. Real virtue is a very expensive article, plated goods look just as well, and are within the reach of all purchasers.

Put yourself under my direction. We will make Doctor Oloroso pay the piper to our dancing, or I am no duenna. By my troth, he shall go the way of Signor Apuntador and all mankind. There is no reason why the forehead of a physician should be smoother than the brow of an apothecary. Poor dear Apuntador! What fun have we had with him, his wife and I! A charming woman, that wife of his! A dear little creature, open to all mankind, and prejudiced by none! Well! she is at peace, and has not left her fellow behind her! Take my word, short as her time was, she made the most of it. Let me see how many rampart chaps have been brought to their bearings in that house, without the dear deluded husband being waked out of his evening's nap! Now, madam, you may see me in my true light; and assure yourself, whatever might be the abilities of your old usher, you will not fare the worse for going further. If he was a benefit to you, I shall be a blessing.

You may judge for yourself, Diego, continued Mergelina, how well I took it of the duenna, that she laid herself open so frankly. I had taken her virtue to be of the impenetrable cast. Look you now, how much women are liable to be scandalized. But her character of plain dealing won my heart at once. I threw my arms about her neck in a rapture, which bespoke my warm and tender feelings at the thoughts of such a mother abbess. I gave her carte blanche of all my private thoughts, and put in for a speedy tête-à-tête with your own dear self. She met me on my own ground. This very morning she engaged the old woman who spoke to you, to take the field: she is an old stager, a veteran in the service of the apothecary's wife, but the best of the joke in this comedy, added she in a paroxysm of laughter, is that Melancia, on my assurance that my husband's habit is to pass the night without stirring, is gone to bed by his side, and drones out my useless office at this moment. So much the worse, madam, said I then to Mergelina; your device is more plausible than profitable. Your husband is very likely to wake, and discover the fraud. He will not discover anything about it, replied she with no little urgency; set your heart at rest about that, and let not an empty fear poison the fountains of a pleasure, which ought to drown every vulgar and earthly consideration in the arms of a young lady who is yours for ever and ever.

The old doctor's help-mate, finding that her assurances had little effect upon my courage, left no stone unturned to put me in heart again; and had so many encouraging ways with her, that a very coward must have plucked up a little. My thoughts were all with Jupiter and Alcmena; but at the very moment that the urchin Cupid, with his train of smiles and antics, was weaving a garland to compliment the crisis of our endeavors, we were stopped in our career by an importunate knocking at the street door. In a moment, away flew love and all his covey, like game at the report of a fowling-piece. Mergelina popped me like an article of household furniture under the hall table, blew out the lamp, and, by previous agreement with her governess, in the event of so unlucky an accident, placed herself at the door of her husband's bed-chamber. In the mean time, the knocking continued with reiterated violence, till the whole house resounded. The physician awoke suddenly, and called Melancia. The duenna flung herself out of bed, though the doctor, taking her for his wife, begged of her not to disturb herself. She ran to her mistress, who, catching hold of her in the dark, began calling Melancia! and told her to go and see who was at the door. Madam, answered the directress, here I am at your service, go to bed again if you please; you shall soon know who it is. During this parley, Mergelina having undressed, got into bed to the doctor, who had not the least suspicion of the farce that was playing. To be sure the stage was darkened, and the actresses had very little occasion for a prompter; one of them was familiar with the boards, and the other wanted only a rehearsal or two to be perfect in her part.

The duenna, in her night-gown, made her appearance soon after, with a candle in her hand—Good doctor, said she to her master, have the goodness to get up. Our neighbor Fernandez de Buendia, the bookseller, is in an apoplectic fit: you are sent for; time presses. The physician got on his clothes as fast as he could, and went out. His wife, in her bed-gown, came into the hall with the duenna. They dragged me from under the table more dead than alive. You have nothing to fear, Diego, said Mergelina, put yourself in proper order. At the same time she told me how things were in two words. She had half a mind to renew our amorous intercourse; but the directress knew better. Madam, said she, your husband may possibly be too late to help the bookseller to the other world, and then he will return immediately. Besides, added she, observing me benumbed with fright, it would be all lost labor upon this poor youth! He is not in a condition to answer your demands. You had better send him home, and defer the debate till to-morrow evening. Donna Mergelina was sorry for the delay, as well knowing that a bird in the hand is worth two in the bush; and I flatter myself she was disappointed at not putting a cuckold's nightcap on the doctor's head.

As for me, less grieved at having drawn a blank in the lottery of love, than rejoiced at getting my neck out of an halter, I returned to my master's, where I passed the remainder of the night in moralizing on the scene I had left. For some time, I was in doubt whether to keep my appointment on the following evening. I thought it was a foolish business from first to last; but the devil, who is always lurking for his prey, or rather taking possession of us as his lawful property, whispered in my ear that I should be a great fool to pack up my alls when the prize was falling into my hands. Mergelina too with opening and unfathomable charms! The exquisite pleasure that awaited me! I determined to stick to my text; and promising myself a larger share of self-possession, took my station the next evening at the doctor's door, between eleven and twelve, in a most spirit-stirring humor. The heavens were completely darkened, not a star to prate of my whereabout. I mewed twice or thrice to give warning of my being in the street; and, as no one answered my signal, I was not satisfied with going over the old ground, but ran up and down the cat's gamut from bass to treble, and from treble to bass, just as I used to sol-fa with a shepherd of Olmédo. I tuned my fundamental bass so musically, that a neighbor, on his return home, taking me for one of those animals whose mewings I counterfeited, picked up an unlucky flint lying at his feet, and threw it at me with all his force, saying—The devil fetch that tom cat! I received the blow on my head, and

was so stunned for the moment, that I was very near falling backwards. I found the skin was broken. This was enough in all conscience to give me a surfeit of gallantry; so that, my passion oozing out with my blood, I made the best of my way homewards,
where I rendered night hideous by my howling, and knocked all
the family up. My master probed my wound, and played the true
surgeon on it; he pronounced the consequences to be uncertain.
He did all he could to make them certain; but flesh will heal in
spite of the faculty; and there was not a scar remaining in three
weeks. During all this time, I heard not a word from Mergelina.
The probability is that Dame Melancia, to wean her impure
thoughts from me, engaged her in some better sport. However,
I did not concern myself about the matter; but left Madrid to
continue my tour of Spain, as soon, as I found myself perfectly
recovered.

CHAPTER VIII.

THE MEETING OF GIL BLAS AND HIS COMPANION WITH A MAN
   SOAKING CRUSTS OF BREAD AT A SPRING, AND THE PAR-
   TICULARS OF THEIR CONVERSATION.

SIGNOR Diego de la Fuenta related some other adventures
which had since happened to him; but they were so little worthy
of preservation, that I shall pass them by in silence. Yet there was
no getting rid of the recital, which was tedious enough: it lasted
as far as Ponte de Duero. We halted in that town the remainder
of the day. Our commons at the inn consisted of a vegetable soup
and a roast hare, whose genus and species we took especial pains
to verify. At daybreak on the following morning we resumed our
journey, after having replenished our flask with some very tolerable wine, and our wallet with some pieces of bread, and half the
hare we had left at supper.

When we had gone about two leagues we waxed hungry; and,
espying at about two hundred yards from the high road some
spreading trees, which threw an agreeable shade over the plain, we
made up to the spot, and rested on our arms. There we met with
a man from seven to eight and twenty, who was dipping crusts of
bread into a spring. He had a long sword lying by him on the
grass, with a soldier's knapsack, of which he had eased his shoulders. We thought his air and person better than his attire. We
accosted him with civility; and he returned our salutation. He then
offered us his crusts, and asked with a smile if we would take pot-
luck with him. We answered in the affirmative, provided he had
no objection to our clubbing our own breakfast, by way of making
the meal more substantial. He agreed to it with the utmost readiness, and we immediately produced our provisions; which were
not unacceptable to the stranger. What is all this, gentlemen, ex-

claimed he in a transport of joy, here is ammunition for an army!
By your forecast, you must be commissaries or quartermasters. I
do not travel with so much contrivance, for my part; but depend a good deal on the chances of the road. At the same time,
though appearances may be against me, I can say, without vanity,
that I sometimes make a very brilliant figure in the world. Would
you believe that princely honors are commonly bestowed on me, and
that I have guards in attendance? I comprehend you, said Diego;

"HE WAS DIPPING CRUSTS OF BREAD INTO A SPRING."

you mean to tell us, you are a player. You guess right, replied the
other; I have been an actor for these fifteen years at least. From
my very infancy, I was sent on the boards in children's parts. To
deal freely, rejoined the barber, shaking his head, I do not believe a
word of it. I know the players; those gentry do not travel on foot,
like you, nor do they mess with St. Anthony. I doubt whether
you are anything better than a candle-snuffer. You may, quoth the

son of Thespis, think of me as you please; but my parts, for all that, are in the first line; I play the lovers. If that be the case, said my companion, I wish you much joy, and am delighted that Signor Gil Blas and myself have the honor of breakfasting with so eminent a character.

We then began to pick our crumbs, and to gnaw the precious relics of the hare, bestowing such harty smacks upon the bottle, as to empty it very shortly. We were all three so deeply engaged in the great affair of eating, that we said very little till we had finished, when we resumed our conversation. I wonder, said the barber to the player, that you should be so much out at elbows. For a the-atrical hero, you have but a needy exterior! I beg pardon if I speak rather freely. Rather freely! exclaimed the actor; ah! by my troth, you are not yet acquainted with Melchoir Zapata. Hea-ven be praised, I have no mind to see things in a wrong light. You do me a pleasure by speaking so confidently: for I love to unbosom myself without reserve. I honestly own I am not rich. Here, pursued he, showing us his doublet lined with playbills, this is the common stuff which serves me for linings; and if you are curious to see my wardrobe, you shall not be disappointed. At the same time he took out of his knapsack a dress, laced with tarnished frip-pery, a shabby head-dress for an hero, with an old plume of feathers; silk stockings full of holes, and red morocco shoes a great deal the worse for wear. You see, said he again, that I am very little bet-ter than a begger. That is astonishing, replied Diego: then you have neither wife nor daughter? I have a very handsome young wife, rejoined Zapata, and yet I might just as well be without her. Look with awe on the lowering aspect of my horoscope. I married a personable actress, in the hope that she would not let me die of hunger, and, to my cost, she is cursed with incorruptible chastity. Who the devil would not have been taken in as well as myself? There was but one virtuous princess in a whole strolling company, and she, plague take her! fell into my hands. It was throwing with bad luck most undoubtedly, said the barber. But then, why did you not look out for an actress in the regular theatre at Madrid? You would have been sure of your mark. You are perfectly in the right, replied the stroller: but the mischief is, we underlings dare not raise our thoughts to those illustrious heroines. It is as much as an actor of the prince's company can venture on; nay, some of them are obliged to match with citizens' daughters. Happily for our fraternity, citizens' daughters now-a-days contract theatrical notions; and you may often meet with characters among them, to the full as eccentric as any bona roba of the green-room.

Well! but have you never thought, said my fellow-traveler, of getting an engagement in that company? Is it necessary to be a Roscius for that purpose? That is very well of you! replied Melchior, you are a wag, with your Roscius! There are twenty performers. Ask the town what it thinks of them, and you will hear a pretty character of their acting. More than half of them deserve to carry a porter's knot. Yet for all that, it is no easy mat-ter to get upon the boards. Bribery or interest must make up for

THE POOR ACTOR.

the defect of talent. I ought to know what I say since my début at Madrid, where I was hissed and cat-called as if the devil had got among the grimalkins, though I ought to have been received with thunders of applause ; for I whined, ranted, and offered all sorts of violence to nature's modesty : nay, I went so far as to clench my fist at the heroine of the piece; in a word, I adopted the conceptions of all the great performers ; and yet that same audience condemned by bell, book, and candle in me, what was thought to be the first style of playing in them. Such is the force of prejudice ! So that, being no favorite with the pit, and not having wherewithal to insinuate myself into the good graces of the manager, I am on my return to Zamora. There we shall all huddle together again, my wife and fellow-comedians, who are making but little of the business. I wish we may not be obliged to beg our way out of town; a catastrophe of too frequent occurrence !

At these words, up rose the stage-struck hero, slung across him his knapsack and his sword, and made his exit with due theatric pomp : Farewell, gentlemen ; may all the gods shower all their bounties on your heads ! And you, answered Diego with corresponding emphasis, may you find your wife at Zamora, softened down in her relentless virtue, and in comfortable keeping. No sooner had Signor Zapata turned upon his heel, than he began gesticulating and spouting as he went along. The barber and myself immediately began hissing to remind him of his first appearance at Madrid. The goose grated harsh upon his tympanum ; he took it for a reception of signals from his old friends. But looking behind him, and seeing that we were diverting ourselves at his expense, far from taking offence at this merry conceit of ours, he joined with good humor in the joke, and went his way laughing as hard as he could. On our part, we returned the complement in kind. After this, we got again into the high road, and pursued our journey.

CHAPTER IX.

THE MEETING OF DIEGO WITH HIS FAMILY; THEIR CIRCUMSTANCES
  IN LIFE ; GREAT REJOICINGS ON THE OCCASION ; THE PARTING
  SCENE BETWEEN HIM AND GIL BLAS.

WE stopped for the night at a little village between Moyados and Valpuesta ; I have forgotten the name : and the next morning, about eleven, we reached the plain of Olmédo. Signor Gil Blas, said my companion, behold my native place. So natural are these local attachments, that I can hardly contain myself at the sight of it. Signor Diego, answered I, a man of so patriotic a soul as you profess to be, might, methinks, have been a little more florid in his descriptions. Olmédo looks like a city at this distance, and you called it a village; it cannot be anything less than a corporate town. I beg its township's pardon, replied the barber; but you are to know that after Madrid, Toledo, Saragossa, and all the other large cities I have passed through in my tour of Spain, these little ones are mere villages to me. As we got further on the plain, there appeared to be a great concourse of people about Olmédo: so that, when we were near enough to distinguish objects, we were in no want of food for speculation.

There were three tents pitched at some distance from each other; and hard by, a bevy of cooks and scullions preparing an en-

J. DIDIER

"AS WE GOT FURTHER ON THE PLAIN, ETC."

tertainment. Here a party was laying covers on long tables set out under the tents; there a detachment was crowning the pitchers of Tellus with the gifts of Bacchus. The right wing was making the pots boil, the left was turning the spits and basting the meat. But what caught my attention more than all the rest, was a temporary stage of respectable dimensions. It was furnished with pasteboard scenes, painted in a tawdry style, and the proscenium was decorated with Greek and Latin mottos. No sooner did the barber spy out these inscriptions, than he said to me—All these Greek words smell strongly of my uncle Thomas's lamp. I would lay a wager he has a hand in them, for between ourselves, he is a man of parts and learning. He knows all the classics by heart. If he would keep them to himself it would be very well, but he is always quoting them in company, and that people do not like. But then to be sure he has a right, because this uncle of mine has translated ever so many of the Latin poets and hard Greek authors with his own hand and pen. He has got all antiquity at his fingers' ends, as you may know by his ingenious and profound criticisms. If it had not been for him, we might never have learned that the Athenian schoolboys cried when they were flogged; we owe that fact in the history of education to his fundamental knowledge of the subject.

After my fellow-traveller and myself had looked about us, we had a mind to inquire what these preparations were for. Going about on the hunt, Diego recognized in the manager Signor Thomas de la Fuenta, to whom we made up with great eagerness. The schoolmaster did not recollect the young barber at first, such a difference had ten years made. But when convinced of his being his own flesh and blood, he gave him a cordial embrace, and said with much appearance of kindness—Ah! here you are, Diego, my dear nephew, here you are, restored after your wanderings to your native land. You come to revisit your household gods, your Penates, and heaven delivers you back safe and sound into the bosom of your family. Oh happy day, happy in all the proportions of arithmetic! A day worthy to be marked with a white stone and inserted among the Fasti! We have annals in abundance for you, my friend; your uncle Pedro, the poetaster, has fallen a sacrifice at the shrine of Pluto: to speak to the comprehension of the vulgar, he has been dead these three months. That miser, in his lifetime, was afraid of wanting necessaries—*Argenti pallebat amore*. Though the great were heaping wealth upon his head, his annual expenditure did not amount to ten pistoles. He had but one miserable attendant, and him he starved. This crazy fellow, more wrong-headed than the Grecian Aristippus, who ordered his slaves to leave all their costly baggage in the heart of Lybia, as an incumbrance on their march, heaped up all the gold and silver he could scrape together. And to what end? for those very heirs whom he refused to acknowledge. He died worth thirty thousand ducats, shared between your father, your uncle Bertrand, and myself. We shall be able to do very well for our children. My brother Nicholas has already married off your sister Theresa to the son of a magistrate in this place—*Connubio junxit stabili propriamque dicavit*. These very hymeneals, greeted auspiciously by all the nuptial powers, have we been celebrating for these two days with all this pomp and luxury. These tents in the plain are of our pitching. Pedro's three heirs have each a booth of his own, and we defray the expenses of the day alternately. I wish you had come sooner, you might have seen the whole progress of our festivities. The day before yesterday, the wedding-day, your father gave his treat. It was a superb entertainment, succeeded by running at the ring. Your uncle, the mercer, regaled us yesterday with a fête champêtre, and paid the piper handsomely. There were

ten of the best grown boys, and ten young girls, dressed out in pastoral weeds; all the frippery in his shop was brought out to prank
them up. This assemblage of Ganymedes and Houris ran through
all the mazes of the dance, and warbled forth a thousand tender and
spirit-stirring lays. And yet, though nothing was ever more genteel, the effect was not thought striking; but that must be owing
to the bad taste of the spectators, the simplicity of pastoral is lost
upon the present age.

To-day, the wheels are greased by your humble servant, and I
mean to present the burgesses of Olmédo with a pageant of my own
invention—*Finis coronabit opus.* I have got a stage erected, on
which, God willing, shall be represented by my scholars a piece of
my own composing, entitled and called—*The Amusements of Muley
Bugentuf, King of Morocco.* It will be played to perfection, for my
pupils declaim like the players of Madrid. They are lads of family
at Penafiel and Segovia, boarders with me. They know how to
touch the passions ! To be sure they have rehearsed under my tuition; their emphasis will seem as if struck in the mint of their
master—*ut ita dicam.* With respect to the piece I shall not say a
word about it, you shall be taken by surprise. I shall simply state
that it must produce a deep impression on the audience. It is one
of those tragic subjects which harrow up the soul, by images of
death presented to the senses in all their fearful forms. I am of
Aristotle's mind, terror is a principal engine. Oh ! if I had written
for the stage, I would have introduced none but bloody tyrants,
and death-dispensing heroes. Not all the perfumes of Arabia should
have sweetened this blood-polluted hand, I would have been up to
my elbows in gore. There would have been tragedy with a vengeance; principal characters ! ay, guards and attendants, should all
have been sprawling together. I would have butchered every man
of them, and the prompter into the bargain. In a word, I refine
upon Aristotle, and border on the horrible, that is my taste. These
plays to tear a cat in, are the only things for popularity ; the actors
live merrily on their own dying speeches, and the authors roll in
luxury on the devastation of mankind.

Just as this harangue was over, we saw a great crowd of both
sexes coming out of town into the plain. Who should it be but
the new-married couple, attended by their families and friends, with
ten or twelve musicians in the van, producing a most obstreperous
din of harmony. We went up to them, and Diego introduced himself. Peals of congratulation were immediately rung through the
assembly, and every one was eager to shake him by the hand. He
had enough upon his shoulders to receive all their fraternal embraces. Relations and strangers were all for having a pull at him.
At length his father said—You are welcome, Diego. You find your
kinsmen living upon the fat of the land, my friend. I shall say no
more at present, a nod is as good as a wink. Meanwhile the company went forward upon the plain, took their stations under the
tents, and sat down to table. I kept close to my companion, and
we both dined with the happy couple, who appeared to be suitably
matched. The meal was not soon over, for the schoolmaster had

the vanity to give three courses, for the purpose of cutting out his
brothers, who had not been so magnificent in their hospitalities.

After the banquet, all the guests expressed their longing to see
Signor Thomas's play, not doubting but the performance of so
extraordinary a genius would deserve all their ears. We came in
front of the stage; the musicians had taken possession of the orchestra, for the overture and act-tunes. While every one was waiting in profound silence for the rising of the curtain, the actors appeared on the boards; and the author, with the piece in his hand,
sat down at the wing, in the prompter's place. Well might he call
it a tragedy, for in the first act the King of Morocco, by way of
diversion, shot an hundred Moorish slaves with arrows; in the second he beheaded thirty Portuguese officers, taken prisoners by one
of his captains : and in the third and last, this monarch, surfeited
with long-indulged libertinism, set fire with his own hands to the
seraglio where his wives were confined, and reduced it to ashes
with its inhabitants. The Moorish slaves, as well as the Portuguese
officers, were puppets on a very curious construction ; and the palace, built of pasteboard, looked very naturally in flames by means
of an artificial firework. This conflagration, accompanied by a
thousand piercing cries, issuing from the ruins, concluded the piece,
and the curtain dropped upon this amiable entertainment. The
whole plain resounded with the applause of this fine tragedy;
which spoke for the good taste of the poet, and proved that he
knew where to look out for a subject.

I did not suppose there was anything more to be seen after *The
Amusements of Muley Bugentuf*, but I was mistaken. Kettle-drums
and trumpets announced a new exhibition—the distribution of
prizes—for Thomas de la Fuenta, to give additional solemnity to
his olympics, had made all his boys, as well day-scholars as boarders,
write exercises ; and on this occasion he was to give to those who
had succeeded best, books bought at Segovia out of his own pocket.
All at once were brought upon the stage two long forms out of the
school, with a press full of old worm-eaten books in fine new bind-
ings. At this signal all the actors returned upon the stage, and
took their places round Signor Thomas, who looked as big as the
head of a college. He had a sheet of paper in his hand, with the
names of the successful candidates. This he gave to the King of
Morocco, who began calling over the list with an authoritative
voice. Each scholar, answering to his name, went humbly to receive a book from the hands of the bum-jerker; after this he was
crowned with laurel, and seated on one of the two benches to be
exposed to the gaze of the admiring company. Yet, desirous as
the schoolmaster might be to send the spectators away in good
humor, he brought his eggs to a bad market; for, having distributed
almost all the prizes to the boarders, according to the usual etiquette of pedagogues, that those who pay most must necessarily be
the cleverest fellows, the mammas of certain day-scholars caught
fire at this instance of partiality, and fell foul of the disciplinarian
thereupon ; so that the festival, hitherto so much to the glory of
the donor, seemed likely to have ended to the same tune as the
carousal of the Lapithæ.

BOOK THE THIRD.

CHAPTER I.

THE ARRIVAL OF GIL BLAS AT MADRID.   HIS FIRST PLACE THERE.

I MADE some stay with the young barber. At my departure, I met with a traveler of Segovia passing through Olmédo. He was returning with four mules from a trading expedition to Valladolid, and took me by way of back carriage. We got acquainted on the road, and he took such a fancy to me that nothing would serve him but I must be his guest at Segovia. He gave me free quarters for two days, and when he found me determined to leave him for Madrid under convoy of a muleteer, he troubled me with a letter, begging me to deliver it in person according to the superscription, without hinting that it was a letter of recommendation. I was punctual in calling on Signor Matheo Melendez. He was a woollen-draper, living at the gate of the Sun, at the corner of Trunkmaker street. No sooner had he broken the cover and read the contents, than he said with an air of complacency—Signor Gil Blas, my correspondent, Pedro Palacio, has written to me so pressingly in your favor, that I cannot do otherwise than offer you a bed at my house; moreover, he desires me to find you a good master, and I undertake the commission with pleasure. I have no doubt of suiting you to a hair.

I embraced the offer of Melendez the more gratefully because my funds were getting much below par ; but I was not long a burden on his hospitality. At the week's end, he told me that he had mentioned my name to a gentleman of his acquaintance, who wanted a valet-de-chambre, and, according to present appearances, the place would be not long vacant. In fact, this gentleman happened to make his appearance in the very nick—Sir, said Melendez, pushing me forward, you see before you the young man as by former advice. He is a pupil of honor and integrity. I can answer for him as if he was one of my own family. The gentleman looked at me with attention, said that my face was in my favor, and hired me at once. He has nothing to do but to follow me, added he, I will put him into the routine of his employment. At these words he wished the tradesman good morning, and took me into the High-street, directly over against St. Philip's church. We went into a very handsome house, of which he occupied one wing ; then going up five or six steps, he took me into a room secured by strong double doors, with an iron grate between. From this room we went into another, with a bed and other furniture, rather neat than gaudy.

If my new master had examined me closely, I had all my wits about me as well as he. He was a man on the wrong side of fifty, with a saturnine and serious air. His temper seemed to be even, and I thought no harm of him. He asked me several questions about my family; and liking my answers—Gil Blas, said he, I take you to be a very sensible lad, and am well pleased to have you in my service. On your part, you shall have no reason to complain. I will give you six rials a day board wages, besides vails. Then I require no great attendance, for I keep no table, but always dine out. You will only have to brush my clothes, and be your own master for the rest of the day. Only take care to be at home early in the evening, and to be in waiting at the door, that is your chief duty. After this lecture, he took six rials out of his purse, and gave them to me as earnest. We then went out, he locked the doors after him, and taking care of the keys—My friend, said he, you need not go with me, follow the devices of your own heart: but on my return this evening, let me find you on that staircase. With this injunction he left me to dispose of myself as seemed best in my own eyes.

In good sooth, Gil Blas, said I in a soliloquy, you have got a jewel of a master. What! fall in with an employer to give you six rials a day for wiping off the dust from his clothes, and putting his room to rights in the morning, with the liberty of walking about and taking your pleasure like a schoolboy in the holidays! By my troth! it is a place of ten thousand. No wonder I was in a hurry to get to Madrid, it was doubtless some mysterious boding of good fortune prepared for me. I spent the day in the streets, diverting myself with gaping at novelties—a busy occupation. In the evening, after supping at an ordinary not far from our house, I squatted myself down in the corner pointed out by my master. He came three quarters of an hour after me, and seemed pleased with my punctuality. Very well, said he, this is right, I like attentive servants. At these words, he opened the doors of his apartment, and closed them upon us again as soon as we had got in. As we had no candle, he took his tinder-box and struck a light. I then helped him to undress. When he was in bed, I lighted, by his order, a lamp in his chimney and carried the wax-light into the antechamber, where I lay in a press-bed without curtains. He got up the next day between nine and ten o'clock; I brushed his clothes. He paid me my six rials, and sent me packing till the evening. My mysterious master went out himself too, not without great caution in fastening the doors, and we parted for the remainder of the day.

Such was our course of life, very agreeable to me. The best of the joke was, that I did not know my master's name. Melendez did not know it himself. The gentleman came to his shop now and then, and bought a piece of cloth. My neighbors were as much at a loss as myself; they all assured me that my master was a perfect stranger, though he had lived two years in the ward. He visited no soul in the neighborhood, and some of them, a little given to scandal, concluded him to be no better than he should be. Suspicions got to be more rife; he was suspected of being a spy of Portugal, and it was thought but fair play to give a hint for my own good. This intimation troubled me. Thought I to myself, should this turn out to be a fact, I stand a chance for seeing the inside of a prison at Madrid. My innocence will be no security; my past ill-usage makes me look on justice with antipathy. Twice have I experienced that if the innocent are not condemned in a lump with the guilty, at least the rights of hospitality are too little regarded in their persons to make it pleasant to pass a summer in the purlieus of the law.

" SIR, SAID I ONE EVENING WHILE HE WAS UNDRESSING."

I consulted Melendez in so delicate a conjecture. He was at a loss how to advise me. Though he could not bring himself to believe that my master was a spy, he had no reason to be confident on the other side of the question. I determined to watch my employer, and to leave him if he turned out to be an enemy of the state; but then prudence and personal comfort required me to be certain of my fact. I began, therefore, to pry into his actions; and to sound him, Sir said I one evening while he was undressing, I do not know how one ought to live so as to be secure from reflections. The world is very scurrilous! We, among others, have neighbors not worth a curse. Sad dogs. You have no notion how they talk of us. Do they indeed, Gil Blas? quoth he. Be it so! but what can they say of us, my friend? Ah! truly, replied I, evil tongues never want a whet. Virtue herself furnishes weapons for her own martyrdom Our neighbors say that we are dangerous people, that we ought to be looked after by government; in a word, you are taken for a spy of Portugal. In throwing out this hint, I looked hard at my master, just as Alexander squinted at his physician, and pursed up all my penetration to remark upon the effect of my intelligence. There seemed to be a hitch in the muscles of my mysterious lord, altogether in unison with the suspicions of the neighborhood; and he fell into a brown study, which bore no very auspicious interpretation. However, he put a better face on the matter and said with sufficient composure: Gil Blas, leave our neighbors to discourse as they please, but let not our repose depend on their judgments. Never mind what they think of us, provided our own consciences do not wince.

Hereupon he went to bed, and I did the like, without knowing what course to take. The next day, just as we were on the point of going out in the morning, we heard a violent knocking at the outer door on the staircase. My master opened the inner, and looked through the grate. A well-dressed man said to him. Please your honor, I am an alguazil, come to inform you that Mr. Corregidor wishes to speak a word with you. What does he want? answered my pattern of secrecy. That is more than I know, sir, replied the alguazil; but you have only to go and wait on him; you will soon be informed. I am his most obedient, quoth my master, I have no business with him. At the tail of this speech, he banged the inner door; then, after walking up and down a little while, like one who pondered on the discourse of the alguazil, he put my six rials into my hand, and said: Gil Blas, you may go out, my friend; for my part, I shall stay at home a little longer, but have no occasion for you. He made an impression on my mind, by these words, that he was afraid of being taken up, and was therefore obliged to remain in his apartments. I left him there; and, to see how far my suspicions were founded, hid myself in a place whence I could see if he went out. I should have had patience to have staid there all the morning, if he had not saved me the trouble. But an hour after, I saw him walk the street with an ease and confidence which dumb-founded my sagacity. Yet far from yielding to these appearances, I mistrusted them; for my verdict went to condemnation. I considered his easy carriage as put on; and his staying at home as a finesse to secure his gold and jewels, when probably he was going to consult his safety by speedy flight. I had no idea of seeing him again, and doubted whether I should attend at his door in the evening; so persuaded was I, that the day would see him on the outside of the city, as his only refuge from impending danger. Yet I kept

my appointment; when, to my extreme surprise, my master returned
as usual. He went to bed without betraying the least uneasiness,
and got up the next morning with the same composure.

Just as he had finished dressing, another knock at the door!
My master looked through the grate. His friend the alguazil was
there again, and he asked him what he wanted. Open the door,
answered the alguazil; here is Mr. Corregidor. At this dreadful
name, my blood froze in my veins. I had a devilish loathing of
those gentry since I had passed through their hands, and could
have wished myself at that moment an hundred leagues from Madrid. As for my employer, less startled than myself, he opened the
door, and received the magistrate respectfully. You see, said the
corregidor, that I do not break in upon you with a whole posse:
my maxim is to do business in a quiet way. In spite of the ugly
reports circulated about you in the city, I think you deserve some
little attention. What is your name, and business at Madrid? Sir,
answered my master, I am from New Castile, and my title is Don
Bernard de Castil Blazo. With respect to my way of life, I lounge
about, frequent public places, and take my daily pleasure in a select
circle of polite company. Of course you have a handsome fortune!
replied the judge. No, sir, interrupted my Mecenas, I have neither
annuities, nor lands, nor houses. How do you live then? rejoined
the corregidor. I will show you, replied Don Bernard. At the
same time he lifted up a part of the hangings, before a door I had
not observed, opened that and one beyond, then took the magistrate
into a closet containing a large chest chuck full of gold.

Sir, said he again, you know that the Spaniards are pro-
verbially indolent; yet, whatever may be their general dislike to
labor, I may compliment myself on bettering the example. I have
a stock of laziness, which disqualifies me for all exertion. If I had
a mind to puff my vices into virtues, I might call this sloth of mine
a philosophical indifference, the work of a mind weaned from all
that worldlings court with so much ardor; but I will frankly own
myself constitutionally lazy, and so lazy, that rather than work for
my subsistence, I would lay myself down and starve. Therefore, to
lead a life befitting my fancy, not to have the trouble of looking
after my affairs, and above all to do without a steward, I have converted all my patrimony, consisting of several considerable estates,
into ready money. In this chest there are fifty thousand ducats;
more than enough for the remainder of my days, should I live
to be an hundred! For I do not spend a thousand a year, and am
already more than fifty years old. I have no fears, therefore, for
futurity, since I am not addicted, heaven be praised, to any one of
the three things which usually ruin men. I care little for the
pleasures of the table; I only play for my amusement; and I have
given up women. There is no chance of my being reckoned, in my
old age, among those libidinous grey-beards to whom jilts sell
their favors by troy weight.

You are a happy man! said the corregidor. They are in the
wrong to suspect you of being a spy: that office is quite out of
character for a man like you. Take your own course, Don Bernard:

continue to live as you like. Far from disturbing your peace, I declare myself your protector; I request your friendship, and pledge my own. Ah! sir, exclaimed my master, thrilled with these kind expressions, I accept with equal joy and gratitude your precious offer. In giving me your friendship you augment my wealth, and carry my happiness to its height. After this conversation, which the alguazil and myself heard from the closet door, the corregidor took his leave of Don Bernard, who could not do enough to express his sense of the obligation. On my part, mimicking my master in doing the honors of the house, I overburdened the alguazil with civilities. I made him a thousand low bows, though I felt for him in my sleeve the contempt and hatred which every honest man naturally entertains for an alguazil.

CHAPTER II.

THE ASTONISHMENT OF GIL BLAS AT MEETING CAPTAIN ROLANDO IN MADRID, AND THAT ROBBER'S CURIOUS NARRATIVE.

Don Bernard de Castil Blazo, having attended the corregidor to the street, returned in a hurry to fasten his strong box, and all the doors which secured it. We then went out, both of us well satisfied, he at having acquired a friend in power, and myself at finding my six rials a day secured to me. The desire of relating this adventure to Melendez made me bend my steps towards his house; but, near my journey's end, whom should I meet but Captain Rolando! My surprise was extreme, and I could not help quaking at the sight of him. He recollected me at once, accosted me gravely, and, still keeping up his tone of superiority, ordered me to follow him. I tremblingly obeyed, saying inwardly: Alas! he means, doubtless, to make me pay my debts! Whither will he lead me? There may, perhaps, be some subterraneous retreat in this city. Plague take it! If I thought so, I would soon show him I have not got the gout. I walked, therefore, behind him carefully looking out where he might stop, with the pious design of putting my best leg foremost, if there was anything in the shape of a trap-door.

Rolando soon dispersed my alarms. He went into a well-frequented tavern; I followed him. He called for the best wine, and ordered dinner. While it was getting ready, we went into a private room, where the captain addressed me as follows: You may well be astonished, Gil Blas, to renew your acquaintance with your old commander; and you will be still more so, when you have heard my tale. The day I left you in the cave, and went with my troop to Mansilla, for the purpose of selling the mules and horses we had taken the evening before, we met the son of the corregidor of Leon, attended by four men on horseback well armed, following his carriage. Two of his people we made to bite the dust, and the other two ran away. On this the coachman, alarmed for his master, cried out to us in a tone of supplication—Alas! my dear gentlemen, in God's name, do not kill the only son of his worship the corregidor of Leon. These words were far from softening my comrades; on the contrary, their fury knew no bounds. Good folks, said one of them, let not the son of a mortal enemy to men like us escape our vengeance. How many ornaments of our profession has his father cut off in their prime! Let us repay his cruelty with interest, and sacrifice this victim to their offended ghosts. The whole troop ap-

"THERE WAS NO WITHSTANDING SUCH A HOST."

plauded the fineness of this feeling, and my lieutenant himself was preparing to act as high priest at this unhallowed altar, when I interdicted the rites. Stop, said I; why shed blood without occasion? Let us rest contented with the youth's purse. As he makes no resistance, it would be against the laws of war to cut his throat. Besides, he is not answerable for his father's misdeeds; nay, his father only does his duty in condemning us to death, as we do ours in rifling travelers.

Thus did I plead for the corregidor's son, and my intercession was not unavailing. We only took every farthing of his money, and carried off with us the horses of the two men whom we had slain. These we sold with the rest at Mansilla. Thence we returned to the cavern, where we arrived the following morning a little before daybreak, We were not a little surprised to find the trap open, and still more so, when we found Leonarda handcuffed in the kitchen. She unraveled the mystery in two words. We wondered how you could have overreached us; no one could have thought you capable of serving us such a trick, and we forgave the effect for the merit of the invention. As soon as we had released our kitchen wench, I gave orders for a good luncheon. In the mean time we went to look after our horses in the stable, where the old negro, who had been left to himself for four-and-twenty hours, was at the last gasp. We did all we could for his relief, but he was too far gone; indeed so much reduced, that, in spite of our endeavors, we left the poor devil on the threshold of another world. It was very sad; but it did not spoil our appetites, and, after an abundant breakfast, we retired to our chambers, and slept away the whole day. On our awaking, Leonarda apprized us that Domingo had paid the debt of nature. We carried him to the charnel-house where you may recollect to have lodged, and there performed his obsequies, just as if he had been one of our own order.

Five or six days afterwards, it fell out that one morning, on a sally, we encountered three companies of the Holy Brotherhood, on the outskirts of the wood. They seemed waiting to attack us. We perceived but one troop at first. These we despised, though superior in number to our party, and rushed forward to the onset. But while we were at loggerheads with the first, two others in ambuscade came thundering down upon us: so that our valor was of no use. There was no withstanding such a host of enemies. Our lieutenant and two of our gang gave up the ghost on this occasion. As for the two others and myself, we were so closely pressed and hemmed in, as to be taken prisoners; and, while two detachments convoyed us to Leon, the third went to destroy our retreat. How it was discovered, I will briefly tell you. A peasant of Luceno, crossing the forest on his way home, by chance espied the trap-door of our subterraneous residence, which a certain young runaway had not shut down after him, for it was precisely the day when you took yourself off with the lady. He had a violent suspicion of its being our abode, without having the courage to go in. It was enough to mark the adjacent parts, by lightly peeling with his knife bark from the nearest trees, and so on, from distance to distance, till he was quite out of the wood. He then betook himself to Leon, with this grand discovery for the corregidor, who was so much the better pleased, as his son had been robbed by our gang. This magistrate collected together three companies to lay hold of us, and the peasant showed them the way.

My arrival in the town of Leon was as good as that of a wild beast to the inhabitants. Even though I had been a Portuguese general made prisoner of war, the people could not have been more anxious to see me. There he goes, was the cry; that is he, the famous captain, the terror of these parts. It would serve him right to tear him piecemeal with pincers, and make his comrades join in the chorus. To the corregidor, was the universal cry; and his worship began insulting me. So, so! said he, scoundrel as you are, the powers of justice, worn to a thread with your past irregularities, hand over the task of punishment to me as their delegate. Sir, answered I, great as my crimes may have been, at least the death of your only son is not to be laid at my door. His life was saved by me; you owe me some acknowledgment on that score. Oh! wretch, exclaimed he, there are no measures to be kept with people of your description. And though it were my wish to save you, my sacred office would not allow me to indulge my feelings. Having spoken to this effect, he committed us to a dungeon, where my companions had no time to lament their hard fate. They got out of confinement, at the end of three days, to expatiate with tragic energy at the place of execution. For my part, I took up my quarters in limbo for three complete weeks. My punishment seemingly was deferred only to render it more terrible; and I was looking for some refinement on the ordinary course of criminal justice, when the corregidor, having summoned me before him, said: Give ear to your sentence. You are free. Had it not been for you, my only son would have been assassinated on the highway. As a father, my gratitude was due for this service; but not being competent to acquit you in my capacity of a magistrate, I have written up to court in your favor; have solicited your pardon, and have obtained it. Go, then, withersoever it may seem good to you. But take my advice; profit by this lucky escape. Look to your paths, and give up the trade of a highwayman for good and all.

I was deeply impressed by this advice, and took my departure for Madrid, in the firm determination of mending my ways, and living quietly in that city. There I found my father and mother dead, and what they left behind them in the hands of an old kinsman, who administered duly and truly, as all trustees of course do. I saved three thousand ducats out of the fire; scarcely a quarter of what I was intitled to. But where was the remedy? There was no standing to the quirks and evasions of the law. Just to be doing something I have purchased an alguazil's place. My colleagues would have set their faces against my admission, for the honor of the cloth, had they known my history. Luckily they did not, or at least affected not to know it, which was just as good as the reality; for, in that illustrious body, it is the bounden duty and interest of every member to wear a mask. The pot cannot call the kettle hard names, thank heaven. The devil would have no great catch in the best of us. And yet, my friend, I could willingly unbosom myself to you without disguise. My present occupation is much against the grain; it requires too circumspect and too mysterious a conduct; there is nothing to be done but by underhand dealings, gravity, and cunning. Oh! for my first trade! The new one is safer, to be sure; but there is more fun in the other, and liberty is my motto. I feel disposed to get rid of my office, and set out some sunshiny morning for the mountains at the source of the Tagus. I know of a retreat thereabouts, inhabited by a numerous gang, composed chiefly of Catalonians: when I have said that, I need say no more. If you will go along with me, we will swell the number of those heroes. I shall be second in command. To make your footing respectable at once, I will swear that you have fought ten times by my side. Your valor shall mount to the very skies. I will tell more good of you than a commander-in-chief of a favorite officer. I will not say a word about the run-away trick, that would render you suspected of turning nose, therefore mum is the word. What say you to it? Are you ready to set off? I am impatient to know your mind.

Every one to his fancy, said I then to Rolando, you were born for bold exploits, and your friend for a serene and quiet life. I understand you, interrupted he; the lady whom love induced you to carry off still preserves her influence over your heart, and you doubtless lead with her that serene life of which you are enamored. Own the truth, master Gil Blas, she is become a thing of your own, and your are both living on the pistoles carried off from the subterraneous retreat. I told him he was mistaken : and, to set him right, related the lady's adventures and my own while we sat at dinner. When our meal was finished he led back to the subject of the Catalonians, and attempted once more to engage me in his project. But finding me inflexible, he looked at me with a terrific frown, and said seriously—Since you are dastard enough to prefer your servile condition to the honor of enlisting in a troop of brave fellows, I turn you adrift to your own grovelling inclinations. But mark me well, a lapse may be fatal. Forget our meeting of to-day, and never prate about me to any living soul ; for if I catch you bandying about my name in your idle talk . . . . . . you know my ways, I need say no more. With these words he called for the landlord, paid the reckoning, and we rose from table to go away.

CHAPTER III.

GIL BLAS IS DISMISSED BY DON BERNARD DE CASTIL BLAZO, AND ENTERS INTO THE SERVICE OF A BEAU.

As we were coming out of the tavern, and taking our leave, my master was passing along the street. He saw me, and I observed him look more than once at the captain. I had no doubt but he was surprised at meeting me in such company. It is certain that Rolando's physiognomy and air were not much in favor of moral qualities. He was a gigantic fellow, with a long face, a parrot's beak, and a very rascally contour, without being absolutely ugly.

I was not mistaken in my guess. In the evening I found Don Bernard harping on the captain's figure, and charmingly disposed to believe all the fine things I could have said of him, if my tongue had not been tied. Gil Blas, said he, who is that great shark I saw with you awhile ago? I told him it was an alguazil, and thought to have got off with that answer, but he returned to the charge; and observing my confusion, from the remembrance of the threats used by Rolando, broke off the conversation abruptly and went to bed. The next morning, when I had performed my ordinary duties, he counted me over six ducats instead of six rials, and said— Here, my friend, this is what I give you for your services up to this day. Go and look out for another place. A servant keeping such high company is too much for me. I bethought myself of saying, in my own defence, that I had known that alguazil, by having prescribed for him at Valladolid, while I was practising medicine. Very good, replied my master, the shift is ingenious enough; you might have thought of it last night, and not have looked so foolish. Sir, rejoined I, in good truth prudence kept me silent, and gave to my reserve the aspect of guilt. Undoubtedly, resumed he, tapping me softly on the shoulder, it was carrying prudence very far, even to the confines of cunning. Go, lad, I have no further occasion for your services.

I went immediately to acquaint Melendez with the bad news, who told me, for my comfort, that he would engage to procure me a better berth. Indeed, some days after, he said—Gil Blas, my friend, you have no notion of the good luck in store for you. You will have the most agreeable post in the world. I am going to settle you with Don Matthias de Silva. He is a man of the first fashion, one of those young noblemen commonly distinguished by the appellation of beaus. I have the honor of his custom. He takes up goods of me, on tick, indeed, but these great men are good pay in the long run, they often marry rich heiresses, and then old scores are wiped off; or, should that fail, a tradesman who understands his business puts such a price upon his article, that if three-fourths of his debts are bad, he is no loser. Don Matthias's steward is my intimate friend. Let us go and look for him. It will be for him to present you to his master, and you may rely upon it, that for my sake he will treat you with high consideration.

As we were on our way to Don Matthias's house, this honest shopkeeper said—it is fit, methinks, that you should be let into the steward's character. His name is Gregorio Rodriguez. Between ourselves, he is a man of low birth, with a talent for intrigue, in which vocation he has labored till a stewardship in two distressed families completed their ruin, and made his fortune. I give you notice, that his vanity is excessive; he loves to see the under-servants creeping and crawling at his feet. It is with him they must make interest if they have any favor to beg of their master, for should they happen to obtain it without his interference, he has always some shift or other at hand to get the boon revoked, or at least to render it of no avail. Regulate your conduct on this hint, Gil Blas; pay court to Signor Rodriguez in preference to your master himself, and leave no stone unturned to get into his good graces. His friendship will be of material service to you. He will pay your wages to the day; and, if you have management enough to worm yourself into his confidence, you may chance to pick up some of the fragments which fall from his table. There are enough for an hungrier dog than you! Don Matthias is a young nobleman, with no thought to throw away but on his pleasures, nor the slightest suspicion how his own affairs are going on. What a house for a steward who knows how to be a steward!

When we got to our journey's end, we asked to speak with Signor Rodriguez. We were told that we should find him in his own apartment. There he was, sure enough, and with him a clownish sort of fellow holding a blue bag, full of money. The steward, looking more wan and yellow than a girl in a hurry for a husband, ran up to Melendez with open arms; the draper was not behindhand with him, and they each hugged the other with a show of friendship, at least as much indebted to art as nature for its plausible effect. After this, the next question was about me. Rodriguez examined me from top to toe; saying very civilly at the same time that I was just such a one as Don Matthias wanted, and that he would with pleasure take upon himself to present me to that nobleman. Thereupon Melendez gave him to understand how deeply he was interested in my behalf; he begged the steward to take me under his protection, and leaving me with him, after plenty of compliments, withdrew. As soon as he was gone out, Rodriguez said, I will introduce you to my master the moment I have dispatched this honest husbandman. He called the countryman to him forthwith, and taking his bag, Talego, said he, let us see if the five hundred pistoles are all right. He counted over the money himself. As the sum was found to be exact, the countryman took a receipt and went away. The cash was put back again into the bag. It was my turn next to be attended to. We may now, said my new patron, go to my master's levee. He usually gets up about noon, it is now near one o'clock, and must be daylight in his apartment.

Don Matthias had indeed just risen. He was still in his morning gown, kicking his heels in a great chair, with a leg tossed over one of the elbows, swinging backwards and forwards, and manufacturing his own snuff. His conversation was addressed to a footman in waiting, who officiated as a temporary valet-de-chambre. My lord, said the steward, here is a young man whom I take the liberty of presenting to your lordship in the place of him you discharged the day before yesterday. Your draper, Melendez, has given him a character; he undertakes for his qualifications, and I believe you will be very well pleased with him. That is enough, answered the young nobleman, since he has your recommendation, I adopt him blindfold into my retinue. He is my valet-de-chambre at once; that business is settled. Let us talk of other matters, Rodriguez, you are come just in time, I was going to send for you. I have a budget of bad news, my dear Rodriguez. I played with ill luck last night, an hundred pistoles in my pocket lost, and two hundred more on credit. You know how indispensable it is for persons of high rank to pay their debts of honor. As for any other, it is no matter when they are paid. Punctuality is all very well between one tradesman and another, but they cannot expect it from one of us. These two hundred pistoles must be raised forthwith and sent to the Countess de Pedrosa. Sir, quoth the steward, that is sooner said than done. Where, prythee, am I to get such a sum? Threaten as I will, I never touch a marvedi from your tenants. And yet your establishment is to be kept up in style, and I am wearing myself to a thread in furnishing the ways and means. It is true that hitherto, heaven be praised, we have rubbed on, but what witch to conjure for a wind now, I know not, the case is desperate. All this prosing is extremely impertinent, interrupted Don Matthias; this counting-house talk makes me hideously nervous. So then, Rodriguez, you really think to undertake my reform, and metamorphose me into a plodding manager of my own estates? A very elegant sort of pastime for a man in my station of life; a man of rank and fashion! Grant me patience, replied the steward; at the rate we are driving now, it is easily calculated how soon you will be released from all those cares. You are a very great bore, resumed the young nobleman rather peevishly, this brutal importunity is downright murder to one's feelings. I hate loud music, be so good as to let me be ruined *pianissimo*. I tell you I want two hundred pistoles, and I must have them. Why, then, said Rodriguez, we must have recourse to the old rascal who has lent you so much already on usurious terms. Have recourse to the devil, if he will do you any good, answered Don Matthias; only let me have two hundred pistoles, and it is the same thing to me how you manage to get them.

While he was uttering these words in a hasty and fretful tone, the steward went out: and Don Antonio Centellés, a young man of quality, came in. What is the matter, my friend? said this last to my master: your atmosphere is overcast; I trace passion in the lines of your countenance. Who can have ruffled that sweet temper? I would lay a wager, it was that booby just gone out. Yes, answered Don Matthias, he is my steward. Every time he comes to speak to me, I am in an agony for a quarter of an hour or twenty minutes. He rings the changes on the state of my affairs; and tells me that I am spending principal and interest. . . . . A beast! He will say next, that I have ruined him into the bargain: My dear fellow, replied Don Antonio, I am exactly in the same situation. My man of business is just such another scarecrow as your steward. When the sneaking scoundrel, after repeated demands, brings me some niggardly supply, it is just as if he was lending me his own. He expostulates most barbarously. Sir, says he, you are going to rack and ruin; there is an execution out against you. I am obliged to cut him short, and beg him to remonstrate in epitome. The worst of it is, said Don Matthias that there is no doing without these fellows; they are the penance attached to our elegant indiscretions. Just so, replied Centellés. . . . . But listen, pursued he, bursting into a fit of laughter; a pleasant idea has just struck me. Nothing was ever more farcically fancied.

We may introduce a *buffo caricato* into our serious opera, and relieve the knell of our departed goods and chattels with an humorous divertisement. The plot is thus: let me try to borrow from your steward whatever you want. You shall do the same with my man of business. Then let them both preach as they please; we shall hearken with the utmost composure. Your steward will come and open his case to me; my man of business will plead the poverty of the land to you. I shall hear of nothing, but your extravagance; and you will see your own in mine as in a glass. It will be vastly entertaining.

A thousand brilliant conceits followed this flight of genius, and put the young patricians into high spirits, so that they kept up the ball with vivacity, if not with wit. Their conversation was interrupted by Gregorio Rodriguez, who brought back with him a little old man with a bald head. Don Antonio was for moving off. Farewell, Don Matthias, said he, we shall meet again anon. I leave you with these gentlemen; you have, doubtless, some state affairs to discuss in council. Oh! no, no, answered my master, you had better stop; you will not interrupt us. This warm old gentleman has the moderation to lend me money at twenty per cent. What! at twenty per cent! exclaimed Centellés in a tone of astonishment. In good truth! I wish you joy on being in such hands. I do not come off so cheaply, for my part: I pay through the nose for every farthing I get. My loans are generally raised at double that per cent. There is usury! said the father of the usurious tribe; unconscionable dogs! Where do they expect to go when they die? I do not wonder there is so strong a prejudice against money-lenders. It is the exorbitant profit which some of them derive from their discounts, that brings reproach and ill-will upon us all. If all my brethren of the blue balls were like me, we should not be treated so scurvily; for my part, I only lend to do my duty towards my neighbor. Ah! if times were as good now as in my early days, my purse should be at your service as a friend; and even now, in the present distress of the money-market, it goes against the grain to take a poor twenty per cent. But one would think the money was all gone back to the mines whence it came: there is no such thing to be had, and the scarcity compels me to depart a little from the disinterested severity of my benevolence, How much do you want? pursued he, addressing my master. Two hundred pistoles, answered Don Matthias. I have four hundred here in a bag, replied the usurer; it is only to give you half of them. At the same time he drew from underneath his cloak a blue bag, looking just like that in which farmer Talego had left five hundred pistoles with Rodriguez. I was not long in forming my judgment of the matter, and saw plainly that Melendez had not bragged without reason of the steward's aptness in the ways of the world. The old man emptied the bag, displayed the cash on a table, and set about counting it. The sight set all my master's extravagant passions in a flame; the sum total proved very striking to his comprehension. Signor Descomulgado, said he to the usurer, I have just made a very sensible reflection; I am a great fool, I only borrow enough to

redeem my credit, without thinking of my empty pockets. I should
be obliged to give you the trouble of coming again to-morrow. I
think, therefore, it will be best to spare your age and infirmities,
and ease you of the four hundred at once. My lord, answered the
old man, I had destined half of this money to a good licentiate, who
lays out the income of his large preferments in those pious and
charitable uses for which they were originally given to the clergy,
as stewards of the poor, and guides to the young and unwary. In
pursuance of this end, it is his great delight to wean young girls
from the seduction of a wicked world, and place them in a snug
well-furnished little box of his own, where they may be obnoxious
to his ghostly admonitions by day and by night. But, since you
have occasion for the whole sum, it is at your disposal. Something
by way of security. . . . . . Oh! as for security, interrupted Rodriguez, taking a paper out of his pocket, you shall have as good as
the bank. Here is a note which Signor Don Matthias has only
just to sign. He makes over five hundred pistoles, due from one
of his tenants, Talego, a wealthy yeoman of Mondejar. That is
enough, replied the usurer, I never split hairs, but deal upon the
square. The steward insinuated a pen between his master's fingers,
who signed his name at the bottom of the note, without reading it ;
and whistled as he signed for want of thought.

That business settled, the old man took his leave of my noble
employer, who shook him cordially by the hand, saying: Till I
have the pleasure of seeing you again, good master pounds, shil-
lings, and pence, I am your most devoted humble servant. I do
not know why you should all be lumped together for a set of blood-
suckers ; you seem to me a necessary link in the chain of well-or-
dered society. You are as good as a physician to us pecuniary invalids of quality, and keep us alive by artificial restoratives in the
last stage of a consumptive purse. You are in the right, exclaimed
Centellés. Usurers are a very gentlemanly order in society, and I
must not be denied the privilege of paying my compliments to this
illustrious specimen, for the sake of his twenty per cent. With
this banter, he came up and threw his arms about the old man's
neck : and these two overgrown children, for their amusement, began sending him backward and forward between them like a shut-
tlecock. After they had tossed him from pillar to post, they suffered him to depart with the steward, who ought to have come in
for his share of the game, and for something a little more serious.

When Rodriguez and his stalking-horse had left the room,
Don Matthias sent, by the lacquey in waiting, half his pistoles to
the Countess de Pedrosa, and deposited the other half in a long
purse worked with gold and silk, which he usually wore in his pocket. Very well pleased to find himself in cash, he said to Don Antonio, with an air of gayety : What shall we do with ourselves to-
day ? Let us call a council. That is talking like a statesman answered Centellés : I am your man : let us ponder gravely. While
they were collecting their deliberative wisdom on the course they
were to pursue for the day, two other noblemen came in ; Don
Alexo Segiar and Don Ferdinand de Gamboa ; both nearly about

my master's age, that is, from eight and twenty to thirty. These four jolly blades began with such hearty salutations, as if they had not met for these ten years. After that, Don Ferdinand, a professed bacchanalian, made his proposals to Don Matthias and Don Antonio: Gentlemen, said he, where do you dine to-day? If you are not engaged, I will take you to a tavern, where you shall quaff celestial liquor. I supped there last night, and did not come away till between five and six this morning. Would to heaven, exclaimed my master, I had done the same! I should not have lost my money.

For my part, said Centellés, I treated myself yesterday evening with a new amusement: for variety has always its charms for me. Nothing but a change of pleasures can make the dull round of human life supportable. One of my friends introduced me neck and heels to one of those gentry ycleped tax-gatherers, who do the government business and their own at the same time. There was no want of magnificence, good taste, or a well-designed set out table; but I found in the family itself an highly seasoned relish of absurdity. The farmer of the revenues, though the most meanly extracted of the whole party, must set up for a great man; and his wife, though hideously ugly, was a goddess in her own estimation, and made a thousand silly speeches, the zest of which was heightened by a Biscayan accent. Add to this, that there were four or five children with their tutor at table. Judge if it must not have been an amusing family party.

As for me, gentlemen, said Don Alexo Segiar, I supped with Arsenia the actress. We were six at table: Arsenia, Florimonde, a coquet of her acquaintance, the Marquis de Zenette, Don Juan de Moncade, and your humble servant. We passed the night in drinking and talking bawdy. What a flow of soul! To be sure, Arsenia and Florimonde are not strong in their upper works; but then they have a facility in their vocation which is more than all the wit in the world. They are the dearest madcaps, gay, romping, and rampant: they are an hundred times better than your modest women of sense and discretion.

CHAPTER IV.

GIL BLAS GETS INTO COMPANY WITH HIS FELLOWS; THEY SHOW
  HIM A READY ROAD TO THE REPUTATION OF WIT, AND IMPOSE
  ON HIM A SINGULAR OATH.

THOSE noblemen pursued this strain of conversation, till Don Matthias, about whose person I was fiddling all the while, was ready to go out. He then told me to follow him; and this bevy of fashionables set sail together for the tavern, whither Don Ferdinand de Gamboa proposed to conduct them. I began my march in the rear rank with three other valets; for each of the gentlemen had his own. I remarked with astonishment that these three servants copied their masters, and assumed the same follies. I introduced myself as a new comer. They returned my salute in form; and one of them, after having taken measure of me very accurately, said—Brother, I perceive, by your gait, that you have never yet lived with a young nobleman. Alas! no, answered I, neither have I been long in Madrid. So it appears, replied he, you smell strong of the country. You seem timid and embarrassed; there is an hitch in your deportment. But no matter, we will soon wear off all stiffness, take my word for it. Perhaps you think better of me than I deserve, said I. No, resumed he, no; there is no such cub as we cannot lick into shape; assure yourself of that.

This specimen was enough to convince me that I had hearty fellows for my comrades, and that I could not be in better hands to initiate me into high life below-stairs. On our arrival at the tavern, we found an entertainment ready which Signor Don Ferdinand had been so provident as to order in the morning. Our masters sat down to table, and we arranged ourselves behind their chairs. The conversation was spirited and lively. My ears tingled to hear them. Their humor, their way of thinking, their mode of expression diverted me. What fire! what sallies of imagination! They appeared like a new order of beings. With the dessert, we sat before them a great choice of the best wines in Spain, and left the room, to go to dinner in a little parlor, where our cloth was laid.

I was not long in discovering that the combatants in our lists had more to recommend them than appeared at first sight. They were not satisfied with aping the manners of their masters, but even copied their phrases; and these varlets gave such a fac-simile, that bating a little vulgarity, they might have passed themselves off very well. I admired their free and easy carriage; still more was I charmed with their wit, but despaired of ever coming up to them in my own person. Don Ferdinand's servant, on the score of his master treating ours, did the honors; and, determined to do the thing genteelly, he called the landlord, and said to him—Master tapster, give us ten bottles of your very best wine; and, as you have an happy knack of doing, make the gentlemen up-stairs believe that they have drank them. With all my heart, answered the landlord; but, Master Gaspard, you know that Signor Don Ferdinand owes me for a good many dinners already. If through your kind intervention I could get some little matter on account. . . . . Oh! interrupted the valet, do not be at all uneasy about your debt: I will take it upon myself; put it down to me. It is true that some unmannerly creditors have preferred legal measures to a reliance on our honor; but we shall take the first opportunity of obtaining a replevy, and will pay you without looking at your bill. To have my master on your books is like so many ingots of gold. The landlord brought us the wine, in spite of unmannerly creditors; and we drank to a speedy replevy. It was as good as a comedy to see us drinking each other's health every minute, under our masters' titles. Don Antonio's servant called Don Ferdinand's plain Gamboa, and Don Ferdinand's servant called Don Antonio's Centellés: they dubbed me Silva; and we kept pace in drunkenness, under these borrowed names, with the noblemen to whom they properly belonged.

Though my wit was less conspicuous than that of the other guests, they lost no opportunity of testifying their pleasure in my acquaintance. Silva, said one of our merriest soakers, we shall make something of you, my friend. I perceive that you have wit at will, if you did but know how to draw upon it. The fear of talking absurdly prevents you from throwing out at all; and yet it is only by a bold push that a thousand people now-a-days set themselves up for good companions. Do you wish to be bright? You have only to give the reins to your loquacity, and to venture indiscriminately on whatever comes uppermost: your blunders will pass for the eccentricities of genius. Though you should utter an hundred extravagancies, let but a single good joke be packed up in the bundle, the nonsense shall be all forgotten, the witticism bandied about, and your talent be puffed into high repute. This is the happy method our masters have devised, and it ought to be adopted by all new candidates. Besides that I had but too strong a wish to pass for a clever fellow, the trick they taught me appeared so easy in the performance, that it ought not to be buried in obscurity. I tried it at once, and the fumes of the wine contributed to my success; that is to say, I talked at random, and had the good luck to strike out of much absurdity some flashes of merriment, very acceptable to my audience. This first essay inspired me with confidence. I redoubled my sprightliness, to sparkle in repartee; and chance gave a successful issue to my endeavors.

Well done! said my fellow-servant who had addressed me in the street, do not you begin to shake off your rustic manners? You have not been two hours in our company, and you are quite another creature: your improvement will be visible every day. This it is to wait on people of quality. It causes an elevation, which the mind can never attain under a plebeian roof. Doubtless, answered I— and for that reason I shall henceforth dedicate my little talents to the nobility. That is bravely said, roared out Don Ferdinand's servant, half seas over, commoners are not entitled to possess such a fund of superior genius as exists in us. Come, gentlemen, let us make a vow never to colleague with any such beggarly fellows; let us swear to that by Styx. We laughed heartily at Gaspard's conceit: the proposal was received with applause: and we took this mock oath with our glass in our hands.

Thus sat we at table till our masters were pleased to get up from it. This was at midnight; an outrageous instance of sobriety, in the opinion of my colleagues. To be sure, these noble lords left the tavern so early only to visit a celebrated wanton, lodging in the purlieus of the court, and keeping open house night and day for the votaries of pleasure. She was a woman from five and thirty to forty, still in the height of her charms, entertaining in her discourse, and so perfect a mistress in the art of pleasure, that she sold the waste and refuse of her beauty at a higher price than the first sample of the unadulterated article. She had always two or three other pieces of damaged goods in the house, who contributed not a little to the great concourse of nobility resorting thither. The afternoon was spent in play; then supper, and the night passed in drinking and making merry. Our masters staid till morning, and so did we, without thinking the time long; for, while they were toying with the mistresses, we attacked the maids. At length, we all parted when daylight peeped in on our festivities, and went to bed each of us at our separate homes.

My master getting up at his usual time, about noon, dressed himself. He went out. I followed him, and we paid a visit to Don Antonio Centellés, with whom we found one Don Alvaro de Acuna. He was an old gentleman, who gave lectures on the sciences of debauchery. The rising generation, if they wanted to qualify themselves for fine gentlemen, put themselves under his tuition. He molded their ductile habits to pleasure, taught them to make a distinguished figure in the world, and to squander their substance: he had no qualms as to running out his own, for the deed was done. After these three blades had exchanged the compliments of the morning, Centellés said to my master—In good faith, Don Matthias, you could not have come at a more lucky time. Don Alvar is come to take me with him to a dinner, given by a citizen to the Marquis de Zenette and Don Juan de Moncade; and you shall be of the party. And what is the citizen's name? said Don Matthias. Gregorio de Noriega, said Don Alvar, and I will describe the young man in two words. His father, a rich jeweler, is gone abroad to attend the foreign markets, and left his son, at his departure, in the enjoyment of a large income. Gregorio is a blockhead, with a turn for every sort of extravagance, and an awkward hankering after the reputation of wit and fashion, in despite of nature. He has begged of me to give him a few instructions. I manage him completely; and can assure you, gentlemen, that I lead him a rare dance. His estate is rather deeply dipped already. I do not doubt it, exclaimed Centellés; I see the vulgar dog in an almshouse. Come, Don Matthias; let us honor the fellow with our acquaintance, and be in at the death of him. Willingly, answered my master, for I delight in seeing the fortune of these plebeian upstarts kicked over, when they affect to mix among us. Nothing, for instance, ever entertained me so much as the downfall of the toll-gatherer's son, whom play, and the vanity of figuring among the great, have stripped, till he has not a house over his head. Oh! as for that, replied Don Alvar, he deserves no pity, he is as great a coxcomb in his poverty as he was in his prosperity.

Centellés and my master accompanied Don Alvar to Gregorio's de Noriega's party. We went there also, that is, Mogicon and myself, both in ecstasy at having an opportunity of spunging on a citizen, and pleasing ourselves with the thought of being in at the death of him. At our entrance, we observed several men employed in preparing dinner; and there issued from the ragouts they were taking up, a vapor which conciliated the palate through the medium of the nostrils. The Marquis de Zenette and Don Juan de Moncade were just come. The founder of the feast seemed a great simpleton. He aped the man of fashion with a most clumsy grace; a wretched copy of admirable originals, or, more properly, an idiot in the chair of wisdom and taste. Figure to yourself a man of this character in the center of five bantering fellows, all intent on making a jest of him, and drawing him into ridiculous expenses. Gentlemen, said Don Alvar, after the first interchange of civilities, give me leave to introduce you to Signor Gregorio de Noriega, a most brilliant star in the hemisphere of fashion. He owns a thousand amiable qualities. Do you know that he has an highly cultivated understanding? Choose your own subject, he is equally at home in every branch, from the subtilty and closeness of logic, to the elementary science of the criss-cross-row. Oh! this is really too flattering, interrupted the scot and lot gentleman with a very uncouth laugh. I might, Signor Alvaro, put you to the blush as you have put me; for you may truly be termed a reservoir as it were, a common sewer of erudition. I had no intention, replied Don Alvaro, to draw upon myself so savory an ecomium; but truly, gentlemen, Signor Gregorio cannot fail of establishing a name in the world. As for me, said Don Antonio, what is so delightful in my eyes, far above the honors of logic or the criss-cross-row, is the tasteful selection of his company. Instead of demeaning himself to the level of tradesmen, he associates only with the young nobility, and sets the expense at nought. There is an elevation of sentiment in this conduct which enchants me: and this is what you may truly call disbursing with taste and judgment.

These ironical speeches were only the preludes to a continual strain of banter. Poor Gregorio was attacked on all hands. The wits shot their bolts by turns, but they made no impression on the fool; on the contrary, he took all they said literally, and seemed highly pleased with his guests, as if they did him a favor by making him their laughing-stock. In short, he served them for a butt while they sat at table, which they did not quit during the afternoon, nor till late at night. We, as well as our masters, drank as we liked, so that the servants'-hall and the dining-room were in equally high order when we took our leave of the young jeweler.

CHAPTER V.

GIL BLAS BECOMES THE DARLING OF THE FAIR SEX, AND MAKES AN INTERESTING ACQUAINTANCE.

AFTER some hours' sleep I got up in fine spirits; and calling the advice of Melendez to mind, went, till my master was stirring, to pay my court to our steward, whose vanity was rather flattered by this attention. He received me with a gracious air, and inquired how I was reconciled to the habits and manners of the young nobility. I answered, that they were strange to me as yet, but that use and good example might work wonders in the end.

Use and good example did work wonders, and that right soon. My temper and conduct were quite altered. From a discreet, sober lad, I got to be a lively, heedless merry andrew. Don Antonio's servant paid me a compliment on my transformation, and told me that there wanted nothing but a tender interest in the lovely part of the creation to shine like a new star dropped from the heavens. He pointed out to me that it was an indispensable requisite in the character of a pretty fellow, that all our set were well with some fine woman or other; and that he himself, to his own share, engrossed the favors of two beauties in high life. I was of opinion that the rascal lied. Master Mogicon, said I, you are doubtless a very dapper, lively little fellow, with a modest assurance; but still I do not comprehend how women of quality, not having your sweet person on their own private establishments, should run the risk of being detected in an intrigue with a footman out of doors. Oh! as for that, answered he, they do not know my condition. To my master's wardrobe, and even to his name, am I indebted for these conquests. I will tell you how it is. I dress myself up as a young nobleman, and assume the manners of one. I go to public places, and tip the wink first to one woman and then to another, till I meet with one who returns the signal. Her I follow, and find means to speak with her. I take the name of Don Antonio Centellés. I plead for an assignation, the lady is squeamish about it; I am pressing, she is kind, *et cætera*. Thus it is, my fine fellow, that I contrive to carry on my intrigues, and I would have you profit by the hint.

I was too ambitious of shining like a new star dropped from the heavens, to turn a deaf ear to such counsel; besides, there was about me no aversion to an amour. I therefore laid a plan to disguise myself as a young nobleman, and look out for adventures of gallantry. There was a risk in assuming my masquerade dress at home, lest it might be observed. I took a complete suit from my master's wardrobe, and made it up into a bundle, which I carried to a barber's, where I thought I could dress and undress conveniently. There I tricked myself out to the best advantage. The barber too lent a helping hand to my attire. When we thought it adjusted to a nicety, I sauntered towards Saint Jerome's meadow, whence I felt morally certain that I should not return without making an impression. But I could not even get thither, without a proof of my own attractions.

As I was crossing a bye-street, a lady of genteel figure, elegantly dressed, came out of a small house, and got into an hired carriage standing at the door. I stopped short to look at her, and bowed significantly, so as to convey an intimation that my heart was not insensible. On her part, to show me that her face was not less lovely than her person, she lifted up her veil for a moment. In the mean time the coach set off, and I stood stock still in the street, not a little stiffened at this vision. A vastly pretty woman! said I to myself, bless us! this is just what is wanting to make me perfectly accomplished. If the two ladies who share Mogicon between them are equally handsome, the scoundrel is in luck! I should be delighted with her for a mistress. Ruminating on these things, I looked by chance towards the house whence that lovely creature had glided, and saw at a window on the ground floor an old woman beckoning me to come in.

I flew like lightning into the house, and found in a very neat parlor, this venerable and wary matron, who, taking me for a marquis at least, dropped a low curtsey, and said—I doubt not, my lord, but you must have a bad opinion of a woman who, without the slightest acquaintance, beckons you out of the street; but you will perhaps judge more favorably of me when you shall know that I do not pay that compliment promiscuously. You look like a man of fashion! You are perfectly in the right, my old girl, interrupted I, stretching out my right leg, and throwing the weight of my body on my left hip; mine is, vanity apart, one of the best families in Spain. It must be so by your looks, replied she, and I will fairly own that I delight in doing a kindness to people of quality, that is my weak side. I watched you through my window. You looked very earnestly at a lady who has just left me. Perhaps you may have taken a fancy to her? tell me so plainly. By the honor of my house, answered I, she has shot me through the heart. I never saw anything so tempting; a most divine creature! Do bring us acquainted, my dear, and rely on my gratitude. It is worth while to do these little offices for us of the beau monde; they are better paid than our bills.

I have told you once for all, replied the old woman, I am entirely devoted to people of condition; it is my passion to be useful to them: I receive here, for example, a certain class of ladies, whom appearances prevent from seeing their favorites at home. I lend them my house, and thus the warmth of their constitutions is indulged, without risk to their characters. Vastly well, quoth I, and you have just done that kindness to the lady in question? No, answered she, this is a young widow of quality, in want of an admirer; but so difficult in her choice, that I do not know whether you will do for her, however great your requisites may be. I have already introduced to her three well-furnished gallants, but she turned up her nose at them. Oh! egad, my life, exclaimed I, confidently, you have only to stick me in her skirts, I will give you a good account of her, take my word for it. I long to have a grapple with a beauty of such peremptory demands, they have not yet fallen in my way. Well, then, said the old woman, you have only to come hither to-morrow at the same hour, your curiosity shall be satisfied. I will not fail, rejoined I; we shall see whether a young nobleman can miss a conquest.

I returned to the little barber's without looking for other adventures, but deeply interested in the event of this. Therefore, on the following day, I went, in splendid attire, to the old woman's an hour sooner than the time. My lord, said she, you are punctual, and I take it kindly. To be sure the game is worth the chase. I have seen our young widow, and we have had a good deal of talk about you. Not a word was to be said; but I have taken such a liking to you that I cannot hold my tongue. You have made yourself agreeable, and will soon be a happy man. Between ourselves, the lady is a relishing morsel, her husband did not live long with her; he glided away like a shadow: she has all the merit of an absolute girl. The good old lady, no doubt, meant one of those clever girls, who contrive not to live single, though they live unmarried.

The heroine of the assignation came soon in an hired carriage, as on the day before, dressed very magnificently. As soon as she came into the room, I led off with five or six coxcombical bows, accompanied by the most fashionable grimaces. After this, I went up to her with a very familiar air, and said—My adored angel, you behold a gentleman of no mean rank, whom your charms have undone. Your image, since yesterday, has taken complete possession of my fancy, you have turned a duchess neck and heels out of my heart, who was beginning to establish a footing there. The triumph is too glorious for me, answered she, throwing off her veil, but still my transports are not without alloy. Young men of fashion love variety, and their hearts are, they say, bandied about from one to the other like a piece of base money. Ah! my sovereign mistress, replied I, let us leave the future to shift for itself, and think only of the present. You are lovely, I am in love. If my passion is not hateful to you, let it take its course at random. We will embark like true sailors, set the storms and shipwreck of a long voyage at defiance, and only take the fair weather of the time present into the account.

In finishing this speech, I threw myself in rapture at the feet of my nymph, and the better to hit off my assumed character, pressed her with some little peevishness not to delay my bliss. She seemed a little touched by my remonstrances, but thought it too soon to yield, and giving me a gentle rebuff—Hold, said she, you are too importunate, this is like a rake. I fear you are but a loose young fellow. For shame, madam, exclaimed I; can you set your face against what women of the first taste and condition encourage? A prejudice against what is vulgarly called vice may be all very well for citizens' wives. That is decisive, replied she, there is no resisting so forcible a plea. I see plainly that with men of your order dissimulation is to no purpose; a woman must meet you half way. Learn then your victory, added she with an appearance of disorder, as if her modesty suffered by the avowal; you have inspired me with sentiments such as are new to my heart, and I only wait to know who you are, that I may take you for my acknowledged lover. I believe you a young lord and a gentleman, yet there is no trusting to appearances; and however prepossessed I may be in your favor, I would not give away my affections to a stranger.

I recollected at the moment how Don Antonio's servant had got out of a similar perplexity; and determining, after his example, to pass for my master—Madam, said I to my dainty widow. I will not excuse myself from telling you my name, it is one that will not disparage its owner. Have you ever heard of Don Matthias de Silva? Yes, replied she; indeed I have seen him with a lady of my acquaintance. Though considerably improved in impudence, I was a little troubled by this discovery. Yet I rallied my forces in an instant, and extricated myself with a happy presence of mind. Well then, my fair one, retorted I, the lady of your acquaintance . . . . . knows a lord . . . . . of my acquaintance . . . . . and I am of his acquaintance ; of his own family, since you must know it. His grandfather married the sister-in-law of my father's uncle. You see we are very near relations. My name is Don Cæsar. I am the only son of the great Don Ferdinand de Ribera, slain fifteen years ago, in a battle on the frontiers of Portugal. I could give you all the particulars of the action ; it was a devilish sharp one . . . . . but to fight it over again would be losing the precious moments of mutual love.

After this discourse I got to be importunate and impassioned, but without bringing matters at all forwarder. The favors which my goddess winked at my snatching, tended only to make me languish for what she was more chary of. The tyrant got back to her coach, which was waiting at the door. Nevertheless, I withdrew, well enough pleased with my success though it still fell short of the only perfect issue. If, said I to myself, I have obtained indulgences but by halves, it is because this lady forsooth, is a high-born dame, and thinks it beneath her quality to play the very woman at the first interview. The pride of pedigree stands in the way of my advancement just now, but in a few days we shall be better acquainted. To be sure, it did not once come into my head that she might be one of those cunning gypsies always on the catch. Yet I liked better to look at things on the right side than on the wrong, and thus maintained a favorable opinion of my widow. We had agreed at parting to meet again on the day after the morrow ; and the hope of arriving at the summit of my wishes gave me a foretaste of the pleasures with which I tickled my fancy.

With my brain full of joyous traces, I returned to my barber. Having changed my dress, I went to attend my master at the tennis-court. I found him at play, and saw that he won , for he was not one of those impenetrable gamesters who make or mar a fortune without moving a muscle. In prosperity he was flippant and overbearing, but quite peevish on the losing side. He left the tennis-court in high spirits, and went for the *Prince's Theatre.* I followed him to the box-door, then putting a ducat into my hand— Here, Gil Blas, said he, as I have been a winner to-day, you shall not be the worse for it ; divert yourself with your friends, and come to me about midnight at Arsenia's, where I am to sup with Don Alexo Segiar. He then went in, and I stood debating with whom I should disburse my ducat according to the pious will of the founder. I did not muse long. Clarin Don Alexo's servant, just then came in my way. I took him to the next tavern, and we amused ourselves there till midnight. Thence we repaired to Arsenia's house, where Clarin had orders to attend A little footboy opened the door, and showed us into a room down-stairs, where Arsenia's waiting-woman, and the lady who held the same office about Florimonde, were laughing ready to split their sides, while their mistresses were above-stairs with our masters.

The addition of two jolly fellows just come from a good supper, could not be unwelcome to abigails, and to the abigails of actresses too, but what was my astonishment when in one of these lowly ladies I discovered my widow, my adorable widow, whom I took for a countess or a marchioness! She appeared equally amazed to see her dear Don Cæsar de Ribera metamorphosed into the valet of a beau. However, we looked at one another without being out of countenance indeed, such a tingling sensation of laughter came over us both, as we could not help indulging in. After which Laura, for that was her name, drawing me aside while Clarin was speaking to her fellow-servant, held out her hand to me very kindly, and said in a low voice—Accept this pledge, Signor Don Cæsar mutual congratulations are more to the purpose than mutual reproaches, my friend. You topped your part to perfection, and I was not quite contemptible in mine. What say you? confess now did not you take me for one of those precious peeresses who are fond of a little smuggled amusement? It is even so, answered I, but whoever you are, my empress, I have not changed my sentiments with my paraphernalia. Accept my services in good part, and let the valet-de-chambre of Don Matthias consummate what Don Cæsar has so happily begun. Get you gone, replied she, I like you ten times better in your natural than in your artificial character. You are as a man what I am as a woman, and that is the greatest compliment I can pay you. You are admitted into the number of my adorers. We have no longer any need of the old woman as a blind, you may come and see me whenever you like. We theatrical ladies are no slaves to form, but live higgledy piggledy with the men. I allow that the effects are sometimes visible, but the public wink hard at our irregularities : the drama's patrons, as you well know, give the drama's laws, and absolve us from all others.

We went no further, because there were bystanders. The conversation became general, lively, jovial, inclining to loose jokes, not very carefully wrapped up. We all of us bore a bob. Arsenia's attendant above all, my amiable Laura, was very conspicuous; but her wit was so extremely nimble, that her virtue could never overtake it. Our masters and the actresses on the floor above, raised incessant peals of laughter, which reached us in the regions below; and probably the entertainment was much alike with the celestials and the infernals. If all the knowing remarks had been written down, which escaped from the philosophers that night assembled at Arsenia's, I really think it would have been a manual for the rising generation. Yet we could not arrest the chaste moon in her progress; the rising of that blab, the sun, parted us. Clarin followed the heels of Don Alexo, and I went home with Don Matthias.

CHAPTER VI.

THE PRINCE'S COMPANY OF COMEDIANS.

MY master getting up the next day, received a note from Don Alexo Segiar, desiring his company immediately. We went, and found there the Marquis de Zenette, and another young nobleman of prepossessing manners, whom I had never seen. Don Matthias, said Segiar to my protector, introducing the stranger, give me leave to present Don Pompeyo de Castro, a relation of mine. He has been at the court of Portugal almost from his childhood. He reached Madrid last night, and returns to Lisbon to-morrow. He can allow me only one day. I wished to make the most of the precious moments, and thought of asking you and the Marquis de Zenette to make out the time agreeably. Thereupon my master and Don Alexo's relation embraced heartily, and complimented one another in the most extravagant manner. I was much pleased with Don Pompeyo's conversation, it showed both acuteness and solidity.

They dined with Segiar; and the gentlemen, after the dessert amused themselves at play till the theatre opened. Then they went all together to the *Prince's House*, to see a new tragedy, called *Th. Queen of Carthage*. At the end of the piece they returned to supper, and their conversation ran first on the composition, then upon the actors. As for the work, cried Don Matthias, I think very lightly of it. Eneas is a more pious blockhead there than in the Eneid. But it must be owned that the piece was played divinely. What does Signor Don Pompeyo think of it? He does not seem to agree with me. Gentlemen, said the illustrious stranger with a smile, you are so enraptured with your actors, and still more with your actresses, that I scarcely dare avow my dissent. That is very prudent, interrupted Don Alexo with a sneer, your criticism would be ill received. You should be tender of our actresses before the trumpeters of their fame. We carouse with them every day, we warrant them sound in their conceptions · we would give vouchers for the justness of their expression if it were necessary. No doubt of it, answered his kinsman, you would do the same kind office by their lives and their manners, from the same motives of companionable feeling.

Your ladies of the sock and buskin at Lisbon, said the Marquis de Zenette, laughing, are doubtless far superior? They certainly are, replied Don Pompeyo. They are some of them at least perfect in their cast. And these, resumed the Marquis, would be warranted by you in their conceptions and expressions? I have no personal acquaintance with them, rejoined Don Pompeyo. I am not of their revels, and can judge of their merit without partiality. Do you, in good earnest, think your company first-rate? No, really, said the Marquis, I think no such thing. and only plead the cause of a few individuals. I give up all the rest. Will you not allow extraordi-

nary powers to the actress who played Dido ? Did she not personate that queen with the dignity, and at the same time with all the
bewitching charms, calculated to realize our idea of the character?
Could you help admiring the skill with which she seizes on the
passions of the spectator, and harmonizes their tone to the vibrations she purposes to produce ? She may be called perfect in the
exquisite art of declaiming. I agree with you, said Don Pompeyo,
that she can touch the string either of terror or of pity: never did
any actress come closer to the heart, and the performance is altogether fine : but still she is not without her defects. Two or three
things disgusted me in her playing! Would she denote surprise ?
she glances her eyes to and fro in a most extravagant manner, altogether unbecoming her supposed majesty as a princess. Add to
this, that in swelling her voice, which is of itself sound and melli-
fluous, she goes out of her natural key, and assumes a harsh rant-
ing tone. Besides, it would seem as if she might be suspected in
more than one passage, of not very clearly comprehending her author. Yet I would in candor rather suppose her wanting in diligence than capacity.

As far as I see, said Don Matthias to the critic, you will never
write complimentary odes to our actresses ! Pardon me, answered
Don Pompeyo. I can discover high talent through all their imperfections. I must say that I was enchanted with the chambermaid in the interlude. What fine natural parts ! With what grace
she treads the stage ! Has she anything pointed to deliver ? she
heightens it by an arch smile, with a keen glance and sarcastic emphasis, which convey more to the understanding than the words to
the ear. It might be objected that she sometimes gives too much
scope to her animal spirits, and exceeds the limits of allowable
freedom, but that would be hypercritical. There is one bad habit
I should strongly advise her to correct. Sometimes in the very
crisis of the action, and in an affecting passage, she bursts in all at
once upon the interest with some misplaced jest, to curry favor
with the mob of barren spectators. The pit, you will say, is caught
by her artifice ; that may be well for her popularity, but not for
their taste.

And what do you think of the men ? interrupted the Marquis ; you
must give them no quarter, since you have handled the women so
roughly. Not so, said Don Pompeyo. There are some promising
young actors, and I am particularly well pleased with that corpu-
lent performer who played the part of Dido's prime minister. His
recitation is unaffected, and he declaims just as they do in Portugal. If you can bear such a fellow as that, said Segiar, you must
be charmed with the representative of Eneas. Did not you think him
a great, an original performer? Very original, indeed, answered
the critic ; his inflections are quite his own, they are as shrill as an
hautboy. Almost always out of nature, he rattles the impressive
words of the sentence off his tongue, while he labors and lingers on
the expletives ; the poor conjunctions are frightened at their own
report as they go off. He entertained me excessively, and especially
when he was expressing in confidence his distress at abandoning

the princess; never was grief more ludicrously depicted. Fair and softly, cousin, replied Don Alexo; you will make us believe at last that good taste is not greatly cultivated at the court of Portugal. Do you know the actor of whom we are speaking is esteemed a phenomenon? Did you not observe what thunders of applause he called down? He cannot therefore be contemptible. That therefore does not prove the proposition, replied Don Pompeyo. But, gentlemen, let us lay aside, I beseech you, the injudicious suffrages of the pit; they are often given to performers very unseasonably. Indeed, their boisterous tokens of approbation are more frequently bestowed on paltry copies than on original merit, as Phedrus teaches us by an ingenious fable. Allow me to repeat it as follows:—

The whole population of a city was assembled in a large square to see a pantomime played. Among the performers there was one whose feats were applauded every instant. This buffoon, at the end of the entertainment, wished to close the scene with a new device. He came alone upon the stage, stooping down, covering his head with his mantle, and began counterfeiting the squeak of a pig. He acquitted himself so naturally as to be suspected of having the animal itself concealed within the folds of his drapery. He stripped, but there was no pig. The assembly rang with more furious applause than ever. A peasant, among the spectators, was disgusted at this misplaced admiration. Gentlemen, exclaimed he, you are in the wrong to be so delighted with this buffoon, he is not so good a mimic as you take him for. I can enact the pig better; if you doubt it, only attend here this time to-morrow. The people, prejudiced in the cause of their favorite, collected in greater numbers on the next day, rather to hiss the countryman than to see what he could do. The rivals appeared on the stage. The buffoon began, and was more applauded than the day before. Then the farmer stooping down in his turn, with his head wrapped up in his cloak, pulled the ear of a real pig under his arm, and made it squeal most horribly. Yet this enlightened audience persisted in giving their preference to their favorite, and hooted the countryman off the boards; who producing the pig before he went, said—Gentlemen, you are not hissing me, but the original pig. So much for your judgment.

Cousin, said Don Alexo, your fable is rather satirical. Nevertheless, in spite of your pig, we will not bate an inch of our opinion. But let us change the subject, this is grown threadbare. Then you set off to-morrow, do what we can to keep you with us longer? I should like, answered his kinsman, to protract my stay with you, but it is not in my power. I have told you already that I am come to the court of Spain on an affair of state. Yesterday, on my arrival, I had a conference with the prime minister; I am to see him to-morrow morning, and shall set out immediately afterwards on my return to Lisbon. You are become quite a Portuguese, observed Segiar, and, to all appearance, we shall lose you entirely from Madrid. I think otherwise, replied Don Pompeyo, I have the honor to stand well with the King of Portugal, and have many motives of attachment to that court; yet with all the kindness that sovereign has testified towards me, would you believe that I have been on the point of quitting his dominions for ever. Indeed! by what strange accident? said the Marquis. Give us the history, I beseech you. Very readily, answered Don Pompeyo, and at the same time my own, for it is closely interwoven with the recital for which you have called.

CHAPTER VII.

HISTORY OF DON POMPEYO DE CASTRO.

DON ALEXO knows, that from my boyish days, my passion was for a military life. Our own country being at peace, I went into Portugal; thence to Africa with the Duke of Braganza, who gave me a commission. I was a younger brother, with as slender a provision as most in Spain; so that my only chance was in attracting the notice of the commander-in-chief by my bravery. I was so far from deficient in my duty, that the Duke promoted me, step by step, to one of the most honorable posts in the service. After a long war, of which you all know the issue, I devoted myself to the court; and the King, on strong testimonials from the general officers, rewarded me with a considerable pension. Alive to that sovereign's generosity, I lost no opportunity of proving my gratitude by my diligence. I was in attendance as often as etiquette would allow me to offer myself to his notice. By this conduct I gained insensibly the love of that prince, and received new favors from his hands.

One day, when I distinguished myself in running at the ring, and in a bull-fight preceding it, all the court extolled my strength and dexterity. On my return home, with my honors thick upon me, I found there a note, informing me that a lady, my conquest over whom ought to flatter me more than all the glory I had gained that day, wished to have the pleasure of my company; and that I had only to attend in the evening, at a place marked out in the letter. This was more than all my public triumphs, and I concluded the writer to be a woman of the first quality. You may guess that I did not loiter by the way. An old woman in waiting, as my guide, conducted me by a little garden-gate into a large house, and left me in an elegant closet, saying—Stay here, I will acquaint my mistress with your arrival. I observed a great many articles of value in the closet, which was magnificently illuminated; but this splendor only caught my attention as confirming me in my previous opinion of the lady's high rank. If appearances strengthened that conjecture, her noble and majestic air on her entrance left no doubt on my mind. Yet I was a little out in my calculation.

Noble sir, said she, after the step I have taken in your favor it were impertinent to disown my partiality. Your brilliant actions of to-day, in presence of the court, were not the inspirers of my sentiments, they only urge forward this avowal. I have seen you more than once, have inquired into your character, and the result has determined me to follow the impulse of my heart. But do not suppose that you are well with a Duchess. I am but the widow of a captain in the King's Guards, yet there is something to throw a radiance round your victory . . . . . the preference you have gained over one of the first noblemen in the kindom. The Duke d'Almeyda loves me, and presses his suit with ardor, yet without success. My vanity only induces me to bear his importunities.

Though I saw plainly, by this address, that I had got in with a coquet, my presiding star was not a wit out of my good graces for involving me in this adventure. Donna Hortensia, for that was the lady's name, was just in the ripeness and luxuriance of youth and dazzling beauty. Nay, more, she had refused the possession of her heart to the earnest entreaties of a duke, and offered it unsolicited to me. What a feather in the cap of a Spanish cavalier! I prostrated myself at Hortensia's feet, to thank her for her favors. I talked just as a man of gallantry always does talk, and she had reason to be satisfied with the extravagance of my acknowledgments. Thus we parted the best friends in the world, on the terms of meeting every evening when the Duke d'Almeyda was prevented from coming and she promised to give me due notice of his absence. The bargain was exactly fulfilled, and I was turned into the Adonis of this new Venus.

But the pleasures of this life are transitory. With all the lady's precautions to conceal our private treaty of commerce from my rival, he found means of gaining a knowledge, of which it concerned us greatly to keep him ignorant . a disloyal chamber-maid divulged the state secret. This nobleman, naturally generous, but proud, self-sufficient, and violent, was exasperated at my presumption. Anger and jealousy set him beside himself. Taking counsel only with his rage he resolved on an infamous revenge. One night when I was with Hortensia, he waylaid me at the little garden-gate, with all his servants provided with cudgels. As soon as I came out, he ordered me to be seized, and beat to death by these wretches. Lay on, said he, let the rash intruder give up the ghost under your chastisement; thus shall his insolence be punished. No sooner had he finished these words, than his myrmidons assaulted me in a body, and gave me such a beating, as to stretch me senseless on the ground · after which they hurried off with their master, to whom this butchery had been a delicious pastime. I lay the remainder of the night, just as they had left me. At daybreak some people passed by, who, finding that life was still in me, had the humanity to carry me to a surgeon. Fortunately my wounds were not mortal; and, falling into skillful hands, I was perfectly cured in two months. At the end of that period I made my appearance again at court, and resumed my former way of life, except that I steered clear of Hortensia, who on her part made no further attempt to renew the acquaintance, because the Duke, on that condition, had pardoned her infidelity.

As my adventure was the town talk, and I was known to be no coward, people were astonished to see me as quiet as if I had received no affront; for I kept my thoughts to myself, and seemed to have no quarrel with any man living. No one knew what to think of my counterfeited insensibility. Some imagined that, in spite of my courage, the rank of the aggressor overawed me, and occasioned my tacit submission. Others, with more reason, mistrusted my silence, and considered my inoffensive demeanor as a cover to my revenge. The King was of opinion with these last, that I was not a man to put up with an insult, and that I should not be wanting to myself at a convenient opportunity. To discover my real intentions, he sent for me one day into his closet, where he said: Don Pompeyo, I know what accident has befallen you, and am surprised, I own, at your forbearance. You are certainly acting a part. Sire, answered I, how can I know whom to challenge? I was attacked in the night by persons unknown: it is a misfortune of which I must make the best. No, no, replied the King, I am not to be duped by these evasive answers. The whole story has reached my ears. The Duke d'Almeyda has touched your honor to the quick. You are nobly born, and a Castilian: I know what that double character requires. You cherish hostile designs. Admit me a party to your purposes; it must be so. Never fear the consequences of making me your confidant.

Since your majesty commands it, resumed I, my sentiments shall be laid open without reserve. Yes, sir, I meditate a severe retribution. Every man, wearing such a name as mine, must account for its untarnished lustre with his family. You know the unworthy treatment I have experienced; and I purpose assassinating the Duke d'Almeyda, as a mode of revenge correspondent to the injury. I shall plunge a dagger in his bosom, or shoot him through the head, and escape, if I can, into Spain. This is my design.

It is violent, said the King: and yet I have little to say against it, after the provocation which the Duke d'Almeyda has given you. He is worthy of the punishment you destine for him. But do not be in a hurry with your project. Leave me to devise a method of bringing you together again as friends. Oh! sir, exclaimed I with vexation, why did you extort my secret from me? What expedient can . . . . If mine is not to your satisfaction, interrupted he, you may execute your first intention. I do not mean to abuse your confidence. I shall not implicate your honor; so rest contented on that head.

I was greatly puzzled to guess by what means the King designed to terminate this affair amicably: but thus it was. He sent to speak with the Duke d'Almeyda in private. Duke, said he, you have insulted Don Pompeyo de Castro. You are not ignorant that he is a man of noble birth, a soldier who has served with credit, and stands high in my favor. You owe him reparation. I am not of a temper to refuse it, answered the Duke. If he complains of my outrageous behavior, I am ready to justify it by the law of arms. Something very different must be done, replied the

King . a Spanish gentleman understands the point of honor too well to fight on equal terms with a cowardly assassin. I can use no milder term ; and you can only atone for the heinousness of your conduct, by presenting a cane in person to your antagonist, and offering to submit yourself to its discipline. Oh heaven ! exclaimed the Duke : what ! sir, would you have a man of my rank degrade, debase himself before a simple gentleman, and submit to be caned ! No, replied the monarch, I will oblige Don Pompeyo to promise not to touch you. Only offer him the cane, and ask his pardon: that is all I require from you. And that is too much, sir, interrupted the Duke d'Almeyda warmly ; I had rather remain exposed to all the secret machinations of his resentment. Your life is dear to me, said the king: and I should wish this affair to have no bad consequences. To terminate it with less disgust to yourself, I will be the only witness of the satisfaction which I order you to offer to the Spaniard.

The King was obliged to stretch his influence over the Duke to the utmost, before he could induce him to so mortifying a step. However, the peremptory monarch effected his purpose, and then sent for me. He related the particulars of his conversation with my enemy, and inquired if I should be content with the stipulated reparation. I answered, yes: and gave my word that, far from striking the offender, I would not even accept the cane, when he presented it. With this understanding, the Duke and myself at a certain hour attended the King, who took us into his closet. Come, said he to the Duke, acknowledge your fault, and deserve to be forgiven by the humility of your contrition. Then my antagonist made his apology, and offered me the cane in his hand. Don Pompeyo, said the monarch unexpectedly, take the cane, and let not my presence prevent you from doing justice to your outraged honor. I release you from your promise not to strike the Duke. No, sir, answered I, it is enough that he has submitted to the indignity of the offer : an offended Spaniard asks no more. Well, then ! replied the King, since you are content with this satisfaction, you may both of you at once assume the privilege of a gentlemanly quarrel. Measure your swords, and discuss the question honorably. It is what I most ardently desire, exclaimed the Duke d'Almeyda in a menacing tone : for that only is competent to make me amends for the disgraceful step I have taken.

With these words, he went away full of rage and shame ; and sent to tell me, two hours after, that he was waiting for me, in a retired place. I kept the appointment, and found this nobleman ready to fight lustily. He was not five and forty ; deficient neither in courage nor in skill: so that the match was fair and equal. Come on, Don Pompeyo, said he, let us terminate our difference here. Our hostility ought to be reciprocally mortal ; yours for my aggression, and mine, for having asked your pardon. These words were no sooner out of his mouth, than he drew upon me so suddenly, that I had no time to reply. He pressed very closely upon me at first, but I had the good fortune to put by all his thrusts. I acted on the offensive in my turn: the encounter was evidently with a man equally skilled in defence or in attack; and there is no knowing what might have been the issue, if he had not made a false step in retiring, and fallen backwards. I stood still immediately, and said to the duke, Recover yourself. Why give me any quarter? he answered. Your forbearance only aggravates my disgrace. I will not take advantage of an accident, replied I; it would only tarnish my glory. Once more recover yourself, and let us fight it out.

Don Pompeyo, said he rising, after this act of generosity, honor allows me not to renew the attack upon you. What would the world say of me, were I to wound you mortally? I should be branded as a coward for having murdered a man, at whose mercy I had just before lain prostrate. I cannot therefore again lift my arm against your life, and I feel my resentful passions subsiding into the sweet emotions of gratitude. Don Pompeyo, let us mutually lay aside our hatred. Let us go still further; let us be friends. Ah! my lord, exclaimed I, so flattering a proposal I joyfully accept. I proffer you my sincere friendship; and, as an earnest, promise never to approach Donna Hortensia, though she herself should invite me. It is my duty, said he, to yield that lady to you. Justice requires me to give her up, since her affections are yours already. No, no, interrupted I; you love her. Her partiality in my favor would give you uneasiness; I sacrifice my own pleasures to your peace. Ah! too generous Castilian, replied the Duke, embracing me, your sentiments are truly noble. With what remorse do they strike me! Grieved and ashamed, I look back on the outrage you have sustained. The reparation in the King's chamber seems now too trifling. A better recompense awaits you. To obliterate all remembrance of your shame, take one of my nieces whose hand is at my disposal, She is a rich heiress, not fifteen, with beauty beyond the attractions of mere youth.

I made my acknowledgments to the Duke in terms such as the high honor of his alliance might suggest, and married his niece a few days afterwards. All the court complimented this nobleman on having made such generous amends to an insulted rival; and my friends took part in my joy at the happy issue of an adventure which might have led to the most melancholy consequences. From this time, gentlemen, I have lived happily at Lisbon. I am the idol of my wife, and have not sunk the lover in the husband. The Duke d'Almeyda gives me new proofs of friendship every day; and I may venture to boast of standing high in the King of Portugal's good graces. The importance of my errand hither sufficiently assures me of his confidence.

CHAPTER VIII.

AN ACCIDENT, IN CONSEQUENCE OF WHICH GIL BLAS WAS OBLIGED
TO LOOK OUT FOR ANOTHER PLACE.

SUCH was Don Pompeyo's story, which Don Alexo's servant
and myself overheard, though we were prudently sent away before
he began his recital. Instead of withdrawing, we skulked behind the
door, which we had left half open, and from that station we did
not miss a word. After this, the company went on drinking; but
they did not prolong their carousals till the morning, because Don
Pompeyo, who was to speak with the prime minister, wished for
a little rest beforehand. The Marquis de Zenette and my master
took a cordial leave of the stranger, and left him with his kinsman.

We went to bed for once before daybreak; and Don Matthias,
when he awoke, invested me with a new office. Gil Blas, said he,
take pen, ink, and paper, and write two or three letters as I shall
dictate: you shall henceforth be my secretary. Well and good!
said I to myself, a plurality of functions. As footman, I follow my
master's heels; as valet-de-chambre, I help him to dress; and write
for him as his secretary. Heaven be praised for my apotheosis!
Like the triple Hecate of the Pantheon, I am to enact three different characters at the same time. Can you guess my intention?
continued he. Thus it is: but take care what you are about; your
life may depend on it. As I am continually meeting with fellows
who boast of their success among the women, I mean, by way of
getting the upper hand, to fill my pockets with fictitious love-
letters, and read them in company. It will be amusing enough.
Happier than my competitors, who make conquests only for the
pleasure of the boasts, I shall take the credit of intrigue, and
spare myself the labor. But vary your writing, so that the manufacture may not be detected by the sameness of the hand.

I then sat down to comply with the commands of Don Matthias,
who first dictated a tender epistle to this tune— *You did not keep
your promise to-night. Ah! Don Matthias, how will you exculpate
yourself? My error was a cruel one! But you punish me deservedly
for my vanity, in fancying that business and amusement were all to
give way before the pleasure of seeing Donna Clara de Mendoza!*
After this pretty note, he made me write another, as if from a lady
who sacrificed a prince to him; and then a third, whose fair writer
offered, if she could rely on his discretion, to embark with him for
the shores of Cytherean enchantment. It was not enough to
dictate these love-sick strains; he forced me to subscribe them with
the most high-flying names in Madrid. I could not forbear hinting at some little hazard in all this, but he begged me to keep my
sage counsels till they were called for. I was obliged to hold my
tongue, and dispatch his orders out of hand. That done, he got up,

and dressed with my assistance. The letters were put into his pocket, and out he went. I followed him to dinner with Don Juan de Moncade, who entertained five or six gentlemen of his acquaintance that day.

There was a grand set-out, and mirth, the best relish was not wanting to the banquet. All the guests contributed to enliven the conversation, some by wit and humor, others by anecdotes of which the relaters were the heroes. My master would not lose so fine an opportunity of bringing our joint performances to bear. He read them audibly, and with so much assurance, that probably the whole party, with the exception of his secretary, was taken in by the device. Among the company, before whom this trick was so impudently played off, there was one person, by name Don Lope de Velasco. This person, a very grave don, instead of making himself merry like the rest with the fictitious triumphs of the reader, asked him coolly if the conquest of Donna Clara had been achieved with any great difficulty? Less than the least, answered Don Matthias; the advances were all on her side. She saw me in public, and took a fancy to my person. A scout was commissioned to follow me, and thus she got at my name and condition. She wrote to me, and gave me an appointment at an hour of the night when the house was sure to be quiet. I was true as the needle to the pole; her bedchamber was the place. . . . . But prudence and delicacy forbid my describing what passed there.

At this instance of tender regard for the lady's character, Signor de Velasco betrayed some very passionate workings in his countenance. It was easy to see the interest he took in the subject. All these letters, said he to my master, looking at him with an eye of indignation and contempt, are infamous forgeries, and above all that which you boast of having received from Donna Clara de Mendoza. There is not in all Spain a more modest young creature than herself. For these two years, a gentleman, at least your equal in birth and personal merit, has been trying every method of insinuating himself into her heart. Scarcely have his assiduities extorted the slightest encouragement: but yet he may flatter himself that, if anything beyond common civility had been granted at all, it would have been to him only. Well! Who says to the contrary? interrupted Don Matthias in a bantering way. I agree with you, that the lady is a very pretty behaved young lady. On my part, I am a very pretty behaved young gentleman. Ergo, you may rest assured that nothing took place between us but what was pretty and well behaved. Indeed! This is too much, interrupted Don Lope in his turn: let us lay aside this unseasonable jesting. You are an impostor. Donna Clara never gave you an appointment by night. Her reputation shall not be blackened by your ribaldry. But prudence and delicacy forbid my describing what must pass between you and me. With this retort on his lips, he looked contemptuously round, and withdrew with a menacing aspect, which anticipated serious consequences to my judgment. My master, whose courage was better than his caue, held the threats of Don Lope in derision. A blockhead! exclaimed he, bursting into a loud fit of laughter. Our knights-errant used to tilt for the beauty of their mistresses, this fellow would engage in the lists for the forlorn hope of virtue in his; he is more ridiculous than his prototypes.

Velasco's retiring, in vain opposed by Moncade, occasioned no interruption to the merriment. The party, without thinking further about it, kept the ball up briskly, and did not part till they had made free with the next day. We went to bed, that is, my master and myself, about five o'clock in the morning. Sleep sat heavy on my eyelids, and, as I thought, was taking permanent possession thereof; but I reckoned without my host, or rather without our porter, who came and waked me in an hour, to say that there was a lad inquiring for me at the door. Oh! thou infernal porter, muttered I indistinctly, through the interstices of a long yawn, do you consider that I have but now got to bed? Tell the little rascal that I am just asleep; he must come again by-and-by. He insists, replied Cerberus, on speaking with you instantly; his business cannot wait. As that was the case I got up, put on nothing but my breeches and doublet, and went down-stairs, swearing and gaping. My friend, said I, be so good as to let me know what urgent affair procures me the honor of seeing you so early? I have a letter, answered he, to deliver personally into the hands of Signor Don Matthias, to be read by him without loss of time; it is of the last consequence to him—pray show me into his room. As I thought the matter serious, I took the liberty of disturbing my master. Excuse me, said I, for waking you, but the pressing nature. . . . . What do you want? interrupted he, just in my style with the porter. Sir, said the lad who was at my elbow, here is a letter from Don Lope de Velasco. Don Matthias looked at the cover, broke it, and after reading the contents, said to the messenger of Don Lope—My good fellow, I never get up before noon, let the party be ever so agreeable; judge whether I can be expected to be stirring by six in the morning for a small-sword recreation. You may tell your master, that if he chooses to kick his heels at the spot till half-past twelve, we will come and see how he looks there—carry him that answer. With this flippant speech he plunged down snugly under the bed-clothes and fell fast asleep again as if nothing had happened.

Between eleven and twelve he got up and dressed himself with the utmost composure, and went out, telling me that there was no occasion for my attendance: but I was too much on the tenterhooks about the result to mind his orders. I sneaked after him to Saint Jerome's meadow, where I saw Don Lope de Velasco waiting for him. I took my station to watch them; and was an eye-witness to all the circumstances of their rencounter. They saluted, and began their fierce debate without delay. The engagement lasted long. They exchanged thrusts alternately, with equal skill and mettle. The victory, however, was on the side of Don Lope: he ran my master through, laid him helpless on the ground, and made his escape, with apparent satisfaction at the severe reprisal. I ran up to the unfortunate Don Matthias, and found him in a most desperate situation. The sight melted me. I could not help weeping at a catastrophe to which I had been an involuntary contributor. Nevertheless, with all sympathy, I had still my little wits about me. Home went I in a hurry, without saying a word. I made up a bundle of my own goods and chattels, inadvertently slipped in some odd articles belonging to my master: and when I had deposited this with the barber, where my dress as a fine gentleman was still lodged, I published the news of the fatal accident. Any gaper might have it for the trouble of listening; and above all, I took care to make Rodriguez acquainted with it. He would have been extremely afflicted, but that his own proceedings in this delicate case required all his attention. He called the servants together, ordered them to follow him, and we went all together to Saint Jerome's meadow. Don Matthias was taken up alive, but he died three hours after he was brought home. Thus ended the life of Signor Don Matthias de Silva, only for having taken a fancy to reading supposititious love-letters unseasonably.

CHAPTER IX.

A NEW SERVICE, AFTER THE DEATH OF DON MATTHIAS DE SILVA.

SOME days after the funeral, the establishment was paid up and discharged. I fixed my head-quarters with the little barber, in a very close connection with whom I began to live. It seemed to promise more pleasure than with Melendez. As I was in no want of money, it was time enough to think of another place: besides, I had got to be rather nice on that head. I would not go into service any more, but in families above the vulgar. In short, I was determined to inquire very strictly into the character of a new place. The best would not be too good; such high pretensions did the late valet of a young nobleman think himself entitled to assume above the common herd of servants.

Waiting till fortune should throw a situation in my way, worthy to be honored by my acceptance, I thought I could not do better than to devote my leisure to my charming Laura, whom I had not seen since the pleasant occurrence of our double discovery. I could not venture on dressing as Don Cæsar de Ribera; it would have been an act of madness to have assumed that style but as a disguise. Besides that my own suit was not much out of condition, all smaller articles had propagated miraculously in the aforesaid bundle. I made myself up, therefore, with the barber's aid, as a sort of middle man between Don Cæsar and Gil Blas. In this demi-character, I knocked at Arsenia's door. Laura was alone in the parlor where we had met last. Ah! is it you? cried she, as soon as she saw me; I thought you were lost. You have had leave to come and see me for this week: but it seems you are modest, and do not presume too much on your license,

I made my apology on the score of my master's death, with my own engagements consequent thereupon : and I added, in the spirit of gallantry, that in my greatest perplexities, my lovely Laura had always been foremost in my thoughts. That being so, said she, I have no more reproaches to make; and I will frankly own that I have thought of you. As soon as I was acquainted with the untimely end of Don Matthias, a plan occurred to me, probably not quite displeasing to you. I have heard my mistress say some time ago, that she wanted a sort of man of business; a good arithmetician, to keep an exact account of our outgoings. I fixed my affections on your lordship; you seem exactly calculated for such an office. I feel myself, answered I, a steward by inspiration. I have read all that Aristotle has written on finance ; and as for reducing it to the modern system of book-keeping . . . . . But, my dear girl, there is one impediment in the way. What impediment? said Laura. I have sworn, replied I, never again to live with a commoner: I have sworn by Styx, or something else as binding. If Jupiter could not burst the links of such an oath, judge whether a poor servant ought not to be bound by it. What do you mean by a commoner? rejoined the impetuous abigail: for what do you take us actresses? Do you take us for the ribs of the limbs of the law? for attorneys' wives? I would have you to know, my friend, that actresses rank with the first nobility; being only common to the uncommon, and therefore, though common, uncommonly illustrious.

On that footing, my uncommon commoner, said I, the post you have destined for me is mine: I shall not lower my dignity by accepting it. No, to be sure, said she : backwards and forwards between a puppy of fashion and a she-wolf of the stage ; why, it is exactly preserving an equilibrium of rank in the creation. We are sympathetic animals, just on a level with the people of quality. We have our equipages in the same style ; we give our little suppers on the same scale; and on the broad ground we are just of as much use in civil society. In fact, to draw a parallel between a marquis and a player through the space of four and twenty hours, they are just on a par. The marquis, for three fourths of the time, ranks above the player by political courtesy and sufferance: the player, during his hour on the stage, overtops the marquis in the part of an emperor or a king, which he better knows how to enact. Thus there seems to be a balance between natural and political nobility, which places us at least on a level with the live lumber of the court. Yes, truly, replied I, you are a match for one another, there is no gainsaying it. Bless their dear hearts ! the players are not men of straw, as I foolishly believed, and you have made my mouth water to serve such a worshipful fraternity. Well, then ! resumed she, you have only to come back again in two days. That time will be sufficient to incline my mistress in your favor ; I will speak up for you. She is a little under my influence ; I do not fear bringing you under this roof.

I thanked Laura for her good dispositions. My gratitude took the readiest way to prove itself to her comprehension ; and my tender thrillings expressed more than words. We had a pretty long conversation together, and it might have lasted till this time, if a little skipping fellow had not come to tell my nymph of the side-scenes that Arsenia was inquiring for her. We parted. I left the house, in the sweet hope of soon living there scot-free; and my face was shown up again at the door in two days. I was looking out for you, said my accomplished scout, to assure you that you are a mess-mate at this house. Come, follow me; I will introduce you to my mistress. At these words, she led me into a suite of five or six rooms on a floor, in a regular gradation of costly furniture and tasteful equipment.

What luxury! What magnificence! I thought myself in pres-ence of a vice-queen, or, to mend the poverty of the comparison, in a fairy palace, where all the riches of the earth were collected. In fact, there were the productions of many people and of many countries, so that one might describe this residence as the temple of a goddess, whither every traveler brought some rare product of his native land, as a votive offering. The divinity was reclining on a voluptuous satin sofa: she was lovely in my eyes, and pampered with the fumes of daily sacrifices. She was in a tempting disha-bille, and her polished hands were elegantly busy about a new head-dress for her appearance that evening. Madam, said the abigail, here is that said steward; take my word for it, you will never get one more to your liking. Arsenia looked at me very inquisitively, and did not find me disagreeable. Why, this is something, Laura, cried she; a very smart youth truly: I foresee that we shall do very well together. Then directing her discourse to me, Young man, added she, you suit me to a hair, and I have only one observation to make: you will be pleased with me, if I am so with you. I an-swered that I should do my utmost to serve her to her heart's con-tent. As I found that the bargain was struck, I went immediately to fetch in my own little accommodations, and returned to take formal possession.

CHAPTER X.

MUCH SUCH ANOTHER AS THE FOREGOING.

It was near the time of the doors opening. My mistress told me to attend her to the theatre with Laura. We went into her dressing-room, where she threw off her ordinary attire, and assum-ed a more splendid costume for the stage. When the performance began, Laura showed me the way, and seated herself by my side where I could see and hear the actors to advantage. They disgust-ed me for the most part, doubtless because Don Pompeyo had pre-judiced me against them. Several of them were loudly applauded, but the fable of the pig would now and then come across my mind.

Laura told me the names of the actors and actresses as they made their entrances. Nor did she stop there, for the hussey gave some highly seasoned anecdotes into the bargain. Her characters were, crack-brain for this, impertinent fellow for that. That delicate sample of sin, who depends on her wantonness for her attractions, goes by the name of Rosarda : a bad speculation for the company! She ought to be sent with the next cargo to New Spain, she may answer the purpose of the viceroy. Take particular notice of that brilliant star now coming forward ; that magnificent setting sun, increasing in bulk as its fires become less vivid. That is Casilda. If from that distant day when she first laid herself open to her lovers, she had required from each of them a brick to build a pyramid, like an ancient Egyptian princess, the edifice by this time would have mounted to the third heaven. In short, Laura tore all character to pieces by her scandal. Heaven forgive her wicked tongue! She blasphemed her own mistress.

And yet I must own my wickedness. I was in love with the wench, though her morals were not strictly pure. She scandalized with so winning a malignity that one liked her the better for it. Off went the jill-flirt between the acts, to see if Arsenia wanted her; but instead of coming straight back to her place, she amused herself behind the scenes, in laying herself out for the little flatteries of all the wheedling fellows. I dogged her once, and found that she had a very large acquaintance. No less than three players did I reckon up, who stopped to chat with her one after the other, and they seemed to be on a very improvable footing. This was not quite so well ; and for the first time in my life I felt what jealousy was. I returned to my seat so absent and out of spirits, that Laura remarked it as soon as she came back to me. What is the matter, Gil Blas, said she with astonishment; what blue devil has perched upon your shoulder in my absence? You look gloomy and out of temper. My fairy queen, answered I, it is not without reason, you have an ugly kick in your gallop. I have observed you with the players. . . . . . . So, so! An admirable subject for a long face, interrupted she with a laugh. What! That is your trouble, is it? Why really! You are a very silly swain ; but you will get better notions among us. You will fall by degrees into our easy manners. No jealousy, my dear creature, you will be completely laughed out of it in the theatrical world. The passion is scarcely known there. Fathers, husbands, brothers, uncles, and cousins, are all upon a liberal plan of community, and often make a strange jumble of relationships.

After having warned me to take no umbrage, but to look at everything like a philosophical spectator, she vowed that I was the happy mortal who had found the way to her heart. She then declared that she should love me always, and only me. On the assurance, which a man might have doubted without criminal scepticism, I promised her not to be alarmed any more, and kept my word. I saw her, on that very evening, whisper and giggle with more men than one. At the end of the play we returned home with our mistress, whither Florimonde came soon after to supper, with three old noblemen and a player. Besides Laura and myself, the establishment consisted of a cook-maid, a coachman, and a little footboy. We all labored in our respective vocations. The lady of the frying-pan, no less an adept than Dame Jacintha, was assisted in her cookery by the coachman. The waiting-woman and the little footboy laid the cloth, and I set out the sideboard, magnificently furnished with plate, offered up at the shrine of our green-room goddess. There was every variety of wines, and I played the cup-bearer, to show my mistress the versatility of my talents. I sweated at the impudence of the actresses during supper; they gave themselves quality airs, and affected the tone of high life. Far from giving their guests all their style and titles, they did not even vouchsafe a simple "Your lordship," but called them familiarly by their proper names. To be sure the old fools encouraged their vanity by forgetting their own distance. The player, for his part, in the habits of the heroic cast, lived on equal terms with them; he challenged them to drink, and in every respect took the upper hand. In good truth, said I to myself, while Laura was demonstrating the equality of the Marquis and the comedian during the day, she might have drawn a still stronger inference for the night, since they pass it so merrily in drinking together.

Arsenia and Florimonde were naturally frolicsome. A thousand broad hints escaped them, intermingled with small favors, and then a coquettish revolt at their own freedom, which were all seasoned exactly to the taste of these old sinners. While my mistress was entertaining one of them with a little harmless toying, her friend, between the other elders, had not taken the cue of Susanna. While I was contemplating this picture, which had but too many attractions for a knowing youth like me, the dessert was brought in. Then I set the bottles and glasses on the table, and made my escape to sup with Laura, who was waiting for me. How now! Gil Blas, said she, what do you think of those noblemen above stairs? Doubtless, answered I, they are deeply smitten with Arsenia and Florimonde. No, replied she, they are old sensualists, who hang about our sex without any particular attachment. All they ask is some little frivolous compliance, and they are generous enough to pay well for the least trifle of amorous endearment. Heaven be praised, Florimonde and my mistress are at present without any serious engagements; I mean that they have no husband-like lovers, who expect to engross all the pleasure of a house, because they stand to the expenses. For my part, I am very glad of it; and maintain that a sensible woman of the world ought to refuse all such monopolies. Why take a master? It is better to support an establishment by retail trade, than to confine one's self to chamber practice on such terms.

When Laura's tongue was wound up, and it was seldom down, words seemed to cost her nothing. What a glorious volubility! She told a thousand stories of the actresses belonging to the prince's company; and I gathered from her whole drift that I could not be better situated to take a scientific view of the cardinal vices. Unfortunately I was at an age when they inspire but little horror; and this abigail had the art of coloring her corruptions so lusciously as to hide their deformities and heighten their meretricious lure. She had not time to open the tenth part of her theatrical budget, for she did not take more than three hours. The senators and the player went away with Florimonde, whom they saw safe home.

When they were gone, my mistress said to me—Here, Gil Blas, are ten pistoles to go to market to-morrow. Five or six of our gentlemen and ladies are to dine here, take care that we are well served. Madam, answered I, with this sum there shall be a banquet for the whole troop. My friend, replied Arsenia, correct your phraseology; you must say company, not troop. A troop of robbers, a troop of beggars, a troop of authors; but a company of comedians, especially when you have to mention the actors of Madrid. I begged my mistress's pardon for having used so disrespectful a term, and entreated her to excuse my ignorance. I protested that henceforward, when I spoke collectively of so august a body, I would always say the company.

CHAPTER XI.

A THEATRICAL LIFE AND AN AUTHOR'S LIFE.

I TOOK the field the next morning, to open my campaign as steward. It was a fish day; for which reason I bought some good fat chickens, rabbits, partridges, and every variety of game. As the gentlemen of the sock and buskin are not on the best possible terms with the church, they are not over-scrupulous in their observance of the rubric. I brought home provisions more than enough for a dozen portly gentlemen to have fasted on during a whole Lent. The cook had a good morning's work. While she was getting dinner ready, Arsenia got up and spent the early part of the day at her toilet. At noon came two of the players, Signor Rosimiro and Signor Ricardo. Afterwards two actresses, Constance and Celinaura; then entered Florimonde, attended by a man who had all the appearance of a most spruce cavalier. He had his hair dressed in the most elegant manner, his hat set off with a fashionable plume, very tight breeches, and a shirt with a laced frill. His gloves and his handkerchief were in the hilt of his sword, and he wore his cloak with a grace altogether peculiar to himself.

With a prepossessing physiognomy and a good person, there was something extraordinary in the first blush of him. This gentleman, said I to myself, must be an original. I was not mistaken; his singularities were striking. On his entrance, he ran with open arms and embraced the company, male and female, one after another. His grimaces were more extravagant than any I had yet seen in this region of foppery. My prediction was not falsified by his discourse. He dwelt with fondness on every syllable he uttered, and pronounced his words in an emphatic tone, with gestures and glances artfully adapted to the subject. I had the curiosity to ask Laura who this strange figure might be. I forgive you, said she, this instance of an inquisitive disposition. It is impossible to see and to hear Signor Carlos Alonso de la Ventoleria for the first time, without having such a natural longing. I will paint him to the life. In the first place, he was originally a player. He left the stage through caprice, and has since repented in sober sadness of the step. Did you notice his dark hair? Every thread of it is pencilled, as well as his eyebrows and his whiskers. He was born in the reign of Saturn's father, in the age before the golden; but as there were no parish registers at that time, he avails himself of the primitive barbarism, and dates at least twenty centuries below the true epoch. Moreover, his self-sufficiency keeps pace with his antiquity. He passed the olympiads of his youth in the grossest ignorance; but taking a fancy to become learned about the Christian era, he engaged a private tutor, who taught him to spell in Greek and Latin. Nay, more, he knows by heart an infinite number of good stories, which he has given so often as genuine, that he actually begins to believe them himself. They are eternally pressed into the service, and it may truly be said that his wit shines at the expense of his memory. He is thought to be a great actor. I am willing to believe it implicitly, but I must own he is not to my taste. He declaims here sometimes; and I have observed, among other defects, an affectation in his delivery, with a tremulousness of voice bordering on the antiquated and ridiculous.

Such was the portrait drawn by my abigail of this honorary spouter; and never was mortal of a more stately carriage. He prided himself too on being an agreeable companion. He never was at loss for a commodity of trite remarks, which he delivered with an air of authority. On the other hand, the Thespian fraternity were not much addicted to silence. They began canvassing their absent colleagues in a manner little consistent with charity, it must be owned; but this is a failing pardonable in players as well as in authors. The fire grew brisk and the satire personal. You have not heard, ladies, said Rosimiro, a new stroke of our dear brother Cesarino. This very morning he bought silk stockings, ribbons, and laces, and sent them to rehearsal by a little page, as a present from a countess. What a knavish trick! said Signor de la Ventoleria, with a smile made up of fatuity and conceit. In my time there was more honesty, we never thought of descending to such impositions. To be sure, women of fashion were tender of our inventive faculties, nor did they leave such purchases to be made out of our own pockets; it was their whim. By the honor of our house, said Ricardo, in the same strain, that whim of theirs is lasting, and if it were allowable to kiss and tell. . . . . But one must be secret on these occasions, above all when persons of a certain rank are concerned.

Gentlemen, interrupted Florimonde, a truce, if you please, with your conquests and successes, they are known over the whole earth. Apropos of Ismene. It is said that the nobleman who has fooled away so much money upon her, has at length recovered his senses. Yes, indeed, exclaimed Constance; and I can tell you besides that she has lost, by the same stroke, a snug little hero of the counting-house, whose ruin would otherwise have been signed and sealed. I have the thing from the first hand. Her Mercury made an unfortunate mistake, for he carried a tender invitation to each, and delivered them wrong. These were great losses, my darling, quoth Florimonde. Oh! as for that of the lord, replied Constance, it is a very trifling matter. The man of blood had almost run through his estate, but the little fellow with the pen behind his ear was but just coming into play. He had never been fleeced before, it is a pity he should have escaped so easily.

Such was the tenor of the conversation before dinner, and it was not much mended in its morality at table. As I should never have done with the recital of their ribaldry and nonsense, the reader will excuse the omission, and pass on to the entrance of a poor devil, yclept an author, who called just before the cloth was taken away.

Our little footboy came and said to my mistress in an audible voice—Madam, a man in a dirty shirt, splashed up to his middle, with very much the look of a poet, saving your presence, wants to speak to you. Let him walk up, answered Arsenia. Keep your seats, gentlemen, it is only an author. To be sure so it was, one whose tragedy had been accepted, and he was bringing my mistress her part. His name was Pedro de Moya. On coming into the room he made five or six low bows to the company, who neither rose nor took the least notice of him. Arsenia just returned his superabundant civilities with a slight inclination of the head. He came forward with tremor and embarrassment. He dropped his gloves and let his hat fall. He ventured to pick them up again, then advanced towards my mistress, and presenting to her a paper with more ceremony than a defendant an affidavit to the judge of the court—Madam, said he, have the goodness to receive under your protection the part I take the liberty of offering you. She stretched out her hand for it with cold and contemptuous indifference; nor did she condescend even to notice the compliment by a look.

But our author was not disheartened. Seizing this opportunity to distribute the cast, he gave one character to Rosimiro and another to Florimonde, who treated him just as genteelly as Arsenia had done. On the contrary, the low comedian, a very pleasant fellow, as those gentlemen for the most part affect to be, insulted him with the most cutting sarcasms. Pedro de Moya was not made of stone. Yet he dared not take up the aggressor, lest his piece should suffer for it. He withdrew without saying a word, but stung to the quick, as it seemed to me, by his reception. He could not fail, in the transports of his anger, mentally to apostrophize the players as they deserved: and the players, when he was gone, began to talk of authors in return with infinite deference and kindness. It should seem, said Florimonde, as if Signor de Moya did not go away very well pleased.

Well! madam, cried Rosimiro, and why should you trouble yourself about that? Are we to study the feelings of authors? If we were to admit them upon equal terms, it would only be the way to spoil them. I know that contemptible squad; I know them of old: they would soon forget their distance. There is no dealing with them but as slaves; and as for tiring their patience, never fear that. Though they may take themselves off in a pet sometimes, the itch of writing brings them back again; and they are raised to the third heaven, if we will but condescend to support their pieces. You are right, said Arsenia; we never lose an author till we have made his fortune. When that is done, as soon as we have provided for the ungrateful devils, they get to be in good case, and then they run restive. Luckily the manager does not break his heart after them, and one is just as good as another to the public.

These liberal and sagacious remarks met with their full share of approbation. It was carried unanimously that authors, though treated rather too scurvily behind the scenes, were on the whole the obliged persons. These fretters of an hour upon the stage ranked the inhabitant of Parnassus below themselves; and malice could not degrade him lower.

CHAPTER XII.

GIL BLAS ACQUIRES A RELISH FOR THE THEATRE, AND TAKES A FULL SWING OF ITS PLEASURES, BUT SOON BECOMES DISGUSTED.

THE party sat at table till it was time to go to the theatre. I went after them, and saw the play again that evening. I took such delight in it, that I was for attending every day. I never missed, and by degrees got accustomed to the actors. Such is the force of habit. I was particularly delighted with those who were most artificial and unnatural; nor was I singular in my taste.

The beauties of composition affected me much on the same principle as the excellence of representation. There were some pieces with which I was enraptured. I liked, among others, those which brought all the cardinals or the twelve peers of France upon the stage. I got hold of striking passages in these incomparable performances. I recollect that in two days I learnt by heart a whole play, called, *The Queen of Flowers*. The Rose, who was the queen, had the Violet for her maid of honor, and the Jessamin for her prime minister. I could conceive nothing more elegant or refined: such productions seemed to be the triumph of our Spanish wit and invention.

I was not content to store my memory and discipline my mind with the choicest selections from these dramatic masterpieces: but I was bent on polishing my taste to the highest perfection. To secure this grand object, I listened with greedy ears to every word which fell from the lips of the players. If they commended a piece, I was ravished by it: but suppose they pronounced it bad? why, then I maintained that it was infernal stuff. I conceived that they must determine the merits of a play, as a jeweler the water of a diamond. And yet the tragedy by Pedro de Moya was eminently successful, though they had predicted its entire miscarriage. This, however, was no disparagement of their critical skill in my estimation ; and I had rather believe the audience to be divested of common sense, than doubt the infallibility of the company. But they assured me, on all hands, that their judgments were usually confirmed by the rule of contraries. It seemed to be a maxim with them, to set their faces point blank against the taste of the public ; and as a proof of this, there were a thousand cases in point of unexpected successes and failures. All these testimonies were scarcely sufficient to undeceive me.

I shall never forget what happened one day at the first representation of a new comedy. The performers had pronounced it uninteresting and tedious ; they had even prophesied that it would not be heard to the end. Under this impression, they got through the first act, which was loudly applauded. This was very astonishing! They played the second act ; the audience liked it still better than the first. The actors were confounded. What the devil, said Rosimiro, this comedy succeeds ! At last they went on in the third act, which rose as a third act ought to rise. I am quite thrown upon my back, said Ricardo ; we thought this piece would not be relished ; and all the world are mad after it. Gentlemen, said one of the players archly, it is because we happened accidentally to overlook all the wit.

From this time I held my opinion no longer of the players as competent judges, and began to appreciate their merit more truly than they had estimated that of the authors. All the lampoons which were current about them were fully justified. The actors and actresses ran riot on the applauses of the town, and stood so high in their own conceit, as to think that they conferred a favor by appearing on the boards. I was shocked at their public misconduct ; but unfortunately reconciled myself too easily to their private manners, and plunged into debauchery. How could I do otherwise ? Every word they uttered was poison in the ears of youth, and every scene that was presented, an alluring picture of corruption. Had I been a stranger to what passed with Casilda, with Constance, and with the other actresses, Arsenia's house alone would have been sufficient for my ruin. Besides the old noblemen of whom I have spoken, there came thither young debauchees of fashion, who forestalled their inheritances by the disinterested mediation of money-lenders : and sometimes we had officers under government, who were so far from receiving fees, as at their public boards, that they paid most exorbitant ones for the privilege of mixing with such worshipful society.

Florimonde, who lived at next door, dined and supped with Arsenia every day. Their long intimacy surprised every one. Coquets were not thought usually to maintain so good an understanding with each other. It was concluded that they would quarrel, sooner or later, about some paramour ; but such reasoners could not see into the hearts of these exemplary friends. They were united in the bonds of indissoluble love. Instead of harboring jealousy, like other women, they had everything in common. They had rather divide the plunder of mankind, than childishly fall out, and contend for trumpery, as hearts and affections.

Laura, after the example of these two illustrious partners, turned the fresh season of youth to the best advantage. She had told me that I should see strange doings. And yet I did not take up the jealous part. I had promised to adopt the principles of the company on that score. For some days I kept my thoughts to myself. I only just took the liberty of asking her the names of the men whom she favored with her private ear. She always told me that they were uncles or cousins. From what a prolific family was she sprung! King Priam had no luck in propagation, compared with her ancestors. Nor did this precious abigail confine herself to her uncles and cousins: she went now and then to lay a trap for unwary aliens, and personate the widow of quality under the auspices of the discreet old dowager above mentioned. In short, Laura, to hit off her character exactly, was just as young, just as pretty, and just as loose as her mistress, who had no other advantage over her than that of figuring in a more public capacity.

I was borne down by the torrent for three weeks, and ran the career of dissipation in my turn. But I must at the same time say for myself, that in the midst of pleasure I frequently felt the still small voice of conscience, arising from the impression of a serious education, which mixed gall in the Circean cup. Riot could not altogether get the better of remorse: on the contrary, the pangs of the last grew keener with the more shameful indulgence of the first; and, by a happy effect of my temperament, the disorders of a theatrical life began to make me shudder. Ah! wretch, said I to myself, is it thus that you make good the hopes of your family? Is it not enough to have thwarted their pious intentions, by not following your destined course of life as an instructor of youth? Need your condition of a servant hinder you from living decently and soberly? Are such monsters of iniquity fit companions for you? Envy, hatred, and avarice are predominant here; intemperance and idleness have purchased the fee-simple there: the pride of some is aggravated into the most barefaced impudence, and modesty is turned out of doors, by the common consent of all. The business is settled: I will not live any longer with the seven deadly sins.

BOOK THE FOURTH.

CHAPTER I.

GIL BLAS NOT BEING ABLE TO RECONCILE HIMSELF TO THE
MORALS OF THE ACTRESSES, QUITS ARSENIA, AND GETS INTO
A MORE REPUTABLE SERVICE.

A SURVIVING spark of honor and of religion, in the midst of so
general depravity, made me resolve not only to leave Arsenia, but
even to abjure all commerce with Laura, whom yet I could not
cease to love, though I was well aware of her daily inconstancy.
Happy the man who can thus profit by those appeals, which occasionally interrupt the headlong course of his pleasures! One fine
morning, I made up my bundle; and, without reckoning with
Arsenia, who indeed owed me next to nothing, without taking
leave of my dear Laura, I burst from that mansion, which smelt of
brimstone and fire reserved for the wicked. I had no sooner taken
so virtuous a step, than providence interfered in my behalf. I met
the steward of my late master, Don Matthias, and greeted him: he
knew me again at once, and stopped to inquire where I lived. I
answered that I had just left my place; that after staying near a
month with Arsenia, whose manners did not at all suit me, I was
come away by a sudden impulse of virtue, to save my innocence.
The steward, just as if he had been himself of a religious cast,
commended my scruples, and offered me a place much to my
advantage, since I was so chaste and honest a youth. He kept
his word, and introduced me on that very day into the family
of Don Vincent de Gusman, with whose agent he was acquainted.

I could not have got into a better service; nor did I repent in
the sequel of having accepted the situation. Don Vincent was a
very rich old nobleman, who had lived many years unincumbered
with lawsuits or with a wife. The physicians had removed the
last plague out of the way, in their attempts to rid her of a cough,
which might have lasted a great while longer, if the remedies had
not been more fatal than the disease. Far from thinking of the
holy state a second time, he gave himself up entirely to the education of his only daughter Aurora, who was then entering her
twenty-sixth year, and might pass for an accomplished person.
With beauty above the common, she had an excellent and highly
cultivated understanding. Her father was a poor creature as to
intellect; but he possessed the happy talent of looking well after
his affairs. One fault he had, of a kind excusable in old men: he
was an incessant talker, especially about war and fighting. If that

string was unfortunately touched in his presence, in a moment he blew his heroic trumpet, and his hearers might think themselves lucky if they compounded for a gazette extraordinary of two sieges and three battles. As he had spent two-thirds of his life in the service, his memory was an inexhaustible depôt of various facts; but the patience of the listeners did not always keep pace with the perseverance of the relater. The stories, sufficiently prolix in themselves, were still further spun out by stuttering; so that the manner was still less happy than the matter. In all other respects, I never met with a nobleman of a more amiable character: his temper was even; he was neither obstinate nor capricious; the general alternative of men in the higher ranks of life. Though a good economist, he lived like a gentleman. His establishment was composed of several men servants and three women in waiting on Aurora. I soon discovered that the steward of Don Matthias had procured me a good post, and my only anxiety was to establish myself firmly in it. I took all possible pains to feel the ground under my feet, and to study the characters of the whole household : then regulating my conduct by my discoveries I was not long in ingratiating myself with my master and all the servants.

I had been with Don Vincent about a month, when it struck me that his daughter was very particular in her notice of me above all the servants in the family. Whenever her eyes happened accidentally to meet mine, they seemed to be suffused with a certain partial complacency, which did not enter into her silent communications with the vulgar. Had it not been for my haunts among the coxcombs of the theatrical tribe and their hangers-on, it would never have entered into my head that Aurora should throw away a thought on me : but my brain had been a little turned among those gentry, from whose libertine suspicions ladies of the noblest birth are not always held sacred. If, said I, those chronicles of the age are to be believed, fancy and high blood lead women of quality a dance, in which they sometimes join hands with unequal partners : how do I know but my young mistress may caper to a tune of my piping ? But no : it cannot be so, neither. This is not one of your Messalinas, who, derogating from the loftiness of ancestry, unworthily let down their regards to the dust, and sully their pure honor without a blush : but rather one of those virtuously apprehensive, yet tender-hearted girls, who encircle their softness within the insurmountable pale of delicacy ; yet think it no tampering with chastity, to inspire and cherish a sentimental flame, interesting to the heart without being dangerous to the morals.

Such were my ideas of my mistress, without knowing exactly whether they were right or wrong. And yet when we met, she was continually caught with a smile of satisfaction on her countenance. Without passing for a fop, a man might give in to such flattering appearances ; and a philosophical apathy was not to be expected from me. I conceived Aurora to have been deeply smitten with my irresistible attractions ; and looked on myself henceforth in the light of a favored attendant, whose servitude was to be sweetened by the balmy infusion of love. To appear in some measure less unworthy of the blessings, which propitious fortune had kept in store for me, I began to take better care of my person than I had done heretofore. I laid out my slender stock of money in linen, pomatums, and essences. The first thing in the morning was to prank up and perfume myself, so as not to be in an undress in case of being sent for into the presence of my mistress. With these attentions to personal elegance and other dexterous strokes in the art of pleasing, I flattered myself that the moment of my bliss was not very distant.

Among Aurora's women there was one who went by the name of Ortiz. This was an old dowager, who had been a fixture in Don Vincent's family for more than twenty years. She had been about his daughter from her childhood, and still held the office of duenna; but she no longer performed the invidious part of the duty. On the contrary, instead of blazoning, as formerly, Aurora's little indiscretions, her skill was now employed in throwing them into shade. One evening, Dame Ortiz, having watched her opportunity of speaking to me without observation, said in a low voice, that if I was close and trustworthy, I had only to be in the garden at midnight, when a scene would be laid open in which I should not be sorry to be an actor. I answered the duenna, pressing her hand significantly, that I would not fail, and we parted in a hurry for fear of a surprise. How the hours lagged from this moment till supper-time, though we supped very early! Then again from supper to my master's bed-time! It should seem as if the march of the whole family was timed to a *largo* movement. By way of helping forward the fidgets, when Don Vincent withdrew to his chamber, the army was put on the war establishment, and we were obliged to fight the campaigns in Portugal over again, though my ears had not recovered from the din of the last cannonade. But a favor, from which I had hitherto made my escape, was reserved for this eventful evening. He repeated the army list from beginning to end, with copious digressions on the exploits of those officers who had distinguished themselves in his time. Oh my poor tympanum! It was almost cracked before we got to the end. Time, however, will wear out even an old man's story, and he went to bed. I immediately went to my own little chamber, whence there was a way into the garden by a private staircase. I depended on my purchase of perfumery for overcoming the effluvia of the day's drudgery, and put on a clean shirt highly scented. When every invention had been pressed into the service to render my person worthy of its destiny, and cherish the fondness of my mistress, I went to the appointment.

Ortiz was not there. I concluded that, tired of waiting for me, she had gone back to her chamber, and that the happy moment of philandering was over. I laid all the blame on Don Vincent, but just as I was singing Te Deum backwards for his campaigns, I heard the clock strike ten. To be sure it must be wrong! It could not be less than one o'clock. Yet I was so egregiously out in my reckoning, that full a quarter of an hour afterwards, I counted ten upon my fingers by the clock at next door. Vastly well, thought I to myself, I have only two complete hours to ventilate my passion here *al fresco*. At least they shall not complain of me for want of punctuality. What shall I do with myself till twelve! Suppose we take a turn about this garden and settle our cues in the delicious drama just going to be brought on the stage; it is my first appearance in so principal a character. I am not yet sufficiently well read in the crotchets of your quality dames. I know how to tickle a girl in a stuff gown, or an actress: You swagger up to them with an easy impudent assurance and pop the question without making any bones of it. But one must take a female of condition on a very different tack. It seems to me, that in this case the happy swain must be well bred, attentive, tender, respectful, without degenerating into bashfulness. Instead of taking his happiness by storm, he must plant his amorous desires in ambuscade, and wait till the garrison is asleep, and the outworks defenceless.

Thus it was that I argued, and such were the preconcerted plans of my campaign with Aurora. After a few tedious minutes, according to my calculation, I was to experience the ecstasy of finding myself at the feet of that lovely creature, and pouring forth a torrent of impassioned nonsense. I scraped together in my memory all the clap-traps in our stock-plays, which were most successful with the audience, and might best set off my pretensions to spirit and gallantry. I trusted to my own adroitness for the application, and hoped, after the example of some players in the list of my acquaintance, bringing only a stock of memory into the trade, to deal upon credit for my wit. While my imagination was engrossed by these thoughts, which kept my impatience at bay much more successfully than the commentaries of my modern Cæsar, I heard the clock strike eleven. This was some encouragement, and I fell back to my meditations, sometimes sauntering carelessly about, and sometimes throwing myself at my length on the turf, in a bower at the bottom of the garden. At length it struck twelve, the long-expected hour, big with my high destiny. Some seconds after, Ortiz, as punctual as myself though less impatient, made her appearance. Signor Gil Blas, said she, accosting me, how long have you been here? Two hours, answered I. Indeed! Truly, replied she, laughing, you are very exact; there is a pleasure in making nocturnal assignations with you. Yet you may assure yourself, continued she more gravely, that you cannot pay too dear for such good fortune as that of which I am the messenger. My mistress wants to have some private talk with you. I shall not anticipate what may be the subject, that is a secret which you must learn from no lips but her own. Follow me; I will show you into her chamber. With these words the duenna took me by the hand, and led me mysteriously into her lady's apartment through a little door of which she had the key.

CHAPTER II.

AURORA'S RECEPTION OF GIL BLAS. THEIR CONVERSATION.

I FOUND Aurora in an undress. I saluted her in the most re-spectful manner, and threw as much elegance into my attitude as I had to throw. She received me with the most winning affability, made me sit down by her against all my remonstrances, and told her ambassadress to go into another room. After this opening, which seemed highly encouraging to my cause, she entered upon the business. Gil Blas, said she, you must have perceived how favorably I have regarded and distinguished you from all the rest of my father's servants, and though my looks had not betrayed my partial dispositions towards you, my proceeding of this night would leave you no room to doubt them.

I did not give her time to say a word more. It struck me, that as a man of feeling, I ought to spare her trembling diffidence the cruel necessity of explaining her sentiments in more direct terms. I rose from my chair in a transport, and, throwing myself at Aurora's feet, like a tragedy hero of the Grecian stage when he supplicates the heroine "by her knees," exclaimed in a declamatory tone —Ah! Madam, could it be possible that Gil Blas, hitherto the whirligig of fortune and football of embattled nature, should have called down upon his head the exquisite felicity of inspiring sentiments . . . . . . Do not speak so loud, interrupted my mistress with a laugh of mingled apprehension and ridicule, you will wake my women who sleep in the adjoining chamber. Get up, take your seat, and hear me out without putting in a word. Yes, Gil Blas, pursued she, resuming her gravity, you have my best wishes; and to show you how deep you are in my good graces, I will confide to you a secret on which depends the repose of my life. I am in love with a young gentleman, possessing every charm of person and face, and noble by birth. His name is Don Lewis Pacheco. I have seen him occasionally in the public walks and at the theatre, but I have never conversed with him. I do not even know what his private character may be, or what bad qualities he may have. It is on this subject that I wish to be informed. I stand in need of a person to inquire diligently into his morals, and give me a true and particular account. I make choice of you. Surely I run no risk in entrusting you with this commission. I hope that you will acquit yourself with dexterity and prudence, and that I shall never repent of giving you my confidence.

My mistress concluded thus, and waited for my answer to her proposal. I had been disconcerted in the first instance at so disagreeable a mistake; but I soon recovered my scattered senses, and surmounting the confusion which rashness always occasions when it is unlucky, I exposed to sale such a cargo of zeal for the lady's interests. I devoted myself with so martyr-like an enthusiasm to her service, that if she did not absolutely forget my silly vanity in the thought of having pleased her, at least she had reason to believe that I knew how to make amends for a piece of folly. I asked only two days to bring her a satisfactory account of Don Lewis. After which Dame Ortiz, answering the bell, showed me the way back into the garden, and said, on taking leave, Good-night, Gil Blas. I need not caution you to be in time at the next appointment. I have sufficient experience of your punctuality on these occasions.

I returned to my chamber, not without some little mortification at finding my voluptuous anticipations all divested of even their ideal sweetness. I was nevertheless sufficiently in my senses to reflect soberly that it was more in my element to be the trusty scout of my mistress than her lover. I even thought that this adventure might lead to something further ; that the middle men in the trade of love usually pocket a tolerable percentage; and went to bed with the resolution of doing whatever Aurora required of me. For this purpose I went abroad the next morning. The residence of so distinguished a personage as Don Lewis was not difficult to find out. I made my inquiries about him in the neighborhood, but the people who came in my way could not satisfy my curiosity to the full, so that it was necessary to resume my search diligently on the following day. I was in better luck. I met a lad of my acquaintance by chance in the street, we stopped for a little gossip. There passed by in the very nick one of his friends, who came up and told him that he was just turned away from the family of Don Joseph Pacheco, Don Lewis' father, about a paltry remnant of wine, which he had been accused of drinking. I would not lose so fair an occasion of learning all I wanted to know, and plied my questions so successfully as to go home with much self-complacency, at my punctual performance of my engagements with my mistress. It was on the coming night that I was to see her again at the same hour and in the same manner as the first time. I was not in such a confounded hurry this evening. Far from writhing with impatience under the prolixity of my old commander, I led him on to the charge. I waited for midnight with the greatest indifference in the world, and it was not till all the clocks within ear-shot had struck that I crept down into the garden, without any nonsense of pomatum and perfumery. That foppery was completely cured.

At the place of meeting I found the very faithful duenna, who sneeringly reproached me with a defalcation in my zeal. I made her no answer, but suffered myself to be conducted into Aurora's chamber. She asked me, as soon as I made my appearance, whether I had gained any intelligence of Don Lewis. Yes, madam, said I, and you shall have the sum total in two words. I must first tell you, that he will soon set out for Salamanca, to finish his studies. The young gentleman is brim full of honor and probity. As for valor, he cannot be deficient there, since he is a man of birth and a Castilian. Besides this, he has an infinite deal of wit, and is very agreeable in his manners ; but there is one thing which can scarcely be to your liking. He is pretty much in the fashion of our young nobility here at court—exemplarily catholic in his devotions to the fair. Have you not heard that at his age he has already been tenant at will to two actresses? What is it you tell me? replied Aurora. What shocking conduct! But do you know, for certain, Gil Blas, that he leads so dissolute a life? Oh! there is no doubt of it, madam, rejoined I. A servant, turned off this morning, told me so, and servants are very plain dealers when the failings of their masters are the topic. Besides, he keeps company with Don Alexo Segiar, Don Antonio Centellés, and Don Fernando de Gamboa; that single circumstance proves his libertinism with all the force of demonstration. It is enough, Gil Blas, said my mistress with a sigh; on your report I am determined to struggle with my unworthy passion. Though it has already struck deep root in my heart, I do not despair of tearing it forcibly from its bed. Go, added she, putting into my hands a small purse, none of the lightest, take this for pains. Beware of betraying my secret. Consider it as intrusted to your silence.

I assured my mistress that she might be perfectly easy on that score, for I was the Harpocrates of confidential servants. After this compliment to myself, I withdrew with no small eagerness to investigate the contents of the purse. There were twenty pistoles. It struck me all at once that Aurora would surely have given me more had I been the bearer of pleasant tidings, since she paid so handsomely for a blank in the lottery. I was sorry not to have adopted the policy of the pleaders in the courts, who sometimes paint the cheek of truth when her natural complexion is inclined to be cadaverous. It was a pity to have stifled an amour in the birth which might in its growth have been so profitable. Yet I had the comfort of finding myself reimbursed the expense so unseasonably incurred in perfumery and washes.

CHAPTER III.

A GREAT CHANGE AT DON VINCENT'S. AURORA'S STRANGE RESOLUTION.

IT happened soon after this adventure that Signor Don Vincent fell sick. Independent of his very advanced age, the symptoms of his disorder appeared in so formidable a shape that a fatal termination was but too probable. From the beginning of his illness he was attended by two of the most eminent physicians in Madrid. One was Doctor Andros, and the other Doctor Oquetos. They considered the case with due solemnity; and both agreed, after a strict investigation, that the humors were in a state of mutiny, but this was the only thing about which they did agree. The proper practice, said Andros, is to purge the humors, though raw, with all possible expedition, while they are in a violent agitation of flux and reflux, for fear of their fixing upon some noble part. Oquetos maintained, on the contrary, that we must wait till the humors were ripened before it would be safe to go upon purgatives. But your method, replied the first speaker, is directly in the teeth of the rules laid down by the prince of medicine. Hippocrates recommends purging in the most burning fever from the very first attack, and says in plain terms that no time is to be lost in purging when the humors are in οργαδμος, that is to say, in a state of fermentation. Ay! there is your mistake, replied Oquetos. Hippocrates by the word οργαδμος does not mean the fermentation, he means rather the concoction of the humors.

Thereupon our doctors got heated. One quotes the Greek text, and cites all the authors who have explained it in his sense; the other, trusting to a Latin translation, takes up the controversy in a still more positive tone. Which of the two to believe? Don Vincent was not the man to decide that question. In the mean time, finding himself obliged to choose, he gave his confidence to the party who had dispatched the greatest number of patients—I mean the elder of the two. Andros, the younger, immediately withdrew, not without flinging out a few satirical taunts at his senior on the ορχαδμος. Here then was Oquetos triumphant. As he was a professor of the Sangrado school, he began by bleeding copiously, waiting till the humors were ripened before he went upon purgatives. But death, fearing, no doubt, lest this reserve of purgatives should turn the fortunes of the day, got the start of the concoction, and secured his victory over my master by a coup-de-main. Such was the final close of Signor Don Vincent, who had lost his life because his physician did not know Greek.

Aurora having buried her father with a pomp suited to the dignity of his birth, administered to his effects. Having the whole arrangement of everything in her own breast, she discharged some of the servants with rewards proportioned to their services, and soon retired to her castle on the Tagus, between Sacedon and Buendia. I was among the number of those whom she kept, and who made part of her country establishment. I had even the good fortune to become a principal agent in the plot. In spite of my faithful report on the subject of Don Lewis, she still harbored a partiality for that bewitching young fellow; or rather, for want of spirit to combat her passion in the first instance, she surrendered at discretion. There was no longer any need of taking precautions to speak with me in private. Gil Blas, said she with a sigh, I can never forget Don Lewis. Let me make what effort I will to banish him from my thoughts, he is present to them without intermission, not as you have described him, plunged in every variety of licentious riot, but just what my fancy would paint him—tender, loving, constant. She betrayed considerable emotion in uttering these words, and could not help shedding tears. My fountains were very near playing from mere sympathy. There was no better way of paying my court than by appearing sensibly touched at her distress. My friend, continued she, after having wiped her lovely eyes, your nature is evidently cast in a benevolent mould; and I am so well satisfied with your zeal that it shall not go unrewarded. Your assistance, my dear Gil Blas, is more necessary to me than ever. You must be made acquainted with a plan which engrosses all my thoughts, though it will appear strangely eccentric. You are to know that I mean to set out for Salamanca as soon as possible. There my design is to assume the disguise of a fashionable young fellow and to make acquaintance with Pacheco under the name of Don Felix. I shall endeavor to gain his confidence and friendship, and lead the conversation incidentally to the subject of Aurora de Guzman, for whose cousin I shall pass. He may perhaps express a wish to see her, and there is the point on which I expect the interest to turn. We will have two apartments in Salamanca. In one I shall be Don Felix, in the other, Aurora; and I flatter myself that by presenting my person before Don Lewis, sometimes under the resemblance of a man, sometimes in all the natural and artificial attractions of my own sex, I may bring him by little and little to the proposed end of my stratagem. I am perfectly aware that my project is extravagant in the highest degree, but my passion drives me headlong; and the innocence of my intentions renders me insensible to all compunctious feelings of virgin apprehension respecting so hazardous a step.

I was exactly in the same mind with Aurora respecting the extravagance of her scheme. Yet, unseasonable as it might seem to reflecting persons like myself, there was no occasion for me to play the schoolmaster, On the contrary, I began to practice all the arts of a thorough-bred special pleader, and undertook to magnify this hair-brained pursuit into a piece of incomparable wit and spirit, without the least tincture of imprudence. This was highly gratifying to my mistress. Lovers like to have their rampant fancies tickled. We no longer considered this rash enterprise in any other light than as a play, of which the characters were to be properly cast, and the business dramatically arranged. The actors were chosen out of our own domestic establishment, and the parts distributed without secret jealousy or open rupture, but then we were not players by profession. It was determined that Dame Ortiz should personate Aurora's aunt, under the name of Donna Kimena de Guzman, with a valet and waiting-maid by way of attendance; and that Aurora, with the swashing outside of a gay spark, was to take me for her valet-de-chambre, with one of her women disguised as a page, to be more immediately about her person. The drama thus filled up we returned to Madrid, where we understood Don Lewis still to be, though it was not likely to be long till his departure for Salamanca. We got up with all possible haste the dresses and decorations of our wild comedy. When they were in complete order, my mistress had them packed up carefully, that they might come out all in their gloss and newness on the rising of the curtain. Then, leaving the care of her family to her steward, she began her journey in a coach drawn by four mules, and traveled towards the kingdom of Leon, with those of her household who had some part to play in the piece.

We had already crossed Old Castile, when the axletree of the coach gave way. The accident happened between Avila and Villaflor, at the distance of three or four hundred yards from a castle near the foot of a mountain. Night was coming on, and the measure of our troubles seemed to be heaped up and overflowing. But there passed accidentally by us a countryman, by whose assistance we were relieved from our difficulties. He acquainted us that the castle yonder belonged to Donna Elvira, widow of Don Pedro de Penarés; at the same time giving us so favorable a character of that lady, that my mistress sent me to the castle with a request of a night's lodging. Elvira did not disgrace the good word of the countryman. She received me with an air of hospitality, and returned such an answer to my compliment as I wished to carry back. We all went to the castle, whither the mules dragged the carriage with considerable difficulty. At the gate we met the widow of Don Pedro, who came out to meet my mistress. I shall pass over in silence the reciprocal civilities which were exchanged on this occasion, in compliance with the usage of the polite world. I shall only say that Elvira was a lady rather advanced in years, but remarkably well bred, with an address superior to that of most women in doing the honors of her house. She led Aurora into a sumptuous apartment, where, leaving her to rest herself for a short time, she looked after everything herself, and left nothing undone which could in the least contribute to our comfort. Afterwards, when supper was ready, she ordered it to be served up in Aurora's chamber, where they sat down to table together. Don Pedro's widow was not of a description to cast a slur on her own hospitalities, by assuming an air of abstraction or sullenness. Her temper was gay, and her conversation lively without levity; for her ideas were dignified, and her expressions select. Nothing could exceed her wit, accompanied by a peculiarly fine turn of thought. Aurora appeared as much to be delighted as myself. They became sworn friends, and mutually engaged in a regular correspondence. As our carriage could not be repaired till the following day, and we should have encountered some perils by setting out late at night, it was determined that we should take up our abode at the castle till the damage was made good. All the arrangements were in the first style of elegance, and our lodgings were correspondent to the magnificence of the establishment in other respects.

The day after, my mistress discovered new charms in Elvira's conversation. They dined in a large hall, where there were several pictures. One among the rest was distinguished for its admirable execution, but the subject was highly tragic. A principal figure was a man of superior mien, lying lifeless on his back, and bathed in his own blood; yet in the very embraces of death he wore a menacing aspect. At a little distance from him you might see a young lady in a different posture, though stretched likewise on the ground. She had a sword plunged in her bosom, and was giving up her last sighs, and at the same time casting her dying glances at a young man who seemed to suffer a mortal pang at losing her. The painter had besides charged his picture with a figure which did not escape my notice. It was an old man of a venerable physiognomy, sensibly touched with the objects which struck his sight, and equally alive with the young man to the impressions of the melancholy scene. It might be said that these images of blood and desolation affected both the spectators with the same astonishment and grief, but that the outward demonstrations of their inward sentiments were different. The old man, sunk in a profound melancholy, look-ed as if he was bowed down to the ground; while the youth min-gled something like the extravagance of despair with the tears of affliction. All these circumstances were depicted with touches so characteristic and affecting, that we could not take our eyes off the performance. My mistress desired to know the subject of the piece. Madam, said Elvira, it is a faithful delineation of the mis-fortunes sustained by my family. This answer excited Aurora's curiosity; and she testified so strong a desire to learn the particu-lars, that the widow of Don Pedro could do no otherwise than promise her the satisfaction she desired. This promise, made be-fore Ortiz, her two fellow-servants, and myself, rooted us to the spot on which we were listening to their former conversation. My mistress would have sent us away; but Elvira, who saw plainly that we were dying with eagerness to be present at the explanation of the picture, had the goodness to desire us to stay, alleging at the same time that the story she had to relate was not of a nature to enjoin secrecy. After a moment's recollection, she began her re-cital to the following effect:—

CHAPTER IV.

THE FATAL MARRIAGE; A NOVEL.

ROGER, king of Sicily, had a brother and a sister. His brother, by name Mainfroi, rebelled against him, and kindled a war in the kingdom, bloody in its immediate effects, and portentous in its fu-ture consequences. But it was his fate to lose two battles, and to fall into the king's hands. The punishment of his revolt extended no further than the loss of liberty. This act of clemency served only to make Roger pass for a barbarian in the estimation of the disaffected party among his subjects. They contended that he had saved his brother's life only to wreak his vengeance on him by tor-tures the more merciless because protracted. People in general, on better grounds, transferred the blame of Mainfroi's harsh treat-ment while in prison to his sister Matilda. That princess had, in fact, cherished a long-rooted hatred against this prince, and was indefatigable in her persecutions during his whole life. She died in a very short time after him, and her premature fate was con-sidered as the retribution of a just providence for her disregard of those sentiments implanted by nature for the best purposes.

Mainfroi left behind him two sons. They were yet in their childhood. Roger had a kind of lurking desire to get rid of them, under the apprehension lest, when arrived at a more advanced age, the wish of avenging their father might hurry them to the revival of a faction which was not so entirely overthrown as to be incapable of originating new intrigues in the state. He communicated his purpose to the senator Leontio Siffredi, his minister, who diverted him from his bloody thoughts by undertaking the education of Prince Enriquez, the eldest, and recommending the care of the younger, by name Don Pedro, to the constable of Sicily, as a trusty counsellor and loyal servant. Roger, assured that his nephews would be trained up by these two men in principles of due submission to the royal authority, gave up the reins of guardianship to their control, and himself took charge of his niece Constance. She was of the same age with Enriquez, and only daughter of the princess Matilda. He allowed her an establishment of female attendants, and of masters in every branch of the politer studies, so that nothing was wanting either to her instruction or her state.

Leontio Siffredi had a castle at the distance of less than two leagues from Palermo, in a spot named Belmonte. There it was that this minister exerted all his talents and diligence, to render Enriquez worthy of one day ascending the throne of Sicily. From the first, he discovered dispositions so amiable in that prince, that his attachment became as strong as if he had no child of his own. He had, however, two daughters—Blanche. the first-born, one year younger than the prince, was armed at all points with the weapons of a most perfect beauty. Her sister Portia was still in her cradle. The mother had died in child-bed of this youngest. Blanche and Prince Enriquez conceived a reciprocal affection as soon as they were alive to the influence of love: but they were not allowed to improve their acquaintance into familiar intercourse. The prince nevertheless found the means of occasionally eluding the prudential vigilance of his guardian. He knew sufficiently well how to avail himself of those precious moments, and prevailed so far with Siffredi's daughter, as to gain her consent to the execution of a project which he meditated. It happened precisely at this time that Leontio was obliged by the king's order to take a journey into one of the most remote provinces in the island. During his absence Enriquez got an opening made in the wall of his · partment, which led into Blanche's chamber. This opening was concealed by a sliding shutter, so exactly corresponding with the wainscot, and so closely fitting in with the ceiling and the floor, that the most suspicious eye could not have detected the contrivance. A skillful workman, whom the prince had gained over to his interests, helped him to this private communication with equal speed and secrecy.

The enamoured Enriquez having obtained this inlet into his mistress's chamber, sometimes availed himself of his privilege; but Le never took advantage of her partiality. Imprudent as it may well be thought, to admit of a secret entrance into her apartment, it was only on the express and reiterated assurance that none but the most innocent favors should be requested at her hands. One night he found her in a state of unusual perturbation. She had been informed that Roger was drawing near his end, and had sent for Siffredi as lord high chancellor of the kingdom, and the legal depository of his last will and testament. Already did she figure to herself her dear Enriquez elevated to royal honors. She was afraid of losing her lover in her sovereign, and that fear had strangely affected her spirits. The tears were standing in her eyes, when the unconscious cause of them appeared before her. You weep, madam, said he, what am I to think of this overwhelming grief? My lord, answered Blanche, it were vain for me to hide my apprehensions. The king your uncle is at the point of death, and you will soon be called to supply his place. When I measure the distance placed between us by your approaching greatness, I will own to you that my mind misgives me. The monarch and the lover estimate objects through a far different medium. What constituted the fondest wish of the individual, while his aspiring thoughts were checked by the control of a superior, fades into insignificance before the tumultuous cares or brilliant destinies of royalty. Be it the misgiving of an anxious heart, or the whisper of a well-founded opinion, I feel distracting emotions succeed one another in my breast, which not all my just confidence in your goodness can allay. The source of my mistrust is not in the suspected steadiness of your attachment, but in a diffidence of my own happy fate. Lovely and beloved Blanche, replied the prince, your fears but bind me the more firmly in your fetters, and warrant my devotion to your charms. Yet this excessive indulgence of a fond jealousy borders on disloyalty to love, and, if I may venture to say so, trenches on the esteem to which my constancy has hitherto entitled me. No, no, never entertain a doubt that my destiny can ever be sundered from yours, but rather indulge the pleasing anticipation, that you, and you alone, will be the arbitress of my fate, and the source of all my bliss. Away, then, with these vain alarms. Why must they disturb an intercourse so charming? Ah! my lord, rejoined the daughter of Leontio, your subjects, when they place the crown upon your head, may ask of you a princess-queen, descended from a long line of kings, whose glittering alliance shall join new realms to your hereditary estates. Perhaps, alas! you will meet their ambitious aims, even at the expense of your softest vows. Nay, why, resumed Enriquez, with rising passion, why too ready a self-tormentor, do you raise so afflicting a phantom of futurity? Should heaven take the king my uncle to itself, and place Sicily under my dominion, I swear to unite myself with you at Palermo, in presence of my whole court. To this I call to witness all which is held sacred and inviolable among men.

The protestations of Enriquez removed the fears of Siffredi's daughter. The rest of their discourse turned on the king's illness. Enriquez displayed the goodness of his natural disposition, for he pitied his uncle's lot, though he had no reason to be greatly affected by it; but the force of blood extorted from him sentiments of regret for a prince whose death held out an immediate prospect of the crown. Blanche did not yet know all the misfortunes which hung over her. The constable of Sicily, who had met her coming out of her father's apartment, one day when he was at the castle of

Belmonte on some business of importance, was struck with admiration. The very next day, he made proposals to Siffredi, who entertained his offer favorably; but the illness of Roger taking place unexpectedly about that time, the marriage was put off for the present, and the subject had not been hinted at in the most distant manner to Blanche.

One morning, as Enriquez had just finished dressing, he was surprised to see Leontio enter his apartment, followed by Blanche. Sir, said this minister, the news I have to announce will in some degree afflict your excellent heart, but it is counteracted by consoling circumstances which ought to moderate your grief. The king your uncle has departed this life; and by his death left you the heir of his sceptre. Sicily is at your feet. The nobility of the kingdom wait your orders at Palermo. They have commissioned me to receive them in person, and I come my liege, with my daughter to pay you the earliest and sincerest homage of your new subjects. The prince, who was well aware that Roger had been for two months sinking under a complaint gradual in its progress but fatal in its nature, was not astonished at this news. And yet, struck with his sudden exaltation, he felt a thousand confused motions raising up by turns in his heart. He mused for some time, then breaking silence, addressed these words to Leontio—Wise Siffredi, I have always considered you as my father. I shall make it my glory to be governed by your counsels, and you shall reign in Sicily with a sway paramount to my own. With these words, advancing to the standish and taking a blank sheet of paper, he wrote his name at the bottom. What are you doing, sir? said Siffredi. Proving my gratitude and my esteem, answered Enriquez. Then the prince presented the paper to Blanche, and said—Accept, madam, this pledge of my faith, and of the empire with which I invest you over my thoughts and actions. Blanche received it with a blush, and made this answer to the prince—I acknowledge with all humility the condescensions of my sovereign, but my destiny is in the hands of a father, and you must not consider me as ungrateful if I deposit this flattering token in his custody, to be used according to his dictates of his sage discretion.

In compliance with these sentiments of filial duty, she gave the sign manual of Enriquez to her father. Then Siffredi saw at once what till that moment had eluded his penetration. He entered clearly into the prince's sentiments, and said: Your majesty shall have no reproaches to make me. I shall not act unworthily of the confidence. . . . . My dear Leontio, interrupted Enriquez, you and unworthiness never can be allied. Make what use you please of my signature. I shall confirm your determination. But go, return to Palermo, prescribe the ceremonies for my coronation there, and tell my subjects that I shall follow you in person immediately, to receive their oaths of allegiance, and assure them of my protection in return. The minister obeyed the commands of his new master, and set out for Palermo with his daughter.

Some hours after their departure, the prince also left Belmonte, with his thoughts more intent on his passion than on the high rank to which he was called. Immediately on his arrival in the city, the air was rent with a thousand cries of joy. He made his entry into the palace amid the acclamations of the people, and everything was ready for the august formalities. The Princess Constance was waiting to receive him in a magnificent mourning dress. She appeared deeply affected by Roger's death. The customs of society required from them a reciprocal compliment of condolence on the late event; and they each of them acquitted themselves with good breeding and propriety. But there was somewhat more coldness on the part of Enriquez than on that of Constance, who could not enter into family quarrels, and resolved on hating the young prince. He placed himself on the throne, and the princess sate beside him, in a chair of state a little less elevated. The great officers of the realm fell into their places, each according to his rank. The ceremony began ; and Leontio, as lord high chancellor of the kingdom, holding in his possession the will of the late king, opened it, and read the contents aloud. This instrument contained in substance that Roger, in default of issue, nominated the eldest son of Mainfroi his successor, on condition of his marrying the Princess Constance : and in the event of his refusing her hand, the crown of Sicilly was to devolve, to his exclusion, on the head of the infant Don Pedro, his brother, on the like condition.

These words were a thunderstroke to Enriquez. His senses were all bewildered even to distraction ; and his agonies became still more acute, when Leontio, having finished the reading of the will, addressed the assembly at large to the following effect : My lords, the last injunctions of the late king having been made known to our new monarch, that pious and excellent prince consents to honor his cousin the princess Constance with his hand. At these words Enriquez interrupted the chancellor. Leontio, said he, remember the writing; Blanche. . . . . Sire, interrupted Siffredi in his turn with precipitation, lest the prince should find an opportunity of making himself understood, here it is. The nobility of the kingdom, added he, exhibiting the blank paper to the assembly, will see by your majesty's august subscription, the esteem in which you hold the princess, and your implicit deference to the last will of the late king your uncle.

Having finished these words, he forthwith began reading the instrument in such terms as he had himself inserted. According to the contents, the new king gave a promise to his people, with formalities the most binding and authentic, that he would marry Constance, in conformity with the intention of Roger. The hall re-echoed with pealing shouts of satisfaction. Long live our high and mighty King Enriquez ! exclaimed all those who were present. As the marked aversion of the prince for the princess had never been any secret, it was apprehended, not without reason, that he might revolt against the condition of the will, and light up the flame of civil discord in the kingdom ; but the public enunciation of this solemn act, quieting the fears of the nobility and the people on that head, excited these universal applauses, which went to the monarch's heart like the stab of an assassin. Constance, who had a nearer interest than any human being in the result, from the double motive of glory and personal affection, laid hold of this opportunity for expressing her gratitude. The prince had much ado to keep his feelings within bounds. He received the compliment of the princess with so constrained an air, and evinced so unusual a disorder in his behavior, as scarcely to reply in a manner suited to the common forms of good breeding. At last, no longer master of his violent passions, he went up to Siffredi, whom the formalities of his office detained near the royal person, and said to him in a low tone of voice—What is the meaning of all this, Leontio? The signature which I deposited in your daughter's hands was not meant for such a use as this. You are guilty of . . . . . .

My liege, interrupted Siffredi again with a tone of firmness, look to your own glory. If you refuse to comply with the injunctions of the king, your uncle, you lose the crown of Sicily. No sooner had he thrown in this salutary hint, than he got away from the king, to prevent all possibility of a reply. Enriquez was left in a most embarrassing situation. A thousand opposite emotions agitated him at once. He was exasperated against Siffredi: to give up Blanche was more than he could endure: so that, balancing between his private feelings and the calls of public honor, he was doubtful to which side he should incline. At length his doubts were resolved, under the idea of having found the means to secure Siffredi's daughter, without giving up his claim to the throne. He affected therefore an entire submission to the will of Roger, in the hope, while a dispensation from his marriage with his cousin was soliciting at Rome, of gaining the leading nobility by his largesses, and thus establishing his power so firmly, as not to be under the necessity of fulfilling the conditions of the obnoxious instrument.

After forming this design, he got to be more composed; and turning towards Constance, confirmed to her what the lord high chancellor had read in presence of the whole assembly. But, at the very moment when he had so far betrayed himself as to pledge his faith, Blanche arrived in the hall of council. She came thither, by her father's command, to pay her duty to the princess; and her ears, on entering, were startled at the expressions of Enriquez. In addition to this shock, Leontio, determined not to leave her in doubt of her misfortune, accompanied her presentation to Constance with these words: Daughter, make your homage acceptable to your queen; call down upon her the blessings of a prosperous reign and a happy marriage. This terrible blow overwhelmed the unfortunate Blanche Vain were all her attempts to suppress her anguish; her countenance changed successively from the deepest blush to a deadly paleness, and she trembled from head to foot. And yet the princess had no suspicion how the matter really stood; but attributed the confused style of her compliment to the awkwardness of a young person brought up in a state of rustication, and totally unacquainted with the manners of a court. But the young king was more in the secret. The sight of Blanche put him out of countenance: and the despair, too legible in her eyes, was enough to drive him out of his senses. Her feelings were not to be misunderstood; and they pointed at him as the most faithless of men. Could he have spoken to her, it might have tranquillized his agitation: but how to lay hold of the happy moment, when all Sicily, at least the illustrious part of it, was fixed in anxious expectation on his proceedings? Besides, the stern and inflexible Siffredi extinguished at once every ray of hope. This minister, who was at no loss to decipher the hearts of the two lovers, and was firmly resolved, if possible, to prevent the evil consequences impending over the state from the violence of this imprudent attachment, got his daughter out of the assembly with the dexterity of a practised courtier, and regained the road to Belmonte with her in his possession, determined, for more reasons than one, to marry her as soon as possible.

When they reached home, he gave her to understand all the horror of her destiny, by announcing his promise to the constable. Just heaven, exclaimed she, transported into a paroxysm of despair, which her father's presence could not restrain, what unparalleled sufferings have you the cruelty to lay up in store for the ill-fated Blanche? Her agony went to such a degree of violence, as to suspend every power of her soul. Her limbs seemed as if stiffened under the icy grasp of death. Cold and pale, she fell senseless into her father's arms. Neither was he insensible to her melancholy condition. Yet, feeling as he did all the alarm and anxiety of a parent, the stern inflexibility of the statesman remained unshaken. Blanche, after a time, was recalled to life and feeling, rather by the keenness of her mental pangs than by the means which Siffredi used for her recovery. Languishingly did she raise her scarcely conscious eyes: when glancing on the author of her misery, as he was anxiously employed about her person; . . . . . . My lord, said she, with inarticulate and convulsive accents, I am ashamed to let you see my weakness; but death, which cannot be long in finishing my torments, will soon rid you of a wretched daughter, who has ventured to dispose of her heart without consulting you. No, my dear Blanche, answered Leontio, your death would be too dear a sacrifice: Virtue will resume her empire over your actions. The constable's proposals do you honor; it is one of the most considerable alliances in the state . . . . . I esteem his person and am sensible of his merit, interrupted Blanche; but, my lord, the king had given me encouragement to indulge . . . . Daughter, vociferated Siffredi, breaking in upon her discourse, I anticipate all you have to say on that subject. Your partiality for the prince is no secret to me, nor would it meet my disapprobation under other circumstances. You should even see me active and ardent to secure for you the hand of Enriquez, if the cause of glory and the welfare of the realm demanded it not indispensably for Constance. It is on the sole condition of marrying that princess, that the late king has nominated him his successor. Would you have him prefer you to the crown of Sicily? Believe me, my heart bleeds at the mortal blow which impends over you. Yet, since we cannot contend with the fates, make a magnanimous effort. Your fame is concerned, not to let the whole nation see that you have nursed up a delusive hope. Your sensibility towards the person of the king might even give birth to ignominious rumors. The only method of preserving yourself from their poison, is to marry the constable. In short, Blanche, there is no time left for irresolution. The king has decided between a throne and the possession of your charms. He has fixed his choice on Constance. The constable holds my words in pledge; enable me to redeem it, I beseech you. Or if nothing but a paramount necessity can fix your wavering resolution, I must make an unwilling use of my parental authority; know then, I command you.

Ending with this threat, he left her to make her own reflections on what had passed. He was in hopes that after having weighed the reasons he had urged to support her virtue against the bias of her feelings, she would determine of herself to admit the constable's addresses. He was not mistaken in his conjecture: but at what an expense did the wretched Blanche rise to this height of virtuous resolution! Her condition was that in the whole world the most deserving of pity. The affliction of finding her fears realized respecting the infidelity of Enriquez, and of being compelled, besides losing the man of her choice, to sacrifice herself to another whom she could never love, occasioned her such storms of passion and alternate tossings of frantic desperation, as to bring with each successive moment a variety of vindictive torture. If my sad fate is fixed, exclaimed she, how can I triumph over it but by death? Merciless powers, who preside over our wayward fortunes, why feed and tantalize me with the most flattering hopes, only to plunge me headlong into a gulf of miseries? And thou too, perfidious lover! to rush into the arms of another, when all those vows of eternal fidelity were mine. So soon then is that plighted faith void and forgotten? To punish thee for so cruel a deception, may it please heaven, in its retribution, to make the conscious couch of conjugal endearment, polluted as it must be by perjury, less the scene of pleasure than the dungeon of remorse! May the fond caresses of Constance distil poison through thy faithless heart! Let us rival one another in the horrors of our nuptials! Yes, traitor, I mean to wed the constable, though shrinking from his ardent touch, to avenge me on myself! to be my own scourge and tormentor, for having selected so fatally the object of my frantic passion. Since deep-rooted obedience to the will of God forbids to entertain the thought of a premature death, whatever days may be allotted me to drag on shall be but a lengthened chain of heaviness and torment. If a sentiment of love still lurks about your heart, it will be revenge enough for me to cast myself into your presence, the devoted bride or victim of another: but if you have thrown off my remembrance with your own vows, Sicily at least shall glory in the distinction of reckoning among its natives a woman who knew how to punish herself for having disposed of her heart too lightly.

In such a state of mind did this wretched martyr to love and duty pass the night preceding her marriage with the constable. Siffredi, finding her the next morning ready to comply with his wishes, hastened to avail himself of this favorable disposition. He sent for the constable to Belmonte on that very day, and the marriage ceremony was performed privately in the chapel of the castle. What a crisis for Blanche! It was not enough to renounce a crown, to lose a lover endeared to her by every tie, and to yield herself up to the object of her hatred. In addition to all this, she must put a constraint on her sentiments before a husband, naturally jealous, and long occupied with the most ardent admiration of her charms. The bridegroom, delighted in the possession of her, was all day long in her presence. He did not leave her to the miserable consolation of pouring out her sorrows in secret. When night arrived, Leontio's daughter felt all her disgust and terror redoubled. But what seemed likely to become of her when her women, after having undressed her, left her alone with the constable? He enquired respectfully into the cause of her apparent faintness and discomposure. The question was sufficiently embarrassing to Blanche, who affected to be ill. Her husband was at first deceived by her pretences; but he did not long remain in such an error. Being, as he was, sincerely concerned at the condition in which he saw her, but still pressing her to go to bed, his urgent solicitations, falsely construed by her, offered to her wounded mind an image so cruel and indelicate, that she could no longer dissemble what was passing within, but gave a free course to her signs and tears. What a discovery for a man who thought himself at the summit of his wishes! He no longer doubted but the distressed state of his wife was fraught with some sinister omen to his love. And yet, though this knowledge reduced him to a situation almost as deplorable as that of Blanche, he had sufficient command over himself to keep his suspicions within his own breast. He redoubled his assiduities, and went on pressing his bride to lay herself down, assuring her that the repose of which she stood in need should be undisturbed by his interruption. He offered of his own accord even to call her women, if she was of opinion that their attendance could afford any relief to her indisposition. Blanche, reviving at that proposal, told him that sleep was the best remedy for the debility under which she labored. He affected to think so too. They accordingly partook of the same bed, but with a conduct altogether different from what the laws of love, sanctioned by the rites of marriage, might authorize in a pair mutually delighted and delighting.

While Siffredi's daughter was giving way to her grief, the constable was hunting in his own mind for the causes which might render the nuptial office so contemptible a sinecure in his hands. He could not be long in conjecturing that he had a rival, but when he attempted to discover him he was lost in the labyrinth of his own ideas. All he knew with certainty, was the peculiar severity of his own fate. He had already passed two thirds of the night in this perplexity of thought, when an undistinguishable noise grew gradually on his sense of hearing. Great was his surprise when a footstep seemed audibly to pace about the room. He fancied himself mistaken; for he recollected shutting the door himself after Blanche's women had retired. He drew back the curtain to satisfy his senses on the occasion of this extraordinary noise. But the light in the chimney corner had gone out, and he soon heard a feeble and melancholy voice calling Blanche with anxious and importunate repetitions. Then did the suggestions of his jealousy transport him into rage. His insulted honor obliging him to rush from the bed to which he had so long aspired, and either to prevent a meditated injury, or take vengeance for its perpetration, he caught up his sword and flew forward in the direction whence the voice seemed to proceed. He felt a naked blade opposed to his own. As he advanced, his antagonist retired. The pursuit became more eager, the retreat more precipitate. His search was vigilant, and every corner of the room seemed to contain its object, but that which he momentarily occupied. The darkness, however, favored the unknown invader, and he was nowhere to be found. The pursuer halted. He listened, but heard no sound, It seemed like enchantment! He made for the door, under the idea that this was the outlet to the secret assassin of his honor; yet the bolt was shot as fast as before. Unable to comprehend this strange occurrence, he called those of his retinue who were most within reach of his voice. As he opened the door for this purpose, he placed himself so as to prevent all egress, and stood upon his guard, lest the devoted victim of his search should escape.

At his redoubled cries, some servants ran with lights. He laid hold of a taper, and renewed his search in the chamber with his sword still drawn. Yet he found no one there, nor any apparent sign of any person having been in the room. He was not aware of any private door, nor could he discover any practicable mode of escape: yet for all this, he could not shut his eyes against the nature and circumstances of his misfortune. His thoughts were all thrown into inextricable confusion. To ask any questions of Blanche was in vain: for she had too deep an interest in perplexing the truth, to furnish any clue whatever to its discovery. He therefore adopted the measure of unbosoming his griefs to Leontio; but previously sent away his attendants with the excuse that he thought he had heard some noise in the room, but was mistaken. His father-in-law having left his chamber in consequence of this strange disturbance, met him, and heard from his lips the particulars of this unaccountable adventure. The narrative was accompanied with every indication of extreme agony, produced by deep and tender feeling, as well as by a sense of insulted honor.

Siffredi was surprised at the occurrence. Though it did not appear to him at all probable, that was no reason for being easy about its reality. The king's passion might accomplish anything; and that idea alone justified the most cruel apprehensions. But it could do no good to foster either the natural jealousy of his son-in-law, or his particular suspicions arising out of circumstances. He therefore endeavored to persuade him, with an air of confidence, that this imaginary voice, and airy sword opposed to his substantial one, were, and possibly could be, but the gratuitous creations of a fancy, under the influence of amorous distrust. It was morally impossible that any person should have made his way into his daughter's chamber. With regard to the melancholy, so visible in his wife's deportment, it might very naturally be attributed to precarious health and delicacy of constitution. The honor of a husband need not be so tremblingly alive to all the qualms of maiden fear and inexperience. Change of condition, in the case of a girl habituated to live almost without human society, and abruptly consigned to the embraces of a man in whom love and previous acquaintance had not inspired confidence, might innocently be the cause of these tears, of these sighs, and of this lively affliction so irksome to his feelings. But it was to be considered that tenderness, especially in the hearts of young ladies, fortified by the pride of blood against the excesses of love-sick abandonment, was only to be cherished into a flame by time and assiduity. He therefore exhorted him to tranquillize his disturbed mind; to be ardently officious in redoubling every instance of affection; to create a soft and seducing interest in the sensibility of Blanche. In short, he besought him earnestly to return to her apartment, and labored to persuade him that his distrust and confusion would only set her on an unconjugal and litigious defence of her insulted virtue.

The constable returned no answer to the arguments of his father-in-law, whether because he began to think in good earnest that his senses were imposed on by the disorder of his mind, or because he thought it more to the purpose to dissemble, than to undertake ineffectually to convince the old man of an event so devoid of all likelihood. He returned to his wife's chamber, laid himself down by her side, and endeavored to obtain from sleep some relief from his extreme uneasiness. Blanche, on her part, the unhappy Blanche, was not a whit more at her ease. Her ears had been but too open to the same alarming sounds, which had assailed her husband's peace; nor could she construe into illusion an adventure of which she well knew the secret and the motives. She was surprised that Enriquez should attempt to find his way into her apartment, after having pledged his faith so solemnly to the Princess Constance. Instead of feeding her soul with vanity, or deriving any flattering omens from a proceeding fraught with personal tenderness, but destructive to self-approbation, she considered it as a new insult, and her heart was only so much the more exasperated with resentment against the author.

While Siffredi's daughter, with all her prejudices excited against the young king, believed him the most guilty of men, that unhappy prince, more than ever ensnared by Blanche, was anxious for an interview, to satisfy her mind on a subject which seemed to make so much against him. For that purpose he would have visited Belmonte sooner, but for a press of business too urgent to be neglected; nor could he withdraw himself from the court before that night. He was perfectly at home in all the turnings of a place where he had been brought up, and therefore was at no loss to slip into the castle of Siffredi. Nay, he was still in possession of the key to a secret door communicating with the gardens. By this inlet did he gain his former apartment, and thence found his way into Blanche's chamber. Only conceive what must have been the astonishment of that prince to find a man in possession, and to feel a sword opposed to his guard. He was just on the point of betraying all, and of punishing the rebel on the very spot, whose sacrilegious hand had dared to lift itself against the person of its lawful sovereign. But then the delicacy due to the daughter of Leontio held his indignation in check. He retreated in the same direction as he had advanced, and regained the Palermo road, in more distress and perplexity than ever. Getting home some little time before day-break, his apartment afforded him the most quiet retreat. But his thoughts were all on the road back to Belmonte. The resting-place of his affections, a sense of honor, in a word, love with all its pretensions and surmises, would never allow him to delay an explanation, involving all the circumstances of so strange and melancholy an adventure.

As soon as it was daylight he gave out that he was going on a hunting expedition. Under cover of sporting, his huntsmen and a chosen party of his courtiers penetrated into the forest of Belmonte under his direction. The chase was followed for some time, as a blind to his real design. When he saw the whole party eagerly driving on, and wholly engrossed by the sport, he galloped off in a different direction, and struck, without any attendants, into the road towards Leontio's castle. The various tracks of the forest were too well known to him to admit of his losing his way. His impatience, too, would not allow him to take any thought of his horse; so that the moments scarcely flitted faster, than his expedition in leaving behind him the distance which separated him from the object of his love. His very soul was on the rack for some plausible excuse to plead for a private interview with Siffredi's daughter, when, crossing a narrow path just at the park gate, he observed two women sitting close by him, in earnest conversation under the shelter of a tree. It might well be supposed that these females belonged to the castle; and even that probability was sufficient to rouse an interest in him. But his emotion was heightened into a feeling beyond his reason to control, for these ladies happened to look round on hearing the trot of a horse advancing in that direction; when at once he recognized his dear Blanche. The fact was, she had made her escape from the castle with Nisa, the person of all others among her women most in her confidence, that she might at least have the satisfaction of weeping over her misfortunes without intrusion or restraint.

He flew, and seeemed rather to throw himself headlong than to fall at her feet. But when he beheld in the expression of her countenance every mark of the deepest affliction, his heart was softened. Lovely Blanche, said he, do not, let me entreat you, give way to the emotions of your grief. Appearances, I own, must represent me as guilty in your eyes: but when you shall be made acquainted with my project in your behalf, what you consider as a crime will be transformed in your thoughts into a proof of my innocence, and an evidence of my unparalleled affection. These words, calculated, according to the views of Enriquez, to allay the grief of Blanche, served only to redouble her affliction. Fain would she have answered, but her sobs stifled her utterance. The prince, thunderstruck at the death-like agitation of her frame, addressed her thus. What, madam, is there no possibility of tranquilizing your agitation? By what sad mischance have I lost your confidence, at the very moment when my crown and even my life are at stake, in consequence of my resolution to hold myself engaged to you? At this suggestion the daughter of Leontio, doing violence to her own feelings, but thinking it necessary to explain herself, said to him—My liege, your assurances are no longer admissible. My destiny and yours are henceforward as far asunder as the poles. Ah! Blanche, interrupted Enriquez with impatience, what cutting words are these, too painful for my sense of hearing? Who dares step in between our loves? Who would venture to stand forward against the headlong rage of a king who would kindle all Sicily into a conflagration, rather than suffer you to be ravished from his long-cherished hopes? All your power, my liege, great as it is, replied the daughter of Siffredi in a tone of melancholy, becomes inefficient against the obstacles in the way of our union. I know not how to tell it you, but . . . . . . I am married to the constable.

Married to the constable! exclaimed the prince, starting back to some distance from her. He could proceed no further in his discourse, so completely was he thunderstruck at the intelligence. Overwhelmed by this unexpected blow, he felt his strength forsake him. His unconscious limbs laid themselves without his guidance against the trunk of a tree just behind him. His countenance was pallid, his whole frame in a tremor, his mind bewildered and his spirits depressed. With no sense or faculty at liberty but that of gazing, and there every power of his soul was suspended on Blanche, he made her feel most poignantly how he himself was agonized by the fatal event she had announced. The expression of countenance on her part was such as to show him that her emotions were not uncongenial with his own. Thus did these two distressed lovers for a time preserve a silence towards each other, which portended something of terror in its calmness. At length the prince, recovering a little from his disorder by an effort of courage, resumed the discourse, and said to Blanche with a sigh—Madam, what have you done? You have destroyed me, and involved yourself in the same ruin by your credulity.

Blanche was offended at the seeming reproaches of the king, when the strongest grounds of complaint were apparently on her side. What! my lord, answered she, do you add dissimulation to infidelity? Would you have me reject the evidence of my own eyes and ears, so as to believe you innocent in spite of their report? No, my lord, I will own to you such an effort of abstraction is not in my power. And yet, madam, replied the king, these witnesses by whose testimony you have been so fully convinced, are but impostors. They have been in a conspiracy to betray you. It is no less the fact that I am innocent and faithful, than it is true that you are married to the constable. What is it you say, my lord? replied she. Did I not overhear you confirming the pledge of your hand and heart to Constance? Have you not bound yourself to the nobility of the realm, and undertaken to comply with the will of the late king? Has not the princess received the homage of your new subjects as their queen, and in quality of bride to Prince Enriquez? Were my eyes then fascinated? Tell me, tell me rather, traitor, that Blanche was weighed as dust in the balance of your heart, when compared with the attractions of a throne. Without lowering yourself so far as to assume what you no longer feel, and what perhaps you never felt, own at once that the crown of Sicily appeared a more tenable possession with Constance than with the daughter of Leontio. You are in the right, my lord. My title to an illustrious throne, and to the heart of a prince like you, stands on an equally precarious footing. It was vanity in the extreme to prefer a claim to either: but you ought not to have drawn me on into error. You well recollect what alarms were my portion at the very thought of losing you, of which I had almost a supernatural foreboding. Why did you lull my apprehensions to sleep? To what purpose was that delusive mockery? I might else have accused fate rather than yourself, and you would at least have retained an interest in my heart, though unaccompanied by a hand which no other suitor could ever have obtained. As we are now circumstanced, your justification is out of season. I am married to the constable. To relieve me from the continuance of an interview, which casts a shade over my purity, hitherto unsullied, permit me, my lord, without failing in due respect, to withdraw from the presence of a prince to whose addresses I am no longer at liberty to listen.

With these words, she darted away from Enriquez in as hurried a step as the agitation of her spirits would allow. Stop, madam, exclaimed he, drive not to despair a prince, inclined to overturn a throne, which you reproach him for having preferred to yourself, rather than yield to the importunities of his new subjects. That sacrifice is under present circumstances superfluous, rejoined Blanche. The bond must be broken between the constable and me, before any effect can be produced by these generous transports. Since I am not my own mistress, little would it avail that Sicily should be embroiled, nor does it concern me to whom you give your hand. If I had betrayed my own weakness, and suffered my heart to be surprised, at least shall I muster fortitude enough to suppress every soft emotion, and prove to the new king of Sicily, that the wife of the constable is no longer the mistress of Prince Enriquez. While this conversation was passing, they reached the park gate. With a sudden spring she and Nisa got within the walls. As they took care to fasten the wicket after them, the prince was left in a state of melancholy and stupefaction. He could not recover from the stunning sensation, occasioned by the intelligence of Blanche's marriage. Unjust may I well call you, exclaimed he. You have buried all remembrance of our solemn engagement! Spite of my protestations and your own, our fates are rent asunder? The long-cherished hope of possessing those charms was an empty phantom! Ah! cruel as you are, how dearly have I purchased the distinction, of compelling you to acknowledge the constancy of my love!

At that moment his rival's happiness, heightened by the coloring of jealousy, presented itself to his mind in all the horrors of that frantic passion. So arbitrary was its sway over him for some moments, that he was on the point of sacrificing the constable, and even Siffredi, to his blind vengeance. Reason, however, calmed by little and little the violence of his transports. And yet the obvious impossibility of effacing from the mind of Blanche her natural conviction of his infidelity, reduced him to despair. He flattered himself with weaning her from her prejudices, could he but converse with her secure from interruption. To attain this end, it seemed the most feasible plan to get rid of the constable. He therefore determined to have him arrested, as a person suspected of treasonable designs, in the then unsettled state of public affairs. This commission was given the captain of his guard, who went immediately to Belmonte, secured the person of his prisoner just as the evening was closing in, and carried him to the castle of Palermo.

This occurrence spread an alarm at Belmonte. Siffredi took his departure forthwith, to offer his own responsibility to the king for the innocence of his son-in-law, and to represent in their true colors the unpleasant consequences attending such arbitrary exertions of power. The prince, who had anticipated such a proceeding on the part of his minister, and was determined at least to secure himself a free interview with Blanche before the release of the constable, had expressly forbidden any one to address him till the next day. But Leontio, setting this prohibition at defiance, contrived so well as to make his way into the king's chamber. My liege, said he, with an air of humility tempered with firmness, if it is allowable for a subject full of respect and loyalty to complain of his master, I have to arraign you before the tribunal of your own conscience. What crime has my son-in-law committed? Has your majesty sufficiently reflected what an everlasting reproach is entailed on my family? Are the consequences of an imprisonment calculated to disgust all the most important officers of the state with the service, a matter of indifference? I have undoubted information, answered the king, that the constable holds a criminal correspondence with the Infant Don Pedro. A criminal correspondence! interrupted Leontio, with surprise. Ah! my liege, give no ear to the surmise. Your majesty is played upon. Treason never gained a footing in the family of Siffredi. It is sufficient security for the constable that he is my son-in-law, to place him above all suspicion. The constable is innocent: but private motives have been the occasion of your arresting him.

Since you speak to me so openly, replied the king, I will adopt the same sincerity with you. You complain of the constable's imprisonment! Be it so. And have I no reason to complain of your cruelty? It is you, barbarous Siffredi, who have wrested my tranquillity from me, and reduced your sovereign, by your officious cares, to envy the lowliest of the human race. For do not so far deceive yourself as to believe that I shall ever enter into your views. My marriage with Constance is quite out of the question . . . . .

What, my liege, interrupted Leontio, with an expression of horror, is there any doubt about your marrying the princess, after having flattered her with that hope in the face of your whole people? If their wishes are disappointed, replied the king, take the credit to yourself. Wherefore did you reduce me to the necessity of giving them a promise my heart would not allow me to make good? Where was the occasion to fill up with the name of Constance an instrument designed for the elevation of your own daughter? You could not be a stranger to my design; need you have completed your tyranny by devoting Blanche to the arms of a man to whom she could not give her heart? And what authority have you over mine to dispose of it in favor of a princess whom I detest? Have you forgotten that she is the daughter of that cruel Matilda, who, trampling the rights of consanguinity and human nature under foot, caused my father to breathe his last under all the rigors of a hard captivity? And should I marry her! No, Siffredi, throw away that hope. Before the lurid torch of such an hymeneal shall be kindled in your presence, ycu shall behold all Sicily in flames, and the expiring embers quenched in blood.

Do not my ears deceive me? exclaimed Leontio. Ah! sovereign, what a scene do you present me with! Who can hear such menances without shuddering? But I am too forward to take the alarm, continued he in an altered voice. You are in too close a union with your subjects to be the instrument of a catastrophe so melancholy. You will not suffer passion to triumph over your reason. Virtues like yours shall never lose their lustre by the tarnish of human and ordinary weakness. If I have given my daughter into the arms of the constable, it was with the design, my liege, of securing to your majesty a powerful subject, able by his own valor, and the army under his command, to maintain your party against that of the Prince Don Pedro. It appeared to me that by connecting him with my family in so close a bond. . . . . . . Yes, yes! This bond, exclaimed Prince Enriquez, this fatal bond has been my ruin. Unfeeling friend, to aim a wound at my vital part! What commission had you to take care of my interests at the expense of my affections? Why did you not leave me to support my pretensions by my own arm? Was there any question about my courage that I should be thought incompetent to reduce my rebellious subjects to their obedience? Means might have been found to punish the constable had he dared to have fallen off from his allegiance! I am well aware of the difference between a lawful king and an arbitrary tyrant. The happiness of our people is our first duty. But are we, on the other hand, to be the slaves of our subjects? From the moment when we are selected by heaven for our high office, do we lose the common privilege of nature, the birthright of the human race, to dispose of our affections in whatsoever current they may flow? Well then! if we are less our own masters than the lowest of the human race, take back, Siffredi, that sovereign authority you affect to have secured to me by the wreck of my personal happiness.

You cannot but be acquainted, my liege, replied the minister.

that it was on your marriage with the princess, the late king, your uncle made the succession of the crown to depend. And by what right, rejoined Enriquez, did even he assume to himself so arbitrary a disposition? Was it on such unworthy terms that he succeeded his brother, King Charles? How came you yourself to be so besotted as to allow of a stipulation so unjust? For a high chancellor, you are not too well versed in our laws and constitutions. To cut the matter short, though I have promised my hand to Constance, the engagement was not voluntary. I do not therefore think myself bound to keep my word; and if Don Pedro founds on my refusal any hope of succeeding to the throne without involving the nation in a bloody and destructive contest, his error will be too soon visible. The sword shall decide between us to whom the prize of empire may more worthily fall. Leontio could not venture to press him further, and confined himself to supplicating on his knees for the liberty of his son-in-law. That boon he obtained. Go, said the king to him, return to Belmonte, the constable shall follow you thither without delay. The minister departed, and made the best of his way to Belmonte, under the persuasion that his son-in-law would overtake him on the road. In this he was mistaken. Enriquez was determined to visit Blanche that night, and with such views he deferred the enlargement of her husband till the next morning.

During this time the feelings of the constable were of the most agonizing nature. His imprisonment had opened his eyes to the real cause of his misfortune. He gave himself up to jealousy without restraint or remorse, and belying the good faith which had hitherto rendered his character so valuable, his thoughts were all bent on his revenge. As he conjectured rightly that the king would not fail to reconnoitre Blanche's apartment during the night, it was his object to surprise them together. He therefore besought the governor of the castle at Palermo to allow of his absence from the prison, on the assurance of his return before daybreak. The governor, who was devoted to his interest, gave his permission so much the more easily, as being already advertised that Siffredi had procured his liberty. Indeed, he even went so far as to supply him with a horse for his journey to Belmonte. The constable on his arrival there fastened his horse to a tree. He then got into the park by a little gate of which he had the key, and was lucky enough to slip into the castle without being recognized by any one. On reaching his wife's apartment he concealed himself in the ante-chamber, behind a screen placed as if expressly for his use. His intention was to observe narrowly what was going forward, and to present himself on a sudden in Blanche's chamber at the sound of any footstep he should hear. The first object he beheld was Nisa, taking leave of her mistress for the night, and withdrawing to a closet where she slept.

Siffredi's daughter, who had been at no loss to fathom the meaning of her husband's imprisonment, was fully convinced that he would not return to Belmonte that night, although she had heard from her father of the king's assurance that the constable

should set out immediately after him. As little could she doubt
but Enriquez would avail himself of the interval to see and converse with her at his pleasure. With this expectation she awaited
the prince's arrival, to reproach him for a line of conduct so pregnant with fatal consequences to herself. As she had anticipated,
a very short time after Nisa had retired the sliding panel opened,
and the king threw himself at the feet of his beloved. Madam,
said he, condemn me not without a hearing. It is true I have
occasioned the constable's imprisonment, but then consider that it
was the only method left me for my justification. Attribute therefore that desperate stratagem to yourself alone. Why did you
refuse to listen to my explanation this morning? Alas! To-
morrow your husband will be liberated, and I shall no longer
have an opportunity of addressing you. Hearken to me then for
the last time. If the loss of you has embittered the remainder of
my days, vouchsafe me at least the melancholy satisfaction of convincing you that I have not called down this misfortune on myself
by my own inconstancy. I did indeed confirm the pledge of my
hand to Constance, but then it was unavoidable in the situation to
which your father's policy had reduced us. It was necessary to
put this imposition on the princess for your interest and for my
own, to secure to you your crown, and with it the hand and heart
of your devoted lover. I had flattered myself with the prospect of
success. Measures were already taken to supersede that engagement, but you have destroyed the bright illusions of my fancy;
and, by disposing of yourself too precipitately, have antedated an
eternity of torment for two hearts, whom a mutual and perfect love
might have conducted to perpetual bliss.

He concluded this explanation with such evident marks of unfeigned agony, that Blanche was affected by his words. She had
no longer any hesitation about his innocence. At first her joy was
bounded at the conviction: but then again a sense of their cruel
circumstances gained the ascendant over her mind. Ah! my honored lord, said she to the prince, after such a determination of our
destinies, you only inflict a new pang by informing me that you
were not to blame. What have I done, wretched as I am? My
keen resentment has betrayed me into error. I fancied myself cast
off; and in the moment of my anger, accepted the hand of the
constable, whose addresses my father promoted. But the crime is
all my own, though the woes are mutual. Alas! In the very conjuncture when I accused you of deceiving me, it was by my own act,
too credulously impassioned as I was, that the ties were broken,
which I had sworn forever to make indissoluble. Take your revenge, my lord, in your turn. Indulge your hatred against the ungrateful Blanche . . . Forget . . . . What! and is it in my power
then, madam? interrupted Enriquez with a dejected air. how is it
possible to tear a passion from my heart, which even your injustice
had not the power of extinguishing? Yet it becomes necessary
for you to make that effort, my liege, replied the daughter of Siffredi, with a deep sigh . . . . And shall you be equal to that effort
yourself? replied the king. I am not confident with myself for

my success, answered she : but I shall spare no pains in the attainment of my object. Ah! unfeeling fair one, said the prince, you will easily banish Enriquez from your remembrance, since you can contemplate such a purpose so steadfastly. Whither then does your imagination lead? said Blanche, in a more decisive tone. Do you flatter yourself that I can permit the continuance of your tender assiduities? No, my lord, banish that hope for ever from your thoughts. If I was not born for royalty, neither has heaven formed me to be degraded by illicit addresses. My husband, like yourself, my liege, is allied to the noble house of Anjou. Though the call of duty were less peremptory, in opposing an insurmountable obstacle to your insidious proposals, a sense of pride would hinder me from admitting them. I conjure you to withdraw : we must meet no more. What a barbarous sentence! exclaimed the king. Ah! Blanche, is it possible that you should treat me with so much severity? Is it not enough then to weigh me down, that the constable should be in possession of your charms? And yet you would cut me off from the bare sight of you, the only comfort which remains to me! For that very reason avoid my presence, answered Siffredi's daughter, not without some tears of tenderness. The contemplation of what we have dearly loved is no longer a blessing, when we have lost all hope of the possession. Adieu, my lord! Shun my very image. You owe that exertion to your own honor and to my good name. I claim it also for my own peace of mind: for to deal sincerely, though my virtue should be steady enough to combat with the suggestions of my heart, the very remembrance of your affection stirs up so cruel a conflict, that it is almost too much for my frail nature to support the shock.

Her utterance of these words was attended with so energetic an action, as to overset the light placed on a table behind her, and its fall left the room in darkness. Blanche picked it up. She then opened the door of the antechamber, and went to Nisa's closet, who was not yet gone to bed, for the purpose of lighting it again. She was now returning, after having accomplished her errand. The king, who was waiting for her impatiently, no sooner saw her approach, than he resumed his ardent plea with her, to allow of his attentions. At the prince's voice, the constable rushed impetuously, sword in hand, into the room, almost at the same moment with his bride. Advancing up to Enriquez with all the indignation which his fury kindled within him: This is too much, tyrant, cried he; flatter not yourself that I am cowardly enough to bear with this affront, which you have offered to my honor. Ay! traitor, answered the king, standing on his guard, lay aside the vain imagination of being able to compass your purpose with impunity. With these mutual taunts, they entered on a conflict, too violent to be long undecided. The constable, fearing lest Siffredi and his attendants should be roused too soon by the piercing shrieks of Blanche, and should interpose between him and his revenge, took no care of himself. His frenzy robbed him of all skill. He fenced so heedlessly, as to run headlong on his adversary's sword. The weapon entered his body up to the hilt. He fell; and the king instantaneously checked his hand.

The daughter of Leontio, touched at her husband's condition, and rising superior to her natural repugnance, threw herself on the ground, and was anxious to afford him every assistance. But that ill-fated bridegroom was too deeply prejudiced against her, to allow himself to be softened by the evidences she gave of her sorrow and pity. Death, whose hand he felt upon him, could not stifle the transports of his jealousy. In these his last moments, no image presented itself to his mind but his rival's success. So insufferable was that idea to him, that, collecting together the little strength he had left, he raised his sword, which he still grasped convulsively, and plunged it deep in Blanche's bosom. Die, said he, as he inflicted the fatal wound; die, faithless bride, since the ties of wedlock were not strong enough to preserve to me the vow which you had sworn upon the altar. And as for you Enriquez, pursued he, triumph not too loudly on your destinies. You are prevented from taking advantage of my forward fortune; and I die content. Scarcely did these words quiver on his lips, when he breathed his last. His countenance, overcast as it was with the shades of death, had still something in it of fierceness and of terror. That of Blanche presented a quite different aspect. The wound she had received was mortal. She fell on the scarcely breathing body of her husband; and the blood of the innocent victim flowed in the same stream with that of her murderer, who had executed his cruel purpose so suddenly, that the king could not prevent it from taking effect.

This ill-fated prince uttered a cry at the sight of Blanche as she fell. Pierced deeper than herself by the stab which deprived her of life, he did his utmost to afford the same relief to her as she had offered, though at so fatal an expense, to one who might have rewarded her better. But she addressed him in these words, while the last breath quivered on her lips: My lord, your assiduities are fruitless, I am the victim. Merciless fate demands me, and I resign myself to death. May the anger of heaven be appeased by the sacrifice, and the prosperity of your reign be confirmed. As she was with difficulty uttering these last words, Leontio, drawn thither by the reverberation of her shrieks, came into the room, and, thunderstruck at the dreadful scene before him, remained fixed to the spot where he stood. Blanche, without noticing his presence, went on addressing herself to the king. Farewell, prince, said she; cherish my memory with the tenderness it deserves. My affection and my misfortunes entitle me at least to that. Harbor no aversion to my father; he is innocent. Be a comfort to his remaining days; assuage his grief; acknowledge his fidelity. Above all, convince him of my spotless virtue. With this I charge you, before every other consideration. Farewell, my dear Enriquez . . . . . I am dying . . . . . Receive my last sigh.

Here her words were intercepted by the approach of death. For some time the king maintained a sullen silence. At length he said to Siffredi, whose senses seemed to be locked up in a mortal trance: Behold, Leontio; feed on the contemplation of your own work. In this tragical event, you may ruminate on the issue of your officious cares, and your overweening zeal for my service. The old man returned no answer, so deeply was he penetrated by his affliction. But wherefore dwell on the description of circumstances, when the powers of language must sink under the weight of such a catastrophe? Suffice it to say, that they mutually poured forth their sorrows in the most affecting terms, as soon as their grief allowed them to give vent to its effusions in speech.

Through the whole course of his life, the king cherished a tender recollection of his mistress. He could not bring himself to marry Constance. The infant Don Pedro combined with that princess, and by their joint efforts, an obstinate attempt was made to carry the will of Roger into execution; but they were compelled in the end to give way to Prince Enriquez, who gained the ascendancy over all his enemies. As for Siffredi, the melancholy he contracted from having been the cause of destruction to his dearest friends, gave him a disgust to the world, and made a longer abode in his native country insupportable. He turned his back on Sicily for ever; and, coming over into Spain with Portia, his surviving daughter, purchased this mansion. He lived here nearly fifteen years after the death of Blanche, and had the consolation, before his own death, of establishing Portia in the world. She married Don Jerome de Silva, and I am the only issue of that marriage. Such, pursued the widow of Don Pedro de Penares, is the story of my family; a faithful recital of the melancholy events represented in that picture, which was painted by order of my grandfather Leontio, as a record to his posterity of the fatal adventure I have related.

CHAPTER V.

THE BEHAVIOR OF AURORA DE GUZMAN ON HER ARRIVAL AT SALAMANCA.

ORTIZ, her companions, and myself, after having heard this tale, withdrew together from the hall, where we left Aurora with Elvira. There they lengthened out the day in a mutual intercourse of confidence. They were not likely to be weary of each other: and on the following morning, when we took our leave, there was as much to do to part them, as if they had been two friends brought up in the closest habits of confidence and affection.

In due time we reached Salamanca without any impediment. There we immediately engaged a ready-furnished house, and Dame Ortiz, as it had been before agreed, assumed the name of Donna Kimena de Guzman. She had played the part of a duenna too long not to be able to shift her character according to circumstances. One morning she went out with Aurora, a waiting-maid and a man-servant and betook herself to a lodging-house, where we had been informed that Pacheco most commonly took up his abode. She asked if there was any lodging to be let there. The answer was in the affirmative; and they showed her into a room in very neat condition, which she hired. She paid down earnest to the landlady, telling her that it was for one of her nephews who was coming from Toledo to finish his studies at Salamanca, and might be expected on that very day.

The duenna and my mistress, after having made sure of this apartment, went back the way they came, and the lovely Aurora, without loss of time, metamorphosed herself into a spruce young spark. She concealed her black ringlets under a braid of light-colored hair, the better to disguise herself; . . . . . manufactured her eye-brows to correspond, and dressed herself up in such a costume, as to look for all the world as if her sex were of a piece with her appearance. Her deportment was free and easy; so that, with the exception of her face, which was somewhat more delicate than became the manly character, there was nothing to lead to a discovery of her masquerading. The waiting-woman who was to officiate as page, got into her paraphernalia at the same time, and we had no apprehension respecting her competency to perform her part. There was no danger of her beauty telling any tales; and besides, she could put on as brazen-faced a swagger as the most impudent dog in town. After dinner, our two actresses, finding themselves in cue to make their first appearance on the stage, where he scene was laid in the ready-furnished lodging, took me along with them. We all three placed ourselves in the coach, and carried with us all the baggage we were likely to have occasion for.

The landlady, Bernarda Ramirez by name, welcomed us with a glut of civility, and led the way to our room, where we began to make arrangements with her. We concluded a bargain for our board by the month, which she undertook should be suitable to our condition. Then we asked if she had her complement of boarders. I have none at all at present, answered she. Not that there would be any want of enough, if I was of the mind to take in all sorts of people: but young men of fashion are the thing for me. I expect one of that description this morning: he is coming hither from Madrid to complete his education. Don Lewis Pacheco! But you must have heard of him before now. No, said Aurora, I have no acquaintance whatever with the gentleman; and since we are to be inmates together, you will do me a kindness by letting me a little into his character. Please your honor, replied the landlady, leering at this outside of a man, his figure is as taking as your own; just the same sort of make, and about the same size. Oh! how well you will do together! By Saint James, though I say it who should not say it, I shall have about me two of the prettiest young fellows in all Spain. Well, but about Don Lewis! for my mistress was in a fidget to ask the grand question. Of course; . . . . he is well with the ladies in your parts! Enough of . . . of love affairs . . . on his hands! Oh! do not you be afraid of that, rejoined the old lady; it is a forward sprig of gallantry, take my word for it. He has but to show himself before the works, and the citadel sends to capitulate. Among the number of his conquests, he has got into the good graces of a lady, with as much youth and beauty as he will know what to do with. Her name is Isabella. Her father is an old doctor of laws. She is over head and ears in love with him, absolutely out of her wits! Well, but do tell me now, my dear little woman, interrupted Aurora, as if she was ready to burst, is he out of his wits too? He used to be very fond of her, answered Bernarda Ramirez, before he went last to Madrid : but whether he holds in the same mind still, I will not venture to say; because on these points he is not altogether to be trusted. He is apt to flirt, first with one woman, and then with another, just as all you young deceivers take pleasure in doing. You are all alike!

The bonny widow had scarcely got to the end of her harangue, before we heard a noise in the court. On looking out at the window, behold! there appeared two young men dismounting from their steeds. Who should it be, but the identical Don Lewis Pacheco, just arrived from Madrid with a servant behind him. The old lady brushed off to go and usher him in; while my mistress was putting herself in order, not without some palpitation of heart, to enact Don Felix to the best of her conceptions. Without waiting for any formalities, in marched Don Lewis to our apartment in his traveling dress. I have just been informed, said he, paying his respects to Aurora, that a young noblemen of Toledo takes up his abode in this house. May I take the liberty of expressing my joy in the circumstance, and hoping that we may be better acquainted? During my mistress's reply to this compliment, it seemed to me as if Pacheco did not know what to make of so smock-faced a young spark. Indeed he could not refrain from declaring a more than ordinary admiration of an air and figure so attractive. After abundance of discourse, with every demonstration of reciprocal good breeding, Don Lewis withdrew to the apartment provided for him.

While he was getting his boots off, and changing his dress and linen, a sort of a page, on the look-out after him to deliver a letter, met Aurora by chance on the staircase. Her he mistook for Don Lewis. Thinking he had found the right owner for this tender message, of which he was the Mercury—Softly! my honored lord and master, said he, though I have not the honor of knowing Signor Pacheco, there can be no occasion for asking whether you are the man. It is impossible to be mistaken in the guess. No, my friend, answered my mistress with a most happy presence of mind, assuredly you are not mistaken. You acquit yourself of your embassies to a marvel. I am Don Lewis Pacheco. You may retire! I will find an opportunity of sending an answer. The page vanished, and Aurora shutting herself up with her waiting-maid and me, opened the letter, and read to us as follows :—" I have just heard of your being at Salamanca. With what joy did I receive the news! I thought I should have gone out of my senses. But do you love Isabella as well as ever? Lose no time in assuring her that your are still the same. In good truth, she will almost expire with pleasure when once she is assured of your constancy."

This is a mighty passionate epistle, said Aurora. The heart that indited it has been caught in a trap. This lady is a rival of no mean capacity. No pains must be spared to wean Don Lewis from her, and even to prevent any future interview. The undertaking is difficult, I acknowledge, and yet there seems no reason to despair of the result. My mistress, taking her own hint, fell into a fit of musing; from which having recovered as soon as she fell into it, she added—I will lay a wager they are at daggers drawn in less than twenty-four hours. It so happened that Pacheco, after a short repose in his apartment, came to look after us in ours, and entered once more into conversation with Aurora before supper. My dapper little knight, said he with a rakish air; I fancy the poor devils of husbands and lovers will have no reason to hug themselves on your arrival at Salamanca. You will make their hearts ache for them. As for myself, I tremble for all my snug arrangements. I tell you what! answered my mistress with congenial spirit, your fears are not without their foundation. Don Felix de Mendoza is rather formidable, so take care what you are about. This is not my first visit in this country, the ladies hereabouts, to my knowledge, are made of penetrable materials. About a month ago my way happened to lie through this city. I halted for eight days, and you are to know . . . . . but you must not mention it . . . . . that I set fire to the daughter of an old doctor of laws.

It was evident enough that Don Lewis was disturbed by this declaration. Might one without impropriety, replied he, just ask the lady's name? What do you mean by impropriety? exclaimed the pretended Don Felix. Why make any secret about such a matter as that? Do you think me more of a Joseph than other young noblemen of my standing? Have a better opinion of my spirit. Besides, the object, between ourselves, is unworthy of any great reserve, she is but a little mushroom of the lower ranks. A man of fashion never quarrels with his conscience about such obscure gallantries, and even thinks it an honor conferred on a tradesman's wife or daughter when he leaves her without any. I shall therefore acquaint you in plain terms, that the name of the doctor's daughter is Isabella. And the doctor himself, interrupted Pacheco impatiently . . . . he possibly may be Signor Murcia de la Llana? Precisely so, replied my mistress. Here is a letter sent me just now. Read it, and then you will see how deeply your humble servant has dipped into her good graces. Don Lewis just cast his eye upon the note, and recognizing the handwriting, was struck dumb with astonishment and vexation. What is the matter? cried Aurora, with an air of surprise, keeping up the spirit of her assumed character. You change color! God forgive me, but you are a party concerned in this young lady. Ah! Plague take my officious tongue for having opened my affairs to you with so much frankness.

I am very much obliged to you for it for my own part, said Don Lewis in a transport made up of spite and rage. Traitress! Jilt! My dear Don Felix, how shall I ever requite you! You have restored me to my senses when they were just on the wing for an eternal flight. I was tickling myself into a fool's paradise of credulous love. But love is too cold a term to express my extravagancies. I fancied myself adored by Isabella. The creature had wormed herself into my heart by feigning to give me her own. But now I know her clearly for a coquet, and as such despise her as she deserves. Your feelings on the occasion do you infinite credit, said Aurora, testifying a friendly sympathy in his resentment. A plodding pettifogger's worthless brood might have gorged to surfeit on the love of a young nobleman so captivating as yourself. Her fickleness is inexcusable. So far from taking her sacrifice of you in good part, it is my determination to punish her by the keenest contempt. As for me, rejoined Pacheco, I shall never set eyes on her again; and if that is not revenge, the devil is in it. You are in the right, exclaimed our masquerading Mendoza. At the same time, that she may fully understand how ineffably we both disdain her, I vote for sitting down, each of us, and writing her a sarcastic farewell. They shall be inclosed in one cover, and serve as an answer to her own letter. But do not let us proceed to this extremity till you have examined your heart; it may be you will repent hereafter of having broken off with Isabella. No, no, interrupted Don Lewis, I am not such a fool as that comes to; let it be a bargain, and we will mortify the ungrateful wretch as you propose.

I immediately sent for pen, ink, and paper, when they sat themselves down at opposite corners of the table, and drew up a most tender bill of indictment against Doctor Murcia de la Llana's daughter. Pacheco, in particular, was at a loss for language forcible enough to convey his sentiments in all their acrimony; away went exordium after exordium, to the tearing and maiming of five or six fair sheets, before the words looked crooked enough to please his jealous eyes. At length, however, he produced an epistle which came up with his most tragical conceptions. It ran thus—"Self-knowledge is a leading branch of wisdom, my little philosopher. As a candidate for a professor's chair, lay aside the vanity of fancying yourself amiable. It requires merit of a far different compass to fix my affections. You have not enough of the woman about you to afford me even a temporary amusement. Yet do not despair, you have a sphere of your own, the beggarly servitors in our university have a keen appetite, but no very distinguishing palate." So much for this elegant epistle! When Aurora had finished hers, which rang the changes on similar topics, she sealed them, wrapped them up together, and giving me the packet—There, Gil Blas, said she, take care that comes to Isabella's hands this very evening. You comprehend me added she, with a glance from the corner of her eye, which admitted of no doubtful construction. Yes my lord, answered I, your commands shall be executed to a tittle.

I lost no time in taking my departure, no sooner in the street than I said to myself—So ho! Master Gil Blas, your part then is that of the intriguing footman in this comedy Well! so be it, my friend! show that you have wit and sense enough to top it over the favorite actor of the day Signor Don Felix thinks a wink as good a nod. A high compliment to the quickness of your apprehension!

Is he then in an error? No. His hint is as clear as daylight.
Don Lewis' letter is to drop its companion by the way. A lucid
exposition of a dark hieroglyphic, enough to shame the dullness of
the commentators. The sacredness of a seal could never stand
against this bright discovery. Out came the single letter of
Pacheco, and away went I to hunt after Doctor Murcia's abode.
At the very threshold, whom should I meet but the little page who
had been at our lodging. Comrade, said I, do not you happen to
live with the great lawyer's daughter? His answer was in the affirmative. I see by your countenance, resumed I, that you know
the ways of the world. May I beg the favor of you to slip this
little memorandum into your mistress' hand?

The little page asked me on whose behalf I was a messenger.
The name of Don Lewis Pacheco had no sooner escaped my lips,
than he told me—Since that is the case, follow me. I have orders
to show you up. Isabella wants to confer with you. I was introduced at once into a private apartment, where it was not long before the lady herself made her appearance. The beauty of her
face was inexpressibly striking; I do not recollect to have seen
more lovely features. Her manner was somewhat mincing and
infantine, yet for all that it had been thirty good years at least
since she had mewled and puked in her nurse's arms. My friend,
said she with an encouraging smile, are you on Don Lewis Pacheco's establishment? I told her I had been in office for these three
weeks. With this I fired off my paper popgun against her peace.
She read it over two or three times, but if she had rubbed her eyes
till doomsday she would have seen no clearer. In point of fact,
nothing could be more unexpected than so cavalier an answer. Up
went her eyes towards the heavens, appealing to their rival lumi-
naries. The ivory * fences of her pretty mouth committed alternate trespass on her soft and suffering lips, and her whole physiognomy bore witness to the pangs of her distressed and disappointed
heart. Then coming to herself a little, and recovering her speech
—My friend, said she, has Don Lewis taken leave of his senses?
Tell me, if you can, his motive for so heroic an epistle. If he is
tired of me, well and good, but he might have taken his leave like
a gentleman.

Madam, said I, my master most assuredly has not acted as I
should have acted in his place. But he has in some sort been compelled to do as he has done. If you would give me your word to
keep the secret, I could unravel the whole mystery. You have it
at once, interrupted she with eagerness, depend on it you shall
be brought into no scrape by me, therefore explain yourself without reserve. Well, then! replied I, the fact is, without paraphrase,
circumlocution, loss of time, or perplexity of understanding, as I
shall distinctly state in two short words—Not half a minute after

---

* Should this phrase appear far-fetched in the person of Gil Blas, it may be recollected, that though not much of a student himself, he had waited on students ; and might
have sucked in, while standing behind their chairs, along with " fates and destinies,
and such old sayings, the sisters three, and such branches of learning," that exquisitely
characteristic Greek metaphor—" a hedge of teeth."—TRANSLATOR.

the receipt of your letter, there came into our house a lady, under a veil as impenetrable as her purpose was dark. She inquired for Signor Pacheco, and talked with him in private for some time. At the close of the conversation, I overheard her saying—You swear to me never to see her more ; but we must not stop there, to set my heart completely at rest you must instantly write her a farewell letter of my dictating. You know my terms. Don Lewis did as she desired, then giving the result into my custody—Acquaint yourself, said he, where Doctor Murcia de la Llana lives, and contrive to administer this love potion to his daughter Isabella.

You see plainly, madam, pursued I, that this uncivil epistle is a rival's handiwork, and that consequently my master is not so much to blame as he appears. Oh, heaven ! exclaimed she, he is more so than I was aware of. His words might have been the error of his hand, but his infidelity is the offence of his heart. Faithless man ! Now he is held by other ties ! . . . But, added she, assuming an air of disdain, let him devote himself unconstrained to his new passion; I shall never cross him. Tell him, however, that he need not have insulted me. I should have left the course open to my rival, without his warning me from the field : for so fickle a lover has not soul enough about him to pay for the degradation of soliciting his return. With this sentiment she gave me my dismissal, and retired in a whirlwind of passion against Don Lewis.

My exit was conducted entirely to my own satisfaction, for I conceived that with due cultivation of my talent I might in time become a consummate hypocrite and most successful cheat. I returned home on the strength of it, where I found my worthy masters, Mendoza and Pacheco, supping together, and rattling away as if they had been playfellows from their cradles. Aurora saw at once, by my self-sufficient air, that her commission had not been neglected in my hands. Here you are again then, Gil Blas, said she, give us an account of your embassy. Wit and invention was all I had to trust to, so I told them I had delivered the packet into Isabella's own hands; who, after having glanced over the contents of the two letters, so far from seeming disconcerted, burst into a fit of laughter, as if she had been mad, and said—Upon my word, our young men of fashion write in a pretty style. It must be owned they are much more entertaining than scribes of plebeian rank. It was a very good way of getting out of the scrape, exclaimed my mistress, she must be an arrant coquet. For my part, said Don Lewis, I cannot trace a feature of Isabella in this conduct. Her character must have been completely metamorphosed in my absence. She struck me too in a very different light, replied Aurora. It must be allowed some women can assume all modes and fashions at will. I was once in love with one of that description, and a fine dance she led me. Gil Blas can tell you the whole story ! She had an air of propriety about her which might have imposed upon a whole synod of old maids. It is true, said I, putting in my oar ; it was a face to play the devil with a sworn bachelor, I could scarcely have been proof against it myself

The personated Mendoza and Pacheco shouted with laughter

at my manner of expressing myself; the one for the false witness I bore against a culprit of my own creation; the other laughed simply at the phrase in which my anathema was couched. We went on talking about the versatility of women, and the verdict, after hearing the evidence, all on one side, was given against Isabella. A convicted coquet! and sentence passed on her accordingly. Don Lewis made a fresh vow never to see her more, and Don Felix, after his example, swore to hold her in eternal abhorrence. By dint of these mutual protestations a sort of friendship was established on the spur of the occasion, and they promised on both sides to keep no secrets from each other. The time after supper passed in ingratiating intercourse, and the time seemed short till they retired to their separate apartments. I followed Aurora to hers, where I gave her a faithful account of my conversation with the Doctor's daughter, not forgetting the most trivial circumstance. She had much ado to help kissing me for joy. My dear Gil Blas, said she, I am delighted with your spirit. When one has the misfortune to be engaged in a passion not to be gratified but by stragagems, what an advantage is it to secure on the right side a lad of so enterprising a genius as yourself. Courage, my friend, we have thrown a rival into the background, whose presence in the scene might have marred our comedy. So far, all is well. But as lovers are subject to strange vagaries, it seems to me that we must make short work of it, and bring Aurora de Guzman on the stage to-morrow. The idea met with my entire approbation; so leaving Signor Don Felix with his page, I withdrew to bed in an adjoining closet.

CHAPTER VI.

AURORA'S DEVICES TO SECURE DON LEWIS PACHECO'S AFFECTIONS.

THE two new friends met as soon as they came down in the morning. The ceremonies of the day began with reciprocal embraces, about which it was impossible for Aurora to be squeamish, for then Don Felix must have dropped the mask altogether. They went out and walked about town arm in arm, attended by Chilindron, Don Lewis's footman, and myself. We loitered about the gates of the university, looking at some posting bills and advertisements of new publications. There were a good many people amusing themselves, like us, with reading over the contents of these placards. Among the rest my eye was caught by a little fellow, who was giving his opinion very learnedly on the works exposed to sale. I observed him to be heard with profound attention, and could not help remarking how amply he deserved it in his own opinion. He was evidently a complete coxcomb, of an arrogant and dictatorial stamp, the common curse of your gentry under size. This new translation of Horace, said he, announced here to

the public in letters of a yard long, is a prose work, executed by an old college author. The students have taken a great fancy to the book; so as to carry off four editions. But not a copy has been bought by any man of taste! His criticisms were scarcely more candid on any of the other books; he mauled them every one without mercy. It was easy enough to see he was an author! I should not have been sorry to have staid out his harangue, but Don Lewis and Don Felix were not to be left in the lurch. Now they took as little pleasure in this gentleman's remarks as they felt interest in the books which he was Scaligerising, so that they took a quiet leave of him and the university.

We returned home at dinner-time. My mistress sat down at table with Pacheco, and dexterously turned the conversation on her private concerns. My father, said she, is a younger branch of the Mendoza family, settled at Toledo, and my mother is own sister to Donna Kimena de Guzman, who came to Salamanca some days ago on an affair of business, with her niece Aurora, only daughter of Don Vincent de Guzman, whom possibly you might be acquainted with. No, answered Don Lewis, but I have often heard of him, as well as of your cousin Aurora. Is it true what they say of her? Her wit and beauty are reported to be unrivaled. As for wit, replied Don Felix, she certainly is not wanting, for she has taken great pains to cultivate her mind. But 'er beauty is by no means to be boasted of; indeed, we are thought to be very much alike. If that is the case, exclaimed Pacheco, she cannot be behindhand with her reputation. Your features are regular, your complexion almost too fine for a man; your cousin must be an absolute enchantress. I should like to see and converse with her. That you shall, if I have any interest in the family, and this very day too, replied the little Proteus of a Mendoza. We will go and see my aunt after dinner.

My mistress took the first opportunity of changing the topic, and conversing on indifferent subjects. In the afternoon, while the two friends were getting ready to go and call on Donna Kimena, I played the scout, and ran before to prepare the duenna for her visitors. But there was no time to be lost on my return, for Don Felix was waiting for me to attend Don Lewis and him on their way to his aunt's. No sooner had they stepped over the threshold than they were encountered by the adroit old lady, making signs to them to walk as softly as possible. Hush! hush! said she, in a low voice, you will waken my niece. Ever since yesterday she has had a dreadful headache, but is just now a little better; and the poor girl has been taking a little sleep for the last quarter of an hour. I am sorry for this unlucky accident, said Mendoza, I was in hopes we should have seen my cousin. Besides, I meant to have introduced my friend Pacheco. There is no such great hurry on that account, answered Ortiz with a significant smile, and if that is all, you may defer it till to-morrow. The gentlemen did not trouble the old lady with a long visit, but took their leave as soon as they decently could.

Don Lewis took us to see a young gentleman of his acquaintance, by name Don Gabriel de Pedros. There we stayed the remainder of the day, and took our suppers. About two o'clock in the morning we sallied forth on our return home. We had got about half-way, when we stumbled against something on the ground, and discovered two men stretched at their length in the street. We concluded they had fallen under the knife of the assassin, and stopped to assist them, if yet within reach of assistance. As we were looking about to inform ourselves of their condition, as nearly as the darkness of the night would allow, the patrol came up. The officer took us at first for the murderers, and ordered his people to surround us; but he mended his opinion of us on the sound of our voices, and by favor of a dark lantern held up to the faces of Mendoza and Pacheco. His myrmidons, by his direction, examined the two men, whom our fancies had painted as in the agonies of death, but it turned out to be a fat licentiate with his servant, both of them overtaken in their cups, and not dead, but dead drunk. Gentlemen, exclaimed one of the posse, this jolly fellow is an acquaintance of mine. What! do you not know Signor Guyomer the licentiate, head of our university? With all his imperfections he is a great character, a man of superior genius. He is as stanch as a hound at a philosophical dispute, and his words flow like a gutter after a hail-storm. He has but three foibles in which he indulges; intoxication, litigation, and fornication. He is now returning from supper at his Isabella's, whence, the more is the pity, the drunk was leading the drunk, and they both fell into the kennel. Before the good licentiate came to the headship this happened continually. Though manners make the man, honors, you perceive, do not always mend the manners. We left these drunkards in custody of the patrol, who carried them safe home, and betook ourselves to our lodgings and our beds.

Don Felix and Don Lewis were stirring about mid-day. Aurora de Guzman was the first topic of their conversation. Gil Blas, said my mistress to me, run to my aunt, Donna Kimena, and ask if there is any admission for Signor Pacheco and me to-day, we want to see my cousin. Off I went to acquit myself of this commission, or rather to concert the plan of the campaign with the duenna. We had no sooner laid our heads together to the purpose intended, than I was once more at the elbow of the false Mendoza. Sir, quoth I, your cousin Aurora has got about wonderfully. She enjoined me from her own lips to acquaint you, that your visit could not be otherwise than highly acceptable, and Donna Kimena desired me to assure Signor Pacheco, that any friend of yours would always meet with an hospitable reception.

These last words evidently tickled Don Lewis's fancy. My mistress saw that the bait was swallowed, and prepared herself to haul the prey to shore. Just before dinner, a servant made his appearance from Signora Kimena, and said to Don Felix—My lord, a man from Toledo has been inquiring after you, and has left this note at your aunt's house. The pretended Mendoza opened it, and read the contents aloud to the following effect—" If your father and family still live in your remembrance, and you wish to hear of their concerns, do not fail, on the receipt of this, to call at the Black

Horse, near the university." I am too much interested, said he, in these proffered communications, not to satisfy my curiosity at once. Without ceremony, Pacheco, you must excuse me for the present; if I am not back again here within two hours, you may find your way by yourself to my aunt's; I will join the party in the evening. You recollect Gil Blas' message from Donna Kimena, the visit is no more than what will be expected from you. After having thrown out this hint, he left the room, and ordered me to follow him.

It can scarcely be necessary to apprize the reader, that instead of marching down to the Black Horse, we filed off to our other quarters. The moment that we got within doors, Aurora tore off her artificial hair, washed the charcoal from her eyebrows, resumed her female attire, and shone in all her natural charms, a lovely dark-complexioned girl. So complete indeed had been her disguise that Aurora and Don Felix could never have been suspected of identity. The lady seemed to have the advantage of the gentleman even in stature, thanks to a good high pair of heels, to which she was not a little indebted. It was her first business to heighten her personal graces with all the embellishments of art; after which she looked out for Don Lewis, in a state of agitation, compounded of fear and of hope. One instant she felt confident in her wit and beauty; the next she anticipated the failure of her attempt. Ortiz, on her part, set her best foot foremost, and was determined to play up to my mistress. As for me, Pacheco was not to see my knave's face till the last act of the farce, for which the great actors are always reserved, to unravel the intricacy of the plot; so I went out immediately after dinner.

In short, the puppet-show was all adjusted against Don Lewis's arrival. He experienced a very gracious reception from the old lady, in amends for whose tediousness he was blessed with two or three hours of Aurora's delightful conversation. When they had been together long enough, in popped I, with a message to the enamored spark. My lord, my master Don Felix begs you ten thousand pardons, but he cannot have the pleasure of waiting on you here this evening. He is with three men of Toledo, from whom he cannot possibly get away. Oh! the wicked little rogue, exclaimed Donna Kimena; as sure as a gun then he is going to make a night of it. No, madam, replied I, they are deeply engaged in very serious business. He is really distressed that he cannot pay his respects, and commissioned me to say everything proper to your ladyship and Donna Aurora. Oh! I will have none of his excuses, pouted out my mistress, he knows very well that I have been indisposed, and might show some slight degree of feeling for so near a relation. As a punishment, he shall not come near me for this fortnight. Nay, madam, interposed Don Lewis, such a sentence is too severe. Don Felix's fate is but too pitiable, in having been deprived of your society this evening.

They bandied about their fine speeches on these little topics of gallantry for some time, and then Pacheco withdrew. The lovely

Aurora metamorphosed herself in a twinkling, and resumed her swashing outside. The grass did not grow under her feet while she was running to the other lodging. I have a million of apologies to make, my dear friend, said she to Don Lewis, for not giving you the meeting at my aunt's; but there was no getting rid of the tiresome people I was with. However, there is one comfort, you have had so much the more leisure to look about you, and criticise my cousin's beauty. Well! and how do you like her? She is a most lovely creature, answered Pacheco. You were in the right to claim a resemblance to her. I never saw more correspondent features; the very same cast of countenance, the eyes exactly alike, the mouth evidently a family feature, and the tone of voice scarcely to be distinguished. The likeness, however, goes no further, for Aurora is taller than you, she is brown and you are fair, you are a jolly fellow, she has a little touch of the demure; so that you are not altogether the male and female Sosias. As for good sense, continued he, if an angel from heaven were to whisper wisdom in one ear, and your cousin her mortal chit-chat in the other, I am afraid the angel might whistle for an audience. In a word, Aurora is all-accomplished.

Signor Pacheco uttered these last words with so earnest an expression, that Don Felix said with a smile—My friend, I advise you to stay away from Donna Kimena's, it will be more for your peace of mind. Aurora de Guzman may set your wits a wandering, and inspire a passion. . . . . .

I have no need of seeing her again, interrupted he, to become distractedly enamored of her. I am sorry for you, replied the pretended Mendoza, for you are not a man to be seriously caught, and my cousin is not to be made a fool of, take my word for it. She would never encourage a lover whose designs were otherwise than honorable. Otherwise than honorable! retorted Don Lewis: who could have the audacity to form such on a lady of her rank and character? As for me, I should esteem myself the happiest of mankind, could she be prevailed on to favor my addresses, and link her fate with mine.

Since those are your sentiments, rejoined Don Felix, you may command my services. Yes, I will go heart and hand with you in the business. All my interest in Aurora shall be yours; and by to-morrow morning I will commence an attack on my aunt, whose good word has more influence than you may think. Pacheco returned his thanks with the best air possible to this young go-between, and we were all agog at the promising appearance of our stratagem. On the following day we found the means of heightening the dramatic effect by entangling the plot a little more. My mistress, after having waited on Donna Kimena, as if to speak a good word in favor of the suitor, came back with the result of the interview. I have spoken to my aunt, said she, but it was as much as I could do to make her hear your proposal with patience. She was primed and loaded against you. Some good-natured friend in the dark has painted you out for a reprobate; but I took your part with some little quickness, and at length succeeded in vindicating your moral character from the attack it had sustained.

This is not all, continued Aurora. You had better enter on the subject with my aunt in my presence, we shall be able to make something of her between us. Pacheco was all impatience to insinuate himself into the good graces of Donna Kimena; nor was the opportunity deferred beyond the next morning. Our amphibious Mendoza escorted him into the presence of Dame Ortiz, where such a conversation passed between the trio as put fire and tow to the combustible heart of Don Lewis. Kimena, a veteran performer, took the cue of sympathy at every expression of tenderness, and promised the enarmored youth that it should not be her fault if his plea with her niece was urged in vain. Pacheco threw himself at the feet of so good an aunt, and thanked her for all her favors. In this stage of the business Don Felix asked if his cousin was up. No, replied the Duenna, she is still in bed, and is not likely to be down-stairs while you stay; but call again after dinner, and you shall have a tête-à-tête with her to your heart's content. It is easy to imagine that so coming on a proposal from the dragon which was to guard this inaccessible treasure, produced its full complement of joy in the heart of Don Lewis, The remainder of the long morning had nothing to do but to be sworn at! He went back to his own lodging with Mendoza, who was not a little enraptured to observe, with the scrutinizing eye of a mistress under the disguise of a friend, all the symptoms of an incurable amorous infirmity.

Their tongues ran on no earthly subject but Aurora. When they had done dinner, Don Felix said to Pacheco—A thought has just struck me. It would not be amiss for me to go to my aunt's a few minutes before you; I will get to speak to my cousin in private, and pry, if it be possible, into every fold and winding of her heart, as far as your interests are concerned. Don Lewis just chimed in with this idea, so that he suffered his friend to set out first, and did not follow him till an hour afterwards. My mistress availed herself so diligently of the interval, that she was tricked out as a lady from heel to point before the arrival of her lover. I beg pardon . . . . . . said the poor abused inamorato, after having paid his compliments to Aurora and the Duenna, . . . I took it for granted Don Felix would be here. You will see him in a few seconds, answered Donna Kimena, he is writing in my closet. Pacheco was easily put off with the excuse, and found his time pass cheerfully in conversation with the ladies. And yet, notwithstanding the presence of all his soul held dear, it seemed very strange that hour after hour glided away but no Mendoza stepped forth from the closet! He could not help remarking, that the gentleman's correspondence must be unusually voluminous, when Aurora's features all at once assumed the broader contour of a laugh, with a delightfully provoking question to Don Lewis—Is it possible that love can be so blind as not to detect the glaring imposition by which it has been deluded? Has my real self made so faint an impression on your senses, that a flaxen peruke and a pen cilled eyebrow could carry the farce to such a height as this? But the masquerade is over now. Pacheco, continued she, resuming an air of gravity; you are to learn that Don Felix de Mendoza and Aurora de Guzman are but one and the same person.

It was not enough to discover to him all the springs and contrivances by which he had been duped; she confessed the motives of tender partiality that led her to the attempt, and detailed the progress of the plot to the winding up of the catastrophe. Don Lewis scarcely knew whether to be most astonished or delighted at the recital; at my mistress's feet he thus uttered the transports of his fond applause—Ah! lovely Aurora, can I believe myself indeed the happy mortal on whom your favors have been so lavished? What can I do to make you amends for them? My affection, were this life eternal, could scarcely pay the price. These pretty speeches were followed by a thousand others of the same quality and texture; after which the lovers descended a little nearer to common sense, and began planning the rational and human means of arriving at the accomplishment of their wishes. It was resolved that we should set out without loss of time for Madrid, where marriage was to drop the curtain on the last act of our comedy. This purpose was executed in the spirit of impatience which conceived it; so that Don Lewis was united to my mistress in a fortnight, and the nuptial ceremonies were graced with the usual accompaniments of music, feasting, balls, and rejoicings, without either end or respite.

CHAPTER VII.

GIL BLAS LEAVES HIS PLACE AND GOES INTO THE SERVICE OF
DON GONZALES PACHECO.

THREE weeks after marriage, my mistress bethought herself of rewarding the services I had rendered her. She made me a present of a hundred pistoles, telling me at the same time—Gil Blas, my good fellow, it is not that I mean to turn you away, for you have my free leave to stay here as long as you please; but my husband has an uncle, Don Gonzales Pacheco, who wants you very much for a valet-de-chambre. I have given you so excellent a character, that he would let me have no peace till I consented to part with you. He is a very worthy old nobleman, so that you will be quite in your element in his family.

I thanked Aurora for all her kindness; and, as my occupation was over about her, I so much the more readily accepted the post that offered, as it was merely a transfer from one branch of the Pachecos to another. One morning, therefore, I called on the illustrious Don Gonzales with a message from the bride. He ought at least to have over-slept himself, for he was in bed at near noon. When I went into his chamber, a page had just brought him a basin of soup which he was taking. The dotard cherished his whiskers, or rather tortured them with curling-papers; though his eyes were sunk in their sockets, his complexion pale, and his visage emaciated. This was one of those old codgers who have been a little whimsical or so in their youth, and have made poor amends for their freedoms by the discretion of their riper age. His reception of me was affable enough, with an assurance that if my attachment to him kept pace with my fidelity to his niece, my condition should not be worse than that of my fellows. I promised to place him in my late mistress's shoes, and became the working partner in a new firm.

A new firm it undoubtedly was, and heaven knows we had a strange head of the house. The resurrection of Lazarus was an ordinary event compared to his getting up. Imagine to yourself a long bag of dry bones, a mere skeleton, a dissection, an anatomy of a man; a study in osteology! As for the legs, three or four pair of stockings one over the other, had no room to make any figure upon them. In addition to the foregoing, this mummy before death was asthmatic, and therefore obliged to divide the little breath he had between his cough and his loquacity. He breakfasted on chocolate. On the strength of that refreshment, he ventured to call for pen, ink, and paper, and to write a short note, which he sealed and sent to its address by the page who had administered the broth. But this henceforth will be your office, my good lad, said he, as he turned his haggard eyes upon me; all my little concerns will be in your hands, and especially those in which Donna Euphrasia takes an interest. That lady is an enchanting young creature, with whom I am distractedly in love, and by whom, though I say it who should not say it, I am met with all the mutual ardor of inextinguishable and unutterable passion.

Heaven defend us! thought I within myself: good now! if this old antidote to rapture can fancy himself an object on which the fair should waste their sweets, is it any wonder that among our young folks each fancies himself the Adonis, for whom every Venus pines? Gil Blas, pursued he with a chuckle, this very day will I take you to this abode of pleasure; it is my house of call almost every evening for a bit of supper. You will be quite petrified at her modest appearance, and the rigid propriety of her behavior. Far from taking after those little wanton vagrants, who are hey-go-mad after striplings, and give themselves up to the fascinations of exterior appearance, she has a proper insight into things, staid, ripe, and judicious: what she wants is the bonâ fide spirit and discretion of a man; a lover who has served an apprenticeship to his trade, in preference to all the flashy fellows of the modern school. This is but an epitome of the panegyric, which the noble dupe Don Gonzales pronounced upon his mistress. He burdened himself with the task of proving her a compendium of all human perfection, but the lecture was little calculated for the conviction of the hearer. I had attended an experimental course among the actresses; and had always found that the elderly candidates had been plucked in their amours. Yet, as a matter of courtesy, it was impossible not to put on the semblance of giving implicit credit to my master's veracity; I even added chivalry to courtesy, and threw down my glove on Euphrasia's penetration and the correctness of her taste. My impudence went the length of asserting, that it was impossible for her to have selected a better-provided crony. The grown-up simpleton was not aware that I was fumigating his nostrils at the expense of his addled brain; on the contrary, he bristled at my praises; so true is it, that a flatterer may play what game he likes against the pigeons of high life! They let you look over their hand, and then wonder that you beat them.

The old crawler, having scribbled through his billet-doux, restrained the luxuriance of a straggling hair or two with his tweezers; then bathed his eyes in the nostrum of some perfumer to give them a brilliancy which their natural gum would have eclipsed. His ears were to be picked and washed, and his hands to be cleansed from the effects of his other ablutions; and the labors of the toilette were to be closed, by pencilling every remaining hair in the disforested domain of his whiskers, pericranium, and eyebrows. No old dowager, with a purse to buy a second husband, ever took more pains to assure herself by the cultivation of her charms, that the person and not the fortune should be the object of attraction. The assassin stab of time was parried by the quart and tierce of art. Just as he had done making himself up, in came another old fogram of his acquaintance, by name the Count of Asumar. This genius made no secret of his grey locks; leant upon a stick, and seemed to plume himself on his venerable age instead of wishing to appear in the hey-day of his prime. Signor Pacheco, said he as he came in, I am come to take pot-luck with you to-day. You are always welcome, count, rejoined my master. No sooner said than done! they embraced with a thousand grimaces, took their seats opposite to one another, and began chatting till dinner was served.

Their conversation turned at first upon a bull-feast which had taken place a few days before. They talked about the cavaliers, and who among them had displayed most dexterity and vigor; whereupon the old count, like another Nestor, whom present events furnish with a topic of expatiating on the past, said with a deep-drawn sigh: Alas! where will you meet with men now-a-days, fit to hold a candle to my contemporaries? The public diversions are a mere bauble, to what they were when I was a young man. I could not help chuckling in my sleeve at my good lord of Asumar's whim; for he did not stop at the handiwork of human invention. Would you believe it? At table, when the fruit was brought in, at the sight of some very fine peaches, this ungrateful consumer of the earth's produce exclaimed: In my time, the peaches were of a much larger size than they are now; but nature sinks lower and lower from day to day. If that is the case, said Don Gonzales with a sneer, Adam's hot-house fruit must have been of a most unwieldy circumference.

The Count of Asumar staid till quite evening with my master, who had no sooner got rid of him, than he sallied forth with me in his train. We went to Euphrasia's, who lived within a stone's throw of our house, and found her lodged in a style of the first elegance. She was tastefully dressed, and for the youthfulness of her air might have been taken to be in her teens, though thirty bonny summers at least had poured their harvests in her lap. She had often been reckoned pretty, and her wit was exquisite. Neither was she one of your brazen-faced jilts with nothing but flimsy balderdash in their talk, and a libertine forwardness in their manners; here was modesty of carriage as well as propriety of discourse; and she threw out her little sallies in the most exquisite manner, without seeming to aspire beyond natural good sense. Oh, heaven! said I, is it possible that a creature of so virtuous a stamp by nature should have abandoned herself to vicious courses for a livelihood? I had taken it for granted, that all women of light character carried the mark of the beast upon their foreheads. It was a surprise therefore to see such apparent rectitude of conduct; neither did it occur to me that these hacks for all customers could go at any pace, and assume the polish of well-bred society, to impose upon their cullies of the higher ranks. What if a lively petulance should be the order of the day? they are lively and petulant. Should modesty take its turn in the round of fashion, nothing can exceed their outward show of prudent and delicate reserve. They play the comedy of love in many masks; and are the prude, the coquet, or the virago, as they fall in with the quiz, the coxcomb, or the bully.

Don Gonzales was a gentleman and a man of taste; he could not stomach those beauties who call a spade a spade. Such were not for his market; the rites of Venus must be consummated in the temple of Vesta. Euphrasia had got up her part accordingly, and proved by her performance that there is no comedy like that of real life. I left my master, like another Numa with his Egeria, and went down into a hall, where whom should fortune throw in my way but an old abigail, whom I had formerly known as maid-of-all-work to an actress? The recognition was mutual. So! well met once more, Signor Gil Blas, said she. Then you have turned off Arsenia, just as I have parted with Constance. Yes, truly, answered I, it is a long while ago since I went away, and exchanged her service for that of a very different lady. Neither the theatre nor the people about it, are to my taste. I gave myself my own discharge, without condescending to the slightest explanation with Arsenia. You were perfectly in the right, replied the new-found abigail, called Beatrice. That was pretty much my method of proceeding with Constance. One morning early, I gave in my accounts with a very sulky air; she took them from me in moody silence, and we parted in a sort of well-bred dudgeon.

I am quite delighted, said I, that we have met again, where we need not be ashamed of our employers. Donna Euphrasia looks for all the world like a woman of fashion, and I am much deceived if she has not reputation too. You are too clear-sighted to be deceived, answered the old appendage to sin. She is of a good family; and as for her temper, I can assure you it is unparalleled for evenness and sweetness. None of your termagant mistresses, never to be pleased, but always grumbling and scolding about everything, making the house ring with their clack, and fretting poor servants to a thread, whose places, in short, are a hell upon earth! I have not in all this time heard her raise her voice on any occasion whatever. When things happen not to be done exactly in her way, she sets them to rights without any anger, nor does any of that bad language escape her lips, of which some high-spirited ladies are so liberal. My master, too, rejoined I, is very mild in his disposition; the very milk of human kindness; and in this respect we are, between ourselves, much better off than when we lived among the actresses. A thousand times better, replied Beatrice; my life used to be all bustle and distraction; but this place is an actual hermitage. Not a creature darkens our doors but this excellent Don Gonzales. You will be my only helpmate in my solitude, and my lot is but too greatly blessed. For this long time have I cherished an affection for you: and many a time and oft have I begrudged that Laura the felicity of engrossing you for her sweetheart; but in the end I hope to be even with her. If I cannot boast of youth and beauty like hers, to balance the account, I detest coquetry, and have all the constancy as well as affection of a turtle-dove.

As honest Beatrice was one of those ladies who are obliged to hawk their wares, and cheapen themselves for want of cheapeners in the market, I was happily shielded from any temptation to break the commandments. Nevertheless, it might not have been prudent to let her see in what contempt her charms were held; for which reason I forced my natural politeness so far, as to talk to her in a style not to cut off all hope of my more serious advances. I flattered myself then, that I had found favor in the eyes of an old dresser to the stage: but pride was destined to have a fall, even on so humble an occasion. The domestic trickster did not sharpen her allurements, from any longing for my pretty person; her design in subduing me to the little soft god was to enlist me for the purposes of her mistress, to whom she had sworn so passive an obedience, that she would have sold her eternal self to the old chapman, who first set up the trade of sin, rather than have disappointed her slightest wishes. My vain conceit was sufficiently evident on the very next morning, when I carried an Ovidian letter from my master to Euphrasia. The lady gave me an affable reception, and made a thousand pretty speeches, echoed from the practised lips of her chambermaid. The expression of my countenance was peculiarly interesting to the one: but that within which passeth show was the flattering theme of the other. According to their account the fortunate Don Gonzales had picked up a treasure. In short, my praises ran so high, that I began to think worse of myself than I had ever done in the whole course of my life. Their motive was sufficiently obvious; but I was determined to play at diamond cut diamond. The simper of a simpleton is no bad countermine to the attack of a sharper. These ladies under favor were of the latter description, and they soon began to open their batteries.

Hark you, Gil Blas, said Euphrasia, fortune declares in your favor if you do not balk her. Let us put our heads together, my good friend. Don Gonzales is old, and a good deal shaken in constitution; so that a very little fever, in the hands of a very great doctor, would carry him to a better place. Let us take time by the forelock, and ply our arts so busily as to secure to me the largest slice of his effects. If I prosper, you shall not starve, I promise you; and my bare word is a better security than all the deeds and conveyances of all the lawyers in Madrid. Madam, answered I, you have but to command me. Give me my commission on your muster-roll, and you shall have no reason to complain either of my cowardice or contumacy. So be it, then, replied she. You must watch your master, and bring me an account of all his comings and goings. When you are chatting together in his more familiar moments, never fail to lead the conversation on the subject of our sex; and then by an artful, but seemingly natural transition, take occasion to say all the good you can invent of me. Ring Euphrasia in his ears till all the house re-echoes. I would counsel you besides to keep a wary eye on all that passes in the Pacheco family. If you catch any relation of Don Gonzales sneaking about him, with a design on the inheritance, bring me word instantly: that is all you have to do, and trust me for sinking, burning, and destroying him in less than no time. I have ferreted out the weak side of all your master's relations long ago; they are each of them to be made ridiculous in some shape or other; so that the nephews and cousins, after sitting to me for their portraits, are already turned with their faces to the wall.

It was evident by these instructions, with many more to the same time and tune, that Euphrasia was one of those ladies whose partialities all lean to the side of elderly inamoratos, with more money than wit. Not long before, Don Gonzales, who could refuse nothing to the tender passion, had sold an estate · and she pocketed the cash. Not a day passed, but she got some little personal remembrance out of him; and besides all this, a corner of his will was the ultimate object of her speculation. I affected to engage hand over head in their infamous plot; and if I must confess all without mental reservation, it was almost a moot point, on my return home, on which side of the cause I should take a brief. There was on either a profitable alternative; whether to join in fleecing my master, or to merit his gratitude by rescuing him from the plunderers. Conscience, however, seemed to have some little concern in the determination; it was quite ridiculous to choose the by-path of villany when there was a better toll to be taken on the highway of honesty. Besides, Euphrasia had dealt too much in generals; an arithmetical definition of so much for so much has more meaning in it than "all the wealth of the Indies;" and to this shrewd reflection, perhaps, was owing my uncorrupted probity. Thus did I resolve to signalize my zeal in the service of Don Gonzales, in the persuasion that if I was lucky enough to disgust the worshiper by befouling his idol, it would turn to very good account. On a statement of debtor and creditor between the right and the wrong side of the action, the money balance was visibly in favor of virtue, not to mention the delights of a fair and irreproachable character,

If vice so often assumes the semblance of its contrary, why

should not hypocrisy now and then change sides for variety? I held myself up to Euphrasia for a thorough swindler. She was dupe enough to believe that I was incessantly talking of her to my master; and thereupon I wove a tissue of frippery and falsehood, which imposed on her for sterling truth. She had so completely given herself up to my insinuations, as to believe me her convert, her disciple, her confederate. The better still to carry on this fraud upon fraud, I affected to languish for Beatrice; and she, in ecstasy at her age to see a young fellow at her skirts, did not much trouble herself about my sincerity, if I did but play my part with vigor and address. When we were in the presence of our princesses, my master in the parlor and myself in the kitchen, the effect was that of two different pictures, but of the same school. Don Gonzales, dry as touchwood, with all its inflammability, and nothing but its smother, seemed a fitter subject for extreme unction than for amorous parley; while my little pet, in proportion to the violence of my flame, niggled, nudged, toyed, and romped, like a school-girl in vacation; and no wonder she knew her lesson so pat, for the old coquet had been upwards of forty years in the form. She had finished her studies under certain professors of gallantry, whose art of pleasing becomes the more critical by practice; till they die under the accumulated experience of two or three generations.

It was not enough for me to go every evening with my master to Euphrasia's; it was sometimes my lounge even in day-time. But let me pop my head in at what hour I would, that forbidden creature man was never there, nor even a woman of any description, that might not be just as easily expressed as understood. There was not the least loop-hole for a paramour! a circumstance not a little perplexing to one who could not readily believe, that so pretty a bale of goods could submit to a strict monopoly, by such a dealer as Don Gonzales. This opinion undoubtedly was formed on a near acquaintance with female nature, as will be apparent in the sequel; for the fair Euphrasia, while waiting for my master's translation, fortified herself with patience in the arms of a lover, with some little fellow-feeling for the frailties of her age.

One morning I was carrying, according to custom, a note to this peerless pattern of perfection. There certainly were, or I was not standing in the room, the feet of a man ensconced behind the tapestry. Out slunk I, just as if I had no eyes in my head; yet, though such a discovery was nothing but what might have been expected, neither was the piper to be paid out of my pocket, my feelings were a good deal staggered at the breach of faith. Ah! traitress, exclaimed I with virtuous indignation, abandoned Euphrasia! Not satisfied to humbug a silly old gentleman with a tale of love, you share his property in your person with another, and add profligacy to dissimulation! But to be sure, on after-thoughts, I was but a green-horn, when I took on so for such a trivial occurrence! It was rather a subject for mirth than for moral reflection, and perfectly justified by the way of the world; the languid, embargoed commerce of my master's amorous moments had need be filipped by a trade in some more merchantable wares. At all events it would have been better to have held my tongue, than to have laid hold on such an opportunity of playing the faithful servant. But instead of tempering my zeal with discretion, nothing would serve the turn but taking up the wrongs of Don Gonzales in the spirit of chivalry. On this high principle, I made a circumstantial report of what I had seen, with the addition of the attempt made by Euphrasia to seduce me from my good faith. I gave it in her own words without the least reserve, and put him in the way of knowing all that was to be known of his mistress. He was struck all in a heap by my intelligence, and a faint flash of indignation on his faded cheek seemed to give security, that the lady's infidelity would not go unpunished. Enough, Gil Blas, said he, I am infinitely obliged by your attachment to my service, and your probity is very acceptable to me, I will go to Euphrasia this very moment. I will overwhelm her with reproaches, and break at once with the ungrateful creature. With these words, he actually bent his way to the subject of his anger; and dispensed with my attendance, from the kind motive of sparing me the awkwardness which my presence during their explanation would have occasioned to my feelings.

I longed for my master's return with all the impatience of an interested person. There could not be a doubt but that with his strong grounds of complaint, he would return completely disentangled from the snares of his nymph. In this thought I extoled and magnified myself for my good deed. What could be more flattering than the thanks of the kindred who were naturally to inherit after Don Gonzales, when they should be informed that their relative was no longer the puppet of a figure-dance so hostile to their interests? It was not to be supposed but that such a friend would be remembered, and that my merits would at last be distinguished from those of other serving-men, who are usually more disposed to encourage their masters in licentiousness, than to draw them off to habits of decency. I was always of an aspiring temper, and thought to have passed for the Joseph or the Scipio of the servants' hall; but so fascinating an idea was only to be indulged for an hour or two. The founder of my fortunes came home. My friend, said he, I have had a very sharp brush with Euphrasia. She insists on it that you have trumped up a cock-and-bull story. If their word is to be taken, you are no better than an impostor, a hireling in the pay of my nephews, for whose sake you have set all your wits to work to bring about a quarrel between her and me. I have seen the real tears, made of water, run down in floods from her poor dear eyes. She has vowed to me as solemnly as if I had been her confessor, that she never made any overtures to you in her life, and that she does not know what man is. Beatrice, who seems a simple, innocent sort of girl, is exactly in the same story, so that I could not but believe them and be pacified, whether I would or no.

How then, sir? interrupted I, in accents of undissembled sorrow, do you question my sincerity? Do you distrust . . . . . No, my good lad, interrupted he again in his turn, I will do you ample justice. I do not suspect you of being in league with my nephews. I am satisfied that all you have done has been for my good, and own myself much obliged to you for it: but appearances are apt to mislead, so that perhaps you did not see in reality what you took it into your head that you saw; and in that case, only consider yourself how offensive your charge must be to Euphrasia. Yet let that be as it will, she is a creature whom I cannot help loving in spite of my senses; so that the sacrifice she demands must be made, and that sacrifice is no less than your dismission. I lament it very much, my poor dear Gil Blas, and if that will be any satisfaction to you, my consent was wrung from me most unwillingly; but there was no saying nay. With one thing, however, you may comfort yourself, you shall not be sent away with empty pockets. Nay, more, I mean to turn you over to a lady of my acquaintance, where you will live to your liking.

I was not a little mortified to find all my noble acts and motives end in my own confusion. I gave a left-handed blessing to Euphrasia, and wept over the weakness of Don Gonzales, to be so foolishly infatuated by her. The kind-hearted old gentleman felt within himself that in turning me adrift at the peremptory demand of his mistress, he was not performing the most manly action of his life. For this reason, as a set-off against his hen-pecked cowardice, and that I might the more easily swallow this bitter dose, he gave me fifty ducats, and took me with him next morning to the Marchioness of Chaves, telling that lady before my face, that I was a young man of unexceptionably good character, and very high in his good graces, but that as certain family reasons prevented him from continuing me on his own establishment, he should esteem it as a favor if she would take me on hers. After such an introduction, I was retained at once as her appendage, and found myself, I scarcely knew how, established in another household.

CHAPTER VIII.

THE MARCHIONESS OF CHAVES: HER CHARACTER, AND THAT OF HER COMPANY.

THE Marchioness of Chaves was a widow of five-and-thirty, tall, handsome, and well-proportioned. She enjoyed an income of ten thousand ducats, without the incumbrance of a nursery. I never met with a lady of fewer words, nor one of a more solemn aspect. Yet this exterior did not prevent her from being set up as the cleverest woman in all Madrid. Her great assemblies, attended by people of the first quality, and by men of letters who made a coffeehouse of her apartments, contributed perhaps more than anything she said to give her the reputation she had acquired. But this is a point on which it is not my province to decide. I have only to relate, as her historian, that her name carried with it the idea of superior genius, and that her house was called, to distinguish it from the ordinary societies in town, The Fashionable Institution for Literature, Taste, and Science.

In point of fact, not a day passed, but there were readings there, sometimes of dramatic pieces, and sometimes in other branches of poetry. But the subjects were always selected from the graver muses; wit and humor were held in the most sovereign contempt. Comedy, however spirited; a novel, however pointed in its satire or ingenious in its fable, such light productions as these were treated as weak efforts of the brain without the slightest claim to patronage; whereas, on the contrary, the most microscopical work in the serious style, whether ode, pastoral, or sonnet, was trumpeted to the skies as the most illustrious effort of a learned and poetical age. It not unfrequently fell out, that the public reversed the decrees of this chancery for genius: nay, they had sometimes the gross ill-breeding to hiss the very pieces which had been sanctioned by this court of criticism.

I was chief manager of the establishment, and my office consisted in getting the drawing-room ready to receive the company, in setting the chairs in order for the gentlemen, and the sofas for the ladies: after which I took my station on the landing-place to bawl out the names of the visitors as they came upstairs, and usher them into the circle. The first day, an old piece of family furniture, who was stationed by my side in the ante-chamber, gave me their description with some humor, after I had shown them into the room. His name was Andrew Molina. He had a good deal of mother's wit, with a flowing vein of satire, much gravity of sarcasm, and a happy knack at hitting off characters. The first comer was a bishop. I roared out his lordship's name, and as soon as he was gone in, my nomenclator told me—That prelate is a very curious gentleman. He has some little influence at court; but wants to persuade the world that he has a great deal. He presses his service on every soul he comes near, and then leaves them completely in the lurch. One day he met with a gentleman in the presence-chamber who bowed to him. He laid hold of him, and squeezing his hand, assured him, with an inundation of civilities, that he was altogether devoted to his lordship. For goodness' sake, do not spare me; I shall not die in my bed without having first found an opportunity of making you my debtor. The gentleman returned his thanks with all becoming expressions of gratitude, and when they were at some distance from one another, the obsequious churchman said to one of his attendants in waiting—I ought to know that man; I have some floating, indistinct idea of having seen him somewhere.

Next after the bishop, came the son of a grandee. When I had introduced him into my lady's room—This nobleman, said Molina, is also an original in his way. You are to take notice that he often pays a visit, for the express purpose of talking over some urgent business with the friend on whom he calls, and goes away again without once thinking on the topic he came solely to discuss. But, added my showman on the sight of two ladies, here are Donna Angela de Penafiel and Donna Margaretta de Montalvan. This pair have not a feature of resemblance to each other. Donna Margaretta prides herself on her philosophical acquirements; she will hold her head as high as the most learned head among the doctors of Salamanca, nor will the wisdom of her conceit ever give up the point to the best reasons they can render. As for Donna Angela, she does not affect the learned lady, though she has taken no unsuccessful pains in the improvement of her mind. Her manner of talking is rational and proper, her ideas are novel and ingenious, expressed in polite, significant, and natural terms. This latter portrait is delightful, said I to Molina; but the other, in my opinion, is scarcely to be tolerated in the softer sex. Not over bearable indeed! replied he with a sneer: even in men it does but expose them to the lash of satire. The good marchioness herself, our honored lady, continued he, she too has a sort of a philosophical looseness. There will be fine chopping of logic there to-day! God grant the mysteries of religion may not be invaded by these disputants.

As he was finishing his last sentence, in came a withered bit of mortality, with a grave and crabbed look. My companion showed him no mercy. This fellow, said he, is one of those pompous, unbending spirits who think to pass for men of profound genius, under favor of a few common-places extracted out of Seneca; yet they are but shallow coxcombs when one comes to examine them narrowly. Then followed in the train a spruce figure, with tolerable person and address, to say nothing of a troubled air and manner, which always supposes a plentiful stock of self-sufficiency. I inquired who this was. A dramatic poet! said Molina. He has manufactured a hundred thousand verses in his time, which never brought him in the value of a groat; but as a set-off against his metrical failure, he has feathered his nest very warmly by six lines of humble prose: you will wonder by what magic touch a fortune could be made . . . . .

And so I did; but a confounded noise upon the staircase put verse and prose completely out of my head. Good again! exclaimed my informer: here is the licentiate Campanario. He is his own harbinger before ever he makes his appearance. He sets out from the very street door in a continued volley of conversation, and you hear how the alarm is kept up till he makes his retreat. In good sooth, the vaulted roof re-echoed with the organ of the thundering licentiate, who at length exhibited the case in which the pipes were contained. He brought a bachelor of his acquaintance by way of accompaniment, and there was not a *sotto voce* passage during the whole visit. Signor Campanario, said I to Molina, is to all appearance a man of very fine conversation. Yes, replied my sage instructor, the gentleman has his lucky hits, and a sort of quaintness that might pass for humor; he does very well in a mixed company. But the worst of it is, that incessant talking is one of his most pardonable errors. He is a little too apt to borrow from himself, and as those who are behind the scenes are not to be dazzled by the tinsel of the property-man, so we know how to separate a certain volubility and buffoonery of manner from sterling wit and sense. The greater part of his good things would be thought very bad ones, if submitted, without their concomitant grimaces, to the ordeal of a jest book.

Other groups passed before us, and Molina touched them with his wand. The marchioness too came in for a magic rap over the knuckles. Our lady patroness, said he, is better than might be expected for a female philosopher. She is not dainty in her likings; and bating a whim or too, it is no hard matter to give her satisfaction. Wits and women of quality seldom approach so near the atmosphere of good sense; and for passion, she scarcely knows what it is. Play and gallantry are equally in her black books: dear conversation is her first and sole delight. To lead such a life would be little better than penance to the common run of ladies. Molina's character of my mistress established her at once in my good graces. And yet, in the course of a few days, I could not help suspecting that, though not dainty in her liking, she knew what passion was, and that a foul copy of gallantry delighted her more than the fairest conversation.

One morning, during the mysteries of the toilette, there presented himself to my notice a little fellow of forty, forbidding in his aspect, more filthy if possible than Pedro de Moya the bookworm, and verging in no marketable measure towards deformity. He told me he wanted to speak with my lady marchioness. On whose business? quoth I. On my own, quoth he, somewhat snappishly. Tell her I am the gentleman; . . . . . she will understand you; . . . . . about whom she was talking yesterday with Donna Anna de Velasco. I went before him into my lady's apartment, and gave in his name. The marchioness all at once shrieked out her satisfaction, and ordered me to show him in. It was not courtesy enough to point to a chair, and bid him sit down: but the attendants, forsooth, her own maids about her person, were to withdraw, so that the little hunchback, with better luck than falls to the lot of many a taller man, had the field entirely to himself, as lord paramount. As for the girls and myself, we could not help tittering a little at this uncouthly concerted duet, which lasted nearly an hour: when my patroness dismissed his little lordship, with such a profusion of farewells and God-be-with-you's, as sufficiently evinced her thankfulness for the entertainment she had received.

The conversation had, in fact, been so edifying, that in the afternoon she seized a private opportunity of whispering in my ear—Gil Blas, when the short gentleman comes again, you may show him up the back stairs; there is no need of parading him along a line of staring servants. I did as I was ordered. When this epitome of humanity knocked at the door, and that hour was no further off than the next morning, we threaded all the bye passages to the place of assignation. I played the same modest part two or three times in the very innocence of my soul, without the most distant guess that the material system could form any part of their philosophy. But that hound-like snuff at an ill construction, with which the devil has armed the noses of the most charitable, put me on the scent of a very whimsical game, and I concluded either that the marchioness had an old taste, or that crookback courted her as proxy to a better man.

Faith and troth, thought I, with all the impertinence of a hasty opinion, if my mistress really likes a handsome fellow behind the curtain, all is well; I forgive her her sins: but if she is stark mad for such a monkey as this, to say the truth, there will be little mercy for her on male or female tongues. But how foully did I defame my honored patroness! The genius of magic had perched herself upon the little conjurer's protuberant shoulder; and his skill having been puffed off to the marchioness, who was just the right food for such jugglers and their tricks, she held private conferences with him. Under his tuition she was to command wealth and treasure, to build castles in the air, to remove from place to place in an instant, to reveal future events, to tell what is done in far countries, to call the dead out of their graves, and terrify the world with many miracles. Seriously, and to give him his deserts, the scoundrel lived on the folly of the public; and it has been confidently asserted, that ladies of fashion have not in all ages and countries been exempt from the credulity of their inferiors.

CHAPTER IX.

AN INCIDENT THAT PARTED GIL BLAS AND THE MARCHIONESS OF CHAVES. THE SUBSEQUENT DESTINATION OF THE FORMER.

FOR six months I lived with the Marchioness of Chaves, and, as it must be admitted, on the fat of the land. But fate, who thrusts footmen as well as heroes into the world, with herself tied about their necks, gave me a jog to be gone, and swore that I should stay no longer in that family or in Madrid. The adventure by which this decree was announced shall be the subject of the ensuing narrative.

In my mistress's female squad there was a nymph named Portia. To say nothing of her youth and beauty, it was her meek demeanor and good repute that captivated me, who had yet to learn that none but the brave deserves the fair. The marchioness's secretary, as proud as a prime minister, and as jealous as the Grand Turk, was caught in the same trap as myself. No sooner did he cast an unlucky squint at my advances, than, without waiting to see how Portia might chance to fancy them, he determined pell-mell to have a tilt with me. To forward this ghostly enterprise, he gave me an appointment one morning in a place sadly impervious to all seasonable interruption. Yet as he was a little go-by-the-ground, scarcely up to my shoulders, and apparently of feeble frame, he did not look like a very dangerous antagonist; so away I went with some little courage to the appointed spot. Thinking to come off with flying colors, I anticipated the effect of my bravery on the heart of Portia; but as it turned out, I was gathering my laurels before they had budded. The little secretary, who had been practising for two or three years at the fencing-school, disarmed me like a very baby, and holding the point of his sword up to my throat, Prepare thyself, said he, to balance thine accounts with this world, and open a correspondence with the next, or give me thy rascally word to leave the Marchioness of Chaves, this very day, and never more to think of my Portia. I gave him my rascally word, and was honest enough not to think of breaking it. There was an awkwardness in showing my face before the servants of the family, after having been worsted; and especially before the high and mighty princess who had been the theme of our tournament, I only returned home to get together my baggage and wages, and on that very day set off towards Toledo, with a purse pretty well lined, and a knapsack at my back with my wardrobe and movables. Though my rascally word was not given to abandon the purlieus of Madrid, I considered it as a matter of delicacy to disappear, at least for a few seasons. My resolution was to make the tour of Spain, and to halt first at one town and then at another. My ready money, thought I, will carry me a good way; I shall not call about me very prodigally. When my stock is exhausted, I can but go into service again. A lad of my versatility will find places in plenty, whenever it may be convenient to look out for them.

It was particularly my wish to see Toledo: and I got thither after three days' journey. My quarters were at a respectable house of entertainment, where I was taken for a gentleman of some figure, under favor of my best clothes, in which I did not fail to bedizen myself. With the pick-tooth carelessness of a lounger, the affectation of a puppy, and the pertness of a wit, it remained with me to dictate the terms of an arrangement with some very pretty women who infested that neighborhood; but, as a hint had been given me that the pocket was the high road to their good graces, my amorous enthusiasm was a little flattered, and, as it was no part of my plan to domesticate myself in any one place, after having seen all the lions at Toledo, I started one morning with the dawn, and took the road to Cuença, intending to go to Arragon. On the second day I went into an inn which stood open to receive me by the roadside. Just as I was beginning to recruit the carnal department of my nature, in came a party belonging to the Holy Brotherhood. These gentlemen called for wine, and set in for a drinking bout. Over their cups they were conning the description of a young man, whom they had orders to arrest. The spark, said one of them, is not above three-and-twenty: he has long black hair, is well grown, with an aquiline nose, and rides a bay horse.

I heard their talk without seeming to be a listener; and, in fact, did not trouble my head much about it. They remained in their quarters, and I pursued my journey. Scarcely had I gone a quarter of a mile, before I met a young gentleman on horseback, as personable as need be, and mounted as described by the officers,

Faith and truth, thought I within myself, this is the very identical man. Black hair and an aquiline nose! One cannot help doing a good office when it comes in one's way. Sir, said I, give me leave to ask you whether you have not some disagreeable business on your hands? The young man, without returning any answer, looked at me from head to foot, and seemed startled at my question. I assured him it was not wanton curiosity that induced me to address him. He was satisfied of that when I related all I had

"COME IN, MY SONS, REPLIED THE HERMIT."

heard at the inn. My unknown benefactor, said he, I will not deny to you that I have reason to believe myself actually the person of whom the officers are in quest: therefore I shall take another road to avoid them. In my opinion, answered I it would be better to look out for a spot where you may be in safety, and under shelter from a storm which is brewing, and will soon pour down upon our heads. Without loss of time we discovered and made for a row of trees, forming a natural avenue, which led us to the foot of a mountain, where we found an hermitage.

There was a large and deep grotto which time had worn away into the heart of the rock; and the hand of man had added a rude front built of pebbles and shell-work, covered all over with turf. The adjacent grounds were strewed with a thousand sorts of flowers, which scattered their perfume; and one was pleased to see hard by the grotto, a small fissure in the mountain whence a spring rippled with a tinkling noise, and poured its pellucid stream along the meadow. At the entrance of this solitary abode stood a venerable hermit, seemingly weighed down with years. He supported himself with one hand upon a staff, and held a rosary of large beads with the other, composed of at least twenty rows. His head was almost lost in a brown woolen cap with long ears; and his beard, whiter than snow, swept down in aged majesty to his waist. We advanced towards him. Father, said I, is it your pleasure to allow us shelter from the threatening storm? Come in, my sons, replied the hermit, after examining me attentively; this hermitage is at your service, to occupy it during pleasure. As for your horse, added he, pointing to the court-yard of his mansion, he will be very well off there. My companion disposed of the animal accordingly, and we followed the old man into the grotto.

No sooner had we got in than a heavy rain fell, with a terrific storm of thunder and lightning. The hermit threw himself upon his knees before a consecrated image, fastened to the wall, and we followed the example of our host. Our devotions ceased with the subsiding of the storm; but as the rain continued, though with diminished violence, and night was not far distant, the old man said to us—My sons, you had better not pursue your journey in such weather, unless your affairs are pressing. We answered with one consent, that we had nothing to hinder us from staying there, but the fear of incommoding him; bnt that if there was room for us in the hermitage, we would thank him for a night's lodging. You may have it without inconvenience, answered the hermit, at least the inconvenience will be all your own. Your accommodation will be rough, and your meal such as a recluse has to offer.

With this cordial welcome to a homely board, the holy personage seated us at a little table, and set before us a few vegetables, a crust of bread, and a pitcher of water. My sons, resumed he, you behold my ordinary fare, but to-day I will make a feast in hospitality towards you. So saying, he fetched a little cheese and some nuts, which he threw down upon the table. The young man, whose appetite was not keen, felt but little tempted by his entertainment. I perceive, said the hermit to him, that you are accustomed to better tables than mine, or rather that sensuality has vitiated your natural relish. I have been in the world like you. The utmost ingenuity of the culinary art, whether to stimulate or soothe the palate, was exerted by turns for my gratification. But since I have lived in solitude, my taste has recovered its simplicity. Now, vegetables, fruit, and milk, are my greatest dainties; in a word, I keep an antediluvian table.

While he was haranguing after this fashion, the young man fell into a deep musing. The hermit was aware of his inattention. My son, said he, something weighs upon your spirits. May we not be informed what disturbs you? Open your heart to me. Curiosity is not my motive for questioning you, but charity, and a desire to be of service. I am at a time of life to give advice, and you perhaps are under circumstances to stand in need of it. Yes, father, replied the gentleman with a sigh, I doubtless do stand in need of it, and will follow yours, since you are so good as to offer it; I cannot suppose there is any risk in unbosoming myself to a man like you. No, my son, said the old man, you have nothing to fear, it is under more stately roofs that confidences are betrayed. On this assurance the cavalier began his story.

CHAPTER X.

THE HISTORY OF DON ALPHONSO AND THE FAIR SERAPHINA.

I WILL attempt no disguise from you, my venerable friend, nor from this gentleman who completes my audience. After the generosity of his conduct towards me, I should be in the wrong to distrust him. You shall know my misfortunes from their beginning. I am a native of Madrid, and came into the world mysteriously. An officer of the German guard, Baron Steinbach by name, returning home one evening, espied a bundle of fair linen at the foot of his staircase. He took it up and carried it to his wife's apartment, where it turned out to be a new-born infant, wrapped up in very handsome swaddling-clothes, with a note containing an assurance that it belonged to persons of condition, who would come forward and own it at some future period; and the further information that it had been baptized by the name of Alphonso. I was that unfortunate stranger in the world, and this is all that I know about myself. Whether honor or profligacy was the motive of the exposure, the helpless child was equally the victim; whether my unhappy mother wanted to get rid of me, to conceal an habitual course of scandalous amours, or whether she had made a single deviation from the path of virtue with a faithless lover, and had been obliged to protect her fame at the expense of nature and the maternal feelings.

However this might be, the Baron and his wife were touched by my destitute condition, and resolved, as they had no children of their own, to bring me up under the name of Don Alphonso. As I grew in years and stature their attachment to me strengthened. My manners, genteel before strangers and affectionate towards them, were the theme of their fondest panegyric. In short, they loved me as if I had been their own. Masters of every description were provided for me. My education became their leading object, and far from waiting impatiently till my parents should come for ward, they seemed, on the contrary, to wish that my birth might always remain a mystery. As soon as the Baron thought me old enough to bear arms, he sent me into the service. With my ensign's commission, a genteel and suitable equipment was provided for me ; and, the more effectually to animate me in the career of glory, my patron pointed out that the path of honor was open to every adventurer, and that the renown of a warrior would be so much the more creditable to me, as I should owe it to none but myself. At the same time he laid open to me the circumstances of my birth, which he had hitherto concealed. As I had passed for his son in Madrid, and had actually thought myself so, it must be owned that this communication gave me some uneasiness. I could not then, nor can I even now, think of it without a sense of shame. In proportion as the innate feelings of a gentleman bear testimony to the birth of one, am I mortified at being rejected and renounced by the unnatural authors of my being.

I went to serve in the Low Countries, but peace was concluded in a short time ; and Spain finding herself without assailants, though not without assassins, I returned to Madrid, where I received fresh marks of affection from the Baron and his wife. Rather more than two months after my return, a little page came into my room one morning, and presented me with a note couched nearly in the following terms :—" I am neither ugly nor crooked, and yet you often see me at my window without the tribute of a glance. This conduct is little in unison with the spirit of your physiognomy, and so far stings me to revenge that I will make you love me if possible."

On the perusal of this epistle, there could be no doubt but it came from a widow, by name Leonora, who lived opposite our house, and had the character of a very great coquet. Hereupon I examined my little messenger, who had a mind to be on the reserve at first, but a ducat in hand opened the floodgates of his intelligence. He even took charge of an answer to his mistress, confessing my guilt, and intimating that its punishment was far advanced.

I was not insensible to a conquest even of this kind. For the rest of the day home and my window-seat were the grand attraction ; and the lady seemed to have fallen in love with her window-seat too. I made signals. She returned them ; and on the very next day sent me word by her little Mercury, that if I would be in the street on the following night between eleven and twelve, I might converse with her at a window on the ground-floor. Though I did not feel myself very much captivated by so coming on a kind of widow, it was impossible not to send such an answer as if I was ; and a sort of amorous curiosity made me as impatient as if I had really been in love. In the dusk of the evening, I went sauntering up and down the Prado till the hour of assignation. Before I could get to my appointment, a man mounted on a fine horse alighted near me, and coming up with a peremptory air—Sir, said he, are not you the son of Baron Steinbach ? I answered in the affirmative. You are the person then, resumed he, who were to meet Leonora at her window to-night? I have seen her letters and your answers, her page has put them into my hands, and I have followed you this evening from your own house hither, to let you know you have a rival whose pride is not a little wounded at a competition with yourself in an affair of the heart. It would be unnecessary to say more. We are in a retired place, let us therefore draw, unless, to avoid the chastisement in store for you, you will give me your word to break off all connection with Leonora. Sacrifice in my favor all your hopes and interest, or your life must be the forfeit. It had been better, said I, to have insured my generosity by good manners, than to extort my compliance by menaces. I might have granted to your request what I must refuse to this insolent demand.

Well, then, resumed he, tying up his horse and preparing for the encounter, let us settle our dispute like men. Little could a person of my condition have stomached the debasement of a request, to a man of your quality. Nine out of ten in my rank would, under such circumstances, have taken their revenge on terms of less honor but more safety. I felt myself exasperated at this last insinuation, so that, seeing he had already drawn his sword, mine did not linger in the scabbard. We fell on one another with so much fury, that the engagement did not last long. Whether his attack was made with too much heat, or my skill in fencing was superior, he soon received a mortal wound. He staggered, and dropped dead upon the spot. In such a situation, having no alternative but an immediate escape, I mounted the horse of my antagonist, and went off in the direction of Toledo. There was no venturing to return to Baron Steinbach's, since, besides the danger of the attempt, the narrative of my adventure from my own mouth would only afflict him the more, so that nothing was so eligible as an immediate decampment from Madrid.

Chewing the cud of my own melancholy reflection, I traveled onwards the remainder of the night and all the next morning. But about noon it became necessary to stop, both for the sake of my horse and to avoid the insupportable fierceness of the mid-day heat. I staid in a village till sun-set, and then, intending to reach Toledo without drawing bit, went on my way. I had already got two leagues beyond Illescas, when, about midnight, a storm like that of to-day overtook me as I was jogging along the road. There was a garden wall at some little distance, and I rode up to it. For want of any more commodious shelter, my horse's station and my own were arranged, as comfortably as circumstances would admit, near the door of a summer-house at the end of the wall, with a balcony over it. Leaning against the door, I discovered it to be open, owing, as I thought, to the negligence of the servants. Having dismounted, less from curiosity than for the sake of a better standing, as the rain had been very troublesome under the balcony, I went into the lower part of the summer-house, leading my horse by the bridle.

My amusement during the storm was in reconnoitring my quarters; and though I had nothing to form an opinion by, but the lurid gleams of the lightning, it was very evident that such a house must belong to some family above the common. I was waiting anxiously till the rain abated, to set forward again on my journey; but a great light at a distance made me change my purpose. Leaving my horse in the summer-house, with the precaution of fastening the door, I made for the light, in the assurance that they were not all gone to bed in the house, and with the intention of requesting a lodging for the night. After crossing several walks, I came to a saloon, and here too the door was left open. On my entrance, from the magnificence so handsomely displayed by the light

"LEAVING MY HORSE IN THE SUMMER-HOUSE."

of a fine crystal lustre, it was easy to conclude that this must be the residence of some illustrious nobleman. The pavement was of marble, the wainscot richly carved and gilt, the proportions of architecture tastefully preserved, and the ceiling evidently adorned by the masterpieces of the first artists in fresco. But what particularly engaged my attention was a great number of busts, and those of Spanish heroes, supported on jasper pedestals, and ranged round the saloon. There was opportunity enough for examining all this splendor, since there was not even a foot-fall, nor the shadow of any one gliding along the passage, though my ears and eyes were incessantly on the watch for some inhabitant of this fairy desert.

On one side of the saloon there was a door a-jar; by pushing it a little wider open, I discovered a range of apartments, with a light only in the furthest. What is to be done now? thought I within myself. Shall I go back, or take the liberty of marching forward, even to that chamber? To be sure, it was obvious that the most prudent step would be to make good my retreat; but curiosity was not to be repelled, or rather, to speak more truly, my star was in its ascendant. Advancing boldly from room to room, at length I reached that where the light was. It was a wax taper on a marble slab, in a magnificent candlestick. The first object that caught my eye was the gay furniture of this summer abode; but soon afterwards, casting a look towards a bed, of which the curtains were half undrawn on account of the heat, an object arrested my attention, which engrossed it with the deepest interest. A young lady, in spite of the thunderclaps which had been pealing round her, was sleeping there, motionless and undisturbed. I approached her very gently, and by the light of the taper I had seized, a complexion and features the most dazzling were submitted to my gaze. My spirits were all afloat at the discovery. A sensation of transport and delight came over me; but however my feelings might harass my own heart, my conviction of her high birth checked every presumptuous hope, and awe obtained a complete victory over desire. While I was drinking in floods of adoration at the shrine of her beauty, the goddess of my homage awoke.

You may well suppose her consternation, at seeing a man, an utter stranger, in her bedchamber, and at midnight. She was terrified at this strange appearance, and uttered a loud shriek. I did my best to restore her composure, and throwing myself on my knees in the humblest posture, Madam, said I, fear nothing. My business here is not to hurt you. I was going on, but her alarm was so great that she was incapable of hearing my excuses. She called her woman with a most vehement importunity, and as she could get no answer, she threw over her a thin night-gown at the foot of the bed, rushed rapidly out of the room, and darted into the apartments I had crossed, still calling her female establishment about her, as well as a younger sister whom she had under her care. I looked for nothing less than a posse of strapping footmen who were likely, without hearing my defence, to execute summary justice on so audacious a culprit; but by good luck, at least for me, her cries were to no purpose: they only roused an old domestic, who would have been but a sorry knight had any ravisher or magician invaded her repose. Nevertheless, assuming somewhat of courage from his presence, she asked me haughtily who I was, by what inlet and to what purpose I had presumptuously gained admission into her house. I began then to enter on my exculpation, and had no sooner declared that the open door of the summer-house in the garden had invited my entrance, than she exclaimed as if thunderstruck—Just heaven! what an idea darts across my mind!

As she uttered these words, she caught at the wax light on the table; then ran through all the apartments one after another, without finding either her attendants or her sister. She remarked, too, that all their personals and wardrobe were carried off. With such a comment on her hasty suspicions, she came up to me and said, in the hurried accent of suspense and perturbation: Traitor! add not hypocrisy to your other crimes. Chance has not brought you hither. You are in the train of Don Ferdinand de Leyva, and are an accomplice in his guilt. But hope not to escape, there are still people enough about me to secure you. Madam, said I, do not confound me with your enemies. Don Ferdinand de Leyva is a stranger to me; I do not even know who you are. You see before you an outcast, whom an affair of honor has compelled to fly from Madrid; and I swear by whatever is most sacred among men, that had not a storm overtaken me, I should never have set my foot over your threshold. Entertain, then, a more favorable opinion of me. So far from suspecting me for an accomplice in any plot against you, believe me ready to enlist in your defence, and to revenge your wrongs. These last words, and still more the sincere tone in which they were delivered, convinced the lady of my innocence, and she seemed no longer to look on me as her enemy; but if her anger abated it was only that her grief might sway more absolutely. She began weeping most bitterly. Her tears called forth my sympathy, and my affliction was scarcely less poignant than her own, though the cause of this contagious sorrow was still to be ascertained. Yet it was not enough to mingle my tears with her; in my impatience to become her defender and avenger, an impulse of terrific fury came over me. Madam, exclaimed I, what outrage have you sustained? Let me know it, and your injuries are mine. Would you have me hunt out Don Ferdinand, and stab him to the heart? Only tell me on whom your justice would fall, and they shall suffer. You have only to give the word. Whatever dangers, whatever certain evils may be attendant on the execution of your orders, the unknown, whom you thought to be in league with your enemies, will brave them all in your cause.

This enraptured devotion surprised the lady, and stopped the flowing of her tears, Ah! sir, said she, forgive this suspicion, and attribute it to the blindness of my cruel fate. A nobility of sentiment like this speaks at once to the heart of Seraphina: and while it undeceives, makes me the less repine at a stranger being witness of an affront offered to my family. Yes, I own my error, and revolt not, unknown as you are, from your proffered aid. But the death of Don Ferdinand is not what I require. Well, then, madam, resumed I, of what nature are the services you would enjoin me? Sir, replied Seraphina, the ground of my complaint is this: Don Ferdinand de Leyva is enamored of my sister Julia, whom he met with by accident at Toledo, where we for the most part reside. Three months since, he asked her in marriage of the Count de Polan, my father, who refused his consent on account of an old grudge subsisting between the families. My sister is not yet fifteen, she must have been indiscreet enough to follow the evil counsels of my woman, whom Don Ferdinand has doubtless bribed; and this daring ruffian, advertised of our being alone at our country-house, has taken the opportunity of carrying off Julia. At least I should like to know what hiding-place he has chosen to deposit her in, that my father and my brother, who have been these two months at Madrid, may take their measures accordingly. For heaven's sake, added she, give yourself the trouble of examining the neighborhood of Toledo, an act so heinous cannot escape detection, and my family will owe you a debt of everlasting gratitude.

The lady was little aware how unseasonable an employment she was thrusting upon me. My escape from Castile could not be too soon effected; and yet how should such a reflection ever enter into her head, when it was completely superseded in mine by a more powerful suggestion? Delighted at finding myself important to the most lovely creature in the universe, I caught at the commission with eagerness, and promised to acquit myself of it with equal zeal and industry. In fact, I did not wait for daybreak, to go about fulfilling my engagement. A hasty leave of Seraphina gave me occasion to beg her pardon for the alarm I had caused her, and to assure her that she should speedily hear somewhat of my adventure. I went out as I came in, but so wrapped up in admiration of the lady, that it was palpable I was completely caught. My sense of this truth was the more confirmed, by the eagerness with which I embarked in her cause, and by the romantic, gaily-colored bubbles which my passion blew. It struck my fancy that Seraphina, though engrossed by her affliction, had remarked the hasty birth of my love, without being displeased at the discovery. I even flattered myself that if I could furnish her with any certain intelligence of her sister, and the business should terminate in any degree to her satisfaction, my part in it would be remembered to my advantage.

Don Alphonso broke the thread of his discourse at this passage, and said to our aged host: I beg your pardon, father, if the fullness of my passion should lead me to dilate too long upon particulars, wearisome and uninteresting to a stranger. No, my son, replied the hermit, such particulars are not wearisome: I am interested to know the state and progress of your passion for the young lady you are speaking of; my counsels will be influenced by the minute detail you are giving me.

With my fancy heated by these seductive images, resumed the young man, I was two days hunting after Julia's ravisher: but in vain were all the inquiries that could be made; by no means I could devise was the least trace of him to be discovered. Deeply mortified at the unsuccessful issue of my search, I bent my steps back to Seraphina, whom I pictured to myself as overwhelmed with uneasiness. Yet she was in better spirits than might have been expected. She informed me that her success had been better than mine; for she had learned how her sister was disposed of. She had received a letter from Don Ferdinand himself, importing that after being privately married to Julia, he had placed her in a convent at Toledo. I have sent his letter to my father, pursued Seraphina. I hope the affair may be adjusted amicably, and that a solemn marriage will soon extinguish the feuds which have so long kept our respective families at variance.

When the lady had thus informed me of her sister's fate, she began making an apology for the trouble she had given me, as well as the danger into which she might imprudently have thrown me, by engaging my services in pursuit of a ravisher without recollecting what I had told her, that an affair of honor had been the occasion of my flight. Her excuses were couched in such flattering terms, as to convert her very oversight into an obligation. As rest was desirable for me after my journey, she conducted me into the saloon, where we sat down together. She wore an undress gown of white taffety with black stripes, and a little hat of the same materials with black feathers; which gave me reason to suppose that she might be a widow. But she looked so young, that I scarcely knew what to think of it.

If I was all impatient to get at her history, she was not less so to know who I was. She besought me to acquaint her with my name, not doubting, as she kindly expressed it, by my noble air, and still more by the generous pity which had made me enter so warmly into her interests, that I belonged to some considerable family. The question was not a little perplexing. My color came and went, my agitation was extreme: and I must own that, with less repugnance to the meanness of a falsehood than to the acknowledgment of a disgraceful truth, I answered that I was the son of Baron Steinbach, an officer of the German guard. Tell me, likewise, resumed the lady, why you left Madrid. Before you answer my question, I will insure you all my father's credit, as well as that of my brother Don Gaspard. It is the least mark of gratitude I can bestow on a gentleman who, for my service, has neglected the preservation even of his own life. Without further hesitation, I acquainted her with all the circumstances of my rencontre: she laid the whole blame on my deceased antagonist, and engaged to interest all her family in my favor.

When I had satisfied her curiosity, it seemed not unreasonable to plead in favor of my own. I inquired whether she was maid, wife, or widow. It is three years, answered she, since my father made me marry Don Diego de Lara; and I have been a widow these fifteen months. Madam, said I, by what misfortune were your wedded joys so soon interrupted? I am going to inform you, sir, resumed the lady, in return for the confidence you have reposed in me.

Don Diego de Lara was a very elegant and accomplished gentleman: but, though his affection for me was extreme, and every day was witness to some attempt at giving me pleasure, such as the most impassioned and most tender lover puts in practice to win the smile of her he loves; though he had a thousand estimable qualities, my heart was untouched by all his merit. Love is not always the offspring either of assiduity or desert. Alas! we are often captivated at first sight by we know not whom, nor why, nor how.

To love, then, was not in my power. More disconcerted than gratified by his repeated offices of tenderness, which I received with a forced courtesy, but without real pleasure, if I accused my-self in secret of ingratitude, I still thought myself an object as much of pity as of censure. To his unhappiness and my own, his deli-cacy more than kept pace with his affection. Not an action or a speech of mine, but he unraveled all its hidden motives, and fath-omed all my thoughts, almost before they arose. The inmost re-cesses of my heart were laid open to his penetration. He com-plained without ceasing of my indifference; and esteemed himself only so much the more unfortunate, in not being able to please me, as he was well assured that no rival stood in his way; for I was scarcely sixteen years old; and, before he paid his addresses to me, he had tampered with my woman, who had assured him that no one had hitherto attracted my attention. Yes, Seraphina, he would often say, I could have been contented that you had pre-ferred some other to myself, and that there were no more fatal cause of your insensibility. My attentions and your own principles would get the better of such a juvenile prepossession; but I despair of triumphing over your coldness, since your heart is impenetrable to all the love I have lavished on you. Wearied with the repetition of the same strain, I told him that instead of disturbing his repose and mine by this excess of delicacy, he would do better in trusting to the effects of time. In fact, at my age, I could not be ex-pected to enter into the refinements of so sentimental a passion; and Don Diego should have waited, as I warned him, for a riper period and more staid reflection. But, finding that a whole year had elapsed, and that he was no forwarder in my favor than on the first day, he lost all patience, or rather, his brain became distracted. Affecting to have important business at court, he took his leave, and went to serve as a volunteer in the Low Countries; where he soon found in the chances of war what he went to seek, the termi-nations of his sufferings and of his life.

After the lady had finished her recital, her husband's uncom-mon character became the topic of our discourse. We were inter-rupted by the arrival of a courier, charged with a letter for Seraph-ina from the Count de Polan. She begged my permission to read it; and as she went on, I observed her to grow pale, and to become dreadfully agitated. When she had finished, she raised her eyes upward, heaved a long sigh, and her face was in a moment bathed with her tears. Her sorrow sat heavily on my feelings. My spirits were greatly disturbed; and, as if it were a forewarning of the blow impending over my head, a death-like shudder crept through my frame, and my faculties were all benumbed. Madam, said I, in ac-cents half choked with apprehension, may I ask of what dire events that letter brings the tidings? Take it, sir, answered Seraphina most dolefully, while she held out the letter to me. Read for your-self what my father has written. Alas! you are but too deeply con-cerned in the contents.

At these words, which made my blood run cold, I took the let-ter with a trembling hand, and found in it the following intelli-gence: "Your brother, Don Gaspard, fought yesterday at the Prado. He received a small sword wound, of which he died this day: and declared, before he breathed his last, that his antagonist was the son of Baron Steinbach, an officer of the German guard. As misfortunes never come alone, the murderer has eluded my vengeance by flight, but wherever he may have concealed himself, no pains shall be spared to hunt him out. I am going to write to the magistrates all round the country, who will not fail to take him into custody, if he passes through any one of the towns in their jurisdiction, and by the notices I am going to circulate, I hope to cut off his retreat in the country or at the sea-ports.—THE COUNT DE POLAN."

Conceive into what a ferment this letter threw all my thoughts. I remained for some moments motionless and without the power of speech. In the midst of my confusion, I too plainly saw the destructive bearing of Don Gaspard's death on the passion I had imbibed. My despair was unbounded at the thought. I threw myself at Seraphina's feet, and offering her my naked sword, Madam, said I, spare the Count de Polan the necessity of seeking further for a man who might possibly withdraw himself from his resentment. Be yourself the avenger of your brother: offer up his murderer as the victim of your own hand: now strike the blow. Let this very weapon which terminated his life, cut short the sad remnant of his adversary's days. Sir, answered Seraphina, a little softened by my behavior, I loved Don Gaspard, so that though you killed him in fair and manly hostility, and though he brought his death upon himself, you may rest assured that I take up my father's quarrel. Yes, Don Alphonso, I am your decided enemy, and will do against you all that the ties of blood and friendship require at my hands. But I will not take advantage of your evil star: in vain has it delivered you into my grasp: if honor arms me against you, the same sentiment forbids to pursue a cowardly revenge. The rights of hospitality must be inviolable, and I will not repay such service as you have rendered me with the treachery of an assassin. Fly! make your escape, if you can, from our pursuit and from the rigor of the laws, and save your forfeit life from the dangers that beset it.

What, then! madam, returned I, when vengeance is in your own hands, do you turn it over to the laws, which may, perhaps, be too slow for your impatience? Nay! rather stab a wretch who is not worthy of your forbearance. No, madam, maintain not so noble and so generous a proceeding with one like me. Do you know who I am? All Madrid takes me for Baron Steinbach's son—yet am I nothing better than a foundling, whom he brought up from charity. I know not even who were guilty of my existence. No matter, interrupted Seraphina, with precipitation, as if my last words had given her new uneasiness, though you were the lowest of mankind I would do what honor bids. Well, madam, said I, since a brother's death is insufficient to excite your thirst after my blood, I will exasperate your hatred still further by a new offence, of which I trust you will never pardon the boldness. I dote on you: I could not behold your charms without being dazzled by them, and, in spite of the cloud in which my destiny was enveloped, I had cherished the hope of being united to you. I was so infatuated by my passion, or rather by my pride, as to flatter myself that heaven, which perhaps conceals from me my birth in mercy, might discover it one day, and enable me without a blush to acquaint you with my real name. After this injurious avowal, can you hesitate a moment about punishing me?

This rash declaration, replied the lady, would doubtless prove offensive at any other season; but I forgive it in consideration of the trouble which bewilders you. Besides, my own condition so engrosses me, as to render me deaf to any strange ideas that may escape you. Once more, Don Alphonso, added she, shedding tears, begone far from a house which you have cast into mourning: every moment of your longer stay adds pungency to my distress. I no longer oppose your will, madam, returned I, preparing to take my leave: absence from you must then be my portion: but do not suppose that, anxious for the preservation of a life which is become hateful to you, I go to seek an asylum where I may be sheltered from your search. No, no, I bare my breast to your resentment, I shall wait with impatience at Toledo for the fate which you design me; and by surrendering at once to my pursuers, shall myself forward the completion of my miseries.

At the conclusion of this speech I withdrew. My horse was returned to me, and I went to Toledo, where I abode eight days, and really with so little care to conceal myself that I know not how or why I have escaped an arrest; for I cannot suppose that the Count de Polan, whose whole soul is set on cutting off my retreat, should not have been aware that I was likely to pass through Toledo. Yesterday I left that town, where it should seem as if I was tired of my liberty, and without betaking myself to any fixed course of traveling, I came to this hermitage, like a man who had no reason to be ashamed of showing himself. Such, father, was the cause of my absence and distraction. I beseech you to assist me with your counsels.

CHAPTER XI.

THE OLD HERMIT TURNS OUT AN EXTRAORDINARY GENIUS, AND GIL BLAS FINDS HIMSELF AMONG HIS FORMER ACQUAINTANCE.

WHEN Don Alphonso had concluded the melancholy recital of his misfortunes, the old hermit said to him—My son, you have been excessively rash in tarrying so long at Toledo. I consider in a very different light from that you affect to place it in, what you have told me of your story; and your love for Seraphina seems to me to be sheer madness. Take my word for it, you will do well to cancel that young lady from your remembrance; she never can be of your communion. Retreat like a skillful general, when you cannot act with effect on the offensive; and pursue your fortune on another field, where success may smile on your endeavors. You will be terribly out of luck to kill the brother of the next young lady who may chance to succeed this only possible object of your affection.

He was going to add many other inducements to resignation, in such a case as Don Alphonso's, when we saw another hermit enter our retreat, with a well-stuffed wallet slung across his shoulders. He was on his return, with the charitable contributions of all the good folks in the town of Cuença; and the gathering did credit to the religion of the age. He looked younger than his companion, in spite of his thick, foxy beard. Welcome home, brother Antony, said the elder of the two recluses; what news do you bring us from town? Bad enough, answered the carroty friar, putting into his hands a paper, folded in the form of a letter; this little instrument will inform you. The hoary sage opened it, and after reading on with an increased attention, as the contents seemed to grow more interesting, exclaimed: Heaven's will be done! Since the combustion is anticipated, we have only to fall in with the humor of our fate. Let us change our dialect, Signor Don Alphonso! pursued he, addressing his discourse to my young companion: you behold in me a man, like yourself, who has been a broad mark for the wantonness of fortune to take aim at. Word is sent me from Cuença, a town at the distance of a league hence, that some backbiter has been blackening my fair fame in the esteem of justice; who is coming with her hue and cry to disturb the repose of these rural scenes, and to lay her paw upon my person. But an old fox is too cunning to be caught in a trap. This is not the first time that I have cut and run before the bloodhounds of the law. But, thanks to myself for having my wits about me, I have always ended the chase in a whole skin, and held myself in readiness for another. It is now time to assume another form; for, whether you like me best in my old skin or my new, I cast my hermit's decrepit slough, to bask in the sunshine of youth and vigor.

To suit the action to the word, he threw off the incumbrance of his ecclesiastical petticoat, and stood forth to view in a doublet of black serge with slashed sleeves. Then off went his cap, and snap went a string, which supported the hoary honors of a beard, and our anchorite was at once transformed to a brawny ruffian of eight-and-twenty or thirty. Brother Antony, following a good example, discarded the outward show of religion, treated his fiery beard as the snowy one had been handled just before, and pulled out of an old worm-eaten trunk a sorry rag of a cassock, with which he invested his person. But what words can express my surprise, when Signor Don Raphael presented himself to my view, like a phœnix from the ashes of the old bead-counter! To complete the trick of the pantomime, brother Antony was turned into my faithful vassal and trusty squire, Ambrose de Lamela. Here are miracles! exclaimed I in a quandary; as far as I can perceive, we are all hail fellow well met! You never were more lucky in your life, Signor Gil Blas, said Don Raphael, with a brazenfaced good humor: you have fallen among old friends when you least expected it. It must be owned you have a crow to pluck with us; but let the past be buried in oblivion, and thank heaven, here we are together again. Ambrose and I will serve under your banner; and let me tell you, you will have subalterns of no contemptible prowess. You may object to our morals; but they are better in the main than many a hypocrite's pretensions. We never assassinate, and rarely maltreat: and that in pure self-defence. The only liberty we take with society is to live at free quarters: and though robbery may be considered as containing some little spice of injustice, the necessity

TAICHON·L·C·

"I CAST MY HERMIT'S DECREPIT SLOUGH."

we labor under of committing it restores its equilibrium to the scale. Even join your fortune with ours: you will lead a life of hazard, but of variety. Our predatory peregrinations have every pastoral beauty except innocence, and the want of that is more than counterpoised by subtlety and stratagem. Not but, with all our forecast, a certain mechanical concatenation of second causes sometimes frustrates our best-concerted projects, and drags our philosophy through the mire. But a ducking now and then only makes us swim the better. The seasons must all be taken in their turns; the blanks as well as the prizes must be drawn in the cheating lottery of life.

Courteous stranger, pursued the pretended hermit, speaking to Don Alphonso, we extend the proposal of partnership to you, and it may be a question whether you will better yourself by rejecting it, in the lamentable condition of your affairs; for, to say nothing of the chance-medley for which you are at hide and seek, your fortune is probably a little out at elbows. Most lamentably so, said Don Alphonso; and hence, since the truth must out, are my forebodings more dark than even my present evils. That is the very thing! replied Don Raphael. You were sent by our better genius to join the party. You will find no such good berth in the honest part of the world. Your wants will all be supplied, and you may laugh at the vigilance of your pursuers. There is not a corner in all Spain which we have not ferreted out; those who are always on the scamper see a great deal of the country. We are perfect connoisseurs in landscape, and affect Salvator Rosa's rugged scenery. There we graze in peace and freedom, secure from the brutality of justice. Don Alphonso expressed himself very much obliged to them for their kind invitation; and finding neither money in his purse, nor contrivance to procure it in his pericranium, made up his mind at once not to stand upon punctilio with morality. I too was led into a looser course than agreed with my rigid principles, by a growing friendship for this young man, whom I could not find in my heart to abandon in so perilous an enterprise.

We all four agreed to set off in a body, and never to part company. The question was put whether we should sound a retreat on the instant, or first give a peremptory summons to a flagon of excellent wine, which brother Antony had invested by regular approaches at Cuença the day before; but Raphael, a more experienced general than any of us, represented that the first thing to be done was to render our own camp impregnable, for which purpose he proposed that we should march all night, to gain a very thick wood between Villardesa and Almodabar, where we should halt, as in a friendly country, and recruit after the fatigues of the campaign. These general orders were approved of in council. Our lay hermits then went about packing up their baggage and provisions, which were swung in two bundles across the back of Don Alphonso's horse. We were not long in our preparations, after which we sheered off from the hermitage, leaving a rich booty to legal rapine in the saintly paraphernalia of the two hermits; including a white beard and a red one, two rickety bedsteads, a table without a leg, a chest without a bottom, two chairs without any seats, and an unmutilated image of St. Pacomo.

Our march was continued the whole night, and we began to chafe and feel other inconveniences, when at daybreak we hailed the wood where our toils were to end. Sailors after a long voyage work the ship with double alacrity at sight of their native land. So it was with us, we pushed forward and got to our journey's end by sunrise. Dashing into the thickest of the wood, we pitched upon a retired and pleasant spot, where the turf was circled in by tall and branching oaks, whose gigantic limbs, interwoven over our heads, formed a natural vault, not to be penetrated even by noonday heat. We took the bridle off the horse to let him feed after he was unloaded. Then down we sat, pulling out of brother Antony's wallet some large pieces of bread and good substantial slices of roast meat, at which we began pegging with all possible pertinacity. Nevertheless, let our appetites be as obstinate as they might, we every now and then suspended the fray to spar a little with the flagon, which returned our blows till it made us reel again.

About the end of the conflict, Don Raphael said to Don Alphonso—My brave comrade, after the confidence you have reposed in me, it is but fair that in my turn I should recount the history of my life to you with the same sincerity. You will do me a great favor, answered the young man; and an equal one to me, chimed in I. My curiosity is all alive to know your adventures, for doubtless they must afford much matter of useful speculation. You may rest assured of that, replied Don Raphael; and I mean to leave behind me a history of my own times. The composition shall be the amusement of my old age, for I am as yet in the prime of life, and mean to furnish in propriâ personâ many new hints for my commonplace-book. But we are all weary, let us recruit with some hours of sleep. While we three lie down, Ambrose shall keep watch for fear of a surprise, and shall then take a nap in his turn. For though, to all appearance, we are here in perfect safety, it is always good to keep a sentry at the out-posts. After this precaution, he stretched himself along upon the grass. Don Alphonso did the same. I followed their example, and Lamela performed the office of a scout.

Don Alphonso, so far from getting any rest, was incessantly brooding over his misfortunes, and I could not get a wink of sleep. As for Don Raphael, he snored most sonorously. But he awoke in little more than an hour, when finding us in a listening mood, he said to Lamela—My friend Ambrose, you may now yield to the gentle influence of Morpheus. No, no, answered Lamela, my sleepy fit is over and though I know all the passages of your life by rote, they are so instructive to the practitioners of our art and mystery, that I do not care how often I hear the tale over again. Without further preface, Don Raphael began the narrative of his adventures in these terms.

BOOK THE FIFTH.

CHAPTER I.

HISTORY OF DON RAPHAEL.

I MADE my entrance on the stage of life at Madrid, where my mother was an actress, famous for dramatic, and infamous for her intriguing talents. Her name was Lucinda. As for my father, every man must have one; but my arithmetic is too scanty to determine the number of mine. It might indeed be a matter of history, that such or such a man of fashion was dangling after my mother at the epoch of my arrival in this system; but then, that mere fact would by no means warrant a deduction that any individual gallant of the mother must therefore be the father of the child. A lady, so eminent as she was in so notorious and wholesale a profession, must have many strings to her bow; where her blandishments are most publicly lavished, her favors are most sparingly bestowed: there is a show article or two for public exhibition, but her everyday wares are cheap, and hackneyed to the meanest purchaser.

There is nothing like taking scandal by the beard, and treating the opinion of the world with heroic indifference. Lucinda, instead of cooping me up in a garret at home, made no scruple about owning her little bastard, but took me in her hand to the theatre with a modest assurance, regardless how the tongue of rumor might babble at her expense, or how the laugh of malice might peal at my unlucky appearance. In short, I was her pet, and came in for the caresses of all the men who frequented the house. One would have sworn that nature pleaded in my favor, and inspired each of them with a father's pride in the brat they had clubbed for. The twelve first years of my life were suffered to waste away in all kinds of frivolous amusements. Scarcely did they teach me to read and write. Still less was it thought of any consequence to initiate me in the principles of my religion. To dance, to sing, to play on the guitar, was the sum total of my early attainments. With these gifts and graces for my only acquisitions, the Marquis of Leganez asked for me to be about his only son, who was nearly of my own age. Lucinda gave her consent without reluctance, and it was then that I began to mind a little what I was about. Young Leganez could not reproach me with my ignorance, his little lordship was not cast in a scientific mold, for he scarcely knew a letter of his alphabet, though he had been under private tuition for fifteen months. None of his masters could make anything of him, patience was never formed to engage in so unequal a match. To be sure, they were expressly forbid to exercise any severity on his noble carcase, their orders were to teach, not to torture him; and this tender precaution, acting on a subject of insufferably untoward dispositions, was the means of throwing to the dogs all the mental physic they poured in; he would none of it.

But the verb-grinder engendered in his noddle a most ingenious device, by which to keep this troublesome young lordling in awe, without trenching on his foolish father's injunctions. This scheme was no other than to flog me whenever that scape-grace Leganez had incurred the penalty of the rod, and this vicarious execution was inflicted with the utmost rigor. My consent to the transfer had never been asked, and there was nothing in the act itself to recommend it; so that my only chance was to run away, and appeal to my mother against so arbitrary a discipline. However her maternal feelings might inwardly revolt, no trace of woman's weakness could be detected in her manner of receiving my complaint. The Leganez connection was too important to be lost for a few whippings; and away went she, dragging her culprit into the presence of his tormentor, who by this act of hers became master of broom field. Experience had convinced him that the success of his invention corresponded with its felicity. He therefore went on improving the mind and manners of the little grandee at the expense of my skin. Remorse for his delinquencies was to be excited only by sympathy; so that whenever it became necessary to make a bloody example, my seat of vengeance was firked most unmercifully. The running account between young Leganez and me was all on one side, and scarcely a day passed but he sinned on tick and suffered by attorney. By the nearest calculation of whole numbers, there went somewhere about a hundred cuts to teach him each single letter of the alphabet; so that if you multiply 100 by 24 for stupidity, and add an o to the amount for moral offences, you will have the sum total of the belaboring that his education cost me.

This thick and threefold companionship with birch was not the only rub; my path through this family was more beset with thorns than sweetened by flowers. As my birth and connections were no secret, the whole of the establishment, to the very refuse of the household, the stable-boys and scullions, twitted me with my shameful origin. This stuck so terribly in my throat that I made my escape once more, but not without borrowing my tutor's ready money, amounting to upwards of a hundred and fifty ducats, for an indefinite period, and without interest. Thus was the account settled between us, since he had made a property of my hide for a scarecrow, it was but fair that I should have a finger in the earnings of his arm. For a first attempt at thieving both the plan and execution were hopeful. A hue and cry was raised for two days, it was hot while it lasted, but I lay snug, and they missed me. Madrid was no longer a fit hiding-place, so I took to cover in Toledo, and the hounds were thrown out.

I was just then entering into my fifteenth year. What a happy fellow, at such an early age, to shape my own conduct and be in a condition of forming a set of morals for myself! I soon scraped acquaintance with some pleasant youths, who rescued me from the dominion of prejudice, and shared liberally with me in the sin of spending what was not my own. By degrees I rose in society and leagued myself with a set of professional sharpers, who found me so fine a subject to work upon, that a short time, with plenty of practice, put me in possession of all the most desperate jobs. At the expiration of five years, an itch for traveling laid hold of me. I therefore took leave of my comrades and got as far as Alcantara, wishing to commence my peregrinations with the province of Estremadura. In this my first excursion, an opportunity of keeping in my hand occurred; and I was too diligent a practitioner to let it escape. As I was on foot, and loaded moreover with a pretty heavy knapsack, I halted from time to time to avail myself of the shade, and recruit a little under the trees which lined the highway. At one of these baits I picked up two young gentlemen, who were chatting at their ease upon the grass, and inhaling the freshness of the breeze. My mode of accosting them was suited to the occasion ; nor did its familiarity seem to be taken in ill part. The eldest could not be more than fifteen—a couple of as practicable greenhorns as ever fell into the hands of a man of genius. Courteous stranger, said the youngest, we are the sons of two rich citizens at Placentia. Longing extremely to see the kingdom of Portugal, we have each of us begged a hundred pistoles from our friends, and are setting out to satisfy our curiosity. Traveling on foot as we do, we shall be able to get a good way with that supply, shall we not? What do you think of it? If I had as much, answered I, they might take me who could catch me. I would scour over the four known quarters of the globe, and then set out on new discoveries. Fire and fury! Two hundred pistoles! Why it is an entail for a dukedom! You ought to lay by out of the interest. If it is agreeable to you, gentlemen, I will club with you as far as Almeria, whither I am going to take possession of an estate left me by an uncle who was settled there for twenty years or upwards.

My young cockneys testified at once the pleasure they should derive from my company. Whereupon, when we were all three a little refreshed, we trudged on towards Alcantara, where we arrived early in the afternoon. No inn but the best was fit to hold such guests. We asked for a room, and were shown into one where there was a press with a good strong lock upon it. Supper was ordered without delay ; but as some time was required to get it ready, I proposed to my traveling companions a gentle saunter about the town. The party seemed perfectly agreeable. We locked up our knapsacks in the press, the key of which one of the citizens put in his pocket, and out sallied we from the inn. The churches were the best lions we met with in our way ; and while we were gaping about the principal, I pretended to have recollected on a sudden some very urgent business. Gentlemen, said I to my companions, it has just come across me that a good man of Toledo gave me a commission to say two words on his behalf to a merchant who lives hard by

this church.   Have the goodness to wait for me here, I will be back
in a moment.   With this excuse, I went off like a shot, in the
direction of our inn.   The press was my point of attack—I forced
the lock, ransacked the baggage of my young citizens, and laid a
sacrilegious hand on their pistoles.   Poor youths!   How they were
to pay their reckoning, it was not for me to presume even to guess,
for most assuredly I stripped them of all the natural means.   After
this feat, I decamped as expeditiously as my legs could carry me
from the town, and took the direction of Merida, without caring a
curse what became of the young brood I had plucked.

Such a windfall as this placed me in a condition of traveling
merrily.   Though in the very blush of youth, a certain forecast was
not wanting to carry me discreetly through the world, and keep my
head above water.   It must be admitted without question, that I
was a youth of forward parts for my age, and unfettered by the prejudices of innocence.   I determined to buy a mule, and cheapened
one at the first market town.   My knapsack was metamorphosed
into a portmanteau, and by degrees I began to put on the man of
consequence.   On the third day a man came across me singing

vespers with lungs like a pair of bellows on the highway. By his air, he seemed to be a musician of the church establishment, and I accosted him accordingly. Well done, my holy howler of the hallelujahs! You sing your penitential ditties at a good jovial pitch. To all appearance you sol-fa with your whole heart and soul. Good sir, replied he, I belong, with your good leave, to the musical department of the Catholic church: and it is my common practice to keep my devotion and my wind in play by the rehearsal of an anthem or two as I travel along the road.

With this disposition to be sociable, we soon got into conversation. It was clear to me that I had fallen in with a character not to be despised in point of shrewdness, nor indisposed to society or merriment. He was four or five-and-twenty. My companion being on foot, I slackened my pace, for the pleasure of chatting with him. Among other things, we talked about Toledo. I am perfectly well acquainted with that city, said the brazen-lunged torturer of anthems. It was my residence for a considerable time, and my connections there are not altogether contemptible. And in what part of the town, interrupted I, did you reside? In the New Street, was his answer. I was hand in glove with Don Vincent de Buena Garra, Don Matthias de Cordello, and two or three other gentlemen of very considerable fashion. We lived together; took our meals at the same mess, and, in short, were scarcely ever asunder. It was a charming society! This avowal was no small surprise to me, for it is to be understood, that the gentlemen whose names he cited with so pompous an air were the very sharpers with whom I had been affiliated at Toledo. Why, thou degenerate vicar choral! exclaimed I, these fine blades of whom thou hast been boasting are among the number of my acquaintance also, for I too have lived with them in the New Street; we were hand in glove, took our meals at the same mess, and, in short, were scarcely ever asunder. You are a wag! replied he, with a knowing wink, that is to say, you got into the gang three years ago, when I left it My motive for quitting such a worshipful fraternity, resumed I, was an itch for traveling. I mean to make the tour of Spain. A little more knowledge of the world will make me quite another thing. Doubtless, said he, there is no possible way but traveling to rub off the rust, or bring wit, talent, and address to perfection. It is for the self-same reason that I too turned my back upon Toledo, though the time glided away there very agreeably. But thanks to a kind providence, which has yoked me with a laborer in my own vineyard, when I least expected it. Let us join our forces, let us travel the same road, let us make a joint-stock out of our neighbors' purses, let us rob, let us cheat, let us avail ourselves of every opportunity that may offer of exemplifying our theory, and improving our practice, in the noble art on which our skill is employed.

The proposal was made in so candid a spirit, so like a citizen of the world, untainted with the selfishness of your honest men, that I closed in with it at once. My confidence was surrendered at the first summons to the frankness with which he volunteered his own. We spoke our free hearts each to the other. I dilated all my pilgrimage, and he spake of most disastrous chances, of moving accidents through which he had passed even from his boyish days to this very moment of his ripe and rampant roguery. It appeared that he was on his way from Portalegre, whence he had been obliged to decamp with the utmost expedition on account of a little swindling transaction in which his luck happened not to keep pace with his ingenuity. The habit he wore was sacrilegiously adopted as a cloak to his person and real character, since he thought it safest to be near the church, however far from God. Thus did we two share all our counsel, and pledge our brother's vows, till we grew together like a double cherry, and determined, with two seeming bodies but one heart, to incorporate our voices and minds in some master-stroke at Merida. If it took, well and good; if not, we had only to cut and run. From this moment, community of goods, that pure and simple feature of patriarchal life, was enacted as a law between us. Moralez, it is true, for that was my fellow-traveler's name, did not find himself in the most splendid condition possible. His funds were limited to five or six ducats, with a few little articles in a bag. I therefore was the moneyed man of the firm; but then there was brass in his forehead for an inexhaustible coinage, and the seeming of a saint when he played the devil most. So on we journeyed on the ride-and-tie principle, and arrived in humble cavalcade at Merida.

We put up at an inn near the skirts of the town, where my comrade changed his dress. When he had rigged himself in layman's attire, we took a turn up and down, to reconnoitre the ground, and see if we could pick out some opportunity of laboring in our vocation. Had it been our good fortune to have lived before Homer that old apologist for sharping by wholesale would have dignified our excursion with a smile.

> Not half so keen, fierce vultures of the chase
> Stoop from the mountains on the feathered race, &c.

To descend into plain prose, we were ruminating on the chapter of accidents, and hammering out some theme for the employment of our industry, when we espied a grey-headed old gentleman in the street, sword in hand, defending himself against three men who were thrusting at him with all their might and main. The unfairness of the match was what stuck in my throat, so that flying, with the spirit of a prize-fighter, to see fair play, I made common cause with the old man. Moralez followed up my blows. We proved ourselves a match for the three assailants, and put them completely to the rout.

Our rescued friend was profuse in his acknowledgments. We are in rapture, said I, at our good luck in being here so seasonably for your assistance: but let us at least know to whom we have been so fortunate as to be serviceable; and what inducement those three men could possibly have for their murderous attempt. Gentlemen replied he, my obligations are too great to hesitate about satisfying your curiosity; my name is Jerome de Moyadas, a gentleman of this town, living on my means. One of these cut-throat rascals, from whom you have rescued me, professes to be in love with my daughter. He asked her of me in marriage within these few days; and for want of gaining my consent in a quiet way, has just attempted to force himself into my daughter's good graces by sending me into the other world. And may we take the liberty, rejoined I, of inquiring further, why you were so obdurate to the proposals of this enamored swain? I will explain the whole to you at once, said he. I had a brother, a merchant in this town; his name was Austin. Two months ago he happened to be at Calatrava, and took up his abode with his correspondent, Juan Velez de la Membrilla. They got to be as loving as turtles; and my brother, to clinch the connection, engaged my daughter Florence to his good friend's son, not doubting but he had influence enough with me to redeem his pledge when he returned to Merida. Accordingly, he no sooner opened himself on the subject than I consented out of pure fraternal affection. He sent Florence's picture to Calatrava; but, alas! he did not live to put the finishing hand to his own work. We laid him with his forefathers three weeks ago! On his death-bed, he besought me not to dispose of my girl but in favor of his correspondent's son. I satisfied his mind on that point; and this is the reason why I have refused Florence to the suitor by whom I was assaulted, though the match would have been a very desirable one. But my word is my idol; and we are in daily expectation of Juan Velez de la Membrilla's heir, who is to be my son-in-law, though I know no more of him, nor of his father neither, than if they were just imported from an undiscovered island. But I beg pardon; this is an old man's garrulity. Yet you yourselves led me into the scrape.

This tale did I swallow with a greedy ear; and pouncing at once upon a part to play, which my fruitful imagination suggested, I put on an air of inordinate surprise, and ventured at all hazards to lift my eyes upward to a purer region. Then turning to my father-in-law, with an expression of feeling which nothing but hypocrisy could personate: Ah! Signor de Moyadas, is it possible that, on my arrival at Merida, I should enjoy the heartfelt triumph of rescuing from foul assassination the honored parent of my peerless love? This exclamation produced all the astonishment it was levelled to excite in the old citizen. Even Moralez himself stared like an honest man, and showed by his face that there was a degree of impudence to which his conceptions had not hitherto risen. What! do not my ears deceive me? exclaimed the old gentleman. And are you really the son of my brother's correspondent? Really and truly, Signor Jerome de Moyadas rejoined I with impregnable effrontery, and a hug around his neck that had nearly sent him after his brother. Behold the selected mortal of his species, to whose arms the adorable Florence is devoted! But these nuptial anticipations, transporting as they are, must yield to the anguish of my soul for the demise of their founder. Poor Austin! He is gone, and we must all follow! I should be ingratitude personified, if my heart was not lacerated and rent by the death of a man to whom I owe all my hopes of bliss.　At the term of this period, I squeezed good Jerome's wezand once more, and drew the back of my hand across my eyes, to wipe away the tears it had not been convenient to shed.　Moralez, who by this time had conned over the pretty pickings to be made out of this juggle, was not wanting to play his underpart.　He passed himself off for my servant, and improved upon his master in lamentation for the untimely death of Signor Austin.　My honored master Jerome, exclaimed he, what a loss have you sustained, since your brother is no more !　He was such an honest man.　Honest men are not to be met with every day.　A superfine sample of commerce !　A dealer in friendship without a percentage !　A dealer in merchandise without an underhand advantage !　A dealer who dealt as dealers very seldom do deal !

We had our hands to play against a man who was a novice at the game.　Simple and cullible, so far from smelling out the rat, he took his stink for a nosegay.　And why, said he, did you not come straight to my house ?　It was not friendly to put up at an inn.　On the footing we are likely to be upon, there should be none of those punctilios.　Sir, said Moralez, helping me out of the scrape, my master is a little too much given to stand upon ceremony.　Though to be sure, in the present instance, he is in some degree excusable for declining to appear before in this uncouth trim.　We have been robbed upon the road, and have lost all our traveling equipage.　My lad, interrupted I, has let the cat out of the bag, Signor de Moyadas.　This unlucky accident has prevented me from paying my respects sooner.　True love is diffident ; nor could I venture in this garb into the presence of a mistress who was unacquainted with my person.　I was therefore waiting the return of a servant whom I have sent to Calatrava.　Such a trifle, rejoined the old man, must not deprive us of your company ; and I insist upon it, that you make my house your home from this very moment.

With such sort of importunity, he forced me into his family : but as we were on our way, the pretended robbery was a natural topic of conversation ; and I should have made light of my baggage, though the loss was very considerable, had not Florence's picture unluckily formed a part of the booty !　The old codger chuckled at that, and observed, that such a loss was easily repaired : the original was worth five hundred per cent more than the copy.　To make me amends, as soon as we got home, he called his daughter, a girl of not more than sixteen, with a person to have reclaimed a libertine, if beauty ever possessed that power except in romance.　You behold, said he, the bale of goods my late brother has consigned to you.　Oh ! my good sir, exclaimed I in an impassioned tone, words are not wanting to assure me that this must be the lovely Florence : those bewitching features are engraven on my memory, their impression is indelible on my heart.　If the portrait I have lost, the mere outline of these embodied charms, could kindle passion by its cold and lifeless likeness, judge what must be my agitation, my transport at this moment.　Such language is too flattering to be sincere, said Florence ; nor am I so weak and vain as to be persuaded that my merits warrant it. That is right! interchange your fine speeches, my children! This was a good-natured encouragement from the father, who at once left me alone with his daughter, and taking Moralez by the hand, said to him, My friend, those who made so free with your baggage, doubtless did not stand upon any ceremony with your money. Very true, sir, answered my colleague, an overpowering band of robbers poured down upon us near Castil-Blazo, and left us not a rag but what we carry on our backs; but we are in momentary expectation of receiving bills of exchange, and then we shall appear once more like ourselves.

While you are waiting for your bills of exchange, replied the old man, taking a purse out of his pocket, here are a hundred pistoles with which you may do as you please. Oh, sir! rejoined Moralez, as if he were shocked, my master will never take them. You do not know him. Heaven and earth! he is a man of the nicest scruples in money matters. Not one of your shabby fellows, always spunging upon his friends, and ready to take up money wherever he can get it! Running in debt is ratsbane to him. If he is to beg his bread or go into an hospital, why there is an end of it! but as for borrowing, he will never be reduced to that. So much the better! said the good burgess: I value him the more for his independence. Running in debt is a mean thing; it ought to be ratsbane to him and everybody else. Your people of quality, to be sure, may plead prescription in their favor, there is a sort of privileged swindling, not incompatible with high honor, in high life. If tradesmen were to be paid, they would be too nearly on a level with their employers. But as your master has such upright principles, heaven forbid they should be violated in this house! Since any offer of pecuniary assistance would hurt his feelings, we must say no more about it. As the point seemed to be settled, the purse was for steering its course back again into the pocket; but my provident partner laid hold of Signor de Moyadas by the arm, and delayed the convoy. Stay, sir, said he, whatever aversion my master may have to borrowing on a general principle, and considered as borrowing, yet there is a light in which, with good management, he may be brought to look kindly on your hundred pistoles. In fact, it is only in a mercantile point of view, as an affair of debtor and creditor between strangers, that he holds this formal doctrine; but he is free and easy enough where he is on a family footing. Why, there is his own father! It is only ask and have; and he does ask and have accordingly. Now you are going to be a second father to him, and are fairly entitled to be put on the same confidential footing. He is a young man of nice discrimination, and will doubtless think you entitled to the compliment.

By thus shifting his ground, Moralez got possession of the old gentleman's purse. As for the girl and myself, we were engaged in a little agreeable flirting; but were soon joined by our honored parent, who interrupted our tête-à-tête. He told Florence how much he was obliged to me, and expressed his gratitude to myself, in terms which left no doubt of our being a very happy family. I made the most of so favorable a disposition, by telling the good man, that if he would bestow on me an acknowledgment the near-est to my heart, he must hasten my marriage with his daughter. My eagerness was not taken amiss. He assured me, that in three days at latest I should be a happy bridegroom, and that instead of six thousand ducats, the fortune he had promised to give my wife, he would make it up ten, as a substantial proof how deeply he felt himself indebted to me for the service I had rendered him.

Here we were, therefore, quite at home with our good friend Jerome de Moyadas, sumptuously entertained, and catching every now and then a vista vision of ten thousand ducats, with which we proposed to march off abruptly from Merida. Our transports, however, were not without their alloy. It was by no means im-probable that within three days the bonâ fide son of Juan Velez de la Membrilla might come and interrupt our sport. This fear had for its foundation more than the weakness of our nerves. On the very next morning, a sort of clodpole, with a portmanteau across his shoulders, knocked at the door of Florence's father. I was not at home at the time, but my colleague had to bear the brunt of it. Sir, said the rustic to our sagacious friend, I belong to the young gentleman at Calatrava who is to be your son-in-law—to Signor de la Membrilla. We have both just come off our journey : he will be here in an instant, and sent me forward to prepare you for his ar-rival. Hardly had these unaccountable tidings been announced, when the master appeared in person ; which stretched the old fel-low's blinkers into a stare, and put Moralez a little to the blush.

Young Pedro was what we call a tall fellow of his inches. He began at once paying his compliments to the master of the house ; but the good man did not give him time to finish his speech ; and turning towards my partner in iniquity, asked what was the mean-ing of all this. Hereupon Moralez, whose power of face was not to be exceeded by any human impudence, boldly asserted our iden-tity, and said to the old gentleman—Sir, these two men here before you belong to the gang which pillaged us on the highway. I have a perfect recollection of their features ; and in particular could swear to him who has the effrontery to call himself the son of Sig-nor Juan Velez de la Membrilla. The old citizen gulped down the lies of Moralez like nectar, and told the intruders, on the supposi-tion of their being the impostors—Gentlemen, you are come the day after the fair the trick was a very good one, but it will not pass ; the enemy has taken the ground before you. Pedro de la Membrilla has been under this roof since yesterday. Have all your wits about you, answered the young man from Calatrava ; you are nursing a viper in your bosom. Be assured that Juan Velez de la Membrilla has neither chick nor child but myself. And what rela-tion is the hangman to you ? replied the old dupe : you are better known than liked in this house Can you look this young man in the face ? or can you deny that you robbed his master ? If I were anywhere but under your roof, rejoined Pedro in a rage, I would punish the insolence of this scoundrel who fancies to pass me off for a highwayman He is indebted for his safety to your presence. which puts a curb upon my choler. Good sir, pursued he, you are grossly imposed on. I am the favored youth to whom your brother Austin has promised your daughter. Is it your pleasure for me to produce the whole correspondence with my father on the subject of the impending match? Will you be satisfied with Florence's picture sent me by him as a present a little while before his death?

No, put in the old burgess crustily; the picture will work just as strongly on my conviction as the letters. I am perfectly aware by what chance they all fell into your hands; and if you will take a stupid fellow's advice, Merida will soon be rid of such rubbish. A quick march may save you a trouncing. This is beyond all bearing, screamed out the young royster with an overwhelming vehemence. My name shall never be stolen from me, and assumed by a common cheat with impunity; neither shall my person be confounded with that of a freebooter. There are those in this town who can identify me: they are forthcoming, and shall expose the fallacy by which you are prejudiced against me. With this assurance he withdrew, attended by his servant, and Moralez kept possession of the field. The adventure had even the effect of determining Jerome de Moyadas to fix the wedding for the very time being. Accordingly he went his way, for the purpose of giving the necessary orders for the celebration.

Though my colleague in knavery was well enough pleased to see Florence's father in a humor so pat for our purposes, he was not without certain scruples of conscience about our safety. It was to be feared, lest the probable proceedings of Pedro might be followed up by awkward consequences; so that he waited impatiently for my arrival, to make me acquainted with what had occurred. I found him over head and ears in a brown study. What is the matter, my friend? said I, seemingly there is something upon your mind. Indeed there is, and something that will be minded, answered he. At the same time he let me into the affair. Now you may judge, added he after a pause, whether we have not some food for reflection. It is your ill star, rash contriver, which has thrown us into this perplexity. The idea, it must be confessed, was full of fire and ingenuity; had it answered in the application, your renown would have been emblazoned in the chronicles of our fraternity; but according to present appearances, the run of luck is against us, and my counsels incline to a prudent avoidance of all explanations, by quietly sneaking off with the market-penny we have made of the silly old fellow's credulity.

Master Moralez, replied I to this desponding speech, you give way to difficulties with more haste than good speed. Such pusillanimity does but little honor to Don Matthias de Cordel, and the other gallant blades with whom you were affiliated at Toledo. After serving a campaign under such experienced generals, it is not soldierly to shrink from the perils of the field. For my part, I am resolved to fight the battles of these heroes over again, or, in more vulgar phrase, to prove myself a chip from the old blocks. The precipice which makes your head turn giddy only stiffens my sinews to surmount the toils of the way, and push forward to the end of our career. If you arrive at your journey's end in a whole skin.

said my companion, I will myself be your biographer, and set your
fame far above all the parallels of Plutarch.

Just as Moralez was finishing this learned allusion, Jerome de
Moyadas came in. You shall be my son-in-law this very evening,
said he. Your servant must have given you an account of what
has just passed. What say you to the impudence of the scoundrel
who wanted to make me believe that he was the son of my brother's correspondent. Honored sir, answered I, with a melancholy air,
and in a tone of voice the most insinuating that ever cajoled the
easy faith of a dotard, I feel within me that it is not in my nature
to carry on an imposition without betraying it in my countenance.
It now becomes necessary to make you a sincere confession. I am
not the son of Juan Velez de la Membrilla. What is it you tell me?
interrupted the old man, out of breath with surprise, and out of his
wits with apprehension. So then! you are not the young man to
whom my brother . . . . . For pity's sake, sir, interrupted I in my
turn, condescend to give me a hearing patiently to the end of my
story. For these eight days have I doted to distraction on your
daughter; and this dotage, this distraction, has riveted me to Merida. Yesterday, after having rescued you from your danger, I was
making up my mind to ask her of you in marriage; but you gave
a check to my passion and put a tie upon my tongue, by the intelligence that she was destined for another. You told me that your
brother, on his death-bed, enjoined you to give her to Pedro de la
Membrilla; that your word was pledged, and that you were the
sworn vassal and bondman of your veracity. These circumstances,
it must be owned, were overwhelming in the extreme; and my romantic passion, at the last gasp of its despair, gained breath by the
stratagem with which the god of love inspired me. I must at the
same time declare that a trick is at the best but a mean thing, and,
however sanctified by the motive, my conscience recoiled at the delusion. Yet I could not but think that my pardon would be granted
on the discovery, when it should come out that I was an Italian
prince traveling through this country as a private gentleman. My
father reigns supreme over a nest of inaccessible valleys, lying between Switzerland, the Milanese, and Savoy. It could not but occur to me that you would be agreeably surprised when I should un-
fold to you my birth, and having married Florence under my fictitious character, should announce to her the rank she had attained,
with all the rapture of an enamored husband, and all the stage effect of a hero in tragedy or romance. But heaven, pursued I, with
an hypocritical softening down of my accents, has visited my sins
by cutting me off from such a perennial stream of joy. Pedro de
la Membrilla was introduced upon the scene; he must have his
name back again, whatever the restitution may cost me. Your
promise binds you hand and foot to fix upon him for your son-in-
law; it is your duty to give him the preference, without taking my
rank and station into the account; without mercy on the forlorn
condition to which you are going to reduce me. To be sure, it
might be said, but then I should say it who ought not to say it,
that your brother had only the authority of an uncle over your

daughter, that you are her father, and that there is more right and reason in discharging an actual debt of gratitude towards your preserver, than in being mealy-mouthed about a verbal promise which would press but lightly on the conscience of the most scrupulous casuist.

Yes, without doubt, that argument is indisputable, exclaimed Jerome de Moyadas ; and on that ground there can no longer be any question between you and Pedro de la Membrilla. If my brother Austin were still living, he would not think it bad morality to give the preference to a man who has saved my life, nor a bad speculation to close the bargain with a prince who has not disdained to court our alliance. It were an absolute suicide on the part of all my opening prospects ; the frantic desperation of an acknowledged incurable, not to dispose of my daughter so illustriously, not to solicit your highness's acceptance of her hand. And yet, sir, resumed I, these things are not to be determined without due deliberation ; look at your own interests and safety with a microscopic eye, for though the illustrious channel through which my blood has flowed for ages . . . . . You are scarcely serious, interrupted he, in supposing that I can hesitate for a moment. No, may it please your highness ; it is my most humble and earnest request that you will deign, on this very evening, to honor the happy Florence with your hand. Well, then ! said I, be it so ; go yourself and be the bearer of the unlooked-for tidings, announce to her the brilliant career of her exalted destiny.

While the good citizen was putting his best foot foremost, to instill into his daughter that she had make the conquest of a prince, Moralez, who had taken in the whole conversation with greedy ear, threw himself upon his knees before me, and did homage in these bantering terms. Most potent, grave, and august Italian prince, son of a sovereign, supreme over a nest of inaccessible valleys, lying between Switzerland, the Milanese, and Savoy, permit me to humble myself at your highness's feet, in humble acknowledgment of the ecstasy into which you have thrown me. By the honor of a swindler, you are one of the wonders of our world. I always thought myself the first man in the line ; but in good truth I doff my bonnet before you, whose genius seems to supersede the lessons of experience. Then you are no longer uneasy about the result, said I to my colleague in iniquity. Oh ! as to that, not in the least, answered he. I no longer care a fig for Master Pedro ; let him come as soon as he pleases, we are a match for him. Here we are, then, Moralez and myself, safe seated on the saddle, and rising in our stirrups. We even went so far as to begin settling the course we should pursue with the fortune, on which we reckoned so securely, that if it had already been in our pockets, we could not have chuckled more triumphantly over the proverb of " a bird in the hand." Yet we were not in actual possession, which is more than legal right : and the sequel of the adventure proved to us, that many things fall out between the cup and the lip.

We very soon saw the young man of Calatrava returning. He was accompanied by two citizens and by an alguazil, whose dignity

was as much supported by his whiskers, and by the lowering overcast of his swarthy aspect, as by the weight of his official character.
Florence's father was of the party. Signor de Moyadas, said Pedro
to him, here are three honest people come to answer for me ; they
are acquainted with my person, and can tell you who I am. Yes,
undoubtedly, exclaimed the alguazil, I can depose to the fact. I
certify to all those whom it may concern, that you are known to
me : your name is Pedro, and you are the only son of Juan Velez de
la Membrilla : whosoever dares to maintain the contrary is an impostor. I believe you implicitly, master alguazil, said the good
creature Jerome de Moyadas, rather drily. Your evidence is gospel
to me, as well as that of these fair and honest tradesmen you have
brought with you. I am fully satisfied that the young gentleman
on whose behalf you come is the only son of my brother's correspondent. But what is that to me? I am no longer in the humor
to give him my daughter, so there is an end of that.

Oh ! then it is quite another matter, said the alguazil. I only
come to your house for the purpose of assuring you that this young
man is no impostor. You have the authority of a parent over your
child, and no one has any right to dictate to you how you are to
marry her, and whether you will or no. Neither do I, on my part,
interrupted Pedro, pretend to lay any force on the inclinations of
Signor de Moyadas ; but he will perhaps allow me to ask him why
he has so suddenly changed his resolution. Has he any reason to
be dissatisfied with me ? Alas ! let me at least understand, that in
losing the sweet hope of becoming his son-in-law, my promised
bliss has not been wrested from me by any misconduct of my own.
I have no complaint to make of you, answered the old man ; nay,
I will even tell you more ; it is with sincere sorrow that I find myself under the necessity of breaking my word with you, and I
heartily beseech you to forgive me for having done so. I am persuaded that you are too generous to bear me any ill-will for having thrown the balance into the scale of a rival, who has saved my
life. You see him here, pursued he, introducing my noble self, this
is the illustrious personage who threw round me the shield of his
protection in my great peril : and, the better still to apologize for
my seemingly harsh treatment of yourself, you are to know that he
is an Italian prince.

At these last words, Pedro was dumbfounded, and looked as if
he could not help it. The two tradesmen opened their eyes as
wide as they could stare, with surprise at finding themselves for the
first time in princely society. But the alguazil, in the habit of looking at things with the cross eye of suspicion, divined most per-
spicuously that this marvelous adventure must be a complete humbug ; and the verification of the prophecy was calculated to put
money into the pocket of the prophet. He therefore conned over
my countenance with a very inquisitive regard ; but as my features,
which were new to justice, threw him out most cruelly from hunting down the game he was in chase of, he had no alternative but
to try his luck on my companion. Unfortunately for my highness
of the inaccessible valleys, he knew again the hang-dog features of

Moralez; and recollecting to have seen him within the purlieus of a jail, Ay, ay! exclaimed he, this is one of my established customers. This gentleman is a particular acquaintance of mine, and you may take his character from me for one of the rankest rascals within the kingdoms and principalities of Spain. Softly, look before you leap, most adventurous alguazil, said Jerome de Moyadas, this lad, of who you draw so unfavorable a picture, is in the traveling retinue of a prince. So much the better, retorted the alguazil; a man would not desire clearer evidence on which to bring in his verdict. If we can but hang the servant, we shall soon send the master to the devil. The case is as undeniable as a feed counsel's plea; these pleasant sparks are a couple of fortune-hunters, who have laid their heads together to take you in. I am an old hound upon this scent; so that, by way of proof presumptive that these merry vagabonds are within the contemplation of the law in that case provided, I shall lodge them where they will be well taken care of. They will have plenty of time for meditation under the chastising philosophy of a turnkey; or should confinement fail to mend their morals, we have a sort of tangible discipline, which insinuates reformation by the inlet of a smarting hide. Stop there, and bethink you in good time, master officer, rejoined the old gentleman; we must not draw the cord tighter than it will bear. You never make any bones, you hangers-on of the law, about hurting the feelings of better men than yourselves. May not this servant be a common cheat, without his master being a swindler? Princes are persons of honor as a matter of course: yet the retainers to a court are inordinate rascals; it requires no conjurer to find that out. Are you playing into the hands of your deluders, with your princes? interrupted the alguazil. This new manufacturer of false pretences is a proficient, take my word for it; but I shall quench his zeal in the service, and gravel the ingenuity of his partner, with a *whereas* and a commitment in due form. The scouts of justice are all round the door, who will worry their game every inch of the chase, if they do not suffer themselves to be taken quietly on their form. So come along, may it please your serene highness, let us proceed to our destination.

This upshot of the business was a death-blow to me, as well as to Moralez; and our confusion did but infuse doubts into the mind of Jerome de Moyadas, or rather burned, sunk, and destroyed us in his esteem. He began rather to think, not without reason, that we had some little design to impose on his credulity. Nevertheless he acted on this occasion in the spirit of a man of honor and a gentleman. My good friend and protector, said he to the alguazil, your conjectures may be without foundation; on the other hand, they may turn out to have too much truth in them. Whichever of these alternatives may be the fact, let us not look too curiously into their characters. They are both young, and have time enough for amendment if they want it; let them go their ways, and withdraw whithersoever it may best please them. Make no opposition, I beseech you, to their safe egress; it is a favor which you may consider as done to me, and my motive for asking it is to acquit myself of my debt to them. If my heart was not too soft for my profession, answered the alguazil, I should lodge these pretty gentlemen in limbo, in defiance of all your pleadings in their favor; but your eloquence and my susceptibility have relaxed the stern demeanor of justice for this evening. Let them, however, leave town on the spur of the occasion: for if I come across them tomorrow, and there is any faith in an alguazil, they shall see such sport as will be no sport to them.

When it was signified to Moralez and me, culprits as we were, that we were to be let off scot free, we polished up the brass upon our foreheads a little. It was time now to bounce and swagger, and to maintain that we were men of undeniable respectability; but the alguazil looked askew at us, and muttered that least said was soonest mended. I do not know how, but those gentry have a strange knack of curbing our genius; they are complete lords of the ascendant. Florence and her dowry therefore were lost to Pedro de la Membrilla by a turn of the dice, and we may conclude that he was received as the son-in-law of Jerome de Moyadas. I took to my heels with my companion. We blundered on the road to Truxillo, with the consolation at our hearts of having at least pocketed a hundred pistoles by our frolic. An hour before nightfall we passed through a little village with the intention of putting up for the evening at the next stage. An inn of very tolerable appearance for the place attracted our notice. The landlord and landlady were sitting at the door, on a long bench such as usually graces a pot-house porch. Our host, a tall man, withered, and with one foot in the grave, was tinkling on a cracked guitar to the unbounded emolument of his wife, whose faculties seemed to hang in rapture on the performance. Gentlemen, cried out the intrepid tavern-keeper, when he found that we were not upon the halt, you will do well to stop here; you may fare worse further off. There is a devil of a three leagues to the nearest village, and you will find nothing to make you amends for what you leave behind; you may assure yourselves of that. Take a work of advice, know when you are well used; I will treat you with the fat of the land, and charge you at the lowest rate. There was no resisting such a plea. We came up to our courteous entertainers, paid them the compliments of course, and sitting down by their side, the conversation was supported by all four on the indifferent topics of the day. Our host announced himself as an officer of the Holy Brotherhood, and his rib was a fat laughing squab of a women, with outward good-nature, but with an eye to make the most of her commodities.

Our discourse was broken in upon by the arrival of from twelve to fifteen riders, some mounted on mules, others on horseback, followed by about thirty sumpter-mules laden with packages. Ah! what a princely retinue! exclaimed the landlord at the sight of so much company: where can I put them all? In an instant the village was crammed full of men and beasts. As luck would have it, there was near the inn an immense barn, where the sumpter-mules and their packages were secured; the saddle-mules and horses were taken care of in other places. As for their masters, they thought less about bespeaking beds than about calling for the bill of fare, and ordering a good supper. The host and hostess, with a servant girl whom they kept, were all upon the alert to make things agreeable. They laid a heavy hand upon all the fowls in the poul-try-yard. These precious roasts, with some undisguised rabbits, cats in the masquerade of a fricassee, and a deluging tureen of soup, stinking of cabbage and greasy with mutton fat, were enough to have given a sickener to the inveterate stomachs of a regiment.

As for Moralez and myself, we cast a scrutinizing eye on these troopers, nor were they behindhand in passing their secret judg-ments upon us. At last we came together in conversation, and it was proposed on our part, if they had no objection, that we should all sup together. They assured us that they should be extremely happy in our company. Here we are, then, all seated round the table. There was one among them who seemed to take the lead; and for whom the rest, though in the main they were on the most intimate terms with him, thought it necessary on some occasions to testify their deference. In case of a dispute, this high gentle-man assumed the umpire, he talked in a tone above the common pitch, going so far sometimes as to contradict in no very courtly phrase the sentiments of others, who, far from giving him back his own, were ready to swear to his assertions and crouch under his rebuke. By accident the discourse turned on Andalusia. Moralez happening to launch out into the praise of Seville, the man about whom I have been talking said to him—My good fellow-traveler, you are ringing the chimes on the city which gave birth to me; at least I am a native of the neighborhood, since the little town of Mayrena is answerable for my appearance in the world. I have the same story to tell you, answered my companion. I am also of Mayrena; and it is scarcely possible but that our families should be acquainted. Whose son are you? An honest notary's, replied the stranger, by name Martin Moralez. As fate will have it, ex-claimed my comrade with emotion, the adventure is very remark-able! You are then my eldest brother, Manuel Moralez? Exactly so, said the other, and if my senses do not deceive me, you your very self are my little brother Lewis, whom I left in the cradle when I turned my back upon my father's house? You are right in your conjectures, answered my honest colleague. At this dis-covery they both got up from table, and almost hugged the breath out of each other's bodies. At last Signor Manuel said to the company—Gentlemen, this circumstance is altogether marvelous. By mere chance, I have met with a brother and have been chal-lenged by him, whom I have not seen for more than twenty years; allow me to introduce him. At once all the travelers, who had risen from their seats out of curiosity and good manners, paid their compliments to the younger Moralez, and made him run the gaunt-let through their salutations. When these were over, the party returned to the table, nor did they think any more of an adjourn-ment. Bed-time never entered into their heads. The two brothers sat next to one another, and talked in a whisper about their family affairs; the other guests plied the bottle, and made merry in a louder key.

Lewis had a long conference with Manuel, and afterwards, taking me aside, said to me: All these troopers belong to the household of the Count de Montanos, whom the king has very lately appointed to the vice-regal government of Majorca. They are convoying the equipage of the viceroy to Alicant, where they are to embark. My brother, who has risen to be steward to that nobleman, proposes to take me along with him; and on the difficulty I started about leaving you, he told me that if you would be of the party, he would procure you a good berth. My dear friend, pursued he, I advise you not to stand out against this proposal. Let us take flight together for the Island of Majorca. If we find our quarters pleasant, we will fix there; and if they are otherwise, we have nothing to do but to return into Spain.

I accepted the proposal with the best grace possible. What a reinforcement, in the person of young Moralez and myself, to the household of the count! We took our departure in a body from the inn, before daybreak. We got to the city of Alicant by long stages, and there I bought a guitar, and arranged my dress in a manner suited to my new destination, before we embarked. Nothing ran in my head but the island of Majorca; and Lewis Moralez was a new man as well as myself. It should seem as though we had bid farewell to the rogueries of this wicked world. Yet, not to play the liar in the ear of so rigorous a confessor as my own conscience, we had a mind not to pass for villains incarnate, now that we had got into company that had some pretensions to decency! and that was the sum total of our honesty. The natural bent of our genius remained much the same; we were still men of business, but just now keeping a vacation. In short, we went on board gallantly and gaily in this lucid interval of innocence, and had no idea but of landing at Majorca under the especial care of Neptune and Æolus. Hardly, however, had we cleared the gulf of Alicant, when a sudden and violent storm arose, enough to have frightened better men. Now is my opportunity, or never, to speak of moving accidents by flood; to set the atmosphere on fire, and give a louder explosion to the thunder-cloud; to compare the whistling of the winds to the factions of a populace, and the rolling of the waves to the shock of conflicting hosts; with other such old-fashioned phraseologies as have been heir-looms of Parnassus from time immemorial. But it is useless to be poetical without invention. Suffice it therefore to say, in slang metaphor, that the storm was a devil of a storm, and obliged us to stand in for the point of Cabrera. This is a desert island, with a small fort, at that time garrisoned by an officer and five or six soldiers. Our reception was hospitable and cordial.

As it was necessary for us to stay there some days, for the purpose of refitting our sails and rigging, we devised various kinds of amusements to keep off the foul fiend, melancholy. Every one did as seemed good in his own eyes: some played at cards, others diverted themselves in other ways; but as for me, I went about exploring the island, with such of our gentry as had either a curiosity or a taste for the picturesque. We were frequently obliged to clamber from rock to rock ; for the face of the country is rugged, and the soil scanty, presenting a scene difficult of access, but interesting from its wildness. One day, while we were speculating on these dry and barren prospects, and extracting a moral from the vagaries of nature, who can swell into the fruitful mother and the copious nurse, or shrink into the lean and loathsome skeleton as she pleases, our sense was all at once regaled with a most delicious fragrance. We turned as with a common impulse towards the east, whence the scented gale seemed to come. To our utter astonishment, we discovered among the rocks a green plat of considerable dimensions, gay with honeysuckles more luxuriant and more odorous than even those which thrive so greatly in the climate of Andalusia. We were not sorry to approach nearer these delicious shrubs, which were wasting their sweetness in such unchecked profusion, when it turned out that they lined the entrance of a very deep cavern. The opening was wide, and the recess in consequence partially illuminated. We were determined to explore ; and descended by some stone steps overgrown with flowers on each side, so that it was difficult to say whether the approach was formed by art or nature. When we had got down, we saw several little streams winding over a sand, the yellow luster of which outrivaled gold. These drew their sources from the continual distillations of the rock within, and lost themselves again in the hollows of the ground. The water looked so clear, that we were tempted to drink of it ; and such was it freshness, that we made a party to return the next day, with some bottles of generous wine, which we were persuaded would acquire new zest from the retreat where they were to be quaffed.

It was not without regret that we left so agreeable a place : nor did we omit, on our return to the fort, boasting among our comrades of so interesting a discovery. The commander of the fortress, however, with the warmest professions of friendship, warned us against going any more to the cavern, with which we were so much delighted. And why so? said I, is there anything to be afraid of? Most undoubtedly, answered he. The corsairs of Algiers and Tripoli sometimes land upon this island, for the purpose of watering at that spring. One day they surprised two soldiers of my garrison there, whom they carried into slavery, It was in vain that the officer assumed a tone of kind dissuasion ; nothing could prevent us from going. We fancied that he meant to play upon our fears ; and the day following I returned to the cavern with three adventurous blades of our establishment. We were even fool-hardy enough to leave our fire-arms behind as a sort of bravado. Young Moralez declined being of the party : the fort and the gaming-table had more charms for him, as well as for his brother.

We went down to the bottom of the cave, as on the preceding day, and set some bottles of the wine we had brought with us to cool in the rivulets. While we were enjoying them in all the luxury of elegant conviviality, our wits set in motion by the novelty of the scene, and the echo reverberating to the music of our guitars, we espied at the mouth of the cavern several abominable faces overgrown with whiskers; neither did their turbans and Turkish dresses render them a wit more amiable in our conceits. We nevertheless took it into our heads that it was a frolic of our own party, set on by the commanding officer of the fort, and that they had disguised themselves for the purpose of playing us a trick, With this impression on our minds, we set up a horse-laugh, and allowed a quiet entrance to about ten, without thinking of making any resistance. In a few moments our eyes were opened to that fatal error, and we were convinced, in sober sadness, that it was a corsair at the head of his crew, come to carry us away. Surrender, you Christian dogs, cried he in most outlandish Castilian, or prepare for instant death. At the same time the men who accompanied him leveled their pieces at us, and our ribs would have been well lined with the contents, if we had resisted in the least. Slavery seemed the better alternative than death, so that we delivered our swords to the pirate. He ordered us to be handcuffed and carried on board his vessel, which was moored not far off; then, setting sail, he steered with a fair wind towards Algiers.

Thus were we punished for having neglected the warning given us by the officer of the garrison. The first thing the corsair did was to put his hand into our pockets and make free with our money. No bad windfall for him! The two hundred pistoles from the greenhorns at Placentia; the hundred which Moralez had received from Jerome de Moyadas, and which, as ill luck would have it, were in my custody; all this was swept away without a single qualm of conscience. My companions too had their purses well lined; and it was all fish that came to the net. The pirate seemed to chuckle at so successful a drag; and the scoundrel, not contented with chousing us of our cash, insulted us with his infernal Moorish witticisms: but the edge of his satire was not half so keen as the dire necessity which made us the subject of it. After a thousand clumsy sarcasms, he called for the bottles which we had set to cool in the fountain; those irreligious Mahometans not having scrupled to load their consciences with the conveyance of the unholy fermentation. The master and his man pledged one another in many a Christian bumper, and drank to our better acquaintance with a most provoking mockery.

While this farce was acting, my comrades wore a hanging look, which testified how pleasantly their thoughts were employed. They were so much the more out of conceit with their captivity, as they thought they had drawn a prize in the lottery of human life. The island of Majorca, with all its luxuries and delights, was a melancholy contrast with their present situation. For my part, I had the good sense to take things as I found them. Less put out of my way by my misfortune than the rest, I joined in conversation with this trans-marine joker, and showed him that wit was the common language of Africa and of Europe. He was pleased with my accommodating spirit. Young man, said he, instead of groaning and sighing, you do well to arm yourself with patience, and to fall in with the current of your destiny. Play us a little air, continued he, observing that I had a guitar by my side; let us have a specimen of your skill. I complied with his command, as soon as my arms were loosened from their confinement, and began to thrum away in a style that drew down the applauses of my discerning audience. It is true that I had been taught by the best master in Madrid, and that I played very tolerably for an amateur upon that instrument. A song was then called for, and my voice gave equal satisfaction. All the Turks on board testified by gestures of admiration the delight with which my performance inspired them; from which circumstance it was but modest to conclude, that vocal music had made no very extraordinary progress in their part of the world. The pirate whispered in my ear, that my slavery should be no disadvantage to me; and that with my talents I might reckon upon an employment, by which my lot would be rendered not only supportable, but happy.

I felt somewhat encouraged by these assurances; but flattering as they were, I was not without my uneasiness as to the employment, which the corsair held out as a nameless, but invaluable boon. When we arrived in the port of Algiers, a great number of persons were collected to receive us; and we had not yet disembarked, when they uttered a thousand shouts of joy. Add to this, that the air re-echoed with a confused sound of trumpets, of Moorish flutes, and of other instruments, the fashion of that country, forming a symphony of deafening clangor, but very doubtful harmony. The occasion of these rejoicings proceeded from a false report, which had been current about the town. It had been the general talk that the renegado Mahomet, meaning our amiable pirate, had lost his life in the attack of a large Genoese vessel; so that all his friends, informed of his return, were eager to hail him with these thundering demonstrations of attachment.

We had no sooner set foot on shore, than my companions and myself were conducted to the palace of the bashaw Soliman, where a Christian secretary, questioning us individually one after another, inquired into our names, our ages, our country, our religion, and our qualifications. Then Mahomet, presenting me to the bashaw, paid my voice more compliments than it deserved, and told him that I played on the guitar with a most ravishing expression. This was enough to influence Soliman in his choice of me for his own immediate service. I took up my abode therefore in his seraglio. The other captives were led into the public market, and sold there at the usual rate of Christian cattle. What Mahomet had foretold to me on shipboard was completely verified: my condition was exactly to my mind. I was not consigned to the stronghold of a prison, nor kept to any works of oppressive labor. My indulgent master stationed me in a particular quarter, with five or six slaves of superior rank, who were in momentary expectation of being ransomed, and were therefore favored in the distribution of our tasks. The care of watering the orange-trees and flowers in the gardens was allotted as my portion. There could not be a more agreeable or less fatiguing employment.

Soliman was a man about forty years of age, well made as to figure, tolerably accomplished as to his mind, and as much of a lady's man as could be expected from a Turk. His favorite was a Cashmirian, whose wit and beauty had acquired an absolute dominion over his affections. He loved her even to idolatry. Not a day but he paid his court to her by some elegant entertainment; at one time a concert of vocal and instrumental music, at another, a dramatic performance after the fashion of the Turks, which fashion implies a loose sort of comedy, where moral and modesty enter about as much into the contemplation of the contriver, as do Aristotle and his unities. The favorite, whose name was Farrukhnaz, was passionately enamored of these exhibitions; she sometimes even got up among her own women some Arabian melodramas to be performed before her admirer. She took some of the parts herself, and charmed the spectators by the abundant grace and vivacity of her action. One day when I was among the musicians at one of these representations, Soliman ordered me to play on the guitar, and to sing a solo between the acts of the piece. I had the good fortune to give satisfaction, and was received with applause. The favorite herself, if my vanity did not mislead me, cast glances towards me of no unfavorable interpretation.

On the next day, as I was watering the orange-trees in the gardens, there passed close by me an eunuch, who, without stopping or saying a word, threw down a note at my feet. I picked it up with an emotion, strangely compounded of pleasure and alarm. I crouched upon the ground, for fear of being observed from the windows of the seraglio; and, concealing myself behind the boxes in which the orange-trees were planted, opened this unexpected enclosure. There I found a diamond of very considerable value, and these words, in genuine Castilian : " Young Christian, return thanks to heaven for your captivity. Love and fortune will render it the harbinger of your bliss : love, if you are alive to the attractions of a fine person, and fortune, if you have the hardihood to confront danger in every direction."

I could not for a moment doubt that the letter was written by the favorite sultana ; the style and the diamond were more than presumptive evidence against her. Besides that nature did not cast me in the mold of a coward, the vanity of keeping up a good understanding with the mistress of a scoundrelly Mahometan in office, and, more than all the temptations of vanity or inclination, the hope of cajoling her out of four times as much as the curmudgeon her master would demand for my ransom, put me into conceit with the intention of trying my luck at a venture, whatever risk might be incurred in the experiment I went on with my gardening, but always harping on the means of getting into the apartment of Farrukhnaz, or rather waiting till she opened a door of communication ; for I was clearly of opinion that she would not stop upon the threshold, but meet me half way in the career of love and danger. My conjecture was not altogether without foundation. The same eunuch who had led me into this amorous reverie passed the same way an hour afterwards, and said to me, Christian, have you communed with your own determinations, and will you win a fair lady, by abjuring a faint heart? I answered in the affirmative. Well, then, rejoined he, heaven sprinkle its dew upon your resolutions! You shall see me betimes to-morrow morning. With this comfortable assurance, he withdrew. The following day, I actually saw him make his appearance about eight o'clock in the morning. He made a signal for me to go along with him: I obeyed the summons; and he conducted me into a hall where was a large wrapper of canvas which he and another eunuch had just brought thither, with the design of carrying it to the sultana's apartment, for the purpose of furnishing a scene for an Arabian pantomime, in preparation for the amusement of the bashaw.

The two eunuchs unrolled the cloth, and laid me at my length on the proscenium; then, at the risk of turning the farce into a tragedy by stifling me, they rolled it up again, with its palpitating contents. In the next place, taking hold of it at each end, they conveyed me with impunity by this device into the chamber devoted to the repose of the beautiful Cashmirian. She was alone with an old slave devoted to her wishes. They helped each other to unroll their precious bale of goods; and Farrukhnaz, at the sight of her consignment, set up such an alarm of delight, as exhibited the woman of the East, without forgetting her prurient propensities. With all my natural bias towards adventure, I could not recognize myself as at once transported into the private apartment of the women, without something like an inauspicious damp upon my joy. The lady was aware of my feelings, and anxious to dissipate the unpleasant part of them, Young man, said she, you have nothing to fear. Soliman is just gone to his country-house; he is safely lodged for the day; so that we shall be able to entertain one another here at our ease.

Hints like these rallied my scattered spirits, and gave a cast to my countenance which confirmed the speculation of the favorite. You have won my heart, pursued she, and it is in my contemplation to soften the severity of your bondage. You seem to be worthy of the sentiments which I have conceived for you. Though disguised under the garb of a slave, your air is noble, and your physiognomy of a character to recommend you to the good graces of a lady. Such an exterior must belong to one above the common. Unbosom yourself to me in confidence; tell me who you are. I know that captives of superior condition and family disguise their real circumstances, to be redeemed at a lower rate; but you have no inducement to practise such a deception on me; and it would even be a precaution revolting to my designs in your favor, since I here pledge myself for your liberty. Deal with sincerity, therefore, and own to me at once that you are a youth of illustrious rank. In good earnest then, madam, answered I, it would ill become me to repay your generous partiality with dissimulation. You are absolutely bent upon it, that I should entrust you with the secret of my quality, and commands like yours are not to be questioned or resisted. I am the son of a Spanish grandee. And so it might actually have been, for anything that I know to the contrary; at all events, the sultana gave me credit for it, so that with considerable self-congratulation, at having fixed her regard on a gentleman of some little figure in the world, she assured me that it only depended on herself, whether or no we should meet pretty often in private. In fact, we were no niggards of our mutual good-will at the very first approaches. I never met with a woman who was more what a man wishes her to be. She was besides an expert linguist, above all in Castilian, which she spoke with fluency and purity. When she conceived it to be time for us to part, I got by her order into a large osier basket, with an embroidered silk covering of her own manufacture; then the two slaves who had brought me in were called to carry me out as a present from the favorite to her deluded lord; for under this pretence it is easy to screen any amorous exports from the inspection of the officers entrusted with the superintendence of the women.

As for Farrukhnaz and myself, we were not slack in other devices to bring us together; and that lovely captive inspired me by degrees with as much love as she herself entertained for me. Our good understanding was kept a profound secret for full two months, notwithstanding the extreme difficulty in a seraglio of veiling the mysteries of love for any length of time from those uninitiated, whose eyes are jaundiced by their own disqualification. Neither was the discovery made at last by the means of envious spies. An unlucky chance disconcerted all our little arrangements, and the features of my fortune were at once aggravated into a frown. One day when I had been introduced into the presence of the sultana, in the body of an artificial dragon, invented as a machine for a spectacle, while we were parleying most amicably together, Soliman, to whom we had given credit for having gone out of town, made his unwelcome appearance. He entered so abruptly into his favorite's apartment, as scarcely to leave time for the old slave to give us notice of his approach. Still less was there any opportunity to conceal me. Thus therefore, with all my enormities on my head, was I the first object which presented itself to the astonished eyes of the bashaw.

He seemed considerably startled at the sight; and his countenance flashed with indignation on the instant. I considered myself as a wretch just hovering on the brink of the grave; and death seemed arrayed in all the paraphernalia of torture. As for Farrukhnaz, it was very evident, in good truth, that she was miserably frightened; but instead of owning her crime and imploring pardon, she said to Soliman: My lord, before you pronounce my sentence, be pleased to hear my defence. Appearances, doubtless, condemn me; and it must strike you that I have committed an act of treason, worthy the most dreadful punishments. It is true, I have brought this young captive hither; it is true that I have introduced him into my apartment, with just such artifices, as I should have used if I had entertained a violent passion for him And yet, I call our great prophet to witness, in spite of these seeming irregularities, I am not faithless to you. It was my wish to converse with this Christian slave, for the purpose of disengaging him from his own sect, and proselyting him to that of the true believers. But I have found in him a principle of resistance for which I was not well prepared. I have, however, conquered his prejudices; and he came to give me an assurance that he would embrace Mahometanism.

I do not mean to deny that it was an act of duty to have contradicted the favorite flatly, without paying the least attention to the dangerous predicament in which I stood : but my spirits were taken by surprise ; the beloved partner of my imprudence was hovering on the brink of perdition; and my own fate was involved with hers. How could I do otherwise than give a silent and perturbed assent to her impious fiction ? My tongue, indeed, refused to ratify it; but the bashaw, persuaded by my acquiescence that his mistress had told him the whole truth and nothing but the truth, suffered his angry spirit to be tranquilized. Madam, answered he, I am willing to believe that you have committed no infidelity towards me; and that the desire of doing a thing agreeable to the prophet has been the means of leading you on to risk so hazardous and delicate a proceeding. I forgive, therefore, your imprudence, on condition that this captive assumes the turban on the spot. He sent immediately for a priest * to initiate me. My dress was changed with all due ceremony into the Turkish. They did just what they pleased with me ; nor had I the courage to object : or, to do myself more justice, I knew not what was becoming of me, in so dreadful a disorder of all my faculties and feelings. There are other good Christians in the world, who have been guilty of apostatizing on less imminent emergencies !

After the ceremony, I took my leave of the seraglio, to go and possess myself, under the name of Sidy Hali, of an inferior office which Soliman had given me. I never saw the sultana more; but an eunuch of hers came one day to look after me. He brought with him, as a present from his mistress, jewels to a very considerable amount, accompanied with a letter, in which the lady assured me she should never forget my generous compliance, in turning Mahometan to save her life. In point of fact, besides these rich gifts, lavished upon me by Farrukhnaz, I obtained through her interest a more considerable employment than my first, and in the course of six or seven years became one of the richest renegadoes in the town of Algiers.

You must be perfectly aware, that if I assisted at the prayers put up by the Mussulmen in their mosques, or fulfilled the other observances of their religion, it was all a mere copy of my countenance. My inclination was always uniform and determined, as to returning before my death into the bosom of our holy church ; and with this view I looked forward to withdrawing some time or other into Spain or Italy with the riches I should have accumulated. But there seemed no reason whatever against enjoying life

---

* These wandering priests are at present known in Africa by the name of Marabut. The first gymnosophists of Ethiopia most probable were nothing more.—TRANSLATOR.

in the interval. I was established in a magnificent mansion, with gardens of extent and beauty, a numerous train of slaves, and a well-appointed equipage of pretty girls in my seraglio. Though the Mahometans are forbidden the use of wine in that country, they are not backward for the most part in their stolen libations. As for me, my orgies were without either a mask or a blush, after the manner of my brother renegadoes. I remember in particular two of my bottle companions, with whom I often drank down the night before we rose from table. One was a Jew, and the other an Arabian. I took them to be good sort of people; and, with that impression, lived in unconstrained familiarity with them. One evening I invited them to sup at my house. On that very day a dog of mine died—it was a pet; we performed our pious ablutions on his lifeless clay, and buried him with all the solemn obsequies attendant on a Mahometan funeral. This act of ours was not designed to turn the religion we outwardly professed into ridicule; it was only to furnish ourselves with amusement, and give loose to a ludicrous whim which struck us in the moment of jollity, that of paying the last offices of humanity to my dog.

This action was, however, very near laying me by the heels. On the following day there came a fellow to my house, saying, Master Sidy Hali, it is no laughing matter that induces me to pay you this visit. My employer, the cadi, wants to have a word in your ear; be so good, if you please, as just to step to his office, without loss of time. An Arabian merchant, who supped with you last night, has laid an information respecting a certain act of irreverence perpetrated by you, on occasion of a dog which you buried. It is on that charge that I summon you to appear this day before the judge; and in case of failure, you are hereby warned that you will be the subject of a criminal prosecution. Away went he, leaving me to digest his discourse, but the citation stuck in my throat, and took away my appetite. The Arabian had no reason whatever to set his face against me; and I could not comprehend the meaning of the dog's trick the scoundrel had played me. The circumstance at all events demanded my prompt attention. I knew the cadi's character: a saint on the outside, but a sinner in his heart. Away went I therefore to wait on this judge, but not with empty pockets. He sent for me into his private room, and began upon me in all the vehemence of pious indignation: You are a fellow rejected out of paradise! a blasphemer of our holy law! a man loathsome and abominable to look upon! You have performed the funeral service of a Mussulman over a dog. What an act of sacrilege! Is it thus, then, that you reverence our most holy ceremonies? Have you only turned Mahometan to laugh at our devotions and our rites? My honored master, answered I, the Arabian who has told you such a cock-and-bull story is a wolf in sheep's clothing; and more than that, he is even an accomplice in my crime, if it is one, to grant such rest as to peace-parted souls to a faithful household servant, to an animal with more good qualities than half the two-legged Mahometans out of Christendom. His attachment besides to people of merit and consideration in the world was at once moral and sensible; and at his death he left several little tokens of remembrance to his friends. By his last will and testament, he bequeathed his effects in the manner therein mentioned, and did me the honor to name me for his executor. This old crony came in for twenty crowns, that for thirty, and another for a cool hundred; but your worship is interested deeply in this instrument, pursued I, drawing out my purse; he has left you residuary legatee, and here is the amount of the bequest. The cadi's gravity could not but relax, after the posthumous kindness of his deceased friend; and he laughed outright in the face of the mock executor. As we were alone, there was no occasion to make wry mouths at the purse, and my acquittal was pronounced in these words: Go, Master Sidy Hali; it was a very pious act of yours, to enlarge the obsequies of a dog, who had so manly a fellow-feeling for honest folks.

By this device I got out of the scrape; and if the hint did not increase my religion, it doubled my circumspection. I was determined no longer to open either my cellar or my soul in presence of Arabian or Jew. My bottle companion henceforward was a young gentleman from Leghorn, who had the happiness of being my slave. His name was Azarini. I was of another kidney from renegadoes in general, who impose greater hardships on their Christian slaves than do the Turks themselves. All my captives waited for the period of their ransom, without any impatient hankering after home. My behavior to them was, in truth, so gentle and fatherly, that many of them assured me they were more afraid of changing their master than anxious after their liberty; whatever magic that word may have to the ears of those who have felt what it is to be deprived of it.

One day the bashaw's corsairs came into port with considerable prizes. Their cargo amounted to more than a hundred slaves of either sex, carried off from the Spanish coast. Soliman retained but a very small number, and all the rest were sold. I happened to go to market, and bought a Spanish girl, ten or twelve years old. She cried as if her heart would break, and looked the picture of despair. It seemed strange, that at her age slavery should make such an impression on her. I told her, in Castilian, to combat with her terrors: and assured her that she was fallen into the hands of a master who had not put off humanity when he took up the turban. The little mourner, not initiated in the trade of grief, pursued the subject of her lamentations without listening to me. Her whole soul seemed to be breathed in her sighs; she descanted on her wretched fate, and exclaimed from time to time in softened accents: O my mother, why were we ever parted? I could bear my lot with patience, might we share it together. With these lamentations on her lips, she turned round towards a woman of from five-and-forty to fifty, standing at the distance of several paces, and waiting with her eyes fixed to the ground, in a determined, sullen silence, till she met with a purchaser. I asked my young bargain if the lady she was looking at was her mother. Alas! she is, indeed, sir, replied the girl; for the love of God, do not let me be parted from her. Well, then, my distressed little damsel, said I, if it will give you any pleasure, there is no more to do than to settle you both in the same quarters, and then you will give over your murmuring. On the very moment I went up to the mother, with the intention of cheapening her but no sooner did I cast my eyes on her face, than I knew again, with what emotion you may guess! the very form and pressure of Lucinda. Just heaven ' said I within myself, this is my mother ; Nature whispered it in my ear, and can I doubt her evidence? On her part, whether a keen resentment of her woes pointed out an enemy in every object on which she glanced, or else it might be my dress that disfigured me ; . . . or else I might have grown a little older in about a dozen years since she had seen me . . . . but however historians may account for it, she did not know me. But I knew her, and bought her; the pair were sent home to my house.

When they were safely lodged, I wished to surprise them with the pleasure of ascertaining who I was. Madam, said I to Lucinda, is it possible that my features should not strike you? 'Tis true, I wear whiskers and a turban but is Raphael less your son for that? My mother thrilled through all her frame at these words, looked at me with an eager gaze, my whole self rushed into her recollection, and into each other's arms we affectionately flew. I then caressed, in moderated ecstacies, her daughter, who perhaps knew as much about having a brother as I did about having a sister. Tell the truth, said I to my mother; in all your theatrical discoveries, did you ever meet with one so truly natural and dramatic as this? My dear son, answered she, in an accent of sorrow, the first sight of you after so long a separation overwhelmed me with joy, but the revulsion was only the more deeply distressing. In what condition, alas! do I again behold you? My own slavery is a thousand times less revolting to my feelings than the disgraceful habiliments . . . . . Heyday! By all the powers, Madam, interrupted I with a hearty laugh, I am quite delighted with your newly-acquired morality : this is excellent in an actress. Well ' well! as heaven is my judge, my honored mamma, you are mightily improved in your principles, if my transformation astounds your religious eyesight. So far from quarreling with your turban, consider me rather as an actor, playing a Turkish character on the stage of the world. Though a conformist, I am just as much a Mussulman as when I was in Spain; nay, in the bottom of my heart, I never was a more firm believer in our Christian creed than at the present moment. When you shall become acquainted with all my hair-breadth escapes, since I have been domesticated in this country, you will not be rigorous in your censure. Love has been the cause of my apostasy, and he who worships at that shrine may be absolved from all other infidelities. I have a little of my mother in me, take my word for it. Another reason besides ought to moderate your disgust at seeing me under my present circumstances. You were expecting to experience a harsh captivity in Algiers, but you find in your protector a son, with all the tenderness and reverence befitting his relation to you, and rich enough to maintain you here in plenty and comfort, till a favorable opportunity offers of returning with safety into Spain. Admit, therefore, the force of the proverb, which says that evil itself is good for something.

My dear son, said Lucinda, since you fully intend one day to go back into your own country, and to throw off the mantle of Mahomet, my scruples are all satisfied. Thanks to heaven, continued she, I shall be able to carry back your sister Beatrice safe and sound into Castile. Yes, madam, exclaimed I, so you may. We will all three, as soon as the season may serve, go and throw ourselves into the bosom of our family for I make no matter of doubt but you have still in Spain other indisputable evidences of your prolific powers. No, said my mother, I have only you two, the offspring of my body; and you are to know that Beatrice is the fruit of a marriage, manufactured in as workmanlike a manner as any within the pale of the church. And pray, for what reason, replied I, might not my little sister have been just as contraband as myself? How did you ever work yourself up to the formidable resolution of marrying? I have heard you say a hundred times, in my childhood, that there was no benefit of clergy for a pretty woman who could commit such an offense as to take up with a husband. Times and seasons ebb and flow, my son, rejoined she. Men of the most resolute character may be shaken in their purposes; and do you require that a woman should be inflexible in hers? But I will now relate to you the story of my life since your departure from Madrid. She then began the following recital, which will never be obliterated from my memory. I will not withhold from you so curious a narrative.

It is nearly thirteen years, if you recollect, said my mother, since you left young Leganez. Just at that time the Duke of Medina Celi told me that he had a mind to sup with me one evening in private. The day was fixed. I made preparations for his reception : he came, and I pleased him. He required from me the sacrifice of all his rivals, past, present, and to come. I came into his terms, in the hope of being well paid for my complaisance. There was no deficiency on that score. On the very next morning, I received presents from him, which were followed up by a long rain of kindred attentions. I was afraid of not being able to hold in my chains a man of his exalted rank; and this apprehension was the better founded, because it was a matter of notoriety, that he had escaped from the clutches of several celebrated beauties, whose chains he had worn, only for the purpose of breaking. But for all that, so far from surfeiting on the relish of my kindness, his appetite grew by what it fed on. In short, I found out the secret of entertaining him, and impounding his heart, naturally roving, so that it should not go astray according to its usual volatility.

He had now been my admirer for three months, and I had every reason to flatter myself that the arrangement would be lasting, when a lady of my acquaintance and myself happened to go to an assembly, where the duchess his wife was of the party. We were invited to a concert of vocal and instrumental music. We accidentally seated ourselves too near the duchess, who took it into her head to be affronted, that I should exhibit my person in a place where she was. She sent me word by one of her women, that she should take it as a favor if I would quit the room immediately. I sent back an answer, just as saucy as the message. The duchess, irritated to fury, laid her wrongs before her husband, who came to me in person, and said : Retire, Lucinda. Though noblemen of the first rank attach themselves to pretty playthings like yourself, it is highly unbecoming in you to forget your proper distance. If we love you better than our wives, we honor our wives more than you : whenever, therefore, your insolence shall go so far as to set yourselves up for their rivals under their very noses, you will always be mortified, and made to know your places.

Fortunately the duke held his cruel language to me in so low a tone of voice as not to have been overheard by the people about us. I withdrew in deep confusion, and cried with vexation at having incurred such an affront. At once, to crown my shame and aggravate my chastisement, the actors and actresses got hold of the story on the very same evening. To do them justice, these gentry must contrive to entertain a familiar spirit, whose business is to fly about, and whisper in the ear of one whatever falls out amiss to the other. Suppose, for instance, that an actor gets drunk and makes a fool of himself, or an actress gets hold of a rich cully and makes a fool of him ! The green-room is sure to ring with all the particulars, and a few more than are true. All my kindred of the sock and buskin were informed at once of what had happened at the concert, and a blessed life they led me with their quips and quiddities. Never was there charity like theirs. Without beginning at home, heaven only knows where it ends ! But I held myself too high to be affected by their jibes and jeers : nor did even the loss of the Duke de Medina Celi hang heavy on my spirits ; for true it was, I never saw him more at my toilette, but learned, a very short time after, that he had got into the trammels of a little warbler.

When a theatrical lady has the good luck to be in fashion, she may change her lover as often as her petticoat : and one noble fool, should he even recover his wits at the end of three days, serves excellently well for a decoy to his successor. No sooner was it buzzed about Madrid, that the duke had raised the siege, than a new host of would-be conquerors appeared before the trenches. The very rivals whom I had sacrificed to his wishes, looking at my charms through the magnifying medium of delay and disappointment, came back again in crowds to encounter new caprices ; to say nothing of a thousand fresh hearts, ready to bargain on the mere report of my being to let. I had never been so exclusively the mode. Of all the men who put in for being cajoled by me, a portly German, belonging to the Duke of Ossuna's household, seemed to bid highest. Not that his personal attractions were by any means the most catching ; but then there were a thousand amiable pistoles on the list of candidates, scraped together by perquisites in his master's service, and turned adrift with the prodigality of a prince, in the hope of becoming my favored lover. This fat pigeon to be plucked was by name Brutandorf. As long as his pockets were lined, his reception was warm ; empty purses meet with fastened doors. The principles on which my friendship rested were not altogether to his taste. He came to the play to look after me during the performance. I was behind the scenes. It was his humor to load me with reproaches; it was mine to laugh in his face. This provoked his boorish wrath, and he gave me a box on the ear, like a clumsy-fisted German as he was. I set up a loud scream: the business of the stage was suspended. I came forward to the front, and, addressing the Duke of Ossuna, who was at the play on that occasion with his lady duchess, begged his protection from the German gallantry of his establishment. The duke gave orders for our proceeding with the piece, and intimated that he would hear the par-

"IT WAS HIS HUMOR TO LOAD ME WITH REPROACHES; IT WAS MINE TO LAUGH IN HIS FACE."

ties after the curtain had dropped. At the conclusion of the play I presented myself in all the dreary pomp of tragedy before the duke, and laid open my griefs in all the majesty of woe. As for my German pugilist, his defence was on a level with his provocation; so far from being sorry for what he had done, his fingers itched to give me another dressing. The cause being heard pro and con, the Duke of Ossuna said to his Scandinavian savage: Brutandorf, I dismiss you from my service, and beg never to see anything more of you, not because you have given a box on the ear to an actress, but for your failure in respect to your master and mistress, in having presumed to interrupt the progress of the play in their presence.

This decision was a bitter pill for me to swallow. It was high treason against my histrionic majesty, that the German was not turned off on the ground of having insulted me. It seemed difficult to conceive the possibility of a greater crime than that of insulting a principal actress: and where crimes are parallel, punishments should tally. The retribution in this case would have been exemplary; and I expected no less. This unpleasant occurrence undeceived me, and proved, to my mortification, that the public distinguished between the actors and the personages they may chance to enact. On this conviction, my pride revolted at the theatre: I resolved to give up my engagements to go and live at a distance from Madrid. I fixed on the city of Valencia for the place of my retreat, and went thither under a feigned character, with a property of twenty thousand ducats in money and jewels: a sum in my mind more than sufficient to maintain me for the remainder of my days, since it was my purpose to lead a retired life. I rented a small house at Valencia, and limited my establishment to a female servant and a page, who were as ignorant of my birth, parentage, and education, as the rest of the town. I gave myself out for the widow of an officer belonging to the king's household, and intimated that I had made choice of Valencia for my residence, on the report that it was one of the most agreeable neighborhoods in Spain. I saw very little company, and maintained so reserved a deportment, that there never was the slightest suspicion of my having been an actress. Yet, notwithstanding all the pains I took to hide myself from the garish eye of day, I had worse success against the piercing ken of a gentleman, who had a country seat near Paterna. He was of an ancient family, in person genteel and manly, from five-and-thirty to forty years of age, nobly connected, but scandalously in debt; a contradiction in the vocabulary of honor, neither more unaccountable nor uncommon in the kingdom of Valencia, than what takes place every day in other parts of the civilized world.

This gentleman of a generation or two before the present, finding my person to his liking, was desirous of knowing if in other respects I was a commodity for his market. He set every engine at work to inquire into the most minute particulars, and had the pleasure to learn from general report, that I was a warm widow with a comfortable jointure, and a person little, if anything, the worse for wear. It struck him that this was just the match; so that in a very short time an old lady came to my house, telling me, from him, that with equal admiration of my virtues and my charms, he laid himself and his fortune at my feet, and was ready to lead me to the altar, if I could condescend so far as to become his wife. I required three days to make up my mind on the subject. In this interval, I made inquiries about the gentleman; and hearing a good character of him, notwithstanding the deranged state of his finances, it was my determination to marry him without more ado, so that the preliminaries were soon ratified by a definitive treaty.

Don Manuel de Xerica, for that was my husband's name, took

me immediately after the ceremony to his castle, which had an air of antiquity highly flattering to his family pride. He told a story about one of his ancestors who built it in days of yore, and because it was not founded the day before yesterday, jumped to a conclusion that there was not a more ancient house in Spain than that of Xerica. But nobility, like perishable merchandise, will run to decay; the castle, shored up on this side and on that, was in the very agony of tumbling to pieces: what a buttress for Don Manuel and for his old walls was his marriage with me! More than half my savings were laid out on repairs, and the residue was wanted to set us going in a genteel style among our country neighbors. Behold me, then, you who can believe it, landed on a new planet, transformed into the presiding genius of a castle, the Lady Bountiful of my parish: our stage machinery could never have furnished such a change! I was too good an actress not to have supported my new rank and dignity with appropriate grace. I assumed high airs, theatrical grandeurs, a most dignified strut and demeanor; all which made the bumpkins conceive a wonderful idea of my exalted origin. How would they not have tickled their fancies at my expense, had they known the real truth of the case! The gentry of the neighborhood would have scoffed at me most unmercifully, and the country people would have been much more chary of the respect they showed me.

It was now near six years that I had lived very happily with Don Manuel, when he ended ways, means, and life together. My legacy consisted of a broken fortune to splice, and your sister Beatrice, then more than four years old, to maintain. The castle, which was our only tangible resource, was unfortunately mortgaged to several creditors, the principal of whom was one Bernard Astuto. Cunning by name, and cunning by nature! He practised as an attorney at Valencia, and bore his faculties in all the infamy of pettifogging; law and equity conspired in his person to push the trade of cozening and swindling to the utmost extremity. To think of falling into the clutches of such a creditor! A gentleman's property under the grip of such a claw as this attorney's affords much the same sport as a lamb to a wolf, or a dove to a kite. Nearly after the fashion of these beasts and birds of prey, did Signor Astuto, when informed of my husband's death, hover over his victim, concealing his fell purpose under the ambush of the law. The whole estate would have been swallowed up in pleadings, affidavits, demurrers, and rejoinders, but for the light thrown upon the proceedings by my lucky star; under whose influence the plaintiff was turned at once into defendant, and was left without a reply to the arguments of these all-powerful eyes. I got to the blind side of him in an interview, which I contrived during the progress of our litigation. Nothing was wanting on my part, I own it frankly, to fill him brimful of the tender passion; an ardent longing to save my goods, chattels, and domain, made me practise upon him, to my own disgust, that system of coquettish tactics and flirtation which had drawn so many former fools into an ambuscade. Yet, with all the resources of a veteran, I was very near letting the attorney escape. He was so barricaded by moldy parchments, so immured in actions and informations, as scarcely to seem susceptible of any love but the love of law. The truth, however, was, that this moping pettifogger, this porer over ponderous abridgments, this scrawler of acts and deeds, had more young blood in him than I was aware of, and a trick of looking at me out of the corner of his eye. He professed to be a novice in the art of courtship. My whole heart and soul, madam, said he, have been wedded to my profession; and the consequence has been, that the uses and costumes of gallantry have seemed weary, stale, flat, and unprofitable to me. But though not a man of outward show, I am well furnished with the stock in trade of love. To come to the point at once, if you can resolve in your mind to marry me, we will make a grand bonfire of the whole lawsuit; and I will give the go-by to those rascally creditors, who have joined issue with me in our attack upon your estate. You shall have the life interest, and your daughter the reversion. So good a bargain for Beatrice and myself would not allow of any wavering: I closed without delay on the conditions. The attorney kept his word most miraculously: he turned short round upon the other creditors, defeated them with the very weapons himself had furnished with their joint campaign, and secured me in the possession of my house and lands. It was probably the first time in his life that he had taken up the cause of the widow and the orphan.

Thus did I become the honored wife of an attorney, without losing my rank as the lady of the manor. But this incongruous marriage ruined me in the esteem of the gentry about Valencia. The women of quality looked upon me as a person who had lowered herself, and refused any longer to visit me. This inevitably threw me on the acquaintance of the tradespeople; a circumstance which could not do otherwise than hurt my feelings a little at first, because I had been accustomed, for the last six years, to associate only with ladies of the higher classes. But it was in vain to fret about it; and I soon found my level. I got most intimately acquainted with the wives of my husband's brethren of the quill and brief. Their characters were not a little entertaining. There was an absurdity in their manners, which tickled me to the very soul. These trumpery fine ladies held themselves up for something far above the common run. Well-a-day! said I to myself, every now and then, when they forgot the blue-bag: this is the way of the world! Every one fancies himself to be something vastly superior to his neighbor. I thought we actresses only did not know our places; women at the lower end of private life, as far as I see, are just as absurd in their pretensions. I should like, by way of check upon their presumption, to propose a law, that family pictures and pedigrees should be hung up in every house. Were the situation left to the choice of the owner, the deuce is in it if these legal gentry would not cram their scrivening ancestors either into the cellar or the garret.

After four years passed in the holy state of wedlock, Signor Bernardo d'Astuto fell sick, and went the way of all flesh. We had no family. Between my settlement and what I was worth before, I found myself a well-endowed widow. I had too the reputation of being so; and on this report, a Sicilian gentleman, by name Colifichini, determined to stick in my skirts, and either ruin or marry me. The alternative was kindly left to my own choice. He was come from Palermo to see Spain, and, after having satisfied his curiosity, was waiting, as he said, at Valencia for an opportunity of taking his passage back to Sicily. The spark was not quite five-and-twenty; of an elegant, though diminutive person; . . . . in short, his figure absolutely haunted me. He found the means of getting to the speech of me in private: and, I will own it to you frankly, I fell distractedly in love with him from the moment of our very first interview. On his part, the little knave flounced over head and ears in admiration of my charms. I do really think, God forgive me for it, that we should have been married out of hand, if the death of the attorney, whose funeral baked meats were scarcely cold enough to have furnished forth the marriage tables, would have allowed me to contract a new engagement at so short a warning. But since I had got into the matrimonial line, it was necessary that where the church makes the feast, the devil should not send cooks; I therefore took care always to season my nuptials to the palate of the world at large.

Thus did we agree to delay our coming together for a time, out of a tender regard to appearances. Colifichini, in the mean time, devoted all his attentions to me: his passion, far from languishing, seemed to become more a part of himself from day to day. The poor lad was not too flush of ready money. This struck my observation; and he was no longer at a loss for his little pocket expenses. Besides being very nearly twice his age, I recollected having laid the men under contribution in my younger days; so that I looked upon what I was then lavishing as a sort of restitution, which balanced my debtor and creditor account, and made me quits with my conscience. We waited, as patiently as our frailty would allow, for the period when widows may in decency so far surmount their grief as to try their luck again. When the happy morning rose, we presented ourselves before the altar, where we plighted our faith to each other by oaths the most solemn and binding. We then retired to my castle, where I may truly say that we lived for two years, less as husband and wife than as tender and unfettered lovers. But alas! such an union, so happy and sentimental, was not long to be the lot of humanity: a pleurisy carried off my dear Colifichini.

At this passage in her history, I interrupted my mother. Heyday! madam, your third husband dispatched already? You must be a most deadly taking. What do you mean? answered she: is it for me to dispute the will of heaven, and lengthen the days parcelled out to every son of earth? If I have lost three husbands, it was none of my fault. Two of them cost me many a salt tear. If I buried any with dry eyes, it was the attorney. As that was merely a match of interest, I was easily reconciled to the loss of him. But to return to Colifichini. I was going to tell you, that

some months after his death, I had a mind to go and take possession of a country house near Palermo, which he had settled on me
as a jointure, by our marriage contract. I took my passage for
Sicily with my daughter; but we were taken on the voyage by
Algerine corsairs. This city was our destination. Happily for us,
you happened to be at the market where we were put up for sale.
Had it been otherwise, we must have fallen into the hands of some
barbarian purchaser, who would have used us ill; and we probably
might have passed our whole life in slavery, nor would you ever
have heard of us.

Such was my mother's story. To return to my own, gentlemen, I gave her the best apartment in my house, with the liberty
of living after her own fashion; which was a circumstance very
agreeable to her taste. She had a confirmed habit of loving,
brought to such a system by so many repeated experiments, that
it was impossible for her to do without either a gallant or a husband. At first she looked with favor on some of my slaves; but
Hali Pegelin, a Greek renegado, who sometimes came and called
upon us, soon drew all her glances on himself. She conceived a
stronger passion for him than she had ever done for Colifichini:
and such was her aptitude for pleasing the men, that she found
the way to wind herself about the heart of this man also. I seemed
as if unconscious of their good understanding; being then intent
only on my return into Spain. The bashaw had already given me
leave to fit out a vessel, for the purpose of sweeping the sea and
committing acts of piracy. This armament was my sole object.
Just a week before it was completed, I said to Lucinda: Madam,
we shall take our leave of Algiers almost immediately; so that
you will bid a long farewell to an abode which you cannot but
detest.

My mother turned pale at these words, and stood silent and
motionless. My surprise was extreme. What do I see? said I to
her: whence comes it that you present such an image of terror and
despair? My design was to fill you with transport; but the effect
of my intelligence seems only to overwhelm you with affliction. I
thought to have been thanked for my welcome news; and hastened
with eagerness to tell you that all is ready for our departure. Are
you no longer in the mind to go back into Spain? No, my son;
Spain no longer has any charms for me, answered my mother. It
has been the scene of all my sorrows, and I have turned my back
on it for ever. What do I hear? exclaimed I in an agony: ah!
tell me rather, that it is a fatal passion which alienates you from
your native country. Just heavens! what a change! When you
landed here, every object that met your eyes was hateful to them,
but Hali Pegelin has given another color to your fancy. I do not
deny it, replied Lucinda: I love that renegado, and mean to take
him for my fourth husband. What an idea! interrupted I with horror:
you, to marry a Mussulman! You forget yourself to be a Christian,
or rather have hitherto been one only in name and not in heart.
Ah! my dear mother, what a futurity do you present to my imagination! You are running headlong to your eternal ruin. You are

going to do voluntarily, and from impure motives, what I have only done under the pressure of necessity.

I urged many other arguments in the same strain, to turn her aside from her purpose: but all my eloquence was wasted; she had made up her mind to her future destiny. Not satisfied with following the bent of her base inclinations, and leaving her son to go and live with this renegado, she had even formed a design to settle Beatrice in her own family. This I opposed with all my might and main. Ah! wretched Lucinda, said I, if nothing is capable of keeping you within the limits of your duty, at least rush on perdition alone; confine within yourself the fury which possesses you; cast not a young innocent headlong over a precipice, though you yourself may venture on the leap. Lucinda quitted my presence in moody silence. It struck me that a remnant of reason still enlightened her, and that she would not obstinately persevere in requiring her daughter to be given up to her. How little did I know of my mother! One of my slaves said to me two days afterwards: Sir, take care of yourself. A captive belonging to Pegelin has just let me into a secret, of which you cannot too soon avail yourself. Your mother has changed her religion; and as a punishment upon you for having refused Beatrice to her wishes, it is her purpose to acquaint the bashaw with your flight. I could not for a moment doubt but what Lucinda was the woman to do just what my slave had said she would. The lady had given me manifold opportunities of studying her character: and it was sufficiently evident that by dint of playing bloody parts in tragedy, she had familiarized herself with the guilty scenes of real life. It would not in the least have gone against her nature to have got me burned alive; nor probably would she have been more affected by my exit after that fashion, than by the winding up of a dramatic tale.

The warning of my slave, therefore, was not to be neglected. My embarkation was hastened on. I took some Turks on board, according to the practice of the Algerine corsairs when going on a piratical expedition but I engaged no more than was necessary to blind the eyes of jealousy, and weighed anchor from the port as soon as possible, with all my slaves and my sister Beatrice. You will do right to suppose, that I did not forget, in that moment of anxiety, to pack up my whole stock of money and jewels, amounting probably to the worth of six thousand ducats. When we were fairly out at sea, we began by securing the Turks. They were easily mastered, as my slaves outnumbered them. We had so favorable a wind, that we made the coast of Italy in a very short time. Without let or hindrance, we got into the harbor of Leghorn, where I thought the whole city must have come out to see us land. The father of my slave Azarini, either accidentally or from curiosity, happened to be among the gazers. He looked with all his eyes at my captives, as they came ashore; but though his object was to discover his lost son among the number, it was with little hope of so fortunate a result. But how powerful is the plea of nature! What transports, expressed by mutual embraces, followed the recognition of a tie so close, but so painfully interrupted for a time!

As soon as Azarini had acquainted his father who I was, and what brought me to Leghorn, the old man obliged me, as well as Beatrice, to accept of an apartment in his house. I shall pass over in silence the description of a thousand ceremonies, necessary to be gone through, in order to my return into the bosom of the church; suffice it to say, that I forswore Mahometanism with much more sincerity than I had pledged myself to it. After having entirely purged myself from my Algerine leaven, I sold my ship, and set all my slaves at liberty. As for the Turks, they were committed to prison at Leghorn, to be exchanged against Christians. I received kind attention in abundance from the Azarini family: indeed, the young man married my sister Beatrice, who, to speak the truth, was no bad match for him, being a gentleman's daughter, and inheriting the castle of Xerica, which my mother had taken care to let out to a rich farmer of Paterna, when she resolved upon her voyage to Sicily.

From Leghorn, after having staid there some time, I departed for Florence, a town I had a strong desire to see. I did not go thither without letters of recommendation. Azarini the father had connections at the grand duke's court, and introduced me to them as a Spanish gentleman related to his family. I tacked don to my name, in honest rivalry of impudence with other low Spaniards, who take up that traveling title of honor without compunction, when far enough from home to set detection at defiance. Boldly then did I dub myself Don Raphael; and appeared at court with suitable splendor, on the strength of what I had brought from Algiers, to keep my nobility from starving. The high personages, to whom old Azarini had written in my favor, gave out in their circle that I was a person of quality; so that with this testimony, and a natural knack I had of giving myself airs, the deuce must have been in it if I could not have passed muster for a man of some consequence. I soon got to be hand in glove with the principal nobility; and they presented me to the grand duke. I had the good fortune to make myself agreeable. It then became an object with me to pay court to that prince, and to study his humor. I sucked in with greedy ear all that his most experienced courtiers said about him, and by their conversation fathomed all his peculiarities. Among other things, he encouraged a play of wit; was fond of good stories and lively repartees. On this hint I formed myself. Every morning I wrote down in my pocket-book such anecdotes as I meant to rack off in the course of the day. My stock was considerably extensive; so that I was a walking budget of balderdash. Yet even my estate in nonsense required economy; and I began to get out at elbows, so as to be reduced to borrow from myself, and mortgage my resources twenty times over; but when the shallow current of wit and wisdom was nearly at its summer drought, a torrent of matter-of-fact lies gave new force to the exhausted stream of quibble. Intrigues which never had been intrigued, and practical jokes which had never been played off, were the tools I worked with, and exactly to the level of the grand duke : nay, what often happens to dull dealers in inextinguishable vivacity, the mornings were spent in financiering those funds of conversation, which were to be drawn upon after dinner, as if from a perennial spring of preternatural wealth.

I had even the impudence to set up for a poet, and made my broken-winded muse trot to the praises of the prince. I allow candidly that the verses were execrable ; but then they were quite good enough for their readers ; and it remains a doubt whether, if they had been better, the grand duke would not have thrown them into the fire. They seemed to be just what he would have written upon himself. In short, it was impossible to miss the proper style on such a subject. But whatever might be my merit as a poet, the prince, by little and little, took such a liking to my person, as gave occasion of jealousy to his courtiers. They tried to find out who I was. This, however, was beyond their compass. All they could learn was, that I had been a renegado. This was whispered forthwith in the prince's ear, in the hopes of hurting me. Not that it succeeded : on the contrary, the grand duke one day commanded me to give him a faithful account of my adventures at Algiers. I obeyed ; and the recital, without reserve on my part, contributed more than any other of my stories to his entertainment.

Don Raphael, said he, after I had ended my narrative, I have a real regard for you, and mean to give you a proof of it, which will place my sincerity beyond a doubt. Henceforth you are admitted into my most private confidence, as the first fruits of which, you are to know that one of my ministers has a wife, with whom I am in love. She is the most enchanting creature at court ; but at the same time the most impregnable. Shut up in her own household, exclusively attached to a husband who idolizes her, she seems to be ignorant of the combustion her charms have kindled in Florence. You will easily conceive the difficulty of such a conquest. And yet this epitome of loveliness, so deaf to all the whispers of common seduction, has sometimes listened to my sighs. I have found the means of speaking to her without witnesses. She is not unacquainted with my sentiments. I do not flatter myself with having warmed her into love; she has given me no reason to form so sweet a conjecture. Yet I will not despair of pleasing her by my constancy, and by the cautious conduct, even to mystery, which I take care to observe.

My passion for this lady, continued he, is known only to herself. Instead of pursuing my game wantonly, and overleaping the rights of my subjects like a true sovereign, I conceal from all the world the knowledge of my love. This delicacy seems due to Mascarini, the husband of my beloved mistress. His zeal and attachment to me, his services and honesty, oblige me to act in this business with the closest secrecy and circumspection. I will not plunge a dagger into the bosom of this ill-starred husband, by declaring myself a suitor to his wife. Would he might for ever be insensible, were it within possibility, to the secret flame which devours me : for I am persuaded that he would die of grief, were he to know the

circumstances, I have just now confided to you. I therefore veiⁱ
my pursuit in impenetrable darkness; and have determined to
make use of you, for the purpose of conveying to Lucretia the
merit of the sacrifices my delicacy imposes on my feelings. Of these
you shall be the interpreter. I doubt not but you will acquit yourself to a marvel of your commission. Contrive to be intimate with
Mascarini; make a point of worming yourself into his friendship.
Then an introduction to his family will be easy; and you will secure to yourself the liberty of conversing freely with his wife. This
is what I require from you, and what I feel assured that you will
execute with all the dexterity and discretion necessary to so delicate an unkertaking.

I promised the grand duke to do my utmost, in furtherance of
his good opinion, and in aid of his success with the object of his
desires. I kept my word without loss of time. No pains were
spared to get into Mascarini's good graces; and the design was not
difficult to accomplish. Delighted to find his friendship sought by
a man possessing the affections of the prince, he advanced half way
to meet my overtures. His house was always open to me, my intercourse with his lady was unrestrained; and I have no hesitation
in affirming my measures to have been taken so well, as to have
precluded the slightest suspicion of the embassy intrusted to my
management. It is true, he had but a small share of the Italian
jealousy, relying as he did on the virtue of his Lucretia; so that he
often shut himself up in his closet, and left me alone with her. I
entered at once into the pith and marrow of my subject. The
grand duke's passion was my topic with the lady; and I told her
that the motive of my visits was only to plead for that prince. She
did not seem to be over head and ears in love with him; and yet,
methought, vanity forbade her to frown decisively on his addresses.
She took a pleasure in listening to his sighs, without sighing in
concert. A certain propriety of heart she had; but then she was a
woman; and it was obvious that her rigor was giving way insensibly to the triumphant image of a sovereign, bound in the fetters
of her resistless charms. In short, the prince had good reason to
flatter himself that he might dispense with the ill-breeding of a
Tarquin, and yet bend Lucretia to a compliance with his longings.
An incident, however, the most unexpected in the annals of romance, blasted his flattering prospects; in what manner you shall
hear.

I am naturally free and easy with the women. This constitu-
tional assurance, whether a blessing or a curse, was ripened into
inveterate habit among the Turks. Lucretia was a pretty woman.
I forgot that I was courting by proxy, and assumed the tone of a
principal. Nothing could exceed the warmth and gallantry with
which I offered my services to the lady. Far from appearing offended at my boldness, or silencing me by a resentful answer, she
only said with a sarcastic smile: Own the truth, Don Raphael; the
grand duke has pitched upon a very faithful and zealous agent.
You serve him with an integrity not sufficiently to be commended.
Madam, said I in the same strain, let us not examine things with

too much nicety. A truce, I beseech you, with moral discussions, they are not of my element: good honest passion tallies better with our natures. I do not believe myself, after all, the first prince's confidant who has ousted his master in an affair of gallantry; your great lords have often dangerous rivals, in more humble messengers than myself. That may be, replied Lucretia: but a haughty temper stands with me in the place of virtue, and no one under the degree of a prince shall ever sully these charms. Regulate your behavior accordingly, added she in a tone of serious severity, and let us change the subject. I willingly bury your presumption in oblivion, provided you never hold similar discourse to me again: if you do, you may repent of it.

Though this was a comment of some importance on my text, and ought to have been heedfully conned over, it was no bar to my still entertaining Mascarini's wife with my passion. I even pressed her with more importunity than heretofore, for a kind consent to my tender entreaties; and was rash enough to feel my ground, by some little personal freedoms. The lady then, offended at my words, and still more at my Mahometan quips and cranks, gave a complete set down to my assurance. She threatened to acquaint the grand duke with my impertinence; and declared she would make a point of his punishing me as I deserved. These menaces bristled up my spirit in return. My love turned at once into hatred, and determined me to revenge myself for the contempt with which Lucretia had treated me. I went in quest of her husband; and after having bound him by oath not to betray me, I informed him of his wife's correspondence with the prince, and failed not to represent her as distractedly enamored of him, by way of heightening the interest of the scene. The minister, lest the plot should become too intricately entangled, shut his wife up, without any law but his own will, in a secret apartment, where he placed her under the strict guard of confidential persons. While she was thus kept at bay by the watch-dogs of jealousy, who prevented her from acquainting the grand duke with her situation, I announced to that prince, with a melancholy air, that he must think no longer of Lucretia. I told him that Mascarini had doubtless discovered all, since he had taken it into his head to keep a guard over his wife: that I could not conceive what had induced him to suspect me, as I flattered myself with having always behaved according to the most approved rules of discretion in such cases. The lady might, I suggested, have been beforehand, and owned all to her husband; and had perhaps, in concert with him, suffered herself to be immured, in order to lie hid from a pursuit so dangerous to her virtue. The prince appeared deeply afflicted at my relation. I was not unmoved by his distress, and repented more than once of what I had done; but it was too late to retract. Besides, I must acknowledge, a spiteful joy tingled in my veins, when I meditated on the distressed condition of the disdainful fair, who had spurned my vows.

I was feeding with impunity on the pleasure of revenge, so palatable to all the world, but most of all to Spaniards, when one day the grand duke, chatting with five or six nobles of his court and myself, said to us: In what manner would you judge it fitting for a man to be punished, who should have abused the confidence of his prince, and designed to step in between him and his mistress? The best way, said one of the courtiers, would be to have him torn to pieces by four horses. Another gave it as his verdict, that he should be soundly beaten, till he died under the blows of the executioner. The most tender-hearted and merciful of these Italians, with comparative lenity towards the culprit, wished only just to admonish him of his fault, by throwing him from the top of a tower to the bottom. And Don Raphael, resumed the grand duke after a pause, what is his opinion? The Spaniards, in all likelihood, would improve upon our Italian severity, in a case of such aggravated treachery.

I fully understood, as you may well suppose, that Mascarini had not kept his oath, or that his wife had devised the means of acquainting the prince with what had passed between her and me. My countenance sufficiently betokened my inward agitation. But for all that, suppressing as well as I could my rising emotion and alarm, I replied to the grand duke in a steady tone of voice—My lord, the Spaniards are more generous; under such circumstances, they would pardon the unworthy betrayer of his trust, and by that act of unmerited goodness, would kindle in his soul an everlasting abhorrence of his own villany. Yes, truly, said the prince, and I feel in my own breast a similar spirit of forbearance. Let the traitor then be pardoned; since I have myself only to blame for having given my confidence to a man of whom I had no knowledge, but, on the contrary, much ground of suspicion, according to the current of common report. Don Raphael, added he, my revenge shall be confined to this single interdict. Quit my dominions immediately, and never appear again in my presence. I withdrew in all haste, less hurt at my disgrace, than delighted to have got off so cheaply. The very next day I embarked in a Barcelona ship, just setting sail from the port of Leghorn on its return.

At this period of his history I interrupted Don Raphael to the following effect. For a man of shrewdness, methinks you were not a little off your guard, in trusting yourself at Florence for even so short a time, after having discovered the prince's love of Lucretia to Mascarini. You might well have foreboded that the grand duke would not be long in getting to the knowledge of your duplicity. Your observation is very just, answered the well-matched son of so eccentric a mother as Lucinda: and for that reason, not trusting to the minister's promise of screening me from his master's indignation, it had been my intention to disappear without taking leave.

I got safe to Barcelona, continued he, with the remnant of the wealth I had brought from Algiers; but the greater part had been squandered at Florence in enacting the Spanish gentleman. I did not stay long in Catalonia. Madrid was the dear place of my nativity, and I had a longing desire to see it again, which I satisfied as soon as possible; for mine was not a temper to stand parleying with its own inclinations. On my arrival in town, I chanced to take up my abode in a ready-furnished lodging, where dwelt a lady, by name Camilla. Though at some distance from her teens, she was a very spirit-stirring creature, as Signor Gil Blas will bear me out in saying; for he fell in with her at Valladolid nearly about the same time. Her parts were still more extraordinary than her beauty; and never had a lady with a character to let a happier talent of in-veigling fools to their ruin. But she was not like those selfish jilts, who put out the cullibility of their lovers to usury. The pillage of the plodding merchant, or the grave family man, was squand-ered upon the first gambler or prize-fighter who happened to find his way into her frolicsome fancy.

We loved one another from the first moment, and the con-formity of our tempers bound us so closely together, that we soon lived on the footing of joint property. The amount, in sober sad-ness, was little better than a cypher, and a few good dinners more reduced it to that ignoble negative of number. We were each of us thinking, as the deuce would have it, of our mutual pleasures, without profiting in the least by those happy dispositions of ours for living at the expense of other folks. Want at last gave a keener edge to our wits, which indulgence had blunted. My dear Raphael, said Camilla, let us carry the war into the enemy's quarters, if you love me; for while we are as faithful as turtles, we are as foolish; and fall into our own snare, instead of laying it for the unwary. You may get into the head and heart of a rich widow: I may con-jure myself into the good graces of some old nobleman: but as for this ridiculous fidelity, it brings no grist to the mill. Excellent Camilla, answered I, you are beforehand with me. I was going to make the very same proposal. It exactly meets my ideas, thou paragon of morality. Yes; the better to maintain our mutual fire, let us forage for substantial fuel. As good may always be extracted out of evil, those infidelities which are the bane of other loves, shall be the triumph of ours.

On the basis of this treaty we took the field. At first, there was much cry but little wool; for we had no luck at finding cullies. Camilla met with nothing but pretty fellows, with vanity in their hearts, tinsel on their backs, and not a maravedi in their pockets; my ladies were all of a kidney to levy, rather than to pay contribu-tions. As love left us in the lurch, we paid our devotions at the shrine of knavery. With the zeal of martyrs to a new religion, did we encounter the frowns of the civil power, whose myrmidons, as like the devil in their nature as their office, were ordered on the look-out after us; but the alguazil, with all the good qualities of which the corregidor inherited the contraries, gave us time to make our escape out of Madrid, for the good of the trade and a small sum of money. We took the road to Valladolid, meaning to set up in that town. I rented a house for myself and Camilla, who passed for my sister, to avoid evil tongues. At first we kept a tight rein over our speculative talents, and begun by reconnoitring the ground before we determined on our plan of operations.

One day a man accosted me in the street, with a very civil salu-tation, to this effect—Signor Don Raphael, do you recollect my face? I answered in the negative. Then I have the advantage of you, replied he, for yours is perfectly familiar to me. I have seen you at the court of Tuscany, where I was then in the grand duke's guards. It is some months since I quitted that prince's service. I came into Spain with an Italian, who will not discredit the politics of his country: we have been at Valladolid these three weeks. Our residence is with a Castilian and a Galician, who are, without dispute, two of the best creatures in the world. We live together by the sweat of our brows, and the labor of our hands. Our fare is not abstemious, nor have we made any vow against the temptations of a life about the court. If you will make one of our party, my brethren will be glad of your company; for you always seemed to me a man of spirit, above all vulgar prejudices, in short, a monk of our order.

Such frankness from this arch-scoundrel was met half-way by mine. Since you talk to me with so winning a candor, said I, you deserve that I should be equally explicit with you. In good truth I am no novice in your ritual; and if my modesty would allow me to be the hero of my own tale, you would be convinced that your compliments were not lavished on an unworthy subject. But enough of my own commendations; proceed we to the point in question. With all possible desire to become a member of your body, I shall neglect no opportunity of proving my title to that distinction. I had no sooner told this sharper at all points, that I would agree to swell the number of his gang, than he conducted me to their place of meeting, and introduced me in proper form. It was on this occasion that I first saw the renowned Ambrose de Lamela. These gentlemen catechized me in the religion of coveting my neighbor's goods, and doing as I would not be done by. They wanted to discern whether I played the villain on principle, or had only some little practical dexterity; but I showed them tricks which they did not know to be on the cards, and yet acknowledged to be better than their own. They were still deeper lost in admiration, when in cool disdain of manual artifice, as an every-day effort of ingenuity, I maintained my prowess in such combinations of roguery as require an inventive brain and a solid judgment to support them. In proof of these pretensions I related the adventure of Jerome de Moyadas; and on this single specimen of my parts, they conceived my genius of so high an order, as to elect me by common consent for their leader. Their choice was fully justified by a host of slippery devices, of which I was the master-wheel, the corner-stone, or according to whatever other metaphor in mechanics you may best express the soul of a conspiracy. When we had occasion for a female performer to heighten the interest, Camilla was sent upon the stage, and played up to admiration in the parts she had to perform.

Just at that period, our friend and brother Ambrose was seized with a longing to see his native country once more. He went for Galicia with an assurance that we might reckon on his return. The visit cured his patriotic sickness. As he was on the road back, having halted at Burgos to strike some stroke of business, an innkeeper of his acquaintance introduced him into the service of

Signor Gil Blas de Santillane, not forgetting to instruct him thoroughly in the state of that gentleman's affairs. Signor Gil Blas, pursued Don Raphael, addressing his discourse to me, you know in what manner we eased you of your movables in a ready-furnished lodging at Valladolid; and you must doubtless have suspected Ambrose to have been the principal contriver of that exploit, and not without reason. On his coming into town, he ran himself out of breath to find us, and laid open every particular of your situation, so that the associated swindlers had nothing to do but to build on his foundation. But you are unacquainted with the consequences of that adventure: you shall therefore have them on my authority. Your portmeanteau was made free with by Ambrose and myself. We also took the liberty of riding your mules in the direction of Madrid, not dropping the least hint to Camilla nor to our partners in iniquity, who must have partaken in some measure of your feelings in the morning, at finding their glory shorn of two such beams.

On the second day we changed our purpose. Instead of going to Madrid, whence I had not sallied forth without an urgent motive, we passed by Zebreros, and continued our journey as far as Toledo. Our first care, in that town, was to dress ourselves in the genteelest style; then assuming the character of two brothers from Galicia on our travels of mere curiosity, we soon got acquainted in the most respectable circles. I was so much in the habit of acting the man of fashion, as not easily to be detected; and as the generality of people are blinded by a free expenditure, we threw dust into the eyes of all the world, by the elegant entertainments to which we invited the ladies. Among the women who frequented our parties, there was one not indifferent to me. She appeared more beautiful than Camilla, and certainly much younger, I inquired who she was; and learned that her name was Violante, and that she was married to an ungrateful spark, who soon grew weary of her chaste caresses, and was running after those of a prostitute, with whom he was in love. There was no need to say any more, to determine me on enthroning Violante the sovereign lady and mistress of my thoughts and affections.

She was not long in coming to the knowledge of her conquest. I began by following her about from place to place, and playing a hundred monkey tricks to instil into her comprehension, that nothing would please me better than the office of making her amends for the ill usage of her husband. The pretty creature ruminated on my proffered kindness, and to such purpose as to let me know in the end that my labor was not wasted on an ungrateful soil. I received a note from her in answer to several I had transmitted by one of those convenient old dowagers, in such high request throughout Spain and Italy. The lady sent me word that her husband supped with his mistress every evening, and did not return home till very late. It was impossible to mistake the meaning of this. On that very night I planted myself under Violante's windows, and engaged her in a most tender conversation. At the moment of parting, it was settled between us that every evening, at the same hour, we should meet and converse on the same ever-lasting topic, without gainsaying any such other acts of gallantry as might safely be submitted to the peering eye of day.

Hitherto Don Balthazar, as Violante's husband was called, had no reason to complain of his forehead; but I was a natural philosopher, and little satisfied with metaphysical endearments. One evening, therefore, I repaired under my lady's windows, with the design of telling her that there was an end of life and every-thing, if we could not come together on more accommodating terms than from the balcony to the street; for I had never yet been able to get into the house. Just as I got thither, a man came within sight, apparently with the view of dogging me. In fact, it was the hus-band returning earlier than usual from his precious bit of amuse-ment; but observing a male nuisance near his nunnery, instead of coming straight home, he walked backwards and forwards in the street. It was almost a moot point with me what I ought to do. At last, I resolved on accosting Don Balthazar, though neither of us had the slightest knowledge of each other. Noble gentleman, said I, you would do me a most particular favor by leaving the street vacant to me for this one night; I would do as much for you. Sir, answered he, I was just going to make the same request to you. I am on the look-out after a girl, over whom a confounded fellow of a brother keeps watch and ward like a jailer; and she lives not twenty yards from this place. I could wish to carry on my project without a witness. We have the means, replied I, of attaining both our ends without clashing; for the lady of my de-sires lives there, added I, pointing to his own house. We had bet-ter even help one another, in case of being attacked. With all my heart, resumed he; I will go to my appointment, and we will make common cause if need be. Under this pretense he went away, but only to observe me the more narrowly; and the darkness of the night favored his doing so without detection.

As for me, I made up to Violante's balcony in the simplicity of my heart. She soon heard my signal, and we began our usual par-ley. I was not remiss in pressing the idol of my worship to grant me a private interview in some safe and practicable place. She was rather coy to my entreaties, as favors hardly earned are the higher valued: at length she took a letter out of her pocket, and flung it down to me. There, said she, you will find in that scrap of paper the promise of what you have teased me so long about. She then withdrew, as the hour approached when her husband usually came home. I put the note up carefully, and went towards the place where Don Balthazar had told me that his business lay. But that stanch husband, with the sagacity of an old sportsman where his own wife was the game, came more than half-way to meet me, with this question: Well, good sir, are you satisfied with you happy for-tunes? I have reason to be so, answered I. And as for yourself, what have you done? has the blind god befriended you? Alas! quite the contrary, replied he; that impertinent brother, who takes such liberties with my beauty, though fit to come back from his country house, whence we hugged ourselves as sure that he would not return till to-morrow. This infernal chance has put all my soft and soothing pleasures out of tune.

Nothing could exceed the mutual pledges of lasting friendship which were exchanged between Don Balthazar and me. To draw the cords the closer, we made an appointment for the next morning in the great square. This plotting gentleman, after we had parted, betook himself to his own house, without giving Violante at all to understand that he knew more about her than she wished him. On the following day he was punctual in the great square, and I was not five minutes after him. We exchanged greetings with all the warmth of old friendship; but it was a vapor to mislead on his part, though a spark of heavenly flame on mine. In the course of conversation, this hypocritical Don Balthazar palmed upon me a fictitious confidence, respecting his intrigue with the lady about whom he had been speaking the night before. He put together a long story he had been manufacturing on that subject, and all this to hook me in to tell him, in return, by what means I had got acquainted with Violante. The snare was too subtle for me to escape; I owned all with the innocence of a new-born babe. I did not even stick at showing the note I had received from her, and read the contents, to the following purport: " I am going to-morrow to dine with Donna Inez. You know where she lives. It is in the house of that confidential friend that I mean to pass some happy moments along with you. It is impossible longer to refuse a boon your patience has so well merited."

Here indeed, said Don Balthazar, is an epistle which promises to crown all your wishes at once. I congratulate you beforehand on your approaching happiness. He could not help fidgeting and wriggling a little, while he talked in these terms of his own household; but all his hitches and wry faces passed off, and my eyes were as fast sealed as ever. I was so full of anticipating titillations, as not to think of noticing my new friend, who was obliged to get off as fast as he could, for fear of betraying his agitation in my presence. He ran to acquaint his brother-in-law with this strange occurrence. I know not what might pass between them : it is only certain that Don Balthazar happened to knock at Donna Inez's door, just when I was at that lady's house with Violante. We were warned who it was, and I escaped by a back door exactly as he went in at the front. As soon as I had got safe off, the women, whom the unexpected visit of this troublesome husband had disconcerted a little, recovered their presence of mind, and with it so large a stock of assurance, as to stand the brunt of his attack, and put him to a nonplus in ascertaining whether they had hid me or smuggled me out. I cannot exactly tell you what he said to Donna Inez and his wife; nor do I believe that history will ever furnish any authentic particulars of the squabbles.

In the mean time, without suspecting yet how completely I was gulled by Don Balthazar, I sallied forth with curses in my mouth, and returned to the great square, where I had appointed Lamela to meet me. But no Lamela was there. He also had his little snug parties, and the scoundrel fared better than his comrade. As

I was waiting for him, I caught a glimpse of my treacherous associate, with a knowing smile upon his countenance. He made up to
me, and inquired, with a hearty laugh, what news of my assignation with my nymph, under the convenient roof of Donna Inez. I
cannot conceive, said I, what evil spirit, jealous of my joys, takes
delight to nip them in their blossom : but after we had embraced,
kissed, protested, and, as it were, spoke the prologue of our comedy, comes the peaking cornuto of a husband (the furies fly away
with him), and knocks at the door at the instant of our encounter.
There was nothing to be done but to secure my retreat as fast
as possible. So I got out at a back door, sending to all the inhabitants of hell and its suburbs the jealous knave, who was so uncivil
as to search another lady's house for his own horns. I am sorry you
sped so ill-favoredly, exclaimed Don Balthazar, who was chuckling
with inward satisfaction at my disappointment. What a mechanical rogue of a husband ! I would advise you to show no mercy to
the wittol. Oh ! you need not teach me how to predominate over
such a peasant, replied I. Take my word for it, a new quarter shall
be added to his coat of arms this very night. His wife, when I went
away, told me not to be faint-hearted for such a trifle; but to place
myself without fail under her window at an earlier hour than usual,
for she was resolved to let me into the house; and as a precaution
against all accidents, she begged me to bring two or three friends
in my train, for fear of a surprise. What a discreet and inventive
lady ! said he. I should have no objection to being of your party.
Ah ! my dear friend, exclaimed I, out of wits with joy, and throwing my arms about Don Balthazar's neck, how infinitely you will
oblige me ! I will do more, resumed he ; I know a young man,
armed like another Cæsar, for either field of love or war; he shall
be of our number, and you may then rely boldly on the sufficiency
of your escort.

I knew not in what words to thank this seeming friend, so that
my gratitude might be equivalent to his zeal. To make short of
the matter, I accepted his proffered aid. Our meeting was fixed
under Violante's balcony early in the evening, and we parted. He
went in quest of his brother-in-law, who was the hero in question.
As for me, I walked about all day with Lamela, who had no more
misgivings than myself, though somewhat astonished at the warmth
with which Don Balthazar engaged in my interests. We slipt our
own necks completely into the noose. I own this was mere infatua-
tion on our parts, whose natural instinct ought to have warned us
of a halter. When I thought it proper time to present myself under Violante's windows, Ambrose and I took care to be armed with
small swords. There we found the husband of my fair dame and
another man, waiting for us with a very determined air. Don Balthazar accosted me, and introducing his brother-in-law, said : Sir,
this is the brave officer whose prowess I have extolled so highly to
you. Make the best of your way into your mistress's house, and
let no fear of the consequences be any bar to the enjoyment of the
most rapturous human bliss.

After a mutual interchange of compliments, I knocked at Violante's door. It was opened by a kind of duenna. In I went, and without looking back after what was passing behind me, made the best of my way to the lady's room. While I was paying her my preliminary civilities, the two cut-throats, who had followed me into the house, and had banged the door after them so violently that Ambrose was left in the street, made their appearance. You may well suppose that then was the appeal to arms. They both fell upon me at the same time, but I showed them some play. I kept them engaged on either side so fiercely, that they were sorry perhaps not to have taken a safer road to their revenge. The husband was run through the body. His brother-in-law, seeing him on his travels to the shades below, made the best of his way to the door, which the duenna and Violante had opened, to make their escape while we were fighting. I ran after him into the street, where I met with Lamela once more, who by dint of not being able to get a word out of the women, running as they did for their very lives, did not know exactly what he was to divine from the infernal noise he had just heard. We got back to our inn. After packing up what was best worth taking with us, we mounted our mules, and got out of town, without waiting for daybreak or fear of robbers.

It was sufficiently clear that this business was not likely to be without its consequences, and that a hue and cry would be set up in Toledo, which we should act like wise men to anticipate by a retreat. We stayed the night at Villarubia. At the inn where we put up, some time after our arrival, there alighted a tradesman of Toledo on his way to Segorba. We clubbed our suppers. He related to us the tragical catastrophe of Violante's husband; and so far was he from suspecting us of being parties concerned, that we inquired into particulars with the curious indifference of common newsmongers. Gentlemen, said he, just as I was setting out this morning, the report of this melancholy event was handed about. Every one was on the hunt after Violante; and they say that the corregidor, a relation of Don Balthazar, is determined on sparing no pains to discover the perpetrators of this murder. So much for my knowledge of the business.

The corregidor of Toledo and his police gave me very little uneasiness. But for fear of the worst, I determined to precipitate my retreat from New Castile. It occurred to me that Violante, when hunted out of her hiding-place, would turn informer, and in that case she might give such a description of my person to the clerks in office, as might enable them to put their scouts upon a right scent. For this reason, on the following day we struck out of the high road, as a measure of safety. Fortunately Lamela was acquainted with three-fourths of Spain, and knew by what cross paths we could get securely into Arragon. Instead of going straight to Cuença, we threaded the defiles of the mountains overhanging that town, and arrived, by ways with which my guide was well acquainted, at a grotto looking very much like a hermitage. In fact, it was the very place whither you came yesterday evening to petition me for an asylum.

While I was reconnoitring the neighborhood, which presented a most delicious landscape to my view, my companion said to me, it is six years since I traveled this way. At that time the grotto before us afforded a retreat to an old hermit who entertained me charitably. He made me fare as he did. I remember that he was a holy man, and talked in such a strain as almost to wean me from the vices and follies of this nether world. He may possibly be still living; I will ascertain whether it be so or not. With these words in his mouth, Ambrose, under the influence of natural curiosity, alighted from his mule, and went into the hermitage. He remained there some minutes, and then returned, calling after me. and saying, Come hither, Don Raphael, come and bear witness to a most effecting event. I dismounted immediately, we tied our mules to a tree, and I followed Lamela into the grotto, where I descried an old anchoret stretched at his length upon a couch, pale and at the point of death. A white beard, very thick, hung down to his middle, and he held a large rosary, most piously ornamented, in his clasped hands. At the noise which we make in coming near him, he opened his eyes, upon which death had already begun to lay his leaden hand; and after having looked at us for a moment, said, "Whosoever you are, my brethren, profit by the spectacle which presents itself to your observation. I have seen out forty years in the world, and sixty in this solitude. But mark! At this eternal crisis, the time I have devoted to my pleasures seems an age, and that on the contrary which has been sacred to repentance, but a minute! Alas! I fear lest the austerities of brother Juan should be found light in the balance with the sins of the licentiate Don Juan de Solis."

No sooner were these words out of his mouth than he breathed his last. We were struck by the solemn scene. Objects of this kind always make some impression even on the greatest libertines; but our serious thoughts were of no long duration. We soon forgot what he had been saying to us, and began making an inventory of what the hermitage contained; an employment which was not oppressively laborious, since the household furniture extended no further than what you remarked in the grotto. Brother Juan was not only in ill-furnished lodgings; his kitchen, too, was in a very rustic plight. All the store laid in consisted of some small nuts and some pieces of crusty barley bread as hard as flint, which had all the appearance of having been impregnable to the gums of the venerable man. I specify his gums, because we looked for his teeth, and found they had all dropped out. The whole arrangement of this solitary abode, every object that met our eyes, made us look upon this good anchoret as a pattern of sanctity. One thing only staggered us in our opinion. We opened a paper folded in the form of a letter, and lying upon the table, wherein he besought the persons who should read the contents, to carry his rosary and sandals to the bishop of Cuença. We could not make out in what spirit this modern recluse of the desert could aim at making such a present to his bishop. It seemed to us to tread somewhat on the heels of his humanity, and to savor of one who was a candidate for a niche in the calendar. Though indeed it might be, that there was nothing in it but a simple supposition, that the bishop was such another as himself; but whether his ignorance was really so extreme, I shall not pretend to decide.

In talking over this subject, a very pleasant idea occurred to Lamela. Let us take up our abode, said he, in this holy retreat. The disguise of hermits will become us. Brother Juan must be laid quietly in the earth. You shall personate him; and for myself, in the character of Brother Anthony, I will go and see what is to be done in the neighboring towns and villages. Besides that we shall be

"NO SOONER WERE THESE WORDS OUT OF HIS MOUTH THAN HE
BREATHED HIS LAST."

too cunningly ensconced for the prying curiosity of the corregidor, since it is not to be supposed that he will think of coming hither to look for us, I have some good connections at Cuença, which may be of essential service to us. I fell in with this odd whim, not so much for the reasons given me by Ambrose, as in compliance with the humor of the thing, and as it were to play a part in a dramatic piece. We made an excavation in the ground at about thirty or forty yards from the grotto, and buried the old anchoret there without any pompous rites, after having stripped him of his wardrobe which consisted of a single gown tied round the middle with a leathern girdle. We likewise despoiled him of his beard to make me an artificial one: and finally, after his interment, we took possession of the hermitage.

The first day our table was but meanly served; the provisions of the deceased were all we had to feed on; but on the following morning, before sunrise, Lamela set off to sell the two mules at Toralva, and returned in the evening, laden with provisions and other articles which he had purchased. He brought everything necessary to metamorphose us completely. For himself he had provided a gown of coarse dark cloth, and a little red horse-hair beard, so ingeniously appended to his ears, that one would have sworn it had been natural. There is not a cleverer fellow in the universe for a frolic. Brother Juan's beard was also new-modeled, and adapted to the plumpness of my face. My brown woolen cap completed the masquerade. In fact, nothing was wanting to make us pass for what we were not. Our equipage was so ludicrously out of character, that we could not look at one another without laughing, under a garb so diametrically at variance with our general complexion. With brother Juan's mantle, I caught and kept his rosary and sandals; taking the liberty of borrowing them for the time being from the bishop of Cuença.

We had already been three days in the hermitage, without having been interrupted by a living soul; but on the fourth, two countrymen came into the grotto. They brought bread, cheese, and onions, for the deceased, whom they supposed to be still living. I threw myself on our miserable couch as soon as they made their appearance; and it was not difficult to impose on them. Besides that it was too dark to distinguish my features accurately, I imitated the voice of brother Juan, whose last words I had heard, to the best of my ability. They had no suspicion of the trick, though a good deal surprised at finding another hermit there. Lamela, taking advantage of their stupid wonder, said in a canting tone: My brethren, be not astonished at seeing me in this solitude. I have quitted a hermitage of my own in Arragon, to come hither and be a companion to the venerable and edifying brother Juan, who, at his advanced age, wants a yoke-fellow to administer to his necessities. The rustics lavished their clumsy panegyrics on the charity of Ambrose, and congratulated themselves that they might triumph over their neighbors, and boast of two holy personages residing in their country.

Lamela, laden with a large wallet which he had not forgotten among the number of his purchases, went for the first time to reconnoitre the town of Cuença, which is but a very short distance from the hermitage. With a mortified exterior, by which nature had dubbed him for a cheat, and the art of making that natural deception go as far as possible, by a most hypocritical and factitious array of features, he could not fail to play upon the feelings of the charitable and humane, and those whom heaven has blessed with affluence. His knapsack bore testimony to the extravagance of their pious liberalities. Master Ambrose, said I on his return, I congratulate you on your happy knack at softening the souls of all good Christians. As we hope to be saved! one would suppose that you had been a mendicant friar among the Capuchins. I have done something else besides bringing in food for the convent, answered he. You must know that I have ferreted out a certain lass called Barbara, with whom I used to flirt formerly. She is as much altered as any of us : for she also has addicted herself to a godly life. She forms a coterie with two or three other sanctified dames, who are an example to the faithful in public, and flounce over head and ears in every sort of private vice. She did not know me again at first. What then, mistress Barbara, said I, is it possible that you should have discharged one of your oldest friends from your remembrance, your servant Ambrose? As I am a true Christian, Signor de La-mela, exclaimed she, I never thought to have turned you up in such a garb as that. By what transformation are you become a hermit? This is more than I can tell you just now, rejoined I. The particulars are rather long; but I will come to-morrow evening and satisfy your curiosity. Nay, more ; I will bring brother Juan, my companion, along with me. Brother Juan, interrupted she, the venerable hermit who has taken up his saintly residence near this town? You do not know what you are saying; he is supposed to be more than a hundred years old. It is very true, said I, that he was of that age some little while ago ; but time, in deference to his sanctity, has gone backward with him; and he is grown considerably younger within these few days. He is at present just about my turn of life. Say you so! Then let us have him too, replied Barbara. I perceive there is something more in this mystery than the church will be able to explain.

We did not miss our appointment with these whited sepulchres on the following night. To make our reception the more agreeable, they had laid out a sumptuous entertainment. Off went our beards and cowls, and vestments of mortification ; and without any squeamishness we confessed our birth, education, and real character to these sisters in hypocrisy. On their part, for fear of being behindhand with us in freedom from prejudice, they fairly let us see of what pretended religionists are capable, when they drop the vail of the sanctuary, and exhibit their unmanufactured faces. We spent almost the whole night at table, and got back to our grotto but a moment before daybreak. We were not long in repeating our visit ; or, if the truth must be told, it was nightly for three months ; till we had ate up more than two-thirds of our ways and means in the company of these delicate creatures. But an unsuccessful candidate for their favor got wind of our proceedings, and prated of our whereabout in the ear of justice, which was to have been in motion towards the hermitage this very day, to lay hold of our persons. Yesterday Ambrose, while picking up eleemosynaries at Cuença, stumbled upon one of our whining sisterhood, who gave him a note, with this caution: A female friend of mine has written me this letter, which I was going to send to you by a man on purpose. Show it to brother Juan, and regulate your proceedings accordingly. It was this very note, gentlemen, that Lamela gave me in your presence, which occasioned us to take so abrupt a leave of our solitary dwelling.

CHAPTER II.

DON RAPHAEL'S CONSULTATION WITH HIS COMPANY, AND THEIR
ADVENTURES AS THEY WERE PREPARING TO LEAVE THE WOOD.

WHEN Don Raphael had finished the narrative of his adventurous life, which, with all the other qualities of a romance, had the
tediousness, Don Alphonso, according to the laws of good breeding, swore himself black in the face that he had been prodigiously
entertained.   After the usual exchange of compliments, Signor
Ambrose put in his oar, with an admonitory hint to the partner of
his exploits and peregrinations.   Consider, Don Raphael, that the
sun is setting.   It would not be amiss, methinks, to take counsel on
what we are to do.   You are in the right, answered his comrade, we
must determine on the place of our destination.   For my own part,
replied Lamela, I am of opinion that we should get upon the road
again without loss of time, reach Requena to-night, and enter upon
the territory of Valencia to-morrow, where we will go to work full
tilt at our old trade.   I have some prognosticating twitches, which
tell me that we shall strike some good strokes in that quarter.   His
colleague, from ample experience of his infallibility in such prophecies, voted on his side of the question.   As for Don Alphonso and
myself, having nothing to do but to follow the lead of these two
worthy gentlemen, we waited, in silent acquiescence, the issue of
this momentous debate.

Thus it was determined that we should take the direction of
Requena; and all hands were piped to make the necessary arrangements.   We made our meal after the same fashion as in the morning, and the horse was laden with the bottle, and with the remnant
of our provisions.   After a time, the approach of night seemed to
promise us that darkness so friendly, and even so necessary, to the
safety of our retreat; and we were beginning our march through
the wood: but before we had gone a hundred paces, a light among
the trees gave us a subject of anxious speculation.   What can be
the meaning of that? said Don Raphael; these surely must be
blood-hounds of the police from Cuença, uncoupled and eager for
the sport, with a fresh scent of us in this forest, and in full cry
after their game.   I am of a very different opinion, said Ambrose;
they are more likely to be benighted travelers taking shelter in the
thicket till daybreak.   Bnt there is no trusting to conjecture: I
will examine into the real truth.   Stay you here all three of you; I
will be back again instantly.   No sooner said than done; he stole,
just as if he had been used to it, towards the light, which was not
far off; no brute or human thief of forest or city could have done it
better.   With a gentle removal of the leaves and branches which
obstructed his passage, the whole scene was laid open to his silent
contemplation; and it afforded sufficient food.   On the grass, round
about a lighted candle with a clod for its candlestick, were seated

four men, just finishing a meat pie, and hugging a pretty large bottle, which was at its last gasp, after having sustained their alternate
embraces for successive rounds. At some paces from these gentry,
he espied a lady and gentleman tied to the trees, and a little further
off, a carriage with two mules richly caparisoned. He determined
at once in his own mind that the fellows carousing on the ground
were banditti; and the tenor of their talk assured him that he had
not belied their trade by his conjecture. The four cut-throats all
avowed a like desire of possessing the female who had fallen into
their hands; and they were proposing to draw lots for her. La-

" ON THE GRASS, ROUND ABOUT A LIGHTED CANDLE WITH A CLOD FOR ITS
CANDLESTICK, WERE SEATED FOUR MEN."

mela, having made himself master of the business, came back to
us, and gave an exact account of all he had seen and heard.

My friends, said Don Alphonso on his recital, that lady and
gentleman whom the robbers have tied to trees, are probably persons of the first condition. Shall we suffer scoundrels like these
to triumph over their honor and take away their lives? Put yourselves under my direction: let us assail the desperate outlaws, and
they will perish under our attack. With all my heart, said Don
Raphael. It is all one to me, I had just as soon engage on the
right side as on the wrong. Ambrose, for his part, protested that
he wished for nothing better than to lend a hand in so moral an enterprise, as it promised to combine much profit with some share of

honor. And indeed, if a man may speak a good word for himself, danger stood better recommended than usual to my comprehension; all the boiling courage of knighthood, pledged up to the knuckles or the chin on the behalf of female innocence, was oozing out at every pore of this chivalrous person. But, if we are to state facts in the spirit of history rather than of romance, the danger was more in imagination than in reality. Lamela having brought us word that the arms of the robbers were all piled up at the distance of ten or twelve paces out of their reach, there was no difficulty in securing the mastery of the field. We tied our horses to a tree, and drew near, as softly as possible, to the spot where the robbers were seated. They were debating with some impetuosity, and their vociferous argument was all in favor of our covert attack. We got possession of their arms before they had any suspicion of us. But the enemy was nearer than they imagined: too near to miss aim, and they were all stretched lifeless on the ground.

During the conflict the candle went out, so that we proceeded in our business by guess-work. We were not remiss, however, in unbinding the prisoners, of whom fear had got such complete possession, that they had not their wits enough about them to thank us for what we had done for them. It must be allowed that they could not at first distinguish whether they were to consider us as their deliverers, or as a fresh gang who had taken them out of one furnace to cast them hissing into another. But we recovered their spirits by the assurance, that we should lodge them safely in a public-house which Ambrose mentioned as not being more than half a mile off, whence they might take all necessary measures to pursue their journey in whatever direction they thought proper. After these words of comfort, which seemed to sink deep, we placed them in their carriage, and conducted them out of the wood, holding their mules by the bridle. Our clerical friends instituted a ghostly visitation to the pockets of the vanquished banditti. Our next step was to recover Don Alphonso's horse. We also took to ourselves the steeds of the robbers, waiting as they were to be released from the trees to which they were tied near the field of battle. With this extensive cavalcade we followed brother Antony, mounted on one of the mules, and conducting the carriage to the inn, whither we did not arrive in less than two hours, though he had pledged his credit that the distance from the wood was very short.

We knocked roughly at the door. Every living creature was napping, except the fleas. The landlord and landlady got on their clothes in a hurry, and were not at all annoyed at finding their rest disturbed by the arrival of an equipage, which promised to do more for the good of the house than it eventually did. The whole inn was lighted up in an instant. Don Alphonso and the stage-bred son of Lucinda lent their assistance to the gentleman and lady in alighting from the carriage, and acted as their ushers in leading the way to the room prepared for them by the landlord. Compliments flew backwards and forwards like shuttlecocks; but we were not a little astonished at discovering the Count de Polan himself and his daughter Seraphina, in the persons we had just rescued.

It would be difficult to represent by words the surprise of that lady, as well as of Don Alphonso, when they recognized each other's features. The count took no notice of it, his attention being engrossed by other matters. He set about relating to us in what manner the robbers had attacked him, and how they secured his daughter and himself, after having killed his postilion, a page, and a valet-de-chambre. He ended with declaring how deeply he felt his obligation; and that if we would call upon him at Toledo, where he should be in a month, we should judge for ourselves whether he felt as a grateful heart ought to feel.

His lordship's daughter was not backward in her acknowledgments for her timely rescue; and as we were of opinion, that is, Raphael and myself, that we should do a good turn to Don Alphonso by giving him an opportunity of a minute's private parley with the young widow, we contrived to keep the Count de Polan in play. Lovely Seraphina, said Don Alphonso to the lady in a low voice, I no longer lament over the lot which obliges me to live like a man banished from civil society, since I have been so fortunate as to assist in the important service just rendered you. What then! answered she, with a sigh, is it you who have saved my life and honor? Is it to you that we are so indebted, myself equally with my father? Ah! Don Alphonso, why were you the instrument of my brother's death? She said no more upon the subject; but he conceived clearly by these words, and by the tone in which they were pronounced, that if he was over head and ears in love with Seraphina, she was equally out of her depth in the same passion.

BOOK THE SIXTH.

CHAPTER I.

THE FATE OF GIL BLAS AND HIS COMPANIONS AFTER THEY TOOK LEAVE OF THE COUNT DE POLAN. ONE OF AMBROSE'S NOTABLE CONTRIVANCES SET OFF BY THE MANNER OF ITS EXECUTION.

THE Count de Polan, after having exhausted half the night in thanking us, and protesting that we might reckon upon his substantial acknowledgments, sent for the landlord to consult him on the best method of getting safely to Turis, whither it was his intention to go. We had nothing to do with this nobleman's further progress, and therefore left him to take his own measures. Our departure from the inn was now resolved on; and we followed Lamela like sheep after the bell-wether.

After two hours' traveling, the day overtook us near Campillo.

We made as expeditiously as possible for the mountains between that hamlet and Requena. There we wore out the day in taking our rest and reckoning up our stock, which the spoil of the robbers had considerably replenished, to the amount of more than three hundred pistoles, the lawful ravage of their pockets. We began our march again with the setting-in of the night; and on the following morning reached the frontier of Valencia in safety. We got quietly into the first wood that offered as a shelter. The inmost recesses of it were best suited to our purpose, and led us on by winding paths to a spot where a rivulet of transparent water was meandering in its slow and silent course, to incorporate with the waters of Guadalaviar. The refreshing shade afforded by the foliage, and the rich pasturage in which our toil-worn beasts so much delighted, would have fixed this for the place of our halting, if our resolution had not been previously taken to that effect.

We therefore alighted, and were preparing to pass the day very pleasantly, but a good breakfast was amongst the foremost of our intended pleasures; and we found that there was very little ammunition left. Bread was beginning to be a nonentity; and our bottle was becoming an evidence of the material system, mere carnal leather without a vivifying soul. Gentlemen, said Ambrose, scenery and the picturesque have but hungry charms for me, unless Bacchus and Ceres preside over the landscape. Our provisions must be lengthened out. For this purpose, away post I to Xelva. It is a very pretty town, not more than two leagues off. I shall soon make this little excursion. Speaking after this manner, he slung the bottle and the wallet over a horse's back, leaped merrily into his seat, and shot out of the wood with a rapidity which seemed to bid fair for a speedy return.

He did not, however, come back quite so soon as he had given us reason to expect. More than half the day had elapsed; nay, night herself was already pranking up her dun and gloomy wings, to overshadow the thicket with a denser horror, when we saw our purveyor once again, whose long stay was beginning to give us some uneasiness. Our extreme wishes were lame and impotent, compared with the abundance of his stores. He not only produced the bottle filled with some excellent wine, and the wallet stuffed with game and poultry ready dressed, to say nothing of bread; the horse was laden besides with a large bundle of stuffs, of which we could make neither head nor tail. He took notice of our wonder, and said with a smile: I will lay a wager, neither Don Raphael nor all the colleges of soothsayers upon earth can guess why I have bought these articles. With this fling at our dullness, we untied the bundle, and lectured on the intrinsic value of what we had been considering only as an empty pageant. In the inventory was a cloak and a black gown of trailing dimensions; doublets, breeches, and hose to correspond; an inkstand and writing paper, such as a secretary of state need not be ashamed of; a key, such as a treasurer might carry; a great seal and green wax, such as a chancellor might affix to his decrees. When he had at length exhausted the display of his bargains, Don Raphael observed in a

bantering tone—Faith and troth, Master Ambrose, it must be confessed that you have made a good sensible speculation. But pray,
how do you mean to turn the penny on your purchase? Let me
alone for that, answered Lamela. All these things cost me only
ten pistoles, and it shall go hard but they bring us in above five
hundred. The tens in five hundred are fifty; a good improvement
of money, my masters! I am not a man to burden myself with a
trumpery peddler's pack; and to prove to you that I have not been
making ducks and drakes of our joint stock, I will let you into the
secret of a plan which has just taken birth in my pericranium.

After having laid in my stock of bread, I went into a cook's
shop, where I ordered a range of partridges, chickens, and young
rabbits, half-a-dozen of each, to be put instantly on the spit.
While these relishing little articles were roasting, in came a man
in a violent passion, open-mouthed against the coarse conduct of
a tradesman to his consequential self. This faggot of fury observed
to the lord paramount of the dripping-pan: By St. James! Samuel
Simon is the most wrong-headed retail dealer in the town of Xelva.
He has just insulted me in his own shop before his customers.
The skinflint would not trust me for six ells of cloth, though he
knows very well that my credit is as good as the bank, and that
no one could say he ever lost anything by me. Are not you delighted with the outlandish monster? He has no objection to
getting people of fashion on his books. He had rather toss up
heads or tails with them, than oblige a plain citizen in an honest
way, and be paid in full at the time appointed. What a strange
whim! But he is an infernal Jew. He will be taken in some day
or other! All the merchants on the Exchange are lying in wait to
catch him upon the hip; and his disgrace or ruin will be nuts to me.

While this reptile of the warehouse was thus spitting his spite
and blurting out many other ill-natured inuendos, there came over
me a sort of astrological anticipation that I should be lord of the
ascendant over this Samuel Simon, My friend, said I to the man
who was complaining against that hawker of damaged goods, of
what character is the strange fellow you are talking about? Of a
confoundedly bad character, answered he in a pet. Lepend on it,
he is one of the most extortionate usurers in existence, though with
the affectation of not letting his left hand know what his right
gives away in charity. He was a Jew, and has turned Catholic;
but rip your way into his heart if he has any, and you will find him
still as inveterate a Jew as ever Pilate was. As for his conversion
it was all in the way of trade.

I took in with greedy ear the whole invective of the shop-
keeping declaimant, and failed not, on coming out of the eating-
house, to inquire for Samuel Simon's residence. A person directed
me to the part of the town, and there was no difficulty in finding
out the house. It was not enough to skim my eye cursorily over
his shop. I peered into every hole and corner of it; and my
imagination, always on the alert when any profit is to be picked
up, has already engendered a rogue's trick, which only waits the
period of gestation, when it may turn out a bantering not un-

worthy to be fathered by the sanctimonious servant of Signor Gil Blas. Straightway went I to the ready-made warehouse, where I bought these dresses, into which we may stuff an inquisitor, a notary, and an alguazil, and play the parts in the spirit of the solemn offices they represent.

Ah! my dear Ambrose, interrupted Don Raphael, transported with rapture at the suggestion, what a wonderful idea! a glorious scheme indeed. I am quite jealous of the contrivance. Willingly would I blot out the proudest quarter from my escutcheon, to have owned an effort of genius so transcendent. Yes, Lamela, I see, my friend, all the rich invention of the design, and you need be at no loss for instruments to carry it into effect. You want two good actors to play up to you; and you have not far to look for them. You have yourself a face that can look sanctified, magisterial, or blood-thirsty at will, and may do very well to represent the inquisition. My character shall be that of the notary; and Signor Gil Blas, if he pleases, may enact the alguazil. Thus are the persons of the drama distributed: to-morrow we will play the piece, and I will pledge myself for its success, bating one of those unlucky chance medleys, which turn awry the currents of the most pithy and momentous enterprises.

As yet Don Raphael's masterpiece of roguery had made but a clumsy impression on my plodding brain; but the argument of the fable was developed at supper-time, and the hinge upon which it turned was, to my mind, of an ingenious contrivance. After having despatched part of our game, and lled our bottle to the last stage of evacuation, we stretched our length upon the grass, and soon fell fast asleep. Up with you! up with you! was the alarum of Signor Ambrose, as the day began to dawn. People who have a great enterprise on hand ought not to indulge themselves in indolence, A plague upon you, master inquisitor, said Don Raphael, rubbing his eyes, you are confounded early on the move! It is as good as an order for execution to master Samuel Simon. Many a true word is spoken in jest, replied Lamela. Nay, you shall know more, added he with a sarcastic grin. I dreamt last night that I was plucking the hairs out of his beard. Was not that a left-handed dream for him, master secretary? These pleasant hits were followed by a thousand others, which called forth new bursts of merriment. Our breakfast passed off with the utmost gayety; and when it was over, we made our arrangements for the pageant we had got up. Ambrose arrayed himself in sables, as befitted so ghostly an instrument for the suppression of vice. We also took to our official habits; nor has the dignity of magistracy been often more gravely represented than by Don Raphael and myself. The making up of our persons was rather a tedious operation; for it was later than two o'clock in the afternoon when we sallied from the wood to attend our call at Xelva. It is true, there was no hurry, since the play was not to begin till the setting-in of the evening. That being the case, we jogged on leisurely, and stopped at the gates of the town till the day was closed

At that eventful hour, we left our horses where they were, to the care of Don Alphonso, who was very well satisfied to have so humble a cast in the distribution. As for Don Raphael, Ambrose, and myself, our first visit was not to Samuel Simon in person, but to a tavern-keeper who lived very near him. His reverence the inquisitor walked foremost. In went he to the bar, and said gravely to the landlord : Master, I want to speak a word with you in private. The obsequious publican showed us into a room, where Lamela, now that we had got him to ourselves, said. I have the honor to be an unworthy member of the holy office, and am come here on a business of very great importance. At this intimation, the man of liquor turned pale, and answered in a tremulous tone that he was not conscious of having given any umbrage to the holy inquisition. True, replied Ambrose with encouraging affability ; neither do we meditate any harm against you. Heaven forbid, that august tribunal, too hasty in its punishments should make no distinction between guilt and innocence. It is unrelenting, but always just : to become obnoxious to its vengeance you must have earned its displeasure by wickedness or contumacy. Be satisfied therefore that it is not you who bring me to Xelva but a certain dealer and chapman, by name Samuel Simon. A very ugly story about him has come round to us. He is still a Jew in his heart, they say ; and has only embraced Christianity from sordid and secular motives. I command you, in the name of the tremendous court I represent, to tell me all you know about that man. Beware how you are induced by good neighborhood or possibly by close friendship, to gloss over and palliate his errors ; for, I warn you authoritatively, if I detect the slightest prevarication in your evidence, you are yourself even as one of the abandoned and accursed. Where is my secretary ? pursued he turning towards Don Raphael. Sit down and do your duty.

Mr. Secretary, with his paper already in his hand and his pen behind his ear, took his seat most pompously, and made ready to take down the landlord's deposition ; who promised solemnly on his part not to suppress one tittle of the real facts. So far so good said the worshipful commissioner ; we have only to proceed in our examination. You will only just answer my questions ; but do not interlard your replies with any comments of your own. Do you often see Samuel Simon at church ? I never thought of looking for him, said the drawer of corks ; but I do not know that I ever saw him there in my life. Very good ! cried the inquisitor. Write down that the defendant never goes to church. I do not say so, your worship, answered the landlord, I only say that I never happened to see him there. We may have been at church together and yet not have come across each other. My good friend, replied Lamela, you forget that you are deposing to facts, and not arguing. Remember what I told you ; contempt of court is a heinous offence. You are to give a sound and discreet evidence ; every iota of what makes against him, and not a word in his favor, if you knew volumes. If that is your practice, O upright and impartial judge, resumed our host, my testimony will scarcely be worth the trouble of taking. I know nothing about the tradesman you are inquiring after; and therefore can tell neither good nor harm of him: but if you wish to examine into the history of his private life, I will run and call Gaspard, his apprentice, whom you may question as much as you please. The lad comes and takes his glass here sometimes with his friends. Bless us, what a tongue! He will rip up all the minutest actions of his master's life, and find employment for your secretary till his wrist aches, take my word for it.

I like your open dealing, said Ambrose with a nod of approbation. To point out a man so capable of speaking to the bad morals of Simon, is an instance of Christian charity as well as of religious zeal. I shall report you very favorably to the inquisition. Make haste, therefore; go and fetch this Gaspard, of whom you speak, but do the thing cautiously, so that his master may have no suspicion of what is going forward. The multiplier of scores acquitted himself of his commission with due diligence and laudable privacy. Our little shopman came along with him. The youth had a tongue with a tang, and was just the sort of fellow that we wanted. Welcome, my good young man! said Lamela. You behold in me an inquisitor, appointed by that venerable body to collect information against Samuel Simon, on an accusation of still adhering to Judaism in his secret devotions. You are an inmate of his family, consequently you must be an eye-witness to many of his most private transactions. It probably may be unnecessary to warn you, that you are obliged in conscience, and by fear of punishment, to declare all you know about him, notwithstanding any promise to the contrary, when I order you so to do on the part of the holy inquisition. May it please your reverence, answered the plodding little rascal, I am quite ready to satisfy your heart's desire on that head, without being commanded thereto in the name of the holy office. If ever my acquittal was to depend on my master's character of me, I am persuaded that my chance would be a sorry one; and for that reason, I shall serve him as he would serve me. And I may tell you in the first place, that he is a fly-by-night whose proceedings it is no easy matter to take measure of; a man who puts on all the starch formalities of an inveterate religionist, but at bottom has not a spark of principle in his composition. He goes every evening dangling after a little girl no better than she should be . . . . I am vastly glad indeed to find that, interrupted Ambrose, because I plainly perceive, by all you have been telling me, that he is a man of corrupt morals and licentious practices. But answer point by point to the questions I shall put you. It is above all on the subject of religion that I am commissioned to inquire into his sentiments and conduct. Pray tell me, do you eat much pork at your house? I do not think, answered Gaspard, that we have seen it at table twice in the year that I have lived with him. Better and better! replied the paragon of inquisitors: write down in legible characters that they never eat pork in Samuel Simon's family. But as a set-off against that, doubtless a joint of lamb is served up every now and then? Yes, every now and then, rejoined the apprentice; we killed one for our own consumption about last Easter. The season is pat and to the purpose, cried the ecclesiastical commissioner. Come, write down, that Simon keeps the passover. This goes on merrily to a complete conviction; and it seems, we have got a good serviceable information here.

Tell me again, my friend, pursued Lamela, whether you have not often seen your master fondle young children. A thousand times, answered Gaspard. When he sees the little urchins playing about before the shop, if they happen to be pretty, he calls them in and makes much of them. Write that down, be sure you write that down! interrupted the inquisitor. Samuel Simon is very grievously suspected of lying in wait for Christian children, and enticing them into his den to circumcise them. Vastly well! vastly well, indeed, Master Simon! you will have an account to settle with the society for the suppression of Judaism, take my word for it. Do not take it into your savage head that such bloody sacrifices are to be perpetrated with impunity. A pretty use you make of baptism and shaving! Cheer up, religious Gaspard, thou foremost of elect apprentices! Make a full confession of all thy master's sins; complete thine honest testimony by telling us how this simular of a Catholic is more than ever wedded to his Jewish customs and ceremonies. Is it not a fact, that one day in the week he sits with his hands before him, and will not even perform the most necessary offices for himself? No, answered Gaspard, I have not exactly observed that. What comes nearest to it is that on some days he shuts himself up in his closet, and stays there a long time. Ay! now we have it, exclaimed the commissary. He keeps the sabbath, or I am not an inquisitor. Note that particularly, officer; note that he observes the fast of the sabbath most superstitiously! Out upon him! What a shocking fellow! One question more, and his business is done. Is not he always parleying about Jerusalem? Pretty often indeed, replied our informer. He knows the Old Testament by heart, and tells us how the temple of Jerusalem was destroyed. The very thing! resumed Ambrose. Secretary! be sure you do not neglect that feature of the case. Write, in letters of an inch long, that Samuel Simon has contracted with the devil for the rebuilding of the temple, and that he is plotting day and night for the re-establishment of his nation. That is all I want to know; and it is labor in vain to pursue the examination any further. What Gaspard, in the spirit of truth and charity, has deposed, would be sufficient to make a bonfire of all Jewry.

When the august mouth-piece of the holy tribunal had sifted the little scoundrelly apprentice after this manner, he told him he might go about his business; at the same time commanding him, under the severest penalties of the inquisition, not to say a word to his master about what was going forward. Gaspard promised implicit obedience, and marched off. We were not long in coming after him: our procession from the inn was as grave and solemn as our pilgrimage thereunto. till we knocked at Samuel Simon's door.

He opened it in person. Three figures such as ours might have dumbfounded a better man; but his face was as long as a lawsuit, when Lamela, our spokesman, said to him in a tone of authority: Master Samuel, I command you in the name of the holy inquisition, whose delegate I have the honor to be, to give me the key of your closet without murmur or delay. I want to see if I cannot find wherewithal to corroborate certain hints which have been communicated to us respecting you.

The son of commerce, aghast at these sounds of melancholy import, reeled two steps backward, just as if some one had given him a blow in the bread-basket. Far from smelling a rat in this pleasant trick of ours, he fancied in good earnest that some secret enemy had made him an object of suspicion to the holy hue-and-cry; and it might possibly have happened that, from being rather clumsy at his new duties as a Christian, he might be conscious of having laid himself open to serious animadversion. However that might be, I never saw a man look more foolish. He did as he was ordered without saying nay; and opened all his lock-up places with the sheepish acquiescence of a man who stood in awe of an ecclesiastical rap on the knuckles. At least, said Ambrose as he went in, at least you are not a contumacious oppugner of our resistless mandates. But withdraw into another room, and leave me to fulfill the duties of my station without profane observers. Samuel did not set his face against this command any more than against the first: but kept himself quiet in his shop, while we went all three of us into his closet, where, without loss of time, we laid an embargo on his cash. It was no difficult matter to find it; for it lay in an open coffer, and in much larger quantity than we could carry away. There were a great many bags heaped up; but all in silver. Gold would have been more to our mind: but, as robbers must not be choosers any more than beggars, we were obliged to yield to the necessity of the case. Not only did we line our pockets with ducats: but the most unsearchable parts of our dress were made the receptacles of our filchings. Yet was there no outward show of the heavy burden under which we tottered; thanks to the cunning contrivance of Ambrose and Don Raphael, who proved that there is nothing like being master of one's trade.

We marched out of the closet, after having feathered our nests pretty warmly; and then, for a reason which the reader will have no great difficulty in guessing, the worshipful inquisitor produced his padlock, and fixed it on the door with his own hands: he affixed moreover his own seal, and then said to Simon: Master Samuel, I forbid you, in the name of the holy inquisition, to touch either this padlock or this seal, which it is your bounden duty to hold sacred, since it is the authentic seal of our holy office. I shall return hither this time to-morrow, then and here to open my commission, and provisionally to take off the interdict. With this injunction, he ordered the street door to be opened, and we made our escape after the processional manner, out of our wits with joy. As soon as we had marched about fifty yards, we began to mend our pace into such a quick step, aggravated by degrees into a leap and a bound, that we were almost like vaulters and tumblers, in spite of the weight we carried. We were soon out of town; and mounting our horses once more, pushed forward towards Segorba, with many a pious ejaculation to the god Mercury, on the happy issue of so bold an attempt.

CHAPTER II.

THE DETERMINATION OF DON ALPHONSO AND GIL BLAS AFTER THIS ADVENTURE.

WE traveled all night, according to our modest and unobtrusive custom; so that we found ourselves at sunrise near a little village two leagues from Segorba. As we were all tired to death, it was agreed unanimously to strike out of the highway, and rest under the shade of some willows, which we saw at the foot of a little hill, about ten or twelve hundred yards from the village, where it did not seem expedient for us to halt. These willows furnished us with an agreeable retreat, by the side of a little brook which bubbled as it washed their roots. The place struck our fancy, and we resolved to pass the day there. We unbridled our horses, and turned them out to grass, stretching our own gentle limbs on the soft sod. There we courted the drowsy god of innocent repose for a while, and then rummaged to the bottom of our wallet and our wine-skin. After an ecclesiastical breakfast, we counted up our ten tithes of Samuel Simon's money; and it mounted to a round three thousand ducats. So that with such a sum and what we had before, it might be said, without boasting, that we knew how to make both ends meet.

As it was necessary to go to market, Ambrose and Don Raphael, throwing off their dresses now the play was over, said that they would take that office conjointly on themselves: the adventure at Xelva had only sharpened their wit, and they had a mind to look about Segorba, just to make the experiment whether any opportunity might offer of striking another stroke. You have nothing to do, added the heir of Lucinda's wit and wisdom, but to wait for us under these willows: we shall not be long before we are with you again. Signor Don Raphael, exclaimed I with a horse-laugh, tell us rather to wait for you under a more substantial tree; the gallows. If you once leave us, we are in a month's mind that we shall not see you again till the day after the fair. This suspicion of our honor goes against the grain, replied Signor Ambrose; but we deserve that our characters should suffer in your esteem. It is but reason that you should distrust our purity, after the affair at Valladolid, and should fancy that we shall make it no more a matter of conscience to play at the devil take the hindmost with you, than with the party that we left in the lurch in that town. Yet you deceive yourselves egregiously. The gang upon whom we turned the tables were people of very bad character, and their company began to be disreputable to us. Thus far justice must be done to the members of our profession, that there is no bond in all civilized life less liable to be broken by personal and private interest; but when there are no feelings in common, our good understanding will be the worse for wear, as it happens among other descriptions of men. Wherefore, Signor Gil Blas, I entreat you, and Signor Don Alphonso as well as you, to be somewhat more liberal in your construction of us, and to set your hearts at rest respecting Don Raphael's and my whim about going to Segorba.

It is the easiest thing in the world, observed Lucinda's hopeful brat, to quash all subject of uneasiness on that score: they have only to remain treasurers of the exchequer, and they will have a sufficient pledge in their hands for our return. You see, Signor Gil Blas, that we are all fair and above-board. You shall both hold security for our reappearance, and you may rest assured that for Ambrose and myself, we shall set off without the slightest misgiving of your taking to your heels with so valuable a deposit. After so substantial a proof of our good faith, will you not place implicit confidence in us? Yes, gentlemen, said I, and you may do at once whatever seems good in your own eyes. They took their departure immediately, carrying the bottle and the wallet along with them, and left me under under the willows with Don Alphonso, who said to me after they were out of sight: Now is the time, Signor Gil Blas, now is the time to open my heart to you. I am angry with myself for having been so easily prevailed on to herd thus far with these two knaves. You have no idea how many times I have quarreled with myself on that score. Yesterday evening, while I was watching the horses, a thousand mortifying reflections rushed upon my mind. I thought it did not become a young man of honorable principles to live among such scurvey fellows as Don Raphael and Lamela; that if by ill-luck some day or other, and many a more unlikely thing has happened, the success of our swindling tricks should throw us into the hands of justice, I might sustain the shame of being tried with them as a reputed thief, and undergoing the disgraceful sentence of the law. These frightful thoughts present themselves incessantly to my imagination, and I will own to you that I have determined, as the only means of escape from the contamination of their bad actions, to part from them for ever. I can scarcely suppose that you will disapprove of my design. No, I promise you, answered I: though you have seen me perform the part of the alguazil in Samuel Simon's comedy, do not fancy that such pieces as those are got up to my taste. I take heaven to witness that while acting in so witty a scene, I said to myself: Faith and troth, master Gil Blas, if justice should come and lay hold of you by the wesand at this moment, you would well deserve the penitential wages of your iniquity. I feel therefore no more disposed than yourself, Don Alphonso, to tarry longer in such bad company; and if you think well of it, I will bear you company. When these gentlemen come back, we will demand a balancing of the accounts, and to-morrow morning, or even to-night, before to-morrow, we will make our bow to them.

The lovely Seraphina's lover approved my proposal. Let us get to Valencia, said he, and we will embark for Italy, where we shall be able to enter into the service of the Venetian republic. Will it not be far better to take up the profession of arms, than to lead such a dastardly and disreputable life as we are now engaged in? We shall even be in a condition to make a very handsome figure with the money that will be coming to us. Not that I appropriate to myself without remorse a fund so unfairly established; but besides that necessity obliges me to it, if ever I acquire any property in my campaigns, I make a vow to indemnify Samuel Simon. I gave Don Alphonso to understand that my sentiments coincided with his own, and we resolved at once to separate ourselves from our companions on the following morning before daybreak. We were above the temptation of profiting by their absence, that is, of marching off in a hurry with the sum total of the finances: the confidence they had reposed in leaving us masters of the whole revenue, did not permit such a thought so much as to pass through our minds.

Ambrose and Don Raphael returned from Segorba just at the close of day. The first thing they told us was, that their journey had been propitious; for they had laid the corner-stone of a rascality which, to all appearance, would turn out still better than that of the evening before. And thereupon the son of Lucinda was going to put us in possession of the details; but Don Alphonso cut him short in his explanation, and declared at once his intention of parting company. I announced my own wish to do the same. To no purpose did they employ all their rhetoric, to prove to us the propriety of our accompanying them in their professional travels: we took leave of them the next morning, after having made an equal division of our cash, and pushed on towards Valencia.

CHAPTER III.

AN UNFORTUNATE OCCURRENCE, WHICH TERMINATED TO THE HIGH DELIGHT OF DON ALPHONSO. GIL BLAS MEETS WITH AN ADVENTURE WHICH PLACES HIM ALL AT ONCE IN A VERY SUPERIOR SITUATION.

WE galloped on gaily as far as Bunol, where, as ill-luck would have it, we were obliged to stop. Don Alphonso was taken ill. His disorder was a high fever, with such an access of alarming symptoms, as put me in fear for his life. By the greatest mercy in the world, the place was not beset by a single physician, and I got clear off without any harm but by fright. He was quite out of danger at the end of three days, and with my nursing, his recovery was rapid and without relapse. He seemed to be very grateful for my attentions; and as we really and truly felt a liking for each other, we swore an eternal friendship.

At length we got on our journey again, in the constant determination, when we arrived at Valencia, of profiting by the first opportunity which might offer to go over into Italy. But heaven disposed of us differently. We saw at the gate of a fine castle some country people of both sexes making merry and dancing in a ring. We went near to be spectators of their revels; and Don Alphonso was never less prepared than for the surprise which all at once came over his senses. He found it was Baron Steinbach, who was

"MY DEAR SON, KNOW IN ME THE AUTHOR OF YOUR BEING."

as little backward in recognizing him, but ran up to him with open arms, and exclaimed, in accents of unbridled joy—Ah, Don Alphonso! is it you? What a delightful meeting! While search was making for you in every direction, chance presents you to my view.

My fellow-traveler dismounted immediately, and ran to embrace the baron, whose joy seemed to me of an extravagant nature. Come, my long-lost son, said the good old man, you shall now be informed of your own birth, and know the happy destiny that awaits you. As he uttered these words, he conducted him into the castle. I went in along with them; for while they were exchanging salutations, I had alighted and tied our horses to a tree. The lord of the castle was the first persons whom we met. He was about the age of fifty, and a very well-looking man. Sir, said Baron Steinbach as he introduced Don Alphonso, behold your son. At these words, Don Cæsar de Leyva, for by that title the lord of the castle was called, threw his arms round Don Alphonso's neck, and weeping with joy, muttered indistinctly, My dear son, know in me the author of your being. If I have for so long left you in ig-

SERAPHINA.

norance of your birth and family, rest assured that the self-denial was mine in the most painful degree. I have a thousand times been ready to burst with anxiety, but it was impossible to act otherwise. I had married your mother from sheer attachment, for her origin was very inferior to mine. I lived under the control of an austere father, whose severity rendered it necessary to keep secret a marriage contracted without his sanction. Baron Steinbach, and he alone, was in my confidence: he brought you up at my request,

and under my directions. At length my father is laid with his ancestors, and I can own you for my son and heir. This is not all;
I can give you for a bride a young lady whose rank is on a level
with my own. Sir, interrupted Don Alphonso, make me not pay
too dear for the happiness you have just been throwing in my lap.
May I not be told that I have the honor of being your son without
being informed at the same time that you are determined to make
me miserable? Ah, sir! be not more cruel than your own father.

DON ALPHONSO.

If he did not consent to the indulgence of your passion, at least
he never compelled you to take another wife. My son, replied Don
Cæsar. I have no wish to exercise a tyranny over your inclinations,
which I spurned at in my own case. But have the good manners
just to see the lady I design for you, that is all I require from
your filial duty. Though a lovely creature and a very advantageous match, I promise never to force you into marriage. She is
now in this castle. Follow me you will be obliged to acknowl-

edge that you have rarely seen a more attractive object. So saying, he led Don Alphonso into a room where I made myself one of the party with Baron Steinbach.

There was the Count de Polan with his two daughters, Seraphina and Julia, and Don Ferdinand de Leyva, his son-in-law, who was Don Cæsar's nephew. Don Ferdinand, as was mentioned before, had eloped with Julia, and it was on the occasion of the marriage between these two lovers that the peasantry of the neighborhood were collected on this day to congratulate the bride and bridegroom. As soon as Don Alphonso made his appearance, and his father had introduced him to the company, the Count de Polan rose from his chair and ran to embrace him, saying—Welcome, my deliverer! Don Alphonso, added he, addressing his discourse to him, observe the power of virtue over generous minds. Though you have killed my son, you have saved my life. I lay aside my resentment for ever, and give you that very Seraphina whose honor you protected from invasion. In so doing, my debt to you is paid. Don Cæsar's son was not wanting in acknowledgment to the Count de Polan, nor could he be otherwise than deeply affected by his goodness; and it may be doubted whether the discovery of his birth and parentage touched his felicity more nearly than the intelligence that he was the destined husband of Seraphina. This marriage was actually solemnized some days afterwards, to the entire satisfaction of all parties concerned.

As I was one of the Count de Polan's deliverers, the nobleman, who knew me again immediately, said that he would take upon himself the care of making my fortune. I thanked him for his liberality, but would not leave Don Alphonso, who made me steward of his household, and honored me with his confidence. A few days after his marriage, still harping upon the trick which had been played to Samuel Simon, he sent me to return to that cozened shopkeeper all the money which had been filched from him. I went therefore to make restitution. This was setting up the trade of a steward, but beginning at the wrong end: they ought all of them to end with restitution; but nine hundred and ninety-nine out of a thousand think it double trouble, and excuse themselves.

BOOK THE SEVENTH.

CHAPTER I.

THE TENDER ATTACHMENT BETWEEN GIL BLAS AND DAME LOR-
ENZA SEPHORA.

AWAY went I to Xelva with three thousand ducats under my charge, as an equivalent to Samuel Simon for the amount of his loss. I will have the honesty to own, that my fingers itched as I jogged along, to transfer these funds to my own account, and begin my stewardship in character, since everything in this life depends upon setting out well. There was no risk in preferring instinct to principle: because it was only to ride about the country for five or six days, and come home upon a brisk trot as if I had done my business and made the best of my way. Don Alphonso and his father would never have believed me capable of a breach of trust. Yet, strange to tell, I was proof against so tempting a suggestion: it would scarcely be too much to say, that honor, not the fear of being found out, was the spring of so praiseworthy a decision; and as times go, that is saying a great deal for a lad, whose conscience had been pretty well seasoned by keeping company with a succession of scoundrels. Many people who have not that excuse, but frequent worshipful society, will wonder how such squeamishness should have prevailed over my good sense: treasurers of charities in particular; persons who have the wills of relations in their custody; and do not exactly like the contents; in short, all those whose characters stand higher than their principles, will find food for reflection in my overstrained scrupulosity.

After having made restitution to the merchant, who little thought ever to have seen one farthing of his property again, I returned to the castle of Leyva. The Count de Polan had taken his departure, and was far on his journey to Toledo with Julia and Don Ferdinand. I found my new master more wrapped up than ever in Seraphina; his Seraphina equally wrapped up in my master, and Don Cæsar just as much wrapped up as either in the contemplation of the happy couple. My object was to gain the good will of this affectionate father, and I succeeded to my wish. The whole house was placed implicitly under my superintendence—nothing was done without my special direction; the tenants paid their rents into my hands; the disbursements of the family were all under my revision; and the subordinate situations in the household were at my disposal without appeal; and yet the power of tyrannizing did not give me the inclination, as it has always hitherto done to my equals and superiors. I neither turned away the male servants, because I did not like the cut of their beards, nor the female ones because they happened not to like the cut of mine. If they made up to Don Cæsar or his son at once, without currying my favor as the channel of all good graces, far from taking umbrage at them on that account, I spoke out officiously in their behalf. In other respects, too, the marks of confidence my two masters were incessantly lavishing on me inspired me with a substantial zeal for their service. Their interest was my real object : there was no slight of hand in my ministry ; I was such a caterer for the general good, as you rarely meet with in private families or in political societies.

While I was hugging myself on the well-earned prosperity of my condition, love, jealous of my dealings with fortune, was bent on sharing my gratitude by the addition of a higher zest. He planted, watered, and ripened in the heart of Dame Lorenza Sephora, Seraphina's confidential woman, an abundant crop of liking for the happy steward. My Helen, not to sink the fidelity of the historian in the vanity of the man, could not be many months short of her fiftieth year. But for all that, a look of wholesomeness, a face none of the ugliest, and two good-looking eyes of which she knew the efficient use, might make her still pass for a decent bit of amusement in a summer evening. I could only just have been thankful for a little more relief to her complexion, since it was precisely the color of chalk ; but that I attributed to maiden concealments, which had eat away all the damask of her cheek.

The lady ogled me for a long time, with ogles that savored more of passion than of chastity ; but instead of communing in the language of the eyes, I made pretence at first not to be sensible of my own happiness. Thus did my gallantry appear as if arrayed in its first blushes, a circumstance which was rather tempting than repulsive to her feelings. Taking it into her head, therefore, that there was no standing upon dumb eloquence with a young man who looked more like a novice than he was, at our very first interview she declared her sentiments in broad, unequivocal terms, that I might have no plea for misinterpretation. She played her part like an old stager. Affected to be overwhelmed with confusion while she was speaking to me ; and after having said all she wanted to say in a good audible voice, put her hand before her face, to hide the shame which was not there, and make me believe that she was incommoded by the delicacy of her own feelings. There was no standing such an attack ; and though vanity had a larger share in my surrender than the tender passion, I did not receive her overtures ungraciously. Nay, more, I presumed to overlook decorum in my vivacity, and acted the impatient lover so naturally as to call down a modest rebuke upon my freedoms. Lorenza chid my fonddess, but with so much fondness in her chidings, that while she prescribed to me the coldness of an anchorite, it was very evident she would have been miserably disappointed if I had taken her prescription. I should have pressed the affair at once to the natural termination of all such affairs, if the lovely object of my ardent wishes had not been afraid of giving me a left-handed opinion of her virtue, by abandoning the works before the siege was regularly formed. This being so, we parted, but with a promise to meet again : Sephora in the full persuasion that her reluctant resistance would stamp her for a vestal in my esteem, and myself full of the sweet hope that the torments of Tantalus would soon be succeeded by an elysium of enjoyment.

My affairs were in this happy train, when one of Don Cæsar's under servants brought me such a piece of news, as gave an ague to my raptures. This lad was one of those inquisitive inmates who apply either an ear or an eye to every keyhole in a house. As he paid his court constantly to me, and served up some fresh piece of scandal every day, he came to tell me one morning, that he had made a pleasant discovery ; and that he had no objection to letting me into the fun, on condition that I would not blab : because Dame Lorenza Sephora was the theme of the joke, and he was afraid of becoming obnoxious to her resentment and revenge. I was too much interested in coming at the story he had to tell, not to swear myself into discretion through thick and thin ; but it was necessary that my motive should seem curiosity and not personal concern, so that I asked him, with an air of as much indifference as I could put on, what was this mighty discovery about which he made such a piece of work. Lorenza, whispered he, smuggles the surgeon of the village every evening into her apartment : he is a tight vessel, well armed and manned ; and the pirate generally stays pretty long upon his cruise. I do not mean to say, added he, with supercilious candor, but that all this may be perfectly innocent on both sides, but you cannot help admitting, that where a young man does insinuate himself slily into a girl's bed-chamber, he takes better care of his own pleasure than of her reputation.

Though this tale gave me as much uneasiness as if I had been verily and romantically in love, I had too much sense to let him know it ; but so far stifled my feelings as to laugh heartily at a story which struck at the very life of all my hopes. But when no witnesses were by, I made myself full amends for having gulped down my rising indignation. I blustered and stormed : muttered blessings on them the wrong way, and swore outright : but all this without coming nearer to a decision on my own conduct. At one time, holding Lorenza in utter contempt, it was my good pleasure to give her up altogether, without condescending so far as to come to any explanation with the coquet. At another time, laying it down as a principle, that my honor was concerned in making the surgeon an example to all intriguers, I spirited up my courage to call him out. Thus dangerous valor prevailed over safe indifference. At the approach of evening I placed myself in ambuscade ; and sure enough the gentleman did slink into the temple of my Vesta, with a fear of being found out that spoke rather unfavorably for the purity of his designs. Nothing short of this could have kept my rage alive against the chilliness of the night air. I immediately quitted the precincts of the castle, and posted myself on the high road, where the gay deceiver was sure to be intercepted on his return. I waited for him with my fighting spirits on the full boil : my impatience increased with the lapse of time, till Mars and Bellona seemed to inhabit my frame, and enlarge it beyond human dimensions. At length my antagonist came in sight. I took a few strides, such as bully Mars or Bellona might have taken; but I do not know how the devil it came to pass, my courage went further off as my body came nearer; my frame was contracted within somewhat less than its human dimensions, and my heart felt exactly like the heart of a coward. The hearts of Homer's heroes felt exactly the same, when the dastardly dogs were not backed by a supernatural drawcansir! In short, I was just as much out of my element as ever Paris was, when he pitted himself against Menelaus in single combat. I began taking measure of this operator in love, war, and anatomy. He appeared to be large limbed and well knit, with a sword by his side of a most abominable length. All this made me consider, that the better part of valor is discretion: nevertheless, whether from the superiority of mind over the nervous system in a case of honor, or from whatever other cause, though the danger grew bigger as the distance diminished, and in spite of nature, which pleaded obstinately that honor is a mere scutcheon, and can neither set a leg nor take away the grief of a wound, I mustered up boldness enough to march forward towards the surgeon sword in hand.

My proceeding seemed to him to be of the drollest. What is the matter, Signor Gil Blas? exclaimed he. Why all this fire and fury? You are in a bantering mood, to all appearance. No, good master shaver, answered I, no such thing; there never was anything more serious since Cain killed Abel. I am determined to try the experiment, whether as little preparation serves your turn in the field of battle as in a lady's chamber. Hope not that you will be suffered to possess without a rival that heaven of bliss in which you have been indulging but this moment at the castle. By all the martyrdoms we phlebotomizers have ever suffered or inflicted! replied the surgeon, setting up a shout of laughter, this is a most whimsical adventure. As heaven is my judge! appearances are very little to be trusted. At this put off, fancying that he had no keener stomach for cold iron than myself, I got to be ten times more overbearing. Teach your parrot to speak better Spanish, my friend, interrupted I: do you think we do not know a hawk from a hernshaw? Imagine not that the simple denial of the fact will settle the business. I see plainly, replied he, that I shall be obliged to speak out, or some mischief must happen either to you or me. I shall therefore disclose a secret to you; though men in our profession cannot be too much on the reserve. If Dame Lorenza sends for me into her apartment under suspicious circumstances, it is only to conceal from the servants the knowledge of her malady. She has an incurable ulcer in her back, which I come every evening to dress. This is the real occasion of those visits which disturb your peace. Henceforward, rest assured that you have her all yourself. But if you are not satisfied with this expectation, and are absolutely bent on a fencing match, you have only to say so; I am not a man to turn my back upon a game at sword play. With these words in his mouth he drew his long rapier, which

made my heart jump into my throat, and stood upon his guard. It
is enough, said I, putting my sword up again in its scabbard, I am
not a wild beast, to turn a deaf ear to reason : after what you have
told me, there is no cause of enmity between us. Let us shake
hands. At this proposal, by which he found out that I was not
such a devil of a fellow as he had taken me for, he returned his
weapon with a laugh, met my advances to be reconciled, and we
parted the best friends in the world.

From that time forward Sephora never came into my thoughts
but with the most disgusting associations. I shunned all the opportunities she gave me of entertaining her in private, and this
with so obvious a study, almost bordering on rudeness, that she
could not but notice it. Astonished at so sudden a reverse, she
was dying to know the cause, and at length, finding the means of
pinning me down to a tête-à-tête, Good Mr. Steward, said she, tell
me, if so please you, why you avoid the very sight of me? It is
true that I made the first advances ; but then you fed the consum-
ing fire. Recall to memory, if it is not too great a favor, the private interview we had together. Then you were a magazine of
combustibles, now you are as frozen as the north sea. What is the
meaning of all this? The question was not a little difficult of
solution, for a man unaccustomed to the violence of amorous interrogatories. The consequence was, that it puzzled me most confoundedly. I do not precisely recollect the identical lie I told the
lady, but I recollect perfectly that nothing but the truth could have
affronted her more highly. Sephora, though by her mincing air
and modest outside one might have taken her for a lamb, was a
tigress when the savage was roused in her nature. I did think,
said she, darting a glance at me full of malice and hideousness, I
did think to have conferred such honor as was never conferred
before, on a little scoundrel like you, by betraying sentiments
which the first nobility of the country would make it their boast
to excite. Fitly indeed am I punished for having preposterously
lowered myself to the level of a dirty, snivelling adventurer.

That was pretty well ; but she did not stop there : I should
have come off too cheaply on such terms. Her fury taking a long
lease of her tongue, that brawling instrument of discord rung a
bob-major of invective, each strain more clamorous and confound-
ing than the former. It certainly was my duty to have received it
all with cool indifference, and to have considered candidly that in
triumphing over female reserve, and then not taking possession of
the conquest, I had committed that sin against the sex, which
would have transformed the most feminine of them into a Sephora.
But I was too irritable to bear abuse, at which a man of sense in
my place would only have laughed ; and my patience was at length exhausted. Madam, said I, let us not rake into each other's personal
misfortunes. If the first nobility in the country had only looked
at your back, they would have forgotten all your other charms,
and have boasted but little of the sentiments they had excited you
to betray. I had no sooner laid in this home stroke, then the enraged duenna visited me with the hardest box on the ear that ever

'vet proceeded from the delicate fingers of a woman scorned. Such favors might pall on repetition; so I did not wait for a second, but took shelter in the nimbleness of my legs from the clatter of castigation she was going to shower down on me.

I returned thanks to the protecting powers for having brought me clear off from this unequal encounter, and fancied that I had nothing further to apprehend, since the lady had taken corporal vengeance. It was likely, too, that she would be wise and hold her tongue, for the honor of her own back: and, in point of fact, a full fortnight had elapsed without my hearing a word upon the subject. The very tingling in my own cheek began to abate, when I was told that Sephora was taken ill. With that forgiveness of injuries so natural to me, I was sincerely afflicted at the news. I really felt for the poor lady. I concluded that, unable to contend with a passion so ill repaid, that hapless victim of her own tenderness was giving up the ghost. It was with exquisite pain that I turned this subject in my thoughts. I was the cruel cause that her heart was breaking; and my pity at least was the duenna's, though love is too wayward to be controlled by advice. But I was miserably mistaken in her nature. Her tenderness had all curdled into acrimonious hatred; and at that very moment was she plotting to be my bane.

One morning while I was with Don Alphonso, that amiable young master of mine was absent, moody, and out of spirits. I inquired respectfully what was the matter. I am vexed to the soul, said he, to find Seraphina weak, unjust, ungrateful. You are not a little surprised at this, added he, remarking the expression of astonishment with which I heard him; yet nothing is more strictly and lamentably true. I know not what reason you have given Dame Lorenza to be at variance with you; but true it is, you are become so unbearably hateful to her, that if you do not get out of this castle as soon as possible, her death, she says, must be the sure consequence. You cannot but suppose that Seraphina, who knows your value, used all her influence at first against a prejudice to which she could not administer without injustice and ingratitude. But though the best of women, she is still a woman. Sephora brought her up, and she loves her like a mother. Should her old nurse die shortly, she would fancy she had her death to answer for, had she refused herself to any of her whims. For my own part, with all my affection towards Seraphina, and it is none of the weakest, I will never be guilty of so mean a compliance as to side with her on this question. Perish our duennas, perish the whole system of our Spanish vigilance! but never let me consent to the banishment of a young man whom I look upon rather as a brother than a servant!

When Don Alphonso had thus expressed his sentiments, I said to him: My good sir, I am born to be the mere whipping-top of fortune. It had been my hope that she would leave off persecuting me when under your roof, where everything held out to me happy days and an unruffled life. Now, the part for honor to take is to tear myself away, whatever hankering I may feel after my continuance. No, no, exclaimed the generous Don Cæsar. Leave me to bring Seraphina to a proper view of things. It shall never be said that you are sacrificed to the caprices of a duenna, who, on every occasion, has but too much influence over the family. All you will get by it, sir, replied I, will only be to put Seraphina in an ill humor by opposing her wishes. I had much rather withdraw than run the risk, by a longer abode here, of sowing division between a married pair, who are a model of conjugal felicity. Such a consequence of my unhappy quarrel would make me miserable for the remainder of my days.

Don Alphonso absolutely forbade me to take any hasty step; and I found him so determined in the intention of standing by me, that Lorenza must infallibly have been thrown into the background, if I had chosen to have stood an election against her. There were moments when, exasperated against the duenna, I was tempted to keep no measures with her; but when I came to consider that to unravel this surgical mystery would be to plunge a dagger into the heart of a poor creature, whose curse had been my fastidious prejudice against an ulcerated back, and whom a physical and mental misfortune were conjointly handing down to the grave, I lost all feeling but that of compassion towards her. It was evident, since I was so potentous a phenomenon, that it was my imperious duty to re-establish the tranquillity of the castle by my absence; and that duty I performed the next morning before daybreak, without taking any leave of my two masters, for fear they should oppose my departure from a misplaced partiality towards me. My only notice was to leave behind in my chamber a memorial, containing an exact account of my receipts and disbursements during the time of my stewardship.

CHAPTER II.

WHAT HAPPENED TO GIL BLAS AFTER HIS RETREAT FROM THE CASTLE OF LEYVA; SHOWING THAT THOSE WHO ARE CROSSED IN LOVE ARE NOT ALWAYS THE MOST MISERABLE OF MANKIND.

I WAS mounted on a good horse, my own property, and was the bearer of two hundred pistoles, the greater part of which arose from the plunder of the vanquished banditti, and the forfeiture of Samuel Simon by the Inquisition; for Don Alphonso, without requiring me to account for any part of the said forfeiture, had made restitution of the entire sum out of his own funds. Thus, considering my effects, however obtained, as converted into lawful property by a sort of vicarious sponsorship, I took them into my good graces without any remorse of conscience. An estate like this rendered it absurd to throw away any thought about the future;

and a certain likelihood of doing well, which always hangs about a young man at my age, held out an additional security against the caprices of fortune. Besides, Toledo offered me a retreat exactly to my mind. There could not be a doubt but the Count de Polan would take a pleasure in giving a kind reception to one of his deliverers, and would insist on his accepting an apartment in his own house. But I only looked upon this nobleman as a very distant resource; and determined, before laying any tax on his grateful recollection, to spend part of my ready cash in traveling over the provinces of Murcia and Grenada, which I had a very particular inclination to see. With this intention I took the Almanza road, and afterwards, following the route chalked out, traveled from town to town as far as the city of Grenada, without stumbling on any sinister occurrence. It should seem as if fortune, wearied out with the school-girl's tricks she had been playing me, was contented at last to leave me as she found me. But she still had her skittish designs upon me, as will be seen in the sequel.

One of the first persons I met in the streets of Grenada was Signor Don Ferdinand de Leyva, son-in-law, as well as Don Alphonso, of the Count de Polan. We were both of us equally surprised at meeting so far from home. How is this, Gil Blas? exclaimed he; to find you in this city! What the devil brings you hither? Sir, said I, if you are astonished at seeing me in this country, you will be ten times more so when you shall know why I have quitted the service of Signor Don Cæsar and his son. Then I recounted to him all that had passed between Sephora and myself, without garbling the facts in any particular. He laughed heartily at the recital; then, recovering his gravity, My friend, said he, my mediation is at your service in this affair. I will write to my sister-in-law . . . . . . No, no, sir, interrupted I, do not write upon the subject, I beseech you. I did not quit the castle of Leyva to go back again. You may, if you please, make another use of the kindness you have expressed for me. If any of your friends should be looking out for a secretary or a steward, I should be much obliged to you to speak a good word in my favor. I will take upon me to assure you that you will never be reproached with recommending an improper object. You have only to command me, answered he: I will do whatever you desire. My business at Grenada is to visit an old aunt in an ill state of health. I shall be here three weeks longer, after which I shall set out on my return to my castle of Lorqui, where I have left Julia. That is my lodging, added he, showing me a house about a hundred yards from us. Call upon me in a few days; probably I may by that time have hit upon some eligible appointment.

And, in fact, so it was; for the very first time that we came together again, he said to me: My Lord Archbishop of Grenada, my relation and friend, is in want of a young man with some little tinge of literature, who can write a good hand and make fair copies of his manuscripts; for he is a great auther. He has composed I know not how many homilies, and still goes on composing more every day, which he delivers to the high edification of his audience.

As you seem to be just the thing for him, I have mentioned your name, and he has promised to take you. Go, and make your bow to him as for me; you will judge, by his reception of you, whether my recommendation has been couched in handsome terms.

The situation was, to all appearance, exactly what I should have picked out for myself. That being the case, with such an arrangement of my air and person as seemed most likely to square with the ideas of a reverend prelate, I presented myself one morning before the archbishop. If this were a gorgeous romance, and not a grave history, here might we introduce a pompous description of the episcopal palace, with architectural digressions on the structure of the building: here would be the place to expatiate on the costliness of the furniture like an upholsterer, to criticise the statues and pictures like a connoisseur; and the pictures themselves would be nothing to the uninformed reader, without the stories they represent, till universal history, fabulous and authentic, sacred and profane, should be pressed into the service. But I shall content myself with modestly stating, that the royal palace itself is scarcely superior in magnificence.

Throughout the suite of apartments, there was a complete mob of ecclesiastics and other officers, consisting of chaplains, ushers, upper and menial servants. Those of them who were laymen were most superbly attired; one would sooner have taken them for temporal nobility than for spiritual understrappers. They were as proud as the devil; and gave themselves intolerably consequential airs. I could not help laughing in my sleeve, when I considered who and what they were, and how they behaved. Set a beggar on horseback! said I. These gentry are in luck to carry a pack without feeling the drag of it; for surely if they knew they were beasts of burden, they would not jingle their bells with so high a toss of the head. I ventured just to speak to a grave and portly personage who stood sentinel at the door of the archbishop's closet, to turn it upon its hinges as occasion might require. I asked him civilly if there was no possibility of speaking with my lord archbishop. Stop a little, said he, with a supercilious demeanor and repulsive tone: his grace will shortly come forth, to go and hear mass: you may snatch an audience for a moment as he passes on. I answered not a single syllable. Patience was all I had for it; and it even seemed advisable to try and enter into conversation with some of the jacks in office: but they began conning me over from the sole of my foot to the crown of my head, without condescending to favor me with a single interjection; after which they winked at one another, whispered, and looked out at the corners of their eyes, in derision of the liberty I had assumed, by intruding upon their select society.

I felt, more fool that I did so, quite out of countenance at such cavalier treatment from a knot of state footmen. My confusion was but beginning to subside, when the closet door opened. The archbishop made his appearance. A profound silence immediately ensued among his officers, who quitted at once their insolent behavior, to adopt a more respectful style before their master. That prelate was in his sixty-ninth year, formed nearly on the model of my uncle, Gil Perez the canon, which is as much as to say, as broad as he was long. But the highest dignitaries should always be the most amply gifted; accordingly his legs bowed inwards to the very extremity of the graceful curve, and his bald head retained but a single lock behind; so that he was obliged to ensconce his pericranium in a fine woolen cap with long ears. In spite of all this, I espied a man of quality in his deportment, doubtless, because I knew that he actually happened to be one. We common fellows, the fungus growth of the human dunghill, look up to great lords with a facility of being overawed, which often furnishes them with a Benjamin's mess of importance, when nature has denied even the most scanty and trivial gifts.

The archbishop moved towards me in a minuet step, and kindly inquired what I wanted. I told him I was the young man about whom Signor Don Ferdinand de Leyva had spoken to him. He did not give me a moment to go on with my story. Ah! is it you, exclaimed he, is it you of whom so fine a character has been given me? I take you into my service at once, you are a mine of literary utility to me. You have only to take up your abode here. Talking thus condescendingly, he supported himself between two ushers, and moved onwards after having given audience to some of his clergy, who had ecclesiastical business to communicate. He was scarcely out of the room, when the same officers who had turned upon their heel, were now cap in hand to court my conversation. Here the rascals are, pressing round me, currying favor, and expressing their sincere joy at seeing me become as it were an heirloom of the archbishopric. They had heard what their master had said, and were dying with anxiety to know on what footing I was to be about him; but I had the ill nature not to satisfy their curiosity, in revenge for their contempt.

My lord archbishop was not long before he returned. He took me with him into his closet for a little private conference. I could not but suppose that he meant to fathom the depth of my understanding. I was accordingly on my guard, and prepared to measure out my words most methodically. He questioned me first in the classics. My answers were not amiss; he was convinced that I had more than a schoolboy's acquaintance with the Greek and Latin writers. He examined me next in logic; nor could I but suppose that he would examine me in logic. He found me strong enough there. Your education, said he, with some degree of surprise, has not been neglected. Now let us see your hand-writing. I took a blank piece of paper out of my pocket, which I had brought for the purpose. My ghostly father was not displeased with my performance. I am very well satisfied with the mechanical part of your qualifications, exclaimed he, and still more so with the powers of your mind. I shall thank my nephew, Don Ferdinand, most heartily, for having sent me so fine a lad; it is absolutely a gift from above.

We were interrupted by some of the neighboring gentry, who were come to dine with the archbishop. I left them together, and withdrew to the second table, where the whole household, with one consent, insisted on giving me the upper hand. Dinner is a busy time at an episcopal ordinary ; and yet we snatched a moment to make our observations on each other. What a mortified propriety was painted on the outside of the clergy ? They had all the look of a deputation from a better world : strange to think how place and circumstance impose on the deluded sense of men ! It never once came into my thoughts that all this sanctity might possibly be a false coin ; just as if there could be nothing but what appertained to the kingdom above, among the successors of the apostles on earth.

I was seated by the side of an old valet-de-chambre, by name Melchoir de la Ronda. He took care to help me to all the nice bits. His attentions were not lost upon me, and my good manners quite enraptured him. My worthy sir, said he, in a low voice after dinner, I should like to have a little private talk with you. At the same time he led the way to a part of the palace where we could not be overheard, and there addressed me as follows : My son, from the very first instant that I saw you, I felt a certain prepossession in your favor. Of this I will give you a certain proof, by communicating in confidence what will be of great service to you. You are here in a family where true believers and painted hypocrites are playing at cross purposes against each other. It would take an antediluvian age to feel the ground under your feet. I will spare so long and so disgusting a study, by letting you into the characters on both sides. After this, if you do not play your cards, it is your own fault.

I shall begin with his grace. He is a very pious prelate, employed without ceasing in the instruction of the people, whom he brings back to virtue, like sheep gone astray, by sermons full of excellent morality, and written by himself. He has retired from court these twenty years, to watch over his flock with the zeal of an affectionate pastor. He is a very learned person, and a very impressive declaimer : his whole delight is in preaching, and his congregation take care he should know that their whole delight is in hearing him. There may possibly be some little leaven of vanity in all this heavenly-mindedness : but, besides that it is not for human fallibility to search the heart, it would ill become me to rake into the faults of a person whose bread I eat. Were it decent to lay my finger on anything unbecoming in my master, I should discommend his starchness. Instead of exercising forbearance towards frail churchmen, he visits every peccadillo, as if it were a heinous offense. Above all, he prosecutes those with the utmost rigor of the spiritual court, who, wrapping themselves up in their innocence, appeal to the canons for their justification, in bar of his despotic authority. There is besides another awkward trait in his character, common to him with many other people of high rank. Though he is very fond of the people about him, he pays not the least attention to their services, but lets them sink into years without a moment's thought about securing them any provision. If at any time he makes them any little presents, they may thank the goodness of some one who shall have spoken up in their behalf : he would never have his wits enough about him to do the slightest thing for them as a volunteer.

This is just what the old valet-de-chambre told me of his master. Next, he let me into what he thought of the clergymen with whom we had dined. His portraits might be likenesses ; but they were too hard-featured to be owned by the originals. It must be admitted, however, that he did not represent them as honest men, but only as very scandalous priests. Nevertheless, he made some exceptions, and was as loud in their praises as in his censure of the others. I was no longer at any loss how to play my part so as to put myself on an equal footing with these gentry. That very evening, at supper, I took a leaf out of their book, and arrayed myself in the convenient vesture of a wise and prudent outside. A clothing of humility and sanctification costs nothing. Indeed it offers such a premium to the wearer, that we are not to wonder if this world abounds in a description of people called hypocrites.

CHAPTER III.

GIL BLAS BECOMES THE ARCHBISHOP'S FAVORITE, AND THE CHANNEL OF ALL HIS FAVORS.

I HAD been after dinner to get together my baggage, and take my horse from the inn where I had put up, and afterwards returned to supper at the archbishop's palace, where a neatly furnished room was got ready for me, and such a bed as was more likely to pamper than to mortify the flesh. The day following, his grace sent for me quite as soon as I was ready to go to him. It was to give me a homily to transcribe. He made a point of having it copied with all possible accuracy. It was done to please him ; for I omitted neither accent, nor comma, nor the minutest tittle of all he had marked down. His satisfaction at observing this was heightened by its being unexpected. Eternal Father! exclaimed he in a holy rapture, when he had glanced his eye over all the folios of my copy was ever anything seen so correct? You are too good a transcriber not to have some little smattering of the grammarian. Now tell me with the freedom of a friend : in writing it over, have you been struck with nothing that grated upon your feelings? Some little careless idiom, or some word used in an improper sense? Oh! may it please your grace, answered I with a modest air, it is not for me, with my confined education and coarse taste, to aim at making critical remarks. And though ever so well qualified, I am satisfied that your grace's works would come out pure from the essay. The successor of the apostles smiled at my answer. He made no observation on it ; but it was easy to see, through all his piety, that he was an arrant author at the bottom : there is something in that dye, that not heaven itself can wash out.

I seemed to have purchased the fee-simple of his good graces by my flattery. Day after day did I get a step further in his esteem; and Don Ferdinand, who came to see him very often, told me my footing was so firm, that there could not be a doubt but my fortune was made. Of this my master himself gave me a proof some little time afterwards : and the occasion was as follows :—One evening in his closet he rehearsed before me, with appropriate emphasis and action, a homily which he was to deliver the next day in the cathedral. He did not content himself with asking me what I thought of it in the gross, but insisted on my telling him what passages struck me most. I had the good fortune to pick out those which were nearest to his own taste, his favorite common-places. Thus, as luck would have it, I passed in his estimation for a man who had a quick and natural relish of the real and less obvious beauties in a work. This, indeed, exclaimed he, is what you may call having discernment and feeling in perfection! Well, well, my friend! it cannot be said of you,

Bæotum in crasso jurares aëre natum.

In a word, he was so highly pleased with me, as to add in a tone of extraordinary emotion—Never mind, Gil Blas! henceforward rake no care about hereafter, I shall make it my business to place you among the favored children of my bounty. You have my best wishes; and to prove to you that you have them, I shall take you into my inmost confidence.

These words were no sooner out of his mouth, than I fell at his grace's feet, quite overwhelmed with gratitude. I embraced his elliptical legs with almost pagan idolatry, and considered myself as a man on the high road to a very handsome fortune. Yes, my child, resumed the archbishop, whose speech had been cut short by the rapidity of my prostration, I mean to make you the receiver-general of all my inmost ruminations. Hearken attentively to what I am going to say. I have a great pleasure in preaching. The Lord sheds a blessing on my homilies : they sink deep into the hearts of sinners; set up a glass in which vice sees its own image, and bring back many from the paths of error into the high road of repentance. What a heavenly sight, when a miser, scared at the hideous picture drawn by my eloquence of his avarice, opens his coffers to the poor and needy, and dispenses the accumulated store with a liberal hand! The voluptuary, too, is snatched from the pleasures of the table; ambition flies at my command to the wholesome discipline of a monastic cell; while female frailty, tottering on the brink of ruin, with one ear open to the siren voice of the seducer, and the other to my saintly correctives, is restored to domestic happiness and the approving smile of heaven, by the timely warnings of the pulpit. These miraculous conversions, which happen almost every Sunday, ought of themselves to goad me on in the career of saving souls. Nevertheless, to conceal no part of my weakness from my monitor, there is another reward on which my heart is intent, a reward which the seraphic scrupulousness of my virtue to little purpose condemns as too carnal; a literary reputation for a sublime and elegant style. The honor of being handed down to posterity as a perfect pulpit orator has its irresistible attractions. My compositions are generally thought to be equally powerful and persuasive; but I could wish of all things to steer clear of the rock on which good authors split, who are too long before the public, and to retire from professional life with my reputation in undiminished lustre.

To this end, my dear Gil Blas, continued the prelate, there is one thing requisite from your zeal and friendship. Whenever it shall strike you that my pen begins to contract, as it were, the ossification of old age, whenever you see my genius in its climacteric, do not fail to give me a hint. There is no trusting to one's self in such a case; pride and conceit were the original sin of man. The probe of criticism must be intrusted to an impartial stander-by, of fine talents and unshaken probity. Both those requisites centre in you: you are my choice, and I give myself up to your direction. Heaven be praised, my lord, said I, there is no need to trouble yourself with any such thoughts yet. Besides, an understanding of your grace's mould and calibre will last out double the time of a common genius; or to speak with more certainty and truth, it will never be the worse for wear, if you live to the age of Methusalem. I consider you as a second Cardinal Ximenes, whose powers, superior to decay, instead of flagging with years, seemed to derive new vigor from their approximation with the heavenly regions. No flattery, my friend! interrupted he. I know myself to be in danger of failing all at once. At my age one begins to be sensible of infirmities, and those of the body communicate with the mind. I repeat it to you, Gil Blas, as soon as you shall be of opinion that my head is not so clear as usual, give me warning of it instantly. Do not be afraid of offending by frankness and sincerity, to put me in mind of my own frailty will be the strongest proof of your affection for me. Besides, your very interest is concerned in it, for if it should, by any spite of chance towards you, come to my ears that the people say in town, "His grace's sermons produce no longer their accustomed impression, it is time for him to abandon his pulpit to younger candidates," I do assure you most seriously and solemnly, you will not only lose my friendship, but the provision for life that I have promised you. Such will be the result of your silly tampering with truth.

Here my patron left off to wait for my answer, which was an echo of his speech, and a promise of obeying him in all things. From that moment there were no secrets from me; I became the prime favorite. All the household, except Melchior de la Ronda, looked at me with an eye of envy. It was curious to observe the manner in which the whole establishment, from the highest to the lowest, thought it necessary to demean themselves towards his grace's confidential secretary; there was no meanness to which they would not stoop to curry favor with me; I could scarcely believe they were Spaniards. I left no stone unturned to be of service to them, without being taken in by their interested assiduities. My lord archbishop, at my entreaty, took them by the hand. He got a company for one, and fitted him out so as to make a handsome figure in the army. Another he sent to Mexico, with a considerable appointment which he procured him; and I obtained a good slice of his bounty for my friend Melchior. It was evident from these facts, that if the prelate was not particularly active in good works, at least he rarely gave a churlish refusal, when any one had the courage to importune him for his benevolence.

But what I did for a priest seems to deserve being noticed more at large. One day a certain licentiate, by name Lewis Garcias, a well-looking man still in the prime of life, was presented to me by our steward, who said—Signor Gil Blas, in this honest ecclesiastic you behold one of my best friends. He was formerly chaplain to a nunnery. Scandal has taken a few liberties with his chastity. Malicious stories have been trumped up to hurt him in my lord archbishop's opinion, who has suspended him, and unfortunately is so strongly prejudiced by his enemies, as to be deaf to any petition in his favor. In vain have we interested the first people in Grenada to get him re-established; our master will not hear of it.

These first people in Grenada, said I, have gone the wrong way to work. It would have been much better if no interest at all had been made for the reverend licentiate. People have only done him a mischief by endeavoring to serve him. I know my lord archbishop thoroughly: entreaties and importunate recommendations do but aggravate the ill condition of a clergyman who lies under his displeasure: it is but a very short time ago since I heard him mutter the following sentiment to himself. The more persons a priest, who has been guilty of any misconduct, engages to speak to me in his behalf, the more widely is the scandal of the church disseminated, and the more severe is my treatment of the offender. That is very unlucky, replied the steward; and my friend would be put to his last shifts if he did not write a good hand. But, happily, he has the pen of a ready scribe, and keeps his head above water by the exercise of that talent. I was curious to see whether this boasted hand-writing was so much better than my own. The licentiate, who had a specimen in his pocket, showed me a sheet which I admired very much: it had all the regularity of a writing-master's copy. In looking over this model of penmanship, an idea occurred to me. I begged Garcia to leave this paper in my hands, saying, that I might be able to do something with it which should turn out to his advantage; that I could not explain myself at that moment, but would tell him more the next day. The licentiate, to whom the steward had evidently talked big about my capacity to serve him, withdrew in as good spirits as if he had already been restored to his functions.

I was in earnest in my endeavor that he should be so, and lost no time in setting to work. Happening to be alone with the archbishop, I produced the specimen. My patron was delighted with it. Seizing on this favorable opportunity, May it please your grace, said I, since you are determined not to put your homilies to the press, I should very much like them at least to be transcribed in this masterly manner.

I am very well satisfied with your performance, answered the prelate, but yet I own that it would be a pleasant thing enough to have a copy of my works in that hand. Your grace, replied I, has only to signify your wishes. The man who copies so well is a licentiate of my acquaintance. It will give him so much the more pleasure to gratify you, as it may be the means of interesting your goodness to extricate him from the melancholy situation to which he has the misfortune at present to be reduced.

The prelate could not do otherwise than inquire the name of this licentiate. I told him it was Lewis Garcias. He is in despair at having drawn down your censure upon him. That Garcias, interrupted he, if I am not mistaken, was chaplain in a convent of nuns, and has been brought into the ecclesiastical court as a delinquent. I recollect some very heavy charges which have been sent me against him. His morals are not the most exemplary. May it please your grace, interrupted I in my turn, it is not for me to justify him in all points ; but I know that he has enemies. He maintains that the authors of the information you have received are more bent on doing him an ill office than on vindicating the purity of religion. That very possibly may be the case, replied the archbishop; there are a great many firebrands in the world. Besides, though we should take it for granted that his conduct has not always been above suspicion, he may have repented of his sins ; in short, the mercies of heaven are infinite, however heinous our transgressions. Bring that licentiate before me, I take off his suspension.

Thus it is that men of the most austere character descend from their altitudes, when interest or a favorite whim reduces them to the level of the frail. The archbishop granted, without a struggle, to the empty vanity of having his works well copied, what he had refused to the most respectable applications. I carried the news with all possible expedition to the steward, who communicated it to his friend Garcias. That licentiate, on the following day, came to return me thanks commensurate with the favor obtained. I presented him to my master, who contented himself with giving him a slight reprimand, and put the homilies into his hand, to copy them out fair. Garcias performed the task so satisfactorily, that he was reinstated in the cure of souls, and was afterwards preferred to the living of Gabia, a large market town in the neighborhood of Grenada.

CHAPTER IV.

THE ARCHBISHOP IS AFFLICTED WITH A STROKE OF APOPLEXY.
HOW GIL BLAS GETS INTO A DILEMMA, AND HOW HE GETS
OUT.

WHILE I was thus rendering myself a blessing first to one and
then to the other, Don Ferdinand de Leyva was making his arrangements for leaving Grenada. I called on that nobleman before his
departure, to thank him once more for the advantageous post he
had procured me. My expressions of satisfaction were so lively,
that he said—My dear Gil Blas, I am delighted to find you in such
good humor with my uncle the archbishop. I am absolutely in
love with him, answered I. His goodness to me has been such as
I can never sufficiently acknowledge. Less than my present happiness could never have made me amends for being at so great a
distance from Don Cæsar and his son. I am persuaded, replied
he, they are both of them equally chargrined at having lost you.
But possibly you are not separated for ever, fortune may some
day bring you together again. I could not hear such an idea
started without being moved by it. My sighs would find vent;
and I felt at that moment so strong an affection for Don Alphonso,
that I could willingly have turned my back on the archbishop and
all the fine prospects that were opening to me, and have gone
back to the castle of Leyva, had but a mortification taken place in
the back of the scarecrow which had frightened me away. Don
Ferdinand was not insensible to the emotions that agitated me,
and felt himself so much obliged by them, that he took his leave
with the assurance of the whole family always taking an anxious
interest in my fate.

Two months after this worthy gentleman had left us, in the
luxuriant harvest of my highest favor, a lowering storm came
suddenly over the episcopal palace; the archbishop had a stroke
of apoplexy. By dint of immediate applications and good nursing,
in a few days there was no bodily appearance of disease remaining.
But his reverend intellects did not so easily recover from their
lethargy. I could not help observing it to myself in the very first
discourse that he composed. Yet there was not such a wide gap
between the merits of the present and the former ones, as to warrant the inference that the sun of oratory was many degrees
advanced in its post-meridian course. A second homily was
worth waiting for; because that would clearly determine the line
of my conduct. Alas, and well-a-day! when that second homily
came, it was a knock-down argument. Sometimes the good prelate
moved forward, and sometimes he moved backwards; sometimes
he mounted up into the garret; and sometimes dipped down into
the cellar. It was a composition of more sound than meaning,
something like a superannuated schoolmaster's theme, when he at-

tempts to give his boys more sense than he possesses of his own, or like a capuchin's sermon, which only scatters a few artificial flowers of paltry rhetoric over a barren desert of doctrine.

I was not the only person whom the alteration struck. The audience at large, when he delivered it, as if they too had been pledged to watch the advances of dotage, said to one another in a whisper all round the church—Here is a sermon, with symptoms of apoplexy in every paragraph. Come, my good Coryphæus of the public taste in homilies, said I then to myself, prepare to do your office. You see that my lord archbishop is going very fast— you ought to warn him of it, not only as his bosom friend, on whose sincerity he relies, but lest some blunt fellow should anticipate you, and bolt out the truth in an offensive manner. In that case you know the consequence; you would be struck out of his will, where no doubt you have a more convertible bequest than the licentiate Sedillo's library.

But as reason, like Janus, looks at things with two faces, I began to consider the other side of the question; the hint seemed difficult to wrap up so as to make it palatable. Authors in general are stark mad on the subject of their own works, and such an author might be more testy than the common herd of the irritable race: but that suspicion seemed illiberal on my part, for it was impossible that my freedom should be taken amiss, when it had been forced upon me by so positive an injunction. Add to this, that I reckoned upon handling the subject skillfully, and cramming discretion down his throat like a high-seasoned epicurean dish. After all my pro and con, finding that I risked more by keeping silence than by breaking it, I determined to venture on the delicate duty of speaking my mind.

Now there was but one difficulty; a difficulty indeed! how to open the business. Luckily the orator himself extricated me from that embarrassment, by asking what they said of him in the world at large, and whether people were tolerably pleased with his last discourse. I answered that there could be but one opinion about his homilies; but that it should seem as if the last had not quite struck home to the hearts of the audience, like those which had gone before. Do you really mean what you say, my friend? replied he, with a sort of wriggling surprise. Then my congregation are more in the temper of Aristarchus than of Longinus! No, may it please your grace, rejoined I, quite the contrary. Performances of that order are above the reach of vulgar criticism; there is not a soul but expects to be saved by their influence. Nevertheless, since you have made it my duty to be sincere and unreserved, I shall take the liberty of just stating that your last discourse is not written with quite the overpowering eloquence and conclusive argument of your former ones. Does not your grace feel just as I do on the subject?

This ignorant and stupid frankness of mine completely blanched my master's cheek; but he forced a fretful smile, and said—Then, good Master Gil Blas, that piece does not exactly hit your fancy? I did not mean to say that, your grace, interrupted I, looking very foolish. It is very far superior to what any one else could produce, though a little below par with respect to your own works in general. I know what you mean, replied he. You think I am going down hill, do not you? Out with it at once. It is your opinion that it is time for me to think of retiring? I should never have had the presumption, said I, to deliver myself with so little reserve, if it had not been your grace's express command. I act in entire obedience to your grace's orders; and I most obsequiously implore your grace not to take offence at my boldness. I were unfit to live in a Christian land! interrupted he, with stammering impatience; I were unfit to live in a Christian land if I liked you the less for such a Christian virtue as sincerity. A man who does not love sincerity sets his face against the distinguishing mark between a friend and a flatterer. I should have given you infinite credit for speaking what you thought, if you had thought anything that deserved to be spoken. I have been finely taken in by your outside show of cleverness, without any solid foundation of sober judgment?

Though completely unhorsed, and at the enemy's mercy, I wanted to make terms of decent capitulation, and to go unmolested into winter quarters: but let those who think to appease an exasperated author, and especially an author whose ear has been long attuned to the music of his own praises, take warning by my fate. Let us talk no more on the subject, my very young friend, said he. You are as yet scarcely in the rudiments of good taste, and utterly incompetent to distinguish between gold and tinsel. You are yet to learn that I never in all my life composed a finer homily than that unfortunate one which had not the honor of your approbation. The immortal part of me, by the blessing of heaven on me and my congregation, is less weighed down by human infirmity than when the flesh was stronger. We all grow wiser as we grow older, and I shall in future select the people about me with more caution; nor submit the castigation of my works but to a much abler critic than yourself. Get about your business! pursued he, giving me an angry shove by the shoulders out of his closet; go and tell my treasurer to pay you a hundred ducats, and take my priestly blessing in addition to that sum. God speed you, good Master Gil Blas! I heartily pray that you may do well in the world! There is nothing to stand in your way. but the want of a little better taste.

CHAPTER V.

THE COURSE WHICH GIL BLAS TOOK AFTER THE ARCHBISHOP HAD
GIVEN HIM HIS DISMISSAL. HIS ACCIDENTAL MEETING WITH
THE LICENTIATE WHO WAS SO DEEPLY IN HIS DEBT, AND A
PICTURE OF GRATITUDE IN THE PERSON OF A PARSON.

I MADE the best of my way out of the closet, cursing the caprice,
or more properly the dotage of the archbishop, and more in dudgeon at his absurdity, than cast down at the loss of his good graces.
For some time it was a moot point whether I should go and lay
claim to my hundred ducats; but after having weighed the matter
dispassionately, I was not such a fool as to quarrel with my bread
and butter. There was no reason why that money, fairly earned,
should deprive me of my natural right to make a joke of this ridiculous prelate; in which good deed I promised myself not to be
wanting, as often as himself or his homilies were brought upon the
carpet in my hearing.

I went therefore and asked the treasurer for a hundred ducats,
without telling a word about the literary warfare between his master and me. Afterwards I called on Melchior de la Ronda, to take
a long leave of him. He was too much my friend not to sympa-
thise with my misfortune. While I was telling my story vexation
was strongly imprinted on my countenance. In spite of all his respect for the archbishop, he could not help blaming him; but, when
in the fever of my resentment I threatened to be a match for the
prelate, and to entertain the whole city at his expense, the prudent
Melchior gave me a salutary caution: Take my advice, my dear
Gil Blas, and rather pocket the affront. Men of a lower sphere in
life should always be cap in hand to people of quality, whatever
may be their grounds of complaint. It must be admitted, there
are some very coarse specimens of greatness, which in themselves
are scarcely deserving of the least respect or attention; but even
such animals have their weapons of annoyance, and it is best to keep
out of their way.

I thanked the old valet-de-chambre for the good counsel he had
given me, and promised to be guided by it. Pleased with my deference to his opinion, he said to me: If you go to Madrid, be sure
you call upon my nephew, Joseph Navarro. He is factotum in the
the family of Signor Don Balthazar de Zunigna, and I can venture
to recommend him as a lad in every respect worthy of your friendship. He is just as nature made him, with all the vivacity of youth,
courteous in his manners, and forward to oblige; I could wish you
to get acquainted with him. I answered that I would not fail to
go and see this Joseph Navarro as soon as I should get to Madrid,
whither I meant to return in due time. Then did I turn my back
on the episcopal palace, never to grace it with my presence again.
If I had kept my horse, I should perhaps have set out for Toledo

immediately; but I had sold it during the period of my administration, supposing that I was in office for life, and should not henceforward be migratory. My final resolution was to hire a ready-furnished lodging, as I had made up my mind to stay another month in Grenada, and then to pay the Count de Polan a visit.

As dinner-hour was drawing nigh, I asked my landlady if there was any eating-house in the neighborhood. She answered that there was a very good one within a few yards of her house, where the accommodations were excellent, and the company select and numerous. I made her show me where it was, and went thither sharp set. I was shown into a large room, resembling a hall of a monastery in everything but good cheer. There were ten or a dozen men sitting at a long table, with a cloth spread over it that fretted in its own grease; but they, with unoffended nostrils, were engaged in general conversation, though they dined individually, each having a miserable scrap for his portion. The people of the house brought me my allowance, which at another time would have turned my stomach, and have made me sigh after the luxuries of the table I had just lost. But at this moment I was so indignant against the archbishop, that the homely fare of a paltry eating-house seemed more palatable than the dainties of his sumptuous board. It was a burning shame to see such a waste of provisions served up in soups and sauces to pamper the appetite. Arguing like a deep examiner in the economy of the human frame, and reasoning medically as well as philosophically, on the disproportion between the simple wants of nature and the complexity of luxurious indulgence; cursed be they, said I, who invented those pernicious dinners and suppers, where one must sit on the tenterhooks of self-denial, for fear of overloading the storehouse and shop of the whole body! Man wants but little here below; and provided he can but keep body and soul together, the less he eats the better. Thus did I, in my surly vein, give utterance to wise saws; which, however just in theory, had hitherto been little recommended by my practice.

While I was dispatching my commons, without any danger of a surfeit from repletion, the licentiate Lewis Garcias, who had got the living of Gabia in the manner above-mentioned, came into the room. The moment he recognized me, he ran into my arms with all the cordiality of friendship, or rather with the extravagant joy of a lover after a long exile from his mistress. He folded me repeatedly within his sincere embrace, and I was compelled to stand the brunt of a long-winded compliment on the unparalleled disinterestedness of my conduct towards him. Gratitude is a fine virtue; and yet it is wearisome when carried beyond due bounds! He took his seat next me, saying: Well! a parson must not swear. though by the mass, my dear patron, since my good fortune has thrown me in your way, we will not part without a jovial glass. But as there is no good wine in this shabby inn, I will take you, if you please, after our make-shift dinner, to a place where I will treat you with a couple of bottles, rich, genuine, and old, in comparison of which the Falernian of Horace was all a farce. The church will give us absolution, in the cause of gratitude! If I could

but get you for a few days down at my parsonage of Gabia! Mæcenas was never more welcome to the poet's Sabine farm, than the
author of all my ease and comfort to the choicest produce of a
glebe which is mine only by your benevolence.

While he was holding this high-flown language, his little slice
of dinner was set before him. He fell to without the fear of indigestion before his eyes, still heightening the luxury of the repast
at intervals, by fine speeches addressed to me in the most fulsome
style of flattery. I took the opportunity, when his mouth was filled
with something more substantial, to edge in a word or two amidst
the torrent; and as he had not forgotten to ask after his friend the
steward, I made no bones about acknowledging that I was no longer a hanger-on of the church. I even went so far as to particular-
ize the most trivial circumstances attending my resignation, to all
of which he listened with an attentive ear. After all his fine professions, who would not have expected to see him moved even to
tears with the throes of resentful gratitude, to hear him thunder
bulls and interdicts against the superannuated archbishop? The
devil a bit! he did neither the one thing nor the other. But his
countenance fell, and his whole air was that of an absent man; the
rest of his dinner was bolted down without the garnish of intermediate talk about Mæcenas; as soon as he had done, he hurried
from table without minding grace or gratitude, wished me good
day with a cold and distant air, and got off as fast as possible. The
unfeeling scoundrel, perceiving that I was no longer in a situation
for him to pump anything out of me, would not even take the
trouble to draw a decent veil over his dirty principles. But such a
blackguard could excite no other sensation than contempt and
laughter. Looking at him with derision, the fittest chastisement
for fellows like these, I called after him loud enough to be heard
by the whole room: Stop there, you nun's priest! Go and put those
two bottles in ice against Mæcenas comes to the Sabine farm!
Be sure they are rich, genuine. and old: or they will be a farce to
Falernian.

CHAPTER VI.

GIL BLAS GOES TO THE PLAY AT GRENADA. HIS SURPRISE AT SEE-
ING ONE OF THE ACTRESSES, AND WHAT HAPPENED THEREUPON.

No sooner had Garcias rid the room of his presence, than two
gentlemen came in, extremely well dressed, and took their seats
close by me. They began talking about the players of the Grenada
company, and about a new piece which just then had a great run.
According to their account, it was quite the town talk. Nothing
would do for me, but to go and see it that very day. I had never
been at the play since my residence at Grenada. As I had lived

nearly the whole time in the archbishop's palace, where all such profane shows were condemned as uncanonical, I had been cut off from every recreation of that sort. All my knowledge of men and manners were drawn from homilies!

I repaired therefore to the theater at the appointed hour, and found a very full house. All around me, discussions were going on about the piece before the curtain drew up; and there was not a soul in the numerous assembly but had some remark to make upon it. One liked it, another could not bear it. Do not you think the dialogue is particularly happy? said a candid critic on my right: Was there ever such miserable stuff! cried a snarling critic on my left. In good truth, if bad authors abound, it must be admitted that the public are at variance about what is good and what is bad; but the bad judges have a right to be pleased for their money; and as they far outnumber the good ones, their favorite writers can never want employment. When one only considers through what an ordeal dramatic poets have to pass, it is a matter of wonder that any should be found hardy enough at once to contend against the ignorance of the multitude, and the random shot of those self-created guides in matters of taste, who always pretend to lead the blindness of the public judgment, and too frequently push it into the mire of absurdity.

At length the buffoon of the piece came forward by way of pro-logue. As soon as his grotesque countenance was visible, there was a general clapping of hands; a sure indication of his being one of those spoiled actors, who are allowed to take any liberties with the pit, and to be applauded through thick and thin. In fact, this player neither opened his lips, nor moved a muscle, without excit-ing the most extravagant raptures. He would have performed better, had he been less conscious what a favorite he was. But he presumed on that circumstance most abominably. I observed that he sometimes forgot what was set down for him, and took the license of adding to his part out of his own free fancy; a common cause of complaint against low comedians, which, though it make the unskillful laugh, cannot but make the judicious grieve. Would the audience but receive such mirth with hisses, instead of crying bravo, they might restrain the absurd practice, and purge the stage from barbarism.

Some of the other performers were greeted with the usual tokens on their entrance, and particularly an actress who played the chambermaid. There was something about her which more than usually attracted my attention; and language must sink under the labor of expressing my astonishment at tracing the features of Laura, that fair, that chaste, that inexpressible she, whom I sup-posed to be still at Madrid, warbling in one key, with hands, sides, voice, and mind incorporate with Arsenia. But there could be no doubt of her identity. The kick in her gallop, the leer in her eye, and the tripping pertness of her tongue, all conspired in evidence that there could be no mistake. Yet, as if I had refused belief to the affidavit of my own eyes and ears, I asked her name of a gentleman who was sitting beside me. What the deuce! Why, where do you come from? said he. You must unquestionably be a new importation, not to have seen or heard of the divine Estella.

The likeness was too perfect for me to be mistaken. It was easy to comprehend why Laura, changing her sphere of action, changed her name also; wherefore from curiosity to know how matters stood with her, since the public always pry into the most private concerns of theatrical persons, I inquired of the same man whether this Estella had any particular affair of gallantry on her hands. He informed me that for the last two months there had been a great Portuguese nobleman at Grenada, his name was the Marquis de Marialva, who had laid out a great deal of money upon her. He might have told me more, if I had not been afraid of becoming troublesome with my questions. I was better employed in musing on the information this good gentleman had given me, than in attending to the play; and if any one had asked me what it was all about, when the piece was over, I should have been puzzled for an answer. I could do nothing but decline Laura and Estella through all cases and numbers, till at length I boldly made up my mind to call at her house the next day. Not but there was some risk as to the reception she might give me; it might be suspected, without excess of modesty, that my appearance would give her no great pleasure in the high tide of her affairs; nor was it at all improbable that so good an actress, to revenge herself on a man, with whom certainly she had an account to settle, might look strange, and swear she had never seen his face before. Yet did none of these apprehensions deter me from my venture. After a light supper, for all the meals at my eating-house were regulated on principles of economy and temperance, I withdrew to my chamber with an anxious longing for the next day.

My sleep was short and interrupted, so that I got up by daybreak. But as it was to be recollected that a mistress in high keep was not likely to be visible early in the morning, I passed three or four hours in dressing, shaving, powdering, and perfuming. it was my business to present myself before her in a trim, not to put her to the blush at acknowledging my acquaintance. I sallied forth about ten o'clock, and knocked at her door, after having inquired her address at the theater. She was living on the first floor of a large and elegant house. I told the chambermaid who opened the door to me, that a young man wanted to speak with her lady. The chambermaid went in to give my message, when all at once I heard her mistress call out, not in the best-tempered tone in the world, Who is the young man? What does he want? Show him up-stairs.

This was a hint to me that my time was ill chosen; that probably her Portuguese lover was at her toilette, and that she spoke so loud, with the laudable design of convincing him that she was not a sort of girl to allow of any impertinent intruders. This conjecture of mine turned out to be the fact; the Marquis de Marialva lounged away almost every morning with her I had made up my mind to be kicked down-stairs by way of welcome; but that admirable actress, never forgetting her cue, ran forward with open arms at the sight of me, exclaiming Ah! my dear brother, is it you that I behold? On the strength of so near a kindred, she was no niggard of her embraces; but recollected herself so far as to say, turning round to the Portuguese, My lord, you must excuse me if nature will put in her claim, and trench upon good breeding. After three years of absence, I cannot see a brother once again, whom I love so tenderly, without expressing my feelings in all their warmth. Come! my dear Gil Blas, continued she, address-ing me afresh, tell me some news of the family; in what circum-stances did you leave it?

This whimsical scene disconcerted me at first; but I was not long in seeing through Laura's intention; and playing up to her with a spirit scarcely less than her own, answered according to the plot: Heaven be praised, sister, all our good folks are in perfect health, and well in the world. I make no doubt, resumed she, but you must be very much surprised to find me an actress in Grena-da; but hear me first and blame me afterwards. It is three years, as you may recollect, since my father thought to have established me advantageously in marriage with Don Antonio Cœllo, an offi-cer in the service, who took me from the Asturias to Madrid, his native place. Six months after our arrival, he got into an affair of honor in consequence of his violent temper. Some attentions in-cautiously paid to me were the cause of the affray, and his an-tagonist was killed. This gentleman was of a family high in rank and interest. My husband, who though well born, had very few connections, made his escape into Catalonia with everything he could get together in jewels and ready money. He embarked at Barcelona, went over into Italy, enlisted in the Venetian service, and finally lost his life in the Morea, fighting against the Turks. In the mean time, a landed estate which constituted our whole revenue was confiscated, and I was left a widow with very little for my support. What was to be done in so pressing an emergency? There was nothing left to pay my traveling expenses back into the Asturias. And then what should I have done there? I should have got nothing from my family but a long string of condolences, which would have furnished me neither with food nor with raiment. On the other hand, I had been too well brought up to fall into those courses, into which too many poor young women are betrayed for the sake of a scandalous subsistence. There was but one thing remaining for me to determine on. I turned actress to preserve my morals.

So tingling a sense of ridicule came over me, when Laura wound up her romance with this pious motive for turning actress, that I could scarcely refrain from relieving myself by a fit of laughter. But gravity was of too much consequence to be dispensed with; and I said to her with an air the counterpart of her own—My dear sister, I entirely approve of your conduct, and am heartily glad to meet with you at Grenada, and moreover settled on so respectable a footing.

The Marquis de Marialva, who had not lost a word of all these fine speeches, swallowed down blindfold whatever Don Antonio's widow thought fit to drench his credulity with. He took part in

the conversation too and asked me whether I had any fixed employment in Grenada or elsewhere. I paused for a moment to consider
whether and a ter what manner I should lie; but as there seemed no
need in the case to draw on my invention, I told the truth by way of
variety. In a plain matter of fact manner did I rehearse my introduction to the archbishop's palace, and my discharge therefrom,
to the infinite amusement of his Portuguese lordship. To be sure,
in telling the truth, I did not keep my word, for I could not help
launching out a little at the archbishop's expense, in spite of my
solemn promise given to Melchior. But the best of the joke was,
that Laura, taking my story for a fiction invented after her example, burst out into peals of laughter · whereas the whimsicality of
the circumstance would have raised a soberer mirth, had she known
it to have been alloyed with the base ingredient of veracity.

After having come to the end of my tale, which closed with just
mentioning the lodging I had taken, dinner was announced. I
instantly motioned to withdraw, as if intending to take that frugal
meal at home; but Laura would not hear of it. Do you mean to
affront me, brother? said she. You must dine here. Indeed, I
cannot think of your staying any longer at a paltry inn. You must
positively board and lodge in my house. Send your trunks hither
this very evening; there is a spare bed for you.

His Portuguese lordship, possibly not altogether relishing this
excess of hospitality even to a brother, then interfered between us,
and said to Laura—No, Estella, you have not sufficient accomo-
dation to give him a bed without inconvenience. Your brother
seems to be a clever young fellow, and the circumstance of his being so nearly related to you, gives him a strong claim on my kindness. He shall be put at once upon my establishment. I am in
want of a secretary, and shall delight in giving him the appointment · he shall be my right-hand man. Let him be sure to come
and sleep at my house this very night; I will order a room to be
got ready for him. I will fix his regular salary at four hundred
ducats · and if on better acquaintance I have reason, as I trust I
shall, to be satisfied with him, I will place him in a situation to
laugh at the consequences of having been a little too plain-spoken
with his patron the archbishop.

My acknowledgments to the marquis for this high honor were
followed by those of Laura, who far exceeded me in powers of
panegyric. Let us drop the subject, interrupted he; it is a settled
point. Settled as it was, he confirmed the contract on the lips of
his green-room Dulcinea, and went his way. She immediately
pulled me by the arm into a closet, where, secure from interruption,
she cried out, Cut my laces! I shall burst if I do not give way at
once to the fit of laughter that is coming over me. And so she
probably would; for she threw herself into an arm-chair, and holding both her sides, shouted out her convulsive peal of mirth like a
mad woman. It was impossible for me to refrain from following
her example. When we had exhausted our risible propensities,
Own, Gil Blas, said she, that we have just been acting a very humorous farce. But I did not look for the concluding scene. My

only thought was to secure you board and lodging under my own roof; and there was no other possibility of making the proposition in a modest way but by passing you off for my brother. But I am heartily glad that the chapter of accidents has opened with so good a berth for you. The Marquis de Marialva is a nobleman of liberal and honorable sentiments, who will be better than his word in what he does for you. But confess now! There is scarcely a woman in existence except myself, would have given so coming-on a reception to a fellow who shirks his friends without saying with your leave or by your leave. I however am one of those simple-hearted girls, who are glad to receive back again the base man they have once loved, though he should have offended and repented seven, or even seven thousand times.

The best way for me was to acknowledge the extreme ill-breeding of which I had been guilty, to blush and beg pardon once for all. After this explanation, she led the way to a very handsome dining-room. We placed ourselves at table, where having a chambermaid and a footboy for eye-witnesses, we kept within the bounds of brother and sister. When we had done dinner, we went back again into the same closet where we had been conversing before. Having our time to ourselves, my paragon of a Laura, giving herself up to her natural love of merriment, and to her no less natural curiosity, required from me a faithful and true narrative of all my pros and cons, my ins and outs, since that unmannerly separation of ours. I gave her a full and particular account: nothing extenuating on my own behalf, nor setting down aught in malice on the other side. When I had quenched her thirst after a story, she slaked mine, by communicating the particulars of her eventful life to the following effect.

CHAPTER VII.

LAURA'S STORY.

I SHALL just run over to you, as briefly as possible, the circumstances which led me to embrace the theatrical profession.

After you took French leave, so much to your credit, great events happened. My mistress Arsenia, more surfeited with a glut of pleasures than scandalized at their immorality, renounced the stage, and took me with her to a fine estate which she had just purchased in the neighborhood of Zenora with the wages of her sinful life. We soon got acquainted in the town. Our visits there were very frequent; and sometimes for a day or two together. With the exception of these little excursions, we were as closely domesticated as probationers in a nunnery, and almost as piously employed.

On one of our high days and holidays, Don Felix Moldonado, the corregidor's only son, saw me by chance, and took a liking to me. He soon found an opportunity of speaking with me in private; and, as it is in vain to affect modesty before one who knows me so well, there was some little contrivance of my own to bring the interview about. The young gentleman was not twenty years of age; the very picture of Venus's sweetheart, or Venus's sweetheart the very picture of him; with a form for a sculptor to work from; with an address so elegant, and with sentiments so generous, as to throw even his personal graces into the background. There was such a winning way with him, so pressing an earnestness to prevail, when he took a large diamond from his own finger, and slid it upon mine, that it would have been quite brutal not to have let it stay there. It was really something like sentiment that I began to entertain towards a swain of so interesting a character. But what an absurd thing it is for wenches of a certain sort to hook themselves upon young men of family, when their surly fathers hold official situations! The corregidor, who had scarcely his equal in the whole tribe of corregidors, got wind of our correspondence, and determined to close it in a summary manner. He sent a host of alguazils to take me into custody, who dragged me away, in spite of my cries and tears, to the house of correction for female penitents.

There, without bill of indictment or form of trial, the lady abbess ordered me to be stripped of my ring and my clothes, and to be dressed in the habit of the institution; a long gown of gray serge tied about the middle with a strap of black leather, whence depended a rosary with large beads swinging down to my heels. After this pleasant reception, they took me into a hall, where there was an old monk, the deuce knows of what order, who set to work preaching up repentance and resignation, pretty much in the same strain as Dame Leonarda, when she exhorted you to patience in the subterraneous cavern. He told me that I was excessively obliged indeed to those good people who had so kindly shut me up, and could never thank them sufficiently for their good deed, in rescuing me from the harpy talons of the world, the flesh, and the devil. But I must frankly own that all my other sins were pressed down and heaped high with ingratitude: far from overflowing with the milk of human kindness towards those who had conferred such a favor upon me, I abused them in terms that would have put any dictionary to the blush.

Eight days thus passed in this wilderness of desolation; but on the ninth, for I had notched the hours and even the minutes on a stick, my fate seemed beginning to take another turn. Crossing a little court, I met the house steward, a personage whose will was absolute: yes, the lady abbess herself was obedient to his will. He rendered an account of his stewardship to none but the corregidor, on whom alone he was dependent, and whose confidence in him was unbounded. His name was Pedro Zendono, and the town of Salsedon in Biscay laid claim to the honor of his birth. Figure to yourself a tall man, with the complexion of a mummy and the bare anatomy of a dealer in mortification; he might have sat for a penitent thief in a picture of the crucifixion. He scarcely ever cast a carnal glance towards us Magdalens. You never saw such a face of rank hypocrisy in all your life, though you have spent some part of it under the same roof with the archbishop, and are not unacquainted with the clergy of his diocese.

But to return from this digression; . . . . I met this Signor Zendono, who said to me slily as he passed—Take comfort, my girl, I am sensibly affected with your wretched case. He said no more, and went on his way, leaving me to make my own comments on so concise and general a text As he looked like a good man, and there was no positive evidence to set against his looks, I was simpleton enough to fancy that he had taken the trouble of inquiring why I was shut up; and meant, not finding me so atrocious a culprit as to deserve such shameful insults, to take my part with the corregidor. But I was not up to the tricks of the Biscayan, he had a much longer head. He was turning over in his mind the scheme of an elopement, and made the proposal to me in profound privacy some days afterwards. My dear Laura, said he, your sufferings have taken such deep possession of my mind, that I have determined to end them. I am perfectly aware that my own ruin is involved in the measure, but needs must when the tender passion drives. To-morrow morning do I intend to take you out of prison, and conduct you in person to Madrid. No sacrifice is too great for the pleasure of being your deliverer.

I was very near fainting with surprise and joy at this promise of Zendono, who, concluding from my acknowledgments that my very life depended on my rescue, had the effrontery to carry me off next day in the face of the whole town, by the following device:—He told the lady abbess that he had orders to take me before the corregidor, who was at his country box a few miles off; and without betraying himself by a single change of countenance, packed me off, with him for my companion, in a post-chaise drawn by two good mules which he had bought for the occasion. Our only attendant was the driver, a servant of his own, and entirely devoted to the steward by stronger ties than those of gratitude. We began bowling away, not in the direction of Madrid, as I had taken for granted, but towards the frontiers of Portugal, whither we got in less time than it took the corregidor of Zamora to receive the deposition of our flight, and uncouple his pack or set them barking at his heels.

Before we entered Braganza, the Biscayan made me put on man's clothes, with which he had taken the precaution of providing himself. Reckoning on me as being fairly launched in the same boat with him, he said to me in the inn where we put up, Lovely Laura, do not take it unkindly of me to have brought you into Portugal. The corregidor of Zenora will make our own country too hot to hold us, for in his eyes we are two criminals, under the weight of whose enormities it is not for Spain to groan. But we may set his malice at defiance in this distant realm, though at the present conjuncture under the dominion of the Spanish monarchy. At least we shall stand a better chance for safety here than at home. League your fortunes with those of a man who would follow you in prosperity or in adversity through the world. Let us fix our residence at Coimbra. There I will get employed as a spy for the inquisition; under the cover of that formidable tribunal, a refreshing shade for us, but Cimmerian darkness to its victims, our days will glide smoothly on in ease and pleasure, we shall fatten on the spoil of religious delinquency.

A proposal so much to the point gave me to understand that I had to do with a knight, who had other motives for officiating as the guardian of distressed damsels, besides the honor of chivalry. I saw at once that he reckoned much on my gratitude, and still more on my distress. Nevertheless, though these two pleas were almost equally eloquent in his favor, I rejected his addresses with disdain. The reason was, that there were two advocates still more eloquent on the side of a refusal; a certainty that he was disagreeable, and a strong suspicion that he was poor. But when he returned to the charge, and offered to say the grace of matrimony before he fell to, proving to me at the same time, by the undeniable evidence of cash in hand, that his stewardship had enabled him to live in clover for a long time to come, the truth must come out in spite of blushes; my heart was softened, and my ears unstopped. I was dazzled by the gold and jewels which he laid out in burning row before me, and became a living monument in my own person, that miraculous transformations are effected by the power of pelf, as well as by the wand of love. My Biscayan became, by little and little, quite another sort of man in my eyes. His tall body and bare bones were plumped up into a shapely and commanding figure; his cadaverous complexion was improved into a manly brown: even that look, as if butter would not melt in his mouth, was no longer hypocrisy, but a staid and decent aspect. Having made these discoveries, I accepted his hand without any material abhorrence, and he plighted the usual vows in all due form. After this, like a good wife, I kept the spirit of contradiction as much as possible under the hatches. We resumed our journey, and Coimbra soon received a new family within its walls.

My husband stocked my wardrobe as became my sex and station, making me a present of several diamonds, among which I fixed my eye on that of Don Felix Moldonado. There were no further documents wanting to give a shrewd guess whence came all the precious stones I had seen, and to be morally certain that I had not married a troublesomely nice observer of the eighth article in the decalogue. Yet, considering myself as the main-spring of all his little deviations from the strict law of propriety, it was not for me to judge harshly on that point. A woman can always find a palliation for the misdeeds which are set in motion by the power of her own beauty. But for that, he certainly would have ranked no higher than one of the wicked in my estimation.

I had no great reason to complain of him for two or three months. His attentions were always polite and kind, amounting apparently to a sincere and tender affection. But no such thing! These proofs of wedded love, this worshiping with the body, and endowing with the worldly goods, were all but a copy of his countenance; for the cheating fellow meant, as men serve a cucumber, to throw me away on the first opportunity. One morning, at my return from mass, I found nothing at home but the bare walls; the movables, not excepting my own apparel, every stick and every thread, had been carried off. Zendono and his faithful servant had taken their measures so adroitly, that in less than an hour the house had been completely gutted; so that with nothing but the gown upon my back, and Don Felix's ring, as good luck would have it, on my finger, here stood I, like another Ariadne, abandoned by the ungrateful rifler of my effects as well as of my charms. But you may take my word for it, I did not beguile the sense of my misfortunes in tragedy, elegy, scene individable, or poem unlimited. I rather fell upon my kness, and blessed my guardian angel, for having delivered me from a rascal who must sooner or later fall into the hands of justice. The time we had passed together I considered in the light of a dead loss, and my spirits were all on the alert to make up for it. If I had been inclined to stay in Portugal, as a hanger-on to some woman of fashion, I should have found no difficulty in suiting myself; but whether it was patriotism, or some astrological conjunction, preparing a better fortune for me under the influence of the planets, my whole heart was bent on getting back into Spain. I applied to a jeweler, who valued my diamond and gave me cash for it, and then took my departure with an old Spanish lady who was going to Seville in a post-chase.

This lady, whose name was Dorothea, had been to see a relation settled at Coimbra, and was on her return to Seville, where she lived. There was such a sympathy between us, as made us fast friends on the very first day of our acquaintance; and the attachment grew so close while we traveled together, that the lady insisted, at our journey's end, on my making her house my home. I had no reason to repent having formed such a connection. Never was there a woman of a more charming character. One might still conclude from the turn of her countenance, and from the spirit not yet quenched in her eyes, that in her youth the catgut of many a guitar must have been fretted under her window. As a proof of this, she had many trials what a state of widowhood was; her husbands had all been of noble birth, and her finances were flourishing on the accumulation of her several jointures.

Among other admirable qualities, she had that of not visiting severely the frailties of her own sex. When I let her into the secret of mine, she entered so warmly into my interests, as to speak of Zendono with more sincerity than good manners. What graceless fellows these men are! said she in a tone from which one might infer that she had met with some light-fingered steward in the passing of her accounts. They would not be worth picking off a dunghill, if one could do without them! There is a large fraternity of sorry scoundrels in the world, who make it their sport to gain the hearts of women, and then desert them. There is, however, one consoling circumstance. my dear child. According to

your account, you are by no means bound fast to that faithless
Biscayan. If your marriage with him was sufficiently formal to
save your credit with the world, on the other hand, it was contracted loosely enough to admit of your trying your luck at a better
match, whenever an opportunity may fall in your way.

I went out every day with Dorothea, either to church, or to visit
among her friends; both likely occasions of picking up an adventure; so that I attracted the notice of several gentlemen. There
were some of them who had a mind to feel how the land lay. They
made their proposals to my venerable protectress; but these had
not wherewithal to defray the expenses of an establishment, and
those were mere unfledged boys under age; an insuperable objection, which left me very little merit in turning a deaf ear to them.
One day a whim seized Dorothea and me, to go and see a play at
Seville. The bills announced a favorite and standard piece: El
Embaxador de Si-mismo, written by Lope de Vega.

Among the actresses who came upon the stage, I discovered
one of my old cronies. It was impossible to have forgotten Phenicia, that bouncing good-humored girl whom you have seen as
Florimonde's waiting-maid, and have supped with more than once
at Arsenia's. I was aware that Phenicia had left Madrid above
two years ago, but had never heard of her turning actress. I
longed so earnestly to embrace her, that the piece appeared quite
tedious. Perhaps, too, there might be some fault in those who
played it, as being neither good enough nor bad enough to afford
me entertainment. For as to my own temper, which is that of
seeking diversion wherever I can find it, I must confess that an
actor supremely ridiculous answers my purpose just as well as the
most finished performer of the age.

At last, the moment I had been waiting for being arrived,
namely the dropping of the curtain on this favorite and standard
piece, we went, for my widow would go with me, behind the scenes,
where we caught a glimpse of Phenicia, who was playing off the
amiable and unaffected simpleton, and listening with all the prim-
ness of studied simplicity to the soft chirping of a young stagefinch,
who had evidently suffered himself to be caught in the birdlime of
her professional or meretricious talents. No sooner did her eye
meet mine, than she quitted him with a genteel apology, ran up to
me with open arms, and lavished upon me all the demonstrations
of strong attachment imaginable. Our expressions of joy at this
unexpected meeting were indeed reciprocal; but neither time nor
place admitting of any very copious indulgence in the privilege of
asking questions, we adjourned till the following day, with a
promise of renewing our mutual inquiries thick and threefold,
under the shelter of her friendly roof.

The pleasure of talking is the inextinguishable passion of
woman, coeval with the act of breathing. I could not get a wink
of sleep all night, for the burning desire of having a grapple with
Phenicia, and closing in upon her in the conflict of curiosity.
Witness all the powers who preside over tattling, whether the love
of lying in bed, another passion of woman, prevented me from get-

ting up and flying to my appointment as early as good manners would allow. She lived with the rest of the company in a large ready-furnished lodging. A female attendant who met me at entrance, on being requested to show me Phenicia's apartment, led the way up-stairs to a gallery, along which were ranged ten or twelve small rooms, divided only by partitions of deal boards, and inhabited by this merry band. My conductress knocked at a door which Phenicia opened; for her tongue was cruelly on the fidget to be let loose, as well as my own. We allowed ourselves no time for the impertinent ceremonies which usually usher in a visit, but plunged at once into a most furious career of loquacity. It seemed as if we should have a tight bout together. They were so many interrogatories to be bandied backwards and forwards, that question and answer rebounded like tennis-balls, only with tenfold velocity.

After having related our adventures each to other, and inquired into the actual condition of affairs, Phenicia asked me how I meant to provide for myself. My reply was, that I purposed, while waiting for something better, to get a situation with some young lady of quality. For shame, exclaimed my other self, you shall not think of such a thing. Is it possible, my darling, that you should not yet be disgusted with menial service? Are you not heartily sick of knocking under to the good or ill pleasure of others, of being cap-in-hand to all their caprices, and after all to be entertained with that unchangeable tune called a scolding, in a word, to be a downright slave? Why do not you follow my example, and turn your thoughts towards the stage? Nothing can be better suited to people of parts, when they happen not to be equally favored in the articles of wealth and birth. It is a sphere of life which holds a middle rank between the nobility and mere tradespeople; a profession exempted from all troublesome restraint, and raised far above the common prejudices of humble and decent society. The public are our bankers, and we draw upon them at sight. We live in a continual round of ecstacy, and spend our money to the full as fast as we earn it.

The theater (for she went on at a great rate) is favorable above all to women. When I lived with Florimonde, it is a misery to think of it, I was reduced to take up with the supernumeraries ơ the prince's company; not a single man of fashion paid the least attention to my figure. How came that about? Because they never got a glimpse of it. The finest picture in the world may escape the admiration of the connoisseurs, if it is not placed in a proper light. But since I have been suitably framed and varnished, which could only happen in consequence of a theatrical finish, what a revolution! The finest young fellows of all the towns we pass through are shuffling at my heels. An actress therefore has all her little comforts about her, without deviating from the line of her duty. If she is discreet, by which we mean that she should not admit more than one lover into her good graces at a time, her exemplary conduct is cried up as without a parallel. She is called a very Niobe for her coldness; and when she changes her favorite, she is reprimanded as slightly by the world, as a lawful widow who marries a few weeks too soon after the death of her first husband. If, however, the widow should look for luck in odd numbers, and take to herself a third, the contempt of all mankind is poured down on her devoted head; she is considered as a monster of indelicacy; whereas we happier women are so much the more in vogue, as we add to the list of our favorites. After having been served up to a hundred different lovers, some battered nobleman finds us a dainty dish for himself.

Do you mean that by way of news? interrupted I as she uttered the last sentiment. Do you imagine me to be ignorant of these advantages? I have often conned them over in my mind, and they are but too alluring to a girl of my character. The attractions of the stage would be irresistible, were inclination all. But some little talent is indispensable; and I have not a spark. I have sometimes attempted to rehearse passages from plays before Arsenia. She was never satisfied with my performance: and that disgusted me with the profession. You are easily put out of conceit with yourself, replied Phenicia. Do not you know that these great actresses are very apt to be jealous? With all their vanity, they are afraid lest some newer face should put them out of countenance. In short, I would not be guided by Arsenia on that subject; she did not give her real opinion. In my judgment, and without meaning to flatter you, the theater is your natural element. You have admirable powers, free and graceful action, a fine-toned voice, volubility of declamation, and such a turn of countenance! Ah! you little rogue! you will bring all the young fellows behind the scenes, if once you take to the boards!

She plied me with many flattering compliments besides; and made me recite some lines, only by way of enabling me to form my own judgment as to my theatrical genius. Now that she was my censor, it seemed quite another thing. She praised me up to the skies, and held all the actresses in Madrid as mere makeweights in the scale. After such a testimony, it would have been inexcusable to hesitate about my own merit. Arsenia stood attainted, nay, convicted of jealousy and treachery. There could be no question about my being everything that was delightful. Two players happened to drop in by accident, and Phenicia prevailed on me to repeat the lines I had already spouted; they fell into a sort of enthusiastic trance, whence they were roused only to launch out fervently in admiration of me. Literally, had they all three been flattering me up for a wager, they could not have adopted a more extravagant scale of panegyric. My modesty was not proof against such praise from those who were themselves praised. I began to think myself really worthy of something; and now was my whole heart and soul turned towards a theatrical life.

Since this is the case, said I to Phenicia, the affair is determined. I will follow your advice and engage in your company, if they will accept me. My friend, transported with joy at this proposal, clasped me in her arms; and her two companions seemed no less delighted than herself at finding me in that humor. It was settled that I should attend the theater on the following day in the morning, and exhibit before the collected body the same sample of my talent as I had just displayed. If I had bought golden opinions from Phenicia and her friends, the actors in general were still more complimentary in their judgment, after I had recited but twenty lines before them. They gave me an engagement with the utmost willingness. Then there was nothing thought of but my first appearance. To make it as striking as possible, I laid out all the money remaining from the sale of my ring; and though my funds would not allow of being splendid in my dress, I discovered the art of substituting taste for glitter, and converting my poverty into a new grace.

At length I came out. What clapping of hands! what general admiration! It would be speaking faintly, my friend, to tell you downright that the spectators were all in an ecstacy. You must have heard with your own ears what a noise I made at Seville, to believe it. The whole talk of the town was about me, and the house was crowded for three weeks successively; so that this novelty restored the theater to its popularity, when it was evidently beginning to decline. Thus did I come upon the stage, and step into public favor at once. But to come upon the stage with such distinction, is generally a prelude to coming upon the town; or at least to putting one's self up at auction to the best bidder. Twenty sparks of all ages, from seventeen to seventy, were on the list of candidates, and would have worn me in my newest gloss. Had I followed my own inclination, I should have chosen the youngest, and the most of a lady's man; but in our profession, interest and ambition must bear the sway, till we have feathered our nest; that is as invariable a rule as any in the prompt book. On this principle, Don Ambrosio de Nisana, a man in whom age and ugliness had done their worst, but rich, generous, and one of the most powerful noblemen in Andalusia, had the refusal of the bargain. It is true that he paid handsomely for it. He took a fine house for me, furnished in the extreme of magnificence, allowed me a man cook of the first eminence, two footmen, a lady's maid, and a thousand ducats a month for my personal expenses. Add to all this a rich wardrobe, and an elegant assortment of jewels.

What a revolution in my affairs! My poor brain was completely turned. I could not believe myself to be the same person. No wonder if girls soon forget the meanness and misery whence some man of quality has rescued them in a fit of caprice. My confession shall be without reserve: public applause, flattering speeches buzzed about on every side, and Don Ambrosio's passion kindled such a flame of self-conceit as kept me in a continual ferment of extravagance. I considered my talents as a patent of nobility. I put on the woman of fashion; and becoming as chary as I had hitherto been lavish of my amorous challenges, determined to look no lower than dukes, counts, or marquises.

My lord of Nisana brought some of his friends to sup with me every evening. It was my care to invite the best companions among our actresses, and we wore away a good part of the night in laughing and drinking. I fell in very kindly with so delicious a life; but it lasted only six months. Men of rank are apt to be whimsical; but for that fault, they would be too heavenly. Don Ambrosio deserted me for a young coquet from Grenada, who had just brought a pretty person to the Seville market, and knew how to set off her wares to the best advantage. But I did not fret after him more than four-and-twenty hours. His place was supplied by a young fellow of two-and-twenty, Don Lewis d'Alcacer, with whom few Spaniards could vie in point of face and figure.

You will ask me, doubtless, and it is natural to do so, why I selected so green a sprig of nobility for my paramour, when my own experience so strongly dissuaded from such a choice. But, besides that Don Lewis had neither father nor mother, and was already in possession of his fortune, you are to know that there is no danger of disagreeable consequences attaching to any but girls in a servile condition of life, or those unfortunate loose fish who are game for every sportsman. Ladies of our profession are privileged persons; we let off our charms like a rocket, and are not answerable for the damages where they fail; so much the worse for those families whose heirs we set in a blaze.

As for Alcacer and myself, we were so strongly attached to one another, that I verily believe, love never yet did such execution as when he took aim at us two. Our passion was of such a violent nature, that we seemed to be under the influence of some spell. Those who knew how well we were together, thought us the happiest pair in the world; but we, who knew best, found ourselves the most miserable. Though Don Lewis had as fine an outside as ever fell to the lot of man, he was at the same time so jealous, that there was no living for vexation at his unfounded surmises. It was of no use, knowing his weakness and humoring it, to lay an embargo on my looks, if ever a male creature peeped into harbor; his suspicious temper, seldom at a loss for some crime to impute, rendered my armed neutrality of no avail. Our most tender moments had always a spice of wrangling. There was no standing the brunt of it; patience could hold out no longer on either side, and we quarreled more peaceably than we had loved. Could you believe that the last day of our being together was the happiest? both equally wearied out by the perpetual recurrence of unpleasant circumstances, we gave a loose to our transports when we embraced for the last time. We were like two wretched captives, breathing the fresh air of liberty after all the horrors of our prison-house.

Since that adventure, I have worn a breastplate against the little archer. No more amorous nonsense for me, at least to a troublesome excess! It is quite out of our line, to sigh and complain like Arcadian shepherdesses. Those should never give way to a passion in private, who hold it up to ridicule before the public.

While these events were passing in my domestic establishment, Fame had not hung her trumpet breathless on the willows; she spread it about universally that I was an inimitable actress. That celestial tattler, though bankrupt times out of number, still contrives to revive her credit; the comedians of Grenada therefore wrote to offer me an engagement in their company; and by way of evidence that the proposal was not to be scorned, they sent me a statement of their daily receipts and disbursements, with their terms, which seemed to be advantageous. That being the case, I closed, though grieved in my heart to part with Phenicia and Dorothea, whom I loved as well as woman is capable of loving woman. I left the first laudably employed in melting the plate of a little haggling goldsmith, whose vanity so far got the better of his avarice that he must needs have a theatrical heroine for his mistress. I forgot to tell you that on my translation to the stage, from mere whim, I changed the name of Laura to that of Estella; and it was under the latter name that I took this engagement at Grenada.

My first appearance was no less successful here than at Seville; and I soon felt myself wafted along by the sighs of my admirers. But resolving not to favor any except on honorable terms, I kept a guard of modesty in my intercourse with them, which threw dust in their eyes. Nevertheless, not to be the dupe of virtues which pay very indifferently, and were not exactly at home in their new mansion, I was balancing whether or not to take up with a young fellow of mean extraction, who had a place under government, and assumed the style of a gentleman in virtue of his office, with a good table and handsome equipage, when I saw the Marquis de Marialva for the first time. This Portuguese nobleman, traveling over Spain from mere curiosity, stopped at Grenada as he passed through it. He came to the play. I did not perform that evening. His examinations of the actresses was very particular, and he found one to his liking. Their acquaintance commenced on the very next day; and the definitive treaty was very nearly concluded when I appeared upon the stage. What with some personal graces, and no little affectation in setting them off, the weather-cock veered about all on a sudden; my Portuguese was mine and mine only till death do us part. Yet, since the truth must be told, I knew perfectly that my sister of the sock and buskin had entrapped this nobleman, and spared no pains to chouse her out of her prize; to my success you are yourself a witness. She bears me no small grudge on that account; but the thing could not be avoided. She ought to reflect that it is the way of all female flesh; that the dearest friends play off the same trick upon one another, and put a good face upon it into the bargain.

CHAPTER VIII.

THE RECEPTION OF GIL BLAS AMONG THE PLAYERS AT GRENADA;
AND ANOTHER OLD ACQUAINTANCE PICKED UP IN THE GREEN-
ROOM.

JUST as Laura was finishing her story, there came in an old actress who lived in her neighborhood, and was come to take her to
the theater as she passed by. This venerable tutelary of the stage
was admirably fitted to play some superannuated strumpet among
the heathen goddesses in a pantomime. My sister was not remiss
in introducing her brother to that stale old harridan, whereupon a
profusion of compliments were bandied about on both sides.

I left them together, telling the steward's relict that I would
join her again at the playhouse, as soon as I had sent my baggage
to the Marquis de Marialva's, to whose residence she directed me.
First I went to the room I had hired, whence, after having settled
with my landlady, I repaired with a porter who carried my luggage
to a large ready-furnished house, where my new master was quartered. At the door I met his steward, who asked me if I was not
the lady Estella's brother. I answered in the affirmative. Then
you are welcome, Signor cavalier, replied he. The Marquis de
Marialva, whose steward I have the honor to be, has commissioned
me to receive you properly. There is a room got ready for you; I
will show you the way to it, if you please, that you may be quite at
home. He took me up to the top of the house, and thrust me into
so small a room, that a very narrow bed, a chest of drawers, and
two chairs completely filled it. This was my apartment. You will
not have much spare room, said my conductor, but as a set-off, I
promise you that you shall be superbly lodged at Lisbon. I locked
up my portmanteau in the wardrobe, and put the key in my pocket,
asking at the same time what was the hour of supper. The answer
was, that his lordship seldom supped at home, but allowed each
servant a monthly sum for board wages. I put several other questions, and learnt that the Marquis's people were a happy set of idle
fellows. After a conversation short and sweet, I left the steward
to go and look for Laura, reflecting much to my own satisfaction
on the happy omens I drew from the opening of my new situation.

As soon as I got to the playhouse door, and mentioned my name
as Estella's brother, there was free admission at once. You might
have observed the forwardness of the guards to make way for me,
just as if I had been one of the most considerable noblemen in
Grenada. All the supernumeraries, door-keepers, and receivers of
checks whom I encountered in my progress, made me their very
best bows. But what I should like best to give the reader an idea
of, is the serious reception which the merry vagrants gave me in
the green-room, where I found the whole dramatis personæ ready
dressed, and on the point of drawing up the curtain. The actors

and actresses, to whom Laura introduced me, fell upon me without mercy. The men were quite troublesome with their greetings; and the women, not to be outdone, laid their plastered faces alongside of mine, till they covered it with a villanous compound of red and white. No one choosing to be the last in making me welcome, they all paid their compliments in a breath. Æolus himself, answering from all the points of the compass at once, would not have been a match for them: but my sister was; for the loan of her tongue was always at the service of a friend, and she brought me completely out of debt.

But I did not get clear off with the squeezes of the principal performers. The civilities of the scene-painters, the band, the prompter, the candle-snuffer, and the call-boy were to be endured with patience; all the understrappers in the theater came to see me run the gauntlet. One would have supposed one's self in a foundling hospital, and that they had none of them ever known what sort of animals brothers and sisters were.

In the mean time the play began. Some gentlemen who were behind the scenes, then ran to get seats in the front of the house; for my part, feeling myself quite at home, I continued in conversation with those of the actors who were waiting to go on. Among the number there was one whom they called Melchior. The name struck me. I looked hard at the person who answered to it, and thought I had seen him somewhere. At last I recollected that it was Melchior Zapata, a poor strolling player, who has been described in the first volume of this true history, as soaking his crusts in the pure element.

I immediately took him aside, and said: I am much mistaken if you are not that Signor Melchior with whom I had the honor of breakfasting one day by the margin of a clear fountain, between Valladolid and Segovia. I was with a journeyman barber. We had some provisions with us which we clubbed with yours, and all three partook of a little rural feast, to which wit and anecdote gave additional relish. Zapata bethought him for a minute or two, and then answered: You tell me of a circumstance which often since came across my mind. I had then just been trying my fortune at Madrid, and was returning to Zamora. I recollect perfectly that my affairs were a little out at elbows. I recollect it too, replied I, by the token of a doublet which you wore, lined with play-bills. Neither have I forgotten that you complained of having a wife cursed with incorruptible chastity. Oh! that misfortune has found its remedy long ago, said Zapata, shaking his ears. By all the powers of womanhood, the jade has effectually reformed that virtue, and given me a warmer lining to my doublet.

I was going to congratulate him on his wife's having shown so much sense, when he was obliged to leave me and go on the stage. Being curious to know what sort of an animal his wife was, I went up to an actor and desired him to point her out. He did so, saying at the same time: There she is, it is Narcissa; the prettiest of all our women except your sister. I concluded that this must be the actress in whose favor the Marquis de Marialva had declared before meeting with his Estella; and my conjecture was but too correct. After the play I attended Laura home, where I saw several cooks preparing a handsome entertainment. You may sup here, said she. I will do no such thing, answered I; the marquis perhaps will like to be alone with you. Not at all, replied she; he is coming with two of his own friends and one of our gentlemen; you will just make the sixth. You know that in our free and easy way there is no impropriety in secretaries sitting down at table with their masters. Very true, said I: but it is rather too soon to assume the privilege of a favorite. I must first get employed in some confidential commission, and then lay in my claim to that honorable distinction. Judging it to be so best, I went out of Laura's house, and got back to my inn, whither I reckoned on repairing every day, since my master had no regular establishment.

CHAPTER IX.

AN EXTRAORDINARY COMPANION AT SUPPER; AND AN ACCOUNT OF THEIR CONVERSATION.

I REMARKED in the coffee-room a sort of an old monk, habited in coarse gray cloth, at supper quite alone in a corner. I went and sat opposite to him out of curiosity; we exchanged a civil bow, and he showed himself to be quite as well bred as I was, notwithstanding my lay education. My commons were brought me, and I fell to with a very catholic appetite. While I was eating, my tongue was mute, but my eyes glanced by snatches towards this singular character, and always caught his at the same employment. Liking better to stare than be stared at, I addressed my speech to him thus: Pray, father, have we ever by any chance met anywhere but here? You peer at me as if you scarcely knew whether I was an acquaintance or a stranger. He answered gravely: If I look at you with fixed attention, it is only to admire the prodigious variety of adventures which are chronicled in the features of your face. It seems, said I in a joking tone, as if your reverence was something of a physiognomist. Far more deeply imbubed in science than a mere physiognomist, answered the monk, I found prophecies on my observations which have never been belied by the event. My skill in palmistry is no less, and I will set my oracles against the surest of antiquity, after comparing the inspection of the hand with that of the face.

Though this old man had all the appearance of profound wisdom, his talk was so like that of a madman, that I could not help laughing at him outright. So far from being offended at my want of manners, he smiled at it, and went on to the following effect, after running his eyes round the coffee-room, to be assured that there were no listeners: I am not surprised at finding you so prejudiced against two sciences which pass at this time of day for mere frivolity; the long and painful study they require disheartens the learned, who turn their backs upon them, and then swear that they are fables out of disgust at having missed their attainment. For my part, I am not to be frightened by the darkness which envelopes them, any more than by the difficulties which are perpetual stumbling-blocks in the pursuit of chemical discoveries, and in the marvelous art of transmuting baser metals into gold.

But I do flatter myself, pursued he, looking steadfastly at me, that I am addressing a young gentleman of good sense, to whom my systems will not appear altogether in the light of idle dreams. A sample of my skill will dispose you better than the most subtle arguments to pass a favorable judgment on my pretensions. After talking in this manner he drew from his pocket a phial full of a lively-looking red liquor, on which he expatiated thus: Here is an elixir which I have distilled this morning from the juices of certain plants; for I have employed almost my whole life like Democritus, in finding out the properties of simples and minerals. You shall make trial of its virtue. The wine we are drinking with our supper is very bad; henceforth it will become excellent. At the same time he put two drops of his elixir into my bottle, which made my wine more delicious that the choicest vintage of Spain.

The marvelous strikes the imagination; and when once that faculty is enlisted, judgment is turned adrift. Delighted with so glorious a secret, and persuaded that he must have out-deviled the devil before he could have got at it, I cried out in a paroxysm of admiration: O reverend father! prythee forgive your servant if he took you at first for an old blockhead. I now abjure my error. There is no need to look further to be assured that it depends only on your own will to turn an iron bar into a wedge of gold in the twinkling of an eye. How happy should I be were I master of that admirable science! Heaven preserve you from ever acquiring it, interrupted the old man with a deep sigh. You know not, my son, what a fatal possession you covet. Instead of envying, rather pity me for having taken such infinite pains to be made unhappy. I am always disturbed in mind. I fear a discovery; and then perpetual imprisonment would be the reward of all my labors. In this apprehension, I lead a vagabond life, sometimes disguised as a priest or a monk, sometimes as a gentleman or a peasant. Where is the benefit of knowing how to manufacture gold on such terms? Are not the goods of this world downright misery to those who cannot enjoy them in tranquillity?

What you say appears to me very sensible, said I to the philosopher. There is nothing like living at one's ease. You have rid me of all hankering after the philosopher's stone. I will rest satisfied with learning from you my future destiny. With all my heart, my good lad, answered he. I have already made my remarks upon your features; now let me see your hand. I gave it him with a confidence which will do my penetration but little credit in the esteem of some readers. He examined it very attentively, and then pronounced, as in a rapture of inspiration: Ah! what transitions from pain to pleasure, and from pleasure to pain! What a whimsical alternation of good and evil chances! But you have already experienced the largest share of your allotted reverses. You have but few more tides of misfortune to stem, and then a great lord will contrive for you an eligible fate, which shall not be subject to change.

After having assured me that I might depend on his prediction, he bade me farewell and went out of the inn, leaving me in deep meditation on the things I had just heard. There could be no doubt of the Marquis de Marialva being the great lord in question; and consequently nothing appeared more within the verge of possibility than the accomplishment of the oracle. But though there had not been the slightest likelihood, that would have been no hindrance to giving the impostor monk unbounded credit, since his elixir had transmuted my sour incredulity into the most tractable digestion of his falsehoods. That nothing might be wanting on my side to play into the hands of my foreboded luck, I determined to attach myself more closely to the marquis than I had ever done to any of my masters. Having taken this resolution, I went home in unusually high spirits; never did foolish woman descend in better humor from the garret of another foolish woman who had told her fortune.

CHAPTER X.

THE MARQUIS DE MARIALVA GIVES A COMMISSION TO GIL BLAS. THAT FAITHFUL SECRETARY ACQUITS HIMSELF OF IT AS SHALL BE RELATED.

THE marquis was not yet returned from his theatrical party, and I found his upper servants playing at cards in his apartment while they were waiting for his arrival. I got to be sociable with them; and we amused ourselves with jocular conversation till two o'clock in the morning, when our master arrived. He was a little surprised at seeing me, and said with an air of kindness which made me conclude that he came home very well satisfied with his evening: How is this, Gil Blas? Are you not gone to bed yet? I answered that I wished to know first whether he had any commands for me. Probably, replied he, I may have a commission to give you to-morrow morning; but it will be time enough then to acquaint you with my wishes. Go to your own room; and henceforward remember that I dispense with your attendance at bedtime; my other servants are sufficient for that occasion.

After this hint, which was much to my satisfaction in the main, since it spared me a slavery which I should have felt very unpleasantly at times, I left the marquis in his apartment, and withdrew to my garret. I went to bed. Not being able to sleep, it seemed good to follow the counsel of Pythagoras, and to examine all the actions of the day by the test of reason; to reprimand severely what had been done amiss, and if anything had been done well, to rejoice in it.

On looking into the day-book of my conscience, the balance was not sufficiently in my favor to keep me in good humor with myself. I felt remorse at having lent myself to Laura's imposition. It was in vain to urge, in self-defence, that I could not, with any decency, give the lie to a girl who had no object in view but to do me a pleasure, and that I was in some sort under the necessity of becoming an accomplice in the fraud. This was a paltry excuse in the darkness of the night, for I pleaded against myself that at all events the matter should be pushed no further, and that it was the summit of impudence to remain upon the establishment of a nobleman whose confidence I so ill repaid. In short, after a severe trial, it was agreed in my own breast, that I was very little short of an arrant knave.

But to have done with the morality of the act, and pass on to the probable issue, it was evidently playing a desperate game, to cozen a man of consequence who might be enabled, as an instrument for the visitation of my sins perhaps, to detect the imposture in its very infancy. A reflection at once so prudent and so virtuous acted as a refrigerator on my spirits; but visions of pleasure and of interest soon raised them above the freezing point. Besides, the prophecy of the man with the elixir would have been enough to put me in heart once more. I therefore gave myself up to the indulgence of the most agreeable fancies. All the rules of arithmetic from simple addition to compound interest were set in array, to cast up what sum my salary would amount to at the end of ten years' service. Then there was a large allowance for presents and gratuities from my master, whose liberal disposition according admirably with my liberal desires, my imagination grew quite fantastical, and extended the landmarks of my fortune over innumerable acres of unsubstantial territory. Sleep overtook me in the calculation, and raised a magnificent aërial mansion on the estate where a new race of grandees was to originate.

I got up the next morning about eight o'clock to go and receive my patron's orders; but as I was opening my door to go out, what was my surprise at meeting him, in his wrapping-gown and night cap. He was quite alone. Gil Blas, said he, on parting with your sister last night, I promised to pass this morning with her; but an affair of consequence will not admit of my keeping my word. Go and assure her from me that I am deeply mortified at the disappointment, but that I shall certainly sup with her to-night. That is not all, added he, putting a purse into my hands and a little sha-green case set round with diamonds; carry her my portrait, and keep this purse of fifty pistoles, which I give you as a mark of my early-conceived friendship. I took the picture in one hand, and in the other the purse to which I was so little entitled. I put my best leg foremost in my way to Laura, muttering to myself in the transports of excessive joy: Good! the prophecy is accomplished in the twinkling of an eye. What a windfall to be the brother of a girl so full of beauty and attraction! It is a pity the credit attached to the relationship is not commensurate with the lucre and the comfort.

Laura, unlike most women in her profession, had a habit of early rising. I caught her at her toilette, where, while waiting for her illustrious foreigner, she was engrafting on her natural beauty all the adventitious charms which the cosmetic art could supply. Lovely Estella, said I, on accosting her, thou absolute loadstone of the tramontanes, I may now sit down at table with my master, since he had honored me with a commission which gives me that prerogative, and which I am just come to fulfill. He cannot have the pleasure of waiting on you this morning, as he had purposed; but to make you amends for the disappointment, he will sup here this evening, and sends you his picture; which to all appearance is inclosed in something more valuable than itself.

I put the box into her hands at once; and the lively sparkling of the brilliants which encompassed it made her eyes sparkle and her mouth water. She opened it out of mere curiosity, looked carelessly at the painting as people perform a duty for which they have little relish, then shut it, and once more fell greedily on the jewelry. Their beauty made her eloquent; and she said to me with the smile of a satirist—These are copies which those mercenary things called actresses value much more highly than originals.

I next acquainted her that the generous Portuguese, when giving me charge of the portrait, recommended it to my care by a purse of fifty pistoles. I beg you accept of my congratulations, said she; this nobleman begins where it is even uncommon for others to leave off. It is to you, my divine creature, answered I, that this present is owing; the marquis only made it on the score of natural affection. I could be well pleased, replied she, that he were to make you a score such presents every day. I cannot express in what extravagance you are dear to me. From the first moment of our meeting, I became attached to you by so strong a tie, as time has not been able to dissolve. When I lost you at Madrid, I did not despair of finding you again; and yesterday, on your sudden appearance, I received you like a deodand. In a word, my friend, heaven has created us for another. You shall be my husband, but we must get plenty of money in the first instance. I shall just lend myself out to three or four silly fellows more, and then you may live like a gentleman on your means.

I thanked her in the most appropriate terms for such an instance of extreme condescension on my behalf, and we got insensibly into a conversation which lasted till noon. At that hour I withdrew, to go and give my master an account of the manner in which his present was received. Though Laura had given me no instructions thereupon, I was not remiss in composing a fine compliment on my way, with which I meant to launch out on her part; but it was just so much flash in the pan. For, when I got home the marquis was gone out; and the fates had decreed that I should never see him more, for reasons which will be methodically stated in the succeeding chapter.

CHAPTER XI.

A THUNDERBOLT TO GIL BLAS.

I REPAIRED to my inn, where meeting with two men of companionable talents, I dined and sat at table with them till the play began. We parted, they as their business and desire pointed them; and, for my own part, my bent was towards the theater. It may be proper to observe by the way, that I had all possible reason to be in good humor. The conversation with my chance companions had been joyous in the extreme; the color of my fortune was gay and animating; yet for all that I could not help giving way to melancholy, without either knowing why, or being able to reason myself out of it. It was doubtless a prophetic warning of the misfortune which threatened me.

As I entered the green-room, Melchior Zapata came up, and told me in a low voice to follow him. He led me to an unfrequented part of the house, and opened his business thus—Worthy sir, I make it a point of conscience to give you a very serious warning. You are aware that the Marquis de Marialva had at first taken a fancy to Narcissa, my wife; he had even gone so far as to fix a day for trying the relish of my rib, when that cockatrice Estella contrived to flyblow the bill of fare, and transfer the banquet to her own untainted charms. Judge then, whether an actress can be gulled instead of gulling, and preserve the sweetness of her temper. My wife has taken it deeply to heart, and there is no species of revenge to which she would not have recourse. A fine opportunity has offered. Yesterday, if you recollect, all our supernumeraries were crowding together to see you. The deputy candle-snuffer told some of the inferior comedians that he recollected you perfectly well, and that you might be anything but Estella's brother.

This report, added Melchior, came to Narcissa's ears to-day: she lost no time in questioning the author; and that grub of the interior stood to the whole story. He says that he knew you as Arsenia's servant, when Estella waited on her at Madrid under the name of Laura. My wife, full of glee at this discovery, means to acquaint the Marquis de Marialva with it, when he comes to the play this evening; so take your measures accordingly, If you are not Estella's brother in good earnest, I would advise you as a friend, and on the score of old acquaintance, to make your escape while your skin is whole. Narcissa, satisfied in her tender mercy with only one victim, and that of her own sex, has allowed me to give you this notice, that you may outrun your ill-luck.

It would have been waste of words to press the subject farther. I returned thanks for the caution to this fretter of his hour, who saw by my terrified aspect that I was not the man to give the deputy candle-snuffer the lie. I did not feel the least temptation to carry my dangerous valor such a length. I had not even the heart to go and bid farewell to Laura, for fear she should insist on me keeping up the farce. I could easily conceive that so excellent an actress might get out of the scrape with flying colors; but there seemed to be nothing for me short of a swinging castigation; and I was not so far gone in love as to stand by my sweetheart at the risk of my own person. I thought of nothing but a precipitate retreat with my household gods, or rather goods, if such a trumpery collection of individual property might be called so. I disappeared from the playhouse in the twinkling of an eye; and in less time than it would have taken to confess my sins, was my portmanteau carried off and safely lodged with a muleteer who was to set out for Toledo at three o'clock next morning. I could have wished myself already with the Count de Polan, whose hospitable roof seemed my only safe asylum. But I was not there yet; and it was impossible to think without dread of the time remaining to be passed in a town where I was afraid they would hunt me out without giving me a night's law.

The smell of supper drew me to my inn notwithstanding; though I was as uneasy as a debtor who knows that a writ is out against him. My stomach, I believe, was not sufficiently well knit that evening for my supper to play its part as it should do. The miserable sport of fear, I watched all the people who came into the coffee-room, and whenever by chance they carried a gallows in their physiognomy, which is no uncommon ensign in such places of resort, I shuddered with horrid forebodings. After having supped the supper of the damned, I got up from table and returned to my carrier's house, where I threw myself on some clean straw till it was time to set out.

My patience was well tried during that interval: for a thousand unpleasant thoughts attacked me in all directions. If I dozed now and then, the enraged marquis stood before me, pounding Laura's fair face to a jelly with his fist, and turning her whole house out at window; or to come nearer home, I heard him giving directions for my death under the operation of a cudgel. At such a vision I started out of my sleep, and waking, which is usually so pleasant after a frightful dream, inspired me with more horror than even the fictions of my entranced fancy.

Happily the muleteer delivered me from so dire a purgatory, by coming to acquaint me that his mules were ready. I was immediately on my legs, and set out radically cured, for which heaven has my best thanks, of Laura and the occult sciences. As we got farther from Grenada, my mind recovered its tone. I began chatting with the muleteer, laughed at his droll stories, and insensibly lost all my apprehensions. I slept undisturbed at Ubeda, where we lay the first night, and on the fourth day we got to Toledo. My first care was to inform myself of the Count de Polan's residence, whither I repaired under the full persuasion that he would not suffer me to lodge elsewhere. But I reckoned without my host. There was no one at home but a person to take care of the house, who told me that his master was just gone to the castle of Leyva, having been sent for on account of Seraphina's dangerous illness.

The count's absence was altogether unexpected: here was no longer any inducement to stay at Toledo, and all my plans were changed at once. Finding myself so near Madrid, I resolved to go thither. It came into my head that I might make my way at court, where talents of the first order, as I had heard, were not absolutely necessary to fill situations of the first consequence. On the very next morning I took advantage of back carriage, to be set down in the renowned capital of Spain. Fortune took me kindly by the hand, and introduced me to a higher cast of parts than those I had hitherto filled.

CHAPTER XII.

GIL BLAS TAKES LODGINGS IN A READY-FURNISHED HOUSE. HE GETS ACQUAINTED WITH CAPTAIN CHINCHILLA. THAT OFFICER'S CHARACTER AND BUSINESS AT MADRID.

ON my first arrival at Madrid, I fixed my headquarters in a lodging-house, where resided, among other persons, an old captain, who was come from the distant part of New Castile, to solicit a pension at court, and he thought his claims but too well founded. His name was Don Annibal de Chinchilla. It was not without much staring that I saw him for the first time. He was a man about sixty, of gigantic stature, and of anatomical leanness. His whiskers were like brushwood, fencing off the two sides of his face as high as his temples. Besides that, he was short in his reckoning by an arm and a leg, there was a vacancy for an eye, which Polypheme would have supplied as he did, had patches of green silk been then in the fashion; and his features were hacked sufficiently to illustrate a treatise of geometry. With these exceptions, his configuration was much like that of another man. As to his mental qualities, he was not altogether without understanding; and what he wanted in quickness he made up by gravity. His principles were rigid in the extreme; and it was his particular boast to be delicate on the point of honor.

After two or three interviews, he distinguished me by his confidence. I soon got into all his personal history; he related on what occasions he had left an eye at Naples, his arm in Lombardy, and a leg in the Low Countries. The most admirable circumstance in all his narratives of battles and sieges, was, that not a single feature of the swaggerer peeped out; not a word escaped him to his own honor and glory; though one could readily have forgiven him for making some little display of the half which was still extant of himself, as a set-off against the dilapidations which had deducted so largely from the usual contexture of a man. Officers who return from their campaigns without a scratch upon their skin or a love-lock out of place. are not always so humble in their pretensions.

But he told me that what gave him most uneasiness was, the having wasted a considerable portion of his private fortune on military objects, so that he had not more than a hundred ducats a year left ; a poor establishment for such a pair of whiskers, a gentleman's lodging, and an amanuensis to multiply memorials by wholesale. For in point of fact, my worthy friend, added he, shrugging his shoulders, I present one, with a blessing on my endeavors, every day, and the last meets with the same attention as the first. You would say that it was an even bet between the prime minister and me, which of us two shall be tired first ; the memorialist or the receiver of the memorials. I have often had the honor, too, of addressing the king on the same subject ; but the rector and his curate say grace in the same key ; and in the mean time, my castle of Chinchilla is falling to ruin for want of necessary repairs.

Faint heart never won fair lady, said I most wisely to the captain ; you are perhaps on the eve of finding all your marches and countermarches repaid with usury. I must not flatter myself with that pleasing expectation, answered Don Annibal. It is but three days since I spoke to one of the minister's secretaries ; and if I am to trust to his representations, I have only to hold up my head and look big. What then did he say to you ? replied I. Had those poor dumb mouths your wounds no eloquence, to wring a hireling pittance for their profuse expense of blood ? You shall judge for yourself, resumed Chinchilla. This secretary told me in good plain terms : My honest friend, you need not boast so much of your zeal and your fidelity ; you have only done your duty in exposing yourself to danger for your country. Naked glory is the true and honorable recompense of gallant actions, and as such is the prize at which a Spaniard aims. You therefore argue on false principles, if you consider the bounty you solicit as a debt. In case it should be granted, you will owe that favor exclusively to the royal goodness, which in its extreme condescension requites those of its subjects who have served the state valiantly. Thus you see, pursued the captain, that if I had a hundred lives they are all pledged, and that I am likely to go back as hungry as I came.

A brave man in distress is the most touching object in this world. I exhorted him to stick close, and offered to write his memorials out fair for nothing. I even went so far as to open my purse to him, and to beg it as a favor that he would draw upon me for whatever he wanted, But he was not one of those folks who never wait to be asked twice on such occasions. So much the reverse, that, with a commendable delicacy on the subject, he thanked me for my kindness, but refused it peremptorily. He afterwards told me that, for fear of spunging upon any one, he had accustomed himself, by little and little, to live with such sobriety that the smallest quantity of food was sufficient for his subsistence ; which was but too true. His daily fare was confined to vegetables, by dint whereof his component parts were confined to skin and bone. That he might have no witnesses how ill he dined, he usually shut himself up in his chamber at that meal. I prevailed so far with him, however, by repeated entreaties, as to obtain that we should dine and sup together; then, undermining his pride by little indirect artifices of compassion, I ordered more provision and wine than I could consume to my own share. I pressed him to eat and drink. At first he made difficulties about it; but in the end there was no resisting my hospitality. After a time, his modesty becoming fainter as his diet was more flush, he helped me off with my dinner and lightened my bottle almost without asking.

One day, after four or five glasses, when his stomach had renewed its intimacy with a more generous system of feeding, he said to me with an air of gayety: Upon my word, Signor Gil Blas, you have very winning ways with you; you make me do just whatever you please. There is something so hearty in your welcome as to relieve me from all fear of trespassing on your generous temper. My captain seemed at that moment so entirely to have got rid of his bashfulness, that if I had been in the humor to have seized the lucky moment, and to have pressed my purse once more on his acceptance, I am much mistaken if he would have refused it. I did not put him to the trial; but rested satisfied with having made him my messmate, and taken the trouble not only to copy out his memorials, but to assist him in their composition. By dint of having written homilies out fair, I had learnt the knack of phraseology, and was become a sort of author. The old officer on his side had some little vanity about writing well. Both of us thus contending for the prize, the bursts of eloquence would have done honor to the most celebrated professors of Salamanca. But it was in vain that we sat on opposite sides of the table, and drained our genius to the very dregs, to nourish the flowers of rhetoric in these memorials; you might as well have planted an orange-grove on the sea-beach. In whatever new light we placed Don Annibal's services, it was all the same at court, the connoisseurs were decided about their merit; so that the battered veteran had no reason to sing the praises of that spirit which leads officers on to spend their family estates in the service. In the virulence of his spleen he cursed the planet under which he was born, and sent Naples, Lombardy, and the Low Countries to the devil.

That his mortification might be pressed down and running over, it happened to his face one day that a poet, introduced by the Duke of Alva, having recited a sonnet before the king on the birth of an infanta, was gratified with a pension of five hundred ducats. I believe the lop-limbed captain would have gone raving mad at it, if I had not taken some pains to recompense his spirit. What is the matter with you? said I, seeing him quite beside himself. There is nothing in all this which ought to go so terribly against the grain. Ever since Mount Parnassus swelled above the subject plain, have not poets pleaded the privilege of laying princes under contribution to their muse? There is not a crowned head in Christendom that has not substituted a pensioned laureate for the household fool of less refined times. And between ourselves, this species of patronage, for the most part galloping down full drive to posterity on the saddle of Pegasus, raises a hue and cry in honor of royal munificence; but bounty to persons who are lost in a crowd, however deserving, adds nothing to the bulk or stature of posthumous renown. Augustus must have drained his treasury by gratuities, and yet how few of the names on his pension-list have come down to us! But distant ages shall be informed, as we are, in all the hyperbole of poetic diction, that his benefits descended on Virgil like the rain from heaven, whose drops arithmetic has no combination to count, no principles by which to reason on their number.

But let me talk ever so classically to Don Annibal, there was a confounded acidity in that sonnet which curdled all the milky ingredients of his moral composition; it was impossible to chew, swallow, and digest such food with human organs; and he was fully determined to give the matter up at once. It seemed right, nevertheless, by way of playing for his last stake, to present one more memorial to the Duke of Lerma, and if that failed there was an end of the game. For this purpose we went together to the prime minister's. There we met a young man who, after saluting the captain, said to him in a tone of affection : My old and dear master, is it your own self that I see? What business brings you to this mart of favor? If you have occasion for any one to speak a good word for you, do not spare my lungs; they are entirely at your service. How is this, Pedrillo? answered the officer; to hear you talk it should seem as if you held some important post in this house. At least, replied the young man, I have influence enough here to put an honest rustic like you into the right train. That being the case, resumed the captain with a smile, I place myself under your protection. I accept the pledge, rejoined Pedrillo. You have only to acquaint me with your particular taste, and I engage to give you a savory slice out of the ministerial pasty.

We had no sooner opened our minds to this young fellow, so full of kind assurances, than he inquired where Don Annibal resided; then, promising that we should hear from him on the following day, he vanished without informing us what he meant to do, or even telling us whether he belonged to the Duke of Lerma's household. I was curious to know what this Pedrillo was, whose turn of mind appeared to be so brisk and active. He is a brave lad, said the captain, who waited on me some years ago, but finding me out at elbows, went away in search of a better service. There was no offense to me in all that; it is very natural to change when one cannot be worse off. The creature is pleasant enough, not deficient in parts, and happy in a spirit of intrigue which would wheedle with the devil. But notwithstanding all his fine pretense, I am not sanguine in my reckoning on the zeal he has just testified for me. Perhaps, said I, there may be some plausibility in his designs. Should he be a retainer, for example, to any of the duke's principal officers, it will be in his power to serve you. You have lived too long in the world not to know that in great houses everything is done by party and cabal; that the masters are governed by two or three upper servants about their persons, who, in their turn, are governed by that multitude of menials attendant upon them.

On the next morning we saw Pedrillo at our breakfast table. Gentlemen, said he, if I did not explain myself yesterday as to my means of serving Captain Chinchilla, it was because we were not in a place where such a communication could be made with safety. Besides, I was disposed to ascertain whether the thing was feasible, before you were made parties in it. Understand, then, that I am the confidential servant of Signor Don Rodrigo de Calderona, the Duke of Lerma's first secretary. My master, who is much addicted to women, goes almost every evening to sup with a little Arragonian nightingale, whom he keeps in a cage near the purlieus of the court. She is quite a young girl from Albarazin, a most lovely creature. She has some wit as well as beauty, and sings enchantingly; they call her the Spanish Syren. I am the bearer of some tender inquiries every morning, and am just come from her. I have proposed to her to pass off Signor Don Annibal for her uncle, and the object of the forgery is to engage her lover in his interests. She is very willing to lend her aid in the business. Besides some little commission to which she looks forward on the profits, it will tickle her vanity to be taken for the niece of a military man.

Signor de Chinchilla looked very grim at this suggestion. He declared his extreme abhorrence of becoming a party concerned in a mere swindling trick, and still more of adopting a female adventurer, no better than she should be, into his family, and thus casting a stain upon its immaculate purity. It was not only for himself that he felt all this soreness; there was a recoil of ignominy on his ancestors, which would lay their honors level with the dust. This morbid delicacy seemed out of season to Pedrillo, who could not help expressing his contempt of it thus. You must surely be out of your wits to take the matter up on that footing. A fine market you bring your morals to, you dictators from the plow, with your ridiculous squeamishness! Now you seem a good sensible man, appealing to me as he spoke these last words. Can you believe your ears when you hear such scruples advanced? Heaven defend us! At court, of all the places in the world, to look at morals through a microscope! Let fortune come under what haggard form she may, they hug her in their arms, and swear she is a beauty.

My way of thinking was precisely with Pedrillo; and we dinned it so stoutly into both the captain's ears, as to make him the Spanish Syren's uncle against nature and inclination. When we had so far prevailed over his pride, we all three set about drawing up a new memorial for the minister, which was revised, with a copious interlacing of additions and corrections. I then wrote it out fair, and Pedrillo carried it to the Aragonian chantress, who that very evening put it into the hands of Signor Don Rodrigo, telling her story so artlessly that the secretary, really supposing her the captain's niece, promised to take up his case. A few days afterwards we reaped the fruits of our little project. Pedrillo came back to our house with the lofty air of a benefactor. Good news, said he to Chinchilla. The king is going to make a new grant of officers, places, and pensions; nor will your name be forgotten in the list. But I am specially commissioned to inquire what present you purpose making to the Spanish Syren, for the piper must be paid. As to myself, I vow and protest that I will not take a farthing; the pleasure of having contributed to patch up my old master's broken fortunes, is more to me than all the ingots of the Indies. But it is not precisely so with our nymph of Albarazin: she has a little Jewish blood to plead, when the Christian precept of loving your neighbor as herself is preached up to her. She would pick her own natural father's pocket; so judge you whether she would be above making a bargain with a traveling uncle.

She has only to name her own terms, answered Don Annibal. Whatever my pension may be, she shall have the third of it annually if she pleases; I will pledge my word for it; and that proportion ought to satisfy her craving, if his Catholic Majesty had settled his whole exchequer on me. I would as soon take your word as your bond, for my own part, replied the nimble-footed messenger of Don Rodrigo; I know that it will stand the assay; but you have to deal with a little creature who knows herself, and naturally supposes that she knows all the rest of the world by the same token. Besides, she would like better to take it in the lump; two-thirds to be paid down now in ready money. Why, how the devil does she mean that I should get the wherewithal? bawled the captain in a quandary. Does she take me for an auditor of public accounts, or treasurer to a charity? You cannot have made her acquainted with my circumstances. Yes, but I have, replied Pedrillo; she knows very well that you are poorer than Job; after what she has heard from me she could think no otherwise. But do not make yourself uneasy, my brain is never at a loss for an expedient. I know an old scoundrel of an usurer, who will take ten per cent if he can get no more. You must assign your first year's pension to him, in acknowledgment for a like valuable consideration from him, which you will in point of fact receive, only deducting the above-mentioned interest. As to security, the lender will take your castle at Chinchilla, for want of better; there will be no dispute about that.

The captain declared his readiness to accept the terms, in case of his being so fortunate as to possess any beneficial interest in the good things to be given away the next morning. It happened accordingly. He got a government with a pension of three hundred pistoles. As soon as the news came, he signed and sealed as required, settled his little concerns in town, and went off again for New Castile with a balance of some few pistoles in his favor.

CHAPTER XIII.

GIL BLAS COMES ACROSS HIS DEAR FRIEND FABRICIO AT COURT. GREAT ECSTACY ON BOTH SIDES. THEY ADJOURN TOGETHER, AND COMPARE NOTES; BUT THEIR CONVERSATION IS TOO CURIOUS TO BE ANTICIPATED.

I HAD contracted a habit of going to the royal palace every morning, where I lounged away two or three good hours in seeing the good people pass to and fro; but their aspect was less imposing there than in other places, as the lesser stars turn pale in the presence of the sun.

One day as I was walking back and fore, and strutting about the apartments, making about as wise a figure there as my neighbors, I spied out Fabricio, whom I had left at Valladolid in the service of a hospital director. It surprised me not a little that he was chatting familiarly with the Duke of Medina Sidonia and the Marquis of Santa Cruz. Those two noblemen, if my senses did not deceive me, were listening with admiration to his prattle. To crown the whole, he was as handsomely dressed as a grandee.

Surely I must be mistaken! thought I. Can this possibly be the son of Nunez the barber? More likely it is some young courtier who bears a strong resemblance to him. But my suspense was of no long duration. The party broke up, and I accosted Fabricio. He knew me at once; took me by the hand, and after pressing through the crowd to get out of the precincts, said with a hearty greeting, My dear Gil Blas, I am delighted to see you again. What are you doing at Madrid? Are you still at service? Some place about the court perhaps? How do matters stand with you? Let me into the history of all that has happened to you since your precipitate flight from Valladolid. You ask a great many questions in a breath, replied I; and we are not in a fit place for story-telling. You are in the right, answered he; we shall be better at home. Come, I will show you the way; it is not far hence. I am quite my own master, with all my comforts about me; perfectly easy as to the main chance, with a light heart and a happy temper: because I am determined to see everything on the bright side.

I accepted the proposal, and Fabricio escorted me. We stopped at a house of magnificent appearance, where he told me that he lived. There was a court to cross; on one side it had a grand staircase leading to a suite of state apartments, and on the other a small flight, dark and narrow, whither we betook ourselves to a residence elevated in a different sense from what he had boasted. It consisted of a single room, which my contriving friend had divided into four by deal partitions. The first served as an ante-chamber to the second, where he lay; of the third he made his closet, of the last his kitchen. The chamber and antechamber were papered with maps, and many a sheet of phil.sophical discussion; nor was the furniture by any means unsuitable to the hangings. There was a large brocade bed much the worse for wear; tawdry old chairs with coarse yellow coverings, fringed with Grenada silk of the same color; a table with gilt feet, and a cloth over it that once aspired to be red, bordered with tinsel and embroidery tarnished by that old corroder, time; with an ebony cabinet, ornamented with figures in a clumsy taste of sculpture. Instead of a convenient desk, he had a small table in the closet; and his library was made up with some few books, and a great many bundles

FABRICIO.

of paper arranged on shelves one above the other the whole length of the wall. His kitchen, too modest to put the rest of the establishment out of countenance, exhibited a frugal assortment of earthenware and other necessary implements of cookery.

Fabricio, when he had allowed me leisure to philosophize on his domestic arrangements, begged to know my opinion of his apartments and his housekeeping, and whether I was enchanted with them: Yes, beyond all manner of doubt, answered I with a roguish smile. You must have applied your wits to a good purpose at Madrid, to have got so well accoutred. Of course you have some post. Heaven preserve me from anything of the sort! replied he. My line of life is far above all political situations. A man of rank, to whom this house belongs, has given me a room in it, whence I have contrived to piece out a suite of four, fitted up in such taste as you may see. I devote my time to no employments but what are just to my fancy, and never feel what it is to want. Explain yourself more intelligibly, said I, interrupting him. You set met all agog to be let into your little arrangements. Well,

"HE BEGGED TO KNOW MY OPINION OF HIS APARTMENTS AND HIS
HOUSEKEEPING."

then! said he, I will rid you of that devil curiosity at once. I have commenced author, have plunged headlong into the ocean of literature; verse and prose run equally glib; in short I am a jack of all trades to the muses.

What! you bound in solemn league and covenant to Apollo? exclaimed I with most intolerable laughter. Nothing under a prophet could ever have anticipated this. I should have been less surprised at any other transformation. What possible delights have you had the ingenuity to detect in the rugged landscape of Parnassus! It should seem as if the laborers there have a very poor taking in civil life, and feed on a course diet without sauce. Out upon you! cried he, in dudgeon at the hint. You are talking of those paltry authors, whose works and even their persons are under the thumbs of booksellers and players. Is it any wonder that writers under such circumstances should be held cheap? But the good ones, my friend, are on a better footing in the world; and I think it may be affirmed, vanity apart, that my name is to be found in their list. Questionless, said I, talents like yours are convertible to every purpose; compositions from such a pen are not likely to be insipid. But I am on the rack to know how this rage for fencing with inky weapons could have seized thee.

Your wonder and alarm has mind in it, replied Nunez. I was so well pleased with my situation in the service of Signor Manuel Ordonnez, that I had no hankering after any other. But my genius, like that of Plautus, being too high-minded to contract itself whithin the sphere of menial occupations, I wrote a play and got it acted by a company then performing at Valladolid. Though it was not worth the paper it was scrawled upon, it had more success than many better pieces. Hence concluded I that the public was a silly bird, and would hatch any eggs that were put under it. That modest discovery, with the consequent madness of incessant composition, alienated my affections from the hospital. The love of poetry being stronger than the desire of accumulation, I determined on repairing to Madrid, as the centre of everything distinguished, to form my taste in that school. The first thing was to give the governor warning, who parted with me to his own great sorrow, from a sort of affection the result of similar prosperities. Fabricio, said he, what possible ground can you have for discontent? None at all, sir, I replied; you are the best of all possible masters, and I am deeply impressed with your kind treatment; but you know one must follow withersoever the stars ordain. I feel the sacred fire within me, on whose aspiring element my name is to be wafted to posterity. What confounded nonsense! rejoined the old fellow, whose ideas were all pecuniary. You are already become a fixture in the hospital, and are made of a metal which may easily be manufactured into a steward, or by good-luck even into a governor. You are going to give up the great object of life, and to flutter about its frippery. So much the worse for you, honest friend!

The governor, seeing how fruitless it was to struggle with my fixed resolve, paid me my wages, and made me a present of fifty ducats as an acknowledgment of my services. Thus, between this supply and what I have been able to scrape together out of some little commissions, which were assigned to me from an opinion of my disinterestedness, I was in circumstances to make a very pretty appearance on my arrival at Madrid; which I was not negligent in doing, though the literary tribe in our country are not over-punctilious about decency or cleanliness. I soon got acquainted with Lope de Vega, Cervantes, and the whole set of them; but though they were fine fellows, and thought so by the public, I chose for my model in preference, Don Lewis de Gongora, the incomparable, a young bachelor of Cordova, decidedly the first geuius that ever

Spain produced. He will not suffer his works to be printed during his life-time; but confines himself to a private communication among his friends. What is very remarkable, nature has gifted him with the uncommon talent of succeeding in every department of poetry. His principal excellence is in satire; there he outshines himself. He does not resemble, like Lucilius, a muddy stream with a slimy bottom; but is rather like the Tagus, rolling its transparent waters over a golden sand.

You give a fine description of this bachelor, said I to Fabricio; and questionless a character of such merit must have attracted an infinite deal of envy. The whole gang of authors, answered he, good and bad equally, are open-mouthed against him. He deals in bombast, says one; aims at double meanings, luxuriates in metaphor, and affects transposition. His verses, says another, have all the obscurity of those which the Salian priests used to chant in their processions, and which nobody was the wiser for hearing. There are others who impute it to him as a fault, to have exercised his genius at one time in sonnets or ballads, at another in play-writing in heroic stanzas, and in minor efforts of wit alternately, as if he had madly taken upon himself to eclipse the best writers each in their own favorite walk. But all these thrusts of jealousy are successfully parried, where the muse, which is their mark, becomes the idol of the great and of the multitude at once.

Under so able a master did I serve my apprenticeship; and, vanity apart, the preceptor was reflected in the disciple. So happily did I catch his spirit, that by this time he would not be ashamed to own some of my detached pieces. After his example, I carry my goods to market at great houses where the bidding is eager, and the sagacity of the bidders not difficult to match. It is true that I have a very insinuating talent at recitation: which places my compositions in no disadvantageous light. In short, I am the dear delight of the nobility, and live in the most particular intimacy with the Duke of Medina Sidonia, just as Horace used to live with his jolly companion Mecenas. By such conjuration and mighty magic have I won the name of author. You see the method lies within a narrow compass. Now, Gil Blas, it is your turn to deliver a round unvarnished tale of your exploits.

On this hint I spake; and unlike most narrators, gave all the important particulars, passing lightly over minute and tiresome circumstances. The action of talking, long continued, puts one in mind of dining. His ebony cabinet, which served for larder, pantry, and all possible uses, was ransacked for napkins, bread, a shoulder of mutton far gone in a decline, with its last and best contents, a bottle of excellent wine; so that we sat down to table in high spirits, as friends are wont to do after a long separation. You observe, said he, this free and independent manner of life. I might find a plate laid for me every day, if I chose it, in the very first houses: but, besides that the muse often pays me a visit and detains me within doors, I have a little of Aristippus in my nature. I can pass with equal relish from the great and busy world to my retreat, from all the researches of luxury to the simplicity of my own frugal board.

The wine was so good, that we encroached upon a second bottle. As a relish to our fruit and cheese, I begged to be favored with the sight of something, the offspring of his inspired moments. He immediately rummaged among his papers, and read me a sonnet with much energy of tone. Yet, with all the advantage of accent and expression, there was something so uncouth in the arrangement, as to baffle all conjecture about the meaning. He saw how it puzzled me. This sonnet then, said he, is not quite level to your comprehension! Is not that the fact? I owned that I should have preferred a construction somewhat less forced. He began laughing at my rusticity. Well, then! replied he; we will say that this sonnet would confuse clearer heads than thine: it is all the better for that. Sonnets, odes, in short all compositions which partake of the sublime, are of course the reverse of the simple and natural: they are enveloped in clouds, and their darkness constitutes their grandeur. Let the poet only fancy that he understands himself no matter whether his readers understand him or not. You are laughing at me, my friend, said I, interrupting him. Let poetry be of what species it may, good sense and intelligible diction are essential to its powers of pleasing, If your peerless Gongora is not a little more lucid than yourself, I protest that his merit will never pass current with me. Such poets may entrap their own age into applause, but will never live beyond it. Now let me have a taste of your prose.

Nunez showed me a preface which he meant to prefix to a dramatic miscellany, then in the press. He insisted on having my opinion. I like not your prose one atom better than your verse, said I. Your sonnet is a roaring deluge of emptiness; and as for your preface, it is disfigured by a phraseology stolen from languages yet in embryo, by words not stamped in the mint of general use, by all the perplexity of a style that does not know what to make of itself. In a word, the composition is altogether a thing of your own. Our classical and standard books are written in a very different manner. Poor tasteless wretch! exclaimed Fabricio. You are not aware that every prose writer who aspires to the reputation of sentiment and delicacy in these days, affects this style of his own, these perplexities and innovations which are a stumbling-block to you. There are five or six of us determined reformers of our language, who have undertaken to turn the Spanish idiom topsy-turvy; and with a blessing on our endeavors, we will pull it down and build it up again in defiance of Lope de Vega, Cervantes, and all the host of wits who cavil at our new modes of speech. Our party is strongly supported in the fashionable world, and we have laid violent hands upon the pulpit.

After all, continued he, our project is commendable; for, to speak without prejudice, we have ten times the merit of those natural writers, who express themselves just like the mob. I cannot conceive why so many sensible men are taken with them. It is all very well at Athens and at Rome, in a wild and undistinguished democracy; and on that principle only could Socrates tell Alci-biades, that the last appeal was to the people in all disputes about language. But at Madrid there is a polite and a vulgar usage; so that our courtiers talk in a different tongue from their tradesmen. You may assure yourself that it is so; in fine, this newly invented style is carrying everything before it, and turning old nature out of doors. Now I will explain to you by a single instance the difference between the elegance of our diction and the flatness of theirs. They would say, for example, in plain terms, " Ballets incidental to the piece are an ornament to a play;" but in our mode of expression, we say more exquisitely, " Ballets incidental to the piece are the very life and soul of the play." Now observe the phrase; *life and soul*. Are you sensible how glowing it is, at the same time how descriptive, setting before you all the motions of the dancers, as on an intellectual stage?

I broke in upon my reformer of language with a burst of laughter. Get along with you, Fabricio, said I, you are a coxcomb of your own manufacture, with your affected finery of phrase. And you, answered he, are a blockhead of nature's clumsy molding, with your starch simplicity. He then went on taunting me with the archbishop of Grenada's angry banter on my dismission. " Get about your business! Go and tell my treasurer to pay you a hundred ducats, and take my blessing in addition to that sum. God speed you, good master Gil Blas! I heartily pray that you may do well in the world! There is nothing to stand in your way, but a little better taste." I roared out in a still louder explosion of laughter at this lucky hit; and Fabricio, easily appeased on the score of impiety, as manifested in the opinion expressed concerning his writings, lost nothing of his pleasant and propitious temper. We got to the bottom of our second bottle; and then rose from the table in fine order for an adventure. Our first intention was to see what was to be seen upon the Prado; but passing in front of a liquor-shop it came into our heads that we might as well go in.

The company was in general tolerably select at this house of call. There were two distinct apartments; and the pastime in each was of a very opposite nature. One was devoted to games of chance or skill; the other to literary and scientific discussion: and there were at that moment two clever men by profession handling an argument most pertinaciously, before ten or twelve auditors deeply interested in the discussion. There was no occasion to join the circle, because the metaphysical thunder of their logic made itself heard at a more respectful distance: the heat and passion with which this abstract controversy was managed made the two philosophers look little better than madmen. A certain Eleazar used to cast out devils, by tying a ring to the nose of the possessed; had these learned swine been ringed in the same manner, how many little imps would have taken wing out of their nostrils? Angels and ministers of grace defend us, said I to my companion: what contortions of gesture, what extravagance of elocution! One might as well argue with the town crier. How little do we know our natural calling in society! Very true indeed, answered he: you have read of Novius, the Roman pawnbroker, whose lungs went as far beyond the rattle of chariot-wheels, as his conscience beyond the rate of legal interest; the Novii must certainly have been transplanted into Spain, and these fellows are lineal descendants. But the hopeless part of the case is, that though our organs of sense are deafened, our understandings are not invigorated at their expense. We thought it best to make our escape from these braying metaphysicians, and by that prudent motion to avoid a headache which was just beginning to annoy us. We went and seated ourselves in a corner of the other room, whence, as we sipped our refreshing beverage, all comers and goers were obnoxious to our criticism. Nunez was acquainted with almost the whole set. Heaven and earth! exclaimed he, the clash of philosophy is as yet but in its beginning; fresh reinforcements are coming in on both sides. Those three men just on the threshold, mean to let slip the dogs of war. But do you see those two queer fellows going out? That little swarthy, leather-complexioned Adonis, with long lank hair parted in the middle with mathematical exactness, is Don Juliano de Villanuno. He is a young barrister, with more of the prig than the lawyer about him. A party of us went to dine with him the other day. The occupation we caught him in was singular enough. He was amusing himself in his office with making a tall gray-hound fetch and carry the briefs in the causes which were so unfortunate as to have him retained; and of course the canine *amicus curiæ* set his fangs indifferently into the flesh of plaintiff or defendant, tearing law, equity, precedent, and principle into shreds. That licentiate at his elbow, with jolly, pimple-spangled nose and cheeks, goes by the name of Don Cherubino Tonto. He is a canon of Toledo, and the greatest fool that was ever suffered to walk the earth without a keeper. And yet, he arrays his features in that sort of not quite unmeaning smile, that you would give him credit for good sense as well as good humor. His eye has the look of cunning if not of wisdom, and his laugh too much of sarcasm for an absolute idiot. One would conclude that he had a turn for mischief, but kept it down from principle and feeling. If you wish to take his opinion upon a work of genius, he will hear it read with so grave and wrapt a silence, as nothing but deep thought and acute mental criticism could justify; but the truth is, that he comprehends not one word, and therefore can have nothing to say. He was of the barrister party. There were a thousand good things said, as there always must be in a professional company. Don Cherubino added nothing to the mass of merriment; but looked such perfect approbation at those who did, was so tractable and complimentary a listener, that every man at table placed him second in the comparative estimate of merit.

Do you know, said I to Nunez, who those two fellows are with dirty clothes and matted hair, their elbows on that table in the corner, and their cheeks upon their hands, whiffing foul breath into each other's nostrils as they lay their heads together? He told me that by their faces they were strangers to him; but that by physical and moral tokens they could only be coffee-house politicians, venting their spleen against the measures of government. But do look at that spruce spark, whistling as he paces up and down the other room, and balancing himself alternately on one toe and on the other. That is Don Augustino Moreto, a young poet sufficiently of nature's mint and coinage to pass current, if flatterers and sciolists had not debased him into a mere coxcomb by their misplaced admiration. The man to whom he is going up with that familiar shake by the hand, is one of the set who write verses and then call themselves poets; who claim a speaking acquaintance with the muses, but never were of their private parties.

Authors upon authors, nothing but authors! exclaimed he, pointing out two dashing blades. One would think they had made an appointment on purpose to pass in review before you. Don Bernardo Deslenguado and Don Sebastian of Villa Viciosa! The first is a vinegar-flavored vintage of Parnassus, a satirist by trade and company; he hates all the world, and is not liked the better for his taste. As for Don Sebastian, he is the milk and honey of criticism; he would not have the guilt of ill-nature on his conscience for the universe. He has just brought out a comedy without a single idea, which has succeeded with an audience of tantamount ideas; and he has just now published it to vindicate his innocence.

Gongora's candid pupil was running on in his career of benevolent explanation, when one of the Duke de Medina Sidonia's household came up and said: Signor Don Fabricio, my lord duke wishes to speak with you. You will find him at home. Nunez, who knew that the wishes of a great lord could not be too soon gratified, left me without ceremony; but he left me in the utmost consternation, to hear him called Don, and thus ennobled, in spite of master Chrysostom the barber's escutcheon, who had the honor to call him father.

CHAPTER XIV.

FABRICIO FINDS A SITUATION FOR GIL BLAS IN THE ESTABLISHMENT OF COUNT GALIANO, A SICILIAN NOBLEMAN.

I WAS too happy in Fabricio's society, not to hunt him out again early the next morning. Good day to you, Signor Don Fabricio, said I on my first approach; it seems you are the picked and chosen flower, or rather, saving your presence, the nondescript excrescence of the Asturian nobility. This sarcasm had no other effect than to set him laughing heartily. Then the title of Don was not lost upon you! exclaimed he. No, indeed, my noble lord, answered I; and you will give me leave to tell you that when you were recounting your transformations to me yesterday, you forgot the most extraordinary. Exactly so, replied he; but to speak sincerely, if I have taken up that prefix of dignity, it is less to tickle my own vanity, than in tenderness to that of others. You know what stuff the Spaniards are made of; an honest man is no honest man to them, if his honor is not bolstered up with escutcheons, pedigree, and patrimony. I may tell you, moreover, that there are so many gentry, and very queer sort of gentry too, dubbed Don Francisco, Don Pedro, Don What-do-you-call-him, or Don Devil, that if they owe their coats of arms to any herald but their own impudence, modern nobility is a mere drug in the market, so that a plebeian of nature's ennobling confers infinite honor on the upstarts of an artificial creation, by herding with their order.

But let us change the subject, added he. Last night, supping at the Duke de Medina Sidonia's, where among other company we had Count Galiano, a great Sicilian nobleman, the conversation turned upon the ridiculous effects of self-love. Delighted at having a case in point by way of illustration, I treated them with the story of the homilies. You may well suppose that there was a hearty laugh, and that the archbishop's dignity was not saved in the concussion; but the effect was not amiss for you, since the company felt for your situation; and Count Galiano, after a long string of questions, which of course I answered to your advantage, commissioned me to introduce you. I was just now going to look after you for that purpose. In all probability he means to offer you a situation as one of his secretaries. I advise you not to hang back. The count is rich, and lives away at Madrid, on the scale of an ambassador. He is said to have come to court on a negotiation with the Duke of Lerma, respecting some crown lands which that minister thinks of alienating in Sicily. In one word, Count Galiano, though a Sicilian, has every feature of generosity, fair dealing, and gentlemanly conduct. You cannot do better than get upon that nobleman's establishment. In all probability, the flattering prophecy respecting you at Grenada is to be fulfilled in his person.

It was my full determination, said I to Nunez, to take my swing about town and look at men and manners a little, before the harness was buckled on my back again; but you paint your Sicilian nobleman in colors which fascinate my imagination and change my purpose. I should like to close with him at once. You will do so very soon, replied he, or I am much deceived. We sallied forth together immediately, and went to the count's, who resided in the house of his friend, Don Sancho d'Avila, the latter being then in the country.

The court-yard was overrun with pages and footmen in rich and elegant liveries, while the ante-chamber was blockaded by esquires, gentlemen, and various officers of the household. They were all as fine as possible, but with so whimsical an assortment of features, that you might have taken them for a cluster of monkeys dressed up to satirize the Spanish fashions. Do what you will, there is a certain class of men and women in nature, whom no art can trick out into anything human.

At the very name of Don Fabricio, a lane was formed for my

patron, and I followed in the rear. The count was in his dressing-gown, sitting on a sofa and taking his chocolate. We made our obeisance in the most respectful manner; while an inclination of the head on his part, accompanied with a condescending smile, won my heart at once. It is very wonderful, and yet very common, how the most trifling notice from the great penetrates the very soul of those who are not accustomed to it! They must have behaved like fiends, before their behavior will be complained of.

After taking his chocolate, he recreated himself with the humors of a large ape, which underwent the name of Cupid: why the ape was made a god, or the god likened to an ape, the parties concerned can best answer; the only point of resemblance seemed to be mischief. At all events, this hairy brat of the sylvan Venus had so gamboled himself into his master's good graces, had established such a character for wit and humor, that the life of society was extinguished in his absence. As for Nunez and myself, though we had a better turn for drollery, we were cunning enough to chime in with the prevailing taste. The Sicilian was highly delighted with this, and tore himself away for a moment from his favorite pastime, just to tell me: My friend, you have only to say whether you choose to be one of my secretaries. If the situation suits you, the salary is two hundred pistoles a year. If Don Fabricio gives you a character, that is enough. Yes, my lord, cried Nunez, I am not such a cowardly fellow as Plato, who introduced one of his friends to Dionysius the tyrant, and then was afraid to back his own recommendation. But I have no anxiety about being reproached on that head.

I thanked the poet of the Asturias with a low bow, for having so much better an opinion of me than Plato had of his friend. Then addressing my patron, I assured him of my zeal and fidelity. No sooner did this good nobleman perceive his proposal to be acceptable, then he rang for his steward, and after talking to him apart, said to me: Gil Blas, I will explain the nature of your post hereafter. Meanwhile, you have only to follow that right-hand man of mine; he has his orders how to bestow you. I immediately retreated, leaving Fabricio behind with the Count and Cupid.

The steward, who came from Messina, and proved by all his actions that he came thence, led the way to his own room, overwhelming me all the while with the kindness of his reception. He sent for the tailor who lived upon the skirts of the household, and ordered him to make me out of hand a suit of equal magnificence with those of the principal officers. The tailor took my measure and withdrew. As to lodging, said the native of Messina, I know a room which will just suit you. But stay! Have your breakfasted? I answered in the negative. Oh! poor shamefaced youth, replied he, why did not you say so? Come this way: I will introduce you where, thank heaven, you have only to ask and have.

So saying, he led me down into the buttery, where we found the clerk of the kitchen, who was a Neapolitan, and of course a complete match for his neighbor on the other side of the water. It might be said of this pair that they were formed to meet by nature. This honest clerk of the kitchen was doing justice to his trade by cram-

"COME NEARER, GIL BLAS, SAID HE; TAKE A CHAIR, AND HEAR
ME ATTENTIVELY."

ming himself and five or six hangers-on with ham, tongue, saus-ages, and other savory compositions, which, besides their own relish, possess the merit of engendering thirst: we made common cause with these jolly fellows, and helped them to toss off some of my lord the count's best wines. While these things were going on in the buttery, kindred exploits were performing in the kitchen. The cook too was regaling three or four tradesmen of his acquaint-ance, who liked good wine as well as ourselves, nor disdained to stuff their craws with meat pasties aud game: the very scullions were at free quarters, and filched whatever they pleased. I fancied myself in a house given up to plunder and yet what I saw was com-paratively fair and honest. These little festivities were laughing matters; but the private transactions of the family were very serious.

CHAPTER XV.

THE EMPLOYMENT OF GIL BLAS IN DON GALIANO'S HOUSEHOLD.

I WENT away to fetch my movables to my new residence. On my return the count was at table with several noblemen and the poet Nunez, who called about him as if perfectly at home, and took a principal share in the conversation. Indeed, he never opened his lips without applause. So much for wit! with that commodity at market, a man may pay his way in any company.

It was my lot to dine with the gentlemen of the household, who were served nearly as well as their employer. After meal-time I withdrew to ruminate on my lot. So far so good, Gil Blas! said I to myself: here you are in the family of a Sicilian count, of whose character you know nothing. To judge by appearances, you will be as much in your element as a duck upon the water. But do not make too sure! you ought to look askew at your horoscope, whose unkindly position you have too often experienced with a vengeance. Independent of that, it is not easy to conjecture what he means you to do. There are secretaries and a steward already: where can your post be? In all likelihood you are intended to manage his little private affairs. Well and good! There is no better luck about the house of a great nobleman, if you would travel post haste to make your fortune. In the performance of more honorable services, a man gets on only step by step, and even at that pace often sticks by the way.

While these philosophical reflections were revolving in my mind, a servant came to tell me that all the company was gone home, and that my lord the count was inquiring for me. I flew immediately to his apartment, where I found him lolling on the sofa, ready to take his afternoon's nap, with his monkey by his side.

Come nearer, Gil Blas, said he; take a chair, and hear me atten-tively. I placed myself in an attitude of profound listening, when he addressed me as follows. Don Fabricio has informed me that, among other good qualities, you have that of sincere attachment to your masters, and incorruptible integrity. These are my inducements for proposing to take you into my service. I stand in need of a friend in a domestic, to espouse my interests and apply his whole heart and soul to the reform of my establishment. My fortune is large, it must be confessed, but my expenditure far exceeds my income every year. And how happens that? Because they rob, ransack, and devour me. I might as well be in a forest infested by banditti, as an inhabitant of my own house. I suspect the clerk of the kitchen and my steward of playing into one another's hands; and unless my thoughts are unjust as well as uncharitable, they are pushing forward as fast as they can to ruin me beyond redemption. You will ask me what I have to do but send them packing, if I think them scoundrels. But then where are others to be got of a better breed? It will be sufficient to place them under the eye of a man who shall be invested with the right of control over their conduct; and you have I chosen to execute this commission. If you discharge it well, be assured that your services will not be repaid with ingratitude. I shall take care to provide you with a very comfortable settlement in Sicily.

With this he dismissed me; and that very evening, in the presence of the whole household, I was proclaimed principal manager and surveyor-general of the family. Our gentlemen of Messina and Naples expressed no particular chagrin at first, because they considered me as a spark of mettle like their own, and took it for granted, that though the loaf was to be shared with a third, there would always be cut and come again for the triumvirate. But they looked inexpressibly foolish the next day, when I declared myself in serious terms a decided enemy to all peculation and underhand dealing. From the clerk of the kitchen I required the buttery accounts without varnish or concealment. I went down into the cellar. The furniture of the butler's pantry underwent a strict examination, particularly in the articles of plate and linen. Next I read them a serious lecture on the duty of acting for their employer at they would for themselves; exhorted them to adopt a system of economy in their expenditure; and wound up my harangue with a protestation, that his lordship should be acquainted with the very first instance of any unfair tricks that I should discover in the exercise of my office

But I had not yet got to the length of my tether. There was still wanting a scout to ascertain whether they had any private understanding. I fixed upon a scullion, who, won over by my promises, told me that I could not have applied to a better person to be informed of all that was passing in the family: that the clerk of the kitchen and the steward were one as good as the other, and agreed to burn the candle at both ends; that half the provisions bought for the table were made perquisites by these gentlemen; that the Neapolitan kept a lady who lives opposite St. Thomas's college, and his colleague, not to be outdone, provided for another next door to the Sungate; that these two nymphs had their larder regularly supplied every morning, while the cook, following a good example, sent a few little nice things to a widow of his acquaintance in the neighborhood : but as he winked at the table arrangements of his dear and confidential friends, it was but fair that he should draw whenever he pleased upon the wine-cellar : in short, by the practices of these three blood-suckers, a most horrible system of extravagance had found its way into my lord the count's establishment. If you doubt my veracity, added the scullion, only take the trouble of going to-morrow morning about seven o'clock into the neighborhood of St. Thomas's college, and you will see me with a load upon my back, which will convert your suspicions into certainty. Then you, said I, are in the confidence of those honest purveyors? I am factor to the clerk of the kitchen, answered he ; and one of my comrades runs on errands for the steward.

I had the curiosity the next day to loiter about St. Thomas's college at the appointed hour. My informer was punctual to time and place. He brought with him a large tray full of butcher's meat, poultry, and game. I took an account of every article; and drew out the bill of fare in my memorandum book, for the purpose of showing it to my master : at the same time telling my little turnspit to execute his commission as usual.

His Sicilian lordship, naturally warm in his temper, would have turned his countryman and the Italian out of doors altogether, in the first fury of his anger ; but after cooling upon it, he got rid of the former only, and gave me his vacant place. Thus my office of supervisor was suppressed very shortly after its creation ; nor did I relinquish it with any reluctance. To define it strictly and properly, it was nothing better than that of a spy with a sounding title ; there was nothing substantial in the nature of the appointment : whereas to the stewardship was tied the key of the strong box, and with that goes the mastery of the whole family. There are so many little perquisites and so much patronage attached to that department of administration, that a man must inevitably get rich, almost in spite of his own honesty.

But our Neapolitan was not so easily to be driven from his strongholds. Observing to what a pitch of savage zeal I carried my integrity, and that I was up every morning time enough to enter in my books the exact quantity of meat that came from market, he abandoned the practice of sending it off by wholesale : yet the plunderer did not therefore contract the scale of his demands on the animal creation. He was cunning enough to make it as broad as it was long, by arranging the services with so much the more profusion. Thus, what was sent down again untouched being his property by culinary common law, he had nothing to do but to pamper up his pet with victuals ready dressed, instead of giving her the trouble of cooking for herself. The devil will levy his due out of every transaction ; so that the count was very little the better for his paragon of a steward. The unbounded prodigality in our style of setting out a table, even to a surfeiting degree, was a plain hint to me of what was going forward ; I therefore took upon myself to retrench the superfluities of every course. This, however, was done with so judicious a hand, that there was nothing like parsimony to be discovered. No one would ever have missed what was taken away; and yet the expense was reduced very considerably by a well-regulated economy. That was just what my employer wanted; good house-wifery, but a magnificent establishment. There was a love of saving at the bottom; but a taste for grandeur was the ostensible passion.

Abuses seldom exist alone. The wine flowed too freely. If, for instance, there were a dozen gentlemen at his lordship's table, the consumption was seldom less than fifty, sometimes sixty bottles. This was strange; and looked as if there was more in it than met the lips of the guests. Hereupon I consulted my oracle of the scullery, whence I derived most of my wisdom; for he brought me a faithful account of all that was said and done in the kitchen, where they had not the least suspicion of him. It seemed that the havoc of which I complained proceeded from a new confederacy between the clerk of the kitchen, the cook, and the under-butler. The latter carried off the bottles half full, and shared their contents with his allies. I spoke to him on the subject, threatening to turn him and all the footmen under him out of doors at a minute's warning, if ever they did the like again. The hint was understood, and the evil remedied. I took especial care lest the slightest of my services should be lost upon my master, who overwhelmed me with commendations, and took a greater liking to me every day. On my part, as a reward to the scullion, he was promoted to the situation next under the cook.

The Neapolitan was furious at encountering me in every direction. The most aggravating circumstance of the whole was the overhauling of his accounts; for, to pare his nails the closer, I had gone into the market, and informed myself of the prices. I followed him through all his doublings, and always took off the market penny which he wanted to add. He must have cursed me a hundred times a day; but the curses of the wicked fall in blessings on the good. I wonder how he could stay in his place under such discipline; but probably something still stuck by the fingers.

Fabricio, whom I saw occasionally, rather blamed my conduct than otherwise. Heaven grant, said he, one day, that all this virtue may meet with its reward! But between ourselves you might as well be a little more practicable with the clerk of the kitchen. What! answered I, shall this freebooter put a bold face upon the matter, and charge a fish at ten pistoles in his bill, which costs only four, and would you have me pass the articles in my accounts? Why not? replied he, coolly. He has only to let you go snacks in the commission, and the books will be balanced in your favor by the customary rule of stewardship arithmetic. Upon my word, my friend, you are enough to overturn all regular systems of housekeeping; and you are likely to end your days in a livery, if you let the eel slip through your fingers without skinning it. You are to learn that fortune is a very woman; ready and eager to surrender, but expecting the formality of a summons.

I only laughed at this doctrine; and Nunez laughed at it too.

when he found that bad advice was thrown away upon an incorrigibly honest subject. He then wished to make me believe it was all a mere joke. At all events, nothing could shake my resolution to act for my employer as for myself. Indeed my actions corresponded with my words on that subject; for I may venture to say that in four months my master saved at least three thousand ducats by my thrift.

CHAPTER XVI.

AN ACCIDENT HAPPENS TO THE COUNT DE GALIANO'S MONKEY; HIS LORDSHIP'S AFFLICTION ON THAT OCCASION. THE ILLNESS OF GIL BLAS, AND ITS CONSEQUENCES.

AT the expiration of the before-mentioned time, the repose of the family was marvelously troubled by an accident, which will appear but a trifle to the reader; and yet it was a very serious matter to the household, especially to me. Cupid, the monkey of whom I was speaking, that animal, so much the idol of our lord and master, attempting to leap from one window to another, performed so ill as to fall into the court and put his leg out of joint. No sooner were the fatal tidings carried to the count, than he sung a dirge which pealed through all the neighborhood. In the extremity of his sufferings, every inmate without exception was taken to task, and we were all within an inch of being packed off about our business. But the storm only rumbled without falling; he gave us and our negligence to the devil, without being by any means select in the terms of the bequest. The most notorious of the faculty in the line of fractures and dislocations were sent for. They examined the poor dear leg, set, and bound it up. But though they all gave it as their opinion that there was no danger, my master could not be satisfied without retaining the most eminent about the person of the animal, till he could be pronounced to be in a state of convalescence.

It would be a manifest injustice to the family affections of his Sicilian lordship, not to commemorate all the agonizing sensations of his soul during this period of painful suspense. Would it be thought possible that this tender nurse did not stir from his darling Cupid's bedside all the live-long day? The bandages were never altered or adjusted but in his presence, and he got up two or three times in the night to inquire after his patient. The most provoking part of the business was, that all the servants, and myself in particular, were required to be eternally on the alert, to anticipate the slightest wishes of this ridiculous baboon. In short, there was no peace in the house, till the cursed beast, having recovered from the effects of its fall, got back again to his old tricks and whirligigs. After this shall we be mealy-mouthed about believing Suetonius, when he tells us that Caligula cared more for his horse than for all the world besides, that he gave him more than the establishment and attendance of a senator, and that he even wanted to make him consul? Our wise master stopped little short of the emperor in his partiality to the monkey; and had serious thoughts of purchasing for him the place of corregidor.

Mine was the worst luck of any in the family; for I had so topped my part above all the other servants, by way of paying my court to his lordship, and had nursed poor dear Cupid with such assiduity, as to throw myself into a fit of illness. A violent fever seized me, so that I was almost at death's door. They did what they pleased with me for a whole fortnight, without my consciousness; for the physicians and the fates were both conspiring against me. But my youth was more than a match for the fever and the prescriptions united. When I recovered my senses, the first use I made of them was to observe myself removed to another room. I wanted to know why; and asked an old woman who nursed me: but she told me that I must not talk, as the physician had expressly forbidden it. When we are well, we turn up our nose at the doctors; but when we are sick, we are as much like old women as themselves.

It seemed best therefore to keep silence, though with an inveterate longing to hold converse with my attendant. I was debating the point in my own mind, when there came in two foppish-looking fellows, dressed in the very extreme of fashion. Nothing less than velvet would serve their turn, with linen and lace to correspond. They looked like men of rank; and I could have sworn that they were some of my master's friends come to see me out of regard for him. Under that impression I attempted to sit up, and flung away my nightcap to look genteel; but the nurse forced me under the bedclothes again, and tucked me up, announcing these gentlemen at the same time, as my physician and apothecary.

The doctor came up to my bedside, felt my pulse, looked in my face; and discovering undeniable symptoms of approaching convalescence, assumed an air of triumph, as if it was all his handiwork; and said there was nothing wanting but to keep the bowels open, and then he flattered himself he might boast of having performed an extraordinary cure. Speaking after this manner, he dictated a prescription to the apothecary, looking in the glass all the time, adjusting the dress of his hair, and twisting his visage into shapes which set me laughing in spite of my debility. At length he took his leave with a slight inclination of the head, and went his way, more taken with the contemplation of his own pretty person, than anxious about the success of his remedies.

After his departure, the apothecary, not to have the trouble of a visit for nothing, made ready to proceed as it is prescribed in certain cases. Whether he was afraid that the old woman's skill was not equal to the exigency, or whether he meant to enhance his own services by assiduity, he chose to operate in person; but in spite of practice and experience, accidents will happen. Haste to return benefits is among the most amiable propensities of our nature; and such was my eagerness not to be behindhand with my

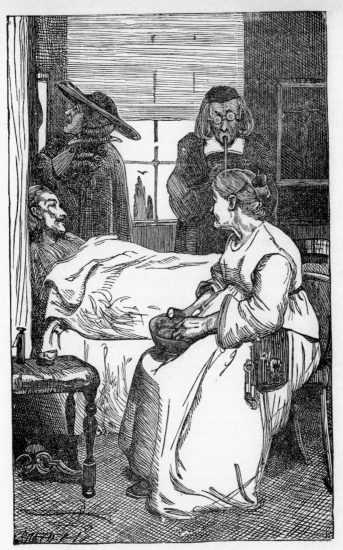

GIL BLAS AND THE DOCTORS.

benefactor, that his velvet dress bore immediate testimony to the profuseness of my gratitude. This he considered merely as one of those little occurrences which chequer the fortunes of the pharmaceutical profession. A napkin is a resource for everything in a sick room, and least said was soonest mended; so he wiped himself quietly, vowing indemnity and vengeance to himself for the necessity under which he unquestionably labored of sending his clothes to the scourer.

On the following morning he returned to the attack more modestly equipped, though there was then no risk of my springing a countermine, as he had only to administer the potion which the doctor had prescribed the evening before. Besides that I felt myself getting better every moment, I had taken such a dislike, since the day before, to the pill-dispensing tribe, as to curse the very universities where these graduated cut-throats kept their exercises in the faculty of slaying. In this temper of mind, I declared, with a round oath, that I would not accept of health through such a medium, but would willingly make over Hippocrates and his myrmidons to the devil. The apothecary, who did not care a doit what became of his compound, if it was but paid for, left the phial on the table, and stalked away in Telamonian silence.

I immediately ordered that bitch of a medicine to be thrown out of window, having set myself so doggedly against it, that I would as soon have swallowed arsenic. Having once drawn the sword, I threw away the scabbard; and erecting my tongue into an independent potentate, told my nurse in a determined tone, that she must absolutely inform me what was become of my master. The old lady, fearing lest the development of the mystery might completely overset me, or thinking possibly that her prey might escape out of her clutches for want of a little irritating contradiction, was most provokingly mute; but I was so pressing in my demand to be obeyed, that she at length gave me a decisive answer: Worthy sir, you have no longer any master but your own will. Count Galiano is gone back into Sicily.

I could not believe my ears; and yet it was fatally the fact. That nobleman, on the second day of my indisposition, being afraid of harboring death under the same roof with him, had the benevolence to send me packing with my little effects to a ready-furnished room, where providence was left to cure, or a nurse to kill me, as it happened. While the alternative was tottering on the balance, he was ordered back into Sicily, and in the headlong haste of his obedience, never thought about me; whether it was that he numbered me already among the dead, or that great lords, like great wits, have short memories.

My nurse gave me these particulars, and informed me that it was she who had called in a physician and an apothecary, that I might not die without professional honors. I fell into profound musing at this fine story. Farewell my brilliant establishment in Sicily! Farewell my budding hopes and blushing honors! When any great misfortune shall have befallen you, says a certain pope, look well to your own conduct, and you will find that there is always something wrong at the bottom of it. With all reverent submission to his holiness, I cannot help thinking myself in this instance an exception to the infallibility of his maxim. How the deuce was I to blame for being visited by a fever? There was more reason for remorse in the monkey or his master than in me.

When I beheld the flattering chimeras with which my head was filled, all vanishing into air, into thin air, the first thing that worried my poor brain was my portmanteau, which I ordered to be laid upon my bed to examine it. I groaned heavily on discovering that it had been opened. Alas! my dear portmanteau, exclaimed I, my only hope, consolation and refuge, you have been, to all appearance, a prisoner in an enemy's country. No, no, Signor Gil Blas, said the old woman, make yourself easy on that head: you have not fallen among thieves. Your baggage is as immaculate as my honor.

I found the dress I had on at my first entrance into the count's service; but it was in vain to look for that which my friend from Messina had ordered for me as a member of the household. My master had not thought fit to leave me in possession of it, or else some one had made free with it. All my other little matters were safe, and even a large leather purse with my coin in it, which I counted over twice, not being able to believe at first that there could be only fifty pistoles remaining out of two hundred and sixty, which was the balance of the account before my illness. What is the meaning of all this, my good lady? said I to the nurse. Here is a leak in the vessel. No living soul but myself has touched a farthing, answered the old woman, and I have been as good an economist for you as possible. But illness is very expensive; one must always have one's money in one's hand. Here! added this excellent economist, taking a bundle of papers out of her pocket, this is a statement of debtor and creditor, as exact as a banker's book, and you will see that I have not laid out the veriest trifle in need-nots.

I ran over the account with a hasty glance; for it extended to fifteen or twenty pages. Mercy on us! The poulterers' shops must have been exhausted, while I was in too weak a state to take sustenance! There must have been at least twelve pistoles stewed down into broths. Other articles were much to the same tune. It was incredible what a sum had been lavished in firing, candles, water, brooms, and innumerable articles of housekeeping and house-cleaning. After all, extortionate as the bill was, the utmost ingenuity could not raise it above thirty pistoles, and consequently there was a deficiency of a hundred and eighty to make the account even. I just ventured to point that out; but the old woman, with a show of simplictly and candor, put all the saints in the calendar into requisition to attest that there were no more than eighty pistoles in the purse when the count's steward gave her charge of the wallet. What say you, my good woman, interrupted I with precipitation: was it the steward who placed my effects in your hands? To be sure it was, answered she: the very man; and with this piece of advice: Here, good mother, when Gil Blas shall be num-

"NO, NO, SIGNOR GIL BLAS, YOU HAVE NOT FALLEN AMONG THIEVES.
YOUR BAGGAGE IS AS IMMACULATE AS MY HONOR."

bered with the dead, do not fail to treat him with a handsome funeral; there is in this wallet wherewithal to defray the expenses.

Ah! most pestiferous Neapolitan! exclaimed I in the bitterness of my heart. I am no longer at a loss to conjecture what is become of the deficiency. You have swept it off as an indemnity for a part of the plunder which I have prevented you from making free with. After relieving my mind by exclamations, I returned thanks to heaven that the scoundrel had been so modest as not to take the whole. Yet whatever reason I had for believing the action to be perfectly in character for the person to whom it was imputed, the nurse had not altogether cleared herself from my suspicions. They hovered sometimes over one and sometimes over the other; but let them light where they would, it was all the same to me. I said nothing about the matter to the old woman; not even so much as to haggle about the items of her fine bill. I should not have been an atom the richer for doing so; and we must all live by our trades. The utmost of my malice was to pay her and send her packing three days afterwards.

I am inclined to think that at her departure she gave the apothecary notice of her quitting the premises, and having left me sufficiently in possession of myself to take French leave without acknowledging my obligations to him; for she had not been gone many minutes before he came in puffing and blowing, with his bill in his hand. There, under names which had escaped my conscription, though as arrant a physician as the worst of them, he had set down all the hypothetical remedies which he insisted that I had taken during the time when I could take nothing. This bill might truly be called the epitome of an apothecary's conscience. Such being the case, we had a bustle about the payment. I pleaded for an abatement of one-half. He swore that he would not take a doit less than his just demand. He kept his oath and yet relaxed; for considering that he had to do with a young man who might run away from Madrid within four-and-twenty hours, he preferred my offer of three hundred per cent on the prime cost of his drugs, though a pitiful profit for an apothecary, to the risk of losing all, I counted out the money with an aching heart, and he withdrew, chuckling over his revenge for the scurvy trick I had played him on the day of evacuation.

The physician made his appearance next; for beasts of prey inhabit the same latitudes. I fee'd him for his visits, which had been quite as frequent as necessary, and his object was answered. But he would not leave me without proving how hardly he had earned his money, for that he had not only expelled the enemy from the interior, but had defended the frontiers from the attack of all the disorders on the army list of the *materia medica.* He talked very learnedly, with good emphasis and discretion; so much so, that I did not comprehend one word he said. When I had got rid of him, I flattered myself that the destinies had now done their worst. But I was mistaken; for there came a surgeon whose face I had never seen in the whole course of my life. He accosted me very politely, and congratulated me on the imminent danger I had escaped; attributing the happy issue of my complaints to those which he had himself cut, with the profuse application of bleeding, cupping, blistering, and all sorts of torments, consequent and inconsequent. Another feather out of my poor wing! I was obliged to pay toll to the surgeon also. After so many purgatives, my purse was brought to such a state of debility, that it might be considered as dead and gone; a mere skeleton, drained of all its vital juices.

My spirits began to flag, on the contemplation of my wretched case. In the service of my two last masters I had wedded myself to the pomps and vanities of this wicked world; and could no longer, as heretofore, look poverty in the face with the sternness of a cynic. It must be owned, however, that I was in the wrong to give way to melancholy, after experiencing so often that fortune had never cast me down, but for the purpose of raising me up again; so that my pitiful plight at the present moment, if rightly considered, was only to be hailed as the harbinger of approaching prosperity.

BOOK THE EIGHTH.

CHAPTER I.

GIL BLAS SCRAPES AN ACQUAINTANCE OF SOME VALUE, AND FINDS WHEREWITHAL TO MAKE HIM AMENDS FOR THE COUNT DE GALIANO'S INGRATITUDE. DON VALERIO DE LUNA'S STORY.

IT seemed so strange to have heard not a syllable from Nunez during this long interval, that I concluded he must be in the country. I went to look after him as soon as I could walk, and found the fact to be, that he had gone into Andalusia three weeks ago, with the Duke of Medina Sidonia.

One morning when rubbing my eyes after a sound sleep, Melchior de la Ronda started into my recollection; and that bringing to mind my promise at Grenada, of going to see his nephew, if ever I should return to Madrid, it seemed advisable not to defer fulfilling my promise for a single day. I inquired where Don Balthazar de Zuniga lived, and went thither straightway. On asking if Signor Joseph Navarro was at home, he made his appearance immediately. We exchanged bows with a well-bred coolness on his part, though I had taken care to announce my name audibly. There was no reconciling such a frosty reception with the glowing portrait ascribed to this paragon of the buttery. I was just going to withdraw in the full determination of not coming again, when assuming all at once an open and smiling aspect, he said with considerable earnestness: Ah! Signor Gil Blas de Santillane, pray forgive the formality of your welcome. My memory ill seconded the warmth of my disposition towards you. Your name had escaped me, and was not at the moment identified with the gentleman, of whom mention was made in a letter from Grenada more than four months ago.

How happy I am to see you! added he, shaking hands with me most cordially. My uncle Melchior, whom I love and honor like

THE DUKE OF LERMA.

my natural father, charges me, if by chance I should have the honor of seeing you, to entertain you as his own son, and in case of need, to stretch my own credit and that of my friends to the utmost in your behalf. He extols the qualities of your heart and mind in terms sufficient of themselves to engage me in your service, though his recommendation had not been added to the other motives. Consider me, therefore, I entreat you, as participating in all my uncle's sentiments. You may depend on my friendship; let me hope for an equal share in yours.

I replied to Joseph's polite assurances in suitable terms of acknowledgment; so that being both of us warm-hearted and sincere, a close intimacy sprung up without waiting for common forms. I felt no embarrassment about laying open the state of my affairs. This I had no sooner done, than he said: I take upon myself the care of finding you a situation; meanwhile, there is a knife and fork for you here every day. You will live rather better than at an ordinary. This offer was sure to be well relished by an invalid just recovering, with a fastidious palate and an empty pocket. It could not but be accepted; and I picked up my crumbs so fast that at the end of a fortnight I began to look like a rosy-gilled son of the church. It struck me that Melchior's nephew larded his lean sides to some purpose. But how could it be otherwise? he had three strings to his bow, as holding the undermentioned pluralities: the butler's place, the clerkship of the kitchen, and the stewardship. Furthermore, without meaning to question my friend's honesty, they do say that the comptroller of the household and he looked over each other's hands.

My recovery was entirely confirmed, when my friend Joseph, on my coming in to dinner as usual one day, said with an air of congratulation: Signor Gil Blas, I have a very tolerable situation in view for you. You must know that the Duke of Lerma, first minister of the crown in Spain, giving himself up entirely to state affairs, throws the burden of his own on two confidential persons. Don Diego de Monteser takes the charge of collecting his rents, and Don Rodrigo de Calderona superintends the finances of his household. These two officers are paramount in their departments, having nothing to do with one another. Don Diego has generally two deputies to transact the business; and finding just now that one of them had been discharged, I have been canvassing for you. Signor Monteser having the greatest possible regard for me, granted my request at once, on the strength of my testimony to your morals and capacity. We will pay our respects to him after dinner.

We did not miss our appointment. I was received with every mark of favor, and promoted in the room of the dismissed deputy. My business consisted in visiting the farms, in giving orders for the necessary repairs, in dunning the farmers, and keeping them to time in their payments; in a word, the tenants were all under my thumb, and Don Diego checked my accounts every month with a minuteness which few receivers could have borne. But this was exactly what I wanted. Though my uprightness had been so ill requited by my late master, it was my only inheritance, and I was determined not to sell the reversion.

One day news came that the castle of Lerma had taken fire, and was more than half burnt down. I immediately went thither to estimate the loss. Informing myself to a nicety, and on the spot, respecting all the particulars of the unlucky accident, I drew up a detailed narrative, which Monteser showed to the Duke of Lerma. That minister, though vexed at the circumstance, was struck with the memorial, and inquired who was the author. Don Diego thought it not enough to answer the question, but spoke of me in such high terms, that his excellency recollected it six months afterwards, on occasion of an incident I shall now relate, had it not been for which I might never, perhaps, have been employed at court. It was as follows:—

There lived at that time in Princes Street an elderly lady, by name Inesilla de Cantarilla. Her birth was a matter of mystery. Some said she was the daughter of a musical instrument-maker, and others gave her a high military extraction. However that might be she was a very extraordinary personage. Nature had gifted her with the singular talent of winning men's hearts in defiance of time, and in contradiction to her own laws; for she was now entering upon the fourth quarter of her century. She had been the reigning toast of the old court, and levied tribute on the passions of the new. Age, though at daggers drawn with beauty, was completely foiled in its assault upon her charms; they might be somewhat faded, but the touch of sympathy they excited in their decline was more pleasing that the vivid glow of their meridian lustre. An air of dignity, a transporting wit and humor, an unborrowed grace in her deportment, perpetuated the reign of passion, and silenced the suggestions of reason.

Don Valerio de Luna, one of the Duke of Lerma's secretaries, a young fellow of five-and-twenty, meeting with Inesilla, fell violently in love with her. He made his sentiments known, enacted all the mummery of despair, and followed up the usual catastrophe of every amorous drama so much according to the unities and rules, that it was difficult, in the very torrent and whirlwind of his passion, to beget a temperance that might give it smoothness. The lady, who had her reason for not choosing to fall in with his humor, was at a loss how to get out of the difficulty. One day she was in hopes to have found the means by calling the young man into her closet, and there pointing to a clock upon the table. Mark the precise hour, said she; just seventy-five years ago was I brought upon the stage of this fantastical world. In good earnest, would it sit well upon my time of life to be engaged in affairs of gallantry? Betake yourself to reflection, my good child; stifle sentiments so unsuitable to your own circumstances and mine. Sensible as this language was, the spark, no longer bowing to the authority of reason, answered the lady with all the impetuosity of a man racked by the most excruciating torments: Cruel Inesilla, why have you recourse to such frivolous remonstrances? Do you think they can change your charms or my desires? Delude not yourself with so false a hope. As long as your loveliness or my delusion lasts, I shall never cease to adore you. Well then, rejoined she, since you are obstinate enough to persist in the resolution of wearying me with your importunities, my door shall henceforth be shut against you. You are banished, and I beg to be no longer troubled with your company.

It may be supposed, perhaps, that after this, Don Valerio, baffled, made good his retreat like a prudent general. Quite the reverse! He became more troublesome than ever. Love is to lovers just what wine is to drunkards. The swain intreated, sighed, looked, and sighed again; when all at once, changing his note from childish treble to the big manly verse of bluster and ravishment, he swore that he would have by foul means what he could not obtain by fair. But the lady, repulsing him courageously, said with a piercing look of strong resentment, Hold, imprudent wretch! I shall put a curb on your mad career. Learn that you are my own son.

Don Valerio was thunderstruck at these words; the tempest of his rage subsided. But, conjecturing that Inesilla had only started this device to rid herself of his solicitations, he answered, That is a mere romance of the moment to steal away from my ardent desires. No, no, said she, interrupting him, I disclose a mystery which should have been for ever buried, had you not reduced me to so painful a necessity. It is six-and-twenty years since I was in love with your father, Don Pedro de Luna, then governor of Segovia; you were the fruit of our mutual passion: he owned you, brought you up with care and tenderness, and having no children born in wedlock, he had nothing to hinder him from distinguishing your good qualities by the gifts of fortune. On my part, I have not forsaken you; as soon as you were of an age to be introduced into the world, I drew you into the circle of my acquaintance, to form your manners to that polish of good company, so necessary for a gentleman, which is only to be gained in female society. I have done more: I have employed all my credit to introduce you to the prime minister. In short, I have interested myself for you as I should have done for my own son. After this confession, take your measures accordingly. If you can purge your affections from their dross, and look on me as a mother, you are not banished from my presence, and I shall treat you with my accustomed tenderness. But if you are not equal to an effort, which nature and reason demand from you, fly instantly, and release me from the horror of beholding you.

Inesilla spoke to this effect. Meanwhile Don Valerio preserved a sudden silence: it might have been interpreted into a virtuous struggle, a conquest over the weakness of his heart. But his purposes were far different; he had another scene to act before his mother. Unable to withstand the total overthrow of all his wild projects, he basely yielded to despair. Drawing his sword, he plunged it in his own bosom. His fate resembled that of Œdipus, with this distinction; that the Theban put out his own eyes from remorse for the crime he had perpetrated, while the Castilian, on the contrary, committed suicide from disappointment at the frustration of his purposes.

The unhappy Don Valerio was not released from his sufferings immediately. He had leisure left for recollection, and for making his peace with heaven, before he rushed into the presence of his Maker. As his death vacated one of the secretaryships on the Duke of Lerma's establishment, that minister, not having forgotten my memoir on the subject of the fire, nor the high character he had heard of me, nominated me to succeed to the post in question,

CHAPTER II.

GIL BLAS IS INTRODUCED TO THE DUKE OF LERMA, WHO ADMITS
HIM AMONG THE NUMBER OF HIS SECRETARIES, AND REQUIRES
A SPECIMEN OF HIS TALENTS, WITH WHICH HE IS WELL SAT-
ISFIED.

MONTESER was the person to inform me of this agreeable circumstance, which he did in the following terms: My friend Gil
Blas, though I do not lose you without regret, I am too much your
well-wisher not to be delighted at your promotion in the room of
Don Valerio. You cannot fail to make a princely fortune, provided
you act upon two hints which I have to give you : the first, to affect
so total a devotion to his excellency's good pleasure, as to leave no
room to conceive it possible that you have any other object or interest in life—the second, to pay your court assiduously to Signor
Don Rodrigo de Calderona; for that personage models and remo-
dels, fashions and touches upon the mind of his master, just as if it
was clay under the hands of the designer. If you are fortunate
enough to chime in with that favorite secretary, you will travel
post to wealth and honor, and find relays upon the road.

Sir, said I to Don Diego, returning him thanks at the same time
for his good advice, be pleased to give some little opening to Don
Rodrigo's character. I have heard a few anecdotes of him. One
would suppose him, from some accounts, not to be the best creature in the world ; but the people at large are inveterate caricatur-
ists when they draw courtiers at full length ; though, after all, the
likeness will strike, in spite of the aggravation. Tell me, therefore,
I beseech you, what is your own sincere opinion of Signor Calderona. That is rather an awkward question, answered my principal,
with an ironical smile. I should tell any one but yourself, without
flinching, that he was a gentleman of the strictest honor, upon
whose fair fame the breath of calumny had never dared to blow;
but I really cannot put off such a copy of my countenance upon
you. Relying as I do on your discretion, it becomes a duty to deal
candidly in the delineation of Don Rodrigo; for without that, it
would be playing fast and loose with you to recommend the cultivation of his good-will.

You are to know then, that when his excellency was no more
than plain Don Francisco de Sandoval, this man had the humility
to serve him as his lackey: since which time he has risen by degrees to the post of principal secretary. A prouder excrescence of
the dunghill never sprung into vegetation on a summer's day. He
considers himself as the Duke of Lerma's colleague ; and in point
of fact, he may truly be said to parcel out the loaves and fishes of
administration, since he gives away offices and governments at the
suggestions of his own caprice. The public grumbles and growls
upon occasion ; but who cares for the grumbling and growling of the
public? Let him steal a pair of gloves from the prostitution of politi-

cal honor, and the bronze upon his forehead will be proof against the peltings of scandal. What I have said will decide your dealings towards so supercilious a compound of dust and ashes. Yes, to be sure, said I; leave me alone for that. It will be strange indeed if I cannot wriggle myself into his good graces. If one can but get on the blind side of a man who is to be made a property, it must be want of skill in the player if the game is lost. Exactly so, replied Monteser; and now I will introduce you to the Duke of Lerma.

We went at once to the minister, whom we found in his audience-chamber. His levee was more crowded than the king's. There were commanders and knights of St. James and of Calatrava, making interests for governments and viceroyalties; bishops who, laboring under oppression of the breath and tightness of the chest in their own dioceses, had been recommended the air of an archbishopric by their physicians; while the sounder lungs of lower dignitaries were strong enough to inhale the Theban atmosphere of a suffragan see. I observed besides some reduced officers dancing attendance to Captain Chinchilla's tune, and catching cold in fishing for a pension, which was never likely to pay the doctor for their cure. If the duke did not satisfy their wants, he put a pleasant face upon their importunities; and it struck me that he returned a civil answer to all applicants.

We waited patiently till the routine of ceremony was dispatched. Then said Don Diego: My lord, this is Gil Blas de Santillane, the young man appointed by your excellency to succeed Don Valerio. The duke now took more particular notice of me, saying obligingly, that I had already earned my promotion by my services. He then took me to a private conference in his closet, or rather to an examination. My birth, parentage, and course of life were the objects of his inquiry; nor would he be satisfied without the particulars, and those in the spirit of sincerity. What a career to run over before a patron! Yet it was impossible to lie, in the presence of a prime minister. On the other hand, my vanity was concerned in suppressing so many circumstances, that there was no venturing on an unqualified confession. What cunning scene had Roscius then to act? A little painting and tattooing might decently be employed to disguise the nakedness of truth, and spare her unsophisticated blushes. But he had studied her complexion, as well as the beauties of her natural form. Monsieur de Santillane, said he with a smile on the close of my narrative, I perceive that hitherto you have had your principles to choose. My lord, answered I, coloring up to the eyes, your excellency enjoined me to deal sincerely; and I have complied with your orders. I take your doing so in good part, replied he. It is all very well, my good fellow: you have escaped from the snares of this wicked world more by luck than management: it is wonderful that bad example should not have corrupted you irreparably. There are many men of strict virtue and exemplary piety, who would have turned out the greatest rogues in existence, if their destinies had exposed them to but half your trials.

Friend Santillane, continued the minister, ponder no longer on the past; consider yourself as to the very bone and marrow the king's; live henceforth but for his service. Come this way; I will instruct you in the nature of your business. He carried me into a little closet adjoining his own, which contained a score of thick folio registers. This is your workshop, said he. All these registers compose an alphabetical peerage, giving the heraldry and history of all the nobility and gentry in the several kingdoms and principalities of the Spanish monarchy. In these volumes are recorded the services rendered to the state by the present possessors and their ancestors, descending even to the personal animosities and rencontres of the individuals and their houses. Their fortunes, their manners, in a word, all the pros and cons of their character are set down according to the letter of ministerial scrutiny; so that they no sooner enter on the list of court candidates, than my eye catches up the very chapter and verse of their pretensions. To furnish this necessary information, I have pensioned scouts everywhere on the look-out, who send me private notices of their discoveries; but as these documents are for the most part drawn up in a gossiping and provincial style, they require to be translated into gentlemanly language, or the king would not be able to support the perusal of the registers. This task demands the pen of a polite and perspicuous writer; I doubt not but you will justify your claim to the appointment.

After this introduction, he put a memorial into my hand, taken from a large portfolio full of papers, and then withdrew from my closet, that my first specimen might be manufactured in all the freedom of solitude. I read the memorial, which was not only stuffed with the most uncouth jargon, but breathed a brimstone spirit of rancor and personal revenge. This was most foul, strange, and unnatural! for the homily was written by a monk. He hacked and hewed a Catalan family of some note most unmercifully; with what reason or truth, it must be reserved for a more penetrating inquirer to decide. It read for all the world like an infamous libel, and I had some scruples about becoming the publisher of the calumny; nevertheless, young as I was at court, I plunged head foremost, at the risk of sinking and destroying his reverence's soul. The wickedness, if there was any, would be put down to his running account with the recording angel; I therefore had nothing to do but to vilify, in the purest Spanish phraseology, some two or three generations of honest men and loyal subjects.

I had already blackened four or five pages, when the duke, impatient to know how I got on, came back and said—Santillane, show me what you have done; I am curious to see it. At the same time, casting his eye over the transcript, he read the beginning with much attention. It seemed to please him; strange that he could be so pleased! Prepossessed as I have been in your favor, observed he, I must own that you have surpassed my expectations. It is not merely the elegance and distinctness of the handwriting! There is something animated and glowing in the composition. You will do ample credit to my choice, and fully make up for the loss of your predecessor. He would not have cut my panegyric so short.

if his nephew the Count de Lemos had not interrupted him in the middle of it. By the warmth and frequency of his excellency's welcome, it was evident that they were the best friends in the world. They were immediately closeted together on some family business, of which I shall speak in the sequel. The king's affairs at this time were obliged to play second to those of the minister.

While they were caballing it struck twelve. As I knew that the secretaries and their clerks quitted office at that hour to go and dine wherever their business and desire should point them, I left my prize performance behind me, and went to the gayest tavern at the court end of the town, for I had nothing further to do with Monteser, who had paid my salary, and taken his leave of me. But a common eating-house would have been a very improper place for me to be seen in. "Consider yourself as to the very bone and marrow the king's." This metaphorical expression of the duke had given birth to a real and tangible ambition in my soul, which put forth shoots like a plantation in a fat and unvexed soil.

CHAPTER III.

ALL IS NOT GOLD THAT GLITTERS. SOME UNEASINESS RESULT-
ING FROM THE DISCOVERY OF THAT PRINCIPLE IN PHIL-
OSOPHY, AND ITS PRACTICAL APPLICATION TO EXISTING
CIRCUMSTANCES.

I TOOK especial care, on my first entrance, to instil into the tavern-keeper's conception that I was secretary to the prime minister ; nor was it easy, in that view of my rank and consequence, to order anything sufficiently sumptuous for dinner. To have selected from the bill of fare, might have looked as if I descended to the meanness of calculation ; I therefore told him to send up the best the house afforded. My orders were punctually obeyed ; and the anxious assiduity of attendance pampered my fancy as much as the dishes did my palate. As to the bill, I had nothing to do with it but to pay it. Down went a pistole upon the table, and the waiters pocketed the difference, which was somewhat more than a quarter. After this display of grandeur I strutted out, practising those obstreporous clearings of the throat which announce, by empty sound, the approach of a substantial coxcomb.

There was at the distance of twenty yards a large house with lodgings to let, principally frequented by foreign nobility. I rented at once a suite of apartments, consisting of five or six rooms elegantly furnished. From my style of living, any one would have thought I had two or three thousand ducats of yearly income. The first month was paid in advance. Afterwards I returned to business, and employed the whole afternoon in going on with what I had begun in the morning. In a closet adjoining mine there were two other secretaries ; but their office was only to copy out fair. I got acquainted with them as we were shutting up for the evening ; and, by way of smoothing the first overtures towards friendship, invited them home with me to my tavern, where I ordered the choicest delicacies of the season, with a profusion of the most exquisite wines.

We sat down to table, and began bandying about more merriment than wit; for with all due deference to my guests, it was but too visible that they owed their official situations to any circumstance rather than to their abilities. They were adepts, it must be confessed, in all the history and mystery of scrivening and clerkship; but as for polite literature and university education, there was not even a suspicion of it in all their talk.

To make amends for that defect, they had a keen eye to the main chance; and though sensible how high an honor it was to be on the prime minister's establishment, there were some dashes of acid in the cup of good fortune. It is now full five months, said one of them, that we have been serving at our own cost. We do not touch one farthing of salary; and, what is worst of all, our very board wages are shamefully in arrear. There is no knowing what footing we are upon. As for me, said the other, I would willingly be tied up to the halbert, and receive a percentage in lashes, for the liberty of changing my berth; but I dare not either take myself off or petition for my discharge, after having transcribed such state secrets as have passed under my inspection. I might chance to become too well acquainted with the tower of Segovia or the castle of Alicant.

How do you manage for a subsistence, then ? said I. You must of course have means of your own. These they represented as very slender; but that, fortunately for them, they lodged with a kind-hearted widow, who boarded them on tick, at the rate of a hundred pistoles a year for each. These anecdotes of a court life, not one of which escaped me, completely ventilated all the rising fumes of pride. It could not be supposed that more consideration would be shown to me than to others, and consequently there was nothing to be so puffed up with in my post; there seemed to be much cry and little wool, a discovery which rendered it expedient to husband my finances with a narrower economy. A picture like this was enough to cure my taste for treating. I repented not having left these secretaries to find their own supper; for they played a most cruel knife and fork at mine! and, when the bill was brought, I squabbled with the landlord about the charges.

We parted at midnight, and the early breaking up was to be laid at my door, for I did not propose another bottle. They went home to their widow, and I withdrew to my magnificent lodgings, which I was now mad with myself for having taken, and was fully determined to give up at the month's end. My bed of down was now converted into a couch of thorns, sleep had abandoned his narcotic tenement, and sold the fee-simple of my repose to the demon of eternal wakefulness. The remainder of the night was passed in contriving not to serve the state too patriotically. For that purpose I bethought me of Monteser's good counsel. I got up with the intention of making my bow to Don Rodrigo de Calderona. My present temper was just pat to the purpose of ingratiating myself with so high and mighty a gentleman: whose patronage was indispensable to my existence. I therefore presented my person in that secretary's ante-chamber.

His apartments communicated with the duke's, and rivaled them in the lustre of their decorations. The field officer could scarcely be distinguished from the subaltern by any outward distinction in his paraphernalia. I sent in my name as Don Valerio's successor; but that did not hinder me from being kept kicking my heels for a good hour. Trusty, but novice officer of the king, said I, while ruminating on court manners, learn a lesson of patience, if so please you. You must begin with showing paces yourself, and afterwards make others bite the bridle.

At length the door of the inner room opened. I went in, and advanced towards Don Rodrigo, who had just been writing an amorous epistle to his charming Siren, and was giving it to Pedrillo at that very moment. I had never manufactured my face and air into such a counterfeit of reverence before the Archbishop of Grenada, nor on my introduction to the Count de Galiano, nor even in presence of the prime minister himself: the crisis of my fawning was reserved for Signor de Calderona. I paid my respects to him with my body bent down to the very ground, as if crouching under the ken of a superior intelligence; and solicited his protection in strains of humble hypocrisy, at which my cheek now burns with shame, to think that man can so debase himself before his fellow-man. My servility would have recoiled to my own undoing, had it been practised towards a compound of any manly and independent ingredients. As for this fellow, he swallowed flattery by the lump without mastication; and assured me, just as if he meant what he said, that he would leave no stone unturned to do me service.

Hereupon, thanking him with unlimited expressions of attachment for his kind and generous sentiments, I sold my very soul and all my little stock of conscience to his free disposal. But as this farce might be tiresome if prolonged, I took my leave, apologizing for having broken in upon his more serious avocations. As soon as I had finished this abominable scene, I slunk back to my desk, where I finished my prescribed task. The duke was at my elbow the next morning. The end of my performance was not less to his mind than the beginning; and he praised it accordingly: This is extremely well indeed! Copy this abridgment in your best hand into the register of Catalonia. You shall not want employment of this kind. I had a very long conversation with his excellency, and was delighted at his mild and familiar deportment. What a contrast to Calderona! They might have sat to a painter for Pan and Apollo.

To-day I dined at a cheap ordinary, and sunk the secretary upon my mess-mates, till I should ascertain what solid profit might accrue from all my bows and scrapes. I had funds for three months, or thereabouts. That interval I allowed myself for casting my bread upon the waters. But as the shortest speculations are the safest, if my salary was not paid by that time, a long farewell to the court, its frippery, and its falsehood! Thus were my plans arranged. For two months I labored hard and fast to stand well with Calderona : but his senses were so callous to all my assiduity, that it seemed labor in vain to build on so hopeless a foundation. This idea produced a change in my conduct. I left some greener fool to fumigate the nostrils of this idol; and placed all my own dependence on making my ground sure with the duke, by the benefit of our frequent conferences.

CHAPTER IV.

GIL BLAS BECOMES A FAVORITE WITH THE DUKE OF LERMA, AND THE CONFIDANT OF AN IMPORTANT SECRET.

THOUGH his grace's interviews with me were short as the fleeting visions of supernatural communication, my turn and character won its way gradually into his excellency's good liking. One day after dinner, he said : Attend to me, Gil Blas. I really like you very much. You are a zealous, confidential lad, full of understanding and discretion. My trust cannot be misplaced in such hands. I threw myself at his feet, at the music of these words; and kissing his outstretched hand, answered thus : Is it possible that your excellency can think so favorably of your servant ? What a host of enemies will such a preference conjure up against me! But Don Rodrigo is the only man whose privy grudge is formidable enough to alarm me.

You have nothing to fear from that quarter, replied the duke. I know Calderona. He has loved me from his cradle. Every movement of his heart is in unison with mine. He cherishes whatever I love, and hates in exact proportion to my dislike. So far from being alarmed at his ill-will, you ought, on the contrary, to hug yourself on his peculiar partiality. This let me at once into the abysses of Don Rodrigo's character. He shuffled and cut the cards to his own deal, and paid his debts of honor out of his excellency's pool. One could not be too wary with this gentleman.

To begin, pursued the duke, with a proof my thorough reliance on your faith, I will open to you a long-projected design. It is necessary for you to be informed of it, to qualify you for the commissions with which I shall hereafter have occasion to intrust to you. For a great length of time have I beheld my authority universally respected, my decisions implicitly adopted, places, pensions, governments, vice-royalties, and church preferments all awaiting my disposal. Without umbrage to my royal master, I may be said to be absolute in Spain. My individual fortunes can be pushed no higher. But I would willingly fix firm the structure I have raised ; for the storms are already beginning to beat about the citadel of my peace. My only safety must consist in nominating my nephew, the Count de Lemos, as my successor in the ministry.

This profound courtier, observing my astonishment, went on thus. I see plainly, Santillane, I see plainly what surprises you. It seems strange and unaccountable that I should prefer my nephew to my own son, the Duke d'Uzeda. But you are to learn that this last has too narrow a genius to fill up my place in politics; and there are other reasons why I set my face against him. He has found out the secret of making himself agreeable to the king, who wants him for his interior cabinet; and back-stairs influence is what I cannot bear. Royal favor is a sort of political mistress; exclusive possession is its only charm. The very existence of the passion is identified with inextinguishable jealousy; nor can we the better endure to share the bliss, because our rival has been nursed in our own bosom.

Thus do I lay bare the very recesses of my soul. I have already tried to ruin the Duke d'Uzeda with the king; but having failed, am pointing my artillery towards another object. I am determined that the Count de Lemos shall stand first with the Prince of Spain. Being gentleman of his bedchamber, he has opportunities of talking with him continually; and, besides that he has a winning manner with him, I know a sure method of enabling him to succeed in his enterprise. By this device, my nephew will be pitted against my son. The cousins harboring unfavorable suspicions of each other, will both be forced to place themselves under my protection; and the necessity of the case will render them submissive to my will. This is my project; nor will your assistance be of slender avail to its success. It is you whom I shall make the private channel of communication between the Count de Lemos and myself.

After this confidence, which sounded for all the world like the clink of current coin, my mind was easy about the future. At length, said I, behold me taking shelter under Plutus's gutter; the golden shower may drench me to the skin, before I shall cry hold, enough! It is impossible that the bosom friend of a man, by whom the whole music of the political machine is tempered, should be left to thrum upon the discord of poverty. Full of these harmonious visions, my fifths and octaves were but little untuned by the sensible declension of my purse.

CHAPTER V.

THE JOYS, THE HONORS, AND THE MISERIES OF A COURT LIFE, IN THE PERSON OF GIL BLAS.

THE minister's growing partiality towards me was soon noticed. He displayed it ostentatiously, by committing his portfolio to my custody, which it was his habit to carry in his own hand when he

"HIS COMPANION, WHO HAD MORE SENSE, SAID WITHIN HIMSELF"

went to council. This novelty causing me to be looked upon as a rising favorite, excited the envy of certain persons, so that I was preciously sprinkled with the hellish dew of court malevolence. My two neighbors the secretaries were not the last to compliment me on my budding honors, and invited me to supper at the widow's, not so much by way of returning my hospitality, as with an eye to business in the cultivation of my acquaintance. Parties were made for me everywhere. Even the haughty Don Rodrigo was cap-in-hand to me. He now called me nothing less than Signor de Santillane, though the moon had scarcely changed her face since he *thee'd* and *thou'd* me, without ever bethinking him that he was talking to something above a pauper. He heaped me up and pressed me down with civilities, especially within eyeshot of our common patron. But the fool was wiser than to be caught with chaff. The good breeding of my returns was nicely proportioned to my thorough detestation of my humble servant: a rascal who had lived in court all his life could not have played the rascal better than I did,

I likewise accompanied my lord duke when he had an audience of the king, which was usually three times a day. In the morning he went into his majesty's chamber as soon as he was awake. There he dropped down on his marrow-bones by the bedside, talked over what was to be done in the course of the day, and put into the royal mouth the speeches the royal tongue was to make. He then withdrew. After dinner he came back again; not for state affairs, but for *what, what?* and a little gossip. He was well instructed in all the tittle-tattle of Madrid, which was sold to him at the earliest of the season. Lastly, in the evening he saw the king again for the third time, put whatever color he pleased on the transactions of the day, and, as a matter of course, requested his instructions for the morrow. While he was with the king, I kept in the ante-chamber, where people of the first quality, sinking that they might rise, threw themselves in the way of my observation, and thought the day not lost if I had deigned to exchange a few words of common civility with them. Was it to be wondered at, if my self-importance fattened upon such food? There are many folks at court, who stalk about on stilts of much frailer materials.

One day my vanity was still more highly pampered. The king, to whom the duke had puffed off my style, was curious to see a sample of it. His excellency made me bring the register of Catalonia and myself into the royal presence; telling me to read the first memorial I had digested. If so catholic a critic overpowered my modesty at first, the minister's encouragement recalled my scattered spirits, and I read with good tone and emphasis what his majesty deigned to hear with some symptoms of approbation. He spoke handsomely of my performance, and recommended my fortunes to the special care of his minister. My humility was not the greater for the augmentation of my consequence; and a particular conversation some days afterwards with the Count de Lemos swelled high the spring tide of all my ambitious anticipations.

I waited on that nobleman from his uncle at the Prince of

Spain's court, and presented credentials from the duke, directing him to deal unreservedly with me, as with a man who was embarked in their design and selected by himself exclusively as their go-between. The count then took me to a room, where he locked the door, and then spoke as follows : Since you are confidential with the Duke of Lerma, I doubt not you deserve to be so, and shall unbosom myself to you without hesitation. You are to know that matters go on just as we could wish. The Prince of Spain distinguishes me above the most assiduous of his courtiers. I had a private conversation with him this morning, wherein he expressed some disgust at being restrained by the king's avarice from following the inclinations of his liberal heart, and living on a scale befitting his august rank. On this head I chimed in with his regrets ; and taking advantage of the opportunity, promised to carry him a thousand pistoles early to-morrow morning, as an earnest of larger sums with which I have engaged to feed his necessities forthwith. He was in ecstasy at my promises ; and I am certain of securing his grace and favor in tail, if I can but fulfill my engagement. Acquaint my uncle with these particulars, and come back in the evening with his sentiments on the subject.

I left the Count de Lemos with the last words still quivering on his lips, and went back to the Duke of Lerma, who, on my report, sent to ask Calderona for a thousand pistoles, which he charged me to carry to the count in the evening. Away went I on my errand, muttering to myself—So, so ! now I have discovered the minister's infallible receipt for the cure of all evils. Faith and troth, he is in the right ; and to all appearance he may draw as copiously as he pleases from the spring, without exhausting the source. I can easily guess what bag those pistoles came from ; but after all, is it not the order of nature that the parent should nurture and maintain the child ? The Count de Lemos, at our parting, said to me in a low voice—Farewell, my good and worthy friend. The Prince of Spain has a little hankering after the women ; we must have a little conversation on that subject one of these days ; I foresee that your agency will be very applicable on that head. I returned with my head full of this last hint, which it was impossible to misinterpret. Neither did I wish to do so, for it suited my talents to a nicety. What the devil is to happen next ? said I. Behold me on the point of becoming pimp to the heir of the monarchy. Whether pimping was a virtue or a vice, I did not stop to inquire : the coarse surtout of morality would have worn but shabbily while the passions of so exalted a gallant were in the glare and glow of all their newest gloss. What a promotion for me to be the provider of pleasure to a great prince ! Fair and softly, Master Gil Blas, some one may say : after all, you will be but second minister. May be so ; but at bottom the honor of both these posts is equal ; the difference lies in the profit only.

While executing these honorable commissions, and getting forward daily in the good graces of the prime minister, what a happy being should I have been if statesmen were born with a set of intestines to turn the cameleon's diet into chyle ! It was more than two months since I had got rid of my grand lodging, and had taken up my quarters in a little room scarcely good enough for a banker's clerk. Though this was not quite as it should be, yet since I went out betimes in the morning, and never returned at night before bedtime, there was not much to quarrel about on that score. All day I was the hero of my own stage, or rather of the duke's. It was a principal part that I was playing. But when I retired from this brilliant theater to my own cockloft, the great lord vanished, and poor Gil Blas was left behind, without a royal image in his pocket, and what was worse, without the means of conjuring up his glorious resemblance. Besides that it would have wounded my pride to have divulged my necessities, there was not a creature of my acquaintance who could have assisted me but Navarro, and him I had too palpably neglected since my introduction at court, to venture on soliciting his benevolence. I had been obliged to sell my wardrobe article by article. There was nothing more left than was absolutely necessary to make a decent appearance. I no longer went to the ordinary, because I had no longer wherewithal to pay my score. How then did I make shift to keep body and soul together? There was every morning, in our offices, a scanty breakfast set out, consisting of a little bread and wine; this was the whole of our commons on the minister's establishment. I never knew what it was to exceed this stint during the day, and at night I most frequently went supperless to bed.

Such was the fare of a man who made a splendid figure at court; but his illustrious fortunes, like those of other courtiers, were more a subject of pity than of grudge. I could no longer resist the pressure of my circumstances, and ultimately resolved on their disclosure at a seasonable opportunity. By good luck such an occasion offered at the Escurial, whither the king and Prince of Spain removed some days afterwards.

CHAPTER VI

GIL BLAS GIVES THE DUKE OF LERMA A HINT OF HIS WRETCHED CONDITION. THAT MINISTER DEALS WITH HIM ACCORDINGLY.

WHEN the king kept his court at the Escurial, all the world was at free quarters: under such easy circumstances I did not feel where the saddle galled. My bed was in a wardrobe near the duke's chamber. One morning that minister, having got up according to his cursed custom at daybreak, made me take my writing apparatus, and follow him into the palace gardens. We went and sat down under an avenue of trees; myself, as he would have it, in the posture of a man writing on the crown of his hat; his attitude was with a paper in his hand, and any one would have supposed he had been reading. At some distance, we must have looked as if the scale of Europe was to turn upon our decision; but between ourselves, who partook of it, the talk was miserably trifling.

For more than an hour had I been tickling his excellency's fancy with all the conceits, engendered by a merry nature and an eccentric course of life, when two magpies perched on the trees above us. Their clack and clatter was so obstreperous, as to force our attention whether we would or no. These birds, said the duke, seem to be in dudgeon with one another. I should like to learn the cause of their quarrel. My lord, said I, your curiosity reminds me of an Indian story in Pilpay or some other fabulist. The minister insisted on the particulars, and I related them in the following terms :

There reigned in Persia a good monarch, who not being blessed with capacities of sufficient compass to govern his dominions in his own person, left the care of them to his grand vizier. That minister, whose name was Atalmuc, was possessed of first-rate talents. He supported the weight of that unwieldy monarchy, without sinking under the burden. He preserved it in profound peace. His art consisted in uniting the love of the royal authority with the reverence of it; while the people at large looked up to the vizier as to an affectionate father, though a devoted servant of his prince. Atalmuc had a young Cachemirian among his secretaries, by name Zeangir, to whom he was particularly attached. He took pleasure in his conversation, invited him frequently to the chase, and opened to him his most secret thoughts. One day as they were hunting together in a wood, the vizier, at the croaking of two ravens on a tree, said to his secretary—I should like to know what those birds are talking about in their jargon. My lord, answered the Cachemirian, your wishes may be fulfilled. Indeed ! How so? replied Atalmuc. Because, rejoined Zeangir, a dervise read in many mysteries, has taught me the language of birds. If you wish it, I will lay my ear close to these, and will repeat to you word for word whatever they may happen to say.

The vizier agreed to the proposal. The Cachemirian got near the ravens, and affected to suck in their discourse. Then, returning to his master, My lord, said he, would you believe it? We are ourselves the topic of their talk. Impossible! exclaimed the Persian minister. Prithee now, what do they say of us? One of the two, replied the secretary, spoke thus: Here he is, the very man; the grand vizier Atalmuc, the guardian eagle of Persia, hovering over her like the parent bird over its nest, watching without intermission for the safety of its brood. For the purpose of unbending from his wearisome toils, he is hunting in this wood with his faithful Zeangir. How happy must that secretary be, to serve so partial and indulgent a master ! Fair and softly, observed the other raven shrewdly, fair and softly ! Make not too much parade about that Cachemirian's happiness. Atalmuc, it is true, talks and jokes familiarly with him, honors him with his confidence, and may very possibly intend to signalize his friendship by a lucrative post; but between the cup and the lip Zeangir may perish with thirst. The poor devil lodges in a ready-furnished apartment, where there is not an article of furniture for his use. In a word, he leads a starving life, with all the paraphernalia of a plump-fed courtier. The grand vizier never troubles his head about inquiring into the right or wrong of his affairs; but satisfied with empty good wishes towards him, leaves his favorite within the ruthless grip of poverty.

I stopped here, to see how the Duke of Lerma would take it; and he asked me with a smile what effect the fable had produced on the mind of Atalmuc; and whether the grand vizier had not felt a little offended at the secretary's presumption. No, my noble lord, answered I, with some little embarrassment at the question; historians say that his ingenuity was amply rewarded. He was more lucky than discreet, replied the duke with a serious air; there are some ministers who would esteem it no joke to be lectured at that rate. But the king will not be long before he is getting up; my duty demands my attendance. After this hint he walked off with hasty strides towards the palace without throwing away a word more upon me, and to all appearance in high dudgeon at my Indian parable.

I followed him up to the very door of his majesty's chamber, and went thence to arrange my papers in the places whence they had been taken. Then I entered a closet where our two copying secretaries were at work; for they also were of the migratory party. What is the matter with you, Signor de Santillane? said they at the sight of me. You are quite down in the mouth! Has anything untoward happened?

I was too much mortified at the ill success of my narrative, to be cautious in the expression of my grief. On the recital of what had passed with the duke, they sympathized in my disappointment. You have some reason to fret, said one of them. Heaven grant you may be better treated than a secretary of Cardinal Spinosa. This unlucky secretary, tired of working for fifteen months without pay, took the liberty of representing his necessities to his Eminence one afternoon, and of asking for a little money towards his subsistence. It is very proper, said the minister, that you should be paid. Here, pursued he, putting into his hands an order on the royal treasury for a thousand ducats; go and receive that sum; but take notice at the same time that it balances accounts between us. The secretary would have pocketed his thousand ducats without remorse, had the thousand ducats been tangible, and the liberty of changing services secure; but just as he stepped down from the cardinal's threshold, he was tapped on the shoulder by an alguazil, and carried away to the tower of Segovia, where he has been a prisoner for a length of time.

This little historical anecdote set my teeth chattering. All was lost and gone! There was no comfort from within nor from without! My own impatience had been my ruin! just as if I had not borne starving, till patience could avail no longer. Alas! said I, wherefore must I have blurted out that ill-starred fable, which went so much against the grain of the minister? He might have been just on the point of extricating me from all miseries; it might have been the moment of that tide in the affairs of men, which sets in for sudden and enormous elevation. What wealth, what honors have slipped through the fingers by my blunder! I ought to have been aware that great folks do not love to be forestalled, but require the common privileges of elementary subsistence to be received as favors at their hands. It would have been more prudent to have kept my lenten entertainment longer without bothering the duke about it, and even to have died with hunger, that he might be blamed for letting me.

Supposing any hope to have remained, my master, when I saw him after dinner, put an extinguisher over it at once. He was very serious with me, contrary to his usual custom, and spoke scarcely at all: an omen of dire dismay for the remainder of the evening. The night did not pass more tranquilly: the chagrin of seeing my agreeable illusions vanish, and the fear of swelling the calendar of state prisoners, left no room but for sighs and lamentations.

The following was the critical day. The duke sent for me in the morning. I went into his chamber, with the ague fit of a criminal before his judge. Santillane, said he, showing me a paper in his hand, take this order. . . . . I shuddered at the word order, and said within myself: Oh heaven! here is the Cardinal Spinosa over again; the carriage is ordered out for Segovia. Such was my alarm at this moment, that I interrupted the minister, and throwing myself at his feet, May it please your lordship, said I, bathed in tears, I most humbly beseech your excellency to forgive me for my boldness; necessity alone impelled me to acquaint you with my wretched circumstances.

The duke could not help laughing at my distress. Be comforted, Gil Blas, answered he, and hearken attentively. Though by betraying your necessities a reproach lights upon me for not having prevented them, I do not take it ill, my friend. I rather ought to be angry with myself for not having inquired how you were going on. But to begin making amends for my want of attention, there is an order on the royal treasury for fifteen hundred ducats, payable at sight. This is not all; I promise you the same sum annually; and moreover, when people of rank and substance shall solicit your interest, I have no objection to your addressing me on their behalf.

In the excess of joy occasioned by such tidings, I kissed the feet of the minister, who, having commanded me to rise, continued in familiar conversation. I endeavored to rally my free and easy humor; but the transition from sorrow to rapture was too instantaneous to be natural. I felt as comical as a culprit, with a pardon singing in his ears, just when he was on the point of being launched into eternity. My master attributed all my flurry to the sole dread of having offended him; though the fear of perpetual imprisonment had its share of influence on my nerves. He owned that he had affected to look cool, to see whether I should be hurt at the alteration: that thereby he formed his opinion with respect to the liveliness of my attachment to his person, and that his own regard for me would always be proportionate.

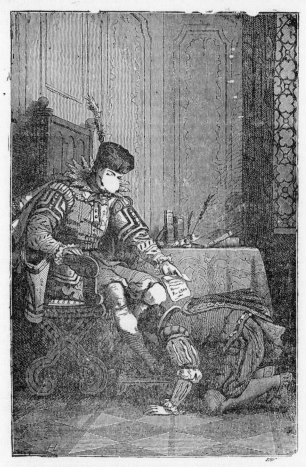

"I KISSED THE FEET OF THE MINISTER."

CHAPTER VII.

A GOOD USE MADE OF THE FIFTEEN HUNDRED DUCATS. A FIRST
INTRODUCTION TO THE TRADE OF OFFICE, AND AN ACCOUNT
OF THE PROFIT ACCRUING THEREFROM.

THE king, as if on purpose to play into the hands of my impatience, returned to Madrid the very next day. I flew like a harpy to the royal treasury, where they paid me down upon the nail the sum drawn for in my order. Ambition and vanity now obtained complete empire over my soul. My paltry lodging was fit only for secretaries of an inferior cast, unpractised in the mysterious language of birds; for which reason, my grand suite of apartments fortunately being vacant, I engaged them for the second time. My next business was to send for an eminent tailor, who arrayed the pretty persons of all the fine gentlemen in town. He took my measure, and then introduced me to a draper, who sold me five ells of cloth, the exact quantity, as he said, to make a suit for a man of my size. Five ells for a light Spanish dress! Whither did this draper and tailor expect to go? . . . . But we must not be uncharitable. Tailors who have a reputation to support require more materials for the exercise of their genius than the vulgar snippers of the shopboard. I then bought some linen, of which I was very bare; an assortment of silk stockings, and a laced hat.

With such an equipage, there was no doing without a footman; so that I desired Vincent Ferrero, my landlord, to look out for one. Most of the foreigners who were recommended to his lodgings, on their arrival at Madrid, were wont to hire Spanish servants; and this was the means of turning his house into a register office. The first who offered was a lad of so mortified and devotional an aspect, that I would have nothing to say to him; he put me in mind of Ambrose de Lamela. I am quite out of conceit, said I to Ferrero, with these pious coat-brushers; I have been taken in by them already.

I had scarcely turned virtue in a livery out of doors, when another came upstairs. This seemed to be a good sprightly fellow, with as little mock modesty as if he had been bred at court, and a certain something about him which indicated that he did not carry principle to any dangerous excess. He was just to my mind. His answers to my questions were pat and to the purpose: he evinced a talent for intrigue beyond my most sanguine hopes. This was exactly the subject for my purpose; so I fixed him at once. Neither had I any reason to repent of my bargain; for it was very soon evident that further off I must have fared worse. As the duke had allowed me to solicit on behalf of my friends, and it was my design to push that permission to the utmost, a stanch hound was necessary to put up the game; or in phrase familiar to dull capacities, an active chap, with a turn for routing out and bringing to my market all palm-tickling petitioners for the loaves and fishes of the prime minister. This was just where Scipio shone most; for my servant's name was Scipio. He had lived last with Donna Anna de Guevara, the Prince of Spain's nurse, where he had ample scope for the exercise of that accomplishment.

As soon as he became acquainted with my credit at court and the use to which I meant to put it, he took the field like his great ancestors, and began the campaign without the loss of a day.

SCIPIO.

Master, said he, a young gentleman of Grenada is just come to Madrid; his name is Don Roger de Rada. He has been engaged in an affair of honor which compels him to throw himself on the Duke of Lerma's protection, and he is well disposed to come down handsomely for any grace and favor he may obtain. I have talked with him on the subject. He had a mind to have made friends with Don Rodrigo de Calderona, whose influence had been represented to him in magnificent terms: but I dissuaded him, by pointing out that secretary's method of selling his good offices for more than their weight in gold; whereas, on the contrary, you would be satisfied with any decent expression of gratitude for yours, and would even do the business for the mere pleasure of doing it, if you were in circumstances to follow the bent of your own generous and disinterested temper. In short, I talked to him in such a strain, that you will see the gentleman early to-morrow morning. How is all this, Master Scipio? said I. You must have transacted a great deal of business in a short time. You are no novice in backstairs influence. It is very strange that you have not feathered your own nest. That ought not to surprise you at all, answered he, I love to make money circulate; not to hoard it up.

Don Roger de Rada came according to his appointment. I received him with a mixture of courtly plausibility and ministerial pride. My worthy sir, said I, before I engage in your interests, I wish to know the nature of the affair which brings you to court; because it may be such as to preclude me from speaking to the minister in your favor. Give me, therefore, if you please, the particulars faithfully, and rest assured that I shall enter warmly into your interests, if they are proper to be espoused by a man who moves in my sphere. My young client promised to be sincere in his representation, and began his narrative in the following words.

CHAPTER VIII.

HISTORY OF DON ROGER DE RADA.

Don Anastasio de Rada, a gentleman of Grenada, was living happily in the town of Antequera, with Donna Estephania his wife, who united every charm of person and mind with the most unquestionable virtue. If her affection was lively towards her husband, his love for her was violent beyond all bounds. He was naturally prone to jealousy; and though wantonness could never assume such a semblance as his wife's, his thoughts were not quite at rest upon the subject. He was apprehensive lest some secret enemy to his repose might make some attempt upon his honor. His eye was turned askance upon all his friends, except Don Huberto de Hordales, who frequented the house without suspicion, in quality of Estephania's cousin, and was the only man in whom he ought not to have confided.

Don Huberto did actually fall in love with his cousin, and ventured to make his sentiments known, in contempt of consanguinity and the ties of friendship. The lady, who was considerate, instead of making an outcry which might have led to fatal consequences, reproved her kinsman gently, represented to him the extreme criminality of attempting to seduce her and dishonor her husband, and told him very seriously that he must not flatter himself with the most distant hope.

This moderation only inflamed the seducer's appetite the more. Taking it for granted that, as a woman who had been accustomed to save appearances, she only wanted to be more strongly urged, he began to adopt little freedoms of more warmth than delicacy; and had the assurance one day to put the question home to her. She repulsed him with unbridled indignation, and threatened to refer the punishment of his offense to Don Anastasio. Her suitor, alarmed at such an intimation, promised to drop the subject; and Estephania in the candor of her soul forgave him for the past.

Don Huberto, a man totally devoid of principle, could not find his passion to be foiled, without entertaining a mean spirit of revenge. He knew the weak side of Don Anastasio's temper. This was enough to engender the blackest design that ever scoundrel plotted. One evening as he was walking alone with this misguided husband, he said with an air of extreme uneasiness: My dear friend, I can no longer live without unburdening my mind; and yet I would be for ever silent, but that you value honor far above a treacherous repose. Your acute feelings and my own, on points which concern domestic injuries, forbid me to conceal what is passing in your family. Prepare to hear what will occasion you as much grief as astonishment. I am going to wound you in the tenderest part.

I know what you mean, interrupted Don Anastasio, in the first burst of agony; your cousin is unfaithful. I no longer acknowledge her for my cousin, replied Hordales with impassioned vehemence; I disown her, as unworthy to share my friend's embraces. This is keeping me too long upon the rack, exclaimed Don Anastasio: say on, what has Estephania done? She has betrayed you, replied Don Huberto. You have a rival to whom she listens in private, but I cannot give you his name; for the adulterer, under favor of impenetrable darkness, has escaped the ken of those who watched him. All I know is, that you are duped: of that fact I am well assured. My own share in the disgrace is a sufficient pledge of my veracity. Her infidelity must be palpable indeed, when I turn Estephania's accuser.

It is to no purpose, continued he, watching the successful impression of his discourse, it is to no purpose to discuss the subject further. I perceive your indignation at the treacherous requital of your love, and your thoughts all aiming at a just revenge. Take your own course. Heed not in what relation to you your victim may stand; but convince the whole city that there is no earthly being whom you would not sacrifice to your honor.

Thus did the traitor exasperate a too credulous husband against an innocent wife; depicting in such glowing colors the infamy in which he would be plunged if he left the insult unpunished, as to heighten his anger into madness. Behold Don Anastasio, with his mind completely overturned; as if goaded by the furies. He returned homewards with the frantic design of murdering his ill-fated wife. She was just going to bed when he came in. He kept his passion under for a time, and waited till the attendants had withdrawn. Then, unrestrained by the fear of vengeance from above, by the vulgar scorn which must recoil upon an honorable family, by natural affection for his unborn child, since his wife was near her time, he approached his victim, and said to her in a furious tone of voice : Now is your hour to die, wretch as you are ! One moment only is your own, which my relenting pity leaves you to make your peace with heaven. I would not that your soul should perish eternally, though your earthly honor is for ever lost.

At these words he drew his dagger. Estephania, just speechless with terror, throwing herself at his feet, besought him with uplifted hands and inarticulate agony, to tell her why he raised his arm against her life. If he suspected her fidelity, she called heaven to attest her innocence.

In vain, in vain, replied the infuriated murderer; your treason is but too well proved. My information is not to be contradicted : Don Huberto. . . . Ah, my lord, interrupted she with eager haste, you must hold your thrust aloof from Don Huberto. He is less your friend than you imagine. If he has said aught against my virtue believe him not. Restrain that infamous tongue, replied Don Anastasio. By appealing against Hordales, you condemn yourself. You would ruin your relation in my esteem, because he is acquainted with your misconduct. You would invalidate his evidence against you ; but the artifice is palpable, and only whets my appetite for vengeance. My dear husband, rejoined the innocent Estephania, while her tears flowed in torrents, beware of this blind rage. If you follow its instigation, you will perpetrate a deed for which you will hate yourself, when convinced of injustice. In the name of heaven, compose your disordered spirits. At least give me time to clear up your suspicions ; you will then deal candidly by a wife who has nothing to reproach herself with.

Any other than Don Anastasio would have been touched by her pleadings, and still more by her agonizing affliction ; but the barbarian, far from being softened, ordered the lady once again to recommend herself briefly to mercy, and lifted his arm to strike the blow. Hold, inhuman as you are, cried she ! If your love for me is as if it had never been, if my lavish fondness in return is all blotted from your memory, if my tears have no eloquence to disarm your hellish purpose, have some pity on your own blood. Launch not your frantic hand against an innocent, who has not yet breathed this vital air. You cannot be its executioner without the curse of heaven and earth. As for myself, I can forgive my murderer ; but the butcher of his own child, think deeply of it, must pay the dreadful forfeit of so detestable a deed.

Determined as Don Anastasio was to pay no attention to anything Estephania could say, he could not help being affected by the frightful images these last words presented to his soul. Wherefore, as if apprehensive lest nature should play the traitress to revenge, he hastened to make sure of his staggering resolves, and plunged his dagger into her bosom. She fell motionless on the ground. He thought her dead; and on that supposition left his house immediately to be no more seen at Antequera.

In the mean time, the unhappy victim of groundless suspicion was so stunned with the blow she had received, as to remain for a short interval on the ground without any signs of life. Afterwards, coming to herself, she brought an old female servant to her assistance by her plaints and lamentations. That good old woman, beholding her mistress in so deplorable a state, waked the whole household and even the neighborhood by her cries. The room was soon filled with spectators. Surgical assistance was sent for. The wound was probed, and pronounced not to be mortal. Their opinion turned out to be correct; for Estephania soon recovered. and was in due time delivered of a son, notwithstanding the cruel circumstances in which she had been placed. That son, Signor Gil Blas, you behold in me: I am the fruit of that dreadful pregnancy.

Women, when chaste as ice, when pure as snow, seldom escape calumny: this plague, however, though virtue's dowry, did not alight upon my mother. The bloody scene passed in common fame for the transport of a jealous husband. My father, it is true, bore the character of a passionate man, prone to kindle into fury on the slightest occasion. Hordales could not but suppose that his kinswoman must suspect him of having sown wild fancies in the mind of Don Anastasio; so that he satisfied himself with this imperfect relish of revenge, and ceased to importune her. But, not to be tedious, I shall pass over the detail of my education. Suffice it to say, that my principal exercise was fencing, which I practised regularly in the most famous schools of Grenada and Seville. My mother waited with impatience till I was of age to measure swords with Don Huberto, that she might instruct me in the grounds of her complaint against him. In my eighteenth year she submitted her cause to my arbitrament, not without floods of tears, and every symptom of the deepest anguish. What must not a son feel, if he has the spirit and the heart of a son, at the sight of a mother in such distressing circumstances? I went immedi-ately and called out Hordales; our place of meeting was private as it should be; we fought long and furiously; three of my thrusts took place, and I threw him to the ground, like a dead dog despised.

Don Huberto, feeling his wound to be mortal, fixed his last looks upon me, and declared that he met his death at my hands as a just punishment for his treason against my mother's honor. He owned that in revenge for the pangs of despised love he had resolved on her ruin. Thus did he breathe his last, imploring pardon from heaven, from Don Anastasio, from Estephania, and from myself. I deemed it imprudent to return home and acquaint my mother of the issue; fame was sure to perform that office for me. I passed the mountains, and repaired to Malaga, where I embarked on board a privateer. My outside not altogether indicating cowardice, the captain consented at once to enrol me among his crew.

We were not long before we went into action. Near the island of Alboutan, a corsair of Millila fell in with us, on his return towards the African coast with a Spanish vessel richly laden, taken off Carthagena. We attacked the African briskly, and made ourselves masters of both ships, with eighty Christians on board, going as slaves to Barbary. Afterwards, availing ourselves of a wind direct for the coast of Grenada, we shortly arrived at Punta de Helena.

While we were inquiring into the birth-place and condition of our rescued captives, a man about fifty, of prepossessing aspect, fell under my examination. He stated himself, with a sigh, to belong to Antequera. My heart palpitated, without my knowing why; and my emotion, too strong to pass unnoticed, excited a visible sympathy in him. I avowed myself his townsman, and asked his family name. Alas! answered he, your curiosity makes my sorrow flow afresh. Eighteen years ago did I leave my home, where my remembrance is coupled with scenes of blood and horror. You must yourself have heard but too much of my story. My name is Don Anastasio de Rada. Merciful heaven! exclaimed I, may I believe my senses? And can this be Don Anastasio? Father! What is it you say, young man? exclaimed he in his turn, with surprise and agitation equal to my own. Are you that ill-fated infant, still in its mother's womb, when I sacrificed her to my fury? Yes, said I; none other did the virtuous Estephania bring into the world, after the fatal night when you left her weltering in her own blood.

Don Anastasio stifled my words in his embraces. For a quarter of an hour we could only mingle our inarticulate sighs and exclamations. After exhausting our tender recollections, and indulging in the wild expression of our feelings, my father lifted his eyes to heaven, in gratitude for Estephania saved; but the next moment, as if doubtful of his bliss, he demanded by what evidence his wife's innocence had been cleared. Sir, answered I, none but yourself ever doubted it. Her conduct has been uniformly spotless. You must be undeceived. Know that Don Huberto was a traitor. In proof of this I unfolded all his perfidy, the vengeance I had taken, and his own confession before he expired.

My father was less delighted at his liberty restored than at these happy tidings. In the forgetfulness of ecstacy, he repeated all his former transports. His approbation of me was ardent and entire. Come, my son, said he, let us set out for Antequera. I burn with impatience to throw myself at the feet of a wife whom I have treated so unworthily. Since you have brought me acquainted with my own injustice, my heart has been torn by remorse.

I was too eager to bring together a couple so near and dear to me, not to expedite our journey as much as possible. I quitted the privateer, and with my share of prize-money bought two mules at Adra, my father not choosing again to incur the hazard of a voyage. He found leisure on the road to relate his adventures, which I inclined to hear as seriously as did the Prince of Ithaca the various recitals of the king his father. At length, after several days, we halted at the foot of a mountain near Antequera. Wishing to reach home privately, we went not into the town till midnight.

You may guess my mother's astonishment at beholding a husband whom she had thought forever lost; and the almost miraculous circumstances of his restoration were a second source of wonder. He entreated forgiveness for his barbarity with marks of repentance so lively, that she could not but be moved. Instead of looking on him as a murderer, she only saw the man to whose will high heaven had subjected her; such religion is there in the name of husband to a virtuous wife! Estephania had been so alarmed about me, that my return filled her with rapture. But her joy on this account was not without alleviation. A sister of Hordales had instituted a criminal prosecution against her brother's antagonist. The search for me was hot, so that my mother, considering home as insecure, was painfully anxious about me. It was therefore necessary to set out that very night for court, whither I come to solicit my pardon, and hope to obtain it by your generous intercession with the prime minister.

The gallant son of Don Anastasio thus closed his narrative; after which I observed, with a self-sufficient physiognomy: It is well, Signor Don Roger; the offense seems to me to be venial. I will undertake to lay the case before his excellency, and may venture to promise you his protection. The thanks my client lavished would have passed in at one ear and out at the other, if they had not been backed by assurances of more substantial gratitude. But when once that string was touched, every nerve and fiber of my frame vibrated in unison. On the very same day did I relate the whole story to the duke, who allowed me to present the gentleman, and addressed him thus: Don Roger, I have been informed of the duel which has brought you to court; Santillane has laid all the particulars before me. Make yourself perfectly easy: you have done nothing but what the circumstances of the case might almost warrant; and it is especially on the ground of wounded honor, that his Majesty is best pleased to extend his grace and favor. You must be committed for mere form's sake; but you may depend on it, your confinement shall be of short duration. In Santillane you have a zealous friend, who will watch over your interests, and hasten your release.

Don Roger paid his respectful acknowledgments to the minister on whose pledge he went and surrendered himself. His pardon was soon made out, owing to my activity. In less than ten days, I sent this modern Telemachus home, to say "how do you do?" to his Ulysses and Penelope; had he stood upon the merits of his case without a protector, he might have whined out a year's imprisonment, and scarcely have got off at last. My commission was but a poor hundred pistoles. It was no very magnificent haul; but I was not as yet a Calderona, to turn up my nose at the small fry.

CHAPTER IX.

GIL BLAS MAKES A LARGE FORTUNE IN A SHORT TIME, AND BE-
HAVES LIKE OTHER WEALTHY UPSTARTS.

THIS affair gave me a relish for my trade; and ten pistoles to
Scipio by way of brokerage, whetted his eagerness to start more
game of the same sort. I have already done justice to his talents
that way; he might as modestly have appended "the great" to the
tail of his name, as the most noted scoundrel of antiquity. The
second customer he brought me was a printer, who manufactured
books of chivalry, and had made his fortune by waging war against
common sense. This printer had pirated a work belonging to a
brother printer, and his edition had been seized. For three hundred ducats I rescued his copies out of jeopardy, and saved him
from a heavy fine. Though this was a transaction beneath the
prime minister's notice, his excellency condescended at my request
to interpose his authority. After the printer, a merchant passed
through my hands; the occasion was thus: A Portuguese vessel
had been taken by a Barbary corsair, and re-taken by a privateer
from Cadiz. Two-thirds of the cargo belonged to a merchant at
Lisbon, who, having claimed his due to no purpose, came to the
court of Spain in search of a protector, with sufficient credit to procure him restitution. I took up his cause, and he recovered his
property, deducting the sum of four hundred pistoles, paid to me in
consideration of my disinterested zeal for justice.

And now most surely the reader will call out to me at this
place: Well said, good master Santillane! Make hay while the
sun shines. You are on the high road to fortune; push forward,
and outstrip your rivals. Oh! let me alone for that. I spy, or my
eyes deceive me, my servant coming in with a new gull that he has
just caught. Even so! It is my very Scipio. Let us hear what
he has to say. Sir, quoth he, give me leave to introduce this eminent practitioner. He wants a license to sell his drugs during the
term of ten years in all the towns of the Spanish monarchy, to the
exclusion of all other quacks; in short, a monopoly of poisons. In
gratitude for this patent to thin mankind, he will present the donor
with a gratuity of two hundred pistoles. I looked superciliously,
like a patron, at the mountebank, and told him that his business
should be done. As lameness and leprosy would have it, in the
course of a few days I sent him on his progress through Spain, invested with full powers to make the world his oyster, and leave
nothing but the shell to his unpatented competitors.

Besides that my avarice outran my accumulating wealth, I had
obtained the four boons just specified so easily from his grace, as
not to be mealy-mouthed about asking for a fifth. The town of
Vera, on the coast of Grenada, wanted a governor; and a knight of
Calatrava wanted the government, for which he was willing to pay

me one thousand pistoles. The minister was ready to burst with laughing, to see me so eager after the scut. By all the powers! my friend Gil Blas, said he, you go to work tooth and nail! You have a most inveterate itch to do as you would be done by. But mark me! When mere trifles stand between us, I shall not stand upon trifles; but when governments or other places of real value are in question, you will have the modesty to be content with half the fee for yourself, and will account to me for the other half. It is inconceivable at what expense I stand, and how it presses on my finances to support the dignity of my station; for though disinterestedness looks vastly well in the eyes of the world, you are to understand between ourselves that I have made a solemn vow against dipping into my private fortune. On this hint, arrange your future plans.

My master, by this discourse, relieving me from the fear of being troublesome, or rather egging me on to run at the ring for every prize, made me still more worldly-minded than ever I had been before. I should not have objected to circulating hand-bills, with an invitation to all candidates for places to apply on certain terms at the secretary's office. My functions were here, Scipio's were there; and we met at the receipt of custom. My client got the government of Tera for his thousand pistoles; and as our price was fixed, a knight of St. James met his brother of Calatrava in the market on an equal footing. But mere governors were paltry fish to fry; I distributed orders of knighthood, and converted some good stupid burgesses into most insufferable gentry by one stroke of the pen, and a lacing across the shoulders with a broad-sword. The clergy, too, were not forgotten in my charities. Lesser preferments were in my gift; everything up to prebendal stalls and collegiate dignities. With regard to bishoprics and archbishoprics, Don Rodrigo de Calderona had the charge of our holy religion. As church and state must always go together, supreme magistracies, commanderies, and viceroyalties were all in his gift; whence the reader will naturally infer, that the upper offices were little better tenanted than the lower ones; since the subjects on whom our election fell, establishing their pretensions on a certain palpable criterion, were not necessarily and unavoidably either the cleverest or the best-principled people in the world. We knew very well that the wits and lampooners of Madrid made themselves merry at our expense; but we borrowed our philosophy from misers, who hug themselves under the hootings of the people, when they count over the accumulation of their pelf.

Isocrates was in the right to insinuate, in his elegant Greek expression, that what is got over the devil's back is spent under his belly. When I saw myself master of thirty thousand ducats, and in a fair way to gain perhaps ten times as much, it seemed to be a necessary of office to make such a figure as became the right hand of a prime minister. I took a house to myself, and furnished it in the immediate taste. I bought an attorney's carriage at second hand: he had set it up at the suggestion of vanity, and laid it down at the suggestion of his banker. I hired a coachman and three footmen. Justice demands that old and faithful servants should be promoted; I therefore invested Scipio with the threefold honor of valet-de-chambre, private secretary, and steward. But the minister raised my pride to its highest pitch, for he was pleased to allow my people to wear his livery. My poor little wits were now completely turned. I was little more in my senses than the disciples of Porcius Latro, who, by dint of drinking cummin, having made themselves as pale as their master, thought themselves every whit as learned; so I could scarcely refrain from fancying myself next of kin and presumptive heir to the Duke of Lerma himself. The populace might take me for his cousin, and people who knew better, for one of his bastards; a suspicion most flattering to my pride of blood.

Add to this, that, after the example of his excellency, who kept a public table, I determined to give parties of my own. Pursuant thereunto, I commissioned Scipio to find me out a professed cook, and he stumbled upon one who might have dished up a dinner for Nomentanus, of dripping-pan notoriety. My cellar was well stored with the choicest wines. My establishment being now complete, I gave my house-warming. Every evening some of the clerks in the public offices came to sup with me, and affected a sort of political high life below-stairs. I did the honors hospitably, and always sent them home half seas over. Like master like man! Scipio, too, had his parties in the servants' hall, where he treated all his chums at my expense. But besides that I felt a real kindness for that lad, he contributed to grease the wheels of my establishment, and was entitled to have a finger in the dissipation. As a young man, some little license was allowable; and the ruinous consequences did not strike me at the time. Another reason, too, prevented me from taking notice of it; incessant vacancies, ecclesiastical and secular, paid me amply in meal and in malt. My surplus was increasing every day. Fortune's curricle seemed to have driven to my door, there to have broken down, and the driver to have taken shelter with me.

One thing more was wanting to my complete intoxication, that Fabricio might be witness to my pomp. He was most probably come back from Andalusia. For the fun of surprising him, I sent an anonymous note, importing that a Sicilian noblemen of his acquaintance would be glad of his company to supper, with the day, hour, and place of appointment, which was at my house Nunez came, and was most inordinately astonished to recognize me in the Sicilian nobleman. Yes, my friend, said I, behold the master of this family. I have a retinue, a good table, and a strong box besides. Is it possible, exclaimed he with vivacity, that all this opulence should be yours? It was well done in me to have placed you with Count Galiano. I told you beforehand that he was a generous nobleman, and would not be long before he set you at your ease. Of course you followed my wise advice, in giving the rein a little more freely to your servants; you find the benefit of it. It is only by a little mutual accommodation, that the principal officers in great houses feather their nests so comfortably.

I suffered Fabricio to go on as long as he liked, complimenting himself for having introduced me to Count Galiano. When he had done, to chastise his ectasies at having procured me so good a post, I stated at full length the returns of gratitude with which that nobleman had recompensed my services. But, perceiving how ready my poet was to string his lyre to satire at my recital, I said to him—The Sicilian's contemptible conduct I readily forgive. Between ourselves, it is more a subject of congratulation than of regret. If the count had dealt honorably by me, I should have followed him into Sicily, where I should still be in a subordinate capacity, waiting for dead men's shoes. In a word, I should not now have been hand in glove with the Duke of Lerma.

Nunez felt so strange a sensation at these last words, that he was tongue-tied for some seconds. Then gulping up his stammering accents like harlequin, Did I hear aright? said he. What! you hand in glove with the prime minister. I on one side, and Don Rodrigo de Calderona on the other, answered I; and according to all appearance, my fortunes will move higher. Truly, replied he, this is admirable. You are cut out for every occasion. What a universal genius! To borrow an expression from the tennis-court, you have a racket for every ball; nothing comes amiss to you. At all events, my lord, I am sincerely rejoiced at your lordship's prosperity. The deuce end all, Master Nunez! interrupted I; good now, dispense with your lords and lordships. Let us banish such formalities, and live on equal terms together. You are in the right, replied he; altered circumstances should not make strange faces. I will own my weakness; when you announced your elevation you took away my breath; but the chill and the shudder are over, and I see only my old friend Gil Blas.

Our conversation was interrupted by the arrival of four or five clerks. Gentlemen, said I, introducing Nunez, you are to sup with Signor Don Fabricio, who writes verses of impenetrable sublimity, and such prose as would not know itself in the glass. Unluckily I was talking to gentry who would have had more fellow-feeling with an Oran Outang than with a poet. They scarcely condescended to look at him. In vain did he pun, parody, rally, or rail to hit their fancies, for they had none. He was so nettled at their indifference, that he assumed the poetic license, and made his escape. Our clerks never missed him, but forgot at once that he had been there.

Just as I was going out the next morning, the poet of the Asturias came into my room. I beg pardon, said he, for having cut your clerks so abruptly last night; but, to deal freely, I was so much out of my element, that I should soon have played old chaos with them. Proud puppies, with their starch and self-important air! I cannot conceive how a clever fellow like you can sit it out with such loutish guests. To-day I will bring you some of more life and spirit. I shall be very much obliged to you, answered I; your introduction is sufficient. Exactly so, replied he. You shall have the feast of reason and the flow of soul. I will go forthwith and invite them, for fear they should engage themselves elsewhere; for happy man be his dole who can get them to dinner or supper; they are such excellent company!

Away went he; and in the evening, at supper-time, returned with six authors in his train, whom he presented one after another with a set speech in their praise. According to his account, the wits of Greece and Italy were nothing in comparison of these, whose works ought to be printed in letters of gold. I received this deputation from the tuneful sisters very politely. My behavior was even in the extravagance of good breeding; for the republic of authors is a little monarchical in its demands upon our flattery. Though I had given Scipio no express direction respecting the number of covers at this entertainment, yet knowing what a hungry and voluptuous race were to be crammed, he had mustered the courses in more than their full complement.

At length supper was announced, and we fell to merrily. My poets began talking of their poems and themselves. One fellow, with the most lyrical assurance, numbered up whole hosts of first-rate nobility and high-flying dames, who were quite enraptured with his muse. Another, though it was not for him to arraign the choice which a learned society had lately made of two new members, could not help saying that it was strange they should not have elected him. All the rest were much in the same story. Amid the clatter of knives and forks, my ears were more discordantly dinned with verses and harangues. They each took it by turns to give me a specimen of their composition. One languishes out a sonnet; another mouths a scene in a tragedy; and a third reads a melancholy criticism on the province of comedy. The next in turn spouts an ode of Anacreon, translated into most un-anacreontic Spanish verse. One of his brethren interrupts him, to point out the unclassical use of a particular phrase. The author of the version by no means acquiesces in the remark; hence arises an argument, in which all the literati take one side or the other. Opinions are nearly balanced; the disputants are nearly in a passion; as argument weakens, invective grows stronger; they get from bad to worse; over goes the table, and up jump they to fisty-cuffs. Fabricio, Scipio, my coachman, my footman, and myself, have scarcely lungs or strength to bring them to their senses. The moment he battle was over, off scampered they as if my house had been a tavern, without the slightest apology for their ill behavior.

Nunez, on whose word I had anticipated a very pleasant party, looked rather blue at this conclusion. Well, my friend, said I, what do you think of your literary acquaintance now? As sure as Apollo is on Parnassus, you brought me a most blackguard set. I will stick to my clerks; so talk no more to me about authors. I shall take care, answered he, not to invite any of them to a gentleman's house again; for these are the most select and well-mannered of the tribe.

CHAPTER X.

THE MORALS OF GIL BLAS BECOME AT COURT MUCH AS IF THEY
HAD NEVER BEEN AT ALL. A COMMISSION FROM THE COUNT
DE LEMOS, WHICH, LIKE MOST COURT COMMISSIONS, IMPLIES
AN INTRIGUE.

WHEN once my name was up for a man after the Duke of
Lerma's own heart, I had very soon my court about me. Every
morning was my ante-chamber crowded with company, and my
levees were all the fashion. Two sorts of customers came to my
shop ; one set, to engage my interposition with the minister, on fair
commercial principles ; the other set, to excite my compassion by
pathetic statements of their cases, and give me a lift to heaven on
the packhorse of charity. The first were sure of being heard patiently and served diligently ; with regard to the second order, I
got rid of them at once by plausible evasions, or kept them dangling till they wore their patience threadbare, and went off in a huff.
Before I was about the court my nature was compassionate and
charitable ; but tenderness of heart is an unfashionable frailty there,
and mine became harder than any flint. Here was an admirable
school to correct the romantic sensibilities of friendship : nor was
my philosophy any longer assailable in that quarter. My manner
of dealing with Joseph Navarro, under the following circumstances,
will prove more than volumes on that head.

This Navarro, the founder of my fortune, to whom my obligations were thick and threefold, paid me a visit one day. With the
warmest expressions of regard such as he was in the habit of lavishing, he begged me to ask the Duke of Lerma for a certain situation
for one of his friends, a young man of excellent qualities and undoubted merit, but incumbered with an inability of getting on in
the world. I am well assured, added Joseph, that with your good
and obliging disposition, you will be enraptured to confer a favor
on a worthy man with a very slender purse ; I am sure you will feel
obliged to me for giving you an opportunity of carrying your benevolent inclinations into effect. This was just as good as telling
me that the business was to be done for nothing. Though such
doctrine was not quite level to my capacity, I still affected a wish
to do as he desired. It gives me infinite pleasure, answered I to
Navarro, to have it in my power to evince my lively sense of all
your former kindness to me. It is enough for you to take any man
living by the hand ; from that moment he becomes the object of
my unwearied care. Your friend shall have the situation you want
for him ; nay, he has it already ; it is no longer any concern of
yours ; leave it entirely to me.

On this assurance Joseph went away in high glee ; nevertheless
the person he recommended had not the post in question. It was
given to another man, and my strong box was the stronger by a

thousand ducats. This sum was infinitely preferable to all the thanks in the world, so that I looked pitifully blank when next we met, saying—Ah, my dear Navarro! you should have thought of speaking to me sooner. That Calderona got the start of me; he has given away a certain thing that shall be nameless. I am vexed to the soul not to meet you with better tidings.

Joseph was fool enough to give me credit, and we parted better friends than ever; but I suspect that he soon found out the truth, for he never came near me again. This was just what I wanted. Besides that the memory of benefits received grated harshly, it would not have been at all the thing for a person in my then sphere to keep company with a certain description of people.

The Count de Lemos has been long in the background, let us bring him a little forwarder on the canvas. We met occasionally. I had carried him a thousand pistoles, as the reader will recollect; and I now carried him a thousand more, by order of his uncle the duke, out of his excellency's funds lying in my hands. On this occasion the Count de Lemos honored me with a long conference. He informed me that at length he had completely gained his end, and was in unrivaled possession of the Prince of Spain's good graces, whose sole confidant he was. His next concern was to invest me with a right honorable commission, of which he had already given me a hint. Friend Santillane, said he, now is the time to strike while the iron is hot. Spare no pains to find out some young beauty, worthy to while away the prince's amorous hours. You have your wits about you: and a word to the wise is sufficient. Go; run about the town; pry into every hole and corner; and when you have pounced upon anything likely to suit, you will come and let me know. I promised the count to leave no stone unturned in the due discharge of my employment, which seemed to require no great force of genius, since the professors of the science are so numerous.

I had not hitherto been much practised in such delicate investigations, but it was more than probable that Scipio had, and that his talent lay peculiarly that way. On my return home I called him in, and spoke thus to him in private: My good fellow, I have a very important secret to impart. Do you know that in the midst of fortune's favors, there is something still wanting to crown all my wishes? I can easily guess what that is, interrupted he, without giving me time to finish what I was going to say; you want a little snug bit of contraband amusement, to keep you awake of evenings, and rub off the dust of business. And, in fact, it is a marvelous thing that you should have played the Joseph in the heyday of your blood, when so many graybeards around you are playing the Elder. I admire the quickness of your apprehension, replied I with a smile. Yes, my friend, a mistress is that something still wanting; and you shall choose for me. But I forewarn you that I am nice hungry, and must have a pretty person, with more than passable manners. The sort of thing that you require, returned Scipio, is not always to be met with in the market. Yet, as luck will have it, we are in a town where everything is to be got

for money, and I am in hopes that your commission will not
hang long on hand.

Accordingly within three days he pulled me by the sleeve: I have
discovered a treasure! a young lady whose name is Catalina, of
good family and matchless beauty, living with her aunt in a small
house, where they make both ends meet by clubbing their little
matters, and set the slanderous world at defiance. Their waiting-
maid, a girl of my acquaintance, has given me to understand that
their door, though barred against all impertinent intruders, would
turn upon its hinges to a rich and generous suitor, if he would only
consent, for fear of prying neighbors, not to pay his visits till after
night-fall, and then in the most private manner possible. Hereupon I magnified you as the properest gentleman in the world, and
intreated piety in pattens to offer your humble services to the ladies.
She promised to do so, and to bring me back my answer to-morrow
morning at an appointed place. That is all very well answered I;
but I am afraid your goddess of bed-making has been running her
rig upon you. No, no, replied he, old birds are not to be caught
with chaff; I have already made inquiry in the neighborhood, and
by the general report of her, Signora Catalina is a second Danae,
on whom you will have the happiness of coming down,

> Like Jove descending from his tower,
> To court her in a silver shower.

Out of conceit as I was with the intrinsic value of ladies' favors,
this was not to be scoffed at; and as our Mercury in petticoats
came the next day to tell Scipio that it only depended on me to be
introduced that very evening, I dropped in between eleven and
twelve o'clock. The knowing one received me without bringing a
candle, and led me by the hand into a very neat apartment, where
the two ladies were sitting on a satin sofa, dressed in the most elegant taste. As soon as they saw me enter, they got up and welcomed me in a style of such superior breeding, as would not have
disgraced the highest rank. The aunt, whose name was Signora
Mencia, though with the remains of beauty, had no attractions for
me. But the niece had a million, for she was a goddess in mortal
form. And yet, to examine her critically, she could not have been
admitted for a perfect beauty; but then there was a charm above
all rules of symmetry, with a tingling and luxurious warmth about
her, that seized on men's hearts through their eyes, and prevented
their brains from being too busy.

Neither were my senses proof against so dazzling a display. I
forgot my errand as proxy, and spoke on my own private individual
account, with the enthusiasm of a raw recruit in the tender passion.
The dear little creature, whose wit sounded in my ears with three
times its actual acuteness, under favor of her natural endowments,
made a complete conquest of me by her prattle. I began to iaunch
out into foolish raptures, when the aunt, to bring me to my bearings, led the conversation to the point in hand: Signor de Santillane, I shall deal very explicitly with you. On the high encomiums
I have heard of your character, you have been admitted here, with-

out the affectation of making much ado about trifles : but do not imagine that your views are the nearer their termination for that. Hitherto I have brought my niece up in retirement, and you are, as it were, the very first male creature on whom she has ever set eyes. If you deem her worthy of being your wife, I shall feel myself highly honored by the alliance : it is for you to consider whether those terms suit you ; but you cannot have her on cheaper.

This was proceeding to business with a vengeance ! It put little Cupid to flight at once : or else he was just going to try one of his sharpest arrows upon me. But a truce with the Pantheon ! A marriage so bluntly proposed dispelled the fairy vision ; I sunk back at once into the count's plodding agent ; and changing my tone, answered Signora Mencia thus : Madam, your frankness delights me, and I will meet it half-way. Whatever rank I may hold at court, lower than the highest is too low for the peerless Catalina. A far more brilliant offer waits her acceptance ; the Prince of Spain shall be thrown into her toils. Surely it was enough to have refused my niece, replied the aunt sarcastically ; such compliments are sufficiently unpleasing to our sex ; it could not be necessary to make us your unfeeling sport. I really am not in so merry a mood, madam ! exclaimed I : it is a plain matter of fact ; I am commissioned to look out for a young lady of merit sufficient to engage the prince's heart, and receive his private visits ; the object of my search is in your house, and here his royal highness shall fix his quarters.

Signora Mencia could scarcely believe her ears ; neither were they grievously offended. Nevertheless, thinking it decent to be startled at the immorality of the proceeding, she replied to the following effect : Though I should give implicit credit to what you tell me, you must understand that I am not of a character to take pleasure in the infamous distinction of seeing my niece a prince's concubine. Every feeling of virtue and of honor revolts at the idea. . . . What a simpleton you are with your virtue and honor ! interrupted I. You have not a notion above the level of a tradesman's wife. Was there ever anything so stupid as to consider affairs of this kind with a view to their moral tendency ? It is stripping them of all their beauty and excellence. In the magic lantern of plenty, pleasure, and preferment, they appear with all their brightest gloss. Figure to yourself the heir to the monarchy at the happy Catalina's feet ; fancy him all rapture and lavish bounty ; nor doubt but that from her shall spring a hero, who shall immortalize his mother's name, by enrolling his own in the unperishable records of eternal fame.

Though the aunt desired no better sport than to take me at my word, she affected not to know what she had best do ; and Catalina, who longed to have a grapple with the Prince of Spain, affected not to care about the matter ; which made it necessary for me to press the siege closer ; till at length Signora Mencia, finding me chop-fallen and ready to withdraw my forces, sounded a parley and agreed to a convention, containing the two following articles, *Imprimis,* if the Prince of Spain, on the fame of Catalina's charms should take fire, and determine to pay her a nightly visit, it should be my care to let the ladies know when they might expect him. *Secondo*, that the prince should be introduced to the said ladies as a private gentleman, accompanied only by himself and his principal purveyor.

After this capitulation, the aunt and niece were upon the best terms possible with me: they behaved as if we had know one another from our cradles; on the strength of which I ventured on some little familiarities, which were not taken at all unkindly; and when we parted, they embraced me of their own accord, and slabbered me over with inexpressible fondness. It is marvelous to think with what facility a tender connection is formed between persons in the same line of trade, but of opposite sexes. It might have been suspected by an eye-witness of my departure, in all the plentitude of warm and repeated salutation, that my visit had been more successful than it was.

The Count de Lemos was highly delighted when I announced the long-expected discovery. I spoke of Catalina in terms which made him long to see her. The following night I took him to her house, and he owned that I had beat the bush to some purpose. He told the ladies, he had no doubt but the Prince of Spain would be fully satisfied with my choice of a mistress, who, on her part, would have reason to be well pleased with such a lover; that the young prince was generous, good-tempered. and amiable; in short, he promised in a few days to bring him in the mode they enjoined, without retinue or publicity. That nobleman then took leave of them, and I withdrew with him. We got into his carriage, in which we had both driven thither, and which was waiting at the end of the street. He set me down at my own door, with a special charge to inform his uncle next day of the new game started, not forgetting to impress strongly how conducive a good bag of pistoles would be to the successful accomplishment of the adventure.

I did not fail on the following morning to go and give the Duke of Lerma an exact account of all that had passed. There was but one thing kept back. I did not mention Scipio's name, but took credit to myself for the discovery of Catalina. One makes a merit of any dirty work in the service of the great.

Abundant were the compliments paid me on this occasion. My good friend Gil Blas, said the minister with a bantering air, I am delighted that with all your talents you have that besides of discovering kind-hearted beauties; whenever I have occasion for such an article, you will have the goodness to supply me. My lord, answered I with mock gravity like his own, you are very obliging to give me the preference; but it may not be unseasonable to observe that there would be an indelicacy in my administering to your excellency's pleasures of this description. Signor Don Rodrigo has been so long in possession of that post about your person, that it would be manifest injustice to rob him of it. The duke smiled at my answer; and then changing the subject, asked whether his nephew did not want money for this new speculation. Excuse my negligence! said I: he will thank you to send him a thousand pistoles. Well and good! replied the minister; you will furnish him accordingly, with my strict injunction not to be niggardly, but to encourage the prince in whatever pleasurable expenses his heart may prompt him to indulge.

CHAPTER XI.

THE PRINCE OF SPAIN'S SECRET VISIT, AND PRESENTS TO CATALINA.

I WENT to the Count de Lemos on the spur of the occasion, with five hundred double pistoles in my hand. You could not have come at a better time, said that nobleman. I have been talking with the prince; he has taken the bait, and burns with impatience to see Catalina. This very night he intends to slip privately out of the palace, and pay her a visit; it is a measure determined on, and our arrangements are already made. Give notice to the ladies, through the medium of the cash you have just brought; it is proper to let them know they have no ordinary lover to receive; and a matter of course that generosity in princes should be the herald of their partialities. As you will be of our party, take care to be in the way at bed-time: and as your carriage will be wanted, let it wait near the palace about midnight.

I immediately repaired to the ladies. Catalina was not visible, having just gone to lie down. I could only speak with Signora Mencia. Madam, said I, forgive my appearance here in the daytime, but there was no avoiding it; you must know that the Prince of Spain will be with you to night; and here, added I, putting my pecuniary credentials into her hand, here is an offering which he lays on the Cytherean shrine, to propitiate the divinities of the temple. You may perceive, I have not entangled you in a sleeveless concern. You have been excessively kind indeed, answered she; but tell me, Signor de Santillane, does the prince love music? To distraction, replied I. There is nothing he so much delights in as a fine voice, with a delicate lute accompaniment. So much the better, exclaimed she in a transport of joy; you give me great pleasure by saying so; for my niece has the pipe of a nightingale, and plays exquisitely on the lute; then her dancing is in the finest style! Heavens and earth! exclaimed I in my turn, here are accomplishments by wholesale, aunt; more than enough to make any girl's fortune! Any one of those talents would have been a sufficient dowry.

Having thus smoothed his reception, I waited for the prince's bed-time. When it was near at hand, I gave my coachman his orders, and went to the Count de Lemos, who told me that the prince, the sooner to get rid of the people about him, meant to feign a slight indisposition, and even to go to bed, the better to cajole his attendants; but that he would get up an hour after-wards, and go through a private door to a back staircase leading into the court-yard.

Conformably with their previous arrangements, he fixed my station. There had I to beat the hoof so long, that I began to suspect our forward sprig of royalty had gone another way, or else, had changed his mind about Catalina; just as if princes ever began to be fickle, till the goad of novelty and curiosity began to be blunted. In short, I thought they had forgotten me, when two men came up. Finding them to be my party, I led the way to my carriage, into which they both got, and I upon the coach-box to direct the driver, whom I stopped fifty yards from the house, whither we walked. The door opened at our approach, and shut again as soon as we got in.

At first we were in absolute darkness, as on my former visit, though a small lamp was fixed to the wall on the present occasion. But the light which it shed was so faint, as only to render itself visible without assisting us. All this served only to heighten the romance in the fancy of its hero, fixed as he was in steadfast gaze at the sight of the ladies as they received him in a saloon whose brilliant illumination was more dazzling, when contrasted with the gloom of the avenue. The aunt and niece were in a tempting undress, where the science of coquetry was displayed in all its luxury and absolute sway. Our prince could have been happy with Signora Mencia, had the dear charmer Catalina been away; but as there was a choice, the younger, according to the rules of precedency in the court of Cupid, had the preference.

Well! prince, said the Count de Lemos, could you have desired a better specimen of beauty? They are both enchanting, answered the prince, and my heart may as well surrender at once; for the aunt would arrest it in its flight, if it attempted to sound a retreat from the niece's all-subduing charms.

After such compliments, as do not fall by wholesale to the share of aunts, he addressed his choicest terms of flattery to Catalina, who answered him in kind. As convenient personages of my stamp are allowed to mingle in the conversation of lovers, for the purpose of making fire hotter, I introduced the subject of singing and play-ing on the lute. This was the signal of fresh rapture! and the nymph, the muse, the anything but mortal, was supplicated to outtune the jingle of the spheres. She complied like a good-humored goddess; played some tender airs, and sung so delicious-ly, that the prince flopped down on his knees in a tumult of love and pleasure. But scenes like these are vapid in description: suffice it to say that hours glided away like moments in this sweet delirium, till the approach of day warned the sober plotters of the lunacy to provide for their patient's safety, and their own. When the parties were all snugly housed, we gave ourselves as much credit for the negotiation as if we had patched up a marriage with a princess.

The next morning the Duke of Lerma desired to know all the particulars. Just as I had finished relating them, the Count de

CATALINA AND HER AUNT ADMIRING THE EARRINGS.

Lemos came in and said – The Prince of Spain is so engrossed by Catalina, he has taken so decided a fancy to her, that he actually proposes to be constant. He wanted to have sent her jewels to the amount of two thousand pistoles to-day, but his finances were aground. My dear Lemos, said he, addressing himself to me, you must absolutely get me that sum. I know it is very inconvenient; you have pawned your credit for me already, but my heart owns itself your debtor; and if ever I have the means of returning your kindness by more than empty words, your fortunes shall not suffer by your complaisance. In answer, I assured him that I had friends and credit, and promised to bring him what he wanted.

There is no difficulty about that, said the duke to his nephew. Santillane will bring you the money; or, to save trouble, he may purchase the jewels, for he is an admirable judge, especially of rubies. Are you not, Gil Blas? This stroke of satire was of course designed to entertain the count at my expense, and it was successful, for his curiosity could not but be excited to know the meaning of the mystery. No mystery at all, replied his uncle with a broad laugh. Only Santillane took it into his head one day to exchange a diamond for a ruby, and the barter operated equally to the advantage of his pocket and his penetration.

Had the minister stopped there, I should have come off cheaply; but he took the trouble of dressing out in aggravated colors the trick that Camilla and Don Raphael played me, with a most provoking enlargement of the circumstances most to the disadvantage of my sagacity. His excellency having enjoyed his joke, ordered me to attend the Count de Lemos to a jeweler's, where we selected trinkets for the Prince of Spain's inspection, and they were intrusted to my care to be delivered to Catalina.

There can be little doubt of my kind reception on the following night, when I displayed a fine pair of drop ear-rings, as the presents of my embassy. The two ladies, out of their wits at these costly tokens of the prince's love, suffered their tongues to run into a gossiping strain, while they were thanking me for introducing them into such worshipful society. In the excess of their joy, they forgot themselves a little. There escaped now and then certain peculiar idioms of speech, which made me suspect that the party in question was no such dainty morsel for royalty to feed upon. To ascertain precisely what degree of obligation I had conferred on the heir-apparent, I took my leave with the intention of coming to a right understanding with Scipio.

CHAPTER XII.

C FALINA'S REAL CONDITION A WORRY AND ALARM TO GIL BLAS.
HIS PRECAUTIONS FOR HIS OWN EASE AND QUIET.

ON coming home, I heard a devil of a noise, and inquired what
was the meaning of it. They told me that Scipio was giving a
supper to half-a-dozen of his friends. They were singing as loud
as their lungs could roar, and threatening the stability of the
house with their protracted peals of laughter. This meal was not
in all respects the banquet of the seven wise men.

The founder of the feast, informed of my arrival, said to his
company: Sit still, gentlemen, it is only the master of the house
come home, but that need not disturb you. Go on with your
merry-making; I will but just whisper a word in his ear, and be
back again in a moment. He came to me accordingly. What an
infernal din! said I. What sort of company do you keep below?
Have you, too, got in among the poets? Thank you for nothing!
answered he. Your wine is too good to be given to such gentry;
I turn it to better account. There is a young man of large property in my party, who wishes to lay out your credit and his own
money in the purchase of a place. This little festivity is all for
him. For every glass he fills, I put on ten pistoles, in addition
to the regular fee. He shall drink till he is under the table. If
that is the case, replied I, go to your presidentship, and do not
spare the cellar.

Then was no proper time to talk about Catalina; but the
next morning I opened the business thus: Friend Scipio, the terms
we are upon entitle me to fair dealing. I have treated you more
like an equal than a servant, consequently you would be much to
blame to cheat me on the footing of a master. Let us, therefore, have
no secrets towards each other. I am going to tell you what will surprise you; and you on your part shall give me your sincere opinion
about the two women with whom you have brought me acquainted. Between ourselves, I suspect them to be no better than
they should be; with so much the more of the knave in their composition, because they affect the simpleton. If my conjecture be
right, the Prince of Spain has no great reason to be delighted
with my activity; for I will own to you frankly, that it was for
him I spoke to you about a mistress. I brought him to see
Catalina, and he is over head and ears in love with her. Sir,
answered Scipio, you have dealt so handsomely by me, that I shall
act upon the square with you. I had yesterday a private interview with the abigail, and she gave me a most entertaining history
of the family. You shall have it briefly, though it did not come
briefly to me.

Catalina was daughter to a sort of gentleman in Arragon. An
orphan at fifteen, with no fortune but a pretty face, she lent a com-

plying ear to an officer who carried her off to Toledo, where he died in six months, having been more like a father than a husband to her. She collected his effects together, consisting of their joint wardrobe and three hundred pistoles in ready money, and then went to housekeeping with Signora Mencia, who was still in fashion, though a little on the wane. These sisters, every way but in blood, began at length to attract the attention of the police. The ladies took umbrage at this, and decamped for Madrid, where they have been living for these two years, without making any acquaintance in the neighborhood. But now comes the best of the joke: they have taken two small houses adjoining each other, with a passage of communication through the cellars. Signora Mencia lives with a servant girl in one of these houses, and the officer's widow inhabits the other, with an old duenna, whom she passes off for her grandmother, so that her versatile child of nature is sometimes a niece brought up by her aunt, and sometimes an orphan under her grandam's fostering wing. When she enacts the niece, her name is Catalina; and when she personates the granddaughter, she calls herself Sirena.

At the grating sound of Sirena I turned pale, and interrupted Scipio, saying—What do you tell me? Alas! it must be so: This cursed imp of Arragon is Calderona's charming Siren. To be sure she is, answered he, the very same! I thought you would be delighted at the news. Quite the reverse, replied I. It portends more sorrow than laughter; do not you anticipate the consequences? None of any ill omen, rejoined Scipio. What is there to be afraid of? It is not certain that Don Rodrigo will rub his forehead; and in case any good-natured friend should show it him in the glass, you had better let the minister into the secret beforehand. Tell him all the circumstances straightforward as they happened; he will see that there has been no trick on your part; and if after that Calderona should attempt to do you an ill office with his excellency, it will be as clear as daylight that he is only actuated by a spirit of revenge.

Scipio removed all my apprehension by this advice, which I followed, in acquainting the Duke of Lerma at once with this unlucky discovery. My aspect, while telling my tale, was sorrowful, and my tone faltering, in evidence of my contrition for having unadvisedly brought the prince and Don Rodrigo into such close quarters; but the minister was more disposed to roast his favorite than to pity him. Indeed, he ordered me to let the matter take its own course, considering it as a feather in Calderona's cap to dispute the empire of love with so illustrious a rival, and not to be worse used than his lawful prince. The Count de Lemos, too, was informed how things stood, and promised me his protection, if the first secretary should come at the knowledge of the intrigue, and attempt to undermine me with the duke.

Trusting to have secured the frail bark of my fortunes by this notable contrivance from the rocks and quicksands that threatened it, my mind was once more at rest. I continued attending the prince on his visits to Catalina, siren-like in nature as in nickname, who was fertile in quaint devices to keep Don Rodrigo away from next door, whenever the course of business required her to devote her nights to his royal competitor.

CHAPTER XIII.

GIL BLAS GOES ON PERSONATING THE GREAT MAN. HE HEARS NEWS OF HIS FAMILY: A TOUCH OF NATURE ON THE OCCA-SION. A GRAND QUARREL WITH FABRICIO.

I MENTIONED some time ago, that in the morning there was usually a crowd of people in my ante-chamber, coming to nego-tiate little private concerns in the way of politics; but I would never suffer them to open their business by word of mouth; but adopting court precedent, or rather giving myself the airs of a jack in office, my language to every suitor was—Send in a memor-ial on the subject. My tongue ran so glibly to that tune, that one day I gave my landlord the official answer, when he came to put me in mind of a twelvemonth's rent in arrear. As for my butcher and baker, they spared the trouble of asking for their memorials, by never giving me time to run up a bill. Scipio, who mimicked me so exactly, that only those behind the scenes could distinguish the double from the principal performer, held his head just as high with the poor devils who curried favor with him, as a step of the ladder to my ministerial patronage.

There was another foolish trick of mine, of which I do not by any means pretend to make a merit ; neither more nor less than the extreme assurance of talking about the first nobility, just as if I had been one of their kidney. Suppose, for example, the Duke of Alva, the Duke of Ossuna, or the Duke of Medina Sidonia were mentioned in conversation, I called them without ceremony, my friend Alva, that good-natured fellow Ossuna, or that comical dog Medina Sidonia. In a word, my pride and vanity had swelled to such a height, that my father and mother were no longer among the number of my honored relatives. Alas ! poor understrappers, I never thought of asking whether you had sunk or were swim-ming in the Asturias. A thought about you never came into my head. The court has all the soporific virtues of Lethe, in the case of poor relations.

My family was completely obliterated from the tablets of my memory, when one morning a young man knocked at my door and begged to speak with me for a moment in private. He was shown into my closet, where, without asking him to take a chair, as he seemed to be quite a common fellow, I desired to know abruptly what he wanted. How ! Signor Gil Blas ? said he, do you not remember me? It was in vain that I perused the lines of his face over and over again; I was obliged to tell him fairly that he had the advantage of me. Why I am one of your old schoolfellows! replied he, bred and born in Oviedo; Bértrand Muscada, the grocer's son, next-door neighbor to your uncle the canon. I recollect you as well as if it was but yesterday. We have played a thousand times together at blind man's buff and prison bars.

My youthful recollections, answered I, are very transient and confused. Blind man's buff and prison bars are but childish amusement! The burden of state affairs leaves me little time to ruminate on the trifles of my younger days. I am come to Madrid, said he, to settle accounts with my father's correspondent. I heard talk of you! Folks say that you have a good berth at court, and are already almost as well off as a Jew broker. I thought I would just call in and say how d'ye do? On my return into the country, your family will jump out of their skins for joy, when they hear how famously you are getting on.

It was impossible in decency to avoid asking how my father, my mother, and my uncle stood in the world; but that duty was performed in so gingerly a manner, as to leave the grocer little room to compliment dame Nature on her liberal provision of instinct. He seemed quite shocked at my indifference for such near kindred, and told me bluntly, with his coarse shopman's familiarity, Methinks you might have shown more heartiness and natural feeling for your kinsfolk! Why, you ask after them just as if they were vermin! Your father and mother are still at service; take that in your dish! And the good canon, Gil Perez, eat up with gout, rheumatism, and old age, has one foot in the grave. People should feel as people ought; and seeing that you are in a berth to be a blessing to your poor parents, take a friend's advice, and allow them two hundred pistoles a year. That will be doing a handsome thing, and making them comfortable, and then you may spend the rest upon yourself with a good conscience. Instead of being softened by this family picture, I only resented the officiousness of unasked advice. A more delicate and covert remonstrance might perhaps have made its impression, but so bold a rebuke only hardened my heart. My sulky silence was not lost upon him, so that while he moralized himself out of charity into downright abuse, my choler began to overflow. Nay, then! this is too much, answered I, in a devil of a passion. Get about your business, Master Muscada, and mind your own shop. You are a pretty fellow to preach to me! As if I were to be taught my duty by you. Without further parley I handed the grocer out of my closet by the shoulder, and sent him off to weigh figs and nutmegs at Oviedo.

The home-strokes he had laid on were not lost to my sober recollection. My neglect of filial piety struck home to my heart, and melted me into tears. When I recollected how much my childhood was indebted to my parents, what pains they had taken in my education, these affecting thoughts gave language for the moment to the still small voice of nature and gratitude; but the language was never translated into solid sense and service. An habitual callousness succeeded this transient sensation, and peremptorily canceled every obligation of humanity. There are many fathers besides mine, who will acknowledge this portrait of their sons.

Avarice and ambition, dividing me between them, annihilated every trace of my former temper. I lost all my gayety, became absent and moping,—in short, a most unsociable animal. Fabricio seeing me so furiously bent on accumulation, and so perfetly indifferent to him, very rarely came to see me. He could not help saying one day: In truth, Gil Blas you are quite an altered man. Before you were about the court, you were always pleasant and easy. Now you are all agitation and turmoil. You form project after project to make a fortune, and the more you realize, the wider your views of aggrandizement extend. But this is not the worst! You have no longer that expansion of heart, those open manners, which form the charm of friendship. On the contrary, you wrap yourself round, and shut the avenues of your heart even to me. In your very civilities, I detect the violence you impose upon yourself. In short, Gil Blas is no longer the same Gil Blas whom I once knew.

You really have a most happy talent for bantering, answered I, with repulsive jocularity. But this metamorphose into the shag of a savage is not perceptible to myself. Your own eyes, replied he, are insensible to the change, because they are fascinated. But the fact remains the same. Now, my friend, tell me fairly and honestly, shall we live together as heretofore? When I used to knock at your door in the morning, you came and opened it yourself, between asleep and awake, and I walked in without ceremony. Now, what a difference! You have an establishment of servants. They keep me cooling my heels in your ante-chamber; my name must be sent in before I can speak to you. When this is got over, what is my reception? A cold inclination of the head, and the insolent strut of office. Any one would suppose that my visits were growing troublesome! Can you suppose this to be treatment for a man who was once on equal terms with you? No, Santillane, it can never be, nor will I bear it longer. Farewell! Let us part without ill blood. We shall both be better asunder; you will get rid of a troublesome censor, and I of a purse-proud upstart who does not know himself.

I felt myself more exasperated than reformed by his reproaches; and suffered him to take his departure without the slightest effort to overcome his resolution. In the present temper of my mind, the friendship of a poet did not seem a catch of sufficient importance to break one's heart about its loss. I found ample amends in the intimacy of some subaltern attendants about the king's person, with whom a similarity of humor had lately connected me closely. These new acquaintance of mine were for the most part men from no one knows where, pushed up to their appointments more by luck than merit. They had all got into warm berths; and, wretches as they were, measuring their own consequence by the excess of royal bounty, forgot their origin as scandalously as I forgot mine. We gave ourselves infinite credit for what told so much and bitterly to our disgrace. O fortune! what a jade you are, to distribute your favors at hap-hazard as you do! Epictetus was perfectly in the right, when he likened you to a jilt of fashion, prowling about in masquerade, and tipping the wink to every blackguard who parades the street.

BOOK THE NINTH.

CHAPTER I.

SCIPIO'S SCHEME OF MARRIAGE FOR GIL BLAS. THE MATCH, A RICH GOLDSMITH'S DAUGHTER. CIRCUMSTANCES CONNECTED WITH THIS SPECULATION.

ONE evening, on the departure of my supper company, finding myself alone with Scipio, I asked him what he had been doing that day. Striking a master-stroke, answered he. I intend that you should marry. A goldsmith of my acquaintance has an only daughter, and I mean to make up a match between you.

A goldsmith's daughter! exclaimed I with a disdainful air: are you out of your senses? Can you think of tying me up to a trinket-maker? People of a certain character in society and on a certain footing at court, ought to have much higher views of things. Pardon me, sir! rejoined Scipio, do not take the subject up in that light. Recollect that nobility accrues by the male side, and do not ride a higher horse than a thousand jockeys of quality whom I could name. Do you know that the heiress in question will bring a hundred thousand ducats in her pocket? Is not that a pretty little sprig of jewelry? To the resounding echo of so large a sum, my ears were instantly symphonious. The day is your own, said I to the secretary; the fortune determines the case in the lady's favor. When do you mean to put me in possession? Fair and softly, sir, answered he, the more haste the worse speed. It will be necessary for me first to communicate the affair to the father, and instill the advantage of it into his capacity. Good! rejoined I with a burst of laughter; is it thereabouts you are? The match is far advanced in its progress towards consummation. Much nearer than you suppose, replied he. But one hour's conversation with the goldsmith, and I pledge myself for his consent. But, before we go any further, let us come to an agreement, if you please. Supposing that I should transfer a hundred thousand ducats to you, what would my commission be? Twenty thousand! was my answer. Heaven be praised therefore! said he. I guessed your gratitude at ten thousand; so that it doubles mine in a similar case. Come on then! I will set this negotiation on foot to-morrow morning; and you may count upon its success, or I am little better than one of the foolish ones.

In fact, he said to me two days afterwards, I have spoken to Signor Gabriel Salero, my friend the goldsmith. On the loud report of your high desert and credit, he has lent a favorable ear to my offer of you for a son-in-law. You are to have his daughter with a hundred thousand ducats, provided you can make it appear clearly that you are in possession of the minister's good graces. Since that is the case, said I confidently to Scipio, I shall soon be married. But, not entirely to forgot the girl, have you seen her? is she pretty? Not quite so pretty as her fortune, answered he. Between ourselves, this heiress' looks are as hard as her cash. Luckily you are perfectly indifferent about that. Stone blind, by the light of the sun, my good fellow! replied I. As for us whimsical fellows about court, we marry merely for the sake of marrying. When we want beauty, we look for it in our friends' wives; and if, by fates and destinies, the sweets are wasted on our own, their flavor is so mawkish to our palate, that there is some merit in their not carrying the commodity to a foreign market.

This is not all, resumed Scipio: Signor Gabriel hopes for the pleasure of your company to supper this evening. By agreement, there is to be no mention of marriage. He has invited several of his mercantile friends to this entertainment, where you will take your chance with the rest, and to-morrow he means to sup with you on the same terms. By this you will perceive his drift of looking before he leaps. You will do well to be a little on your guard before him. Oh! for the matter of that, interrupted I with an air of confidence, let him scrutinize me as closely as he pleases, the result cannot fail to be in my favor.

All this happened as it was foretold. I was introduced at the goldsmith's, who received me with the familiarity of an old acquaintance. A vulgar dog, but warm; and as troublesome with his civility as a prude with her virtue. He presented me to Signora Eugenia his wife, and the youthful Gabriela his daughter. I opened wide my budget of compliments, without infringing the treaty, and prattled soft nothings to them, in all the vacuity of courtly dialogue.

Gabriela, with submission to my secretary's better taste, was not altogether so repulsive; whether by dint of being outrageously bedizened, or because I looked at her in the raree-show box of her fortune. A charming house this of Signor Gabriel! There is less silver, I verily believe, in the Peruvian mines, than under his roof. That metal presented itself to the view in all directions, under a thousand different forms. Every room, and especially that where we were entertained, was a fairy palace. What a bird's eye view for a son-in-law! The old codger, to do the thing genteelly, had collected five or six merchants about him, all plodding spirit-wearing personages. Their tongues could only talk of what their hearts were set upon; it was high change all supper-time; but unfortunately wit was at a discount.

Next night, it was my turn to treat the goldsmith. Not being able to dazzle him with my sideboard, I had recourse to another

"HE PRESENTED ME TO SIGNORA EUGENIA HIS WIFE."

artifice. I invited to supper such of my friends as made the finest figure at court; hangers-on of state, noted for the unwieldiness of their ambition. These fellows could not talk on common topics: the brilliant and lucrative posts at which they aimed were all canvassed in detail; this too made its way. Poor counting-house Gabriel, in amazement at the loftiness of their ideas, shrunk into insignificance, in spite of all his hoards, on a comparison with these wonderful men. As for me, in all the plausibility of moderation, I professed to wish for nothing more than a comfortable fortune; a snug box and a competence: whereupon these gluttons of the loaves and fishes cried out with one voice that I was wrong, absolutely criminal; for the prime minister would do anything upon earth for me, and it was an act of duty to anoint my fingers with bird-lime. My honored papa lost not a word of all this; and seemed, at going away, to take his leave with some complacency.

Scipio went of course the next morning, to ask him how he liked me. Extremely well indeed, answered the knight of the ledger; the lad has won my very heart. But, good master Scipio, I conjure you by our long acquaintance to deal with me as a true friend. Tell me where Signor de Santillane is fallible. Is he fond of play? does he wench? On what lay are his snug little vices? Do not fight shy, I beseech you. It is very unkind, Signor Gabriel, to put such a question, retorted the go-between. Your interest is more to me than my master's. If he had any slippery propensities, likely to make your daughter unhappy, would I ever have proposed him as a son-in-law? The deuce a bit! I am too much at your service. But, between ourselves, he has but one fault; that of being faultless. He is too wise for a young man. So much the better, replied the goldsmith; he is the more like me. You may go, my friend, and tell him he shall have my daughter, and should have her though he knew no more of the minister than I do.

As soon as my secretary had reported this conversation, I flew to thank Salero for his partiality. He had already told his mind to his wife and daughter, who gave me to understand by their reception, that they yielded without disgust. I carried my father-in-law to the Duke of Lerma, whom I had informed the evening before, and presented him with due ceremony. His excellency gave him a most gracious reception, and congratulated him on having chosen a man for his son-in-law, for whom he himself had so great a regard, and meant to do such great things. Then did he expatiate on my good qualities, and, in fact, said so much to my honor, that honest Gabriel thought he had met with the best match in Spain. His joy oozed out at his eyes. On parting, he pressed me in his arms, and said: My son, I am so impatient to see you Gabriela's husband, that the affair shall be finally settled within a week at latest.

CHAPTER II.

IN THE PROGRESS OF POLITICAL VACANCIES, GIL BLAS RECOLLECTS THAT THERE IS SUCH A MAN IN THE WORLD AS DON ALPHONSO DE LEYVA; AND RENDERS HIM A SERVICE FROM MOTIVES OF VANITY.

LET us leave my marriage to take care of itself for a season. The order of events requires me to recount a service rendered to my old master Don Alphonso. I had entirely forgotten that gentleman's existence; but a circumstance recalled it to my recollection.

The government of Valencia became vacant at this time; and put me in mind of Don Alphonso de Leyva, I considered within myself that the employment would suit him to a nicety; and determined to apply for it on his behalf, not so much out of friendship as ostentation. If I could but procure it for him, it would do me infinite honor. I told the Duke of Lerma that I had been steward to Don Cæsar de Leyva and his son; and that having every reason in the world to feel myself obliged to them, I should take it as a favor if he would give the government of Valencia to one or other of them. The minister answered: Most willingly, Gil Blas. I love to see you grateful and generous. Besides, the family stands very high in my esteem. The Leyvas are loyal subjects; so that the place cannot be better bestowed. You may take it as a wedding present, and do what you like with it.

Delighted at the success of my application, I went to Calderona in a prodigious hurry, to get the patent made out for Don Alphonso. There was a great crowd, waiting in respectful silence till Don Rodrigo should come and give audience. I made my way through, and the closet door opened as if by sympathy. There were no one knows how many military and civil officers, with other people of consequence, among whom Calderona was dividing his attentions. His different reception of different people was curious. A slight inclination of the head was enough for some; others he honored with a profusion of courtly grimace, and bowed them out of the closet. The proportions of civility were weighed to a scruple. On the other hand, there were some suitors who, shocked at his cold indifference, cursed in their secret soul the necessity for their cringing before such a monkey of an idol. Others, on the contrary, were laughing in their sleeve at his gross and self-sufficient air. But the scene was thrown away upon me; nor was I likely to profit by such a lesson. It was exactly the counterpart of my own behavior: and I never thought of ascertaining whether my deportment was popular or offensive, so long as there was no violation of outward respect.

Don Rodrigo accidentally casting a look towards me, left a gentleman, to whom he was speaking, without ceremony, and came to pay his respects with the most unaccountable tokens of high consideration. Ah, my dear colleague! exclaimed he, what occasion procures me the pleasure of seeing you here! Is there anything we can do for you? I told him my business; whereupon he assured me, in the most obliging terms, that the affair should be expedited within four-and-twenty hours. Not satisfied with these overwhelming condescensions, he conducted me to the door of his ante-chamber, whither he never attended any but the nobility of first rank. His farewell was as flattering as his reception.

What is the meaning of all this palaver? said I while retreating; has any raven croaked my entrance, and prophesied promotion to Calderona by my overthrow? Does he really languish for my friendship? or does he feel the ground giving way under his feet, and wish to save himself by clinging to the branches of my favor and protection? It seemed a moot point, which of these conjectures might be the right. The following day, on my return, his behavior was of the same stamp; caresses and civilities poured in upon me in torrents. It is true that other people who attempted to speak to him, were rumped in exact proportion with the blandishments of his face towards me. He snarled at some, petrified others, and made the whole circle run the gauntlet of his displeasure. But they were all amply avenged by an occurrence, the relation of which may give a gentle hint to all the clerks and secretaries on the list of my readers.

A man very plainly dressed, and certainly not looking at all like what he was, came up to Calderona and spoke to him about a memorial, stated to have been presented by himself to the Duke of Lerma. Don Rodrigo, without looking from his clothes up to his face, said in a sharp, ungracious tone—Who may you happen to be, honest man? They called me Francillo in my childhood, answered the stranger unabashed; my next style and title was that of Don Francillo de Zuniga; and my present name is the Count de Pedrosa. Calderona was all in a twitter at this discovery, and attempted to stammer out an excuse, when he found that he had to do with a man of the first quality. Sir, said he to the Count, I have to beg you ten thousand pardons; but not knowing whom I had the honor to . . . . . . I want none of your apologies, interrupted Francillo with proud indignation; they are as nauseous as your rudeness was unbecoming. Recollect henceforth, that a minister's secretary ought to receive all descriptions of people with good manners. You may be vain enough to affect the representative of your master, but the public know you for his menial servant.

The haughty Don Rodrigo blushed blue at this rebuke. Yet it did not mend his manners one whit. On me it made a salutary impression. I determined to take care and ascertain the rank of my petitioners, before I gave a loose to the insolence of office, and to inflict torture only upon mutes. As Don Alphonso's patent was made out, I sent it by a purpose messenger, with a letter from the Duke of Lerma, announcing the royal favor. But I took no notice of my own share in the appointment, nor even accompanied it with a line, in the fond hope of announcing it by word of mouth, and surprising him agreeably, when he came to the court on occasion of taking the customary oaths,

CHAPTER III.

PREPARATIONS FOR THE MARRIAGE OF GIL BLAS. A SPOKE IN
THE WHEEL OF HYMEN.

AND now once more for my lovely Gabriela! We were to be married in a week. Preparations were making on both sides for the ceremony. Salero ordered a rich wardrobe for the bride, and I hired a waiting-woman for her, a footman, and a gentleman usher of decent aspect and advanced years. The whole establishment was provided by Scipio, who longed more longingly than myself for the hour when we were to be fingering the fortune.

On the evening before the happy day, I was supping with my father-in-law, the rest of the company being made up of uncles, aunts, and cousins of either sex and every degree. The part of a supple-visaged son-in-law sat upon me to perfection. Nothing could exceed my profound respect for the goldsmith and his wife, or the transports of my passion at Gabriela's feet, while I smoothed my way into the graces of the family, by listening with impregnable patience to their witless repartees and irrational ratiocinations. Thus did I gain the great end of all my forbearance, the pleasure of pleasing my new relations. Every individual of the clan felt himself a foot taller for the honor of my alliance.

The repast ended, the company moved into a large room, where we were entertained with a concert of vocal and instrumental music, not the worst that was ever heard, though the performers were not selected from the choicest bands at Madrid. Some lively airs put us in mind of dancing. Heaven knows what sort of performers we must have been, when they took me for the coryphæus of the opera, though I never had but two or three lessons from a petty dancing-master, who taught the pages on the establishment of the Marchioness de Chaves. After we had tired our tendons, it was time to think of going home. There was no end of my bows and God-bless-you's. Farewell, my dear son-in-law, said Salero as he squeezed my hand, I shall be at your house in the morning with the portion in ready money. You will be welcome, come when you list, my dear father-in-law, answered I. Afterwards, wishing the family good-night, I jumped into my carriage, and ordered it to drive home.

Scarcely had I got two hundred yards from Signor Gabriel's house, when fifteen or twenty men, some on foot and some on horseback, all with swords and fire-arms, surrounded and stopped the coach, crying out, *In the name of our sovereign lord the king.* They dragged me out by main force, and thrust me into a hack-chaise, when the leader of the party got in with me, and ordered the driver to go for Segovia. There could be no doubt but the honest gentleman by my side was an alguazil. I wanted to know something about the cause of my arrest, but he answered in the language of those gentry, which is very bad language, that he had other things to do than to satisfy my impertinent curiosity. I suggested that he might have mistaken his man. No, no, retorted he, the fool is wiser than that. You are Signor de Santillane: and in that case you are to go along with me. Not being able to deny that fact, it became an act of prudence to hold my tongue. For the remainder of the night we traversed Mancanarez in sulky silence, changed horses at Colmenar, and arrived the next evening at Segovia, where the lodging provided for me was in the tower

---

CHAPTER IV.

THE TREATMENT OF GIL BLAS IN THE TOWER OF SEGOVIA. THE CAUSE OF HIS IMPRISONMENT.

THEIR first favor was to clap me up in a cell, where they left me on the straw like a criminal, whose only earthly portion was to con over his dying speech in solitude. I passed the night, not in bewailing my fate, for it had not yet presented itself in all its aggravation, but in endeavoring to divine its cause. Doubtless it must have been Calderona's handiwork. And yet though his branching honors might have pressed thick upon his senses, I could not conceive how the Duke of Lerma could have been induced to treat me so inhumanly. Sometimes I apprehended my arrest to have been without his excellency's knowledge; at other times I thought him the contriver of it, for some political reasons, such as weigh with ministers when they sacrifice their accomplices at the shrine of state policy.

My mind was vibrating to and fro with these various conjectures, when the dawn peeping in at my little grated window, presented to my sight all the horror of the place where I was confined. Then did I vent my sorrows without ceasing, and my eyes became two springs of tears, flowing inexhaustibly at the remembrance of my prosperous state. Pending this paroxysm of grief, a turnkey brought me my day's allowance of bread and water. He looked at me, and on the contemplation of my tear-besprinkled visage, jailer as he was, there came over him a sentiment of pity: Do not despair, said he. This life is full of crosses, but mind them not. You are young; after these days, you will live to see better. In the mean time, eat at the king's mess, with what appetite you may.

My comforter withdrew with this quaint invitation, answered by my groans and tears. The rest of the day was spent in cursing my wayward destiny, without thinking of my empty stomach. As for the royal morsel, it seemed more like the message of wrath than the boon of benevolence; the tantalizing protraction of pain, rather than the solace of affliction.

Night came, and with it the rattle of a key in my keyhole. My dungeon door opened, and in came a man with a wax-light in his hand. He advanced towards me, saying—Signor Gil Blas, behold in me one of your old friends. I am Don Andrew de Tordesillas, in the Archbishop of Grenada's service while you enjoyed that prelate's favor. You may recollect engaging his interest in my behalf, and thereby procuring me a post in Mexico; but instead of embarking for the Indies, I stopped in the town of Alicant. There I married the governor's daughter, and by a series of adventures, of which you shall hereafter have the particulars, I am now warden of this tower. It is expressly forbidden me to let you speak to any living soul, to give you any better bed than straw, or any other suste-

nance than bread and water. But besides that your misfortunes interest my humanity, you have done me service, and gratitude countervails the harshness of my orders. They think to make me the instrument of their cruelty, but it is my better purpose to soften the rigor of your capacity. Get up and and follow me.

Though my humane keeper was entitled to some acknowledgment, my spirits were so affected as to interdict my speech. All I could do was to attend him. We crossed a court, and mounted a narrow staircase to a little room at the top of the tower. It was no small surprise, on entering, to find a table with lights on it, neatly

set out with covers for two. They will serve up immediately,
said Tordesillas. We are going to sup together. This snug retreat
is appointed for your lodging; it will agree better with you than
your cell. From your window you will look down on the flowery
banks of the Eréma, and the delicious vale of Coca, bounded by
the mountains which divide the two Castiles. At first you will
care little for prospects: but when time shall have softened

"LET US SAY GRACE, AND FALL TO."

your keener sensations into a composed melancholy, it will be a
pleasure to feast your eyes on such engaging scenes. Then, as for
linen and other necessaries befitting a man accustomed to the comforts of life, they shall be always at your service. Your bed and
board shall be such as you could wish, with a plentiful supply of
books. In a word, you shall have everything but your liberty.

My spirits were a little tranquilized by these obliging offers. I
took courage and returned my best thanks, assuring him that his

generous conduct restored me to life, and that I hoped at some time or other to find an opportunity of testifying my gratitude. To be sure! and why should you not? answered he. Did you fancy yourself a prisoner for life? Nothing less likely! and I would lay a wager that you will be released in a very few months. What say you, Signor Don Andrew? exclaimed I. Then surely you are acquainted with the occasion of my misfortune. You guess right, replied he. The alguazil who brought you hither told me the whole story in confidence. The king, hearing that the Count de Lemos and you were in the habit of escorting the Prince of Spain by nigh: to a house of suspicious character, as a punishment for your loose morals, has banished the count, and sent you hither, to be treated in the style of which you have had a specimen. And how, said I did that circumstance come to the king's knowledge? That is what I am most curious to ascertain. And that, answered he, is precisely what the alguazil did not tell, apparently because he did not know.

At this epoch of our conversation, the servants brought in supper. When everything was set in order, Tordesillas sent away the attendants, not wishing our conversation to be overheard. He shut the door, and we took our seats opposite to each other. Let us say grace, and fall to, said he. Your appetite ought to be good after two days of fasting. Under this impression he loaded my plate as if he had been cramming the craw of a starveling. In fact, nothing was more likely than that I should play the devil among the ragouts; but what is likely does not always happen. Though my intestines were yearning for support, their staple stuck in my throat, for my heart loathed all pleasurable indulgence in the present state of my affairs. In vain did my warden, to drive away the blue devils, pledge me continually, and expatiate on the excellence of his wine; imperishable nectar would have been pricked according to the fastidious report of my palate. This being the case, he went another way to work, and told me the story of his marriage, with as much humor as such a subject would admit. Here he was still less successful. So wandering was my attention, that before the end I had forgotten the beginning and the middle. At length he was convinced that there was no diverting my gloomy thoughts for that evening. After finishing his solitary supper, he rose from table, saying: Signor de Santillane, I shall leave you to your repose, or rather to the free indulgence of your own reveries. But, take my word for it, your misfortune will not be of long continuance. The king is naturally good. When his anger shall have passed away, and your deplorable estate shall occur to his milder thoughts, your punishment will appear sufficient in his eyes. With these words, my kind-hearted jailer went down stairs, and sent the servants to take away. Not even the brass candlesticks were left behind; and I went to bed by the palpable darkness of a glimmering lamp suspended against the wall.

CHAPTER V.

HIS REFLECTIONS BEFORE HE WENT TO SLEEP THAT NIGHT, AND
THE NOISE THAT WAKED HIM.

TWO hours at least were my thoughts employed on what Tordesillas had told me. Here, then, am I, for having lent myself to the
pleasures of the heir-apparent! It was certainly not having my
wits about me, to pander for so young a prince. Therein consists
my crime; had he been arrived at a more knowing age, the king
perhaps might only have laughed at what has now made him so
angry. But who can have given such counsel to the monarch,
without dreading the prince's resentment or the Duke of Lerma's?
That minister will doubtless take ample vengeance for his nephew
the Count de Lemos. How can the king have made the discovery?
That is above my comprehension.

This last was the eternal burden of my song. But the idea most
afflictive to my mind, what drove me to despair, and laid fiend-like
hold upon my fancy, was the unquestioned plunder of my effects.
My strong box, exclaimed I, my dear wealth, what is become of
you? Into what hands have you fallen? Alas! you are lost in
less time than you were gained. The ruinous confusion of my
household was the perpetual death's-head of my imagination. Yet
this wilderness of melancholy ideas sheltered me from absolute distraction; sleep, which had shunned my wretched straw, now paid
his readier visit to my soft and gentlemanly couch. Watching and
wine, too, imparted a strong narcotic to his poppies. My slumbers
were profound; and to all appearance, the day might have peeped
in upon my repose, if I had not been awakened all at once by such
sounds as rarely perforate a prison wall. I heard the thrum
of a guitar, accompanying a man's voice. My whole attention was
absorbed; but the invisible musician paused, and left the fleeting
impression of a dream. An instant afterwards, my ear was soothed
with the sound of the same instrument, and the same voice.

> Wisely the ant against poor winter hoards
> The stock which summer's wealth affords;
> In grasshoppers, that must at autumn die,
> How vain were such an industry!
>
> Of love or fortune the deceitful light
> Might half excuse our cheated sight,
> If it of life the whole small time would stay,
> And be our sunshine all the day.*

These verses, which sounded as if they had been sung expressly
for the dirge of my departed happiness, were only an aggravation of

---

* To have substituted, with a slight variation, these two stanzas from Cowley for a
translation of the common-place couplet in the original, will probably not be thought
to require any apology. They necessarily involve a change in the consequent reflections of our hero.   TRANSLATOR.

my feelings. The truth of the sentiment, said I, is but too well exemplified in me. The meteor of court favor has but plunged me in substantial darkness; the summer sunshine of ambition is quenched in these autumnal glooms. Now did I sink again into cold and comfortless meditation; my miseries began to flow afresh, as if they fed and grew upon their own vital stream. Yet my wailings ended with the night; and the first rays which played upon my chamber wall amused my mind into composure. I got up to open my window, and let the vivid air of morning into my room. Then I glanced over the country, so attractively depicted in the description of my keeper. It did not seem to justify his panegyric. The Erêma, a second Tagus in my magnifying fancy, was little better than a brook. Its flowery banks were fringed with nettles, and arrayed in all the majesty of thistles; the delicious vale in this fairy prospect was a barren wilderness, untamed by human labor. It therefore was very evident that my keener sensations were not yet softened into such a composed melancholy, as could give any but a jaundiced coloring to the landscape.

I began dressing, and had already half finished my toilet, when Tordesillas ushered in an old chambermaid, laden with shirts and towels. Signor Gil Blas, said he, here is your linen. Do not be saving of it; there shall always be as many changes as you can possibly want. Well now! and how have you passed the night? Has the drowsy god administered his anodyne? I could have slept till this time, answered I, if I had not been awakened by a voice singing to a guitar. The cavalier who has disturbed your repose, resumed he, is a state prisoner; and his chamber is contiguous to yours. He is a knight of the military order of Calatrava, and is a very accomplished person. His name is Don Gaston de Cogollos. You may meet as often as you like, and take your meals together. It will afford reciprocal consolation to compare your fortunes. There can be no doubt of your being agreeable to one another. I assured Don Andrew how sensible I was of his indulgence in allowing me to blend my sorrows with those of my fellow-sufferer; and, as I betrayed some impatience to be acquainted with him, our accommodating warden met my wishes on the very same day. He fixed me to dine with Don Gaston, whose prepossessing physiognomy and symmetry of feature struck me sensibly. Judge what it must have been, to make so strong an impression on eyes accustomed to encounter the dazzling exterior of the court. Figure to yourself a man fashioned in the mold of pleasure; one of those heroes in romance, who has only to show his face, and banish the sweet sleep from the eyelids of princesses. Add to this, that nature, who is generally bountiful with one hand and niggardly with the other, had crowned the perfections of Cogollos with wit and valor. He was a man, whose like, take him for all in all, we might not soon look upon again.

If this fine fellow was mightily to my taste, it was my good luck not to be altogether offensive to him. He no longer sang at night for fear of annoying me, though I begged him by no means to restrain his inclinations on my account. A bond of union is soon formed between brethren in misfortune. A close friendship succeeded to mere acquaintance, and strengthened from day to day. The liberty of uninterrupted intercourse contributed greatly to our mutual support; our burden become lighter by division.

One day after dinner I went into his room, just as he was tuning his guitar. To hear him more at my ease, I sat down on the only stool; while he, reclining on his bed, played a pathetic air, and sang to it a ditty, expressing the despair of a lover and the cruelty of his mistress. When he had finished, I said to him with a smile, Sir knight, such strains as these could never be applicable to your own successes with the fair. You were not made to cope with female repulse. You think too well of me, answered he. The verses you have just heard were composed to fit my own case; to soften a heart of adamant. You must hear my story, and in my story, my distresses.

CHAPTER VI.

HISTORY OF DON GASTON DE COGOLLOS AND DONNA HELENA DE GALISTEO.

IT will be very soon four years since I left Madrid to go and see my aunt Donna Eleonora de Laxarilla at Coria: she is one of the richest dowagers in Old Castile, with myself for her only heir. Scarcely had I got within her doors, when love invaded my repose. The windows of my room faced the lattice of a lady living opposite: but the street was narrow, and her blinds pervious to the eye. It was an opportunity too delicious to be lost; and I found my neighbor so lovely that my heart was captivated. The subject of my sentry-watch could not be mistaken. She marked it well; but she was not a girl to glory in the detection, still less to encourage my fooleries.

It was natural to inquire the name of this mighty conqueror. I learnt it to be Donna Helena, only daughter of Don George de Galisteo, lord of a large domain near Coria. She had innumerable offers of marriage; but her father repulsed them all, because he meant to bestow her hand on his nephew, Don Austin de Olighera, who had uninterrupted access to his cousin while the settlements were preparing. This was no bar to my hopes; on the contrary, it whetted my eagerness: and the insolent pleasure of supplanting a favored rival was, perhaps, at bottom equally my motive with a more noble passion. My visual artillery was obstinately planted against my unyielding fair. Her attendant Felicia was not without the incense of a glance, to soften her rigid constancy in my favor; while nods and becks stood for the current coin of language. But all these efforts of gallantry were in vain—the maid was impregnable like her mistress—never was there such a pair of cold and cruel ones.

The commerce of the eyes being so unthrifty, I had recourse to different agents. My scouts were on the watch to hunt out what acquaintance Felicia might have in town. They discovered an old lady, by name Theodora, to be her most intimate friend, and that they often met. Delighted at the intelligence, I went point blank to Theodora, and engaged her by presents in my interest. She took my cause up heartily, promised to contrive an interview for me with her friend, and kept her engagement the very next day.

I am no longer the wretch of yesterday, said I to Felicia, since my sufferings have melted you to pity. How deep is my debt to your friend for her kind interference in my behalf. Sir, answered she, Theodora can do what she pleases with me. She has brought me over to your side of the question; and if I can do you a kindness, you shall soon be at the summit of your wishes; but, with all my partiality in your favor, I know not how far my efforts may be successful. It would be cruel to mislead you : the prize will not be gained without a severe conflict. The object of your passion is betrothed to another gentleman, and her character most inauspicious to your designs. Such is her pride, and so closely locked are her secrets within her own breast, that if, by constancy and assiduities, you could extort from her a few sighs, fancy not that her haughty spirit would indulge your ears with their music. Ah ! my dear Felicia, exclaimed I in an agony, why will you thus magnify the obstacles in my way? To set them in array will kill me. Lead me on with false hopes, if you will ; but do not drive me to despair. With these words I took one of her hands, pressed it between mine, and slid a diamond on her finger value three hundred pistoles, with such a moving compliment as made her weep again.

Such speeches and corresponding actions deserve some scanty comfort. She smoothed a little the rugged path of love. Sir, said she, what I have just been telling you need not quite quench your hope. Your rival, it is true, is in possession of the ground. He comes back and fore as he pleases. He toys with her as often as he likes, but all that is in your favor. The habit of constant intercourse sheds a languor over their meetings. They part without pain, and come together without emotion. One would take them for man and wife. In a word, my mistress has no marks of violent love for Don Austin. Besides, in point of person, there is such a difference between you and him as cannot fail to catch the eye of a nice observer like Donna Helena. Therefore do not be cast down. Continue your particular attentions. You shall have a second in me. I shall let no opportunity escape of pointing out to my mistress the merit of all your exertions to please her. In vain shall she intrench herself behind reserve. In spite of guard and garrison, I will ransack the muster-roll of her sentiments.

Now were my open attacks and secret ambuscades more fiercely pointed against the daughter of Don George. Among the rest, I entertained her with a serenade. After the concert Felicia, to sound her mistress, begged to know how she had been entertained. The singer had a good voice, said Donna Helena. But how did you like the words? replied the abigail. I scarcely noted them returned the lady; the music engrossed my whole attention. The poetry excited as little curiosity as its author. If that is the case, exclaimed the chambermaid, poor Don Gaston de Cogollos is reckoning without his host; and a miserable spendthrift of his glances, to be always ogling at our lattice-work. Perhaps it may not be he, said the mistress with petrifying indifference, but some other spark, announcing his passion by this concert. Excuse me, answered Felicia, it is Don Gaston himself, who accosted me this morning in the street, and implored me to assure you how he adored, in defiance of your rigorous repulses: but that he should esteem himself the most blest of mortals, if you would allow him to soothe his desponding thoughts by all the most delicate and impassioned attentions. Judge now if I can be mistaken, after so open an avowal.

Don George's daughter changed countenance at once, and said to her servant with a severe frown, You might well have dispensed with the relation of this impertinent discourse. Bring me no more such idle tales; and tell this young madman, when next he accosts you, to play off his shallow artifices on some more accommodating fool; but, at all events, let him choose a more gentlemanly recreation than that of lounging all day at his window, and prying into the privacy of my apartment.

This message was faithfully delivered at my next interview with Felicia, who assured me that her mistress's modes of speech were not to be taken in their literal construction, but that my affairs were in the best possible train. For my part, being little read in the science of coquetry, and finding no favorable sense on the face of the author's original words, I was half out of humor with the wiredrawn comments of the critic. She laughed at my misgivings, and asked her friend for pen, ink, and paper, saying: Sir knight of the doleful countenance, write immediately to Donna Helena as dolefully as you look. Make echo ring with your sufferings; outsigh the river's murmur; and, above all, let rocks and woods resound with the prohibition of appearing at your window. Then pawn your existence on obeying her, though without the possibility ever to redeem the pledge. Turn all that nonsense into pretty sentences, as you gay deceivers so well know how to do, and leave the rest to me. The event, I flatter myself, will redound more than you are aware to the honor of my penetration.

He must have been a strange lover who would not have profited by so opportune an occasion of writing to his mistress. My letter was couched in the most pathetic terms. Felicia smiled at its contents; and said, that if the women knew the art of infatuating men, the men in return had borrowed their influence over women from the arch wheedler himself. My privy councilor took the note, and went back to Don George's, with a special injunction that my windows should be fast shut for some days.

Madam, said she, going up to Donna Helena, I met Don Gaston. He must needs endeavor to come round me with his flattering speeches. In tremulous accents like a culprit pleading against his sentence, he begged to know whether I had spoken to you on his behalf. Then, in prompt and faithful compliance with your orders, I snapped up the words out of his mouth. To be sure, my tongue did run at a fine rate against him. I called him all manner of names, and left him in the street like a stock, staring at my termagant loquacity. I am delighted, answered Donna Helena, that you have disengaged me from that troublesome person. But there was no occasion to have snubbed him so unmercifully. A creature of your degree should always keep a good tongue in its mouth. Madam, replied the domestic, one cannot get rid of a determined lover by mincing one's words, though it comes to much the same thing when one flies into a passion. Don Gaston, for instance, was not to be bullied out of his senses. After having given it him on both sides of his ears, as I told you, I went on that errand of yours to the house of your relation. The lady, as ill-luck would have it, kept me longer than she ought. I say longer than she ought, because my plague and torment met me on my return. Who the deuce would have thought of seeing him? It put me all in a twitter; but then my tongue, which at other times is apt to be in a twitter, stuck motionless in my mouth. While my tongue stuck motionless in my mouth, what did he do? He slid a paper into my hand without giving me time to consider whether I should take it or no, and made off in a moment.

After this introduction, she drew my letter from under her stays, and gave it with half a banter to her mistress, who affected to read it in humorous scorn, but digested the contents most greedily, and then put on the starch, offended prude. In good earnest, Felicia, said she with all the gravity she could assume, you were extremely off your guard, quite bewildered and fascinated, to have taken the charge of an epistle. What construction would Don Gaston put upon it? What must I think of it myself? You give me reason, by this strange behavior, to mistrust your fidelity, while he must suspect me of encouraging his odious suit. Alas! he may, perhaps, lay that flattering unction to his soul, that my love is legible in these characters, and not his trespass. Only consider how you lay my towering pride. Oh! quite the reverse, madam, answered the petticoated pleader; it is impossible for him to think that; and if he did, he would soon be convinced with a flea in his ear. I shall tell him, when next we meet, that I have delivered his letter, that you glanced at the superscription with petrifying indifference, and then, without reading a word, tore it into a thousand pieces. You may swear that I did not read it with a safe conscience, replied Donna Helena. I should be puzzled to retrace a single sentiment. Don George's daughter, not contented with these words, suited the action to them, tore my letter, and imposed silence on my advocate.

As I had promised no longer to play the lover at my window, the farce of obedience was kept up for several days. Ogling being interdicted, my courtship was doomed to enter in at my Helena's obdurate ears. One night I attended under her balcony with musicians; the first bars of the serenade were already playing, when a swaggering blade, sword in hand, rushed in upon our harmony, laying about him to the right and left, to the utter discomfiture of the troop. Such mad warfare fired my tilting propensities to equal fury. The affray became serious. Donna Helena and her maid were disturbed by the clash of swords. They looked out at their lattice, and saw two men engaged. Their cries roused Don George and his servants. The whole neighborhood was assembled to part the combatants. But they came too late; on the field of battle, bathed in his own blood and almost lifeless, lay my unfortunate body. They carried me to my aunt's and sent for the best surgical assistance in the place.

All the world was merciful, and wished me well, especially Donna Helena, whose heart was now unmasked. Her forced severity yielded to her natural feelings. Would you believe it? The cold, relentless, insensible, was kindled into the warmest of love's votaries. She wore out the remainder of the night in weeping with her faithful confidante, and giving her cousin, Don Austin de Olighera, to perdition: for him they taxed with the plotted massacre, and the bill was a true one. He could hide his heart as well as his cousin; he therefore watched my motions, without seeming to suspect them; and fancying them not to be without a corresponding impulse, he resolved not to be sacrificed with impunity. The accident was an awkward one to me, but it ended in overpowering rapture. Dangerous as my wound was, the surgeons soon brought me about. I was still confined to my chamber, when my aunt, Donna Eleonora, went over to Don George, and made proposals for Donna Helena. He consented the more readily to the marriage, as he never expected to see Don Austin again. The good old man was afraid of his daughter's not liking me, because cousin Olighera had kept her company; but she was so tractable to the parental behest, as to furnish grounds for believing that in Spain, as in other countries, the species, not the individual, is the object with the sex.

Felicia, at our first private meeting, communicated the emotions of her mistress on my misfortune. Now, like another Paris, I thought Troy well lost for my Helen, and blessed the happy consequences of my wound. Don George allowed me to speak with his daughter in presence of her attendant. What a heavenly interview! I begged and prayed the lady so earnestly to tell me whether her sufferance of my vows was forced upon her by her father, that she at length professed her obedience to be in unison with her inclinations. After so delicious a declaration, my whole soul was given up to love and pleasurable gratifications. Our nuptials were to be graced by a magnificent procession of all the principal people in Coria and the neighborhood.

I gave a splendid party at my aunt's country-house, in the suburbs on the side of Manroi. Don George, his daughter, the family, and friends on both sides were present. There was a concert of vocal and instrumental music, with a company of strolling players, to represent a comedy. In the middle of the festivities, some one whispered me that a man wanted to speak with me in the hall. I got up from table to go and see who it was. The stranger looked like a gentleman's servant. He put a letter into my hand, containing these words: "If you have any sense of honor, as a knight of your order ought to have, you will not fail to attend to-morrow morning in the plain of Manroi. There you will find an antagonist, ready to give you your revenge for his former attack upon your person, or, what he rather hopes and meditates, to spoil your connubial transports with Donna Helena. "DON AUSTIN DE OLIGHERA."

If love is a Spanish passion, revenge is the Spanish lunacy. Such a note as this was not to be read with composure. At the mere subscription of Don Austin, there kindled in my veins a fire, which almost made me forget the claims of hospitality. I was tempted to steal away from my company, and seek my antagonist on the instant. For fear of disturbing the merriment, however, I bridled in my rage, and said to the messenger: My friend, you may tell your employer that I shall meet him on the appointed spot at sun-rise, and resume the contest with obstinacy equal to his own.

After sending this answer, I resumed my seat at table with so composed a mien, that no creature had the least suspicion of what had occurred. During the rest of the day, I gave myself up to the pleasures of the festival, which ended not till midnight. The guests then returned to town, but I staid behind, under pretext of taking the air on the following morning. Instead of going to bed, I watched for the dawn with maddening impatience. With the first ray I got on horseback, and rode alone towards Manroi. On the plain was a horseman, riding up to me at full speed. I pushed forward, and we met half-way. It was my rival. Knight, said he, superciliously, it is against my will that I meet you a second time on the same occasion, but you have brought your fate on yourself. After the adventure of the serenade, you ought to have waived your pretensions to Don George's daughter, or at least to have been assured that the support of them must cost you dearer than a single encounter. You are too much elated, answered I, with an advantage which is less owing, perhaps, to your superior skill, than to the darkness of the night. Remember, that victory is of the same blind family with fortune. It shall be my lot to teach you, replied he with insulting scorn, that I have unsealed the eyes of both.

At this proud defiance, we both dismounted, tied our horses to a tree, and engaged with equal fury. I must candidly acknowledge the prowess of my antagonist, who was a consummate master of fencing. My life was exposed to the greatest possible danger. Nevertheless, as the strong is often vanquished by the weak, my rival, in spite of all his science, received a thrust through the heart, and fell a lifeless corpse.

I immediately returned, and told a confidential servant what had happened, requesting him to take horse and acquaint my aunt, before the officers of justice could get intelligence of the event. He was also to obtain from her a supply of money and jewels, and then join me at the first inn as you enter Plazencia.

All this was performed within three hours. Donna Eleonora rather triumphed than mourned over a catastrophe, which restored my injured honor; and sent me large remittances for my travels abroad, till the affair had blown over.

Not to dwell on indifferent circumstances, suffice it to say, that I embarked for Italy, and equipped myself so as to make a respectable figure at the several courts.

While I was endeavoring to beguile the weary hours of absence, Helena was weeping at home from the same cause. Instead of joining in the family resentment, her heart was panting for a compromise, and for my speedy return. Six months had already elapsed, and I firmly believe that her constancy would have been proof against the track of time, had time been seconded by no more powerful ally. Don Blas de Combados, a gentleman from the western coast of Galicia, came to Coria, to take possession of a rich inheritance unsuccessfully contested by a near relation. He liked that country so much better than his own, that he made it his principal residence. Combados was a personable man. His manners were gentle and well-bred, his conversation most insinuating. With such a passport, he soon got into the best company, and knew all the family concerns of the place.

It was not long before he heard of Don George's daughter, and of her extraordinary beauty. This touched his curiosity nearly; he was eager to behold so formidable a lady. For this purpose, he endeavored to worm himself into the good graces of her father, and succeeded so well, that the old gentleman already looking, on him as a son-in-law, gave him free admission to the house, and the liberty of conversing with Donna Helena in his presence. The Galician soon became deeply enamored of her : indeed, it was the common fate of all who had ever beheld her charms. He opened his heart to Don George, who consented to his paying his addresses, but told him that so far from offering violence to her inclinations, he should never interfere in her choice. Hereupon Don Blas pressed every device that impassioned ingenuity could suggest into his service, to melt and warm the icicles of reserve ; but the lady was impenetrable to his arts, fast bound in the fetters of an earlier love. Felicia, however, was in the new suitor's interest, convinced of his merit by the universal argument. All the faculties of her soul were called forth in his cause. On the other hand, the father urged his wishes and entreaties. Thus was Donna Helena tormented for a whole year with their importunities, and yet her faith continued unshaken.

Combados finding that Don George and Felicia took up his cause with very little success, proposed an expedient for conquering prejudice to the following effect. We will suppose a merchant of Coria to have received a letter from his Italian correspondent, in which, among the news of the day, there shall be the following paragraph : " A Spanish gentleman, Don Gaston de Cogollos, has lately arrived at the court of Parma. He is said to be nephew and sole heir to a rich widow of Coria. He is paying his addresses to a nobleman's daughter ; but the family wishes to ascertain the validity of his pretensions. Send me word, therefore, whether you know this Don Gaston, together with the amount of his aunt's fortune. On your answer the marriage will depend. Parma, . . . day of, etc."

The old gentleman considered this trick as a mere ebullition of humor, a lawful stratagem of amorous warfare; and the jade of a go-between, with conscience still more callous than her master's, was delighted with the probability of the manœuvre. It seemed to be so much the more happily imagined, as they knew Helena to be a proud girl, capable of taking decisive measures, in the moment of surprise and indignation. Don George undertook to be the herald of my fickleness, and by way of coloring the contrivance more naturally, to confront the pretended correspondent with her. This project was executed as soon as formed. The father, with counterfeit emotions of displeasure, said to Donna Helena : Daughter, it is not enough now to tell you that our relations inveigh against an alliance with Don Austin's murderer ; a still stronger reason hencefoward presses, to detach you from Don Gaston. It may well overwhelm you with shame, to have been his dupe so long. Here is an undeniable proof of his inconstancy. Only read this letter just received by a merchant of Coria from Italy. The trembling Helena caught at this forged paper; glanced over the writing; then weighed every expression, and stood aghast at the import of the whole. A keen pang of disappointment wrung from her a few reluctant tears ; but pride came to her assistance; she wiped away the falling drops of weakness, and said to her father in a determined tone : Sir, you have just been witness of my folly ; now bear testimony to my triumph over myself. The delusion is past ; Don Gaston is the object of my utter contempt. I am ready to meet Don Blas at the altar, and be beforehand with the traitor in the pledge of our transferred affections. Don George, transported with joy at this change, embraced his daughter, extolled her spirit to the skies, and hastened the necessary preparations, with all the self-complacency of a successful plotter.

Thus was Donna Helena snatched from me. She threw herself into the arms of Combados in a pet, not listening to the secret whispers of love within her breast, nor suspecting a story which ought to have seemed so improbable in the annals of true passion. The haughty are always the victims of their own rash conclusions. Resentment of insulted beauty triumphed wholly over the suggestions of tenderness. And yet, a few days after marriage, there came over her some feelings of remorse for her precipitation; it struck her that the letter might have been a forgery; and the very possibility disturbed her peace. But the enamored Don Blas left his wife no time to nurse up thoughts injurious to their newfound joys; a succession of gayety and pleasure kept her in a thoughtless whirl, and shielded her from the pangs of unavailing repentance.

She appeared to be in high good humor with so spirit-stirring a husband ; so that they were living together in perfect unanimity, when my aunt adjusted my affair with Don Austin's relations. Of this she wrote me word to Italy. I returned on the wings of love. Donna Eleonora not having announced the marriage, informed me of it on my arrival ; and remarking what pain it gave me, said : You are in the wrong, nephew, to show so much feeling for a faithless fair. Banish from your memory a person so unworthy to share in its tender recollections.

As my aunt did not know how Donna Helena had been played upon, she had reason to talk as she did · nor could she have given me better advice. To affect indifference, if not to conquer my passion, was my bounden duty. Yet there could be no harm in just inquiring by what means this union had been brought to bear. To get at the truth, I determined on applying to Felicia's friend Theodora. There I met with Felicia herself who was confounded at my unwelcome presence, and would have escaped from the necessity of explanation. But I stopped her. Why do you avoid me ? said I. Has your perjured mistress forbidden you to give ear to my complaints ? or would you make a merit with the ungrateful woman, of your voluntary refusal.

Sir, answered the plotting abigail, I confess my fault, and throw myself on your mercy. Your appearance here has filled me with remorse. My mistress has been betrayed, and unhappily in part by my agency. The particulars of their infernal device followed this avowal, with an endeavor to make me amends for its lamentable consequence. To this effect, she offered me her services with her mistress, and promised to undeceive her ; in a word, to work night and day, that she might soften the rigor of my sufferings, and open the career of hope.

I pass over the numberless contradictions she experienced, before she could accomplish the projected interview. It was at length arranged to admit me privately, while Don Blas was at his hunting-seat. The plot did not linger. The husband went into the country, and they sent for me to his lady's apartment.

My onset was reproachful in the extreme, but my mouth was soon shut upon the subject. It is useless to look back upon the past, said the lady. It can be no part of our present intention to work upon each other's feelings; and you are grievously mistaken, if you fancy me inclined to flatter your aspiring hopes. My sole inducement for receiving you here was to tell you personally, that you have only henceforth to forget me. Perhaps I might have been better satisfied with my lot, had it been united with yours ; but since heaven has ordered it otherwise, we must submit to its decrees.

What ! madam, answered I, is it not enough to have lost you, to see my successful rival in quiet possession of all my soul holds dear, but I must also banish you from my thoughts ? You would tear from me even my passion, my only remaining blessing ! And think you that a man, whom you have once enchanted, can recover his self-possession ? Know yourself better, and cease to enforce impracticable behests. Well, then ! if so, rejoined she with hurried importunity, do you cease to flatter yourself with interesting my gratitude or my pity. In one short word, the wife of Don Blas shall never be the mistress of Don Gaston. Let us at once end a conversation at which delicacy revolts in spite of virtue, and peremptorily forbids its longer continuance.

I now threw myself at the lady's feet in despair. All the powers of language and of tears were called forth to soften her. But even this served only to excite some inbred sentiments of compassion, stifled as soon as born, and sacrificed at the shrine of duty. After having fruitlessly exhausted all my stories of tender persuasion, rage took possession of my breast. I drew my sword, and would have fallen on its point before the inexorable Helena, but she saw my design and prevented it. Stay your rash hand, Cogollos, said she. Is it thus that you consult my reputation? In dying thus and here, you will brand me with dishonor. and my husband with the imputation of murder.

In the agony of my despair, far from yielding to these suggestions, I only struggled against the preventive efforts of the two women, and should have struggled too successfully, if Don Blas had not appeared to second them. He had been apprized of our assignation; and instead of going into the country, had concealed himself behind the hangings, to overhear our conference. Don Gaston, cried he, as he arrested my uplifted arm, recall your scattered senses, and no longer give a loose to these mad transports.

Here I could hold no longer. Is it for you, said I, to turn me from my resolution? You ought rather yourself to plunge a dagger in my bosom. My love, with all its train of miseries, is an insult to you. Have you not surprised me in your wife's apartment at this unseasonable hour? what greater provocation can you want for your revenge? Stab me, and rid yourself of a man who can only give up the adoration of Donna Helena with his life. It is in vain, answered Don Blas, that you endeavor to interest my honor in your destruction. You are sufficiently punished for your rashness; and my wife's imprudence, in giving you this opportunity of indulging it, is sanctified by the purity of her sentiments. Take my advice, Cogollos; shrink not effeminately from your wayward destiny, but bear up against it with the patient courage of a hero.

The prudent Galician, by such language, gradually composed the ferment of my mind, and waked me once more to virtue. I withdrew in the determination of removing far from the scene of my folly, and went for Madrid, two days afterwards. There, pursuing the career of fortune and preferment, I appeared at court, and laid myself out for connections. But it was my ill luck to attach myself particularly to the Marquis of Villareal, a Portuguese grandee, who, lying under a suspicion of intending to emancipate his country from the Spanish yoke, is now in the castle of Alicant As the Duke of Lerma knew me to be closely connected with this nobleman, he gave orders for my arrest and detention here. That minister thought me capable of engaging in such a project—he could not have offered a more outrageous affront to a man of noble birth and a Castilian.

Don Gaston thus ended his story. By way of consolation I said to him, Illustrious sir, your honor can receive no taint from this temporary detainer, and your interest will probably be promoted by it in the end. When the Duke of Lerma shall be convinced of your innocence, he will not fail to give you a considerable post, and thus retrieve the character of a gentleman unjustly accused of treason.

CHAPTER VII.

SCIPIO FINDS GIL BLAS OUT IN THE TOWER OF SEGOVIA, AND
BRINGS HIM A BUDGET OF NEWS.

OUR conversation was interrupted by Tordesilla, who came into
the room, and addressed me thus: Signor Gil Blas, I have just
been speaking with a young man at the prison gate. He inquired
if you were not here, and looked much mortified at my refusal to
satisfy his curiosity. Noble governor, said he, with tears in his
eyes, do not reject my most humble petition. I am Signor de
Santillane's principal domestic, and you will do an act of charity
by allowing me to see him. You pass for a kind-hearted gentleman
in Segovia; I hope you will not deny me the favor of conversing
for a few minutes with my dear master, who is unfortunate rather
than criminal. In short, continued Don Andrew, the lad was so
importunate, that I promised to comply with his wishes this evening.

I assured Tordesillas that he could not have pleased me better
than by bringing this young man to me, who could probably communicate tidings of the last importance. I waited with impatience
for the entrance of my faithful Scipio; since I could not doubt him
to be the man, nor was I mistaken in my conjecture. He was introduced at the time appointed; and his joy, which only mine
could equal, broke forth into the most whimsical demonstrations.
On my side, in the ecstasy of delight, I stretched out my arms to
him, and he rushed into them with no courtly measured embrace.
All distinctions of master and dependant were leveled in the sympathetic rapture of our meeting.

When our transports had subsided a little, I inquired into the
state of my household. You have neither household nor house,
answered he: to spare you a long string of questions, I will sum
up your worldly concerns in two words. Your property has been
pillaged at both ends, both by the banditti of the law and by your
own retainers, who, regarding you as a ruined man, paid themselves their own wages out of whatever they found that was portable. Luckily for you, I had the dexterity to save from their harpy
clutches two large bags of double pistoles. Salero, in whose custody I deposited them, will make restitution on your release, which
cannot be far distant, as you were put upon his majesty's pension
list of prisoners without the Duke of Lerma's knowledge or consent.

I asked Scipio how he knew his excellency to have had no share
in my arrest. You may depend on it, answered he, my information
is undeniable. One of my friends in the Duke of Uzeda's confidence acquainted me with all the circumstances of your imprisonment. Calderona, having discovered by a spy that Signora Sirena,
with the handle of an alias to her name, was receiving night visits

from the Prince of Spain, and that the Count de Lemos managed that intrigue by the panderism of Signor de Santillane, determined to be revenged on the whole knot. To this end he waited on the Duke of Uzeda, and discovered the whole affair. The duke, overjoyed at such a fine opportunity of ruining his enemy, did not fail to bestir himself. He laid his information before the king, and painted the prince's danger in the most lively colors. His majesty was much angered, and showed that he was so, by sending Sirena to the nunnery provided for such frail sisters, banishing the Count de Lemos, and condemning Gil Blas to perpetual imprisonment.

This, pursued Scipio, is what my friend told me. Hence, you gather your misfortune to be the Duke of Uzeda's handiwork, or rather Calderona's.

Thus it seemed probable that my affairs might be reinstated in time; that the Duke of Lerma, chagrined at his nephew's banishment, would move heaven and earth for that nobleman's recall; and it might not be too much to expect that his excellency would not forget me. What a delicate gipsy is hope! She wheedled me out of all anxiety about my shattered fortunes, and made me as light-hearted as if I had good reason to be so. My prison looked not like the dungeon of perpetual misery, but like the vestibule to a more distinguished station. For thus ran the train of my reasoning: Don Fernando Borgia, Father Jerome of Florence, and more than all, Friar Louis of Aliaga, who may thank him for his place about the king's person, are the prime minister's partisans. With the aid of such powerful friends, his excellency will bear down all opposition, even supposing no change to take place in the political barometer. But his majesty's health is very precarious. The first act of a new reign would be to recall the Count de Lemos; he would not feel himself at home in the young monarch's presence till he had introduced me at court; and the young monarch would not sit easy on his throne till he had showered benefits on my head. Thus, feasting by anticipation on the pleasures of futurity, I became callous to existing evils. The two bags, snug in the goldsmith's custody, were no bad doubles to the part which hope acted in this shifting pantomime.

It was impossible not to express my gratitude to Scipio for his zeal and honesty. I offered him half the salvage, but he rejected it. I expect, said he, a very different acknowledgment. Astonished as much at his mysterious claim as at his refusal, I asked what more I could do for him. Let us never part, answered he. Allow me to link my fate with yours. I feel for you what I never felt for any other master. And on my part, my good fellow, said I you may rest assured that your attachment is not thrown away. You caught my fancy at first sight. We must have been born under Libra or Gemini, where friendship is lord of the ascendant. I willingly accept your proffered partnership, and will commence business by prevailing with the warden to immure you along with me in this tower. That is the very thing, exclaimed he. You were beforehand with me, for I was just going to beg that favor. Your company is dearer to me than liberty itself, I shall only just go

to Madrid now and then, to snuff the gale of the ministerial atmosphere, and try whether any scent lies which may be favorable for
your pursuit. Thus will you combine in me a bosom friend, a
trusty messenger, and an unsuspected spy.

These advantages were too important for me to forego them.
I therefore kept so useful a person about me, with leave of the
obliging warden, who would not stand in the way of so soothing a
relief to the weariness of solitude.

CHAPTER VIII.

SCIPIO'S FIRST JOURNEY TO MADRID: ITS OBJECT AND SUCCESS.
GIL BLAS FALLS SICK. THE CONSEQUENCE OF HIS ILLNESS.

IF it is a common proverb that our direst enemies are those of
our own household, the converse ought equally to be admitted
among the saws of a more candid experience. After such incon-
testable proofs of Scipio's zeal, he became to me like another self.
All distinction of place was confounded between Gil Blas and his
secretary: all insolence was dropped on the one hand, all cringing
on the other. Their lodging, bed, and board were in common.

Scipio's conversation was of a very lively turn; he might have
been dubbed the Spanish Momus, without any derogation to the
Punch of the Pantheon. But he had a long head, as well as a
fanciful brain, combining the characters of councilor and jester.
My friend, said I, one day, what do you think of writing to the
Duke of Lerma? It could, methinks, do no harm. Why, as to
that, answered he, the great are such chameleons, that there is no
knowing where to have them. At all events you may risk it;
though I would not lay the postage of your letter on its success.
The minister loves you, it is true; but then political love lacks
memory, as much as personal love lacks visual discrimination.
Out of sight, out of mind! is at once the motto and the stigma of
these gentry.

True as this may be in general, replied I, my patron is a glorious
exception. His kindness lives in my recollection. I am persuaded
that he suffers for my sufferings, and that they are incessantly
preying on his spirits. We must give him credit for only waiting
till the king's anger shall pass away. Be it so, resumed he; I wish
you may not reckon without your host. Assail his excellency
then, with an epistle to stir the waters. I will engage to deliver it
into his own hands. Pen, ink, and paper being brought, I composed
a specimen of eloquence which Scipio declared to be a paragon of
pathos, and Tordesillas preferred, for the cant of sermonizing prolixity, to the old archbishop's homilies.

I flattered myself that there would be tears in the Duke of
Lerma's eyes, and distraction in his aspect, at the detail of miseries

which existed only on paper. In that assurance, I despatched my messenger, who no sooner got to Madrid, than he went to the minister's. Meeting with an old domestic of my acquaintance, he had no difficulty in gaining access to the duke. My lord, said Scipio to his excellency, as he delivered the packet, one of your most devoted servants, lying at his length on straw, in a damp and dreary dungeon at Segovia, most humbly supplicates for the perusal of his letter, which a tender-hearted turnkey has furnished him with the means of writing. The minister opened the letter, and glanced over the contents. But though he found there a motive and a cue for passion, enough to amaze all his faculties at once, far from drowning the floor with briny secretions, he cleaved the ear of his household, and smote the heart of my courier with horrid speech : Friend, tell Santillane that he has a great deal of impudence to address me, after so rank an offense, worthily confronted by the severe sentence of the king. Under that sentence let the wretch drag out his days, nor look to my mediation for a respite.

Scipio, though neither dull nor muddy-mettled, began to be unpregnant of this defeated cause. Yet he was not so pigeon-livered as to retire without an effort in my favor. My lord, replied he, this poor prisoner will give up the ghost with grief, at the recital of your excellency's displeasure. The duke answered like a prime minister, with a supercilious corrugation of features, and a decisive revolution of his front to some more prosperous suitor. This he did, to cover his own share in the shame of pimping ; and such treatment must all those hireling scavengers expect, who rake in the filth and ordure of rotten statesmen, courtiers, and politicians.

My secretary came back to Segovia and delivered the result of his mission. And now behold me, sunk deeper than on the first day of my imprisonment, in the gulf of affliction and despair ! The Duke of Lerma's turning king's evidence gave a hanging posture to my affairs. My courage was run out ; and though they did all they could to keep up my spirits, the agitation and distress of my mind threw me into a fever.

The warden, who took a lively interest in my recovery, fancying in his unmedical head that physicians cured fevers, brought me a double dose of death in two of that doleful deity's most practised executioners. Signor Gil Blas, said he, as he ushered in their grisly forms, here are two godsons of Hippocrates, who are come to feel your pulse, and to augment the number of their trophies in your person. I was so prejudiced against the whole faculty, that I should certainly have given them a very discouraging reception, had life retained its usual charms in my estimation ; but being bent on my departure from this vale of tears, I felt obliged to Tordesillas for hastening my journey, by a safer conveyance than the crime of suicide.

My good sir, said one of the pair, your recovery will, under Providence, depend on your entire confidence in our skill. Implicit confidence ! answered I : with your assistance, I am fully persuaded that a few days will place me beyond the reach of fever, and all the shocks that flesh is heir to. Yes! with the blessing of Heaven, rejoined he, it is a consummation devoutly to be wished, and easily to be effected. At all events, our best endeavors shall not be wanting. And indeed it was no joke: for they got me into such fine training for the other world, that few of my material particles were left in this. Already had Don Andrew, observing me fumble with the sheets, and smile upon my fingers' ends, and thinking there was but one way, sent for a Franciscan to show it me: already had the good father, having mumbled over the salvation of my soul, retired to the refection of his own body; and my own opinion leaned to the immediate necessity of making a good end. I beckoned Scipio to my bedside. My dear friend, said I, in the faint

"HE BATHED MY HAND IN SILENT TEARS."

accents of a tortured and evacuated patient, I give and bequeath to you one of the bags in Gabriel's possession; the other you must carry to my father and mother in the Asturias, who, if still living, must be in narrow circumstances. But, alas! I fear, they have not been able to bear up against my ingratitude. Muscada's report of my unnatural behavior must have brought their gray hairs with sorrow to the grave. Should Heaven have fortified their tender hearts against my indifference, you will give them the bag of doubloons, with assurances of my dying remorse: and, if they are no more, I charge you to lay out the money in masses for the repose of their souls and of mine. Then did I stretch out my hand, which he bathed in silent tears. It is not always true, that the mourning of an heir is mirth in masquerade.

For some hours I fancied myself outward-bound, and on the point of sailing; but the wind changed. My pilots having quitted the helm, and left the vessel to the steerage of nature, the danger of shipwreck disappeared. The fever, mutinying against its commanding officers, gave all their prognostics the lie, and acted contrary to general orders. I got better by degrees, in mind as well as in body. My consolation was all derived from within. I looked at wealth and honors with the eye of a dying anchorite, and blessed the malady which restored my soul. I abjured courts, politics, and the Duke of Lerma. If ever my prison doors were opened, it was my fixed resolve to buy a cottage, and live like a philosopher.

My bosom friend applauded my design, and to further its execution, undertook a second journey to solicit my release, by the intervention of a clever girl about the person of the prince's nurse. He contended that a prison was a prison still, in spite of kind indulgence and good cheer. In this I agreed, and gave him leave to depart, with a fervent prayer to Heaven that we might soon take possession of our hermitage.

CHAPTER IX.

SCIPIO'S SECOND JOURNEY TO MADRID. GIL BLAS IS SET AT LIBERTY ON CERTAIN CONDITIONS. THEIR DEPARTURE FROM THE TOWER OF SEGOVIA, AND CONVERSATION ON THEIR JOURNEY.

WHILE waiting for Scipio's return from Madrid, I began a course of study. Tordesillas furnished me with more books than I wanted. He borrowed them from an old officer who could not read, but had fitted up a magnificent library, that he might pass for a man of learning. Above all, I delighted in moral essays and treatises, because they abounded in common-places according with my antipathy to courts and philosophic relish of solitude.

Three weeks elapsed before I heard a syllable from my negotiator, who returned at length with a cheerful countenance, and news to the following effect: By the intercession of a hundred pistoles with the chambermaid, and her intercession with her mistress, the Prince of Spain has been prevailed with to plead for your enlargement with his royal father. I hastened hither to announce these happy tidings, and must return immediately to put the last hand to my work. With these words, he left me, and went back to court.

At the week's end my expeditious agent returned, with the intelligence that the prince had procured my liberty, not without some difficulty. On the same day my generous keeper confirmed the assurance in person, with the kindest congratulations, and the following notice:—Your prison doors are open, but on two conditions, which I am sorry that my duty obliges me to announce, because they will probably be disagreeable to you. His majesty expressly forbids you to show your face at court, or to be found within the limits of the two Castiles on this day month. I am extremely sorry that you are interdicted from court. And I am delighted at it, answered I. Witness all the powers above! I asked the king for only one favor; he has granted me two.

With my liberty thus confirmed, I hired a couple of mules, on which we mounted the next day, after taking leave of Cogollos, and thanking Tordesillas a thousand times for all his instances of friendship. We set forward cheerfully on the road to Madrid, to draw our deposit out of Signor Gabriel's hands, amounting to a thousand doubloons. On the road my fellow-traveler observed: If we are not rich enough to purchase a splendid property, we can at least secure ease and competency to ourselves. A cabin, answered I, would be large enough for my most ambitious thoughts. Though scarcely at the middle period of life, the world has lost its charms for me, its hopes, its fears, its cares, its duties, are all absorbed in the selfishness of philosophical retirement. Independently of these principles, I can assure you I have painted for myself a rural landscape, with a foreground of innocent pleasures, and pastoral simplicity in the perspective. Already does the enamel of the meadows glitter under my eyes; already does the river's murmur accord with the winged chorus of the grove: hunting exasperates the manly virtues, and fishing preaches patience. Only figure to yourself, my friend, what a continual round of amusement solitude may furnish, and you will pant to be admitted of her crew. Then for the economy of our table, the simplest will be the cheapest, and of course the best. Unadulterated Ceres shall be our official caterer: when hunger shall have tamed our fastidious appetites into sobriety, a mumbled crust will relish like an ortolan. The supreme delight of eating is not in the thing ate, but in the palate of him who eats; a proposition in culinary philosophy, proved by the frequent loathing of my own stomach, through a long series of ministerial dinners. Abstemiousness is a luxury of the most exquisite refinement, and the best recipe in the materia medica.

With your good leave, Signor Gil Blas, interrupted my secretary, I am not altogether of your mind respecting the luscious treat of abstemiousness. Why should we mess like the bankrupt sages of antiquity? Surely we may indulge the carnal man a little, without any reasonable offense to the spiritual. Since we have, by the blessing of Providence and my forecast, wherewithal to keep the spit and the spigot in exercise, do not let us take up our abode with famine and wretchedness. As soon as we get settled, we must stock our cellar, and establish a respectable larder, like people who know what is what, and do not separate themselves from the vulgar crowd to renounce the good things of this life, but to taste them with a more exquisite relish. As Hesiod says,

> Enjoy thy riches with a liberal soul;
> Plenteous the feast, and smiling be the bowl.

And again,

> To stint the wine a frugal husband shows,
> When from the middle of the cask it flows.

What the devil, master Scipio, interrupted I in my turn, you can cap verses out of the Greek poets! And pray where did you get acquainted with Hesiod? In very learned company, answered he. I lived some time with a walking dictionary at Salamanca, a fellow up to the elbows in quotation and commentary. He could put a large volume together like a house of cards. His library furnished him with a hodge-podge of Hebrew, Greek, and Latin commonplaces, which he translated into buckram Castilian. As I was his transcriber, some tags of verses, stings of epigrams, and sage truisms stuck by the way. With such an apparatus, replied I, your memory must be most philosophically stocked. But not to lose sight of our future prospects, whereabouts in Spain had we best fix our Socratic abode? My voice is for Arragon, resumed my counsellor. We shall there enjoy all the beauties of nature, and lead the life of Paradise. Well, then, for Arragon! said I. May it teem with all the dear delights that youthful poets fancy when they dream!

CHAPTER X.

THEIR DOINGS AT MADRID. THE RENCONTRE OF GIL BLAS IN THE STREET, AND ITS CONSEQUENCES.

ON our arrival in Madrid, we alighted at a little public-house where Scipio had been accustomed to put up, whence our first visit was to my banker, Salero. He received us very cordially, and expressed the highest satisfaction at my release. Indeed, added he, your untoward fate touched me so nearly as to change my views of a political alliance. The fortunes of courtiers are like castles in the air: so I have married my daughter Gabriela to a wealthy trader. You have acted very wisely, answered I; for besides that a bird in the hand is worth two in a bush, when a plodding citizen aspires to the honor of bringing a man of fashion into his family, he very often has an impertinent puppy for his son-in-law.

Then changing the topic, and coming to the point: Signor Gabriel, pursued I, we came to talk a little about the two thousand pistoles which . . . . Your money is all ready, said the goldsmith, interrupting me. He then took us into his closet, and delivered the two bags, carefully labeled with my name on them.

I thanked Salero for his exactness, and heaven in my sleeve for my escape from his daughter. At our inn we counted over the money and found it right, deducting fifty doubloons for the expenses of my enlargement. Our thoughts were now wholly bent upon Arragon. My secretary undertook to buy a carriage and two mules. It was my office to provide household and body linen,

"HE WAS PLAYING AT CHESS WITH BARONESS STEINBACH."

During my peregrinations for the purpose, I met Baron Steinbach, the officer in the German Guards with whom Don Alphonso had been brought up.

I touched my hat to him ; he knew me again, and returned my greeting warmly. My joy is extreme, said I, at seeing your lordship in such fine health, to say nothing of my wish to inquire after Don Cæsar and Don Alphonso de Leyva. They are both in Madrid, answered he, and staying at my house. They came to town about three months ago, to be presented on occasion of Don Alphonso's promotion. He has been appointed Governor of Valencia, on the score of old family claims, without having in any shape pushed his interest at court. Nothing could be more grateful to his feelings, or prove more strongly our royal master's goodness, who delights to recognize the merits of ancestry in the persons of their descendants.

Though I knew more of this matter than Steinbach, I kept my knowledge in the background. Yet so lively was my impatience to hail my old masters, that he would not damp my ardor by delay. I had a mind to try Don Alphonso, whether he still retained his regard for me. He was playing at chess with Baroness Steinbach. On my entrance, he started up from his game, ran towards me, and squeezing me tight in his embrace: Santillane, said he, with demonstrations of the sincerest joy, at length, then, you are restored to my heart. I am delighted at it ! It was not my fault that we ever parted. You may remember how strongly I urged you not to withdraw from the Castle of Leyva. You were deaf to my entreaties. But I must not chide your obstinacy, because its motive was the peace of the family. Yet you ought to have let me hear from you, and to have spared my fruitless inquiries at Grenada, where my brother-in-law, Don Ferdinand, sent me word that you were.

And now tell me what you are doing at Madrid. Of course you have some situation here. Be assured that I shall always take a lively interest in your concerns. Sir, answered I, it is but four months since I occupied a considerable post at court. I had the honor of being the Duke of Lerma's confidential secretary. Can it be possible ? exclaimed Don Alphonso, as if he could scarcely believe his ears. What, were you so near the person of the prime minister ? I then related how I had gained and lost his favor, and ended with avowing my determination to buy a cottage and garden with the wreck of my shattered fortunes.

The son of Don Cæsar heard me attentively, and made this answer : My dear Gil Blas, you know how I have always loved you ; nor shall you longer be fortune's puppet. I will set you above her vagaries, by securing you an independence. Since you declare for a country life, a little estate of ours near Lirias, about four leagues from Valencia, shall be settled on you. You are acquainted with the spot. Such a present we can make, without putting ourselves to the least inconvenience. I can answer for my father's joining in the act, and for Seraphina's entire approbation.

I threw myself at Don Alphonso's feet, who raised me immediately. More penetrated by his affection than by his bounty, I pressed his hand and said, Sir, your conduct charms me. Your noble gift is the more welcome, as it precedes the knowledge of a service it has been in my power to render you; and I had rather owe it to your generosity, than to your gratitude. This governor of my making did not know what to understand by the hint, and pressed for an explanation. I gave it in full, to his utter astonishment. Neither he nor Baron Steinbach could ever have the slightest suspicion that the government of Valencia was owing to my interest at court. Yet having no reason to doubt the fact, my friend proposed to grant me an annuity of two thousand ducats, in addition to the little farm at Lirias.

Hold your hand, Signor Don Alphonso! exclaimed I at this offer. You must not set my avarice afloat again. I am myself a living witness, that fortune may give superfluities to her favorites, but has no competence to bestow. With pleasure will I accept of the estate at Lirias, where my present property will be sufficient for all my wants. Rather than increase my cares with my possessions, I would build a hospital out of my existing funds. Riches are a burden: and it must be a foolish animal that would bear fardels in the manger or the field.

While we were talking after this fashion, Don Cæsar came in. His joy was not less than his son's at the sight of me; and being informed of the family obligations, he again pressed me to accept of the annuity, which I again refused. When the writings were drawn, the father and son made the assignment their joint act and deed, transferring to me the fee simple, and putting me in immediate possession. My secretary half stared the eyes out of his head, when I told him we had a landed estate of our own, and how we came by it. What is the value of this little freehold? said he. Five hundred ducats per annum, answered I, and the farm in high cultivation, within a ring fence. I have often been there during my stewardship. There is a small house on the banks of the Guadalaviar, in a little hamlet, surrounded by a charming country.

What pleases me better than all, cried Scipio, is that we shall have plenty of sporting, rare living, and excellent wine. Come, master, let us leave this crowded city, and hasten to our hermitage. I long to be there as much as you can do, answered I; but I must first go to the Asturias. My father and mother are not in comfortable circumstances. They shall therefore end their days with me at Lirias. Heaven, perhaps, has thrown this windfall in my way to try my filial duty, and would punish me for the neglect of it. Scipio approved my purpose, and urged its speedy execution. Yes, my friend, said I, we will set out as soon as possible. I shall consider it as my dear delight to share the gifts of fortune with the authors of my existence. We shall soon be settled in our country retreat; and then will I write these two Latin verses over the door of my farm-house in letters of gold, for the pious edification of my rustic neighbors:

Inveni portum. Spes et fortuna, valete.
Sat me lusistis; ludite nunc alios.

BOOK THE TENTH.

CHAPTER I.

GIL BLAS SETS OUT FOR THE ASTURIAS; AND PASSES THROUGH
VALLADOLID, WHERE HE GOES TO SEE HIS OLD MASTER, DOCTOR
SANGRADO.   BY ACCIDENT, HE COMES ACROSS SIGNOR MANUEL
ORDONNEZ, GOVERNOR OF THE HOSPITAL.

JUST as I was arranging matters to take my departure from
Madrid, and go with Scipio to the Asturias, Paul V. gave the Duke
of Lerma a cardinal's hat.   This pope, wishing to establish the inquisition in the kingdom of Naples, invested the minister with the
purple, and by that means hoped to bring King Philip over to so
pious and praiseworthy a design.   Those who were best acquainted
with this new member of the sacred college, thought much like
myself, that the church was in a fair way for apostolical purity, after
so ghostly an acquisition.

Scipio, who would have liked better to see me once more blazing
at court, than either cloistered or rusticated, advised me to show
my face at the cardinal's audience.   Perhaps, said he, his eminence,
finding you at large by the king's order, may think it unnecessary
to affect any further displeasure against you, and may even rein-
state you in his service.   My good friend Scipio, answered I, you
seem to forget that my liberty was granted only on condition of
making myself scarce in the two Castiles.   Besides, can you suppose me so soon inclined to become an absentee from my domain
of Lirias?   I have told you before, and I tell it you once again:
Though the Duke of Lerma should restore me to his good graces,
though he should even offer me Don Rodrigo de Calderona's place,
I would refuse it.   My resolution is taken: I mean to go and find
out my parents at Oviedo, and carry them with me to Valencia.
As for you, my good fellow, if you repent of having linked your
fate with mine, you have only to say so : I am ready to give you
half of my ready money, and you may stay at Madrid, where fortune puts on her kindest smiles to those who woo her lustily.

What then! replied my secretary, a little affected by these
words, can you suspect me of any unwillingness to follow you into
your retreat?   The very idea is an injury to my zeal and my attachment.   What, Scipio ! that faithful appendage, who would willingly have passed the remnant of his days with you in the tower
of Segovia, rather than abandon you to your wretched fate, can he
feel sorrowful at the prospect of an abode, where a thousand rural
delights are waiting to smile on his arrival?   No, no, I have not a
wish to turn you aside from your resolution.   Nor can I refrain
from owning my malicious drift; when I advised you to show your

face at the Duke of Lerma's audience, it was for the purpose of ascertaining whether any seedlings of ambition were scattered among the fallows of your philosophy. Since that point is settled, and you are mortified to all the pomps and vanities of the world ; let us make the best of our way from court, to go and suck in with Zephyrus and Flora the innocent, delicious pleasures so luxuriant in the nursery of our imaginations.

In fact, we soon afterwards took our departure together, in a chaise drawn by two good mules, driven by a postilion whom I had added to my establishment. We stopped the first day at Alcala de Henarès, and the second at Segovia, whence, without stopping to see our generous warden, Tordesillas, we went forward to Peñafiel on the Duero, and the next day to Valladolid. At sight of this large town, I could not help fetching a deep sigh. My companion, surprised at that conscientious ventilation, inquired the reason of it. My good fellow, said I, it is because I practised medicine here for a long time. It gives me the horrors, even now, to think of my unexpiated murders. The whole list of killed and wounded are mustered in battle array yonder: the tomb and the hospital yawn with their disgorged inhabitants, who are rushing on to tear me piece-meal, and exact the vengeance due to the drenched crew. What a dreadful fancy! said my secretary. In truth, Signor de Santillane, your nature is too tender. Why should you be shocked at the common course of exchange in your branch of trade? Look at all the oldest physicians: their withers are unwrung. What can exceed the self-complacency with which they view the exits of patients, and the entrances of diseases? Natural constitution bears the brunt of all their failures, and medical infallibility takes the credit of lucky accidents.

It is very true, replied I, that Doctor Sangrado, on whose practice I formed myself, was like the rest of the old physicians in point of self-complacency. It was to little purpose that twenty people in a day yielded to his prowess ; he was so persuaded that bleeding in the arm and copious libations of warm water were specifics for every case, that instead of doubting whether the death of his patients might not possibly invalidate the efficacy of his prescriptions, he ascribed the result to a vacillating compliance with his system. By all the powers! cried Scipio with a burst of laughter, you open to me an incomparable character. If you have any curiosity to be better acquainted with him, said I, it may be gratified to-morrow, should Sangrado be still living, and resident at Valladolid : but it is highly improbable ; for he had one foot in the grave when I left him several years ago.

Our first care, on putting up at the inn, was to inquire after this doctor. We were told that he was not dead ; but being incapacitated by age from paying visits or any other vigorous exertions, he had been superseded by three or four other doctors who had risen into repute by a new practice, accomplishing the same end by different means. We determined on lying by for a day at Valladolid, as well to rest our mules, as to call on Signor Sangrado. About ten o'clock next morning we knocked at his door ; and found him sitting in his elbow-chair, with a book in his hand. He rose on our entrance; advanced to meet us with a firm step for a man of seventy, and begged to know our business. My worthy and approved good master, said I, have you lost all recollections of an old pupil? There was formerly one Gil Blas, as you may remember, a boarder in your house, and for some time your deputy. What! is it you, Santillane? answered he, with a cordial embrace. I should not have known you again. It, however, gives me great pleasure to see you once more. What have you been doing since we parted? Doubtless you have made medicine your profession? It was very strongly my inclination so to do, replied I; but imperious circumstances made me reluctantly abandon so illustrious a calling.

So much the worse, rejoined Sangrado; with the principles you sucked in under my tuition, you would have become a physician of the first skill and eminence, with the guiding influence of heaven to defend you from the dangerous allurements of chemistry. Ah, my son! pursued he with a mournful air, what a change in practice within these few years! The whole honor and dignity of the art is compromised. That mystery, by whose inscrutable degrees the lives of men have in all ages been determined, is now laid open to the rude, untutored gaze of blockheads, novices, and mountebanks. Facts are stubborn things; and ere long the very stones will cry aloud against the rascality of these new practitioners: *lapides clamabunt!* Why, sir, there are fellows in this town, calling themselves physicians, who drag their degraded persons at the *currus triumphalis antimonii*, or as it should properly be translated, the cart's tail of antimony. Apostates from the faith of Paracelsus idolaters of filthy *kermes*, healers at hap-hazard, who make all the science of medicine to consist in the preparation and prescription of drugs. What a change have I to announce to you! There is not one stone left upon another in the whole structure which our great predecessors had raised. Bleeding in the feet, for example, so rarely practised in better times, is now among the fashionable follies of the day. That gentle, civilized system of evacuation which prevailed under my auspices is subverted by the reign of anarchy and emetics, of quackery and poison. In short, chaos is come again! Every one orders what seems good in his own eyes; there is no deference to the authority of ancient wisdom; our masters are laid upon the shelf, and their axioms not one tittle more regarded, for being delivered in languages as defunct as the subjects of their application.

However desirable it might seem to laugh at so whimsical a declamation, I had the good manners to resist the impulse; and not only that, but to inveigh bitterly against *kermes*, without knowing whether it was a vegetable or an animal, and to pour forth a commination of curses against the authors and inventors of so diabolical an engine. Scipio, observing my by-play in this scene, had a mind to come in for his share in the banter. Most venerable prop of the true practice, said he to Sangrado, as I am descended in the third generation from a physician of the old school, give me leave to join you in your philippic against chemical conspiracies. My late illustrious progenitor, heaven forgive him all his sins! was so warm a partisan of Hippocrates, that he often came to blows with ignorant pretenders, who vomited forth blasphemies against that high priest of the faculty. What is bred in the bone will not come out of the flesh: I could willingly inflict tortures and death with my own hands on those rash innovators whose daring enormities you have characterized with such accuracy of discrimination and such force of language. When wretches like these gain an ascendancy in civilized society, can we wonder at the disjointed condition of the world.

The times are even more out of joint than you are aware of, said the doctor. My book against the vanities and delusions of the new practice might as well have fallen still-born from the press; it seems, if anything, to have acted by contraries, and to have exasperated heresy. The apothecaries, like the Titans of old, heaping potion upon pill, and invading the Olympus of medicine, think themselves fully qualified to usurp and maintain the throne, now that it is only thought necessary to set open the doors, and to drive the enemy out at the portal or the postern by main force. They go to the length of infusing their deadly drugs into apozems and cordials, and then set themselves up against the most eminent of the fraternity. This contagion has spread its influence even among the cloisters. There are monks in our convents who unite surgery and pharmacy to the labors of the confessional. Those medical baboons are always dipping their paws into chemistry, and inventing compositions strong enough to lay a scene of ecclesiastical mortality in the temperate abodes of peace and religion. Now there are in Valladolid above sixty religious houses for both sexes; judge what ravage must be made there by unmerciful pumping and the lancet misapplied. Signor Sangrado, said I, you are perfectly in the right to give these poisoners no quarter. I utter groan for groan with you, and heave the philanthropic sigh over the invaded lives of our fellow-creatures, sinking under the fell attack of so heterodox a practice. It fills me with horror to think what a dead weight chemistry may one day be to medicine, just as adulterated coin operates on national credit. Far be that evil day from this generation.

Just at this climax of our discourse, in came an old female servant, with a salver for the doctor, on which was a little light roll and a glass with two decanters, the one filled with water and the other with wine. After he had eaten a slice, he washed it down with the diluted beverage, two parts water to one of wine; but this temperate use of the good creature did not at all save him from the acrimony of my ridicule. So so, good master doctor, said I, you are fairly caught in the fact. You a wine-bibbler! you, who have entered the lists like a knight-errant against that unauthenticated fermentation? you, who reached your grand climacteric on the strength of the pure element? How long have you been so at odds with yourself? Your time of life can be no excuse for the alteration; since, in one passage of your writings, you define old age to be a natural consumption, which withers and attenuates the sys-

tem; and as an inference from that position, you reprobate the ig-norance of those writers who dignify wine with the appellation of old men's milk. What can you say, therefore, in your own defense?

You belabor me most unjustly, answered the old physician. If I drank neat wine, you would have a right to treat me as a deserter from my own standard; but your eyes may convince you that my wine is well mixed. Another heresy, my dear apostle of the wells and fountains! replied I. Recollect how you rated the canon Se-dillo for drinking wine, though plentifully dashed with the salubri-fous fluid. Own modestly and candidly that your theory was un-founded and fanciful, and that wine is not a poisonous liquor, as you have so falsely and scandalously libeled it in your works, any further than, like any other of nature's bounties, it may be abused to excess.

This lecture sat rather uneasily on our doctor's feelings, as a candidate for consistency. He could not deny his inveteracy against the use of wine in all his publications; but pride and vanity not al-lowing him to acknowledge the justice of my attack on his apostasy, he was left without a word to say for himself. Not wishing to push my sarcasm beyond the bounds of good humor, I changed the sub-ject; and after a few minutes' longer stay, took my leave, gravely exhorting him to maintain his ground against the new practitioners. Courage, Signor Sangrado! said I: never be weary of setting your wits against *kermes;* and deafen the health-dispensing tribe with your thunders against the use of bleeding in the feet. If, spite of all your zeal and affection for medical orthodoxy, this empiric gen-eration should succeed in supplanting true and legitimate practice, it will be at least your consolation to have exhausted your best en-deavors in the support of truth and reason.

As my secretary and myself were walking to the inn, making our observations in high glee on the doctor's entertaining and orig-inal character, a man from fifty-five to sixty years of age happened to pass near us in the street, walking with his eyes fixed on the ground, and a large rosary in his hand. I conned over the distinc-tive cut of his appearance most cunningly, and was rewarded in the recognition of Signor Manuel Ordonnez, that faithful trustee for the affairs of the hospital, of whom so honorable mention is made in the first volume of these true and instructive memoirs. Accost-ing him with the most profound and unquestionable tokens of re-spect, I paid my compliments in due form and order to the venera-ble and trust-worthy Signor Manuel Ordonnez, the man of all the world in whose hands the interests of the poor and needy are most safely and beneficially placed. At these words he looked me stead-fastly in the face, and answered that my features were not altogether strange to him, but that he could not recollect where he had seen me. I used to go backwards and forwards to your house, replied I, when one of my friends, by name Fabricio Nunez, was in your service. Ah! I recollect the circumstance at once, rejoined the worthy director with a cunning leer, and have good reason to do so; for you were a brace of pleasant lads, and were by no means backward in the little scape-grace tricks of youth and inexperience.

Well! and what is become of poor Fabricio? Whenever he comes across my thoughts, I cannot help feeling a little uneasy about his temporal and eternal welfare.

It was to relieve your mind upon that subject, said I to Signor Manuel, that I have taken the liberty of stopping you in the street. Fabricio is settled at Madrid, where he employs himself in publishing miscellanies and collections. What do you mean by miscellanies and collections? replied he. I mean, resumed I, that he writes in verse and prose, from epic poems and the highest branches of philosophy, down to plays, novels, epigrams, and riddles. In short, he is a lad of universal genius, and most exemplary benevolence; sometimes modestly taking to himself the credit of his own compositions, and sometimes lending out his talents to the literary ambition of those noblemen who write for their own amusement, but wish their names to be concealed, except from a chosen circle. By traffic like this he sits at the very first tables. But how does he sit at his own? said the director: upon what terms does he live with his baker? Not quite so confidentially as with people of fashion, answered I; for between ourselves, I take him to be quite as much out at elbows as ever Job was. More bonds and judgments against him than ever Job had, take my word for it! replied Ordoinez. Let him lick the spittle of his titled friends and patrons till his stomach heaves at the nauseating saliva; his printed dedications and his oral flattery, in spite of all the cringing and all the toad-eating, which constitute the stock-in-trade of his profession, with all the profits of his works, whether by subscription or ordinary publication, will not bring grist enough to his mill to keep hunger from the door. Mind if what I say does not turn out to be true! He will come to the dogs at last.

Nothing more likely! replied I; for he cohabits with the muses already; and many a plain man has found, to his cost, that there is no keeping company with the sisters, without being worried by their bullying brethren. My friend Fabricio would have done much better by remaining quietly with your lordship; he would now have been lying on a bed of roses, and everything he had touched would have turned to gold. He would at least have been in a very snug berth, said Manuel. He was a great favorite of mine; and I meant, by a regular gradation from subaltern to principal situations, to have established him in ease and affluence on the basis of public charity; but the foolish fellow took it into his head to set up for a wit. He wrote a play, and brought it out at the theater in this town: the piece went off tolerably well, and nothing thenceforth would serve his turn but commencing author by profession. Lope de Vega, in his estimation, was but a type of him: preferring, therefore, the intoxicating vapor of public applause to the plain roast and boiled of this substantial ordinary, he came to me for his discharge. It was to no purpose for me to argue the point, or to prove to him what a silly cur he was, to drop the bone and run after the shadow: the mad blockhead was so suffocated by the smother of authorship, that the instinctive dread of fire could not rouse his alacrity to escape burning. In short, he was miserably unconscious of his own interest, as his successor can testify : for he, possessing practical good sense, though without half Fabricio's quickness and versatility, makes it his whole study and delight to go through his business in a workmanlike manner, and to fall in with all my little ways. In return for such good conduct, I pushed him forward in a manner corresponding with his deserts ; and he unites in his own person, even at this time of day, two offices in the hospital, the least lucrative of which would be more than suffi-cient to place any honest man at his ease, though encumbered with a yearly teeming wife.

CHAPTER II.

GIL BLAS CONTINUES HIS JOURNEY, AND ARRIVES IN SAFETY AT OVIEDO. THE CONDITION OF HIS FAMILY. HIS FATHER'S DEATH, AND ITS CONSEQUENCES.

FROM Valladolid we got to Oviedo in four days, without any un-toward accident on the road, in spite of the proverb, which says, that robbers lay their ears to the ground, when pilgrims are going with rich offerings, and traders are riding with fat purses. It would have been a feasible, as well as a tempting speculation. Two ten-ants of a subterraneous abode might have presented an aspect to have frightened our doubloons into a surrender, for courage was not one of the qualities I had imbibed at court ; and Bertrand, my mule-driver, seemed not to be of a temper to get his brains blown out in defending a purse into which he had no free ingress. Scipio was the only one of the party who was anything of a bully.

It was night when we came into town. Our lodgings were at an inn near my uncle, Gil Perez, the canon. I was very desirous of ascertaining the circumstances of my parents before my first in-terview with them, and, in order to gain that information, it was impossible to make my inquiries in a better channel than through my landlord and landlady, into the lines of whose faces you could not look without being satisfied that they knew every tittle of their neighbors' concerns. As it turned out, the landlord kenned me after a diligent perusal of my features, and cried out: By Saint Antony of Padua! this is the son of the honest usher, Blas of San-tillane. Ay, indeed! said the hostess; and so it is : without a sin-gle muscle altered! just for all the world that same little stripling Gil Blas, of whom we used to say that he was as saucy as he was high. It brings old times to my memory! when he used to come hither with his bottle under his arm, to fetch wine for his uncle's supper.

Madam, said I, you have a most inveterate memory; but for goodness sake change the subject, and tell me the modern news of my family. My father and mother are doubtless in no very envia-ble situation. In good truth, you may say that, answered the landlady; you may rack your brains as long as you like, but you will never think of anything half so miserable as what they are suffering at this present moment. Gil Perez, good soul! is defunct all down one side by a stroke of the palsy, and the other half of him is little better than a corpse; we cannot expect him to last long; then your father, who went to live with his reverence a little while ago, is troubled with an inflammation of the lungs, and is standing, as a body may say, quavery-mavery between life and death; while your mother, who is not over and above hale and hearty herself, is obliged to nurse them both.

On this intelligence, which made me feel some compunctious yearnings of nature, I left Bertrand with my stud and baggage at

"HERE IS YOUR SON, GIL BLAS."

the inn; then, with my secretary at my heels, who would not desert me in my time of need, I repaired to my uncle's house. The moment I came within my mother's reach, a natural emotion of maternal instinct unfolded to her who I was, before her eyes could possibly have run over the traces of my countenance. Son, said she, with a melancholy expression, after having embraced me, come and be present at your father's death; your visit is just in time to take in all the piteous circumstances of so deplorable an event. With this heart-rending reception, she led me by the hand into a chamber where the wretched Blas of Santillane, stretched on a comfortless bed, in cold and dismal accord with the thinness of his fortunes, was just entering on the last great act of human nature. Though surrounded by the shades of death, he was not quite unconscious of what was passing about him. My dearest friend, said my mother, here is your son Gil Blas, who entreats your forgiveness for all his undutiful behavior, and is come to ask your blessing before you die. At these tidings my father opened his eyes, which were on the point of closing for ever: he fixed them upon me: and reading in my countenance, notwithstanding the awful brink on which he stood, that I was a sincere mourner for his loss, his feelings were recalled to sympathy by my sorrow. He even made an attempt to speak, but his strength was too much exhausted. I took one of his hands in mine, and while I bathed it with my tears, in speechless agony of soul, he breathed his last, as if he had only waited my arrival to pay the debt of nature, and wing his way to scenes of untried being.

This event had been too long present to my mother's mind to overwhelm her with any unparalleled affliction. Perhaps it sat more heavily on me than on her, though my father had never in his life given me any reason to feel for him as a father. But besides that mere filial instinct would have made me weep over his cold remains, I reproached myself with not having contributed to the comfort of his latter days; then, when I considered what a hard-hearted villain I had been, I seemed to myself like a monster of ingratitude, or rather like an impious parricide. My uncle, whom I afterwards saw lying at his length on another wretched couch, and in a most lamentable pickle, made me experience fresh agonies of upbraiding conscience. Unnatural son! said I, communing with my own uneasy thoughts, behold the chastisement of heaven upon thy sins, in the disconsolate condition of thy nearest relations. Hadst thou but thrown to them the superflux of that abundance, in which before thy imprisonment thou rolledst, thou mightest have procured for them those little comforts which thy uncle's ecclesiastical pittance was too scanty to furnish, and perhaps have lengthened out the term of thy father's life.

Gil Perez had fallen into a state of second childhood, and was, though numerically upon the list of the living, in every individual organ a mere corpse. His memory, nay, his very senses had retired from their allotted stations in his system. Bootless was it for me to strain him in my pious arms, and lavish outward tokens of affection on him; they might as well have been wasted on the desert air. To as little purpose did my mother ring in his unnerved ear, that I was his nephew Gil Blas; he gazed at me with a vacant, stupid stare, and gave neither sign nor answer. Had the ties of consanguinity and gratitude been all too weak, to awaken my tender sympathy for an uncle, to whom I owed the means of my first launch into the world, the impression of helpless dotage on my senses must have softened me into something like the counterfeit of virtuous emotion.

While this scene was passing, Scipio preserved a melancholy silence, sharing in all my sorrows, and mingling his sighs with mine in the chastised luxury of friendship. But concluding that my mother, after so long an absence, might wish to have some such conversation with me, as the presence of a stranger must rather repress than promote, I drew him aside, saying, Go, my good fellow, sit down quietly at the inn, and leave me here with my only surviving parent, who might consider your company as an intrusion, while talking over family affairs. Scipio withdrew, for fear of being a clog upon our confidence; and I sat down with my mother to an interchange of communication, which lasted all night. We reciprocally gave a faithful account of all that had happened to each of us, since my first sally from Oviedo. She related, in full measure and running over, all the petty insults, disappointments, and mortifications, which she had undergone in her pilgrimage from house to house as a duenna. A great number of these little anecdotes it would have hurt my pride that my secretary should have noted down in his biographical budget, though I had never concealed from him the ups and downs in the lottery of my own life. With all the respect I owe to my mother's sainted memory, the good lady had not the knack of going the shortest road to the end of a story; had she but pruned her own memoirs of all luxuriant circumstances, there would not have been materials for more than a tithe of her narrative.

At length she got to the end of her tether, and I began my career. With respect to my general adventures, I passed them over lightly; but when I came to speak of the visit which the son of Bertrand Muscada, the grocer of Oviedo, had paid me at Madrid, I enlarged with decent compunction on that dark article in the history of my life. I must frankly own, said I to my mother, that I gave that young fellow a very bad reception; and he, doubtless, in revenge, must have drawn a hideous outline of my moral features. He did you more than justice, I trust, answered she; for he told us that he found you so puffed and swollen with the good fortune thrust upon you by the prime minister, as scarcely to acknowledge him among your former acquaintance; and when he gave you a moving description of our miseries, you listened as if you had no interest in the tale, or knowledge of the parties. But as fathers and mothers can always find some clue for palliation in the conduct of their graceless children, we were loth to believe that you had so bad a heart. Your arrival at Oviedo justifies our favorable interpretation, and those tears which are now flowing down your cheeks, are so many pledges either of your innocence or your reformation.

Your constructions were too partial, replied I; there was a great deal of truth in young Muscada's report. When he came to see me all my faculties were engrossed by vanity and mammon; ambition, the prevailing devil which possessed me, left not a thought to throw away on the desolate condition of my parents. It therefore could be no wonder, if in such a disposition of mind I gave rather a freezing reception to a man who, accosting me in a peremptory style, took upon him to say, without mincing the matter, that it was well known I was as rich as a Jew, and therefore he advised me to send you a good round sum, seeing that you were very much put to your shifts: nay, he went so far as to reproach me, in phrase of more sincerity than good manners, with my unfeeling negligence of my family. His confounded personality stuck in my throat; so that losing my little stock of patience, I shoved him fairly by the shoulders out of my closet. It must be confessed that I took the administration of justice a little too much into my own hands, being judge and party in the same cause; neither was it proper that you should bear the brunt, because the grocer was a little anti-saccharine in his phraseology; nor was his advice the less pertinent or just, though couched in homely terms, or urged with plodding vulgarity.

All this came plump in the teeth of my conscience, the moment I had turned Muscada out of doors. The voice of natural instinct contrived to make its way: my duty to my parents brought the blood into my face; but it was the blush of shame for its neglect, and not the glow of triumph at its performance. Yet even my remorse can give me little credit in your eyes, since in was soon stifled in the fumes of avarice and ambition. But some time afterwards, having been safely lodged in the tower of Segovia by royal mandate, I fell dangerously ill there; and that timely remembrancer was the cause of bringing back your son to you. So true is it, that sickness and imprisonment were my best moral tutors; for they enabled nature to resume her rights, and weaned me effectually from the court. Henceforth all my dear delight is in solitude; and my only business in the Asturias is to entreat that you would share with me in the mild pleasures of a retired life. If you reject not my earnest petition, I will attend you to an estate of mine in the kingdom of Valencia, and we will live there together very comfortably. You are of course aware that I intended to take my father thither also; but since heaven has ordained it otherwise, let me at least have the satisfaction of affording an asylum to my mother, and making amends by all the attentions in my power for the fallow seasons in the former harvest of my filial duty.

I accept your kind intentions in very good part, said my mother; and would take the journey without hesitation, if I saw no obstacles in the way. But to desert your uncle in his present condition would be unpardonable; and I am too much accustomed to this part of the country, to like living elsewhere: nevertheless, as the proposal deserves to be maturely weighed, I will consider further of it at my leisure. At present, your father's funeral requires to be ordered and arranged. As for that, said I, we will leave it to the care of the young man whom you saw with me; he is my secretary, with as clever a head and as good a heart as you have often been acquainted with; let the business rest with him; it cannot be in better hands.

Hardly had I pronounced these words, when Scipio came back; for it was already broad day. He inquired whether he could be of any service in our present distresses. I answered that he was come just in time to receive some very important directions. As soon as he was made acquainted with the business in hand: A word to the wise! said he: the whole procession with its appropriate heraldry is already marshalled in this head of mine; you may trust me for a very pretty funeral. Have a care, said my mother, to make it plain and decent without anything like pomp or parade. It can scarcely be too humble for my husband, whom all the town knows to have been low in rank, and indigent in circumstances. Madam, replied Scipio, though he had been the meanest and most destitute of the human race, I would not bate one button in the array of his posthumous honors. My master's credit is at stake in the proper conduct of the ceremony; he has been in an ostensible situation under the Duke of Lerma, and his father ought to be buried with all the forms of state and nobility.

I thought exactly as my secretary did upon the subject; and even went so far as to bid him spare no expense on the occasion. A little leaven of vanity still fermented in the mass of my philosophy, and rose in my bosom with all the effervescence of its original lightness. I flattered myself that by lavishing posthumous honors on a father who had blessed the day of his decease by no lucrative bequest, I should instil into the conceptions of the bystanders a high sense of my generous nature. My mother, on her part, whatever airs of humility she might put on, had no dislike to seeing her husband carried out with due observance of funeral pomp and ceremony. We therefore left Scipio to do just as he pleased; and he, without a moment's delay, adopted all the necessary measures for the display of the undertaker's liveliest fancy.

The genius of that artist was called forth but too successfully. His emblems, devices, and draperies, were so ostentatious, as to disgust instead of cajoling the natives : every individual, whether of the town or the suburbs, whether high or low, rich or poor, felt shocked and insulted by this after-thought parade. This ministerial beggar on horseback, said one, can put his hand into his pocket for his father's funeral baked meats, but never found in his heart wherewithal to furnish his living table with common necessaries. It would have been much more to the purpose, said another, to have made the old gentleman's latter days comfortable, than to have wasted such thriftless sums on a post obit act of filial munificence. In short, quips of the brain and peltings of the tongue pattered round our execrated heads. It would have been well had the storm been only a whirlwind of passion, or hurricane of words; but we were all, Scipio, Bertrand, and myself, corporally admonished of our misdeeds, on our coming out of church; they abused us like pickpockets, made mouths and odious noises as we passed, and followed Bertrand at his heels to the inn with a copious volley of stones and mud. To disperse the mob which had collected before my uncle's house, my mother was obliged to show herself at the window, and to declare publicly, that she was thoroughly satisfied with my proceedings. Another detachment had filed off to the stable-yard where my carriage stood, in the full determination of breaking it to pieces; and this they would inevitably have done, if the landlord and lady had not found some means of quieting their perturbed spirits, and turning them aside from their outrageous purpose.

All these affronts, so revolting to my dignity, the effect of the tales which the young grocer had been spreading about town, inspired me with such a thorough hatred for my native place, that I determined on quitting Oviedo almost immediately, though but for this bustle I might have made it my residence for some time. I announced my intention, with the reasons of it, to my mother, who, considering my uncouth reception as no very flattering compliment to herself, did not urge my longer stay among people

so little inclined to treat me civilly. The only point remaining now to be discussed was her future destiny and provision. My dear mother, said I, since my uncle stands so much in need of your attendance, I will no longer urge you to go along with me: but, as his days seem likely to be very few on earth, you must promise to come and take up your abode with me at my farm, as soon as the last duties are performed to his honored remains.

I shall make no such promise, answered my mother, for I mean to pass the remnant of my days in the Asturias, and in a state of perfect independence. Will you not on all occasions, replied I, be absolute mistress in my household? May be so, and may be not! rejoined she: you have only to fall in love with some flirt of a girl, and then you will marry: then she will be my daughter-in-law, and I shall be her stepmother; and then we shall live together as step-mothers and daughters-in-law usually do. Your prognostics, said I, are fetched from a great distance. I have not at present the most remote intention of entering into the happy state: but even though such a whim should take possession of my brain, I will pledge myself for instructing my wife betimes in an implicit sub-mission to your will and pleasure. That is giving security, with-out the means of making good your contract, replied my mother: you would scarcely be able to justify bail. I would not even swear that in our sparring-matches, you might not take your wife's part in preference to mine, however ill she might behave, or however unreasonably she might argue.

You talk very excellent sense, madam, cried my secretary, com-ing in for his share of the conversation: I think just as you do, that docility is about as much the virtue of a donkey as of a daughter-in-law. As the matter stands, that there may be no dif-ference of opinion between my master and you, since you are ab-solutely determined to live asunder, you in the Asturias, and he in the kingdom of Valencia, he must allow you an annuity of a hundred pistoles, and send me hither every year for the payment. By thus arranging matters, mother and son will be very good friends, with an interval of two hundred leagues between them. The parties concerned fell in at once with the proposal: I paid the first year in advance, and stole out of Oviedo, the next morning before dawn, for fear of vying with Saint Stephen in popular favor. Such were the charms of my return to my native place. An admirable lesson this for those successful upstarts, who having gone abroad to make their fortunes, come home to be purse-proud tyrants of their birth-place.

CHAPTER III.

GIL BLAS SETS OUT FOR VALENCIA, AND ARRIVES AT LIRIAS; DESCRIPTION OF HIS SEAT; THE PARTICULARS OF HIS RE-CEPTION, AND THE CHARACTERS OF THE INHABITANTS HE FOUND THERE.

WE took the road for Leon, afterwards that of Palencia; and, continuing our journey by short stages, arrived on the evening of the tenth day at the town of Segorba, whence early on the morrow we repaired to my seat, at the distance of very little more than three leagues. In proportion as we approached nearer, it was amusing to see with what a longing eye my secretary looked at all the estates which lay in our way, to the right and left of the road. Whenever he caught a glimpse of any which bespoke the rank and opulence of its owner, he never missed pointing at it with his finger, and wishing that were the place of our retreat.

I know not, my good friend, said I, what idea you have formed of our habitation; but if you have taken it into your head that ours is a magnificent house, with the domain of a great landed proprietor, I warn you in time that your are laying much too flattering an unction to your vanity.

If you have no mind to be the dupe of a warm imagination. figure to yourself the little ornamented cottage which Horace fitted up near Tibur in the country of the Sabines, on a small farm, the fee-simple of which was given him by Mæcenas. Don Alphonso has made me just such another present, more as a token of affection than for the value of the thing. Then I must expect to see nothing but a dirty hovel! exclaimed Scipio. Bear in mind, replied I, that I have always given you quite an unvarnished description of my place; and now, even at this moment, you may judge for yourself whether I have not stuck to truth and nature in my representations. Just carry your eye along the course of the Guadalaviar, and observe at a little distance from the further bank, near that hamlet, consisting of nine or ten tenements, a house with four small turrets; that is my mansion.

The deuce and all! stammered out my secretary, short-breathed with sudden admiration: why, that house is one of the prettiest things in nature. Besides the castellated air which those turrets give it, all the beauties of situation and architecture, fertility of soil, and perfection of landscape, combine to rival or excel the immediate neighborhood of Seville, complimented as it is for its picturesque attractions by the appellation of an earthly paradise. Had we chosen the place of our settlement for ourselves, it could not have been more to my taste: a river meanders through the grounds, distilling plenty and verdure from its fertilizing bosom; the leafy honors of an umbrageous wood invite the mid-day walk, and qualify the temperature of the seasons. What a heavenly abode of solitude and contemplation! Ah! my dear master, we shall act very foolishly if we are in a hurry to run away from our happiness. I am delighted, answered I, that you are so well satisfied with the retreat provided for us, though yet acquainted with only a small part of its attractions.

As we were chatting in this strain, we got nearer and nearer to the house, where the door opened. as by magic, the moment Scipio announced Signor Gil Blas de Santillane, who was coming to take possession of his estate. At the mention of this name, received with reverential homage by the people who had been instructed in the transfer of their obedience, my carriage was admitted into a large court, where I alighted; then leaning with all my weight upon Scipio, as if walking was a derogation from my dignity, and putting on the great man after the most consequential models, I reached the hall, where, on my entrance, seven or eight servants made their obeisances. They told me they were come to welcome their new master with their best loves and duties : that Don Cæsar and Don Alphonso de Leyva had chosen them to form my establishment, one in quality of cook, another as under-cook, a third as scullion, a fourth as porter, and the rest as footmen; with an express injunction to receive no wages or perquisites, as those two noblemen meant to defray all the expenses of my household. The cook, Master Joachim by name, was commander-in-chief of this battalion, and announced to me the whole array of the campaign; he declared that he had laid in a large stock of the choicest wines in Spain, and insinuated that for the solid supply of the table, he flattered himself a person of his education and experience, who had been six years at the head of my Lord Archbishop of Valencia's kitchen, must know how to dish up a dinner so as to meet the ideas of the most fastidious layman in Christendom. But the proof of the pudding is in the eating, added he, so I will just go and give you a specimen of my talent. You had better take a walk, my lord, while dinner is getting ready : look about the premises ; and see whether you find them in tenantable condition for a person of your lordship's dignity.

The reader may guess whether I did not stir my stumps ; and Scipio, still more eager than myself to take a bird's eye inventory of our goods and chattels, dragged me back and fore from room to room. There was not a corner of the house that we did not peep into, from the garret to the cellar ; not a closet or a cranny, at least as we supposed, could escape our prying curiosity ; and in every fresh room we went into, I had occasion to admire the kindness of Don Cæsar and his son towards me. I was struck, among other things, with two apartments, which were as elegantly furnished as they could be, without misplaced magnificence. One of them was hung with tapestry, the celebrated manufacture of the Low Countries ; the velvet bed and chairs were still very handsome, though in the fashion of the time when the Moors possessed the kingdom of Valencia. The furniture of the other room was in the same taste ; to wit, an old suit of hangings, made of yellow Genoa damask, with a bed and arm-chairs to match, fringed with blue silk. All these effects, which would have furnished but a sorry display in an upholsterer's shop, made no contemptible appearance in their present situation.

After having rummaged over every article of the paraphernalia, my secretary and myself returned to the dining-room, where the cloth was laid for two, we sat down ; and in an instant they served up so delicious an olla podrida, that we could not help revolving on the various turns of the fate below which had parted the good Archbishop of Valencia from his cook. We had in truth a most catholic and ravenous appetite ; a circumstance which added new zest to our praises and enjoyments. Between every succeeding help my servants, with all the alacrity of fresh and holiday service, filled our large glasses to the brim with wine, the choicest vintage of La Mancha. Scipio not thinking it genteel to express aloud the inward chucklings of his heart at our dainty fare, winked and nodded his delight, and spoke by signs, which I returned with the like dumb eloquence of overflowing satisfaction. The remove was a dish of roast quails, flanking a little leveret in high order, just kept long enough; for this we left our hash, good as it was, and gorged ourselves to a surfeit on the game. When we had eaten as if we had never eaten before, and pledged one another in due proportion, we rose from table and went into the garden to look out for some cool, pleasant spot, and take our afternoon's nap voluptuously.

If hitherto my secretary had goggled satisfaction at what he had

"THEY CELEBRATE MY ARRIVAL."

seen, he stared wider and grinned broader at this vista vision of the garden. He scarcely allowed the comparison to be in favor of the Escurial. The reason of its extreme niceness was that Don Cæsar, who came backwards and forwards to Lirias, took pleasure in improving and ornamenting it. All the walks well graveled and lined with orange trees, a large reservoir of white marble, with a lion in bronze spouting water like a dolphin's deputy in the middle, the beauty of the flower borders, the profusion and variety of the fruit trees; such pretty particulars as these made Scipio smack his lips and snuff the air; but his raptures reached their summit at the gradual descent of a long walk, leading to the bailiff's cottage and overarched by the interwoven boughs of the trees planted on each side. While eulogizing a place so well adapted for a refuge from the intenseness of the heat, we made a halt, and sat down at the foot of an elm, where sleep required very little cunning to entangle two high-fed, half-tipsy blades, just risen from so voluptuous and varacious a repast.

In about two hours we were startled out of our sleep by the report of musketry, popping so near the head-quarters of our repose that we apprehended the camp to be attacked. On the alert! was the first idea that invaded our dozing minds. That we might procure the most authentic intelligence, in what direction the enemy was approaching, we directed our march towards the bailiff's tenement. There were collected eight or ten clodhoppers, all friends and neighbors, assembled on the green for the purpose of honoring my arrival, just communicated to the vacant senses of the said clodhoppers, by a discharge of fire-arms, whose barrels and furniture might thank me for the unusual favor of a thorough cleaning. The greater part of them were acquainted with my person, having seen me more than once at the castle, while engaged in the business of my stewardship. No sooner did they set eyes on me, than they all shouted in unison: Long life to our new lord and master! welcome to Lirias! Then they loaded once again, and fired another volley in honor of the occasion. My habits and manners were softened down to the most condescending urbanity, though with a decorous infusion of distance, lest any degrading constructions might be put upon too unlimited a freedom of address. With respect to my protection, I promised it according to the customary charter of newly-installed possessors; and went so far as to throw them a purse of twenty pistoles: and this, in my opinion, was the point of all others in my conduct which touched their hearts most nearly. After this benefaction, I left them at liberty to waste as much powder as they pleased, and withdrew with my secretary into the wood, where we walked to and fro till night-fall, without being at all tired of our rural prospect: so many charms had the view of a landscape, heightened by the substantial beauties of ownership in fee-simple, to our elevated and delighted imaginations.

The cook, the under-cook, and the scullion were not resting upon their oars all this time: they were working hard to fit up for us an artifice of belly timber more magnificent than what we had already demolished; so that we were over head and ears in amazement, when on our return to the room where we had dined, we saw on the table a dish of four roast partridges, with a smothered rabbit on one side, and a fricasseed capon on the other. The second course consisted of pigs' ears, jugged game, and chocolate cream. We drank deeply of the most delicious wines, and began to think of going to bed, when it became a matter of doubt whether we could sit up any longer. Then my people, with lighted candles before me, led the way to the best bedroom, where they were all most officious in assisting to undress me : but when they had tendered me my gown and nightcap, I dismissed them with an authoritative undulation of my hand, signifying that their services were dispensed with for the remainder of that night.

Thus I sent them all about their business, keeping Scipio for a little private conference between ourselves ; and I led to it by asking him what he thought of my reception, as arranged by order of my noble patrons. Indeed and indeed, answered he, the human heart could not devise anything more delicious; I only wish we may go on as we have begun. I have no wish of the kind, replied I : it is contrary to my principles to allow that my benefactors should put themselves to so much expense on my account; it would be a downright fraud upon their benevolence. Besides, I could never feel myself at home with servants in the pay of other people ; it is just like living in a lodging or an inn. Then it is to be remembered, that I did not come hither to live upon so expensive a scale. What occasion have we for so large an establishment of servants ? Our utmost want, with Bertrand, is a cook, a scullion, and a footman. Though my secretary would not have been at all sorry to table for a continuance at the governor of Valencia's expense, he did not oppose his own luxurious taste to my moral delicacy, but conformed at once to my sentiments, and approved the reduction I was meditating to introduce. That point being decided, he left my chamber, and betook himself to his pillow in his own.

CHAPTER IV.

A JOURNEY TO VALENCIA, AND A VISIT TO THE LORDS OF LEYVA.
THE CONVERSATION OF THE GENTLEMEN, AND SERAPHINA'S
DEMEANOR.

I GOT my clothes off as soon as possible, and went to bed, where, finding no great inclination to sleep, I communed with my own thoughts. The mutual attachment between the lords of Leyva and myself was uppermost in the various topics of my contemplation. With my heart full of their late kindness, I determined on setting out for their residence the next day, and quenching my impatience to thank them for their favors. Neither was it a slender gratification to anticipate another interview with Seraphina ; though there was somewhat of alloy in that pleasure : it was impossible to reflect without shuddering, that I should at the same time have to encounter the glances of Dame Lorenza Sephora, who might not be greatly delighted at the renewal of our acquaintance, should her memory happen to stumble upon the circumstances connected with a certain box on the ear. With my mind exhausted by all these differ-ent suggestions, my eyelids at length closed, and the sun had peep-ed in at my window long before they turned upon their hinges.

I was soon out of bed; and dressed myself with all possible expedition, in the earnest desire of prosecuting my intended jour-ney. Just as I had finished my hasty operations, my secretary came into the room. Scipio, said I, you behold a man on the point of setting out for Valencia. I ought to lose no time in paying my respects to those noblemen to whom I am indebted for my little independence. Every moment of delay in the performance of this duty throws a new weight of ingratitude on my conscience. As for you, my friend, there is no necessity for your attendance; stay here during my absence; I shall come back to you within the space of a week. Heaven speed you, sir! answered he—be sure you do not slight Don Alphonso and his father—they seem to me to thrill with the kindly vibrations of friendship, and to be unbounded in their acknowledgment of obligation : gratitude and benevolence are so uncommon in people of rank, that they deserve to be made the most of where found. I sent a message to Bertrand, to hold him-self in readiness for setting out, and took my chocolate while he was harnessing the mules. When all was prepared, I got into my carriage, after having directed my people to consider my secretary as master of the house in my absence, and to obey his orders as if they were my own.

I got to Valencia in less than four hours, and drove at once to the governor's stables, where I alighted and left my equipage. On going to the house, I was informed that Don Cæsar and his son were together. I did not wait for an introduction, but went in with-out ceremony ; and addressing myself to both of them, Servants, said I, never send in their names to their masters; here is an old piece of family furniture, not ornamental indeed, but of a fashion when gratitude was neither out of date nor out of countenance. These words were accompanied with an effort to throw myself on my knees ; but they anticipated my purpose, and embraced me one after the other with all possible evidence of sincere affection. Well, then, my dear Santillane, said Don Alphonso, you have been at Lirias to take possession of your little property. Yes, my lord, answered I ; and my next request is, that you would be pleased to take it back again. What is your reason for that? replied he. Is there anything about it at all offensive to your taste? Not in the place itself, rejoined I : on the contrary, that is everything that my heart can wish, the only fault I have to find with it is, that the kitchen smells too strongly of the hierarchy ; a lay Christian should not live like an archbishop; besides that, there are three times as many servants as are necessary, and consequently you are put to an expense at once enormous and useless.

Had you accepted the annuity of two thousand ducats which we offered you at Madrid, said Don Cæsar, we should have thought it enough to give you the mansion furnished as it is : but you know, you refused it ; and we felt it but right to do what we have done as an equivalent. Your bounty has been too lavish, answered

: the gift of the estate was the utmost limit to which it should ave been extended, and that was more than sufficient to crown ly largest wishes. But to say nothing about what it has cost you to eep up so great and expensive an establishment, I declare to you lost solemnly that these people stand in my way, and are a great nnoyance. In one word. gentlemen, either take back your boon, r give me leave to enjoy it in my own way. I pronounced these st words so much as if I was in earnest, that the father and son, ot meaning to lay me under any unpleasant restraint, at length ave me their permission to manage my household as it should eem expedient to my better judgment.

I was thanking them very kindly for having granted me that rivilege, without which a dukedom would have been but splendid lavery, when Don Alphonso interrupted me by saying: My dear il Blas, I will introduce you to a lady who will be extremely appy to see you. Thus preparing me for the interview, he took le by the hand and led the way to Seraphina's apartment, who et up a scream of joy on recognizing me. Madam, said the governor, I flatter myself that the visit of our friend Santillane at Valencia is not less acceptable to you than myself. On that head, nswered she, he may rest confidently assured; time has not obliterated the remembrance of the service which he once rendered me, nd to that must be added a new debt of gratitude incurred on the core of your obligations. I told the governor's lady that I was lready too well requited for the dangei hich I had shared in ommon with her deliverers, in exposing my life for her sake: ompliments to the like effect were bandied about for some time n both sides, when Don Alphonso motioned to quit Seraphina's oom. We then went back to Don Cæsar, whom we found in the aloon with a fashionable party, who were come to dinner.

All these gentlemen were introduced, and paid their compliments to me in the politest manner; nor did their attentions relax n assiduity, when Don Cæsar told them that I had been one of he Duke of Lerma's principal secretaries. In all likelihood several of them might not be unacquainted that Don Alphonso had been promoted to the government of Valencia by my interest, for political secrets are seldom kept. However that might be, while we were at table, the conversation principally turned on the new cardinal. Some of the company either were, or affected to be, his unqualified admirers, while others allowed his merit upon the whole, but thought it had been rather overrated. I plainly saw through their design of drawing me on to enlarge on the subject of his eminence, and to gratify their taste for scandal with court anecdotes at his expense. I could have been well enough pleased to have delivered my real sentiments on his character, but I kept my tongue within my teeth, and thereby passed in the estimation of the guests for a close, confidential, politic, trustworthy young statesman.

The party respectively retired home after dinner to take their usual nap, when Don Cæsar and his son, yielding to a similar inclination, shut themselves up in their apartments.

For my own part, full of impatience to see a town which I ha
so often heard extolled for its beauty, I went out of the governo
palace with the intention of walking through the streets. At t
gate a man accosted me with the following address: Will Sign
de Santillane allow me to take the liberty of paying my respects
him? I asked him who and what he was. I am Don Cæsa
valet-de-chambre, answered he, but was one of his ordinary foo
men during your stewardship; I used to make my court to yo
every morning, and you used to take a great deal of notice of m
I regularly gave you intelligence of what was passing in the hous
Do you recollect my apprising you one day that the village surge
of Leyva was privately admitted into Dame Lorenza Sephora
bed-chamber? It is a circumstance which I have by no means fo
gotten, replied I. But now that we are talking of that formidab
duenna, what is become of her? Alas! resumed he, the po
creature moped and dwindled after your departure, and at lengt
gave up the ghost, more to the grief of Seraphina than of Do
Alphonso, who seemed to consider her death as no great evil.

Don Cæsar's valet-de-chambre, having thus acquainted me wi
Sephora's melancholy end, made an humble apology for havin
presumed to stop my walk, and then left me to continue my pro
ress. I could not help paying the tribute of a sigh to the memo
of that ill-fated duenna; and her decease affected me the mor
because I taxed myself with that melancholy catastrophe, thoug
a moment's reflection would have convinced me, that the grav
owed its precious prey to the inroads of her cancer rather than t
the cruel charms of my person.

I looked with an eye of pleasure upon everything worth notic
in the town. The archbishop's marble palace feasted my eyes wit
all the magnificence of architecture; nor were the piazzas whic
surounded the exchange much inferior in commercial grandeu
but a large building at a distance, with a great crowd stand'n
before the doors, attracted all my attention. I went nearer, t
ascertain the reason why so great a concourse of both sexes wa
collected, and was soon let into the secret by reading the followin
inscription in letters of gold on a tablet of black marble over th
door: *La Posada de los Representantes.** The play-bills announce
for that day a new tragedy, never performed, and gave the name o
Don Gabriel Triaquero as the author.

---

* The theater.

CHAPTER V.

GIL BLAS GOES TO THE PLAY, AND SEES A NEW TRAGEDY. THE
SUCCESS OF THE PIECE. THE PUBLIC TASTE AT VALENCIA.

I STOPPED for some minutes before the door, to make my
remarks on the people who were going in. There were some of
all sorts and sizes. Here was a knot of genteel-looking fellows,
whose tailors at least had done justice to their fashionable pretensions; there a mob of ill-favored and ill-mannered mortals, in a
garb to identify vulgarity. To the right was a bevy of noble
ladies, alighting from their carriages to take possession of their
private boxes; to the left a tribe of female traders in lubricity, who
came to sell their wares in the lobby. This mixed concourse of
spectators, as various in their minds as in their faces, gave me an
itching inclination to increase their number. Just as I was taking
my check, the governor and his lady drove up. They spied me
out in the crowd, and having sent for me, took me with them to
their box, where I placed myself behind them, in such a position
as to converse at my ease with either.

The theater was filled with spectators from the ceiling downwards, the pit thronged almost to suffocation, and the stage crowded
with knights of the three military orders. Here is a full house!
said I to Don Alphonso. You are not to consider that as anything
extraordinary, answered he; the tragedy now about to be produced
is from the pen of Don Gabriel Triaquero, the most fashionable
dramatic writer of his day. Whenever the play-bill announces any
novelty from this favorite author, the whole town of Valencia is in
a bustle. The men as well as the women talk incessantly on the
subject of the piece: all the boxes are taken; and, on the first night
of performance, there is a risk of broken limbs in getting in, though
the price of admission is doubled, with the exception of the pit,
which is too authoritative a part of the house for the proprietors to
tamper with its patience. What a paroxysm of partiality! said I to
the governor. This eager curiosity of the public, this hot-headed
impatience to be present at the first representation of Don Gabriel's
pieces, gives me a magnificent idea of that poet's genius.

At this period of our conversation the curtain rose. We immediately left off talking, to fix our whole attention on the stage. The
applauses were rapturous even at the prologue: as the performance
advanced, every sentiment and situation, nay, almost every line of
the piece called forth a burst of acclamation; and at the end of
each act the clapping of hands was so loud and incessant, as almost
to bring the building about our ears. After the dropping of the
curtain, the author was pointed out to me, going about from box
to box, and with all the modesty of a successful poet, submitting
his head to the imposition of those laurels, which the genteeler,
and especially the fairer part of the audience had prepared for his
coronation.

We returned to the governor's palace, where we were met by a party of three or four gentlemen. Besides these mere amateurs there were two veteran authors of considerable eminence in their line, and a gentleman of Madrid with tolerably fair claims to critical authority and judgment. They had all been at the play. The new piece was the only topic of conversation during supper-time Gentlemen, said a knight of St. James, what do you think of this tragedy? Has it not every claim to the character of a finished work? Thoughts that breathe, and words that burn, a hand to touch the true chords of pity, and sweep the lyre of poetry; requisites how rarely, and yet how admirably united! In a word, it is the performance of a person mixing in the higher circles of society. There can be no possible difference of opinion on that subject, said a knight of Alcantara. The piece is full of strokes which Apollo himself might have aimed, and of perplexities contrived so that none but the author himself could have unraveled them. I appeal to that acute and ingenious stranger, added he, addressing his discourse to the Castilian gentleman; he looks to me like a good judge, and I will lay a wager that he is on my side of the question. Take care how you stake on an uncertainty, my worthy knight, answered the gentleman with a sarcastic smile. I am not of your provincial school; we do not pass our judgment so hastily at Madrid. Far from sentencing a piece on its first representation, we are jealous of its apparent merit while aided by scenic deception; our fancies and our feelings may be carried away for the moment, but our serious decision is suspended till we have read the work; and the most common result of its appeal to the press is a defalcation from its powers of pleasing on the stage.

Thus you perceive, pursued he, that it is our practice to examine a work of genius closely before we stamp on it the mark of a stock piece: its author's fame, let it ring as loudly as is may, can never confound our exactness of discrimination. When Lope de Vega himself or Calderona ventured on the boards, they encountered rigid critics, though in an audience which doted on them: critics who would not sign their passport to the regions of immortality till they had sifted their claims to be admitted there.

That is a little too much, interrupted the knight of St. James. We are not quite so cautious as you. It is not our custom to wait for the printing of a piece in order to decide on its reputation. By the very first performance it sinks or swims. It does not even seem necessary to be inconveniently attentive to the business of the stage. It is sufficient that we know it for a production of Don Gabriel, to be persuaded that it combines every excellence. The works of that poet may justly be considered as commencing a new era, and fixing the criterion of good taste. The school of Lope and Calderona was the mere cart of Thespis, compared with the polished scenes of this great dramatic master. The gentleman, who looked up to Lope and Calderona as the Sophocles and Euripides of the Spaniards, could not easily be brought to acknowledge such wild canons of criticism. This is dramatic heresy with a vengeance! exclaimed he. Since you compel me, gentlemen, to decide like you on the fallacious evidence of a first night, I must tell you that I am not at all satisfied with this new tragedy of your Don Gabriel. As a poem it abounds more with glittering conceits than with passages of pathos or delineations of nature. The verses, three out of four, are defective either in measure or rhyme; the characters, clumsily imagined or incongruously supported; and the thoughts have often the obscurity of a riddle without its ingenuity.

The two authors at table, who, with a prudence equally commendable and unusual, had said nothing for fear of lying under the imputation of jealousy, could not help assenting to the last speaker's opinions by their looks; which warranted me in concluding that their silence was less owing to the perfection of the work than to the dictates of personal policy. As for the military critics, they got to their old topic of ringing the changes on Don Gabriel, and exalted him to a level with the under-tenants of Olympus. This extravagant association with the demi-gods, this blind and stiff-necked idolatry, divorced the Castilian from his little stock of patience, so that, raising his hands to heaven, he broke out abruptly into a volley of enthusiasm : O divine Lope de Vega, sublime and unrivaled genius, who has left an immeasurable space between thee and all the Gabriels who would light their tapers from thy bright effulgence ! and thou, mellow, soft-voiced Calderona, whose elegance and sweetness, rejecting buskined rant and tragic swell, reign with undisputed sway over the affections, fear not, either of you, lest your altars should be overturned by this tongue-tied nursling of the muses ! It will be the utmost of his renown, if posterity, before whose eyes your works shall live in daily view, and form their dear delight, shall enroll his name, as matter of history and curious record, on the list of obsolete authors.

This animated apostrophe, for which the company was not at all prepared, raised a hearty laugh, after which we all rose from table and withdrew. An apartment had been got ready for me by Don Alphonso's order, where I found a good bed ; and my lordship, lying down in luxurious weariness, went to sleep upon the tag of the Castilian gentleman's impassioned vindication, and dreamed most crustily of the injustice done to Lope and Calderona by ignorant pretenders.

CHAPTER VI.

GIL BLAS, WALKING ABOUT THE STREETS OF VALENCIA, MEETS
WITH A MAN OF SANCTITY, WHOSE PIOUS FACE HE HAS SEEN
SOMEWHERE ELSE. WHAT SORT OF MAN THIS MAN OF
SANCTITY TURNS OUT TO BE.

As I had not been able to complete my view of the city on the preceding day, I got up betimes in the morning with the intention of taking another walk. In the street I remarked a Carthusian friar, who doubtless was thus early in motion to promote the interests of his order. He walked with his eyes fixed on the ground, and a gait so holy and contemplative, as to inspire every passenger with religious awe. His path was in the same direction as mine. I looked at him with more than ordinary curiosity, and could not help fancying it was Don Raphael, that man of shifts and expedients, who has already secured so honorable a niche in the temple of fame. (*See Books I. to VI. of my Memoirs.*)

I was so utterly astonished, so thrown off my balance by this meeting, that instead of accosting the monk, I remained motionless for some seconds, which gave him time to get the start of me. Just heaven! said I, were there ever two faces more exactly alike? I do not know what to make of it! It seems incredible that Raphael should turn up in such a guise! And yet how is it possible to be any one else? I felt too great a curiosity to get at the truth not to pursue the inquiry. Having ascertained the way to the monastery of the Carthusians, I repaired thither immediately, in the hope of coming across the object of my search on his return, and with the full intent of stopping and parleying with him. But it was quite unnecessary to wait for his arrival to enlighten my mind on the subject: on reaching the convent gate, another physiognomy, such as few persons had read without paying for their lesson, resolved all my doubts into certainty; for the friar who served in the capacity of porter was unquestionably my old and godly-visaged servant, Ambrose de Lamela.

Our surprise was equal on both sides at meeting again in such a place. Is not this a play upon the senses? said I, paying my compliments to him. Is it actually one of my friends who presents himself to my astonished sight? He did not know me again at first, or probably might pretend not to do so; but reflecting within himself that it was in vain to deny his own identity, he assumed the start of a man who all at once hits upon a circumstance which had hitherto escaped his recollection. Ah, Signor Gil Blas! exclaimed he, excuse my not recognizing your person immediately. Since I have lived in this holy place, every faculty of my soul has been absorbed in the performance of the duties prescribed by our rules, so that by degrees I lose the remembrance of all worldly objects and events.

After a separation of ten years, said I, it gives me much pleasure to find you again in so venerable a garb. For my part, answered he, it fills me with shame and confusion to appear in it before a man who has been an eye-witness of my guilty courses. These ghostly weeds are at once the charm of my present life, and the condemnation of my former. Alas! added he, heaving a righteous sigh, to be worthy of wearing it, my earlier years should have been passed in primitive innocence. By this discourse, so rational and edifying, replied I, it is plain, my dear brother, that the finger of the Lord has been upon you, that you are marked out for a vessel of sanctification. I tell you once again, I am delighted at it, and would give the world to know in what miraculous manner you and Raphael were led into the path of the righteous; for I am persuaded that it was his own self whom I met in the town, habited as a Car-thusian. I was extremely sorry afterwards not to have stopped and spoken to him in the street; and I am waiting here to apologize for my neglect on his return.

You were not mistaken, said Lamela, it was Don Raphael him-self whom you saw; and as for the particulars of our conversion, they are as follow: After parting with you near Segorba, we struck into the Valencia road, with the design of bettering our trade by some new speculation. Chance or destiny one day led our steps into the church of the Carthusians, while service was performing in the choir. The demeanor of the brethren attracted our notice, and we experienced in our own persons the involuntary homage which vice pays to virtue. We admired the fervor with which they poured forth their devotions, their looks of pious mortification, their dead-ness to the pleasures of the world and the flesh, and in the settled composure of their countenances, the outward sign of an approving conscience within.

While making these observations, we fell into a train of thought which became like manna to the hungry and thirsty soul: we com-pared our habits of life with the employments of these holy men, and the wide difference between our spiritual conditions filled us with confusion and affright. Lamela, said Don Raphael, as we went out of church, how do you stand affected by what we have just seen? For my part, there is no disguising the truth, my mind is ill at ease. Emotions, new and indescribable, are rushing upon my mind: and, for the first time in my life, I reproach myself with the wickedness of my past actions. I am just in the same temper of soul, answered I; my iniquities are all drawn up in array against me, they beset me, they stare me in the face; my heart, hitherto proof against all the arrows of remorse, is at this moment shot through, torn and disfigured, tormented and destroyed. Ah! my dear Ambrose, resumed my partner, we are two stray sheep, whom our Heavenly Father, in mercy, would lead back gently to the fold. It is he himself, my child, it is he who warms and guides us. Let us not be deaf to the call of his voice; let us abandon all our wicked courses, let us begin from this day to work out our salvation with diligence and in the spirit of repentance: we had better spend the remainder of our days in this convent, and consecrate them to penitence and devotion.

I applauded Raphael's sentiment, continued brother Ambrose; and we formed the glorious resolution of becoming Carthusians. To carry it into effect, we applied to the venerable prior, who was no sooner made acquainted with our purpose, than to ascertain whether our call was from the world above or the world beneath, he appointed us to cells, and all the strictness of monkish disci-pline, for a whole year. We acted up to the rules with equal regu-larity and fortitude, and, by way of reward, were admitted among the novices. Our condition was so much what we wished it, and our hearts were so full of religious zeal, that we underwent the toils of our novitiate with unflinching courage. When that was over, we professed; after which, Don Raphael, appearing admirably well qualified, both by natural talent and various experience, for the management of secular concerns, was chosen assistant to an old friar who was at that time proctor. The son of Lucinda would infinitely have preferred dedicating every remaining moment of his existence to prayer; but he found it necessary to sacrifice his taste for devotion, in furtherance of the general prosperity. He entered with so much zeal and knowledge into the interests of the house, that he was considered as the most eligible person to succeed the old proctor, who died three years afterwards. Don Raphael accordingly fills that office at present; and it may be truly said that he discharges his duty to the entire satisfaction of all our fathers, who praise in the highest terms his conduct in the administration of our temporalities. What is most of all miraculous, and shows the hand of heaven in his conversion, is that, with such an accumulation of business rushing in upon him in his bursarial department, his regards are inalienably fixed on the world to come. When business leaves him but a moment to recruit nature, instead of lavishing the short period in indulgence, his thoughts wing their way into the regions of devout and holy meditation. In short, he is the most exemplary member of this body.

At this period of our conversation I interrupted Lamela by an ebullition of joy to which I gave vent at the sight of Raphael coming in. Here he is! exclaimed I: behold that righteous bursar for whom I have been so impatiently waiting. With a leap and a bound did I run to meet and embrace him. He submitted to the hug with his newly-acquired resignation; and, without betraying the slightest shock at meeting with an old companion of his profaner hours, his words were dictated by the spirit of gentleness and humility: The powers above be praised, Signor de Santillane, the powers be praised for this kind providence whereby we meet again. In good truth, my dear Raphael, replied I, your happy destiny pleases me as much as if it had been my own good luck; brother Ambrose has told me the whole story of your conversion, and the tale almost moved me to a similar change. What a glorious lot for you two, my friends, when you have reason to flatter yourselves with being among that picked number of the elect, who have eternal happiness thrust upon them whether they will or no!

Two miserable sinners like ourselves, resumed the son of Lucinda, with an air which marked the extreme of sanctified morality, must not hope that our own merits are of weight enough to save our souls; but even the wicked one who repenteth, findeth grace with the Father of mercies. And you, Signor Gil Blas, added he, is it not time to lay in a claim for pardon of the offenses which you have committed? What is your business here in Valencia? Are you not hankering after some office of devil's deputy, and making shipwreck of your voyage to another world? Not so, by the blessing of heaven, answered I; since I turned my back on the court, I have led a very moral sort of life: sometimes enjoying rural recreations on an estate of mine at a few leagues distance from this town, and sometimes coming hither to pass my time with my friend the governor, whom you both of you must know perfectly well.

On this cue I related to them the story of Don Alphonso de Leyva. They heard the particulars with attention; and on my telling them that I had carried to Samuel Simon, on the part of that nobleman, the three thousand ducats of which we had robbed him, Lamela interrupted the thread of my narrative, and addressing his discourse to Raphael, said: Father Hilary, if this be true, the honest vender of wares has no reason to quarrel with a robbery which has paid him fifty per cent.; and our consciences, as far as that indictment goes, may bask in the sunshine of acquitted innocence. Brother Ambrose and I, said the bursar, did actually, on the assumption of the habit, send Samuel Simon fifteen hundred ducats privately, by a pious ecclesiastic who made a pilgrimage to Xelva for the sole purpose of accomplishing this restitution; but it will go hard with Samuel at the general reckoning, if he for filthy lucre could soil his fingers with that sum, after having been reimbursed in full by Signor de Santillane. But, said I, how do you know that your fifteen hundred ducats were faithfully paid into his hands? Unquestionably they were! exclaimed Don Raphael; I would answer for the disinterested purity of that ecclesiastic as soon as for my own. I would be your collateral security, said Lamela; he is a priest of the strictest sanctity, a sort of universal almoner; and though many times cited for sums of money, deposited with him for charitable uses, he has always non-suited the plaintiffs, and gone out of court with an augmentation of alms-giving notoriety.

Our conversation continued for some time longer: at length we parted, with many a pious exhortation on their side, always to have the fear of the Lord before my eyes, and with many an earnest entreaty on mine, that they would remember me constantly in their prayers. Don Alphonso was now the first object of my search. You will never guess, said I, with whom I have just had a long conference. I am but now come from two venerable Carthusians of your acquaintance, the name of the one is father Hilary, that of the other, brother Ambrose. You are mistaken, answered Don Alphonso; I am not acquainted with a single Carthusian. Pardon me, replied I; you have seen brother Ambrose at Xelva in the capacity of commissary, and father Hilary as register to the Inquisition. Oh heaven! exclaimed the governor with surprise, can it be within the bounds of possibility that Raphael and Lamela should have turned Carthusians? It is even so, answered I; they professed several years ago. The former is bursar and proctor to the convent; the latter, porter.

The son of Don Cæsar rubbed his forehead twice or thrice, then shaking his head, These worshipful officers of the Inquisition, said he, most assuredly purpose playing over the old farce on a new stage here. You judge of them by prejudice, answered I, from the impression of their characters as men of sin: but had you been edified by their lectures as I have been, you would think more favorably of their holiness. To be sure, it is not for mortal men to fathom the depth of other men's hearts; but to all appearance they are two prodigals returned home. It possibly may be so, replied Don Alphonso: there are many instances of libertines, who hide their heads in cloisters, after having scandalized human nature by their obliquities, to expiate their offenses by a severe penance: I heartily wish that our two monks may be such libertines restored.

Well! and why not? said I. They have embraced the monastic life of their own accord, and have squared their conduct for a length of time according to the maxims of their order. You may say what you please, retorted the governor; but I do not like the convent's rents being received by this father Hilary, of whom I cannot help entertaining a very untoward opinion. When the fine story he told us of his adventures comes across my mind, I tremble for the reverend brotherhood. I am willing to believe with you, that he has taken the vow with the pious intention of keeping it; but the blaze of gold may be too much for the weakness of his regenerated eye-sight. It is bad policy to lock up a reformed drunkard in a wine cellar.

In the course of a few days Don Alphonso's misgivings were fully justified; these two official props and stays of the establishment ran away with the year's revenue. This news, which was immediately noised about the town, could not do otherwise than set the tongues of the wits in motion; for they always make themselves merry at the crosses and losses of the well-endowed religious orders. As for the governor and myself, we condoled with the Carthusians, but kept our acquaintance with the apostate pilferers in the background.

CHAPTER VII.

GIL BLAS RETURNS TO HIS SEAT AT LIRIAS. SCIPIO'S AGREE-
ABLE INTELLIGENCE, AND A REFORM IN THE DOMESTIC
ARRANGEMENTS.

I PASSED a week at Valencia in the first company, living on equal terms with the best of the nobility. Plays, balls, concerts, grand dinners, ladies' parties, all things that heart could wish or vanity grow tall upon, were provided for me by the governor and his lady, to whom I paid my court so dexterously, that they were heartily sorry to see me set out on my return to Lirias. They even obliged me, before they would let me go, to engage for a division of my time between them and my hermitage. It was determined that I should spend the winter in Valencia, and the summer at my seat. After this bargain, my benefactors left me at liberty to tear myself from them, and go where their kindness would be always 'taring me in the face.

Scipio, who was waiting impatiently for my return, was ready to jump out of his skin for joy at the sight of me; and his ecstasies were doubled at my circumstantial account of the journey. And now for your history, my friend, said I, taking breath: to what moral uses have you turned the solitary period of my absence? Has the time passed agreeably? As well, answered he, as it could with a servant to whom nothing is so dear as the presence of his master. I have walked over our little domain, circuitously and diagonally: sometimes seated on the margin of a fountain in our wood, I have taken pleasure in beholding the transparency of its waters, which are as pellucid as those of the sacred spring, whose projection from the rock made the vast forest of Albunea to resound with the roar of the cascade: sometimes lying at the foot of a tree, I have listened to the song of the linnet or the nightingale. At other times I have hunted or fished; and, what has given me more rational delight than all these pastimes, I have whiled away many a profitable hour in the improvement of my mind.

I interrupted my secretary in a tone of eager inquiry, to ask where he had procured books. I found them, said he, in an elegant library here in the house, whither master Joachim took me. Heyday! in what corner, resumed I, can this said library be? Did we not go over the whole building on the day of our arrival? You fancied so, rejoined he; but you are to know that we only explored three sides of the square, and forgot the fourth. It was there that Don Cæsar, when he came to Lirias, employed part of his time in reading. There are in this library some very good books, left as a never-failing phylactery against the blue devils, when our gardens despoiled of Flora's treasure, and our woods of their leafy honors, shall no longer challenge those miscreant invaders to combat in the forest or the bower. The lords of Leyva have not done things by halves, but have catered for the mind as well as for the body.

This intelligence filled me with sincere rapture. I was shown to the fourth side of the square, and feasted with an intellectual banquet. Don Cæsar's room I immediately determined to make my own. That nobleman's bed was still there, with correspondent furniture, consisting of historical tapestry, representing the rape of the Sabine woman by the Romans. From the bed-chamber, I went into a closet fitted up with low book-cases well filled, and over them the portraits of the Spanish kings. Near a window whence you command a prospect of a most bewitching country, there was an ebony writing-desk and a large sofa, covered with black morocco. But I gave my attention principally to the library. It was composed of philosophers, poets, historians; and abounded in romances. Don Cæsar seemed to give the preference to that light reading, if one might judge by the profusion of supply. I must own, to my shame, that my taste was not at all above the level of those productions, notwithstanding the extravagances they delight in stringing together: whether it was owing to my not being a very critical reader at that time, or because the Spaniards are naturally addicted to the marvellous. I must nevertheless plead in my own justification, that I was alive to the charms of a sprightly and popular morality, and that Lucian, Horace, and Erasmus became my favorite and standard authors.

My friend, said I to Scipio, when my eyes had coursed over my library, here is wherewithal to feed and pamper our minds; but our present business is to reform our household. On that subject I can spare you a great deal of trouble, answered he. During your absence I have sifted your people thoroughly, and flatter myself it is no empty boast to say that I know them. Let us begin with master Joachim: I take him to be as great a scoundrel as ever breathed, and have no doubt but he was turned away from the archbishop's for errors which were too great to be excepted in the passing of his accounts. Yet we must keep him for two reasons: the first, because he is a good cook; and the second, because I shall always have an eye over him; I shall peep into his actions like a jackdaw into a marrow-bone, and he must be a more cunning fellow than I take him for, to evade my vigilance. I have already told him that you intended discharging three-fourths of your establishment. This declaration stuck in his stomach; and he assured me that, owing to his extreme desire of living with you, he would be satisfied with half his present wages rather than be turned off, which made me suspect that he was tied to the string of some petticoat in the hamlet, and did not like to break up his quarters. As for the under-cook, he is a drunkard, and the porter a foul-mouthed Cerberus, of whose guardianship our gates are in no want; neither is the gamekeeper a necessary evil. I shall take the latter office myself, as you may see to-morrow, when we have got our fowling-pieces in order, and are provided with powder and shot. With regard to the footmen, one of them is an Arragonese, and to my mind a very good sort of fellow. We will keep him; but all the rest are such rapscallions, that I would not advise you to harbor one of them, if you wanted an army of attendants.

After having fully debated the point, we resolved to keep well with the cook, the scullion, the Arragonese, and to get rid of the remainder as decently as we could: all which was planned and executed on the same day, mollifying the bitter dose by the application of a few pistoles, which Scipio took from our strong box, and distributed among them as from me. When we had carried this reform into effect, order was soon established in our mansion; we divided the business fairly among our remaining people, and began to look into our expenses. I could willingly have been contented with very frugal commons; but my secretary, loving high dishes and relishing bits, was not a man who would suffer master Joachim to hold his place as a sinecure. He kept his talents in such constant play, working double tides at dinner and at supper, that any one would have thought we had been converted by father Hilary, and were working out the term of our probation.

CHAPTER VIII.

THE LOVES OF GIL BLAS AND THE FAIR ANTONIA.

Two days after my return from Valencia to Lirias, clodpole Basil, my farming man, came at my dressing-time, to beg the favor of introducing his daughter Antonia, who was very desirous, as he said, to have the honor of paying her respects to her new master. I answered that it was very proper, and would be well received. He withdrew, and in a few minutes returned with his peerless

"IN A FEW MINUTES RETURNED WITH HIS PEERLESS ANTONIA."

Antonia. That epithet, though bold, will not be thought extravagant, in the case of a girl from sixteen to eighteen years of age, uniting to regular features the finest complexion and the brightest eyes in the world. She was dressed in nothing better than a stuff gown; but a stature somewhat above the female standard, a dignified deportment, and such graces as soared higher than the mere freshness and glow of youth, communicated to her rustic attire the simplicity of classical costume. She had no cap on her head; her hair was fastened behind with a knot of flowers, according to the chaste severity of the Spartan fashionables.

When she illumined my chamber with her presence, I was struck as much on a heap by her beauty, as ever were the princes, knights, nobles, and strangers assembled at the solemn feast and tournament of Charlemain, by the personal charms of Angelica. Instead of receiving Antonia with modish indifference, and paying her compliments of course, instead of ringing the changes on her father's happiness in possessing so lovely a daughter, I stood stock-still, staring, gaping, stammering: I could not have uttered an articulate sound for the universal world. Scipio, who saw clearly what was the matter with me, took the words out of my mouth, and accepted those bills of admiration which my affairs were in too much disorder to admit of my duly honoring. For her part, my figure being shrouded by a dressing-gown and night-cap, like the orb of day by a winter fog, she accosted me without being shame-faced, and paid her duty in terms which fired all the combustibles in my composition, though her words were but the holiday expressions of commonplace salutation. In the mean time, while my secretary, Basil, and his daughter, were engaged in reciprocal exchange of civility, I found my senses again; and passed from one extreme of absurdity to another, just as if I had thought that a hare-brained loquacity would be a set-off against the idiotic silence of my first encounter. I exhausted all my stock of well-bred rodomontade; and expressed myself with so unguarded a freedom, as to make Basil look about him: so that he, with his eye upon me as a man who would set every engine at work to seduce Antonia, was in a hurry to get her safely out of my apartment, with a resolved purpose, probably, of withdrawing her for ever from my pursuit.

Scipio finding himself alone with me, said with a smile: Here is another defense for you against the blue devils! I did not know that your farming man had so pretty a daughter; for I had never seen her before, though I have been twice at his house. He must have taken infinite pains to keep her out of the way, and it is impossible to be angry with him for it. What the plague! here is a morsel for a liquorish palate! But there seems to be no necessity for blazoning her perfections to you; their very first glance dazzled you out of countenance. I do not deny it, answered I. Ah! my beloved friend, I have surely seen an inhabitant of the realms above; the electrical spark now thrills through all my frame, it scorches like lightning, yet tingles like the vivifying fluid at my heart.

You delight me beyond measure, replied my secretary, by giving me to understand that you have at length fallen in love. Nothing but a mistress was wanting to complete your rural establishment at all points. Thanks to Heaven, you are now likely to be accommodated in every way. I am well aware that we shall have a hard matter to elude Basil's vigilance, but leave that to me, and I will

undertake before the end of three days to manage a private meeting
for you with Antonia. Master Scipio, said I, it is not so sure that
you will be able to keep your word; but at all events, I have not
the least desire to make the experiment. I will have nothing to do
with the ruin of that girl; for she is an angel, and does not deserve
to be numbered among the fallen ones. Therefore, instead of
laying the guilt upon your soul of assisting me in her dishonor, I
have made up my mind to marry her with your kind help, supposing her heart not to be preoccupied by a prior attachment. I
had no idea, said he, of your directly plunging headlong into the
cold bath of matrimony. The generality of landlords, in your place,
would stand upon the ancient tenure of manorial rights : they would
not deal with Antonia upon the square of modern law and gospel,
till after failure in the establishment of their feudal privileges. But
though this may be the way of the world, do not suppose that I am
by any means against your honorable passion, or at all wish to dissuade you from your purpose. Your bailiff's daughter deserves the
distinction you design for her, if she can give you the first-fruits of
her heart, an offering of sensibility and gratitude; that is what I
shall ascertain this very day by talking with her father, and possibly
with her.

My agent was a man to transact his business according to the
letter. He went to see Basil privately, and in the evening came to
me in my closet, where I waited for him with impatience, somewhat exasperated by apprehension. There was a slyness in his
countenance, whence my prognostic inclined to the brighter side.
Judging, said I, by that look of suppressed merriment, you are
come to acquaint me that I shall soon be at the summit of human
bliss. Yes, my dear master, answered he, the heavens smile upon
your vows. I have talked the matter over with Basil and his
daughter, declaring your intentions without reserve. The father
is delighted at the idea of your asking his blessing as a son-in-law;
and you may set your heart at rest about Antonia's taste in a husband. Darts and flames ! cried I in an ecstasy of amorous transport; what ! am I so happy as to have made myself agreeable to
that lovely creature ? Never question it, replied he; she loves you
already. It is true, she has not owned so much by word of mouth ;
but my assurance rests on the tale-telling sparkle of her eye, when
your proposals were made known to her. And yet you have a
rival ! A rival ! exclaimed I, with a faltering voice, and a cheek
blanched with fear. Do not let that give you the least uneasiness,
said he; your competitor cannot bid very high, for he is no other
man than Master Joachim your cook. Ah ! the hangdog ! said I,
with an involuntary shout of laughter: this is the reason, then, why
he had so great an objection to being turned out of my service.
Exactly so, answered Scipio; within these few days he made proposals of marriage to Antonia, who politely declined them. With
submission to your better judgment, replied I it would be expedient, at least so it strikes me, to get rid of that strange fellow,
before he is informed of my intended match with Basil's daughter :
a cook, as you are aware, is a dangerous rival. You are perfectly

in the right, rejoined my trusty counselor; we must clear the premises of him—he shall receive his discharge from me to-morrow morning, before he puts a finger in the fricandeaus; thus you will have nothing more to fear either from his poisonous sauces or bewitching songue. Yet it goes rather against the grain with me to part with to good a cook; but I sacrifice the interests of my own belly to the preservation of your precious person. You need not, said I, take on so for his loss: he had no exclusive patent; and I will send to Valencia for a cook, who shall outcook all his fine cookery. According to my promise I wrote immediately to Don Alphonso, to let him know that our kitchen wanted a prime minister; and on the following day he filled up the vacancy in so worthy a manner, as reconciled Scipio at once to the change in culinary politics.

Though my adroit and active secretary had assured me of Antonia's secret self-congratulation on the conquest of her landlord's heart, I could not venture to rely solely on his report. I was fearful lest he should have been entrapped by false appearances. To be more certain of my bliss, I determined on speaking in person to the fair Antonia. I therefore went to Basil's house, and confirmed to him what my embassador had announced. This honest peasant, of patriarchal simplicity and golden-aged frankness, after having heard me through, did not hesitate to own that it would br the greatest happiness of his life to give me his daughter; bue added he, you are by no means to suppose that it is because you are lord of the manor. Were you still steward to Don Cæsar and Don Alphonso, I should prefer you to all other suitors who might apply: I have always felt a sort of kindness towards you: and nothing vexes me, but that Antonia has not a thumping fortune to bring with her. I want not the vile dross, said I; her person is the only dowry that I covet. Your humble servant for that, cried he; but you will not settle accounts with me after that fashion; I am not a beggar, to marry my daughter upon charity. Basil de Buenotrigo is in circumstances, by the blessing of Providence, to portion her off decently; and I mean that she should set out a little supper, if you are to be at the expense of dinners. In a word, the rental of this estate is only five hundred ducats: I shall raise it to a thousand on the strength of this marriage.

Just as you please, my dear Basil, replied I; we are not likely to nave any dispute about money matters. We are both of a mind: all that remains is to get your daughter's consent. You have mine, said he, and that is enough. Not altogether so, answered I; though yours may be absolutely necessary, no business can be done without hers. Hers follows mine of course, replied he; I should like to catch her murmuring against my sovereign commands! Antonia, rejoined I, with dutiful submission to paternal authority, is ready without question to obey your will implicitly in all things; but I know not whether in the present instance she would do so without violence to her own feelings; and should that be the case, I could never forgive myself for being the occasion of unhappiness to her; in short, it is not enough that I obtain her hand from you, if her heart is to heave a sigh at the decision of her destiny. Oh, blessed virgin! said Basil, all these fine doctrines of philosophy are far above my reach; speak to Antonia your own self, and you will find, or I am very much mistaken, that she wishes for nothing better than to be your wife. These words were no sooner out of his mouth than he called his daughter, and left me with her for a few short minutes.

Not to trifle with so precious an opportunity, I broke my mind to her at once: Lovely Antonia, said I, it remains with you to fix the color of my future days. Though I have your father's consent, do not think so meanly of me as to suppose that I would avail myself of it to violate the sacred freedom of your choice. Rapturous as must be the possession of your charms, I waive my pretentions if you but tell me that your duty and not your will complies. It would be affectation to put on such a repugnance, answered she; the honor of your addresses is too flattering to excite any other than agreeable sensations, and I am thankful for my father's tender care of me, instead of demurring to his will. I am not sure whether such an acknowledgment may not be contrary to the rules of female reserve in the polite world; but if you were disagreeable to me, I should be plain-spoken enough to tell you so; why, then, should I not be equally free in owning the kind feelings of my heart?

At sounds like these, which I could not hear without being enraptured, I dropped on my knee before Antonia, and in the excess of my tender emotions, taking one of her fair hands, kissed it with an affectionate and impassioned action. My dear Antonia, said I, your frankness enchants me; go on, let nothing induce you to depart from it; you are conversing with your future husband; let your soul expand itself, and reveal all its inmost emotions in his presence. Thus, then, may I entertain the flattering hope that you will not frown on the union of our destinies! The coming in of Basil at this moment prevented me from giving further vent to the delightful sensations which thrilled through me. Impatient to know how his daughter had behaved, and ready primed for scolding in case she had been perverse or coy, he made up to me immediately. Well, now! said he, are you satisfied with Antonia? So much so, answered I, that I am going this very moment to set forward the preparations for our marriage. So saying, I left the father and daughter, for the purpose of taking counsel with my secretary thereupon.

CHAPTER IX.

NUPTIALS OF GIL BLAS WITH THE FAIR ANTONIA; THE STYLE AND MANNER OF THE CEREMONY; THE PERSONS ASSISTING THEREAT; AND THE FESTIVITIES ENSUING THEREUPON.

THOUGH there was no occasion to consult with the lords of Leyva about my marriage, yet both Scipio and myself were of opinion that I could not decently do otherwise than communicate to them my purpose of connecting myself with Basil's daughter, and just pay them the compliment of asking their advice, after the act was finally determined on.

I immediately went off for Valencia, where my visit was a matter of surprise, and still more the purport of it. Don Cæsar and Don Alphonso, who were acquainted with Antonia, having seen her more than once, wished me joy on my good fortune in a wife. Don Cæsar, in particular, made his speech upon the occasion with so much youthful fire, that if there had not been reason to suppose his lordship weaned, by that icy moralist, time, from certain naughty propensities, I should have suspected him of going to Lirias now and then, not so much to look after his concerns there, as after his little empress of the dairy. Seraphina, too, with the kindest assurances of a lively interest in whatever might befall me, said that she had heard a very favorable character of Antonia; but, added she, with a malicious fling, as if to taunt me with my supercilious reception of Sephora's amorous advances, even though her beauty had not been so much the talk of the country, I could have depended on your taste, from former experience of its delicacy and fastidiousness.

Don Cæsar and his son did not stop at cold approbation of my marriage, but declared that they would defray all the expenses of it. Measure back your steps, said they, to Lirias, and stay quietly there till you hear further from us. Make no preparation for your nuptials, for we shall make that our concern. To meet their kind intentions with becoming gratitude, I returned to my mansion, and acquainted Basil and his daughter with the projected kindness of our patrons. We determined to wait their pleasure with as much patience as falls to the lot of poor human nature under such circumstances. Eight long days dragged out their tedious measure, and brought no tidings of our bliss. But the rewards of self-control are not the less assured for being slow: on the ninth, a coach drawn by four mules drove up, with a cargo of mantua-makers for the bride, and an assortment of rich silks on which to exercise their art. Several livery servants, mounted on mules, accompanied the cavalcade. One of them brought me a letter from Don Alphonso. That nobleman sent me word that he would be at Lirias next day with his father and his wife, and that the marriage ceremony should be performed on the day after that, by the vicar-general of Valencia. And just so it came to pass: Don Cæsar, his son, and Seraphina, with that venerable dignitary, were punctual to their appointment; all four of them in a coach and six; none of your mules, like the mantua-makers! preceded by another coach and four, with Seraphina's women; and the rear was brought up by a company of the governor's guards.

The governor's lady had hardly entered the house, before she testified an ardent longing to see Antonia, who on her part no sooner knew that Seraphina was arrived, than she ran forward to bid her welcome, with a respectful kiss upon her hand, so gracefully and modestly impressed, that all the company were enchanted at the action. And now, madam! said Don Cæsar to his daughter-in-law, what do you think of Antonia? Could Santillane have made a better choice? No, answered Seraphina, they are worthy each of the other; there can be no doubt but their union will be most happy. In short, every one was lavish in the praise of my intended; and if they felt her beams so powerfully under the eclipse of a stuff gown, what must they not have endured from her

ANTONIA.

brightness, in the meridian sunshine of her wedding finery? One would have fancied she had been clothed in silks, jewels, and fine linen from her cradle, by the dignity of her air and the ease of her deportment.

The happy moment which was to unite two fond lovers in the bands of Hymen being arrived, Don Alphonso took me by the hand and led me to the altar, while Seraphina conferred the like honor on the bride elect. Our procession had marched in fit and decent order through the hamlet to the chapel, where the vicar-general was waiting to go through the service; and the ceremony was performed amidst the heartfelt congratulations of the inhabitants, and of all the wealthy farmers in the neighborhood, whom Basil had invited to Antonia's wedding. Their daughters too came in their train, tricked out in ribbons and in flowers, and dancing to the music of their own tambourines. We returned to the mansion under the same escort: and there, by the provident attentions of Scipio, who officiated as high steward and master of the ceremonies, we found three tables set out; one for the principals of the party, another for their household, and the third, which was by far the largest, for all invited guests promiscuously. Antonia was at the first, the governor's lady having made a point of it; I did the honors of the second, and Basil was placed at the head of that where the country people dined. As for Scipio, he never sat down, but was here, there, and everywhere, fetching and carrying, changing plates and filling bumpers, urging the company to call freely for what they wanted, and egging them on to mirth and jollity.

The entertainment had been prepared by the governor's cooks; and that is as much as to say, that there were all the delicacies imaginable, in season or out of season. The good wines laid in for me by master Joachim, were set running at a furious rate; the guests were beginning to feel their jovial influence, pleasantry and repartee gave a zest and conviviality, when on a sudden our harmony was interrupted by an alarming occurrence. My secretary, being in the hall where I was dining with Don Alphonso's principal officers and Seraphina's women, suddenly fainted. I started up and ran to his assistance; and while I was employed in bringing him about, one of the women was taken ill also. It was evident to the whole company that this sympathetic malady must involve some mysterious incident, as in effect it turned out almost immediately, that thereby hung a tale; for Scipio soon recovered, and said to me in a low voice, Why must one man's meat be another man's poison, and the most auspicious of your days the curse of mine? But every man bears the bundle of his sins upon his back, and my pack-saddle is once more thrown across my shoulders in the person of my wife.

Powers of mercy! exclaimed I, this can never be; it is all a romance. What! you the husband of that lady whose nerves were so affected by the disturbance? Yes, sir, answered he, I am her husband; and fortune, if you will take the word of a sinner, could not have done me a dirtier office than by conjuring up such a grievance as this. I know not, my friend, replied I, what reasons you may have for thus belaboring your rib with wordy buffets, but however she may be to blame, in mercy keep a bridle on your tongue; if you have any regard for me, do not displace the mirth and spoil the pleasure of this nuptial meeting, by ominous disorder or enraged questions of past injuries. You shall have no reason to complain on that score, rejoined Scipio; but shall see presently whether I am not a very apt dissembler.

With this assurance he went forward to his wife, whom her

companions had also brought back to life and recollection; and, embracing her with as much apparent fervor as if his raptures had been real, Ah, my dear Beatrice, said he, heaven has at length united us again after ten years of cruel separation! But this blissful moment is well purchased by whole ages of torturing suspense! I know not, answered his spouse, whether you really are at all the happier for having recovered a part of yourself: but of this at least I am fully certain, that you never had any reason to run away from me as you

did. A fine story indeed! You found me one night with Signor Don Ferdinand de Leyva, who was in love with my mistress Julia, and consulted me on the subject of his passion; and only for that, you must take it into your stupid head, that I was caballing with him against your honor and my own: thereupon that poor brain of yours was turned with jealousy; you quitted Toledo in a huff, and ran away from your own flesh and blood as you would from a monster of the deserts, without leaving word why or wherefore. Now which of us two, be so good as to tell me, has most reason to take on and be pettish ? Your own dear self, beyond all question, replied Scipio. Beyond all question, re-echoed she, my own ill-used self. Don Ferdinand, very shortly after you had taken yourself off from Toledo, married Julia, with whom I continued as long as she lived; and, after we had lost her by sudden death, I came into my lady her sister's service, who, as well as all her maids, and I would do as much for them, will give me a good character; honest and sober, and a very termagant among the impertinent fellows.

My secretary, having nothing to allege against such a character from my lady and her maids, was determined to make the best of a bad bargain. Once for all, said he to his spouse, I acknowledge my bad behavior, and beg pardon for it before this honorable assembly. It was now time for me to act the mediator, and to move Beatrice for an act of amnesty, assuring her that her husband from this time forward would make it the great object of his life to play the husband to her satisfaction. She began to see that there was reason in roasting of eggs, and all present were loud in their congratulations, on the triumph of suffering virtue, and the renovated pledge of broken vows. To bind the contract firmer, and make it memorable, they were seated next to one another at table; their healths were drank according to the laws of toasting; wish you joy! many returns of this happy day! rang round on every side: one would have sworn that the dinner was given for their reconciliation, and not on account of my marriage.

The third table was the first to be cleared. The young villagers jumped up in a body; the lads took out their blooming partners; the tambourines struck up a merry beat; spectators flocked from the other tables, and caught the enlivening spirit from the gay bustle of the scene. Every limb and muscle of every individual was in motion: the household of the governor and his lady formed a set, apart from the rustics of the company, while their superiors did not disdain to mingle with the homelier dancers. Don Alphonso danced a saraband with Seraphina, and Don Cæsar another with Antonia, who afterwards took me for her partner. She did not perform much amiss, considering that she never got much further than the five positions, in learning which she had her ankles kicked to pieces by a provincial dancing-master at Albarazin, while on a visit to a tradesman's wife, one of her relations. As for me, who, as I have already said, had taken lessons at the Marchioness de Chaves's, I figured away as the principal man in this rural ballet. With regard to Beatrice and Scipio, they preferred a little private conversation to dancing, that they might compare notes on the subject of wear and tear during the painful period of separation: but their billing and cooing was interrupted by Seraphina, who, having been informed of this dramatic discovery, sent for them to pay the customary compliments of congratulation. My good people, said she, on this day of general joy, it gives me additional pleasure to see you two restored to one another. My friend Scipio, I return you your wife under a firm belief that she has always conducted herself as became a woman; take up your abode with her here, and be a good husband to her. And you, Beatrice, attach yourself to Antonia, and let her be as much the object of your devoted service as Signor de Santillane is that of your husband. Scipio, who could not possibly, after this, think of Penelope as fit to hold a candle to his own wife, promised to treat her with all the deference due to such a paragon of conjugal fidelity.

The country people, having kept up the dance till late, withdrew to their own homes; but the rejoicings were prolonged by the company in the house. There was a grand supper, and at bed-time the vicar-general pronounced the blessing of consummation. Seraphina undressed the bride, and the lords of Leyva did me the same honor. The ridiculous part of the business was, that Don Alphonso's officers and his lady's attendants took it into their heads, by way of diverting themselves, to perform the same ceremony: they also undressed Beatrice and Scipio, who, to render the scene supremely farcical, gravely allowed themselves to be untrussed, and put to bed with all nuptial pomp and state.

CHAPTER X.

THE HONEY-MOON (A VERY DULL TIME FOR THE READER AS A THIRD PERSON) ENLIVENED BY THE COMMENCEMENT OF SCIPIO'S STORY.

> "'Tis heaven itself, 'tis ecstasy of bliss,
> Uninterrupted joy, untired excess;
> Mirth following mirth, the moments dance away;
> Love claims the night, and friendship rules the day."

ON the day after the wedding the lords of Leyva returned to Valencia, after having lavished on me a thousand marks of friendship. There was such a general clearance, that my secretary and myself, with our respective wives, and our usual establishment, were left in undisturbed possession of our own home.

The efforts which we both made to please our ladies were not thrown away: I breathed by degrees into the partner of my joys and sorrows as much love for me as I entertained for her; and Scipio made his better part forget the woes and privations he had occasioned her. Beatrice, who had very winning ways with her, and was all things to all women, had no difficulty about worming herself into the good graces of her new mistress, and gaining her complete confidence. In short, we all four agreed admirably well together, and began to enjoy a bliss above the common lot of humanity. Every day rolled along more delightfully than the last. Antonia was pensive and demure; but Beatrice and myself were enlisted in the crew of mirth; and even though we had been constitutionally sedate, Scipio was among us, and he was of himself a pill to purge melancholy. The best creature in the world for a snug little party! one of those merry drolls who have only to show their comical faces, and set the table in a roar of inextinguishable laughter.

One day, when we had taken a fancy to go after dinner, and doze away the usual interval in the most sequestered spot about the grounds, my secretary got into such exuberant spirits, as to chase away the drowsy god by his exhilarating sallies. Do hold your tongue, my loquacious friend, said I : or else, if you are determined to wage war against this lazy custom of our afternoons, at least tell us something which we shall be the wiser for hearing. With all my heart and soul, sir, answered he. Would you have me go through all fabulous histories of wandering knights, distressed damsels, giants, enchanted castles, and the whole train of legendary advent es? I had much rather hear your own true history, replied I ; but that is a pleasure which you have not thought fit to give me so long as we have lived together, and I seem likely to go without it to the end of the chapter. How happens that? said he. If I have not told you my own story, it is because you never expressed the slightest wish to be troubled with the recital : therefore it is not my fault if you are in the dark about my past life ; but if you are really at all curious to be let into the secret, my loquacity is very much at your service on the occasion. Antonia, Beatrice, and myself, unanimously took him at his word, and arranged ourselves for listening like an attentive audience. The speculation was a safe one on our parts ; for the tale was sure to answer, either as a stimulant or a soporific.

I certainly ought to have been descended, said Scipio, from some family of the highest rank and earliest antiquity ; or in default of such parentage, from the most distinguished orders of personal merit, such as that of St. James or Alcantara, if a man may be permitted to decide on the fittest circumstances for his own birth : but as it is not among the privileges of human nature to elect one's own father, you are to know that mine, by name Torribio Scipio, was a subaltern myrmidon of the Holy Brotherhood. As he was going back and fore on the king's highway, and looking after business in his own line, he met once on a time, between Cuença and Toledo, with a young Bohemian babe of chance, who appeared very pretty in his eyes. She was alone, on foot, and carried her whole patrimony at her back in a kind of knapsack. Whither are you going, my little darling? said he in a philandering tone of voice, unlike the natural hoarseness of his accents. Good worthy gentleman, answered she, I am going to Toledo, where I hope to gain an honest livelihood by hook or by crook. Your intentions are highly commendable, retorted he ; and I doubt not but you may have many a hook and many a crook among the implements of your trade. Yes, with a blessing on my endeavors, rejoined she : I have several little ways of doing for myself : I know how to make washes and creams for the ladies' faces, perfumes for their noses and their chambers ; then I can tell fortunes, can search for things lost with a sieve and shears, and erect figures for the taking in of shadows with a glass.

Torribio, concluding that so well-provided a girl would be a very advantageous match for a man like himself, who could scarcely scrape wherewithal to support life by his own profession, though he was as good a thief-taker as the best of them, made her an offer of marriage, and she was nothing loth, nor prudishly coy. They flew on the wings of inclination and convenience to Toledo, where they were joined together; and you behold in me the happy pledge of holy and lawful matrimony. They fixed themselves in a shop on the outskirts of the town, where my mother commenced her career by selling the said washes, creams, tapes, laces, silk, thread, toys, and peddler's ware; but trade not being brisk enough to live comfortably by it, she turned fortune-teller. This drew her customers, got her countenance, credit, crowns, and pistoles: a thousand dupes of either sex soon trumpeted up the reputation of Coselina; for so my gypsy mamma had the honor to be named. Some one or other came every day to bargain for the exercise of her skill in the black art: at one time a nephew at his wit's and purse's end, wanting to know how soon his uncle was to set off post for the other world, and leave behind him wherewithal to piece his worn-out fortunes: at another, some yielding, love-sick girl, to inquire whether the swain who kept her company, and had promised to marry her, would keep his word or be false-hearted.

You will take notice, if you please, that my mother always sold good luck for good money; if the accomplishment trod on the heels of the prediction, well and good; if it was fulfilled according to the rule of contraries, she always cool, though the parties were ever so violently in a passion, and told them plainly that it was her familiar's fault, not hers; for though she paid him the highest wages, and bound him by potent spells to stir up the caldron of futurity from the bottom, like earthly cooks, he would sometimes be careless or out of humor, and apportion the ingredients wrongly.

When my mother thought the conjuncture momentous enough to raise the devil without cheapening him in the eyes of the vulgar, Torribio Scipio enacted his infernal majesty, and played the part just as if he had been born to it, humoring the hideous features of the character by a very small aggravation of his own natural face, and practicing the pandemonian note of elocution in the lower octave of his voice. A person in the slightest degree superstitious would be scared out of his senses at my father's figure. But one day, as his satanic prototype would have it, there came a savage rascal of a captain, who asked to see the devil, for no earthly purpose but to run him clean through the body. The inquisition, having received notice of the devil's death, sent to take charge of his widow, and administer to his effects; as for poor little me, just seven years old at the time, I was sent to the foundling hospital. There was some charitable ecclesiastics on that establishment, who, being liberally paid for the education of the poor orphans, were so zealous in their office as to teach them reading and writing. They fancied there was something particularly promising about me, which made them pick me out from all the rest, and send me on their errands. I was letter-carrier, messenger, and chapel clerk. As a token of their gratitude, they undertook to teach me Latin; but their mode of tuition was so harsh, and their discipline so severe, though I was a sort of pet with them, that, not being able to stand it any longer, I ran away one morning, while out on an errand ; and, so far from returning to the hospital, got out of Toledo through the suburbs on the Seville side.

Though I had not then completed my ninth year, I already felt the pleasure of being free, and master of my own actions. I was without money and without food ; no matter ! I had no lessons to say by heart, no themes to hammer out. After having pushed on for two hours, my little legs began to refuse their office. I had never before made so long a trip. It became necessary to stop and take some rest. I sat myself down at the foot of a tree close by the highway ; there, by way of amusement, I took my grammar out of my pocket, and began conning it over by way of a joke ; but at length, coming to recollect the raps on the knuckles, and the castigations on the more classical seat of punishment which it had cost me, I tore it leaf by leaf with an apostrophe of angry import. Ah ! you odious thing of a book ! you shall never make me shed tears any more. While I was assuaging my vindictive spirit, by strewing the ground about me with declensions and conjugations, there passed that way a hermit with a white beard, with a large pair of spectacles on his nose, and altogether an outside of much sanctity. He came up to me ; and, if I was an object of speculation to him, he was no less so to me. My little man, said he with a smile, it should seem as if we had both taken a sudden liking to each other, and in that case we cannot do better than to live together in my hermitage, which is not two hundred yards distant. Your most obedient for that, answered I pertly enough ; I have not the least desire to turn hermit. At this answer, the good old man set up a roar of laughter, and said with a kind embrace : You must not be frightened at my dress ; if it is not becoming, it is useful ; it gives me my title to a charming retreat, and to the good-will of the neighboring villages, whose inhabitants love or rather idolize me. Come this way, and I will clothe you in a jacket of the same stuff as mine. If you think well of it, you shall share with me the pleasures of the life I lead ; and, if it does not hit your fancy, you shall not only be at liberty to leave me, but you may depend on it that in the event of our parting, I shall not fail to do something handsome by you.

I suffered myself to be persuaded, and followed the old hermit, who put several questions to me, which I answered with a truth-telling simplicity, not always to be found in a more advanced stage of morality. On our arrival at the hermitage he set some fruit before me, which I devoured, having eaten nothing all day but a slice of dry bread, on which I had breakfasted at the hospital in the morning. The recluse, seeing me play so good a part with my jaws, said : Courage, my good boy, do not spare my fruit ; there is plenty of it, Heaven be praised. I have not brought you hither to starve you. And indeed that was true enough ; for an hour after our coming in, he kindled a fire, put a leg of mutton down to roast ; and while I turned the spit, laid a small table for himself and me, with a very dirty napkin upon it.

When the meat was done enough he took it up, and cut some

slices for our supper, which was no dry bargain, since we quaffed a delicious wine, of which he had laid in ample store. Well! my chicken, said he, as he rose from table, are you satisfied with my style of living? You see how we shall fare every day, if you fix your quarters here. Then with respect to liberty, you shall do just as you please in this hermitage. All I require of you is to accompany me whenever I go begging to the neighboring villages; you will be of use in driving an ass laden with two panniers, which the charitable peasants usually fill with eggs, bread, meat, and fish. I ask no more than that. I will do, said I, whatever you desire, provided you will not oblige me to learn Latin. Friar Chrysostom, for that was the old hermit's name, could not help smiling at my school-boy frowardness, and assured me once more that he should not pretend to interfere either with my studies or my inclinations.

On the very next day we went on a foraging party with the donkey, which I led by the halter. We made a profitable gleaning; for all the farmers took a pleasure in throwing somewhat into our panniers. One chucked in an uncut loaf, another a large piece of bacon; here a goose, there a pair of giblets, and a partridge to crown the whole. But without entering further into particulars, we carried home provender enough for a week; and hence you may infer the esteem and friendship in which the country people held the holy man. It is true that he was a great blessing to the neighborhood: his advice was always at their service when they came to consult him : he restored peace where discord had reigned in families, and made up matches for the daughters; he had a nostrum for almost any disease you could mention, with an assortment of pious rituals, to avert the curse of barrenness,

Hence you perceive that I was in no danger of starving in my hermitage. My lodging, too, was none of the worst: stretched on good fresh straw, with a cushion of rattan under my head, and a coverlet over me of the same stuff. I made but one nap of it all night. Brother Chrysostom, who had promised me a hermit's dress, made up an old gown of his own for me, and called me little brother Scipio. No sooner did I appear in my religious uniform, than the ass's back suffered for my genteel appearance in the eyes of the villagers. It was who should give most to the little brother! so much were they delighted with his spruce figure.

The easy, slothful life I led with the old hermit could not be very revolting to a boy of my age. On the contrary, it suited my taste so exactly, that I should have continued it to this time, but that the fates and destinies were weaving a more complicated tissue for my future years. It was cast in the figure of my nativity, early to rouse myself from the effeminacy of a religious life, and to take leave of brother Chrysostom after the following manner.

I often observed the old man at work upon his pillow, unsewing and sewing it up again; and one day, I saw him put in some money. This circumstance excited a tingling curiosity, which I promised myself to satisfy the first time he went to Toledo, as he generally did once a week. I waited impatiently for the day, but as yet, without any other motive than the mere desire of prying.

At last the good man went his way, and I unpicked his pillow, where I found, among the stuffing, the amount of about fifty crowns in all sorts of coin.

This treasure must have accumulated from the gratitude of the peasantry, whom the hermit had cured by his nostrums, and of their wives, who had become pregnant by virtue of his spiritual interference. But however it got there, I no sooner set my eyes on the money, which might be mine without any one near me to say nay, than the gypsy voice of nature and pedigree spoke within me. An inextinguishable itch of pilfering tingled in my veins, and proved that we come into the world with the mark of our descent, and with our characters about us. I yielded to the temptation without a struggle; tied up my booty in a canvas bag where we kept our combs and night-caps: then, having laid aside the hermit's and resumed my foundling's dress, got clear off from the hermitage, and hugged my bag as though it had contained the boundless treasure of the Indies.

You have heard my first exploit, continued Scipio; and I doubt not but you will expect a succession of similar practices. Your anticipations will not be disappointed; for there are many such evidences of genius behind, before I come to those of my actions which prove me good as well as clever; but I shall come to them, and you will be convinced by the sequel, that a scoundrel born may be licked into virtue, as the cub of a bear into shape.

Child as I was, I knew better than to take the Toledo road; it would have been exposing myself to the hazard of meeting friar Chrysostom, who would have balanced accounts with me on a very thriftless principle. I therefore traveled in another direction leading to the village of Galves, where I stopped at an inn, kept by a landlady who was a widow of forty, and hung out the bunch of grapes to a very good purpose. This good woman no sooner kenned me, than, judging by my dress that I must be a truant from the orphan school, she asked who I was and whither I was going. I answered that, having lost my father and mother, I was looking for a place. Can you read, my dear? said she. I assured her that I could read, and write too, with the best of them. In point of fact, I could just form my letters, and join them so as to look a little like writing; and that was clerkship enough for a village pothouse. Then I will take you into my service, replied the hostess. You may earn your board easily enough, by scoring up the customers, and keeping my ledger. I shall give you no wages, because this inn is frequented by very genteel company, who never forget the waiters. You may reckon upon very considerable perquisites.

I clinched the bargain, reserving to myself, as you may suppose, the right of emigration whenever my abode at Galves should cease to be pleasant. No sooner was I settled in my place, than a weight lay heavy on my mind. I did not wish it to be known that I had money; and it was no easy matter to devise where it could be hidden, so as that what was sauce for the goose should not be sauce for the gander. I was not yet well enough acquainted with the house to trust the places obviously most proper for such a deposit.

What a source of embarrassment is great wealth! I determined, however, on a corner of our granary under some straw; and believing it to be safer there than anywhere else, made myself as easy about it as I well could.

The household consisted of three servants: a lubberly ostler, a young Galician chambermaid, and myself. Each of us sponged what we could upon travelers, whether on foot or on horseback. I always came in for some small change, when the bill was paid. Then the equestrians gave something to the ostler, for taking care of their beasts: but as for our female fellow-servant, the muleteers who passed that way chucked her under the chin, and gave her more crowns than we got farthings. I had no sooner realized a penny, than away it went to the granary, and slept with its precursors; so that the higher rose my heap, the more greedy did my little heart become. Sometimes would I kiss the hallowed images of my idolatry, and look at them with a devotional glow, which few worshipers feel, but those whose religion is their gold.

This inordinate passion sent me back and fore to gratify it, at least thirty times a day. I often met the landlady on the staircase. She, being naturally of a suspicious temper, had a mind to find out one day what could carry me every minute to the corn-loft. She therefore went up and began rummaging about everywhere, supposing perhaps that it was my receptacle for articles purloined in the house. Of course she did not forget to pull the straw about; and behold, there was my bag! Two hands in a dish and one in a purse, was not one of her proverbs; so that finding the contents in crowns and pistoles, she thought, or seemed to think, that the money was lawfully and honestly hers. At least she had possession, and that is nine points of the law, though scarcely one of honesty. But to do the thing decently, after calling me little wretch, little rascal, and so forth, she ordered the ostler, a fellow without any will but hers, to give me a hearty flogging; and then turn me out-of-doors, with this salt eel for my breakfast, and a lady-like oath that no light-fingered gentry should ever darken her doors. In vain did I protest and vow that I never wronged my mistress: she affirmed the direct contrary, and her word would go further than mine at any time. Thus were friar Chrysostom's savings transferred from one thief to a greater thief in the thief-taker.

I wept over the loss of my money, as a father over the death of his only son: and though my tears could not bring back what I had lost, they at least answered the purpose of exciting pity in some people, who saw how bitterly they flowed, and among others in the parson, who was accidentally going by. He seemed affected by my sad plight, and took me home with him. There, to gain my confidence, or rather to pump me, he began soothing my sorrows. How much this poor child is to be pitied! said he. Is it any wonder if, thrown upon the wide world at so tender an age, he has committed a bad action? Grown-up men are not always proof against the flesh or the devil. Then, addressing me, Child, added he, from what part of Spain do you come, and who are your parents? You have the look of family about you. Open your heart to me confidentially, and depend upon it, I never will desert you.

His reverence, by this kind and insinuating language, engaged me by degrees to tell him all my history, without falsification or reserve. I owned everything; and thus he moralized on the leading article of my confession: My little friend, though hermits ought to lay up such treasures as neither force nor fraud can wrest from them, that was no excuse for your taking the measure of punishment into your own hands: by robbing brother Chrysostom, you nevertheless sinned against that article of the decalogue, which tells you not to steal; but I will engage to make the hostess return the money, and will punctually remit it to the reverend friar at his hermitage: you may therefore make your conscience perfectly easy on that score. Now, between ourselves, my conscience was perfectly callous to everything like compunction with respect to the crime in question. The parson, who had his own ends to answer, had not done with me yet. My lad, pursued he, I mean to take you by the hand, and find a good birth for you. I shall send you to-morrow morning, by the carrier, to my nephew, a canon of Toledo. He will not refuse, at my request, to admit you upon his establishment, where they live like so many sons of the church, rosily, merrily, and fatly, upon the rents of his prebendal stall: you will be perfectly comfortable there, take my word for it.

Patronage like this gave me so much encouragement, that I did not throw away another thought either upon my bag or my whipping. My mind was wholly occupied with the idea of living rosily, merrily, and fatly, like a son of the church. The following day, at breakfast-time, there came, according to orders, a muleteer to the parsonage, with two mules saddled and bridled. They helped me to mount one, the muleteer flung his leg over the other, and we trotted on for Toledo. My fellow-traveler was a good, pleasant companion, and desired nothing better than to indulge his humor at the expense of his neighbor. My little volunteer, said he, you have a good friend in his reverence, the minister of Galves. He could not give you a better proof of his kindness, than by placing you with his nephew the canon, whom I have the honor of knowing, far beyond all question or comparison, to be the cock of the chapter, and a hearty one he is. None of your lantern-jawed saints, with Lent in his face, a cat-of-nine-tails on his back, and a cholera morbus in his belly. No such thing! Our doctor is rubicund in the jowl, efflorescent on the nose, with a wicked eye at a bumper or a girl; militant against no earthly pleasure, but most addicted to the good things of the table. You will be as snug there as a bug in a blanket.

This hangman of a muleteer, perceiving with what exquisite satisfaction I took in all this, went on tantalizing me with the joys of an ecclesiastical life. He never dropped the subject till we got to the village of Obisa, and stopped there to refresh our mules. Then, while bustling about the inn, he accidentally dropped a paper from his pocket, which I was cunning enough to pick up without his seeing me, and took an opportunity of reading while he was in the stable. It was a letter addressed to the governors and super-intendents of the orphan school, conceived in these terms: "Gen-tlemen, I consider it as an act at once of charity and of duty, to send you back a little truant; he seems a shrewd lad enough, and may do very well with good looking after. By dint of hard and frequent chastisement, I doubt not but you will ultimately bring him to a sense of his own unworthiness and your benevolence. May a blessing be vouchsafed on your pious and charitable labors, for the early extirpation of sin and wickedness! (Signed)

"THE MINISTER OF GALVES."

When I had finished reading this pleasant letter, which let me into the good intentions of his reverence the rector, it required little deliberation to determine what I was to do: from the inn to the banks of the Tagus, a space of three good miles, was but a hop, step, and jump. Fear lent me wings to escape from the governors of the foundling hospital, whither I was absolutely resolved never to return, having formed principles of taste diametrically opposite to their method of teaching the classics. I went into Toledo with as light a heart as if I had known where to get my daily bread. To be sure, it is a town of ways and means, where a man who can live by his wits need never die of hunger. Scarcely had I reached the high street, when a well-dressed gentleman by whom I brushed, caught me by the arm, saying: My little fellow, do you want a place? You are just such a smart lad as I was looking for. And you are just the master for my money, answered I. Since that is the case, rejoined he, you are mine from this moment, and have only to follow me, which I did without asking any more questions.

This spark, about the age of thirty, and bearing the name of Don Abel, lodged in very handsome ready-furnished apartments. He was by profession a blacklegs; and the following was the nature of our engagement. In the morning I got him as much tobacco as would smoke five or six pipes; brushed his clothes, and ran for a barber to shave him and trim his whiskers; after which he made the circle of the tennis-courts, whence he never returned home till eleven or twelve at night. But every morning, at going out, he gave me three reels for the expenses of the day, leaving me master of my own time till ten o'clock in the evening; and provided I was within-doors by his return, all was well. He gave me a livery be-sides, in which I looked like a little lackey of illicit love. I took very kindly to my condition, and certainly could not have met with any more congenial with my temper.

Such and so happy had been my way of life for nearly a month, when my employer inquired whether I liked his service; and on my answer in the affirmative, Well, then, resumed he, to-morrow we shall set out for Seville, whither my concerns call me. You will not be sorry to see the capital of Andalusia. "He that hath not Seville seen," says the proverb, "Is no traveller I ween." I engaged at once to follow him all over the world. On that very day, the Seville carrier fetched away a large trunk with my master's ward-robe, and on the next morning we were on the road for Andalusia.

Signor Don Abel was so lucky at play, that he never lost but when it was convenient; but then it was seldom convenient to stay long in a place, because those who are always losers find out at last, that though chance is a dangerous antagonist, certainly it is a desperate one; and that accounted for our journey.   On our arrival at Seville, we took lodgings near the Cordova gate, and resumed the same mode of life as at Toledo.   But my master found some difference between the two towns.   The Seville tennis-courts could produce players equally in fortune's good graces with himself; so that he sometimes came home a good deal out of humor. One morning, when he was biting the bridle for the loss of a hundred pistoles the day before, he asked why I had not carried his linen to the laundress.   I pleaded forgetfulness.   Thereupon, flying into a passion, he gave me half-a-dozen boxes on the ear, in such a style, as to kindle an illumination in my blinking eyes, to which the glories of Solomon's temple were no more to be compared, than the torches in a Candlemas procession to a rushlight.   There is for you, you little scoundrel! said he; take that, and learn to mind your business.   Must I be eternally at your heels to remind you of what you are to do?   Are your brains in your belly, and all your wits in your grinders?   You are not a downright idiot!   Then why not prevent my wants and anticipate my orders?   After this experimental lecture, he went out for the day, leaving me in high dudgeon, at a reprimand so much in the manner of my friend the ostler, for such a trifle as not getting up his things for the wash.

I could never learn what happened to him a short time after at a tennis-court; but one evening he came home in a terrible heat. Scipio, said he, I am bent on going to Italy, and must embark the day after to-morrow on board a vessel bound for Genoa.   I have my reasons for making this little excursion; of course you will be glad to attend me, and to profit by so fine an opportunity of seeing the loveliest country on the face of the earth.   My tongue gave consent; but with a salvo in my heart and a bargain with my revenge, to give him the slip just at the moment of embarkation. This was so delightful a scheme, that I could not help imparting it to a bully by profession, whom I met in the street.   During my abode in Seville, I had picked up some awkward acquaintance, and this was one of the most ungainly.   I told him how and why my ears had been boxed, and then communicated my project of running away from Don Abel just before the ship was to sail, begging to know what he thought of the plan.

My bluff adviser puckered his eyebrows while he listened, and fiddled with his fingers about his whiskers : then, blaming my master very seriously, My little hero, said he, you are eternally disgraced, can never show your face again, if you sit down quietly with so paltry a satisfaction as what you propose.   To let Don Abel go off by himself, would be a poor revenge for wrongs like yours; the punishment should be proportioned to his crime.   Let us fine him to the full amount of his purse and effects, which we will share like brothers after he is gone.   Now it is to be noted, that though thieving fell in very naturally with the bent of my genius, the pro-

posal rather startled me, as the robbery was upon a large scale for
so young an apprentice.

And yet the arch deceiver of my innocence found the means of
working me up to the perpetration, so that the result of our enterprise was as follows. This glorious ruffian, a tall, brawny fellow,
came in the evening about twilight to our lodging. I showed my
master's traveling trunk ready packed, and asked him whether he
could carry so heavy a load upon his shoulders. So heavy as that!
said he: show me where a transfer of property is to be made in my
favor, and I could run with Noah's ark to the top of mount Ara-
rat. To prove his words, he felt the trunk, flung it carelessly over
his back, and scampered down-stairs. I followed nimbly; and we
had just got to the street door, when Don Abel, brought home in
the nick of time by the ascendency of his lucky stars, stood like an
apparition, to appall our guilty souls.

Whither are you going with that trunk? said he. I was so
taken by surprise that my assurance failed me; and broad-shoulders,
finding that he had drawn a blank in the lottery, threw down his
booty, and took to his heels, rather than be troubled for an explanation. Once more, whither are you going with that trunk? said
my master. Sir, answered I, with all the honest simplicity of a
criminal, pleading in arrest of judgment, I was going to put it on
board the vessel, that we might have the less to do to-morrow,
before we embark ourselves. Indeed! Then you know, retorted
he, in what ship I have taken my passage? No, sir, replied I! but
those who can talk Latin may always find their way to Rome: I
should have inquired at the port, and somebody would have informed me. At this explanation, which left his opinion where it
found it, he darted a furious glance at me. I thought for all the
world, he was going to cuff me again about the head. Who
ordered you, cried he, to take my trunk out of this house? You,
your own self, said I. Can you possibly have forgotten how you
rated me but a few days ago? Did you not tell me, with a flea in
my ear, that you would have me prevent your wants, and do beforehand from my own head whatever your service might require?
Now, not to be thrashed a second time for want of forethought, I
was seeing your trunk safe and soon enough on board. On this
the gamester, finding that I had cut my teeth of wisdom sooner
than suited his purpose, turned me off very coolly, saying: Go
about your business, master Scipio, and speed as you may deserve.
I do not like to play with folks who are in the habit of revoking.
Get out of my sight, or I shall set your *solfeggio* in a crying key.

I spared him the trouble of telling me to go twice. Off I shot
like an arrow, for fear he should unfledge me, by taking away my
livery. When distant enough to slacken my pace, I walked along
in the streets, musing whither I might betake myself for a night's
lodging, with only two reals in my pocket. The gate of the archbishop's palace at length stared me in the face; and, as his grace's
supper was then dressing, a savory odor exhaled from the kitchens, impregnating the gale with soup and sauce for a mile round.
Ods haricots and cutlets! thought I, it would be no hard matter

for me to dispense with one of those little side dishes, which will be of no use to the archbishop but to make out the figure of his table: nay, I would be contented only just to dip in my four fingers and thumb, and then to sup like a bear upon suckings. But how to accomplish it! Is there no way of bringing these choice morsels to a better test than that of smell? And why not? Hunger, they say, will break through stone walls. On this idea did I set my wits to work; and, by dint of conning over the subject, a stratagem struck me, which set my lungs as well as appetite in motion, just as the old carpenter kept bawling, "I have found it," like a madman, when he had hit the right nail of his proposition on the head. I ran into the court of the palace, and made the best of my way to the kitchens, calling out with all my might, "Help! help!" as if some assassin had been at my heels.

At my reiterated cries master Diego, the archbishop's cook, ran with three or four kitchen drudges to learn what was the matter; and seeing only me, asked why I roared so loud. Ah! good sir, answered I, with every token of exquisite distress, for mercy's sake and for St. Polycarp's! save me, I beseech you, from the fury of a blusterer, who swears he will kill me. But where is this disturber of the public peace? cried Diego. You have no one to quarrel with but yourself; for I do not see so much as a cat to spit at you. Go your ways, my little man, and do not be afraid; it is evidently some wag who has been playing upon your cowardice for his diversion; but he knew better than to follow you within these walls, for we would have cut his ears off at the least. No, no, said I, it was for no laughing matter that he ran after me. He is a noted footpad, and meant to rob me; I am certain that he is now waiting for me at the corner of the street. Then he may wait long enough, replied the knight of the iron spit; for you shall stay here till to-morrow. You shall sup with us, and we will give you a bed.

I was out of my little wits with joy at the mention of these last tidings; and it was like the turnpike road to paradise after crossing an Arabian desert, when being led by master Diego through the kitchens, I there saw my lord archbishop's supper, and the stewpans in the last throes of parturition. There were fifteen accountable souls, for I reckoned them up, in attendance on the labor; but the litter of dishes far outnumbered the fecundity of nature in her most prolific mood: so much more gracious and bountiful is providence to the heads of the church in the indulgence of their appetites, than mindful of the worthless brute creation in the propagation of its kind. Here it was, at the fountain-head of prelacy, inhaling an atmosphere of gravy, instead of just snuffing the scent as it lay upon the breeze, that I first shook hands with sensuality. I had the honor of supping with the scullions, and of sleeping in their room; an initiation of friendship so sincere and strong, that on the following day, when I went to thank master Diego for his goodness in vouchsafing me a refuge, he said: Our kitchen lads have been with me in a body, to declare how excessively delighted they are with your manners, and to propose having you among them as a fellow-servant. How should you, on your part, like to make one of the society? I answered that, with such a feather in my cap, I should be the vainest and the happiest of mortals. Then so it be, my friend, replied he, consider yourself henceforth as a buttress of the hierarchy. With this invitation, he introduced me to the major-domo, who thought he saw talent enough in me for a turnspit.

No sooner was I in possession of so honorable an office, than master Diego, following the practice of cooks in great houses, who pamper up their pretty dears in private with all sorts of good things, selected me to supply a lady in the neighborhood with a regular table of butcher's meat, poultry, and game. This good friend of his was a widow on the right side of thirty, very pretty, very lively, and to all appearance contenting herself with cupboard love for her cook. His generous passion was not confined to furnishing her with bread, meat, and garnish; she drank her wine too, and the archbishop was her wine-merchant.

The improvement of my parts kept pace with that of my carnal condition in his grace's palace: where I gave a specimen of rising genius, still ringing on the trump of fame at Seville. The pages and some others of the household had a mind to get up a play on my lord archbishop's birthday. They chose a popular Spanish tragedy; and wanting a boy about my age to personate the young King of Leon, cast me for the part. The major-domo, a great spouter, undertook to train me for the stage; and after a few lessons, pronounced that I should not be the worst actor of the company. His grace not wishing to starve so handsome a compliment to himself, no expense was spared in getting it up magnificently. The largest hall in the palace was fitted up as a theatre, with appropriate decorations. At the side scene there was a bed of turf, on which I was to be discovered asleep, when the Moors were to rush in and take me prisoner. When we had got so forward with our rehearsals as to be sure of being ready by the time fixed, the archbishop sent out cards of invitation to all the principal families in the city.

At length the great, the important day arrived; and each performer was big with the contrivance and adjustment of his dress. Mine was brought by a tailor, accompanied by our major-domo, who, after taking the trouble of drilling me at rehearsal, wished to see justice done to my outward appearance. The tailor put me on a rich robe of blue velvet, with hanging sleeves, gold lace, fringe, and buttons: the major-domo himself crowned me with a paste-board crown, studded with false diamonds and real pearls. Moreover, they gave me a sash of pink silk worked in silver; so that every new ornament was like a quill-feather in the wing of a bird. At last, about dusk, the play began. The curtain drew up for my soliloquy; the purport of which was to express, in a roundabout, poetical way, that not being able to defend myself from the influence of sleep, I was going to lie down and take it as it came. To suit the action to the word, I sidled off to the corner between the flat and the wings, and squatted down on my bed of turf, but instead of going to sleep, according to promise, I was hammering upon the means of getting into the street, and running away with my coronation finery. A little private staircase, leading under the theatre into the lower saloon, seemed to furnish the probability of success. I slid away slyly, while the audience were considering some necessary question of the play, and ran down the staircase, through the saloon, to the door, calling out, "Make way! make way! I must change my dress, and run up again in a moment!" They all made a lane, for fear of hindering me; so that in less than two minutes I got clear out of the palace, under cover of the darkness, and scampered to the house of my friend who saw gentlemen's trunks safe on board.

He stared like a stuck pig at my equipment! But when I let him into the why and the wherefore, he laughed ready to split his sides. Then, shaking hands in the sincerity of his heart, because he flattered himself with the hope of a pension on the King of Leon's civil list, he wished me joy of so successful a first appearance, and joined issue with the major-domo in the prognostic, that with encouragement and practice I should turn out a first-rate actor, and make no little noise in the world. After we had diverted ourselves for some time at the expense of my manager and audience, I said to the bully—What shall we do with this magnificent dress? Do not make yourself uneasy about that, answered he. I know an honest broker, without an atom of curiosity in his composition, who will buy or sell anything with any person, provided that he gets the turn of the market upon the transaction. I will fetch him to you to-morrow morning. The knowing fellow was as good as his word; for he went out early the next day, leaving me in bed, and returned two hours afterwards with the broker, carrying a yellow bundle under his arm. My friend, said he, give me leave to introduce Signor Ybagnez of Segovia, who, in spite of the bad example set him by the trade in general, trusts to fair dealing and small profits for a moderate pittance and an unblemished character. He will tell you to a fraction what the dress you want to part with is really worth, and you may take his calculation as the balance of justice, between man and man. Oh yes! to a nicety, said the broker. Else wherefore live I in a Christian land, but to appraise for my neighbor as for myself? To take a mean advantage never was, thank heaven! and at these years never shall be, imputed to Ybagnez of Segovia. Let us look a little at those articles! You are the seller; I am the buyer! We have only to agree upon an equitable price. Here they are, said the bully, pulling them out: now own the truth, was there ever anything more magnificent? You do not often see such velvet: and then the trimmings! You cannot say too much of it, answered the salesman, examining the suit with the prying eye of a dealer, it is of the very first quality. And what think you of the pearls upon this crown? resumed my friend. A little rounder, observed Ybagnez, and there would be no setting a price upon them! however, take them as they are, it is a very fine set, and I do not want to find fault about trifles. Now your common run of appraisers, under my circumstances, would affect to disparage the goods for the sake of getting them cheaper; one of those fellows would have the conscience to offer twenty pistoles; but there is nothing like bargaining with an upright, downright man! I will give forty at a word; take them or leave them!

Had Ybagnez ventured up to a hundred, he would not have burned his fingers; for the pearls alone would have fetched two hundred anywhere. The bully, who went snacks, then said—Now only look! what a mercy it is, to fall into the hands of a man not of this world. Signor Ybagnez estimates money as dross, in comparison of his principles and his soul. He may die to-night, and yet not be taken unprepared! That is too much! You make me blush, said the salesman of principle and soul; but so far is true, that my price is always fixed. Well, now, is it a bargain? The money down upon the nail too! Stop a moment! answered the bully; my little friend must first try on the clothes you have brought for him by my order: I am very much mistaken if they will not just fit him. The salesman then, untying his bundle, showed me a second-hand suit of dark cloth with silver buttons. I got up, and got into it; too big for me every way! but these gentlemen could have sworn it had been made to my measure. Ybagnex put it at ten pistoles; and as he was an upright, downright man, of fixed principle and soul, estimating money as dross in comparison of integrity, his first price was of course his last. He therefore took out his purse, and counted down thirty pistoles upon a table; after which he packed up the King of Leon's regalia, and went his way.

When he was gone, the bully said—I am very well satisfied with that broker. And so he well might be; for I am certain he must have received at least a hundred pistoles as hush-money. But there was no reason why the broker's benevolence should pay the debts of my gratitude: so he took half the money on the table, without saying with your leave or by your leave, and suffered me to pocket the remainder, with the following advice: My dear Scipio, with that balance of fifteen pistoles, I would have you get out of this town as fast as you can; for you may suppose that my lord archbishop will ferret you out if you are above-ground. It would grieve me to the heart if, after having risen so superior to the prejudice of honesty, you had the weakness to fall foul of what alone keeps it afloat, the house of correction. I answered that it was my fixed purpose to make myself scarce at Seville, and accordingly, after buying a hat and some shirts, I traveled through vineyards and olive groves to the ancient city of Carmona; and in three days afterwards arrived at Cordova.

I put up at an inn close by the market-place, giving myself out for the heir of a good family at Toledo, traveling for his pleasure. My appearance did not belie the story, and a few pistoles, which I contrived carelessly to chink within the landlord's hearing, pinned his faith upon my veracity. Probably my unfledged youth might lead him to take me for some graceless little truant who had robbed his parents and run away. But that was no concern of his: he took the thing just as I gave it him, for fear lest his curiosity should clash with my continuance at his house. For six reals a day one could live like a gentleman at this inn, where there was generally a considerable concourse of company. About a dozen people sat down at supper. It was whimsical enough; but the whole party plied their knives and forks without speaking a word, except one man, who talked incessantly, right or wrong, and made up for the silence of the rest by his eternal babble. He affected to be a wit, to tell a good story, and took great pains to make the good folks merry by his puns; and accordingly they did laugh most inextinguishably; but it was at him, not with him.

For my part, I paid so little attention to the talk of this rattle, that I should have got up from table without knowing what it was all about, if he had not brought it home to my business and my bosom. Gentlemen, cried he, just as supper was over, I have kept my best story for the last; a very droll thing happened within these few days at the archbishop of Seville's palace. I had it from a young fellow of my acquaintance, who assures me that he was present at the time. These words made my heart jump up into my throat, for I had no doubt of this being my exploit—and so it turned out. This pleasant gentleman related the facts as they actually happened, and even carried the adventure to its conclusion, of which I was as yet ignorant: but now you shall be made as wise as myself.

No sooner had I absconded, than the Moors, who were, according to the progress of the fable and the rising of the interest, to lay violent hands on me, appeared upon the stage, for the fell purpose of surprising me on my bed of turf, where the author had given them reason to expect me fast asleep; but when they thought they were just going to capot the King of Leon, they found, to their surprise, that both the king and the knave made a trick against them. Here was a hole in the ballad! The actors all lost their cue; some of them called me by name, others ran to look for me; here is a fellow bawling as though his bellows would burst, there stands another, muttering to himself about the devil, just as if that reptile could stand upright in such a presence! The archbishop, perceiving trouble and confusion to lord it behind the scenes, asked what was the matter. At the sound of the prelate's voice, a page, who was the fiddle of the piece, came to the front and spoke thus: My lord archbishop, ladies, and gentlemen! We are extremely sorry to inform you, as players, but extremely glad, as men and Christians, that the King of Leon is at present in no danger whatever of being taken prisoner by the Moors: he has adopted effectual measures for the security of his royal person; and to the royal person, as liberty avails little without property, he has irrevocably attached the crown, insignia, and robes. And a happy deliverance for himself and Christendom! exclaimed the archbishop. He has done perfectly right to escape from the enemies of our religion, and to burst from the bonds in which their malice would have laid him. By this time, probably, he has reached the confines of his kingdom, or may have entered the capital. May no unlucky accident have retarded him on his journey! And that the sin of none such may lie heavy on my conscience, I beg leave very positively to make my pleasure known, that he may proceed unmolested by any interruption from this quarter; I should be highly mortified indeed, if his majesty's pious endeavors were to be frustrated by the slightest indignity from the ministers of that religion in whose cause he labors and suffers. The prelate, having thus declared his acquiescence in the motives of my flight, ordered my part to be read, and the play to be resumed.

CHAPTER XI.

CONTINUATION OF SCIPIO'S STORY.

As long as I had money in my purse, my landlord was cap in hand; but the moment he began to suspect that the funds were low, he became high and mighty, picked a German quarrel with me, and one morning, before breakfast, begged it as a favor of me to march out of his house. I followed his counsel as proudly as you please, and betook me to a church belonging to the fathers of St. Dominic, where, while mass was performing, an old beggar accosted me on the usual topic of alms. I dropped some small change into his hat, which was truly the orphan's mite, saying at the same time: My friend, remember in your prayers to mention a situation for me; if your petition is heard with favor, it shall be all the better for you; hearty thanks, and a handsome poundage!

At these words, the beggar surveyed me up and down from head to foot, and answered in a grave tone: What place would you wish to have? I should like, replied I, to be footman in some family where I should do well. He inquired whether the matter pressed. With all possible importunity, said I, for unless I have the good luck to get settled very soon, the alternative will be horrible; death by the gripe of absolute famine, or a livelihood in the ranks of your fraternity. If the latter were, after all, to be your lot, resumed he, it certainly would be rather hard upon you, who have not been brought up to our habits of life; but, with a little use and practice, you would prefer our condition to service, which, partiality apart, is far less respectable than the beggar's vocation. Nevertheless, since you like a menial occupation better than leading a free and independent life like me, you shall have a berth without more ado. Mean as my appearance is, you must not measure my power by it. Meet me here at the same hour tomorrow.

I took care to keep the appointment. Though at the spot before the time, I had not long to wait before the beggar joined me, and told me to follow him. I did so. He led me to a cellar not far from the church where he resided. We went in together; and sitting down on a long bench, at least a hundred years the worse for wear, the conversation took this turn on his part: A good action, as the proverb says, always meets with its reward you gave me alms yesterday, and that has determined me to get you a place, which shall be soon done, with a blessing on my endeavors. I know an old Dominican, by name Father Alexis, a holy monk, a ghostly confessor. I have the honor to do all his little odd jobs, performing my task with so much discretion and good faith, that he always lends his interest to me and my friends. I have spoken to him about you, and in such terms as to prepossess him in your favor. You may be introduced to his reverence whenever you please.

There is not a moment to be lost, said I to the old beggar; let us go to the good monk immediately. The mendicant agreed, and led me by the arm to Father Alexis, whom we found in his room, hard at work, writing spiritual letters. He broke off to talk with me. As it was the wish of the mendicant, he would do all in his power to serve me. Having learnt, pursued he, that Signor Balthasar Velasquez is in want of a footboy, I wrote to him this morning on your behalf, and he just sent me for answer, that he would take you without further inquiry on my recommendation. This very day you may call on him from me; he is one of my flock, and my very good friend. Thereupon the monk preached to me for three quarters of an hour on my moral and religious duties, and how to fulfill them in conscience and honor. He enlarged principally on the obligation of serving Velasquez with diligence and devotion; and then assured me that he would take care and keep me in my place, provided my master had no very material fault to find with me.

After having thanked the holy person for his goodness towards me, I left the convent with the beggar, who told me that Signor Balthasar Velasquez was an old woolen-draper, but with much simplicity and good nature in his character. I doubt not, added he, but you will be perfectly comfortable in his house. I begged to know his place of residence, and repaired thither immediately, after promising to make my gratitude manifest, as soon as I had taken root in my new soil. I went into a large shop, where two fashionable young apprentices were walking up and down, practicing new grimaces against the entrance of the next customer. I inquired whether their master was at home, saying that I wanted to speak with him from Father Alexis. At that venerable name they showed me into the counting-house, where their principal was turning over the ledger. I made a low bow, and coming up to him, Sir, said I, Father Alexis ordered me to call here and offer myself as a servant to your honor. Ah! my smart lad, answered he, you are heartily welcome. It is enough that the holy man sent you; and I shall take you in preference to three or four others who have been recommended. It is a clear case; your wages begin from this day.

A very short time in the family convinced me that the head of it was just such a man as he had been described. In point of simplicity, he was everything that could be wished; so exquisite a subject for imposition, that it seemed next to an impossibility not to exercise my craft upon such a handle. He had been a widower four years, and had two children, a son five-and-twenty, and a daughter in her eleventh year. The girl, brought up by a severe duenna, under the spiritual conduct of Father Alexis, walked in the high road of virtue; but her brother, Gaspard Valasquez, though no pains had been spared to make a good man of him, picked out for himself all the vices of a young profligate. Sometimes he stayed away from home two or three days together; and if, on his return, his father ventured to remonstrate in the least against his proceedings, Gaspard shut his mouth at once, with a haughty toss of 'the head, and an impertinent anwer.

Scipio, said the old man one day, my son is the plague of my life. He is over head and ears in all kinds of debauchery: and yet there is no accounting for it, since his education was by no means neglected. I have given him the very best masters; and my friend Father Alexis has done his utmost to train him up in the way he should go; but there was no breaking him in; Master Gaspard ran restive, and bolted into downright libertinism. You may perhaps tell me, that I spared the rod and spoiled the child. Quite otherwise! he was punished whenever the occasion seemed to demand it; for, though good-tempered at bottom, I am not to be played upon. I have even gone so far as to lock him up, but that only made him more headstrong than before. In short, he is one of those impracticable beings, on whom good example, good advice, and a good horsewhip, are equally thrown away. If ever he makes any figure in the world, it must be by a miracle from heaven.

Though my heart was not grievously wrung by the sorrows of this unhappy father, sympathy was expected from me, and I condoled with him accordingly. How much to be pitied you are, sir! said I. Virtues like yours deserved to have been handed down in your progeny. The event is quite the reverse, my good lad, answered he. Heaven heard my prayer, and gave me a son, but converted the blessing into an affliction. Among other grounds of complaint against Gaspard, I may tell you in confidence, there is one which gives me a great deal of uneasiness; a vast longing to rob his old father, which he too often find the means of satisfying, in spite of all my caution. Your predecessor played into his hands, and was turned away in consequence. As for you, I flatter myself that my son will never be able to tamper with your honesty. You will take my side of the question; for doubtless Father Alexis has given you your lesson on that head. You may rest assured of that, said I; for a good long hour did his reverence lecture me on doing your will and pleasure without let or hindrance; but I can assure you, there was no need of his saying anything about the matter. I feel within myself a sort of call to serve you faithfully, and I promise to do it with a zeal beyond all the temptations of the world to shake or lessen.

He who only hears one side is in danger of deciding partially. Young Velasquez, a mixture of the fribble and the braggart, concluding from the cut of my countenance that I was made up of mortal frailty like my dear predecessor, drew me aside to a snug corner, and there talked to me after this fashion. Now mind what is said to you, my dear fellow; you may think I do not know that you are set as a spy upon me by my father; but take especial care how you proceed, for I can assure you most sincerely, that the office is not without very considerable inconvenience to those who undertake it. If ever I find that you tell tales out of school, I will give you such a basting as you never had in your life; but if you will make common cause with me, and a fool of my father, you may buy golden returns of gratitude from your humble servant. Do you wish me to deal with you upon the nail? You shall go snacks in all that we can squeeze out of the old fellow. You have only to take your choice. fall at once into the ranks either of father or son; for neutrals will come worse off where the contending parties fight for their existence.

Sir, answered I, you make the shoe pinch very tight; it is self-evident that there is nothing for me to do but to enlist under your banners, though in my conscience it seems like crying sin to betray Signor Velasquez. That is no concern of yours, rejoined Gaspard; he is an old hunks, who wants to keep me under his thumb; a curmudgeon who refuses me the rights of nature, in refusing to stand to the expenses and repairs of my pleasures; for pleasures are the necessaries of life at five-and-twenty. It is in this point of view that you must form your opinion of my father. If that is the case, so be it, sir, said I; there is no standing against so just a subject of complaint. I am quite at your service to play second fiddle in all your laudable enterprises; but let us take especial care to conceal our good understanding, for fear your faithful, humble servant should be kicked out-of-doors. It will not be amiss, in my poor opinion, for you to affect an extreme antipathy against me: some good round of abuse would have a very pretty effect; you need not be nice; all the blackguard terms in the dictionary will come at your call. Nay, a box on the ear now and then, or a kick on the breech, will break no squares; on the contrary, the more you express your thorough dislike, the more Signor Balthasar will pin his faith upon my sleeve. My cue will be, apparently to avoid speaking to you if possible. In waiting at table, I shall perform my little attentions to you at arm's length; and whenever your honor may happen to be called over the coals by the shopmen, you must not take it amiss if I abuse you worse than a pickpocket.

As plain as chalk from cheese! cried young Valasquez at this last hint; this is admirable, my friend; at your early age, it is uncommon to meet with such a talent for intrigue; I consider it as a most happy omen for my purpose. With such a performer to play up to me, I flatter myself the old codger will be pinched to the bone and left penniless. You really carry your good opinion of me beyond what my merit will justify, said I; some industry may fall to my share, but not such exalted genius. But I shall do my utmost; and if my honest endeavors fail, your candor must find excuses for my imbecility.

It was not long before Gaspard had proof positive that I was to a hair's breadth the very man he wanted; and the following was precisely the first trick I played into his hand. Balthasar's strong box was in the good man's chamber, by his bedside, a sort of oratory, with a prayer-book always lying upon it. Every time I looked that way, my eyes glistened with hope and pleasure; my heart chuckled over the very idea of what might happen: Fair, sweet, cruel box, will you for ever be coy to my addresses? May I never experience the heart-felt delight of possessing all your charms for better, for worse? As I went into the room at pleasure, and only Gaspard was warned off the premises, it happened one day that I watched his father. The old gentleman, fancying himself unobserved of human eye, after having opened his treasury and closed it fast again, hid the key behind the hangings. I took an accurate observation of the place, and communicated the discovery to my young master, who said with an approving hug: Ah! my dear Scipio, what glorious news you bring! Our fortune is made, my dear fellow. I will furnish you with wax; you shall take the impression of the key, and then our business is done. There will be no difficulty in finding a benevolent locksmith in Cordova, where, to do the place justice, there are as many rogues as in any part of Spain.

Well! but why, said I to Gaspard, do you want a false key? We may find our account in the proper one. Yes, answered he; but I am afraid lest my father, through mistrust or whim, should take a fancy to hiding it elsewhere; and the safest way is, to have one of our own. I commended his precaution, and falling in with all his principles, got ready for taking the impression of the key: this was effected one morning early, while my old master was paying a visit to Father Alexis, with whom he for the most part held very long conferences. I did not stop here; but availed myself of the key to open the strong box, wherein an ample range of large and small bags threw me into the most delightful perplexity imaginable. I did not know which to choose, there was such a family likeness among them; nevertheless, as the fear of being caught did not allow of any long deliberation, I laid hands, hap-hazard, on the largest. Then, locking the box carefully, and putting the key back again behind the hangings, I got away out of the chamber with my booty, and hid it under my bed, in a small closet where I lay.

Having performed this exploit so successfully, I ran back as fast as my legs would carry me to young Velasquez, who was waiting at a house where he had given me notice to meet him, and his delight was extreme at the recital of what I had just done. He was so fully satisfied with me, as to lavish caresses without number, and to offer me thrice, in the fullness of his heart, half the contents of the bag, which I did thrice refuse. No, no, sir, said I, this first bag is yours and yours only; apply it to your own uses and occasions. I shall return forthwith to the strong box, where, as our lucky stars have contrived it, there is money enough for both of us. Accordingly, three days afterwards I carried off a second bag, containing, like the first, five hundred crowns, of which I would only handle the fourth part, let Gaspard be as pressing as he pleased to force upon me a brotherly division, share and share alike.

As soon as this young man found himself so flush of money, and consequently in a condition to gratify his hankering after women and play, he gave himself up entirely to the devices of his own imagination; nay, his evil genius pursued him so far, as to make him fall desperately in love with one of those female harpies, who devour without remorse or intermission, and swallow up the largest fortunes. His disbursements at her instigation were frightful; and thus it became necessary for me to pay so many visits to the strong box, that old Velasquez at length found out he had been robbed. Scipio, said he one morning, I must give you a piece of information; some one robs me, my friend; my strong box has been opened; several bags have been taken out, that is a certain fact. Whom ought I to accuse of this theft? or rather, who else but my son can have committed it? Gaspard must have got by stealth into my chamber, or else you yourself must have played booty with him; for I am tempted to believe you are in league with him, though to outward appearance you do not set up your horses together. And yet I am unwilling to harbor that suspicion, because Father Alexis undertook to answer for your honesty. I gave him to understand that, by the blessing of heaven on a good natural disposition, my neighbors' goods had no temptation in my sight; and I so happily suited the action to the lie, and the lie to the action, that my judge pronounced a verdict of acquittal on the evidence of grimace and hypocrisy.

Accordingly the old man dropped the subject; but for all that, there was a general misgiving in his breast, and it would sometimes light upon me; taking precautions, therefore, against our further attacks, he had a new lock put to his strong box, and always carried the key in his pocket. By these means, an embargo being laid on our traffic with the bags, we looked excessively foolish, especially Gaspard, who, being unable any longer to keep his nymph in her usual style, knew very well that he was likely to be tossed out of her window. He had, however, invention enough to devise an expedient for keeping his head above water a few days longer, and that was neither more nor less than to get into his clutches, in the form of a loan, my dividend on the joint stock of the strong box. I refunded to the last farthing; and this restitution, it is to be hoped, may be set off as an anticipated act of justice to the old draper, in the person of his heir.

The young man, having exhausted this scanty supply, and desperate of any other, fell into a deep melancholy, and into ultimate derangement. He no longer looked on his father in any other light than as the bane of his life. His frenzy broke out into the most dreadful projects; so that, without listening to the voice of consanguinity or nature, the wretch conceived the impious design of poisoning him. He was not content with making me privy to the atrocious design, but even proposed to render me the instrument of parricide. At the very thought, my blood ran cold within me. Sir, said I, is it possible that you are so rejected of heaven as to have formed this horrid plot? What! is it in your nature to murder the author of your existence? Shall Spain, the favored abode of the Christian faith, bear witness to the commission of a crime, at the first blush of which transatlantic savages would recoil with horror? No, my dear master, added I, throwing myself on my knees, no, you will not be guilty of an action which would raise the hand of all mankind against you, and be overtaken by an infamous punishment.

I pressed many arguments beside on Gaspard, to dissuade him from so fearful an enterprise. How the deuce I came by all the moral and religious topics, which I brought to act against the fortress of his despair, is more than I can account for; but it is certain that I preached like a doctor of Salamanca, though a mere stripling, born of a gypsy fortune-teller. And yet it was to no purpose that I suggested the duty of communing with his own better resolutions, and stoutly wrestling with the fiend, who was lying in wait for his immortal soul; my pious eloquence was dissipated into air. His head hung sullenly on his bosom, and his tongue uttered no sound, in answer to all my mollifying exhortations, so that there was every reason to conclude he would not swerve from his purpose.

Hereupon, taking my own measures, I requested a private interview with my old master; and being closeted with him, Sir, said I, allow me to throw myself at your feet, and to implore your pity. In pathetic accord with my moving accents, I prostrated myself before him, with my face all bathed in tears. The merchant, surprised at what he saw and heard, asked the cause of my distress. Remorse of conscience and repentance, answered I; but neither repentance nor remorse can ever wash out my guilt. I have been weak enough to give ear to your son, and to be his accomplice in robbing you. To this confession I added a sincere acknowledgment of all that had happened, with the particulars of my late conversation with Gaspard, whose design I laid open without the least reserve.

Bad as was the opinion which old Velasquez entertained of his son, he could scarcely believe his ears. Nevertheless, finding no good reason to distrust the truth of my account, Scipio, said he, raising me from the ground, where I had till now been prostrate at his feet, I forgive you in consideration of the important notice you have communicated. Gaspard! pursued he, raising his voice up to the loudness of anguish, does Gaspard aim a blow at my life? Ah! ungrateful son, unnatural monster! better thou hadst never been born, or stifled at thy birth, than to have been reared for the destruction of thy father! What plea, what object, what palliation of the atrocious deed? I furnished thee annually with a reasonable allowance for thy pleasures, and what wouldst thou have more? Must I have drained my fortune to the dregs to support thee in thy extravagance? Having vented his feelings in this bitter apostrophe, he enjoined secrecy on me, and told me to leave him alone, while he considered how to act in so delicate a conjuncture.

I was very anxious to know what resolution this unhappy father would take, when on that very day he sent for Gaspard, and addressed him thus without betraying the inward emotions of his heart: My son, I have received a letter from Merida, purporting that if you are disposed to marry, you may make a match with a very fine girl of fifteen, with a handsome fortune in her pocket. If you have not forsworn that happy and holy estate, we will set out to-morrow morning by daybreak for Merida: you will see the lady in question, and if she hits your fancy, the business may soon be settled. Gaspard, pricking up his ears at a handsome fortune, and already fingering the cash by anticipation, answered unhesitatingly that he was ready to undertake the journey; and accordingly they departed the following day at sunrise, without attendants, mounted on good mules.

Having reached the mountains of Fesira, in a delightful spot for the operations of banditti, but terror-stirring to the timid souls of travelers, Balthasar dismounted, and desired his son to do likewise. The young man obeyed, but expressed his surprise at such a requisition, in so lonely a place. I will tell you the reason presently, answered the old man, darting at him a look of mingled grief and anger: We are not going to Merida; and the alleged courtship was only an invention of mine, for the purpose of drawing you hither. I am not ignorant, ungrateful and unnatural son, I am not uninformed of your meditated crime. I am aware that a poison, prepared by your hands, was to have been administered to me; but, mad as you are, could it enter into your contemplation that my life could have been invaded with impunity by such means? How fatally mistaken! Your crime would soon have been detected, and you would have perished under the hands of the executioner. There is a safer way of glutting your fell malice, without exposing yourself to an ignominious death; we are here without witnesses, and in a place where daily murders are perpetrated; since you are so thirsty after my blood, plunge your dagger into my bosom: the assassination will naturally be laid at the door of some banditti. After these words, Balthasar, laying his breast bare, and pointing to his heart, ended with this challenge: Here, Gaspard, strike deep enough, strike home; make me pay that forfeit for having engendered such a disgrace to human nature, and no more than what is due to so monstrous a production.

Young Velasquez, struck by this reproach as by a thunderbolt, far from pleading in his own justification, fell instantly lifeless at his father's feet. The good old man, hailing the germ of repentance in this unfeigned testimony of shame, could not help yielding to paternal weakness; he made all possible haste to give his assistance; but Gaspard had no sooner recovered the use of his senses, than unable to stand in the presence of a father so justly offended, he made an effort to raise himself from the ground, then sprang upon his mule, and galloped out of sight without saying one word. Balthasar suffered him to take his own course, and returned to Cordova, little doubting but conscience would play its part in revenging his wrongs. Six months afterwards it appeared that the culprit had thrown himself into the Carthusian convent at Seville, there to pass the remnant of his days in penance,

CHAPTER XII.

CONCLUSION OF SCIPIO'S STORY.

BAD example sometimes produces the converse of itself. The behavior of Young Velasquez made me think seriously on my own predicament. I began to wrestle with my thievish propensities, and to live like one of the better sort. A confirmed habit of pouncing upon money wherever I could get it, had been contracted by such a long succession of individual acts, that it was no easy matter to say where it should stop. And yet I was in hopes to accomplish my own reformation, under the idea that to become virtuous a man had nothing to do but to contract the desire of being so. I therefore undertook this great work, and heaven seemed to smile upon my efforts: I left off eying the old draper's strong box with the carnal regard of avaricious longing: nay, I verily believe, that if it had depended on my own will and pleasure to have turned over the contents to my own use, I should have abstained from the crime of picking and stealing. It must, however, be admitted, that it would have been an unadvisable measure to tempt my new-born integrity with meats too strong for its stomach: and Velasquez was nurse enough to keep me on a proper diet.

Don Manriquez de Medrano, a young gentleman, knight of Alcantara, was in the habit of coming backwards and forwards to our house. He was a customer, one of our principal in point of rank, if not punctual in point of pay. I had the happiness to find favor with this knight, who never met me without that sort of notice which encouraged conversation, and with that conversation he appeared always to be very much pleased. Scipio, said he, one day, if I had a footman of your kidney, it would be as good as a fortune to me, and if you were not in the service of a man who stands so high in my regards, I should make no scruple about enticing you away. Sir, answered I, you would have very little trouble in succeeding; for I am distractedly partial to people of fashion; it is my weak side; their free and easy manners fascinat me to the extreme of folly. That being the case, replied Don Manriquez, I will at once beg Signor Balthasar to turn you over from his household to mine: he will scarcely refuse me such a request. Accordingly Velasquez was kind and complying, with so much the less violence to his own private feelings, as there seemed no reason to think, that if a man parted with one knavish servant, he might not easily get another in his place. To me the change was all for the better, since a tradesman's service appeared but a beggarly condition in comparison with the office of own man to a knight of Alcantara.

To draw a faithful likeness of my new master, I must describe him as a gentleman possessing every requisite of person, figure, manners, and disposition. Nor was that all; for his courage and honor were equal to his other qualities: the goods of fortune were the only good things he wanted, but being the younger son of a family more distinguished by descent than opulence, he was obliged to draw for his expenses on an old aunt living at Toledo, who loved him as her own child, and administered to his occasions with affectionate liberality. He was always well dressed, and everywhere well received. He visited the principal ladies in the city, and among others the Marchioness of Almenara. She was a widow of seventy-two, but the centre of attraction to all the fashionable society of Cordova, by the elegance of her manners and the sprightliness of her conversation: men as well as women laid themselves out for an introduction, because her parties conferred at once on the frequenters the patent of good company.

My master was one of that lady's most assiduous courtiers. After leaving her one evening, his spirits seemed to be more elevated than was natural to him. Sir, said I, you are evidently in a good deal of agitation; may your faithful servant ask on what account? Has anything happened out of the common way? The young gallant smiled at so home a question, and owned candidly that he had just been engaged in a serious conversation with the Marchioness of Almenara. I will lay a wager, said I, laughing outright, that this moppet of threescore and ten, this girl in her second childhood, has been unfolding to you all the secret movements of a tender, susceptible heart. Do not make a jest of it, answered he; for the fact is, my friend, that the Marchioness is seriously in love with me. She told me that the narrowness of my circumstances was as well known to her as the nobility of my birth; that she had taken a liking to me, and was determined to place me at my ease by marriage, since she could not decently lay her fortune at my feet on any other terms. That this marriage would expose her to public ridicule, she professed to have considered; that scandal would be busy at her expense; in short, that she should pass for an old fool with an ambitious eye and a liquorish constitution. No matter for that! She was not to be awed from the career of her humor by quips and sentences: her only alarm was, lest I should either make sport of her intentions, or torment her more grievously by my aversion.

Such, continued the knight, was the substance of the Marchioness's declaration, and I am the more astonished at it, because she is the most prudent and sensible woman in Cordova; wherefore I answered by expressing my surprise at her honoring me with the offer of her hand, since she had hitherto persisted in her resolution of remaining in a state of widowhood. To this she replied, that having a considerable fortune, it would give her pleasure to share it in her life-time with a man of honor to whom she was attached. To all appearance then, rejoined I, you have made up your mind to take a lover's leap. Can you doubt about that? answered he. The Marchioness is immensely rich, with excellent qualities both of head and heart. It would be the extreme of folly and fastidiousness to let so advantageous a settlement slip through my fingers.

I entirely approved my master's purpose of profiting by so fine an opportunity to make his fortune, and even advised him to bring the matter to a short issue, for fear of a change in the wind. Happily the lady had the business more at heart than myself; her orders were given so effectually, that the necessary forms and ceremonies were soon got over. When it became known in Cordova that the old Marchioness of Almenara was getting herself ready to be the bride of young Don Manriquez de Medrano, the wits began breaking their odd quirks and remnants in derision of the widow; but though she heard her own detractions, she did not put them to mending; the town might talk as they pleased; for when she said she would die a widow, she did not think to live till she were married. The wedding was solemnized with a publicity and splendor which furnished fresh food for evil tongues. The bride, said they, might at least have had the modesty to dispense with noise and ostentation, so unbecoming in an old widow who marries a young husband.

The Marchioness, far enough from yielding to the suggestions of shame at her own inconsistency, or the disparity of their ages, yielded herself up without constraint to the expression of the most lively joy. She gave a grand concert and supper, with a ball afterwards, and invited all the principal families in Cordova. Just before the close of the ball, the new-married couple disappeared, and were shown to an apartment, where, with no other witnesses but her own maid and myself, she spoke to my master in these terms:—Don Manriquez, this is your apartment; mine is in another part of the house: we will pass the night in separate rooms, and will live together by day like mother and son. At first the knight did not know what to make of this; he thought that the lady was only trying his temper, as if her coldness must be wooed to kindness, and her love, like her pardon, not unsought, be won. Imagining, therefore, that good manners required, at least, the show of passion, he made his advances, and offered, according to the laws of amorous suit enacted in such cases, to assist in the disencumbering duties of her toilet; but, so far from allowing him to interfere with the province of her servant, she pushed him back with a serious air, saying: Hold, Don Manriquez; if you take me for one of those sweet-toothed old women who marry a second time from mere incontinence, you do me a manifest injustice: my proposals were not fraught with conditions of hard service as the tenure of our nuptial contract; the gift of my heart was unmixed with sensual dross, and your gratitude is only drawn upon for returns of pure and platonic friendship. After this explanation, she left my master and me in our apartment, and withdrew to her own with her attendant, forbidding the bridegroom, in the most positive manner, to attempt retiring with her.

After her departure, it was some time before we recovered from our surprise at what we had just heard. Scipio, said my master, could you ever have believed that the Marchioness would have talked in such a strain? What think you of so philosophic a bride? I think, sir, answered I, that she is a phenix among the brood of Hymen. It is for all the world like a good living without parochial duties. For my part, replied Don Manriquez, there is nothing so much to my taste as a wife of modest pretensions; and I mean to make her amends for the trophy she has raised to unadulterated esteem, by all the delicate attentions in my power to pay. We kept up the subject of the lady's moderation till it was full time to separate. My quarters were fixed in an ante-room with a book-case bedstead; my master's in an elegant bed-chamber with every appurtenance expect one: but however necessary it might be to play the disappointed bridegroom, I am much mistaken if in the bottom of his soul he was half so much afraid of sleeping by himself as of being encumbered with a bed-fellow.

The rejoicings began again on the following day, and the bride was so jocund on the occasion, that the bolts of the fools among her visitors were not soon shot. She was the first to laugh at all their pointless jokes; nay, she even set the little wits to work, by giving them an example of pleasantry, which they were very little able to follow. The happy man, on his part, seemed to be very little less happy than his partner; and one would have sworn, judging by the glance of satisfaction which accompanied his language and deportment, that he liked mutton better than lamb. This well-matched pair had a second conversation in the evening; and then it was decided that without interfering in the least with one another, they should live together just on the same footing as they had lived before marriage. At all events, much credit must be given to Don Manriquez on one account: he did, from delicate consideration towards his wife, what few husbands would have done under his circumstances, for he discarded a little seamstress of whom he was very fond, and who was very fond of him, because he did not choose to keep up a connection insulting to the feelings of a lady so studious of his.

While he was furnishing such unusual testimonies of gratitude to his elderly benefactress, she overpaid and doubly paid her debt of obligation, even without diving into its nature or extent. She gave him the master key of her strong box, which was better provided than that of Velasquez. Though she had reduced her establishment during widowhood, it was now replaced upon the same footing as in the life-time of her first husband; the complement of household servants was enlarged, the stud and equipages were in the very first style; in a word, by her generosity and kindness, the most beggarly knight belonging to the order of Alcantara became the most moneyed member of the fraternity. You may perhaps be disposed to ask me, how much I was in pocket by all that; and my answer is, fifty pistoles from my mistress, and a hundred from my master, who, moreover, appointed me his secretary, with a salary of four hundred crowns; nay, his confidence was so unbounded, that I was fixed on to fill the office of treasurer.

Treasurer! cried I, interrupting Scipio at the very idea, and bursting into an immoderate fit of laughter. Yes, sir, replied he, with a cool, unflinching seriousness; you are perfectly right, treasurer was the word; and I may venture to say that the duties of the office were executed without the slightest occasion for a committee of inquiry. True it is that the balance may be somewhat against me for I was always in the habit of overdrawing my wages; and as the firm was dissolved somewhat suddenly, it is by no means impossible that the balance of my cash account might be on the wrong side; but, at all events, it was my last slip; and since that time my ways have been ways of uprightness and honesty.

Thus was I, continued this son of a gypsy, secretary and treasurer to Don Manriquez, who, to all appearance, was as happy in me as I in him, when he received a letter from Toledo, announcing that his aunt, Donna Theodora Moscoso, was on her last legs. He was so much affected by the news, as to set out instantly and pay his duty to that lady, who had been more than a mother to him for several years. I attended him on the journey with only two under-servants; we were all mounted on the best horses in the stable, and reached Toledo without loss of time, where we found Donna Theodora in a state to warrant our hopes that she would not, at present, weigh anchor on her outward-bound voyage; and, in fact, our judgment on her case, though point blank in contradiction to that of an old physician who attended her, proved by the event that we knew at least as much of the matter as he did.

While the health of our venerable relative was improving from day to day, less, perhaps, from the effect of the prescriptions than in consequence of her dear nephew's presence, your worthy friend the treasurer passed his time in the pleasantest manner possible, with some young people whose acquaintance was admirably calculated to ventilate the confined cash in his pocket. Sometimes they enticed me to the tennis-court, and took me in for a game: on those occasions, not being quite so steady a player as my master, Don Abel, I lost much oftener than I won. By degrees play became a passion with me; and if the taste had been suffered to gain complete possession, it would doubtless have laid me under the necessity of drawing bills of accommodation on the family bank; but happily love stepped in, and saved the credit both of the bank and of my principles. One day, passing along near the church of the Epiphany, I espied through a lattice with the drapery drawn up, a young girl who might well be called a thing divine, for nothing natural was ever seen so lovely. I would lay on my compliment still thicker, if words were not wanting to express the effect of her first appearance upon my mind. I set my wits to work, and by dint of diligent inquiry, learned that her name was Beatrice, and that she was waiting-maid to Donna Julia, younger daughter of the Count de Polan.

Beatrice broke in upon the thread of Scipio's story by laughing immoderately: then, directing her speech to my wife, Charming Antonia, said she, do but just look at me, I beseech you, and then say truly, whether I could be likened to a thing divine. You might at that time, to my enamored sight, said Scipio; and, since your conjugal faith is no longer under a cloud, my visual appetite increases by what it feeds on. It was a pretty compliment! and my secretary, having fired it off, pursued his narrative as follows:

This intelligence kindled the flame of passion within me; but not, it must be confessed, a flame which could be acknowledged without a blush. I took it for granted that my triumph over her scruples would be easy if my biddings were high enough to command the ordinary market of female chastity; but Beatrice was a pearl beyond price. In vain did I solicit her, through the channel of some intriguing gossips, with the offer of my purse and of my most tender attentions; she rejected all my proposals with disdain. I had recourse to the lover's last remedy, and offered her my hand, which she deigned to accept on the strength of my being secretary and treasurer to Don Manriquez. As it seemed expedient to keep our marriage secret for some time, the ceremony was performed privately, in presence of Dame Lorenza Sephora, Seraphina's governess, and before some others of the Count de Polan's household. After our happy union, Beatrice contrived the means of our meeting by day, and passing some part of every night together in the garden, whither I repaired through a little gate of which she gave me a key. Never were man and wife better pleased with each other than Beatrice and myself: with equal impatience did we watch for the hour of our appointment; with congenial emotions of eager sensibility did we hasten to the spot, and the moments which we passed together, though countless from their number in the calendar of cold indifference, to us were few and fleeting, in comparison with that eternity of mutual bliss for which we panted.

One night, a night which should be expunged from the almanac, a night of darkness and despair, contrasted with the brightness of all our former nights, I was surprised on approaching the garden, to find the little gate open. This unusual circumstance alarmed me; for it seemed to augur something inauspicious to my happiness: I turned pale and trembled, as if with a foreknowledge of what was going to happen. Advancing in the dark towards a bower, where our private meetings had usually taken place, I heard a man's voice. I stopped on the instant to listen, when the following words struck like the sound of death upon my ear: Do not keep me languishing in suspense, my dear Beatrice; make my happiness complete, and consider that your own fortunes are closely connected with mine. Instead of having patience to hear further, it seemed as if more had been said than blood could expiate; that devil, jealousy, took possession of my soul; I drew my sword, and breathing only vengeance, rushed into the bower. Ah! base seducer, cried I, whoever you are, you shall tear this heart from out my breast, rather than touch my honor on its tenderest point. With these words on my lips, I attacked the gentleman who was talking with Beatrice. He stood upon his guard without more ado, like a man much better acquainted with the science of arms than myself, who had only received a few lessons from a fencing-master at Cordova. And yet, strong as his sword-arm was, I made a thrust which he could not parry, or what is more likely, his foot slipped: I saw him fall, and fancying that I had wounded him mortally, ran away as hard as my legs could carry me; without deigning to answer Beatrice, who would have called me back.

Yes, indeed! said Scipio's wife, resolved to have her share in the development of the story; I called out for the purpose of unde-ceiving him. The gentleman conversing with me in the arbor was Don Ferdinand de Leyva. This nobleman, who was in love with my mistress Julia, had laid a plan for running away with her, from despair of being able to obtain her hand by any other means; and I had myself made this assignation with him in the garden, to con-cert measures for the elopement, and with his fortune he assured me that my own was closely linked; but it was in vain that I screamed after my husband; he darted from me as if my very touch were contamination.

In such a state of mind, resumed Scipio, I was capable of any-thing. Those who know by experience what jealousy is, into what extravagance it drives the best-regulated spirits, will be at no loss to conceive the disorder it must have produced in my weak brain. I passed in a moment from one extreme to another: emotions of hatred succeeded instantaneously to all my former sentiments of affection for my wife. I took an oath never to see her more, and to banish her for ever from my memory. Besides, the supposed death of a man lay upon my conscience; and under that idea, I was afraid of falling into the hands of justice; so that every torment which could be accumulated on the head of guilt and misery by the fury of despair and the demon of remorse, was the remediless com-panion of my wretched flight. In this dreadful situation, thinking only of my escape, I returned home no more, but immediately quitted Toledo, with no other provision for my journey but the clothes on my back. It is true, I had about sixty pistoles in my pocket; a tolerable supply for a young man, whose views in life pointed no higher than a good service.

I walked forward all night, or rather ran, for the phantom of an alguazil always dogging me at the heels made me perform wonders of pedestrian activity. The dawn overtook me between Rodillas and Maqueda. When I was at the latter town, finding myself a little weary, I went into the church which was just opened, and having put up a short prayer, sat down on a bench to rest. I began musing on the state of my affairs, which were sufficiently out at elbows to require all my skill in patchwork, but the time for re-flection as well as for repentance were cut short. The church echoed on a sudden with three or four smacks of a whip, which made me conclude that some carrier was on the road. I immedi-ately got up to go and see whether I was right or wrong. At the door I found a man, mounted on a mule, leading two others by the halter. Stop, my friend, sa'd I, whither are those two mules going? To Madrid, answered he. I came hither with two good Domini-cans, and am now setting out on my return.

Such an opportunity of going to Madrid gave me an itching desire for the expedition: I made my bargain with the muleteer, jumped upon one of his mules, and away we scampered towards Illescas, where we were to put up for the night. Scarcely were we out of Maqueda before the muleteer, a man from five-and-thirty to forty, began chanting the church service with a most collegiate twang. This trial of his lungs began with matins, in the drowsy tone of a canon between asleep and awake; then he roared out the Belief, alternately in contralto, tenor, and bass, in all the harmonious confusion of high mass; and not content with that, he rang the bell for vespers, without sparing me a single petition or so much as a bar of the *magnificat*. Though the scoundrel almost cracked the drum of my ear, I could not help laughing heartily; and even egged him on to make the welkin reverberate with his hallelujahs, when the anthem was suspended a few rests, for the necessary purpose of supplying wind to the organ. Courage, my friend! said I; go on and prosper. If heaven has given you a good capacious throat, you are neither a niggard nor a perverter of its precious boon. Oh! certainly not for the matter of that, cried he; happily for my immortal soul, I am not like carriers in general, who sing nothing but profane songs about love or drinking: I do not even defile my lips with ballads on our wars against the Moors: such subjects are at least light and unedifying, if not licentious and impure. You have, replied I, an evangelical purity of heart which belongs only to the elect among muleteers. With this excessive squeamishness of yours about the choice of your music, have you also taken a vow of continence, wherever there is a young barmaid to be picked up at an inn? Assuredly, rejoined he, chastity is also a virtue by which it is my pride to ward off the temptations of the road, where my only business is to look after my mules. I was in no small degree astonished at such pious sentiments from this prodigy of psalm-singing mule-drivers; so that looking upon him as a man above the vanities and corruptions of this nether world, I fell into chat with him after he had gone the length of his tether in singing.

We got to Illescas late in the day. On entering the inn-yard, I left the care of the mules to my companion, and went into the kitchen, where I ordered the landlord to get us a good supper, which he promised to perform so much to my satisfaction as to make me remember all the days of my life what usage travelers meet with at his house. As, added he, now only ask your carrier what sort of a man I am. By all the powers of seasoning! I would defy the best cook in Madrid or Toledo to make an olio at all to be compared to mine. I shall treat you this evening with some stewed rabbit after a receipt of my own; you will then see whether it is any boast to say that I know how to send up a supper. Thereupon, showing me a stew-pan with a young rabbit, as he said, cut up into pieces: There, continued he, is what I mean to favor you with. When I shall have thrown in a little pepper, some salt, wine, a handful of sweet herbs, and a few other ingredients which I keep for my own sauces, you may depend on sitting down to such a dish as would not disgrace the table of a chancellor or an archbishop.

The landlord, having thus done justice to his own merits, began to work upon the materials he had prepared. While he was laboring in his vocation, I went into a room, where lying down on a sort of couch, I fell fast asleep through fatigue, having taken no rest the night before. In the space of about two hours, the muleteer came and awakened me, with the information that supper was ready, and a pressing request to take my place at table. The cloth was laid for two, and we sat down to the hashed rabbit. I played my knife and fork most manfully, finding the flavor delicious, whether from the force of hunger in communicating a candid mode of interpretation to my palate, or from the natural effect of the ingredients compounded by the cook. A joint of roast mutton was next served up. It was remarkable that the carrier only paid his respects to this last article; and I asked him why he had not taken his share of the other. He answered with a suppressed smile, that he was not fond of made dishes. This reason, or rather the turn of countenance with which it was alleged, seemed to imply more than was expressed. You have not told me, said I, the real meaning of your not eating the fricassee: do have the goodness to explain it at once. Since you are so curious to be made acquainted with it, replied he, I must own that I have an insuperable aversion to cramming my stomach with meats in masquerade, since one evening at an inn on the road between Toledo and Cuença, they served me up, instead of a wild rabbit, a hash of tame cat; enough, of all conscience, ever after to set my intestines in battle-array against all minces, stews, and force-meats.

No sooner had the muleteer let me into this secret, than in spite of the hunger which raged within me, my appetite left me completely in the lurch. I conceived, in all the horrors of extreme loathing, that I had been eating a cat dressed up as the double of a rabbit; and the fricassee had no longer any power over my senses, except by producing a strong inclination to retch. My companion did not lessen my tendency that way, by telling me that the inn-keepers in Spain, as well as the pastry-cooks, were very much in the habit of making that substitution. The drift of the conversation was, as you may perceive, very much in the nature of a lenitive to my stomach; so much so, that I had no mind to meddle any more with the dish of undefinables, nor even to make an attack upon the roast meat, for fear the mutton should have performed its duty by deputy as well as the rabbit. I jumped up from table, cursing the cookery, the cook, and the whole establishment; then, throwing myself down upon the sofa, I passed the night with less nausea than might reasonably have been expected. The day following with the dawn, after having paid the reckoning with as princely an air as if we had been treated like princes, away went I from Illescas, bearing my faculties so strongly impregnated with fricassee, that I took every animal which crossed the road, of whatever species or dimensions, for a cat.

We got to Madrid betimes, where I had no sooner settled with my carrier than I hired a ready-furnished lodging near the Sun-gate. My eyes, though accustomed to the great world, were nevertheless dazzled by the concourse of nobility which was ordinarily seen in the quarter of the court. I admired the prodigious number of carriages, and the countless list of gentlemen, pages, gentlemen's gentlemen, and plain, downright footmen in the train of the grandees. My admiration exceeded all bounds, on going to the king's levee, and beholding the monarch in the midst of his court. The effect of the scene was enchanting, and I said to myself, It is no wonder they should say that one must see the court of Madrid to form an adequate idea of its magnificence : I am delighted to have directed my course hither, and feel a sort of prescience within me that I shall not come away without taking fortune by surprise. I caught nothing napping, however, but my own prudence, in making some thriftless, expensive acquaintance. My money oozed away in the rapid thaw of my propriety and better judgment, so that it became a measure of expedient degradation to throw away my transcendent merit on a pedagogue of Salamanca, whom some family lawsuit or other concern had brought to Madrid, where he was born, and where chance, more whimsical than wise, thrust me within the horizon of his knowledge. I became his right hand, his prime principal agent ; and dogged him at the heels to the university when he returned thither.

My new employer went by the name of Don Ignacio de Ipigna. He furnished himself with the handle of don, inasmuch as he had been tutor to a nobleman of the first rank, who had recompensed his early services with an annuity for life : he likewise derived a snug little salary from his professorship in the university ; and in addition to all this, laid the public under a yearly contribution of two or three hundred pistoles for books of uninstructive morality, which he protruded from the press periodically by weight and measure, The manner in which he worked up the shreds and patches of his composition deserves a notice somewhat more than cursory. The heavy hours of the forenoon were spent in muzzing over Hebrew, Greek, and Latin authors, and in writing down upon little squares of card every pithy sentence or striking thought which occurred in the morning's reading. According to the progress of this literary Pam, in winning tricks from the ancients, he employed me to score up his honors in the form of an Apollo's wreath : these metaphysical garlands were strung upon wire, and each garland made a pocket volume. What an execrable hash of wholesome viands did we cook up ! The commandments set at loggerheads with an utter confusion of tables ; Epicurean conclusions grafted on stoical premises ! Tully quoting Epictetus, and Seneca supporting his antitheses on the authority of monkish rhyme ! Scarcely a month elapsed without our putting forth at least two volumes, so that the press was kept continually groaning under the weight of our transgressions. What seemed most extraordinary of all, was that these literary larcenies were palmed upon the purchasers for spick and span new wares, and if, by any strange and improbable chance, a thick-headed critic should stumble with his noddle smack against some palpable plagiarism, the author would plead guilty to the indictment, and make a merit of serving up at second-hand

> What Gellius or Stobæus hash'd before,
> Though chewed by blind old scholiasts o'er and o'er.

He was also a great commentator ; and filled his notes chock-full of so much erudition, as to multiply whole pages of discussion upon

what homely common-sense would have consigned to the brief
alternative of a query:

> Disputes of Me or Te, or Aut at At,
> To sound or sink in cano O or A,
> Or give up Cicero to C or K.

As almost every author, ethical and didactic, from Hesiod down
to himself, took his turn to dangle on some one or other of our
manuscript garlands, it was impossible for me not to suck in somewhat of sage nurture from so copious a stream of philosophy: it
would be rank ingratitude to shift off my obligation. My handwriting
also became strictly and decidedly legible, by dint of continual tran-
scription; my estate was more that of a pupil than of a servant, and
my morals were not neglected, while my mind was polished, and my
faculties raised above their former level. Scipio, he used to say,
when he chanced to hear of any serving lad with more cunning
than honesty in his dealings, beware, my good boy, how you take
after the evil example of that graceless villain. "The honor of a
servant is his fidelity; his highest virtues are submission and obedience. Be studious of thy master's interests, be diligent in his
affairs, and faithful to the trust which he reposeth in thee. Thy
time and thy labor belong unto him. Defraud him not thereof, for
he payeth thee for them." To sum up all, Don Ignacio lost no
opportunity of leading me on in the path of virtue, and his prudent counsels sank so deep into my heart, as to keep under anything like even the slightest wish of playing him a rogue's trick
during the fifteen months which I spent in his service.

I have already mentioned that Doctor de Ipigna was a native of
Madrid. He had a relation there, by name Catalina, waiting-maid
to the lady who officiated as nurse to the heir-apparent. This
abigail, the same through whose intervention I got Signor de Santillane released from the tower of Segovia, intent on rendering a
service to Don Ignacio, prevailed with her mistress to petition the
Duke of Lerma for some preferment. The minister named him for
the archdeaconry of Grenada, which, as a conquered country, is in
the king's gift. We repaired immediately to Madrid on receiving
the intelligence, as the doctor wished to thank his patronesses
before he took possession of his benefice. I had more than one
opportunity of seeing Catalina, and conversing with her. The
cheerful turn of my temper and a certain easy air of good company
were altogether to her taste; for my part, I found her so much to
my liking, that I could not help saying yes to the little advances of
partiality which she made in my favor: in short, we got to feel very
kindly towards each other. You must not write a comment with
your nails, my dear Beatrice, on this episode in the romance of my
amours, beause I was firmly persuaded of your inconstancy, and
you will allow that heresy, though impious, being also blind, my
penance may reasonably be remitted on sincere conversion.

In the mean time Doctor Ignacio was making ready to set out
for Grenada. His relation and myself, out of our wits at the
impending separation, had recourse to an expedient which rescued

us from its horrors: I shammed illness, complained of my head, complained of my chest, and made a characteristic wry face for every pain and ache in the catalogue of human infirmities. My master called in a physician, who told me with a grave face, after putting his questions in the usual course, that my complaint was of a much more serious nature than might appear to unprofessional observation, and that, aacording to all present likelihood, I should keep my chamber a long time. The doctor, impatient to take possession of his preferment, did not think it quite so well to delay his departure, but chose rather to hire another boy; he therefore contented himself with handing me over to the care of a nurse, with whom he left a sum of money to bury me if I should die, or to remunerate me for my services if I should recover.

As soon as I knew Don Ignacio to be safe on the road for Grenada, I was cured of all my maladies. I got up, made my final bow to the physician who had evinced so thorough a knowledge of my case, and fairly turned my nurse out-of-doors, who made her retreat good with baggage and ammunition, to the amount of more than half the sum for which she ought to have accounted with me. While I was enacting the sick man, Catalina was playing another part about the person of her mistress, Donna Anna de Guévra, into whose conception having by dint of many a wordy process inserted the notion, that I was the man of all others ready cut and dry for an intrigue, she induced her to choose me for one of her agents. The royal and most catholic nurse, whose genius for great undertakings was either produced or exasperated by the love of great possessions, having occasion for suitable ministers, received me among her hangers-on, and lost no opportunity of ascertaining how far I was for her purpose. She confided some commissions to my care, which, vanity apart, called for no little address, and what they called for was ready at hand: accordingly, she gave me all possible credit for the diligent execution of my office, while my discontent swelled high against her for fobbing me off with the cold recompense of approbation. The good lady was so abominably avaricious, as not to give me a working partner's share in the profits of my industry, nor to allow for the wear and tear of my conscience. She seemed inclined to consider, that by paying me my wages, all the requisitions of Christian charity were made good between us. This excess of illiberal economy would soon have parted us, had it not been for the fascination of Catalina's gentle virtues, who became more desperately in love with me from day to day, and completed the paroxysm by a formal proposal of marriage.

Fair and softly, my pretty friend, said I: we must look before we leap into that bottomless gulf: the first point to be settled is to ascertain the death of a young woman, who obtained the refusal before you, and made me supremely happy, for no other purpose but to anticipate the purgatory of an intermediate state in the present. All a mere sham, a put off! answered Catalina: you swear you are married only by way of throwing a genteel veil over your abhorrence of my person and manners. In vain did I call all the powers to witness, that what I said was solemnly true: my sincere avowal was considered as a mere copy of my countenance; the lady was grievously offended, and changed her whole behavior in regard to me. There was no downright quarrel; but our tender intercourse became visibly more rigid and unaccommodating, so that nothing further took place between us but cold formality and commonplace attentions.

Just at the nick of time, I heard that Signor Gil Blas de Santillane, secretary to the prime minister of the Spanish monarchy, wanted a servant; and the situation was the more flattering, as it bore the bell among all the vacancies of the court register office. Signor de Santillane, they told me, was one of the first men, high in favor with the Duke of Lerma, and consequently in the direct road to fortune: his heart, too, was cast in the mold of generosity: by doing his business, you most assuredly did your own. The opportunity was too good to be neglected: I went and offered myself to Signor Gil Blas, to whom I felt my heart grow from the first; for my sentiments were fixed by the turn of his physiognomy. There could be no question about leaving the royal and most catholic nurse for him; and it is to be hoped, I shall never have any other master.

Here ended Scipio's story. But he continued speaking, and addressed himself to me. Signor de Santillane, do me the favor to assure those ladies that you have always known me for a faithful and zealous servant. Your testimony will stand me in good stead, and vouch for a sincere reformation in the son of Coselina.

Yes, ladies, said I, it is even so. Though Scipio in his childhood was very scape-grace, he has been born anew, and is now the exact model of a trusty domestic. Far from having any complaints to make against him, my debt is infinite. On the fatal night when I was carried off to the tower of Segovia, he saved my effects from pillage, and refunded what he might have taken to himself with impunity: not contented with rescuing my worldly pelf, he came out of pure friendship and shut himself up with me in my prison, preferring the melancholy sympathies of adverse fortune to all the charms of lusty, buoyant liberty.

BOOK THE ELEVENTH

CHAPTER I.

CONTAINING THE SUBJECT OF THE GREATEST JOY THAT GIL
BLAS EVER FELT, FOLLOWED UP, AS OUR GREATEST PLEAS-
URES TOO GENERALLY ARE, BY THE MOST MELANCHOLY
EVENT OF HIS LIFE. GREAT CHANGES AT COURT, PRODUC-
ING, AMONG OTHER IMPORTANT REVOLUTIONS, THE RETURN
OF SANTILLANE.

I HAVE observed already that Antonia and Beatrice understood
one another perfectly well; the latter falling meekly and modestly
into the trammels of an humble attendant on her lady, and the
former taking very kindly to the rank of a mistress and superior.
Scipio and myself were husbands too rich in nature's gifts and in
the affections of our spouses, not very soon to have the satisfaction
of becoming fathers : our lasses were as women wish to be who love
their lords, almost at the same moment. Beatrice's time was up
first : she was safely delivered of a daughter; and in a few days
afterwards Antonia completed the general joy, by presenting me
with a son. I sent my secretary to Valencia with the welcome tidings : the governor came to Lirias with Seraphina and the Marchioness de Pliego, to be present at the baptismal ceremony; for
he made it his pleasure to add this testimony of affection to all his
former kindnesses. As that nobleman stood godfather, and the
Marchioness godmother to my son, he was named Alphonso ; and
the governor's lady, wishing to draw the bonds of sponsorship still
closer in this friendly party, stood for Scipio's daughter, to whom
we gave the name of Seraphina.

The rejoicings at the birth of my son were not confined to the
mansion-house ; the villagers of Lirias celebrated the event by
festivities, which were meant as a grateful token, to prove how much
the little neighborhood partook in all the satisfactions of their landlord. But, alas ! our carousals were of short continuance ; or, to
speak more suitably to the subject, they were turned into weeping,
wailing, and lamentation, by a catastrophe which more than twenty
years have not been sufficient to blot from my memory, nor will
future time, however distant, make me think of it but with the bitterest retrospect. My son died ; and his mother, though perfectly
recovered from her confinement, very soon followed him : a violent
fever carried off my dear wife, after we had been married fourteen
months. Let the reader conceive, if he is equal to the task, the
grief with which I was overwhelmed : I fell into a stupid insensibility; and felt my loss so severely, as to seem not to feel it at all.

I remained in this condition for five or six days, in an obstinate determination to take no nourishment; and I verily believe that, had it not been for Scipio, I should either have starved myself, or my heart would have burst; but my secretary, well knowing how to accommodate himself to the turnings and windings of the human heart, contrived to cheat my sorrows by falling in with their tone and tenor: he was artful enough to reconcile me to the duty of taking food, by serving up soups and lighter fare with so disconsolate an arrangement of features that it looked as if he urged me to the revolting employment, not so much to preserve my life, as to perpetuate and render immortal my affliction.

This affectionate servant wrote to Don Alphonso, to let him know of the misfortune which had happened to me, and my lamentable condition in consequence. That tender-hearted and compassionate nobleman, that generous friend, very soon repaired to Lirias. I cannot recall the moment when he first presented himself to my view without even now being sensibly affected. My dear Santillane, said he, embracing me, I am not come to offer you impertinent consolation; but to weep over Antonia with you, as you would have wept with me over Seraphina, had the hand of death snatched her from me. In good truth, his tears bore testimony to his sincerity, and his sighs were blended with mine in the most friendly sympathy. Though overwhelmed with my affliction, I felt in the most lively manner the kindness of Don Alphonso.

The governor had a long conversation with Scipio respecting the measures to be taken for overcoming my despair. They judged it best to remove me for some time from Lirias, where every object incessantly brought back to my mind the image of Antonia. On this account the son of Don Cæsar proposed carrying me back with him to Valencia; and my secretary seconded the plan with so many unanswerable arguments, that I made no further opposition. I left Scipio and his wife on my estate, where my longer stay could have produced no other effect but that of aggravating and enhancing all my sorrows, and took my own departure with the governor. On my arrival at Valencia, Don Cæsar and his daughter-in-law spared no exertions to divert my sorrows from perpetual brooding; they plied me alternately with every sort of amusement, the most proper to turn the current of my thoughts to passing objects; but, in spite of all their pains, I remained plunged in melancholy, whence they were incompetent to draw me out. Nor was it for want of Scipio's kind attentions that my peace of mind was still so hopeless: he was continually going back and fore between Lirias and Valencia to inquire after me; and his journey home was cheeful or gloomy, in proportion as he found more or less disposition in me to listen to the words of comfort, and to reward the affectionate solicitude of my friends.

He came one morning into my room. Sir, said he, with a great deal of agitation in his manner, a report is current about town, in which the whole monarchy is deeply interested: it is said that Philip the Third has departed this life, and that the prince, his son, is actually seated on the throne. To this it is added, that the Cardinal Duke of Lerma has lost the premiership, that he is even forbidden to appear at court, and that Don Gaspard de Guzman, Count of Olivarez, is actually at the head of the administration. I felt a little agitated by this sudden change, without knowing why. Scipio caught at this manifestation, and asked whether the veering of the wind in the political horizon might not blow me some good. How is that possible? What good can it blow me, my worthy friend? answered I. The court and I have shaken hands once for all: the revolutions which may take place there are all alike indifferent to me.

For a man at your time of life, replied that cunning son of a diviner, you are uncommonly mortified to all the uses of this world. Under your circumstances my curiosity would be all alive; I should go to Madrid and show my face to the young monarch, just to see whether he would recollect it, merely for the amusement of the thing. I understand you, said I; you would have me return to court and try my fortune again, or rather you would plunge me back into the gulf of avarice and ambition. Why should such baleful passions any more take possession of your breast? rejoined Scipio. Do not so much play the calumniator on your own virtue. I will answer for your firmness to yourself. The sound moral reflections which your disgrace has occasioned you to make on the vanities of a court life, are a sufficient security against all the dangers to be feared from that quarter. Embark boldly once again upon an ocean where you are acquainted with every shoal and rock in the dangerous navigation. Hold your tongue, you flatterer, said I, with a smile of no very positive discouragement; are you weary of seeing me lead a retired and tranquil life? I thought my repose had been more dear to you.

Just at this period of our conversation, Don Cæsar and his son came in. They confirmed the news of the king's death, as well as the Duke of Lerma's misfortune. It appeared, moreover, that this minister, having requested permission to retire to Rome, had not been able to obtain it, but was ordered to confine himself to his marquisate at Denia. On this, as if they had been in league with my secretary, they advised me to go to Madrid and offer my congratulations to the new king, as one of his former acquaintances, with the merit of having rendered him even such services, as the great are apt to regard more willingly than some which are performed with cleaner hands. For my part, said Don Alphonso, I have no doubt but they will be liberally acknowledged: Philip the Fourth is bound in honor to pay the Prince of Spain's debts. I consider the affair just in the same light as you do, said Don Cæsar; and Santillane's visit to court will doubtless prove the occasion of his arriving at the very first employments.

In good truth, my noble friends, exclaimed I, you do not consider what you are talking about. It should seem, were one to give ear to the soothing words of you both, as if I had nothing to do but to show my face at Madrid, and receive the key of office, or some foreign government for my pains; but you are egregiously mistaken. I am, on the contrary, well persuaded that the king would pass me over as a stranger, were I to throw myself in his way. I will make the experiment if you wish it, merely for the sake of undeceiving you. The lords of Leyva took me at my word, so that I could not help promising them to set out without loss of time for Madrid. No sooner did my secretary perceive my mind fully made up to the prosecution of this journey, than his ecstasies were wound up to the highest pitch : he was satisfied within himself that if I did but present my excellent person before the new monarch, he would immediately single me out from the crowd of political candidates, and weigh me down under a load of dignities and emoluments. On the strength of these conjectures, puffing himself out and amusing his fancy with the most splendid extravagances of device, he raised me up to the first offices of the state, and pushed forward his own preferment in the path of my exaltation.

I therefore made my arrangements for returning to court, without the most distant intention of again sacrificing at the shrine of fortune, but merely to convince Don Cæsar and his son of their error, in imagining that I was at all likely to ingratiate myself with the sovereign. It is true that there was some little lurking vanity at the bottom of all my philosophy, sprouting up in the shape of a desire to ascertain whether my royal master would throw away a thought on me, now in the spring-time of his new and blushing honors. Led out of that course solely by that tempter, curiosity, without a dream of hope, or any practical contrivance for turning the new reign to my own individual advantage, I set out for Madrid with Scipio, consigning the management of my household to Beatrice, who was well skilled in all the arts of domestic economy.

CHAPTER II.

GIL BLAS ARRIVES IN MADRID, AND MAKES HIS APPEARANCE AT COURT : THE KING IS BLESSED WITH A BETTER MEMORY THAN MOST OF HIS COURTIERS, AND RECOMMENDS HIM TO THE NOTICE OF HIS PRIME MINISTER. CONSEQUENCES OF THAT RECOMMENDATION.

WE got to Madrid in less than eight days, Don Alphonso having given us two of his best horses, that we might lose no time on the road. We alighted at a ready-furnished lodging, where I had lived formerly, kept by Vincent Ferrero, my old landlord, who was uncommonly glad to see me again.

As this man prided himself on being in the secret of whatever was going forward either in court or city, I asked him after the best news. There is plenty of it, whether best or worst, answered he. Since the death of Philip the Third, the friends and partisans of the Cardinal Duke of Lerma have been moving heaven and earth to support his eminence on the pinnacle of ministerial authority, but their efforts have been ineffectual: the Count of Olivarez has carried the day, in spite of all their industry. It is alleged that Spain will be no loser by the exchange, and that the present premier is possessed of a genius so extensive, a mind so capacious, that he would be competent to wield the machine of universal government. New brooms, they say, sweep clean! But, at all events, you may take this for certain, that the public is fully impressed with a very favorable opinion of his capacity: we shall see by and by whether the Duke of Lerma's situation is well or ill filled up. Ferrero, having got his tongue into the right train for wagging, gave me all the particulars of all the changes which had taken place at court, since the Count of Olivarez had taken his seat at the helm of the state vessel.

Two days after my arrival at Madrid, I repaired to the royal palace after my dinner, and threw myself in the king's way as he was crossing the lobby to his closet; but his notice was not at all attracted by my appearance. Next day, I returned to the same place, but with no better success, On the third day he looked me full in the face as he passed by, but the stare was perfectly vacant, as far as my interest or my vanity was concerned. This being the case, I resolved in my own mind what was proper to be done: You see, said I to Scipio, who accompanied me, that the king is grown out of my recollection; or if his memory is not become more frail with the elevation of his circumstances, he has some private reasons for not choosing to renew the acquaintance. I think we cannot do better than make our way back as fast as possible for Valencia Let us not be in too great a hurry for that, sir, answered my secretary: you know better than myself, having served a long apprenticeship, that there is no getting on at court without patience and perseverance. Be indefatigable in exhibiting your person to the prince's regards: by dint of forcing yourself on his observation, you will oblige him to ask himself the question who this assiduous frequenter of his haunts can possibly be, when memory must come to his aid, and trace the features of his cheapener in the purchase of the lovely Catalina's good graces.

That Scipio might have nothing to reproach me with, I so far lent myself to his wishes as to continue the same proceeding for the space of three weeks; when at length it happened one day that the monarch, noticing the frequency of my appearance, sent for me into his presence. I went into the closet, not without some perturbation of mind at the idea of a private interview with my sovereign. Who are you? said he: your features are not altogether strange to me. Where have I seen you? Please your majesty, answered I trembling, I had the honor of escorting you one night with the Count of Lemos to the house of . . . . Ah! I recollect it perfectly, cried the prince, as if a sudden light had broke in upon him: you were the Duke of Lerma's secretary; and if I am not mistaken, your name is Santillane. I have not forgotten that on the occasion alluded to you served me with a most commendable zeal, but received a left-handed recompense for your exertions. Did you not get into prison at the conclusion of the adventure? Yes, please your majesty, replied I: my confinement in the tower of Segovia lasted six months; but your goodness was exercised in procuring my release. That, replied he, does not cancel my debt to my faithful servant Santillane: it is not enough to have restored him to liberty, for I ought to make him ample amends for the evils which he has suffered on the score of his alacrity in my concerns.

Just as the prince was uttering these words, the Count of Olivarez came into the closet. The nerves of favorites are shaken by every breath, their irritability excited by every trifle: he was as much astonished as any favorite need be at the sight of a stranger in that place, and the king redoubled his wondering propensities by the following recommendation—Count, I consign this young man to your care, employ him, and let me find that you provide for his advancement. The minister affected to receive this order with the most gracious acquiescence, but looked me over from head to foot, with a glance from the corner of his eye, and was on tenter-hooks to find out who had been so strangely saddled upon him. Go, my friend, added the sovereign, addressing himself to me, and waving his hand for me to withdraw; the count will not fail to avail himself of your services in a manner the most conducive to the interests of my government, and the establishment of your own fortunes.

I immediately went out of the closet and made the best of my way to the son of Coselina, who, being overrun with impatience to inquire what the king had been talking about, fumbled at his fingers' ends, and was all over in an agitation. His first question was, whether we were to return to Valencia or become a part of the court. You shall form your own conclusions, answered I; at the same time delighting him with an account word for word of the little conversation I had just held with the monarch. My dear master, said Scipio at once in the excess of his joy, will you take me for your almanac-maker another time? You must acknowledge that we were not in the wrong! the lords of Leyva and myself have our eye-teeth about us! a journey to Madrid was the only measure to be adopted in such a case. Already I anticipate your appoint-ment to an eminent post: you will turn out to be some time or other a Calderona to the Count of Olivarez. That is by no means the object of my ambition, observed I in return; the employment is placed on too rugged an eminence to excite any longings in my mind. I could wish for a good situation where there could be no inducement to do what might go against my conscience, and where the favors of my prince are not likely to be bartered away for filthy lucre. Having experienced my own unfitness for the possession of patronage, I cannot be sufficiently on my guard against the inroads of avarice and ambition. Never think about that, sir! replied my secretary, the minister will give you some handsome appointment, which you may fill without any impeachment of your integrity or independence.

Induced more by Scipio's importunity than my own curiosity, I repaired the following day before sunrise to the residence of the Count d'Olivarez, having been informed that every morning, whether in summer or winter, he gave audience by candle-light to all comers. I ensconced myself modestly in a corner of the saloon, and from my lurking-place took especial notice of the count when he made his appearance; for I had marked his person but cursorily in the king's closet. He was above the middle stature, and might pass for fat in a country where it is a rarity to see any but lean subjects. His shoulders were so high, as to look exactly as if he was humpbacked, but appearances were slanderous; for his blade-bones, though inelegant, were a pair; his head, which was large enough to be capacious, dropped down upon his chest by the unwieldiness of its own weight; his hair was black and unconscious of a curl, his face lengthened, his complexion olive-colored, his mouth retiring inwards, with the sharp-pointed, turn-up chin of a pantaloon.

This whole arrangement of structure and symmetry did not exactly make up the complete model of a nobleman according to the ideas of ancient art; nevertheless, as I believed him to be in a temper of mind favorable to the gratification of my wishes, I looked at his defects with an indulgent eye, and found him a man very much to my satisfaction. One of the best points about him was, that he received the public at large with the utmost affability and complacency, holding out his hand for petitions with as much good humor as if he were the person to be obliged, and this was a sufficient set-off against anything untoward in the expression of his countenance. In the mean time, when in my turn I came forward to pay my respects and make myself known to him, he darted at me a glance of rude dislike and frightful menace; then turning his back, without condescending to give me audience, retired into his closet. Then it was that the ugliness of this nobleman's features appeared in all the extravagance of caricature: so that I made the best of my way out of the saloon, thunderstruck at so savage a reception, and quite at a loss how to conjecture what might be the consequence.

Having got back to Scipio, who was waiting for me at the door —Can you guess at all, said I, what sort of a greeting mine was? No, answered he, not as to the minute particulars; but with respect to the substance, easily enough : the minister, ready upon all occasions to fall in with the fancies of his royal master, must of course have made you a handsome offer of an ostensible and lucrative situation. That is all you know about the matter, replied I; and then went on to acquaint him circumstantially with all that passed. He listened to me with serious attention, and then said—The count could not have recollected your person; or rather, he must have been deceived by a fortuitous resemblance between you and some impertinent suitor. I would advise you to try another interview; I will lay a wager he will look on you more kindly. I adopted my secretary's suggestion, and stood for a second time in the presence of the minister; but he, behaving to me still worse than at first, puckered up his features the moment my unlucky countenance came within his ken, just as if it was connected with some lodged hate and certain loathing, which of force swayed him to offend, himself being offended; after this significant demonstration, he turned away his glaring eyeballs, and withdrew without uttering a word.

I was stung to the quick by so hostile a treatment, and in a humor to set out immediately on my return to Valencia; but to that project Scipio uniformly opposed his steady objections, not knowing how for the life of him to part with those flattering hopes which fancy had engendered in his brain. Do you not see plainly, said I, that the count wishes to drive me away from court? The monarch has testified in his presence some sort of favorable intention towards me, and is not that enough to draw down upon me the thorough hatred of the monarch's favorite? Let us drive before the wind, my good comrade; let us make up our minds to put quietly into port, and leave the open sea and the honors of the flag in the possession of an enemy with whom we are too feeble to contend. Sir, answered he, in high resentment against the Count of Olivarez, I would not strike so easily. I would go and complain to the king of the contempt in which his minister held his recommendation. Bad advice, indeed, my friend, said I; to take so imprudent a step as that, would soon bring bitter repentance in the train of its consequences. I do not even know whether it is safe for me to remain any longer in this town.

At this hint, my secretary communed a little with his own thoughts; and, considering that in point of fact we had to do with a man who kept the key of the tower of Segovia in his pocket, my fears became naturalized in his breast. He no longer opposed my earnest desire of leaving Madrid, and I determined to take my measures accordingly on the very next day.

CHAPTER III.

THE PROJECT OF RETIREMENT IS PREVENTED, AND JOSEPH NAVARRO BROUGHT UPON THE STAGE AGAIN, BY AN ACT OF SIGNAL SERVICE.

ON my way home to my lodgings I met Joseph Navarro, whom the reader will recollect as on the establishment of Don Balthasar de Zuniga, and one of my old friends. I made my bow first at a distance, then went up to him, and asked whether he knew me again, and if he would still be so good as to speak to a wretch who had repaid his friendship with ingratitude. You acknowledge then, said he, that you have not behaved very handsomely by me? Yes, answered I; and you are fully justified in laying on your reproaches thick and threefold: I deserve them all, unless indeed my guilt may be thought to have been atoned by the remorse of con-

science attendant on it. Since you have repented of your misconduct, replied Navarro, embracing me, I ought no longer to hold it
in remembrance. For my part, I knew not how to hug Joseph
close enough in my arms ; and we both of us resumed our original
kind feelings towards one another.

He had heard of my imprisonment and the derangement of my
affairs; but of what followed he was totally ignorant. I informed
him of it; relating word for word my conversation with the king,
without suppressing the minister's late ungracious reception of me,
any more than my present purpose of retiring into my favorite obscurity. Beware of removing from the scene of action, said he:
since the sovereign has shown a disposition to befriend you, there
are always uses to be made of such a circumstance. Between ourselves, the Count of Olivarez has something rather unaccountable
in his character: he is a very good sort of nobleman, but rather
whimsical withal: sometimes, as on the present occasion, he acts in
a most offensive manner, and none but himself can furnish a clue
to disentangle the intricate thread of his motives and their results.
But however this may be, or whatever reasons might have swayed
him to give you so scurvy a reception, keep your footing here, and
do not budge ; he will not be able to hinder you from thriving under
the royal shelter and protection ; take my word for that ! I will
just give a hint upon the subject this evening to Signor Don Balthasar de Zuniga, my master ; he is uncle to the Count of Olivarez,
and shares with him in the toils and cares of office. Navarro having given me this assurance, inquired where I lived, and then we
parted.

It was not long before we met again ; for he came to call on me
the very next day. Signor de Santillane, said he, you are not without a protector ; my master will lend you his powerful support : on
the strength of the good character which I have given your lordship, he has promised to speak to his nephew, the Count of Olivarez, in your behalf ; and I doubt not but he will effectually prepossess him in your favor. My friend Navarro not meaning to
serve me by halves, introduced me two days afterwards to Don
Balthasar, who said with a gracious air : Signor de Santillane, your
friend Joseph has pronounced your panegyric in terms which have
won me over completely to your interest. I made a low obeisance
to Signor de Zuniga, and answered, that to the latest period of my
life I should entertain the most lively sense of my obligation to
Navarro, for having secured to me the protection of a minister,
who was considered, and that for the best reasons possible, as the
presiding genius, the greater luminary, or, as it were, the eye and
mind of the ministerial council. Don Balthasar, at this unexpected
stroke of flattery, clapped me on the shoulder with an approving
chuckle, and returned my compliment by a more significant intimation : You may call on the Count of Olivarez again to-morrow,
and then you will have more reason to be pleased with him.

For the third time, therefore, did I make my appearance before
the prime minister, who, picking me out from among the mob of
suitors, cast upon me a look conveying with it a simper of wel-

come, from which I ventured to draw a good omen. This is all as it should be, said I to myself; the uncle has brought the nephew to his proper bearings. I no longer anticipated any other than a favorable reception, and my confidence was fully justified. The count, after having given audience to the promiscuous crowd, took me with him into his closet, and said with a familiar address: My friend Santillane, you must excuse the little disquietude I have occasioned you merely for my own amusement; it was done in sport, though it was death to you, for the sole purpose of practicing on your discretion, and observing to what measures your disgust and disappointment would incite you. Doubtless you must have concluded that your services were displeasing to me; but on the contrary, my good fellow, I must confess frankly, that, as far as appears at present, you are perfectly to my mind. Though the king my master had not enjoined me to take charge of your fortunes, I should have done so of my own free choice. Besides, my uncle, Don Balthasar de Zuniga, to whom I can refuse nothing, has requested me to consider you as a man for whom he particularly interests himself: that alone would be enough to fix my confidence in you, and make me most sincerely your friend.

This outset of my career produced so lively an impression on my feelings, that they became unintelligibly tumultuous. I threw myself at the minister's feet, who insisted on my rising immediately, and then went on to the following effect: Return hither to-day after dinner, and ask for my steward: he will acquaint you with the orders which I shall have given him. With these words his excellency broke up the conference to hear mass, according to his constant custom every day after giving audience: he then attended the king's levee.

CHAPTER IV.

GIL BLAS INGRATIATES HIMSELF WITH THE COUNT OF OLIVAREZ.

I DID not fail returning after dinner to the prime minister's house, and asking for his steward, whose name was Don Raymond Caporis. No sooner had I made myself known, than paying his civilities to me in the most respectful manner, Sir, said he, follow me if you please: I am to do myself the honor of showing you the way to the apartment which is ordered for you in this family. Having spoken thus, he led me up a narrow staircase to a gallery communicating with five or six rooms, which composed the second story belonging to one wing of the house, and were furnished neatly, but without ostentation. You behold, resumed he, the lodging assigned you by his lordship, where you will always have a table of six persons, kept at his expense. You will be waited on by his own servants; and there will always be a carriage at your command. But that is not all: his excellency insisted on it in the most pointed manner, that you should be treated in every respect with the same attention as if you belonged to the house of Guzman.

What the devil is the meaning of all this? said I within myself. What construction ought I to put upon all these honors? Is there not some humorous prank at the bottom of it? and must it not be more in the way of diversion than anything else, that the minister is flattering me up with so imposing an establishment? While I was ruminating in this uncertainty, fluctuating between hope and fear, a page came to let me know that the count was asking for me. I waited instantly on his lordship, who was quite alone in his closet. Well! Santillane, said he, are you satisfied with your rooms, and with my orders to Don Raymond? Your excellency's liberality, answered I, seems out of all proportion with its object, so that I receive it with fear and trembling. Why so? replied he. Can I be too lavish of distinction to a man whom the king has commended to my care, and for whose interests he especially commanded me to provide? No, that is impossible; and I do no more than my duty in placing you on a footing of respectability and consequence. No longer, therefore, let what I do for you be a subject of surprise; but rely on it that splendor in the eye of the world, and the solid advantages of accumulating wealth, are equally within your grasp, if you do but attach yourself as faithfully to me as you did to the Duke of Lerma.

But now that we are on the subject of that nobleman, continued he, it is said that you lived on terms of personal intimacy with him. I have a strong curiosity to learn the circumstances which led to your first acquaintance, as well as in what department you acted under him. Do not disguise or gloss over the slightest particular, for I shall not be satisfied without a full, true, and circumstantial recital. Then it was that I recollected in what an embarrassing predicament I stood with the Duke of Lerma on a similar occasion, and by what line of conduct I extricated myself; that same course I adopted once again with the happiest success; whereby the reader is to understand that throughout my narrative I softened down the passages likely to give umbrage to my patron, and glanced with a superficial delicacy over transactions which would have reflected but little lustre on my own character. I likewise manifested a considerate tenderness for the Duke of Lerma; though by giving that fallen favorite no quarter, I should better have consulted the taste of him whom I wished to please. As for Don Rodrigo de Calderona, there I laid about me with the religious fury of a bishop in a battle. I brought together, and displayed in the most glaring colors, all the anecdotes I had been able to pick up respecting his corrupt practices and underhand dealing in the sale of promotions, military, ecclesiastical, and civil.

What you have told me about Calderona, cried the minister with eagerness, exactly squares with certain memorials which have been presented to me, containing the heads of charges still more seriously affecting his character. He will very soon be put upon his trial, and if you have any wish to glut your revenge by his ruin, I am of opinion that the object of your desire is near at hand. I am far from thirsting after his blood, said I, though had it depended on him, mine might have been shed in the tower of Segovia, where he was the occasion of my taking lodgings for a pretty long term. What! inquired his excellency, was it Don Rodrigo who procured you that sudden journey? this a part of the story of which I was not aware before. Don Balthasar, to whom Navarro gave a summary of your adventures, told me indeed that the late king gave orders for your commitment, as a mark of his indignation against you for having led the Prince of Spain astray, and taken him to a house of suspicious character in the night: but that is all I know of the matter, and cannot for the life of me conjecture what part Calderona could possibly have had to play in that tragicomedy. A principal part, whether on the stage or in real life, answered I: that of a jealous lover, taking vengeance for an injury, sustained in the tenderest point. At the same time I related minutely all the facts with which the reader is already acquainted, and touched his risible propensities, difficult as they were of access, so exactly in the right place, that he could not help wagging his underhung jaw in a paroxysm of humor-stricken ecstasy, and laughing till he cried again. Catalina's double cast in the drama delighted him exceedingly; her sometimes playing the niece and sometimes personating the granddaughter seemed to tickle his fancy more than anything; nor was he altogether inattentive to the appearance which the Duke of Lerma made in this undignified farce of state.

When I had finished my story, the count gave me leave to depart, with an assurance that on the next day he would not fail to make trial of my talents for business. I ran immediately to the family hotel of Zuniga, to thank Don Balthasar for his good offices, and to acquaint my friend Joseph with the favorable dispositions of the prime minister, and my brilliant prospects in consequence.

CHAPTER V.

THE PRIVATE CONVERSATION OF GIL BLAS WITH NAVARRO, AND HIS FIRST EMPLOYMENT IN THE SERVICE OF THE COUNT D'OLIVAREZ.

As soon as I got to the ear of Joseph, I told him with much trepidation of spirits what a world of topics I had to deposit in his private ear. He took me where we might be alone, when I asked him, after having communicated a key to the whole transaction up to the present time, what he thought of the business as it stood. I think, answered he, that you are in a fair way to make an enormous fortune. Everything turns out according to your wishes: you have made yourself acceptable to the prime minister; and what must be taken for something in the account, I can render you the same service as my uncle Melchior de la Ronda, when you attached yourself to the archiepiscopal establishment of Grenada. He spared you the trouble of finding out the weak side of that prelate and his principal officers, by discovering their different characters to you; and it is my purpose, after his example, to bring you perfectly acquainted with the count, his lady countess, and their only daughter, Donna Maria de Guzman.

The minister's parts are quick, his judgment penetrating, and his talents altogether calculated for the formation of extensive projects. He affects the credit of universal genius, on the strength of a showy smattering in general science; so that there is no subject, in his own opinion, too difficult to be decided on his mere authority. He sets himself up for a practical lawyer, a complete general, and a politician of thorough-paced sagacity. Add to all this, that he is so obstinately wedded to his own opinions, as unchangeably to persevere in the path of his own chalking out, to the absolute contempt of better advice, for fear of seeming to be influenced by any good sense or intelligence, but what he would be thought to engross in the resources of his own mind. Between ourselves, this blot in his character may produce strange consequences, which it may be well for the monarchy should indulgent heaven for the defect of human means avert! As for his talents in council, he shines in debate by the force of natural eloquence, and would write as well as he speaks, if he did not injudiciously affect a certain dignity of style, which degenerates into affectation, quaintness, and obscurity. His modes of thinking are peculiar to himself; he is capricious in conduct, and visionary in design. Here you have the picture of his mind, the light and shade of his intellectual merits: the qualities of his heart and disposition remain to be delineated. He is generous and warm in his friendships. It is said that he is revengeful; but would he be a Spaniard if he were otherwise? In addition to this, he has been accused of ingratitude, for having driven the Duke of Uzeda and Friar Lewis Aliaga into banishment, though he owed them, according to common report, obligations of the most binding nature; and yet even this must not be looked into so narrowly under his circumstances: there are few breasts capacious enough to afford house-room for two such opposite inmates as political ambition and gratitude.

Donna Agnes de Zuniga é Velasco, Countess of Olivarez, continued Joseph, is a lady to whom it is impossible to impute more than one fault, but that is a huge one; for it consists in making a market, and a market the most exorbitant in its terms, of her natural influence over the mind of her husband. As for Donna Maria de Guzman, who beyond all dispute is at this moment the very first match in Spain, she is a lady of first-rate accomplishments, and absolutely idolized by her father. Regulate your conduct upon these hints: make your court with art and plausibility to these two ladies, and let it appear as if you were more devoted to the Count of Olivarez than ever you were to the Duke of Lerma before your forced excursion to Segovia; you will become a leading and powerful member of the administration.

I should advise you, moreover, added he, to see my master, Don Balthasar, from time to time; for though you have no longer any occasion for his interest to push you forward, it will not be amiss to waste a little incense upon him. You stand very high in his good opinion; preserve your footing there, and cultivate his friendship; it may stand you in some stead on any emergency. I could not help observing, that as the uncle and nephew were in a certain sort partners in the government of the state, there might possibly be some little symptom of jealousy between brothers near the throne. On the contrary, answered he, they are united by the most confidential ties. Had it not been for Don Balthasar, the Count of Olivarez might probably never have been prime minister; for you are to know, that after Philip the Third had paid the debt of nature, all the adherents and partisans belonging to the house of Sandoval made a great stir, some in favor of the cardinal, and others on his son's behalf; but my master, a greater adept in court intrigue than any of them, and the count, who is nearly as great an adept as himself, disconcerted all their measures, and took their own so judiciously for the purpose of stepping into the vacant place, that their rivals had no chance against them. The Count of Olivarez, being appointed prime minister, divided the duties with his uncle, Don Balthasar, leaving foreign affairs to him, and taking the home department to himself; the consequence is, that the bonds of family friendship are drawn closer between these two noblemen, than if political influence had no share in their mutual interests: they are perfectly independent in their respective lines of business, and live together on terms of good understanding which no intrigue can possibly affect or alter.

Such was the substance of my conversation with Joseph, and the advantage to be derived from it was my own to make the most of: at all events, it was my duty to thank Signor de Zuniga for all the influence he had the goodness to exert in my favor. He assured me with infinite good-breeding that he should avail himself of every opportunity as it arose to promote my wishes, and that he was very glad his nephew had behaved so as to meet my ideas, because he meant to refresh his memory in my behalf, being determined, as he was pleased to say, to place it beyond all manner of doubt how far he himself participated in all my views, and to make it evident that, instead of one fast friend, I had two. In terms like these did Don Balthasar, through mere friendship for Navarro, take the molding of my fortunes on himself.

On that same evening did I leave my paltry lodging to take up my abode at the prime minister's, where I sat down to supper with Scipio in my own suite of apartments. There were we both waited on by the servants belonging to the household, who as they stood behind our chairs, while we were affecting the pomp and circumstance of political elevation, were more likely than not to be laughing in their sleeves at the pantomime they had been ordered by their manager to play in our presence. When they had taken away and left us to ourselves, my secretary being no longer under restraint, gave vent to a thousand wild imaginations which his sprightly temper and inventive hopes engendered in his fancy. On my part, though by no means cold or insensible to the brilliant prospects which were opening on my view, I did not as yet yield in the least degree to the weakness of being thrust aside from the right line of my philosophy by temporal allurements. So much otherwise, that on going to bed I fell into a sound sleep, without being haunted in my dreams by those phantoms of flattering delusion which might have gained admittance with no severe question from a corruptible door-keeper. The ambitious Scipio, on the contrary, tossed and tumbled all night in the agitation of restless contrivance. Whenever he dozed a little imp took possession of his brain, with a pen behind its ear, working out by all the rules of arithmetic the bulky sum total of his daughter Seraphina's marriage portion.

No sooner had I got my clothes on the next morning, than a message came from his lordship. I flew like lightning at the summons, when his excellency said : Now then, Santillane, suppose you give us a specimen of your talents for business. You say that the Duke of Lerma used to give you state papers to bring into official form ; and I have one, by way of experiment, on which you shall try your skill. The subject you will easily comprehend : it turns upon an exposition of public affairs, such as to throw an artificial light on the first appearance of the new ministry, and to prejudice the public in its favor. I have already whispered it about by my emissaries, that every department of the state was completely disorganized, that the talents which preceded us were no talents at all ; and the object at present is to impress both court and city by a formal declaration with the idea, that our aid is absolutely necessary to save the monarchy itself from sinking. On this theme you may expatiate till the populace become lock-jawed with astonishment, and the sober part of the public are gravely argued out of all prepossession in favor of the discarded party. By way of contrast, you will talk of the *dignus vindice nodus*, taking care to translate it into Spanish ; and boast of the measures adopted under the new order of things, to secure the permanent glory of the king's reign, to give perpetual prosperity to his dominions, and to confer perfect, unchangeable happiness on his good people.

His lordship, having given out the general subject of my thesis, left me with a paper containing the heads of charges, whether just or unjust, against the late administration : and I remember perfectly well, that there were ten articles, whose lightest word, even of the lightest article, would harrow up the soul of a true Spaniard, and make his knotted and combined locks to part. That the current of my fancy might experience no interruption, he shut me into a little closet near his own, where the spirit of poetry might possess me in all its freedom and independence. My best faculties were called forth, to compose a statement of affairs commensurate with my own concern in the sweeping of the new brooms. My first object was to lay open the nakedness and abandonment of the kingdom · the finances in a state of bankruptcy, the civil list and immediate resources of the crown pawned fifty times over, the navy unpaid, dismantled, and in mutiny. All this hideous delineation was referred for its justice and accuracy to the wrongheadedness and stupidity of government at the close of the last reign, and the doctrine most strongly enforced, that unexampled wisdom and patriotism only could ward off the fatal consequences. In short, the monarchy could only be sustained on the shoulders of our political sufficiency and reforming prudence. The ex-ministry were so cruelly belabored, that the Duke of Lerma's ruin, according to the terms of my syllogism, was the salvation of Spain. To own the truth, though my professions were in the spirit of Christian charity towards that nobleman, I was not sorry to give him a sly rub in the exercise of my function. Oh man! man! what a compound of candor-breathing satire and splenetic impartiality art thou!

Towards the conclusion, having finished my frightful portraiture of overhanging evils, I endeavored to allay the storm my art had raised by making futurity as bright as the past had been gloomy. The Count of Olivarez was brought in at the close, like the tutelary deity of an ancient commonwealth in the crisis of its fate. I promised more than paganism ever feigned or chivalry fancied in the wildest of its crusading projects. In a word, I so exactly executed what the new minister meant, that he seemed not to know his own hints again, when drawn out in my emphatic and appropriate language. Santillane, said he, do you know that this is more like the composition one might expect from a secretary of state, than like that of a private secretary? I can no longer be surprised that the Duke of Lerma was fond of calling your talents into action. Your style is concise, and by no means inelegant; but it creeps rather too much in the level paths of nature. At the same time, pointing out the passages which did not hit his fancy, he corrected them; and I gathered from the touches he threw in, that Navarro was right in saying he affected sententious wit, but mistook for it quaint and stale conceits. Nevertheless, though he preferred the stately, or rather the grotesque in writing, he suffered two thirds of my performance to stand without alteration; and by way of proving how entirely he was satisfied, sent me three hundred pistoles by Don Raymond after dinner.

CHAPTER VI.

THE APPLICATION OF THE THREE HUNDRED PISTOLES, AND SCIPIO'S COMMISSION CONNECTED WITH THEM. SUCCESS OF THE STATE PAPER MENTIONED IN THE LAST CHAPTER.

THIS handsome present of the minister furnished Scipio with a new subject of congratulation, by reason of our second appearance at court. You may remark, said he, that fortune is preparing a load of aggrandizement to lay on your lordship's shoulders. Are you still sorry for having turned your back on solitude? May the Count of Olivarez live for ever! he is a very different sort of a master from his predecessor. The Duke of Lerma, with all your devotion to his service, left you to live upon suction for months without a pistole to bless yourself with; and the count has already made you a present which you could have had no reason to expect but after a course of long service.

I should very much like, added he, that the lords of Leyva should be witnesses of your great success, or at least that they should be informed of it. It is high time indeed, answered I, and I meant to speak with you on that subject. They must doubtless be impatient to hear of my proceedings, but I waited till my fate was fixed, and till I could decide for certain whether I should stay at court or not. Now that I am sure of my destination, you have only to set out for Valencia whenever you please, and to acquaint those noblemen with my present situation, which I consider as their doing, since it is evident that, but for them, I should never have resolved on my journey to Madrid. My dear master, cried the son of Bohemian accident, what joy shall I communicate by relating what has happened to you! Why am I not already at the gates of Valencia? But I shall be there forthwith. Don Alphonso's two horses are ready in the stable. I shall take one of my lord's livery servants with me. Besides that company is pleasant on the road, you know very well the effect of official parade, in making impression on the natives of a provincial town.

I could not help laughing at my secretary's foolish vanity; and yet, with vanity perhaps more than equal to his own, I left him to do as he pleased. Go about your business, said I, and make the best of your way back; for I have another commission to give you. I mean to send you to the Asturias with some money for my mother. Through neglect I have suffered the time to elapse when I promised to remit her a hundred pistoles, and pledged you to make the payment in person. Such engagements ought to held sacred by a son; and I reproach myself with inaccuracy in the observance of mine. Sir, answered Scipio, within six weeks I shall bring you an account of both your commissions; having opened my budget to the lords of Leyva, looked in at your country-house, and taken a peep at the town of Oviedo, the recollection of which I cannot admit into my mind, without turning over three fourths of the inhabitants, and one half of the remaining quarter, to the corrective discipline of that infernal executioner, who is supposed to be kept on foot for the purpose of castigating sinners. I then counted down one hundred pistoles to that same son of a wandering mother for my honored parents' annuity, and another hundred for himself; meaning that he should perform his long journey without grumbling on my account by the way.

Some days after his departure his lordship sent our memorial to press; and it was no sooner published than it became the topic of conversation in every circle throughout Madrid. The people, enamored of novelty, took up this well-written statement of their own wretchedness with fond partiality; the derangement and exhaustion of the finances, painted with a mixture of truth and poetry, excited a strong feeling of popular indignation against the Duke of Lerma; and if these paper bullets of the brain, cast in the political armory of a rival, failed to carry victory with them in the opinions of all mankind, they were at all events hailed with triumph by the most clamorous of our own partisans. As for the magnificent promises which the Count of Olivarez threw in, and among others that of keeping the machine of state in motion, by a system of economy, without adding to the public burdens, they were caught at with avidity by the citizens at large, and considered as pledges of an enlightened and patriotic policy, so that the whole city resounded with the acclamation of panegyric and congratulation on the opening of new prospects.

The minister, delighted to have gained his end so easily, which in that publication had only been to draw popularity upon himself, was now determined to seize the substance as well as catch at the shadow, by an act of unquestionable credit with the subject, and high utility to the king's service. For that purpose, he had recourse to the emperor Galba's contrivance, consisting in a forced regurgitation of ill-gotten spoils from individuals who had made large fortunes, hell and their own consciences knew best how, in the superintendence of the royal expenditure. When he had squeezed these sponges till they were dry again, and had filled the king's coffers with the drainings, he undertook to render the reform permanent by abolishing all pensions, not excepting his own, and curtailing the gratuities too frequently bestowed on favorites out of the prince's privy purse. To succeed in this design, which he could not carry into effect without changing the face of the government, he charged me with the composition of a new state paper, furnishing the substance and the form from his own idea. He then advised me to raise my style as much as possible above the level of my ordinary simplicity, and to give an air of more eloquence to my phraseology, A hint is sufficient, my lord, said I; your excellency wishes to unite sublimity with illumination, and it shall be so. I shut myself up in the same closet where I had already worked so successfully, and sat down stiffly to my task, first calling to my aid the lofty and clear perceptions, the noble and sonorous expressions, of my old instructor, the archbishop of Grenada.

I began by laying it down as a first maxim of political philosophy, that the vital functions, the respiration as it were of all monarchy, depended on the strict administration of the finances; that in our particular case that duty became imperiously urgent, irresistibly impressing on our consciences; and that the revenue should be considered as the nerves and sinews of Spain, to hold her rivals in check and keep her enemies in awe. After this general declamation, I pointed out to the sovereign, for to him the memorial was addressed, that by cutting down all pensions and perquisites dependent on the ordinary income, he would not thereby deprive himself of that truly royal pleasure, a princely munificence towards those of his subjects who had established a fair claim to his favors;

because without drawing upon his treasury, he had the means of distributing more acceptable rewards; that for one branch of service, there were viceroyalties, lieutenancies, orders of merit, and all sorts of military commissions: for another, high judicial situations with salaries annexed, civil offices of magistracy with sounding titles to give them consequence; and though last, not least, all the temporal possessions of the church to animate the piety of its spiritual pastors.

This memorial, which was much longer than the first, occupied me nearly three days; but as luck would have it, my performance was exactly to my master's mind, who finding it written with sententious cogency, and bristled up with metaphors in the declamatory parts, complimented me in the highest terms. That is vastly well expressed indeed! said he, laying his finger on a passage here and there, and picking out all the most inflated sentences he could find: that language bears the stamp of fine composition, and might pass for the production of a classic. Courage, my friend! I foresee that your services will be worth their weight in gold. And yet, notwithstanding the applauses he lavished on my classical composition, a few of his own heightening touches, he thought, would make it read still better. He put a good deal of his own stuff into it, and the medley was manufactured into a piece of eloquence which was considered as unanswerable by the king and all the court. The whole city joined in opinion with the higher orders, deriving the most flattering hopes of the future from these grand promises, and concluding that the monarchy must recover its pristine splendor during the ministry of so illustrious a character. His excellency, finding that my sermon on economy was fraught with practical inferences of utility to him, was kind enough to wish that I should profit by the exercise of my own talents. In conformity therefore with his new system of patronage, he gave me an annuity of five hundred crowns on the commandery of Castile; and the acceptance of it was so much the more palatable, as no dirty work had been done for it, but it was honestly, though cheaply, earned.

CHAPTER VII.

GIL BLAS MEETS WITH HIS FRIEND FABRICIO ONCE MORE; THE
ACCIDENT, PLACE, AND CIRCUMSTANCES DESCRIBED; WITH
THE PARTICULARS OF THEIR CONVERSATION TOGETHER.

NOTHING gave his lordship greater pleasure than to hear the general decision of Madrid on the conduct of his administration. Not a day passed but he inquired what they were saying of him in the political world. He kept spies in pay, to bring him an exact account of what was going on in the city. They particularized the most trivial discourses which they overheard; and their orders being to suppress nothing, his self-love was grazed now and then, for the people have a way of bolting out home truths, without any nice calculation where they may glance.

Finding that the count loved political small talk, I made it my business to frequent places of public resort after dinner, and to chime in with the conversation of genteel people whenever opportunity offered. Should the measures of government happen to be canvassed among them, I pricked up my ears, and greedily took in their discourse; if anything worth repeating was said, his excellency was sure to hear of it. It can scarcely be necessary to hint, that I never carried home anything which was not likely to pay for the porterage.

One day, returning from one of these little conversational parties, my road lay in front of an hospital. It occurred to me to go in. I walked through two or three wards, filled with diseased patients, and examined their beds to see that they were properly taken care of. Among these unhappy wretches, whom I could not look at without the most painful feelings, I observed one whose features struck me: it surely could be no other than Fabricio, my countryman and chum! To look at him more closely, I drew near his bedside, and finding beyond a possibility of doubt that it was the poet Nunez, I stopped to look at him for a few seconds without saying a word. He also fixed his regards on me. At length breaking silence: Do not my eyes deceive me? said I. Is it indeed Fabricio, and here? It is indeed, answered he, coldly, and you need not wonder at it. Since we parted, I have been working indefatigably at the trade of an author: I have written novels, plays, and works of genius in every department. My brain is fairly spun out, and here I am.

I could not help laughing at such a sketch of literary biography; and still more at the serious air of the accompanying action. What! cried I, has your muse brought you to this pass? Has she played you such a jade's trick as this? Even as you witness, answered he; this establishment is a sort of half-pay receptacle for invalids on the muster-roll of disabled wit. You have acted discreetly, my good friend, to lay yourself out for promotion in a different line. But they tell me, you are no longer a courtier, and that your prospects in political life were all blasted; nay, they went so far as to affirm that you were committed to close custody by the king's order. They told you no more than the truth, replied I: the delightful vision of political eminence wherein you left me last, soon shifted the scene of my incoherent dreams to a prison and complete destitution. But for all that, my friend, here you behold me again in a better plight than ever. That is quite out of the question, said Nunez: your deportment is discreet and decent, you have not that supercilious and devil-take-the-hindermost sort of aspect, which good keep communicates to the human face. The reverses of this checkered life, replied I, have brought me down to the level of the more modest virtues; I have taken a lesson in the school of adversity, to enjoy the possession of a good stud without riding the great horse.

Tell me then candidly, cried Fabricio, raising his head upon his hand with his elbow upon the pillow, what your present occupation can possibly be. A steward perhaps to some nobleman out at elbows, or man of business to some rich widow! Something bette than either the one or the other, rejoined I, but excuse me from saying more at present: another time your curiosity shall be satisfied. It is enough at present to assure you that my means are equal to my inclination, and that you may command independence through me; but then you must submit to an embargo on your wit, and a non-intercourse act between you and the faculty of writing, whether in verse or prose. Can you make this sacrifice to my friendship? I have already made it to the powers above, said he, in my last critical sickness. A Dominican made me forswear poetry, as an amusement bordering on criminality, but at all events beside the turnpike-road of good sense. I wish you joy, my dear Nunez, replied I; beware of a revoke. There is not the least danger on that head, rejoined he: the Muses and I have agreed on terms of separation: just as you came in at that door, I was conning over a farewell ode. Good master Fabricio, said I, with a wise swagging to and fro of my head, it is a doubtful question whether your vow of abjuration ought to pass current with the Dominican and myself: you seem over head and ears in love with those virgins incarnate. No, no, contended he peevishly, I have cut the connection asunder. Nay, more, I have quarreled with their keepers, the public. The readers of these days do not deserve an author of more genius than themselves: I should be sorry to write down to their comprehension. You are not to suppose that this is the language of disgust; it is my sincere and well-weighed opinion. Applause and hisses are just the same to me. It is a toss up who fails and who succeeds; the wit of to-day is the blockhead of to-morrow. What cursed fools our dramatists must be, to care for anything but their poundage when their plays happen to be received! It is all very well for a few nights! But only fancy a revival at the end of twenty years, and what a figure they will cut then! The audiences of the present day turn up their noses at the stock pieces of the last age, and it is a question whether their taste will fare better with their more critical descendants. If that conjecture be probable, the inventors of clap-traps now will be the butt of cat-calls hereafter. It is just the same with novel writers, and all other manufacturers of unnecessary literature: they strut and fret for an hour, and then are no more seen or heard of. The glories of successful authorship are the mere vapors of a murky atmosphere, meteors of a marsh, foul coruscations of a dunghill, cathedral tapers to put out the galaxy, blue flames of coarse paper held over a candle.

Though these caricatures of rival renown were the mere creations of jealousy in the poet of the Asturias, it was not my business to correct his ill temper. I am delighted, said I, that wit and you have had so serious a quarrel; and that the diarrhea of your inventive faculties has been cured by an astringent. You may depend on it, I will put you in the way of a good livelihood, without drawing deep upon your intellectual credit. So much the better, cried he; wit smells like carrion in my nostrils, or rather like a pungent and deleterious perfume; fragrant to the sense, but corrosive to the vitals. I heartily wish, my dear Fabricio, resumed I, that you may always keep in that mind. Only wash your hands completely of poetry, and you may depend on it, I will enable you to keep your head above water without picking or stealing. In the mean while, added I, slipping a purse of sixty pistoles into his hand, accept this as a slight instance of my regard.

O friend like the friends in days of yore, cried the son of barber Nunez, out of his wits with joy and gratitude, it was heaven itself which sent you into this hospital, whence your goodness is now discharging me! Before we parted, I gave him my address, and invited him to come and see me as soon as his health would permit. He opened his eyes as an oyster does its shell, when I told him that I lodged under the minister's roof. O illustrious Gil Blas! said he, great as Pompey and fortunate as Sylla, whose lot it is to be hand in glove with the dictators of modern times! I rejoice most disinterestedly in your good fortune, because it is so very evident what a noble use you make of it.

CHAPTER VIII.

GIL BLAS GETS FORWARD PROGRESSIVELY IN HIS MASTER'S AFFECTIONS. SCIPIO'S RETURN TO MADRID, AND ACCOUNT OF HIS JOURNEY.

THE Count of Olivarez, whom I shall henceforward call my lord duke, because the king was pleased to confer that dignity on him about this time, was infested with a weakness which I did not suffer to pass without taking toll: it was a furious desire of being beloved. The moment he fancied that any one really liked him, his heart was caught in a trap. This was not lost upon my keen sense of character. It was not enough to do precisely as he ordered; I superadded a zeal in the execution which made him mine. I laid myself out to his liking in everything, and provided beforehand for his most eccentric wishes.

By conduct like this, which almost always answers, I became by degrees my master's favorite; and he, on the other hand, as if he had got round to my blind side also, wormed himself into my affections, by giving me his own. So forward did I get into his good graces, as to halve his confidence with Signor Carnero, his principal secretary.

Carnero had played my game; and that so successfully as to be intrusted with the greater mysteries. We two therefore were the keepers of the prime minister's conscience, and held the keys of all his secrets: with this difference, that Carnero was consulted on state affairs, myself about his private concerns, dividing the busi-

ness into two separate departments; and we were each of us equally
pleased with our own. We lived together without jealousy, and
certainly without attachment. I had every reason to be satisfied
with my quarters, where continual intercourse gave me an opportunity of prying into the duke's inmost soul, which was a masked
battery to all mankind beside, but plain as a pikestaff to me, when
he no longer questioned the sincerity of my attachment to him.

Santillane, said he one day, you were witness to the Duke of
Lerma's possession of an authority, more like that of an absolute
monarch than a favorite minister; and yet I am still happier than
he was at the very summit of his good fortune. He had two formidable enemies in his own son, the Duke of Uzeda, and in the
confessor of Philip the Third : but there is no one now about the
king who has credit enough to stand in my way, or even, as I am
aware, the slightest inclination to do me mischief.

It is true, continued he, that on my accession to the ministry, it
was my first care to remove all hangers-on from about the prince
but those of my own family or connections. By means of viceroyalties or embassies I got rid of all the nobility who, by their
personal merit, could have interfered with me in the good graces of
the sovereign, whom I mean to engross entirely to myself; so that
I may say at the present moment, no statesman of the time holds
me in check by the ascendency of his personal influence. You see,
Gil Blas, I open my mind to you. As I have reason to think that
you are mine heart and soul, I have chosen to put you in possession
of everything. You are a clever youth; with reflection, penetration, and discretion : in short, you are just the very creature to
acquit yourself of all possible little offices in all possible directions;
you are also a young fellow of very promising parts, and must in
the nature of things be in my interests.

There was no standing the attack which these flattering representations were calculated to make upon the weakly defended fortress of my philosophy. Unauthorized whims of avarice and ambition mounted suddenly into my head, and brought forward certain
sentiments of political speculation which were supposed to have
been in abeyance. I gave the minister an assurance that I should
fulfill his intentions to the utmost of my power, and held myself in
readiness to execute without examination or interference all the
orders it might be his pleasure to give me.

While I was thus disposed to take fortune in her affable fit,
Scipio returned from his peregrination. I have no long story
for you, said he. The lords of Leyva were delighted at your reception from the king, and at the manner in which the Count of Olivarez and you came to understand one another.

My friend, said I, you would have delighted them still more,
had you been able to tell them on what a footing I am now with
my lord. My advances since your departure have been prodigious.
Happy man be his dole, my dear master, answered he : my mind
forebodes that we shall cut a figure.

Let us change the subject, said I, and talk of Oviedo. You have
been in the Asturias. How did you leave my mother ? Ah, sir !

replied he, with an undertaker's decency of countenance, I have a melancholy tale to tell you from that quarter. O heaven! exclaimed I, my mother then is dead! Six months since, said my secretary, did the good lady pay the debt of nature, and your uncle, Signor Gil Perez, about the same period.

My mother's death preyed upon my susceptible nature, though in my childhood I had not received from her those little fondling indications of maternal love, so necessary to amalgamate with the more serious convictions of filial duty. The good canon, too, came in for his share in bringing me up according to the rules of godliness and honesty. My serious grief was not lasting : but I never lost sight of a certain tender recollection, whenever the idea of my dear relations shot across my mind.

CHAPTER IX.

HOW MY LORD DUKE MARRIED HIS ONLY DAUGHTER, AND TO WHOM: WITH THE BITTER CONSEQUENCES OF THAT MARRIAGE.

VERY shortly after the son of Coselina's return, my lord duke fell into a brown study, and it lasted a complete week. I conceived, of course, that he was brooding over some great measure of government; but family concerns were the object of his musings. Gil Blas, said he one day after dinner, you may perceive that my mind is a good deal distracted. Yes, my good friend, I am pondering over an affair of the utmost consequence to my feelings. You shall know all about it.

My daughter, Donna Maria, pursued he, is marriageable, and of course beset with suitors. The Count de Niéblés, eldest son of the Duke de Medina Sidonia, head of the Guzman family, and Don Lewis de Haro, eldest son of the Marquis de Carpio and my eldest sister, are the two most likely competitors. The latter in particular is superior in point of merit to all his rivals, so that the whole court has fixed on him for my son-in-law. Nevertheless, without entering into private motives for treating him, as well as the Count de Niéblés, with a refusal, my present views are fixed upon Don Ramires Nunez de Guzman, Marquis of Toral, head of the Guzmans d'Abrados, another branch of the family. To that nobleman and his progeny by my daughter I mean to leave all my property, and to entail on them the title of Count d'Olivarez, with the additional dignity of grandee ; so that my grandchildren and their descendants, issue of the Abrados and Olivarez branch, will be considered as taking precedence in the house of Guzman.

Tell me now, Santillane, added he, do you not like my project ? Excuse me, my lord, pleaded I, with a shrug, the design is worthy of the genius which gave birth to it: my only fear is, lest the Duke of Medina Sidonia should think fit to be out of humor at it. Let him take it as he list, resumed the minister ; I give myself very little concern about that. His branch is no favorite with me : they have choused that of Abrados out of their precedence and many of their privileges. I shall be far less affected by his ill humors than by the disappointment of my sister, the Marchioness de Carpio, when she sees my daughter slip through her son's fingers. But let that be as it may. I am determined to please myself, and Don Ramires shall be the man ; it is a settled point.

My lord duke, having announced this firm resolve, did not carry it into effect without giving a new proof of his singular policy. He presented a memorial to the king, entreating him and the queen in concert, to do him the honor of taking the choice of a husband for his daughter on themselves, at the same time acquainting them with the pretensions of the suitors, and professing to abide by their election ; but he took care, when naming the Marquis de Toral, to evince clearly whither his own wishes pointed. The king, therefore, with a blind deference for his minister, answered thus : " I think that Don Ramires Nunez deserves Donna Maria : but determine for yourself. The match of your own choosing will be most agreeable to me." 　　(Signed)　　　　　　THE KING.

The minister made a point of showing this answer everywhere ; and affecting to consider it as a royal mandate, hastened his daughter's marriage with the Marquis de Toral ; a death-blow to the hopes of the Marchioness de Carpio, and the rest of the Guzmans who had been speculating on an alliance with Donna Maria. These rival players of a losing game, not being able to break off the match, put the best face they could upon it, and made the fashionable world to resound with their costly celebrations of the event. A superficial observer might have fancied that the whole family was delighted with the arrangement ; but the pouters and ill-wishers were soon revenged most cruelly at my lord duke's expense. Donna Maria was brought to bed of a daughter at the end of ten months ; the infant was still-born, and the mother died a few days afterwards.

What a loss for a father who had no eyes, as one may say, but for his daughter, and in her loss felt the miscarriage of his design to quash the right of precedence in the branch of Medina Sidonia! Stung to the quick by his misfortune, he shut himself up for several days, and was visible to no one but myself ; a sincere sympathizer, from the recollection of my own experience in his sorrow. The occasion drew forth fresh tears to Antonia's memory. The death of the Marchioness de Toral, under circumstances so similar, tore open a wound imperfectly skinned over, and so exasperated my affliction, that the minister, though he had enough to do with his own sufferings, could not help taking notice of mine. It seemed unaccountable how exactly his feelings were echoed. Gil Blas, said he one day, when my tears seemed to feed upon indulgence, my greatest consolation consists in having a bosom friend so much alive to all my distresses. Ah ! my lord, answered I, giving him the full credit of my amiable tenderness, I must be ungrateful and degenerate in my nature if I did not lament as for myself,

Can I be aware that you mourn over a daughter of accomplished merit, whom you loved so tenderly, without shedding tears of fellow-feeling! No, my lord, I am too much naturalized to you on the side of obligation, not to take a permanent interest in all your pleasures and disappointments.

CHAPTER X.

GIL BLAS MEETS WITH THE POET NUNEZ BY ACCIDENT, AND LEARNS THAT HE HAS WRITTEN A TRAGEDY, WHICH IS ON THE POINT OF BEING BROUGHT OUT AT THE THEATER ROYAL. THE ILL FORTUNE OF THE PIECE, AND THE GOOD FORTUNE OF ITS AUTHOR.

THE minister began to pick up his crumbs, and myself consequently to get into feather again, when one evening I went out alone in the carriage to take an airing. On the road I met the poet of the Asturias, who had been lost to my knowledge ever since his discharge from the hospital. He was very decently dressed. I called him up, gave him a seat in my carriage, and we drove together to Saint Jerome's meadow.

Master Nunez, said I, it is lucky for me to have met you accidentally; for otherwise I should not have had the pleasure. . . . . No severe speeches, Santillane, interrupted he with considerable eagerness: I must own frankly that I did not mean to keep up your acquaintance, and I will tell you the reason. You promised me a good situation provided I abjured poetry, but I have found a very excellent one, on condition of keeping my talents in constant play. I accepted the latter alternative, as squaring best with my own humor. A friend of mine got me an employment under Don Bertrand Gomez del Ribero, treasurer of the king's galleys. This Don Bertrand, wanting to have a wit in his pay, and finding my turn for poetical composition very much in unison with his own sense of what is excellent, has chosen me in preference to five or six authors who offered themselves as candidates for the place of his private secretary.

I am delighted at the news, my dear Fabricio, said I, for this Don Bertrand must be very rich. Rich indeed! answered he; they say that he does not know himself how much he is worth. However that may be, my business under him is as follows. He prides himself on his turn for gallantry, at the same time wishing to pass for a man of genius: he therefore keeps up an epistolary intercourse of wit with several ladies who have an infinite deal, and borrows my brain to indite such letters as may amplify the opinion of his sprightliness and elegance. I write to one for him in verse, to another in prose, and sometimes carry the letters myself, to prove the agility of my heels as well as the ingenuity of my head,

But you do not tell me, said I, what I most want to know. Are you well paid for your epigrammatic cards of compliment? Yes, most plentifully, answered he. Rich men are not always open-handed; and I know some who are downright curmudgeons; but Don Bertrand has behaved in the most handsome manner. Besides a salary of two hundred pistoles, I receive some little occasional perquisites from him, sufficient to set me above the world, and enable me to live on an equal footing with some choice spirits of the literary circles, who are willing, like myself, to set care at defiance. But then, resumed I, has your treasurer critical skill enough to distinguish the beauties of a performance from its blemishes? The least likely man in the world, answered Nunez : a flippant-tongued smatterer, with a miserable assortment of materials for judging. Yet he gives himself out for chief justice and lord president of Apollo's tribunal. His decisions are adventurous, if not always lucky; while his opinions are maintained in so high a tone and with so bullying a challenge of infallibility, that nine times out of ten the issue of an argument is silence, though not conviction, on the part of the opponent, as a measure of precaution against the gathering storm of foul language and contemptuous sneers.

You may readily suppose, continued he, that I take especial care never to contradict him, though it almost exceeds human patience to forbear : for, to say nothing of the unpalatable phrases that might be hailed down on my defenseless head, I should stand a very good chance of being shoved by the shoulders out of doors. I therefore am discreet enough to approve what he praises, and to condemn without mitigation or appeal whatever he is pleased to find fault with. By this easy compliance, for poets are compelled to acquire a knack of knocking under to those by whom they live, not even excepting their booksellers, I have gained the esteem and friendship of my patron. He has employed me to write a tragedy on a plot of his own. I have executed it under his inspection ; and if the piece succeeds, a percentage on the laud and honor must accrue to him.

I asked our poet what was the title of his tragedy. He informed me that it was "The Count of Saldagna," and that it would come out in two or three days. I told him that I wished it all possible success, and thought so favorably of his genius, as to entertain considerable hopes. So do I, said he, but hope never tells a more flattering tale than in the ear of a dramatic author. You might as well attempt to fix the wind by nailing the weathercock, as speculate on the reception of a new piece with an audience.

At length, the day of performance arrived. I could not get to the play, being prevented by official business. The only thing to be done was to send Scipio, that he might bring me back word how it went off, for I was sincerely interested in the event. After waiting impatiently for his return, in he came with a long face which boded no good. Well, said I, how was "The Count of Saldagna" welcomed by the critics? Very roughly, answered he ; never was there a play more brutally handled ; I left the house in high anger at the injustice and insolence of the pit. It serves him right, rejoined I. Nunez is no better than a madman, to be always running his head against the stone walls of a theater. If he was in his senses, could he have preferred the hisses and catcalls of an unfeeling mob, to the ease and dignity he might have commanded under my patronage? Thus did I inveigh with friendly vehemence against the poet of the Asturias, and disturb the even tenor of my mind for an event, which the sufferer hailed with joy, and inserted among the well-omened particulars of his journal.

He came to see me within two days, and appeared in high spirits. Santillane, cried he, I am come to receive your congratulations. My fortune is made, my friend, though my play is marred. You know what a mistake they made on the first and last night of " The Count of Saldagna;" hissed instead of applauding! You would have thought all the wild beasts of the forest had been let loose, with their ears fortified against the softening power of poetry : but the more they bellowed, the better I fared, and they have roared me into a provision for life.

There was no knowing what to make of this incident in the drama of our poet's adventures. What is all this, Fabricio? said I : how can theatrical damnation have conjured up such Elysian ecstasy? It is exactly so, answered he : I told you before that Don Bertrand had thrown in some of the circumstances; and he was fully convinced that there was no defect but in the taste of the spectators. They might be very good judges; but, if they were, he was no judge at all! Nunez! said he this morning :

Victrix causa Diis placuit, sed victa Catoni.*

Your piece has been ill-received by the public ; but against that you may place my entire approbation ; and thus you ought to set your heart at rest. By way of something to balance the bad taste of the age, I shall settle an annuity of two thousand crowns on you : go to my solicitor, and let him draw the deed. We have been about it : the treasurer has signed and sealed ; my first quarter is paid in advance . . . . .

I wished Fabricio joy on the unhappy fate of " The Count of Saldagna," and probably most authors would have envied his failure more than all the success that ever succeeded. You are in the right, continued he, to prefer my fortune to my fame. What a lucky peal of disapprobation in double choir ! If the public had chosen to ring the changes on my merits rather than my misdeeds, what would they have done for my pocket? A mere paltry nothing. The common pay of the theatre might have kept me from starving; but the wind of popular malice has blown me a comfortable pension, engrossed on safe and legal parchment.

---

* Members of parliament, and the ladies, will probably expect a translation of these hard words ; but I refer the former to their dictionaries, to which they bade a long farewell on leaving Eton or Harrow ; and the latter to an extended paraphrase of five acts in the tragedy of Cato. Those of the softer sex who may think the Stoic philosophy rude and uncouth, will feel their nerves vibrate in unison with the love scenes.—*Translator.*

CHAPTER XI.

SANTILLANE GIVES SCIPIO A SITUATION : THE LATTER SETS OUT FOR NEW SPAIN.

MY secretary could not look at the unexpected good luck of Nunez the poet without envy : he talked of nothing else for a week. The whims of that baggage, Fortune, said he, are most unaccountable : she delights to turn her lottery wheel into the lap of a sorry author, while she deals out her disappointments like a step-mother to the race of good ones. I should have no objection, though, if she would throw me up a prize in one of her vertical progresses. That is likely enough to happen, said I, and sooner than you imagine. Here you are in her temple ; for it is scarcely too presumptuous to call the house of a prime minister the temple of Fortune, where favors are conferred by wholesale, and votaries grow fat on the spoils of her altar. That is very true, sir, answered he ; but we must have patience, and wait till the happy moment comes. Take my advice while it is worth having, Scipio, replied I, and make your mind easy : perhaps you are on the eve of some good appointment. And so it turned out ; for within a few days an opportunity offered of employing him advantageously in my lord duke's service ; and I did not suffer the happy moment to pass by.

I was engaged in chat one morning with Don Raymond Caporis, the prime minister's steward, and our conversation turned on the sources of his excellency's income. My lord, said he, enjoys the commanderies of all the military orders, yielding a revenue of forty thousand crowns a year ; and he is only obliged to wear the cross of Alcantara. Moreover, his three offices of great chamberlain, master of the horse, and high chancellor of the Indies, bring him in an income of two hundred thousand crowns ; and yet all this is nothing in comparison of the immense sums which he receives through other transatlantic channels ; but you will be puzzled to guess how. When vessels clear out from Seville or Lisbon for those parts of the world, he ships wine, oil, grain, and other articles, the produce of his own estate ; and his consignments are duty free. With that perquisite in his pocket, he sells his merchandise for four times its current price in Spain, and then lays out the money in spices, coloring materials, and other things which cost next to nothing in the new world, and are sold very dear in Europe. Already has he realized some millions by this traffic, without detracting from the dues of his royal master.

You will easily account for it, continued he, that the people concerned in carrying on this trade return with great fortunes in their pockets ; for my lord thinks it but reasonable that they should divide their diligence between his business and their own.

That shrewd son of chance and opportunity, of whom we are speaking, overheard our conversation, and could not help interrupting Don Raymond to the following purport. Upon my word, Signor Caporis, I should like to be one of those people ; for I am fond of traveling, and have long wished to see Mexico. Your inclinations as a tourist shall soon be gratified, said the steward, if Signor de Santillane will not stand in the way of your wishes. However particular I may think it my duty to be about the persons whom I send to the West Indies in that capacity, and they are all of my appointment, you shall be placed on the list at all adventures, if your master wishes it. You will confer on me a particular favor, said I to Don Raymond; be so good as to do it in kindness to me. Scipio is a young fellow much in my good graces, very capable in business, and will be found irreproachable in his conduct. In a word, I would as soon answer for him as myself.

That being the case, replied Caporis, he has only to repair immediately to Seville : the ships are to sail for South America in a month. I shall give him a letter at his departure for a man who will put him in the way of making a fortune, without the slightest interference in his excellency's dues and profits, which ought to be held sacred by him.

Scipio, delighted with his berth, was in haste to set out for Seville with a thousand crowns with which I furnished him, to make purchases of wine and oil in Andalusia, and enable him to trade on his own bottom in the West Indies. And yet, overjoyed as he was to make a voyage, and as he hoped his fortune therewithal, he could not part from me without tears : and the separation raised the waters even from my dry fountains.

CHAPTER XII.

DON ALPHONSO DE LEYVA COMES TO MADRID ; THE MOTIVE OF HIS JOURNEY A SEVERE AFFLICTION TO GIL BLAS, AND A CAUSE OF REJOICING SUBSEQUENT THEREON.

No sooner had I parted with Scipio than one of the minister's pages brought me a note conceived in the following terms : "If Signor de Santillane will take the trouble of calling at the sign of Saint Gabriel, in the street of Toledo, he will there see a friend who is not indifferent to him."

Who can this nameless friend possibly be? said I to myself. What can be the meaning of all this mystery ? Obviously to occasion me the pleasure of a surprise. I attended the summons immediately, and on my arrival at the place appointed, was not a little astonished to find Don Alphonso de Leyva there. Is it possible! exclaimed I : you here, my lord? Yes, my dear Gil Blas, answered he with a close compression of my hand in his, it is Don Alphonso himself. Well ! but what brings you to Madrid ? said I. You will be not a little startled, rejoined he, and no less vexed at the occasion of my journey. They have taken my government of Valencia from me, and the prime minister has sent for me to give an account of my conduct. For a whole quarter of an hour I was like a man stupefied; then recovering the powers of speech: Of what, said I, are you accused? I know nothing at all about it, answered he; but my disgrace is probably owing to a visit paid about three weeks ago to the Cardinal Duke of Lerma, who was banished about a month since to his seat at Denia.

Yes, indeed! cried I in a pet, you may well attribute your misfortune to that imprudent visit: there is no occasion to look out for causes and effects elsewhere; but give me leave to say that you have not acted with your usual good sense, in claiming acquaintance with that favorite out of favor. The leap is taken, and the neck broken, said he; and I have nothing to do but to make the best out of a bad bargain: I shall retire with my family to our paternal estate at Leyva, where the remnant of my days will glide away in peace and obscurity. What taunts and teases me, is the requisition of appearing before a haughty minister, who may receive me with all the insolence of office. How humiliating to the pride of a Spaniard! And yet it is a measure of necessity; but before the degrading ceremony took place, I wanted to talk it over with you. Sir, said I, do not announce your arrival to the minister, till I have ascertained the nature of the reports to your discredit; for there are few evils without a remedy. Whatever may be your alleged crimes, you will give me leave, if you please, to act in the affair as gratitude and friendship shall dictate. With this assurance, I left him at his inn, and promised to let him hear from me soon.

As I had taken no active part in state affairs since the two memorials, in which my eloquence was so signally displayed, I went to look for Carnero, with a view to inquire whether Don Alphonso's government was really taken from him. He answered in the affirmative, but professed not to know the reason. Finding how things stood, I determined to apply at head-quarters, and to learn the grounds of grievance from his lordship's own mouth.

My spirits were really harassed; so that there was no need of putting on the trappings and the suits of woe, to attract my lord duke's notice. What is the matter, Santillane? said he, as soon as he saw me. I perceive a marked unhappiness on your countenance, and tears just ready to trickle down your cheeks. Has any one behaved ill to you? Tell me, and you shall have your revenge. My lord, answered I, in a melancholy tone, even though my grief would seek to hide itself, it must have vent: my despair is past endurance. The report goes that Don Alphonso is no longer Governor of Valencia; a severer stroke could not have been inflicted on me. What say you, Gil Blas? replied the minister in astonishment: what interest can you take in this Don Alphonso and his government? On this question, I detailed at length my obligations to the Lords of Leyva, and modestly stated my own interference with the Duke of Lerma, to obtain the appointment for my friend.

When his excellency had heard me through with the most polite and kind attention, he spoke thus: Make yourself easy, Gil Blas. Besides my entire ignorance of what you have just told me, I must own that I considered Don Alphonso as the cardinal's creature. Only put yourself in my place: was not the visit to his eminence a most suspicious circumstance? Yet I am willing to believe that owing his preferment to that minister, he might have remembered him in his adversity from a motive of pure gratitude. I am sorry for having displaced a man who owed his elevation to you; but if I have pulled down your handiwork I can build it up again. I mean to do still more than the Duke of Lerma for you. Your friend Don Alphonso was only Governor of Valencia; I appoint him Viceroy of Arragon: you may send him word so yourself, and order him hither to take the oaths.

At these words, my feelings changed from extreme grief to an excess of joy, which completely caricatured the mediocrity of common sense, and made me utter an incoherent rhapsody of thanks: but the want of method in the madness of my discourse was not taken amiss; and on my hinting that Don Alphonso was already at Madrid, he told me that I might present him this very day. I ran to the sign of Saint Gabriel, and communicated my own raptures to Don Cæsar's son, by informing him of his new appointment. He could not believe what I told him; but found it a hard matter to persuade himself, that the prime minister, though likely enough to be very well disposed towards me, should extend his friendship so far as to dispose of viceroyalties at my instance. I carried him with me to my lord duke, who received him very affably, complimented him on his uniform good conduct in his government of Valencia, and finished by saying that the king, considering him as qualified for a higher station, had named him for the viceroyalty of Arragon. Besides, added he, your family is of a rank not to disparage the dignity of the office; so that the Arragonese nobility will have no plea for excepting against the choice of the court.

His excellency made no mention of me, and the public was kept in the dark as to my share in the business; indeed, this prudent silence was lucky both for Don Alphonso and the minister, since the tongues of defamers would have been busy in taking to pieces the pretensions of a viceroy who owed his preferment to my patronage.

As soon as Don Cæsar's son could speak with certainty of his new honors, he sent off an express for Valencia with the information to his father and Seraphina, who soon arrived in Madrid. Their first object was to find me out, and ply me thick and threefold with acknowledgments. What a proud and affecting sight for me, to behold the three persons in the world nearest my heart, vying with each other in their testimonies of affection and gratitude! The pleasure my zeal seemed personally to give them, was equal to the dignity conferred on their house by the post of viceroy. They even talked with me on a footing of equality, and scarcely remembered my original distance or servitude in the fervor of their present feelings. But not to dwell on unnecessary topics, Don Alphonso, having taken the oaths and returned thanks, left Madrid with his family, to take up his abode at Saragossa. He made his public entry with appropriate magnificence; and the Arragonese caused it to appear, by their cordial reception, that I had a very pretty knack at picking out a viceroy.

CHAPTER XIII.

GIL BLAS MEETS DON GASTON DE COGOLLOS AND DON ANDREW DE TORDESILLAS AT THE DRAWING-ROOM, AND ADJOURNS WITH THEM TO A MORE CONVENIENT PLACE. THE STORY OF DON GASTON AND DONNA HELENA DE GALISTEO CONCLUDED. SANTILLANE RENDERS SOME SERVICE TO TORDESILLAS.

I WAS up to the hilts in joy at having so marvelously metamorphosed an ex-governor into a viceroy; the Lords of Leyva themselves were not primed and loaded so near to bursting. But very soon I had another opportunity of employing my credit in the beaten track of friendship; and there is the more occasion to quote these instances, that my readers may clearly discern with how different a man they are in company, from that graceless Gil Blas who, under the former ministry, carried on a shameless traffic in the honors and emoluments of the state.

One day I was waiting in the king's ante-chamber, in conversation with some noblemen, who, knowing me to stand well with the prime minister, were not ashamed of taking me by the hand. In the crowd was Don Gaston de Cogollos, whom I had left a prisoner in the tower of Segovia. He was with Don Andrew de Tordesillas, the warden. I readily quitted my company to go and renew my acquaintance with my two friends. If they were astonished at the sight of me, I was no less so to find them here. After mutual greetings, Don Gaston said: Signor de Santillane, we have many inquiries to make of each other, and this place affords little opportunity for private intercourse; allow me to request your company where we may open our hearts freely. I made no objection; we pushed our way through the crowd, and left the palace. Don Gaston's carriage was ready waiting in the street; we all three got into it, and drove to the great market-place, where the bull-fights are exhibited. There Cogollos lived in a very handsome house.

Signor Gil Blas, said Don Andrew on our entrance, at your departure from Segovia you seemed to have conceived a thorough hatred against the court, and to have formed a settled purpose of abandoning it forever. Such was, in fact, my design, answered I; nor were my sentiments at all changed during the lifetime of the late king; but when the prince his son came to the throne, I had a mind to see whether the new monarch would know me again. He did so, and received me favorably, with a strong recommendation to the prime minister, who admitted me to his friendship, and took me more into his confidence than ever did the Duke of Lerma. This, Signor Don Andrew, is my story. And now tell me whether you still hold your office in the tower of Segovia. No, indeed! answered he; my lord duke has removed me, and put another in my room. He probably considered me as entirely devoted to his predecessor. And I, said Don Gaston, was set at liberty for the contrary reason; the prime minister was no sooner informed that my imprisonment was by the Duke of Lerma's order, than he ordered me to be released. The present business, Signor Gil Blas, is to relate the subsequent particulars of my adventures.

The first thing I did, continued he, after thanking Don Andrew for his kind attentions during my confinement, was to repair to Madrid. I presented myself before the Count Duke of Olivarez, who said: You need not be apprehensive of any blemish on your character in consequence of your late misfortune; you are honorably acquitted: nay, your innocence is so much the more satisfactorily established, as the Marquis of Villareal, with whom you were supposed to be implicated, was not guilty. Though a Portuguese, and related to the Duke of Braganza, he is less in his interests than in those of the king my master. That connection, therefore, ought not to have been imputed to you as a crime; but, to repair your wrongs, the king has given you a lieutenant's commission in the Spanish guards. This I accepted, begging it as a favor of his excellency to allow me, before I joined my regiment, to go and see my aunt, Donna Eleonora de Laxarilla, at Coria. The minister gave me leave of absence for a month, and I departed with only one servant.

We had got beyond Colmenar, and were threading a narrow pass between two mountains, when we came within sight of a gentleman defending himself bravely against three men, who all fell upon him together. I did not hesitate about going to his aid; but hastened forward and planted myself by his side. I remarked while we were fighting, that our enemies were masked, and that we had to do with expert swordsmen. But we triumphed over the united advantages of their skill and disparity. I ran one of the three through the body; he fell from his horse, and the two others immediately betook themselves to flight. The victory indeed was scarcely less fatal to us than to the wretch whom I had killed, for we were both dangerously wounded. But conceive my surprise, when I discovered the gentleman to be Combados, the husband of Donna Helena. He was no less astonished at recognizing me as his defender. Ah, Don Gaston! exclaimed he, was it you, then, who came to my assistance? When you took my part so generously, you little thought it was the person who had snatched your mistress from you. I really did not know it, answered I; but though I had, do you think I could have wavered about doing as I have done? Can you entertain so ill an opinion of me, as to believe my soul so sordid? No, no, replied he; I think better of you; and should I die of my wounds, it will be my prayer that yours may not disable you from profiting by my death. Combados, said I, though I have not yet forgotten Donna Helena, know that I do not pant after the possession of her charms at the expense of your life; so far from it, that I congratulate myself on having contributed to your rescue from assassination, since by so doing I have performed an acceptable service to your wife.

While we were communing together, my servant dismounted; and drawing near to the gentleman stretched at his length, took off his mask, when Combados, with sensations of gratitude for his deliverance, distinctly traced the features. It is Caprara, exclaimed he; that treacherous cousin who, in mere disgust at having missed a rich inheritance which he had unjustly disputed with me, has long since cherished a murderous design against my life, and fixed on this day to put it in execution; but heaven has turned him over to its determined vengeance, and made him the victim of his own attempt.

While this conversation was going on, our blood was flowing at the same rate, and we were becoming more exhausted every minute. Nevertheless, disabled as we were, we had strength enough to reach the town of Villaréjo, which lies within gun-shot or two from the field of battle. At the very first house of call we sent for surgeons. The most expert came at our summons. He examined our wounds, and reported them as dangerous. After taking off the bandages and dressing them a second time, he pronounced those of Don Blas to be mortal. Of mine he thought more favorably, and the event corresponded with his prognostic.

Combados, finding himself consigned to the grave, thought only of due preparation for a most serious event. He sent an express to his wife, with an account of what had happened, particularizing his present sad condition. Donna Helena soon arrived at Villaréjo. Her mind was drawn different ways by two opposite occasions of distress; the hazard of her husband's life, and the fear of feeling the revival of a half-extinguished flame at the sight of me. This sight occasioned her to experience a terrible agitation. Madam, said Don Blas, when she appeared in his presence, you are come just in time to receive my farewell. I am at the point of death, and I consider my fate as a punishment from heaven for having taken you from Don Gaston by a feint: far from murmuring at it, I exhort you with my last breath to restore to him a heart which I had stolen from him. Donna Helena answered him only by her tears: and indeed it was the best answer she could make; for she had neither forgotten her first love, nor the artifices whereby she had been influenced to renounce her plighted faith.

It happened as the surgeon had anticipated, that in less than three days Combados died of his wounds, while mine on the contrary wore the appearance of convalescence. The young widow, whom no earthly considerations could detach from the care of transporting her late husband's remains to Coria, that they might be deposited with due honors in the family vault, left Villaréjo on her return, after inquiring, merely as a matter of course, how I was going on. As soon as I was well enough to be removed, I bent my course to Coria, where my recovery was soon ascertained. My aunt, Donna Eleonora, and Don George de Galisteo, were determined that my marriage with Helena should take place forthwith, lest some new caprice of fortune should part us once more. The ceremony was privately performed, on account of the late melancholy event, and within a few days I returned to Madrid with Donna Helena. As my leave of absence had expired, I was afraid lest the minister should have superseded me in my lieutenancy; but he had not filled up the vacancy, and received my apologies very graciously.

Thus am I, continued Cogollos, lieutenant of the Spanish guards, and my situation is exactly to my mind. The circle of my friends is respectable and pleasant, and I live at my ease among them. Would I could say as much! exclaimed Don Andrew: but I am very far from being satisfied with my lot; I have lost my appointment, which was not without its advantages, and have no friends of sufficient interest to procure me a better berth. Excuse me, Signor Don Andrew, cried I, with a sort of upbraiding smile, you have a friend in me, who may chance to be better than no friend at all. I have told you already that I am a greater favorite with my lord duke than with the Duke of Lerma; and will you tell me to my face that you have no interest at court? Have you not already experienced the contrary? Recollect that, through the archbishop of Grenada's powerful recommendation, I procured you a nomination for Mexico, where you would have made your fortune, if love had not stepped in and marred it at Alicant. My means are now more extensive, since I have the ear of the prime minister. I give myself up to you then, replied Tordesillas; but do not send me into New Spain, though the first appointment in the colonies were at your disposal.

Here we were interrupted by Donna Helena, who came into the room, and improved even upon the visions of my fancy by the reality of her charms. Cogollos introduced me as the companion who had solaced the tedious hours of his imprisonment. Yes, madam, said I to Donna Helena, my conversation did indeed soothe his sorrows, for it turned on you. The compliment was not thrown away, and I took my leave with repeated congratulations. With respect to Tordesillas, I assured him that within a week he should know how far my power as well as will extended.

Nor were these mere words. On the very next day, the opportunity occurred. Santillane, said his excellency, the place of governor in the royal prison of Valladolid is vacant: it is worth more than three hundred pistoles a year; and is yours if you will accept of it. Not if it were worth ten thousand ducats, answered I, for it would carry me away from your lordship. But, replied the minister, you may fill it by deputy, and only visit occasionally. That is as it may be, rejoined I; but I shall only accept it on condition of resigning in favor of Don Andrew de Tordesillas, a brave and loyal gentleman; I should like to give him this place in acknowledgment of his kindness to me in the tower of Segovia.

This plea made the minister laugh heartily, and say: As far as I see, Gil Blas, you mean to make yourself a general patron. Even so be it, my friend; the vacancy is yours for Tordesillas; but tell me unfeignedly what fellow-feeling you have in the business, for you are not such a fool as to throw away your interest for nothing. My lord, answered I, Don Andrew charged me nothing for all his acts of friendship, and should not a man repay his obligations? You are become highly moral and self-mortified, replied his excellency; rather more so than under the last administration. Precisely so, rejoined I; then evil communication corrupted my principles; bargain and sale were the order of the day, and I conformed to the established practice: now, all preferment is allotted on the footing of a meritorious free gift, and my integrity shall not be the last to fall in with the fashion.

CHAPTER XIV.

SANTILLANE'S VISIT TO POET NUNEZ, THE COMPANY AND CONVERSATION.

ONE day, after dinner, a fancy seized me to go and see the poet of the Asturias, feeling a sort of curiosity to know on what floor he lodged. I repaired to the house of Signor Don Bertrand Gomez del Ribero, and asked for Nunez. He does not live here now, said the porter, but over the way, in apartments at the back of the house. I went thither, and crossing a small court, entered an unfurnished parlor, where my friend Fabricio was sitting at table, doing the honors to five or six guests from the hamlet and liberty of Parnassus.

They were at the latter end of a feast, and of course at the beginning of an affray; but as soon as they perceived me, a dead silence succeeded to their obstreperous argumentation. Nunez rose from his seat with much pomp and circumstance of politeness to receive me, saying: Gentlemen, Signor de Santillane! He does me the honor to visit me under this humble roof; as the favorite of the prime minister, you will all join with me in tendering your humble services. At this introduction, the worshipful company got up and made their best bows; for my rank could not fail of procuring me respect from the manufacturers of dedications. Though I was neither hungry nor thirsty, it was impossible not to sit down and drink a toast in such society.

My presence appearing to be a restraint, Gentlemen, said I, it should seem that I have interrupted your conversation: resume it, or you drive me away. My learned friends, said Fabricio, were discussing the "Iphigenia" of Euripides. The bachelor, Melchior de Villégas, a clever man of the first rank in the republic of letters, resumed the topic by asking Don Jacinto de Romerate which was the point of interest in that tragedy. Don Jacinto ascribed it to the imminent danger of Iphigenia. The bachelor contended, offering to prove his proposition by all the evidence admissible at the bar of logic or criticism, that the danger of a trumpery girl had nothing to do with the real sympathy of that affecting piece. What has to do with it then? bawled the old licentiate Gabriel of Leon indignantly. It turns with the wind, replied the bachelor.

The whole company burst into a shout of laughter at this assertion, which they were far from considering as serious; and I myself thought that Melchoir had only launched it by way of adding the zest of wit to the severity of critical discussion. But I was out in my calculation respecting the character of that eminent scholar: he had not a grain of sprightliness or pleasantry in his whole composition. Laugh as you please, gentlemen, replied he, very coolly; I maintain that there is no circumstance but the wind, unless it be the weather-cock, to interest, to strike, to rouse the passions of the spectator. Figure to yourselves a multitudinous army assembled for the purpose of laying siege to Troy; take into account the eager haste of the officers and common men to carry their enterprise into execution, that they may return with their best legs foremost into Greece, where they have left everything most dear to them, their household gods, their wives and their children: all this while a mischievous wind from the wrong quarter keeps them portbound at Aulis, and, as it were, drives a nail into the very head of the expedition; so that till better weather, it was impossible to go and lay siege to Priam's town. Wind and weather therefore make up the interest of this tragedy. My good wishes are with the Greeks: my whole faculties are wrapped up in the success of their design; the sailing of their fleet is with me the only hinge of the fable, and I look at the danger of Iphigenia with somewhat of a self-interested complacency, because by her death the winding up of the story into a brisk and favorable gale was likely to be accelerated.

As soon as Villégas had finished his criticism, the laugh burst out more than ever, at his expense. Nunez was sly enough to side with him, that a fairer scope and broader mark might be presented to the shafts of malicious wit which were let fly from all the quarters in the shipman's card, at this poster of the sea and land. But the bachelor, eying them all with sublime indifference and supreme contempt, gave them to understand how low in the list of the ignorant and vulgar they ranked in his estimation. Every moment did I expect to see these vaporing spirits kindle into a blaze, and wage war against the hairy honors of each other's brainless skulls: but the joke was not carried to that length; they confined their hostilities to opprobrious epithets, and took their leave when they had eaten and drunk as much as they could get.

After their departure, I asked Fabricio why he had separated himself from his treasurer, and whether they had quarreled. Quarreled! answered he: Heaven defend me from such a misfortune! I am on better terms than ever with Signor Don Bertrand, who gave his consent to my living apart from him; here therefore I receive my friends, and take my pleasure with them unmolested. You know very well that I am not of a temper to lay up treasures for those who are to come after me; and as it happens luckily, I am now in circumstances to give my little classical entertainments every day. I am delighted at it, my dear Nunez, replied I, and once more wish you joy on the success of your last tragedy: the great Lope, by his eight hundred dramatic pieces, never made a quarter of the money which you have got by the damnation of your "Count de Saldagna."

BOOK THE TWELFTH.

CHAPTER I.

GIL BLAS SENT TO TOLEDO BY THE MINISTER. THE PURPOSE OF HIS JOURNEY AND ITS SUCCESS.

FOR nearly a month his excellency had been saying to me every day: Santillane, the time is approaching when I shall call your choicest powers of address into action; but the time that was coming never came. It is a long lane, however, where there is no turning; and his excellency at length spoke to me nearly as follows They say that there is, in the company of comedians at Toledo, a young actress of much note for her personal and professional fascinations; it is affirmed that she dances and sings like all the muses and graces put together, and that the whole theatre rings with applause at her performance: to these perfections is added matchless and irresistible beauty. Such a star should only shine within the circle of a court. The king has a taste for the stage, for music, and for dancing: nor must he be debarred from the pleasure of seeing and hearing such a prodigy. I have determined on sending you to Toledo, that you may judge for yourself whether she really is so extraordinary an actress · on your feeling of her merit my measures shall be taken ; for I have unlimited confidence in your discernment.

I undertook to bring his lordship a good account of this business, and made my arrangements for setting out with one servant, but not in the minister's livery, by way of conducting matters more warily; and that precaution relished well with his excellency. On my arrival at Toledo, I had scarcely alighted at the inn, when the landlord, taking me for some country gentleman, said · Please your honor, you are probably come to be present at the august ceremony of an Auto da Fé to-morrow. I answered in the affirmative, the more completely to mislead him, and keep my own counsel. You will see, replied he, one of the prettiest processions you ever saw in your life: there are said to be more : han a hundred prisoners, and ten of them are to be roasted.

In good truth, next morning, before sunrise, I heard all the bells in the town peal merrily; and the design of their bob-majors was to acquaint the people that the pastime was about to begin. Curious to see what sort of a recreation it was, I dressed in a hurry, and posted to the scene of action. All about that quarter, and along the streets where the procession was to pass, were scaffolds, on one of which I purchased a standing. The Dominicans walked first, preceded by the banner of the Inquisition. These Christian fathers were immediately followed by the hapless victims of the holy office, selected for this day's burnt-offering. These devoted wretches walked one by one, with their head and feet bare, each of them with a taper in his hand, and a fiery, not baptismal god-father by his side. Some had large yellow scapularies, worked with crosses of St. Andrew, in red; others wore sugar-loaf caps of paper, illustrated with flames, and diabolical figures of all sorts by way of emblem.

As I looked narrowly at these objects of religious gaze, with a compassion in my heart which might have been construed criminal, had it run over from my eyes, I fancied that the reverend Father Hilary and his companion brother Ambrose were among those who figured in the sugar-loaf caps. They passed too near for me to be deceived. What do I see? thought I inwardly: heaven, wearied out with the wicked lives of these two scoundrels, has given them up to the justice of the Inquisition! My whole frame trembled at the thought, and my spirits were scarcely equal to support me from fainting. My connection with these knaves, the adventure at Xelva, all our pranks in partnership rushed upon my memory, and I did not know how sufficiently to thank God for having pre-served me from St. Andrew's crosses and the painted devils on the paper caps.

When the ceremony was over, I returned to the inn, with my heart sickening at the dreadful sight; but painful impressions soon wear away, and I thought only of my commission and its due accomplishment. I waited with impatience for play-time, as the moment and scene of my commencing operations. On the open-ing of the doors I repaired to the theatre, and took my seat next to a knight of Alcantara. We soon got into chat. Sir, said I, the players here have been represented to me in very favorable terms: may I give credit to general report? The company is not con-temptible, replied the knight: they have some first-rate per-formers; among the rest, the peerless Lucretia, an actress of four-teen, who will astonish you: and she plays one of her best parts to-night.

On the drawing up of the curtain, two actresses came on, with every advantage of dress and stage effect: but neither of them could possibly be the object of my search. At length Lucretia made her appearance at the back scene, and walked forwards amidst a thunder of applause. Ah! this is she, indeed! thought I? and a delicate specimen of loveliness, as I am a sinner! In her very first speech she proved herself a child of nature, with energy and conception far above her years; and the approbation of a provincial audience was confirmed by my metropolitan judgment. The knight was happy to find I liked her, and assured me that if I had heard her sing, my ears might have rejoiced to the sorrow of my heart. Her dancing, too, he represented as not less formidable to the free will of lordly man. I inquired what youth, blessed as the immortal gods, had the exquisite happiness of bringing himself to beggary for so sweet a girl. She is under no avowed protection, said he; and scandal has not coupled her name with private license; but Lucretia must take care of herself, for she is under the wing of her aunt Estella; and there is not an actress in the company so warmly fledged for hatching the tender passions into life.

At the name of Estella, I inquired with some eagerness who she was. One of our best performers, said my informant. She does not play to-night, to our great loss, for her cast is that of abigails, and she humors them to perfection. A little too broad, perhaps, but that is a fault on the right side. From the features of the description, there could be no doubt but this must be Laura; that lady so notorious in these memoirs, whom I left at Grenada.

To make assurance doubly sure, I went behind the scenes after the play. There she was, in the green-room, flirting with some men of fashion, who probably endured the aunt for the sake of the niece. I came up to pay my devotions; but whim, or perhaps revenge for my cutting and running from Grenada, determined her to put on the stranger, and receive my compliments with so discouraging a coldness, as to throw me into some little confusion. Instead of laughing it off, I was fool enough to be angry, and withdrew in a choleric determination to return next day. Laura shall smart for this! said I; her niece shall not appear at court; I will tell the minister that she dances like a she bear, has formed her *bravura* between the scream of a pea-hen and the cackle of a goose, acts like a puppet, and comprehends like an idiot.

Such was my scheme of revenge, but it proved abortive. Just as I was going out of town, a footboy brought me the following note: "Forget and forgive, and follow the bearer." I obeyed, and found Laura at her dressing-table in very elegant apartments near the theater.

She rose to welcome me, saying: Signor Gil Blas, you have every reason to be offended at your reception behind the scenes, which was out of character between such old friends, but I really was most abominably disconcerted. Just as you came up, one of our gentlemen had brought me some scandalous stories about my niece, whose honor has always been dearer to me than my own. On coming to myself, I immediately sent my servant to find you out, with the intention of making you amends to-day. You have done so already, my dear Laura, said I, let us therefore talk over old times. You may remember that I left you in a very ticklish predicament, when conscience and the fear of punishment drove me so precipitately from Grenada. How did you get off with your Portuguese lover? Easily enough, answered Laura: do not you know that in those cases men are mere fools, and acquit us women without even calling for our defence?

I faced the Marquis of Marialva out, that you were my very brother, and drew upon my impudence for the support of my credit. Do you not see, said I to my Portuguese dupe, that this is all the contrivance of jealousy and rage? My rival, Narcissa, infuriated at my possession of a heart which she had vainly attempted to gain, has bribed the candle-snuffer to assert that he has seen me as Arsenia's waiting-woman at Madrid. It is an abominable falsehood; the widow of Don Antonio Coello has always been too high in her notions, to be the hanger-on of a theatrical mistress. Besides, what completely disproves the whole allegation, is my brother's precipitate retreat: if he were here, it would be a subject of evidence; but Narcissa must have devised some stratagem to get him out of the way.

These reasons, continued Laura, were not the most convincing in the world, but they did very well for the marquis; and that good, easy nobleman continued his confidence till his return to Portugal. This happened soon after your departure; and Zapata's wife had the pleasure of seeing me lose what she could not win. After this, I stayed some years longer at Grenada, till the company was broken up in consequence of some squabbles, which will take place in mimic as well as in real life: some went to Seville, others to Cordova; and I came to Toledo, where I have been for these ten years with my niece Lucretia, whose performance you must have seen last night.

This was too much to be taken gravely. Laura inquired why I laughed. Can that be a question? said I. You have neither brother nor sister, one or other of which is a necessary ingredient in an aunt. Besides, when I calculate in my mind the lapse of time since our last separation, and compare that period with the age of your niece, it is more than possible that your relationship may be in a nearer degree of kin.

I understand you, replied Don Antonio's widow, with something like a moral tinge of red in her cheek; you are an accurate chronologist! There is no garbling facts in defiance of your memory. Well, then! Lucretia is my daughter by the Marquis of Marialva: it was extremely wrong, but I cannot conceal it from you. The confession must indeed be a shock to your modesty, said I, after telling me yourself what pranks you played with the hospital steward at Zamora. I must tell you moreover that Lucretia is an article of so superior a quality as to render you a public benefactor by having thrown her into the market. It were to be wished that the stolen embraces of all your fraternity might be blessed with fruitfulness, if they could secure to themselves a patent for breeding after your sample.

Should any sarcastic reader, comparing this passage with some circumstances related while I was the marquis's secretary, suspect me of being entitled to dispute the honors of paternity with that nobleman, I blush to say, that my claims are entirely out of the question.

I laid open my principal adventures to Laura in my turn, as well as the present state of my affairs. She listened with interest, and said: Friend Santillane, you seem to play a principal part on the stage of the world, and I congratulate you most heartily. Should Lucretia be engaged at Madrid, I flatter myself she will find a powerful protector in Signor de Santillane. Doubt it not, answered I: your daughter may have her engagement whenever you please; I can promise you that, without presuming too much on my interest. I take you at your word, replied Laura, and would set out to-morrow, were I not under articles to this company. An order from court will cut the knot of any articles, rejoined I; and that I take upon myself: you shall have it within a week. It is an act of chivalry to rescue Lucretia from Toledo: such a pretty little actress belongs to the royal court, as parcel of the manor.

Lucretia came into the room just as I was talking of her. The goddess Hebe herself never looked better in her best days: it was nature in the bud, exhaling the sweets of her earliest bloom, but promising a more luxuriant waste of treasure. She was just up; and her natural beauty, without the aid of art, communicated the most rapturous sensations. Come, niece, said her mother, thank the gentleman for all his kindness to us: he is an old friend of mine, who ranks high at court, and undertakes to get us both an engagement at the theater royal. The little girl seemed to be much pleased, and made me a low courtesy, saying with an enchanting smile: I most humbly thank you for your obliging intention; but, by taking me from a partial audience, are you certain that I shall not be looked down upon by that of Madrid? I may but lose by the exchange. I remember hearing my aunt say, that she has seen players most favorably received in one town, and hissed off the stage in another, this absolutely frightens me; beware therefore of exposing me to the derision of the court, and yourself to its reproaches. Lovely Lucretia, answered I, we have neither of us anything to fear; I am rather apprehensive lest, by the havoc you will make among hearts, you should excite rivalships and kindle discord among the courtiers. My niece's fears, said Laura, are better founded than yours; but I hope they will both prove vain: however feeble may be Lucretia's charms of person, her talents as an actress are at least above mediocrity.

We continued the conversation for some time: and I could gather, from Lucretia's share in it, that she was a girl of superior talents. On taking leave, I assured them that they should immediately receive a summons to Madrid.

CHAPTER II.

SANTILLANE MAKES HIS REPORT TO THE MINISTER, WHO COM-
MISSIONS HIM TO SEND FOR LUCRETIA. THE FIRST APPEAR-
ANCE OF THAT ACTRESS BEFORE THE COURT.

ON my return, I found my lord duke impatient to be informed
of my success. Have you seen her? said he: is she worth trans-
planting? My lord, answered I, fame, which generally runs beyond
all discretion in its report of beauty, has erred on the side of parsimony in its estimate of the matchless young Lucretia; she is all
that youthful poets fancy when they feign, for personal attractions,
and all that veteran managers seek when they sign articles, in
scenic qualifications.

Is it possible? exclaimed the minister with a satisfaction which
involuntarily peeped out at his eyes, and made me think he had some
selfish hankerings after the article of my marketing at Toledo; is
it possible? and is she really so charming a creature? When you
see her, replied I, you will own that any verbal picture of her perfections must be altogether inadequate to their due description.
His excellency then requiring a minute account of my journey, I
gave him all the particulars, not excepting Laura's story, and
Lucretia's parentage. His lordship was delighted at the latter circumstance, and enjoined me, with a cordial compliment on my skill
in such delicate negotiations, to finish as auspiciously as I had
begun my undertaking.

I went to look for Carnero, and told him that it was his excellency's pleasure he should make out an order for the admission of
Estella and Lucretia, actresses from the Toledo theater, into his
majesty's company. Say you so, Signor de Santillane? answered
Carnero with a sarcastic leer; you shall not be kept long in suspense, since you take so marked an interest in the fortunes of
these two ladies. He expedited the order in my presence, and
within a week the mother and daughter sent me notice of their
arrival. I immediately hastened to their lodging near the theater,
and after an interchange of thanks on their part, and assurances of
continued support on mine, left them with my best wishes for a
brilliant career of success.

Their names were announced in the bills as two new actresses,
engaged by the special mandate of the court. They made their first
appearance in a play, which they had been accustomed to perform
in at Todelo with loud and unanimous applause.

Novelty is the very life and soul of theatrical entertainments.
The house was uncommonly crowded, and I of course was among
the audience. I was rather frightened before the curtain drew up.
Prejudiced as I was in favor of the candidates, my alarm was in
proportion to my interest. But when once they were fairly on the
boards, the din of welcome quieted all my apprehensions. Estella

was considered as a first-rate actress in comic parts, and Lucretia as a female Roscius in heroines and love-sick damsels. But the love which she feigned herself, she really kindled in the hearts of the spectators. Some admired the beauty of her eyes, others were touched with the plaintive sweetness of her voice, and all, bowing to the triumph of youth, vivacity, and elegance, went away in raptures with her person.

My lord duke, who took an uncommon interest in this theatrical event, was at the play that evening. I saw him leave his box at the end of the piece, with evident approbation of our new performers. Curious to know whether they equalled his expectations, I followed him home, and into his closet, saying : Well, my lord, is your excellency well pleased with little Marialva? My excellency, answered he with a sly smile, must be very difficult to be pleased, not to confirm the public voice: yes, indeed, my good friend, I am enraptured with your Lucretia, and firmly believe that the king will not see her without emotion.

CHAPTER III.

LUCRETIA'S POPULARITY; HER APPEARANCE BEFORE THE KING; HIS PASSION, AND ITS CONSEQUENCES.

GREAT was the noise about the court on this double acquisition to the theater; it became the topic of conversation next day at the king's levee. The young Lucretia was most in the mouths of the nobility, who described her so feelingly, that his majesty could not but imbibe the impression, though he was too politic to express his interest either in words or by looks.

To make amends for that restraint, he questioned the minister as soon as he was alone with him, who stated the success of a young actress from Toledo on the evening before. Her name, added he, is Lucretia; and it is really a pity that ladies of her profession should ever have been christened by any less chaste appellative. She is an acquaintance of Santillane, who spoke so highly of her, that I thought it right to engage her for your majesty's company. The king smiled at the mention of my name, recollecting, perhaps, through what channel he became acquainted with Catalina, and foreboding a like assistance on the present occasion. Count, said he to the minister, I mean to see this Lucretia act to-morrow, and will thank you to let her know it.

I was of course sent with this intelligence to the two actresses. Great news! said I to Laura, whom I saw first: you will have the sovereign of the Spanish monarchy among your audience to-morrow, as the minister has desired me to inform you. I cannot doubt but you will both of you do your best to prove yourselves worthy of a royal command; but I would advise you to choose a piece with music and dancing, that all Lucretia's accomplishments may be displayed at one view. We will take your counsel, answered Laura, and it shall not be our faults if his majesty is disappointed. That can scarcely happen, said I, seeing Lucretia come into the room in an undress, which showed her person to more advantage than all the wardrobe of the theater: he will be the more delighted with your lovely niece, because dancing and music are his principal pleasures: he may even be tempted to throw her the handkerchief. I do not at all wish, replied Laura, that he should be that way inclined; all-powerful monarch as he is, he might not find the accomplishment of his desires so easy. Lucretia, though brought up behind the scenes, is not without virtuous principles; whatever pleasure she may take in applause and professional reputation, she had much rather preserve the character of a good girl, than establish that of a great actress.

Aunt, said little Marialva, joining in the conversation, why conjure up monsters only to lay them again? I shall never be at a loss to repel the king's advances, because his taste is too refined to stoop so low. But, charming Lucretia, said I, if such a thing should happen, would you be cruel enough to let him languish like a common lover? Why not? answered she. Setting virtue aside, my vanity would be more flattered by my own resistance than by the tribute of his affection. I was not a little surprised to hear a pupil of Laura's school talk so properly, and to find that with so free an education she imbibed such unusual principles of morality.

The king, impatient to see Lucretia, went to the play next evening. The piece was got up with music and dancing, to show our young actress off to the best advantage. My eyes were fixed on his majesty; but he completely eluded my penetration by an obstinate gravity. On the following day, the minister said: Santillane, I have just been with the king, who has been talking about Lucretia, with so much animation, that I doubt not but he is smitten: and, as I told him that you had sent for her from Toledo, he expressed a wish to confer with you in private on the subject: orders are given for your admittance; run, and bring me back an account of what passes.

I flew to the palace, and found the king alone. He was walking up and down, in much apparent perplexity. He put several questions to me about Lucretia, made me relate her history, and then asked whether the little jade had not been tampering with chastity already. I boldly assured him to the contrary, though such pledges were somewhat hazardous in general; but mine was taken, and gave the prince much pleasure. If so, replied he, I select you for my agent with Lucretia; let her become acquainted with her triumph from your lips. He then put a box of jewels into my hand, worth fifty thousand crowns, with a message begging her acceptance of them, and promising more substantial proofs of his affection.

Before I went on my errand, I reported progress to my lord duke. That minister, I thought, would be more vexed than rejoiced at it; supposing that he had his own views of gallantry towards

Lucretia, and would learn with regret the rivalship of his master; but I was mistaken. Far from appearing chagrined, his joy was so excessive, that it would ooze out at his tongue, in words which were not quite lost on the hearer. "Indeed, friend Philip! then I have you in my clutches: while your pleasures lead you, your business must be left to me!" This side speech explained to me the plot; an amorous prince, and a long-headed minister! My orders were to execute my commission as speedily as possible, with the assurance that the first lord in the land would be proud to stand in my shoes. Besides, there was no pimp of rank, as in the former case, to seize the profit and leave the infamy with me; the honor and emolument were now exclusively my own.

Thus did his excellency relish the ingredients of pandarism to my palate; and I tasted them with the greediness, but not without the qualms of an epicure; for since my imprisonment I had become regenerated, and did not take pride in dirty work, because my employer washed his hands in perfumed water. But though conscience was awake, interest was not asleep. I was no longer a villain for the fun of it; but my compliance would confirm my footing with the minister, and him it was my duty, at all events, to please

My first appeal was to Laura in private. I opened the negotiation delicately, and presented my credentials in the form of the jewel-box. The lady was thrown off her guard by the display. Signor Gil Blas, cried she, you are one of my oldest friends, and I must not play the hypocrite: straitlaced morals are inconsistent with the discipline of my sect. Nothing can be more delightful to me than a conquest, which throws such a game into our hands. But, between ourselves, I am afraid Lucretia is not so enlightened as we are; though a daughter of Thalia, she has taken the better-behaved goddesses for her school-mistresses, and given a rebuff to two young noblemen of amiable manners and large fortunes. They were not kings, you will say, and truly we may hope that Lucretia's virtue will be too undisciplined to stand a royal siege; but you must remember the event is hazardous, and I shall not interpose my authority to compel her. If, far from thinking herself honored by the fleeting passion of the king, she should revolt from his advances with disdain, let not our illustrious sovereign be offended at her reserve. But do you come back hither to-morrow, and carry back either the jewels, or a return of affection.

I had no doubt but Laura would tutor Lucretia in the school of time-serving morality, and depended much on her instruction. It was therefore no small surprise to find that Laura worked as much against wind and tide to launch her daughter into the trade-wind of evil, as other maternal pilots to set the sails of theirs in the contrary monsoon of good; and what is still more unaccountable, Lucretia, after tasting of royal delights, was so completely surfeited with the banquet as to throw herself at once into the arms of the church, where she professed, fell sick, and died of grief. Laura, disconsolate for the loss of her daughter, and the part she herself had acted in the tragedy, retired into a convent of female penitents, and did penance for the unhallowed pleasures of her former life. The king was affected by his sudden loss, but soon found comfort in some other pursuit. The premier talked little on the subject, but thought so much the more, as the reader will easily believe.

CHAPTER IV.

SANTILLANE IN A NEW OFFICE.

MY feelings were all alive to Lucretia's ill fate, and my own infamy in having contributed to it. The royal wants of the lover were no excuse for my taking the post of cheapener, and I determined to resign the staff of office in that department, entreating the minister to employ me in some other. He was charmed with my nice sense of honor, and promised to comply with my scruples, laying open his inmost heart in the following speech.

Some years before I was in office, chance threw me across a lady of such shape and beauty as induced me to trace her home. I learned that she was a Genoese, by name Donna Margarita Spinola, supporting herself at Madrid on the income arising from her beauty. It was reported that Don Francisco de Valéasar, an officer about the court, a rich man, an old man, and a married man, laid out his money very freely on this hazardous speculation. These rumors ought to have deterred me; but they only whetted my desires to share with Valéasar. To gain my end, I had recourse to a female broker of tenderness, who adjusted the terms of a private interview with the Genoese; and the price current being settled, the traffic was frequently repeated; it was an open market for my rival and me, or possibly for many other bidders.

Let that be as it may, a choice boy was in the fullness of time produced to the club, and the mother complimented every member individually in private with the credit : but we were each of us too modest to acknowledge a bantling which had so probable a claim upon a better father; so that the Genoese was compelled to maintain him on the profits of her profession: this she did for eighteen years, and dying at the end of that period, has left her son without a farthing, and what is worse, without an idea or an accomplishment

Such, continued his lordship, is the confidence I meant to repose in you, and I shall now lay open the great design I have formed, to draw this unfortunate child from his obscurity, reverse the color of his fate, raise him to the highest honors, and acknowledge him as my son.

At so extravagant a project it was impossible not to be openmouthed. What, sir, exclaimed I, can your excellency have adopted so strange a resolution? Excuse my freedom; but my zeal can not restrain itself. You will be of my mind, replied he with eagerness, when I shall have explained to you my motives. I have no mind that my estates should descend in the collateral line. You will tell me, that I am not so old as to despair of having children by Madame d'Olivarez. But every one is best judge of his own condition: know therefore that there is not a receipt in the whole extent of chemistry which I have not tried, but without effect, to appear once again in the character of a father. Wherefore, since fortune, stepping in to cover the defects of nature, presents me with a child whose parent after all I may actually be, he is mine by adoption; that is a settled point.

When I found the minister determined, I no longer argued against his resolution, as knowing him to be a man who would rather do a foolish act of his own, than adopt a wise suggestion of another. It only remains now, added he, to educate Don Henry Philip de Guzman; for by that name I intend him to be known in the world, till the time arrives when he may aspire to higher dignities. You, my dear Santillane, I have chosen to superintend his conduct· I have full confidence in your talents and friendship, to regulate his household, direct his studies, and make him an accomplished gentleman. I would willingly have declined the office, as never having exercised the craft of a pedagogue, which required much more genius and solidity than mine; but he shut my mouth by saying it was his absolute determination that I should be tutor to this adopted son, whom he designed for the first offices of the monarchy. As a bribe for my compliance, his lordship increased my little income with a pension of a thousand crowns on the commandery of Mambra.

CHAPTER V.

THE SON OF THE GENOESE IS ACKNOWLEDGED BY A LEGAL INSTRUMENT, AND NAMED DON HENRY PHILIP DE GUZMAN. SANTILLANE ESTABLISHES HIS HOUSEHOLD, AND ARRANGES THE COURSE OF HIS STUDIES.

THE act of adoption was soon legalized with the king's consent and good pleasure. Don Henry Philip de Guzman, as this descendant from a committee of fathers was named, became acknowledged successor to the earldom of Olivarez and the duchy of San Lucar. The minister, to give the act all possible publicity, communicated it through Carnero to the ambassadors and grandees of Spain, who were somewhat startled. The jokers of Madrid were not insensible to the ridicule, and the satirical poets made their harvest of so fine a subject for their pen.

I asked my lord duke where my pupil was. Here in town, answered he, with an aunt from whom I shall remove him as soon as you have got a house ready. This I did immediately, and furnished it magnificently. When my establishment was complete in servants and officers. his excellency sent for this equivocal production, this spurious offset from the renowned stock of the Guzmans. The lad was tall and personable. Don Henry, said his lordship, pointing to me, this gentleman is to be your tutor and introduce you into the world; he has my entire confidence, and an unlimited authority over you. After much good advice, and many compliments to me, the minister retired, and I took Don Henry home.

As soon as we got thither, I introduced him to his household, and explained the nature of each individual's employment. He did not seem at all disconcerted at the change of circumstances, but received the obeisances of his dependants as if he had been a lord by nature, and not by chance. He was not without mother-wit, but ignorant in a deplorable degree; he could scarcely read and write. I gave him masters for the Latin grammar, geography, history, and fencing. A dancing-master of course was not forgotten; but in an affair of the first consequence, selection was difficult, for there were more eminent professors of that art in Madrid than of all the languages and sciences put together.

While I was pondering on this difficulty, a man gaudily dressed came into the court-yard and inquired for me. I went down, supposing him to be at least a knight of some military or privileged order. Signor de Santillane, said he, with a profusion of bows which anticipated his line in life, I am come to offer you my services as Don Henry's governor. My name is Martin Ligero, and I have, thank heaven, some reputation in the world. I have no occasion to canvass for scholars; that is all very well for petty dancing-masters! My custom is to wait till I am sent for; but being a sort of appendage to the house of Guzman, and having taught its various branches for a long period, I thought it a point of respect to wait on you first. I perceive, answered I, that you are just the man we want. What are your terms? Four double pistoles a month, answered he, and I give but two lessons a week. Four doubloons a month! cried I, that is an exorbitant price. Exorbitant! rejoined he with astonishment; why, it is not more than eight times as much as you would give to a mathematical master or a Greek professor.

There was no resisting so ludicrous a comparison of merit; I laughed outright, and asked Signor Ligero whether he really thought his talents worth more than those of the first proficients in learning and science. Most assuredly, said he; at least, if you measure our pretensions by their respective utility. What sort of machines may those be which are fashioned under their hands? Jointless puppets, unlicked cubs, open-mouthed and impenetrable shell-fish; but our lessons supple and render pliant the intractable stiffness of their component parts, and bring them insensibly into shape: in short, we communicate to them a graceful motion, a polite address, the carriage of good company, and the outward marks of elevated rank.

I could not but give way to such cogent arguments in favor of the dancing-master's occupation, and engaged him about Don Henry's person without haggling as to terms, since those specified were only at the rate established by the leading professors of the art.

CHAPTER VI.

SCIPIO'S RETURN FROM NEW SPAIN. GIL BLAS PLACES HIM
ABOUT DON HENRY'S PERSON. THAT YOUNG NOBLEMAN'S
COURSE OF STUDY. HIS CAREER OF HONOR, AND HIS FATH-
ER'S MATRIMONIAL SPECULATION ON HIS BEHALF. A PATENT
OF NOBILITY CONFERRED ON GIL BLAS AGAINST HIS WILL.

I HAD not yet half arranged Don Henry's household, when Scipio returned from Mexico. He brought with him three thousand
ducats in cash, and merchandise to double the amount. I wish you
joy, said I; the foundation of your fortune is laid; and if you prefer
a snug berth at Madrid to the risk of going back, you have only to
tell me so. There is no question about that, said the son of Coselina: a genteel situation at home is far preferable to a second
voyage.

After relating the birth and adventures of the little adopted
Guzman, and my own appointment as tutor, I offered him the situation of upper servant to this babe of chance: Scipio, who could
have devised nothing better for himself, readily accepted the office,
and within the small space of three or four days got the length of
his new master's foot.

I had taken it for granted that the verb-grinders and con-
cord-manufacturers to whom I had given the plant of this Genoese
bastard would lose stock and block, under the idea that he was of
an intractable and profitless age; but my forebodings were completely reversed. He not only comprehended, but easily retained
the lessons of his masters, and they were very well satisfied with
him. I was in an enormous hurry to greet the ears of my lord
duke with this intelligence, and he received it with abundant joy.
Santillane, exclaimed he with delight, you give me new life by the
assurance of Don Henry's capacity and application: it runs in the
blood of the Guzmans; and I am the more confirmed in his being
unquestionably my own, because I am just as fond of him as if
Madame d'Olivarez herself had lain in of the brat in due form under this very roof. The voice of nature, you perceive, will make
itself heard. I thought it unnecessary to give his lordship any
opinion on that subject; but with a delicate deference to his credulity, left him to enjoy his fancied paternity in peace, whether well
or ill founded.

Though all the Guzmans held this clod of newly turned up nobility in utter scorn, they were politic enough to smooth over the
corrugations of their contempt; nay, some of them even affected to
languish for his good opinion: the ambassadors and principal nobility then at Madrid waited on him, with all the ceremony apper-
taining to the rank of a legitimate son. The minister, intoxicated
with the fumes of incense offered to his idol, began to build a temple worthy of the worship. The cross of Alcantara was the foun-

dation, with a commandery of ten thousand crowns. The next step was to a high office in the royal household, and the completion of the whole was matrimony. Wishing to connect him with a family of the first rank, he picked out Donna Johanna de Velasco, daughter to the Duke of Castile, and had influence enough to accomplish the alliance, though against the will of the duke and of all his kindred.

Some days before the nuptial ceremony, his lordship put some papers into my hand, saying: Here, Gil Blas, is a patent of nobility which I have procured as the reward of your services. My lord, answered I, in much astonishment, your excellency knows very well that I am the son of an usher and a duenna: it would be caricaturing the peerage to confer it on me; and besides, of all the boons in his majesty's power to bestow, it is that which I deserve and desire the least. Your birth, replied the minister, is a slight objection. You have been employed on affairs of state under the Duke of Lerma's administration and under mine: besides, added he with a smile, have you not rendered some things to Cæsar, which Cæsar is bound, on the honor of a prince, to render back in another shape? To deal candidly, Santillane, you will make just as good a lord as the best of them; nay, more than that, your high office about my son is incompatible with plebeian rank, and therefore have I procured you to be created. Since your excellency will have it so, replied I, there is no more to be said. So, saying no more, I put my new-blown honors in my pocket, and walked off.

Now can I make any Joan a lady! said I to myself when I had got into the street: but it was not the handy-work of my parents that made me a gentleman. I may add a foot of honor to my name whenever I please; and if any of my acquaintance should snuff or snigger when they call me Don, I may suck my teeth, lean upon my elbow, and draw out my credentials of heraldry. But let us see what they contain; and how the corporeal particles, which have accrued during my artificial contact with the court, are distinguished by genealogical metaphysics from the native clay of my original extraction. The instrument ran thus in substance: That the king, in acknowledgment of my zeal in more than one instance for his service and the good of the state, had been graciously pleased to confer this mark of distinction on me. I may safely say that the recollection of the act for which I was promoted effectually kept down my pride. Neither did the bashfulness of low birth ever forsake me; so that nobility to me was like a hair shirt to a penitent: I determined therefore to lock up the evidences of my shame in a private drawer, instead of blazoning them to dazzle the eyes of the foolish and corrupt.

CHAPTER VII.

AN ACCIDENTAL MEETING BETWEEN GIL BLAS AND FABRICIO.
THEIR LAST CONVERSATION TOGETHER, AND A WORD TO THE
WISE FROM NUNEZ.

THE poet of the Asturias, as the reader, if he thought of him,
may have remarked, was very negligent in his intercourse with me.
It was not to be expected, that my employments would leave me
time to go and look after him. I had not seen him since the critical discussion touching the Iphigenia of Euripides, when chance
threw me across him, as he came out of a printing-house. I accosted him, saying: So! so! Master Nunez, you have got among the
printers: this looks as if we were threatened with some new production.

You may indeed prepare yourselves for such an event, answered
he : I have a pamphlet just ready for publication which is likely to
make some noise in the literary world. There can be no question
about its merit, replied I: but I cannot conceive why you waste
your time in writing pamphlets: it should seem as if such squibs
and rockets were scarcely worth the powder expended in their manufacture. It is very true, rejoined Fabricio: and I am well aware
that none but the most vulgar gazers are caught by such holiday
fireworks: however, this single one has escaped me, and I must
own that it is a child of necessity. Hunger, as you know, will bring
the wolf out of the forest.

What! exclaimed I, is it the author of the " Count of Saldagna"
who holds this language? A man with an annuity of two thousand
crowns? Gently, my friend, interrupted Nunez: I am no longer a
pensioned poet. The affairs of the treasurer Don Bertrand are all
at sixes and sevens: he has been at the gaming-table, and played
with the public money: an extent has issued, and my rent-charge
is gone post-haste to the devil. That is a sad affair, said I: but
may not matters come round again in that quarter? No chance of
it, answered he: Signor Gomez del Ribero, in plight as destitute as
that of his poor bard, is sunk forever; nor can he, as they say, by
any possible contrivance be set afloat again.

In that case, my good friend, replied I, we must look out for
some post which may make you amends for the loss of your annuity. I will ease your conscience on that score, said he : though you
should offer me the wealth of the Indies as a salary in one of your
offices, I would reject the boon: clerkships are no object to a partner in the firm of the Muses ; a literary berth, or absolute starvation
for your humble servant! If you must have it plump, I was born
to live and die a poet, and the man whose destiny is hanging, will
never be drowned.

But do not suppose, continued he, that we are altogether forlorn and destitute : besides that we accommodate the requisites of
independence to our finances, we do not look far beyond our noses

in calculating the average of our fortunes. It is insinuated that we often dine with the most abstemious orders of the religious; but our sanctity in this particular is too credulously imputed. There is not one of my brother wits, without excepting the calculators of almanacs, who has not a plate laid for him at some substantial table: for my own part, I have the run of two good houses. To the master of one I have dedicated a romance; and he is the first commissioner of taxes who was ever associated with the Muses: the other is a rich tradesman in Madrid, whose lust is to get wits about him· he is not nice in his choice, and this town furnishes abundance to those who value wit more by quantity than quality.

Then I no longer feel for you, said I to the poet of the Asturias, since you are satisfied in your condition. But be that as it may, I assure you once more, that you have a friend in Gil Blas, however you may slight him · if you want my purse, come and take it: it will not fail you at a pinch; and you must not stand between me and my sincere friendship.

By that burst of sentiment, exclaimed Nunez, I know and thank my friend Santillane: in return, let me give you a salutary caution. While my lord duke is in his meridian, and you are all in all with him, reap, bind, and gather in your harvest: when the sun sets, the gleaners are sent home. I asked Fabricio whether his suspicions were surely founded; and he returned me this answer. My information comes from an old knight of Calatrava, who pokes his nose into secrets of all sorts; his authority passes current at Madrid, much as that of the Pythian newsmongers did through Greece, and thus his oracle was pronounced in my hearing: My lord duke has a host of enemies in battle-array against him; he reckons too securely upon his influence with the king; for his majesty, as the report goes, begins to take in hostile representations with patience. I thanked Nunez for his friendly warning, but without much faith in his prediction: my master's authority seemed rooted in the court, like the tempest-scoffing firmness of an oak in the native soil of the forest.

CHAPTER VIII.

GIL BLAS FINDS THAT FABRICIO'S HINT WAS NOT WITHOUT FOUNDATION. THE KING'S JOURNEY TO SARAGOSSA.

THE poet of the Asturias was no bad politician. There was a court plot against the duke, with the queen at the bottom; but their plans were too deeply laid to bubble at the surface. During the space of a whole year, my simplicity was insensible to the brewing of the tempest.

The revolt of the Catalans, with France at their back, and the ill success of the war for their suppression, excited the murmurs of the people, and whetted their tongues against government. A council was held in the royal presence, and the Marquis de Grana, the emperor's ambassador, was specially requested to assist. The subject in debate was whether the king should remain in Castile, or go and take command of his troops in Arragon. The minister spoke first, and gave it as his opinion that his majesty should not quit the seat of government. All the members supported his arguments, with the exception of the Marquis de Grana, whose whole heart was with the house of Austria, and the sentiments of his soul on the tip of his tongue, after the homely honesty of his nation. He argued so forcibly against the minister, that the king embraced his opinion from conviction, though contrary to the vote of council, and fixed the day when he would set out for the army.

This was the first time that ever the sovereign had differed from his favorite, and the latter considered it as an inexpiable affront. Just as the minister was withdrawing to his closet, there to bite upon the bridle, he espied me, called me in, and told me with much discomposure what had passed in debate: Yes, Santillane, observed he, the king, who for the last twenty years has spoken only through my mouth, and seen with my eyes, is now to be wheedled over by Grana; and that on the score of zeal for the house of Austria, as if that German had a more Austrian soul in his body than myself.

Hence it is easy to perceive, continued the minister, that there is a strong party against me, with the queen at the head. Heaven forbid it, said I. Has not the queen for upwards of twelve years been accustomed to your paramount authority, and have you not taught the king the knack of not consulting her? The desire of making a campaign may for once have enlisted his majesty on the side of the Marquis de Grana. Say rather that the king, argued my lord duke, will be surrounded by his principal officers when in camp; and then the disaffected will find their opportunity for poisoning him against my administration. But they overreach themselves; for I shall completely insulate the prince from all their approaches; and so he did, in a manner which, for example, deserves not to be passed over.

The day of the king's departure being arrived, the monarch, leaving the queen regent, proceeded for Saragossa by way of Aranjuez; a delightful residence, where he whiled away three weeks. Cuença was the next stage, where the minister detained him still longer by a succession of amusements. A hunting party was contrived at Molina in Arragon, and hence there was no choice of road but to Saragossa. The army was near at hand, and the king was preparing to review it: but his keeper sickened him of the project, by making him believe that he would be taken by the French, who were in force in the neighborhood; so that he was cowed by a groundless apprehension, and consented to be a prisoner in his own court. The minister, from an affectionate regard to his safety, secluded him from all approach: so that the principal nobility, who had equipped themselves at enormous charges to be about his person, could not even procure an occasional audience. Philip, weary of bad lodgings and worse recreation at Saragossa, and perhaps feeling himself scarcely his own master, soon returned to Madrid. Thus ended the royal campaign, and the care of maintaining the honor of the Spanish colors was left to the Marquis de los Velez, commander-in-chief.

CHAPTER IX.

THE REVOLUTION OF PORTUGAL, AND DISGRACE OF THE PRIME MINISTER.

A FEW days after the king's return, an alarming report prevailed at Madrid, that the Portuguese, considering the Catalan revolt as an opportunity offered them by fortune for throwing off the Spanish yoke, had taken arms, and chosen the Duke of Braganza for their king, with a full determination of supporting him on the throne. In this they conceived that they did not reckon without their host; because Spain was then embroiled in Germany, Italy, Flanders, and Catalonia. They could not in fact have hit upon a crisis more favorable for their deliverance from so galling a yoke.

It was a strange circumstance, that while both court and city were struck with consternation at the news, my lord duke attempted to joke with the king, and make the Duke of Braganza his butt; Philip, however, far from falling in with this ill-timed pleasantry, assumed a serious air, of ill omen to the minister, who felt his seat to totter under him. The queen was now his declared enemy, and openly accused him of having caused the revolt of Portugal by his misconduct. The nobility in general, and especially those who had been at Saragossa, when they saw a cloud gathering about the minister, joined the queen's party:* but the decisive blow was the return of the duchess dowager of Mantua from her government of Portugal to Madrid; for she proved clearly to the king's conviction that the counsels of his own cabinet produced the revolution.

His majesty, deeply impressed with what he had heard, was now completely recovered from every symptom of partiality towards his favorite. The minister, finding that his enemies were in possession of the royal ear, wrote for permission to resign his employments, and retire from court, since all the political mischances of the time were ascribed to his personal delinquency. He expected a letter like this to produce a wonderful effect, reckoning as he did upon the prince's private friendship, which could scarcely brook a separation: but his majesty's answer undeceived him, by laconically complying with his ostensible wish to withdraw.

Such a sentence of banishment in the king's own handwriting

---

* At length his sovereign frowns—the train of state
Mark the keen glance, and watch the sign to hate.
Johnson's Imitation of Juvenal's Tenth Satire.

came like a thunder-storm in harvest; but though destruction to his long-cherished hopes, he affected the serene look of constancy, and asked me what I would do in his circumstances. I would drive before the wind, said I; renounce the ungrateful court, and pass the remainder of my days in peace on my own estate. You counsel wisely, replied my master, and I shall set out for Loeches, there to finish my career, after one more interview with his majesty: for I could wish just to convince him that I have done what man can do to support the heavy load of state upon my shoulders, and that it was not within the compass of possibility to prevent the unfortunate events which are imputed to me as a crime. It were equally reasonable to charge the pilot with the wrecking fury of the storm, and make him answerable for the uncontrolled power of the elements. Thus did the minister inwardly flatter himself that he could set things to rights again, and once more fix firm the seat which was shaking under him; but he could not procure an audience, and was even commanded to resign his key of private admission into his majesty's closet.

This last requisition convinced him that there was no hope; and he now made up his mind in earnest for retirement. He looked over his papers, and had the prudence to burn a good number; he then selected a small house holdfor his retreat, and publicly announced his departure for the next day. Apprehending insult from the mob, if the time and manner of his setting out were public, he escaped early in the morning through the kitchens out at the back door, got into a shabby, hired carriage, with his confessor and me, and reached in safety the road leading to Loeches, a village on his own estate, where his countess had founded a magnificent convent of Dominican nuns.

CHAPTER X.

A DIFFICULT, BUT SUCCESSFUL, WEANING FROM THE WORLD. THE MINISTER'S EMPLOYMENTS IN HIS RETREAT.

MADAME D'OLIVAREZ stayed behind her husband some few days, with the intention of trying what her tears and entreaties might do towards his recall; but in vain did she prostrate herself before their majesties: the king paid not the least attention to her pleadings and remonstrances, though artfully adapted for effect; and the queen, who hated her mortally, took a savage pleasure in her tears. The minister's lady, however, was not easily discouraged: she stooped so low as to solicit their good offices from the ladies of the bed-chamber; but the fruit of all this meanness was only the sad conviction that it excited more contempt than pity. Heart-broken at having degraded herself by supplications so humiliating, and yet so unavailing, she departed to her husband, and mourned with him the loss of a situation, which under a reign like that of Philip the Fourth, was little short of sovereign power.

The accounts her ladyship brought from Madrid were wormwood to the duke. Your enemies, said she, sobbing, with the Duke of Medina Celi at their head, are loud in the king's praises for your removal; and the people triumph in your disgrace with an insolent joy, as if the cloud of adversity were to be dispelled by the breath which dissolved your administration. Madame, said my master, follow my example; suppress your discontent: we must drive before the storm, when we cannot weather it. I did think, indeed, that my favor would only be eclipsed with the lamp of life: a common illusion of ministers and favorites, who forget that they breathe but at the good pleasure of their sovereign. Was not the Duke of Lerma as much mistaken as myself, though fondly relying on his purple, as a pledge for the lasting tenure of his authority?

Thus did my lord duke preach patience to the partner of his cares, while his own bosom heaved under the direst pressure of anxiety. The frequent dispatches from Don Henry, who was staying about the court to pick up information, kept him continually on the fret. Scipio was the messenger; for he was still about the person of that young nobleman, though I had relinquished my post on his marriage. Sometimes we heard of changes in the inferior departments of office, solely for the purpose of wreaking vengeance on his creatures, and filling up the vacancies with his enemies. Then Don Lewis de Haro was represented as advancing in favor, and likely to be made prime minister. But the most mortifying circumstance of all was the change in the viceroyalty of Naples, which was taken from his friend, the Duke de Medina de las Torres, and bestowed on the High Admiral of Castile, who was his bitterest enemy. For this there was no other motive but the pleasure of giving pain to a fallen favorite.

For the first three months, his lordship gave himself up in his solitude a prey to disappointment and regret: but his confessor, a holy and pious Dominican, supporting his religious zeal with manly eloquence, succeeded in pouring the balm of consolation into his soul. By continually representing to him, with apostolic energy, that his eternal salvation was now the only object worth his care, he weaned him gradually from the uses of this world. His excellency was no longer panting for news from Madrid, but learning a new and important lesson, how to die. Madame d'Olivarez too, making a virtue of necessity, sought refuge for herself in the maternal guardianship of her convent, where Providence had reared up, for her edification in faith and good works, a sisterhood of holy maidens, whose spiritual discourses fed her soul, as if with manna in the wilderness. My master's peace within his own bosom advanced, as he withdrew more backward from sublunary things. The employment of his day was thus laid out: almost the whole morning was devoted to religious duties, till dinner-time; and after dinner, for about two hours, he played at different games with me and some of his confidential domestics: he then generally retired alone into his closet till sunset, when he walked round his garden, or rode out into the neighborhood either with his confessor or me.

One day when I was alone with him, and was particularly struck with his apparent self-complacency, I took the liberty of congratulating his lordship on his complete reconciliation to retirement. Use, however late acquired, is second nature, answered he : for though I have all my life been accustomed to the bustle of business, I assure you that I become every day more and more attached to this calm and peaceful mode of life.

CHAPTER XI.

A CHANGE IN HIS LORDSHIP FOR THE WORSE. THE MARVELOUS CAUSE, AND MELANCHOLY CONSEQUENCES, OF HIS DEJECTION.

HIS excellency sometimes amused himself with gardening, by way of variety. One day as I was watching his progress, he said jokingly : You see, Santillane, a fallen minister can turn gardener at last. Nature will prevail, my lord, answered I. You plant and water something useful at Loeches, while Dionysius of Syracuse whipped school-boys at Corinth. My master was not displeased either with the comparison or the compliment.

We were all delighted at the castle to see our protector, rising above the cloud of adversity, take pleasure in so novel a mode of life : but we soon perceived an alarming change. He became gloomy, thoughtful, and melancholy. Our parties at play were all given up, and no efforts could succeed to divert his mind. From dinner-time till evening he never left his closet. We thought the dreams of vanished greatness had returned to break his rest ; and in this opinion the reverend Dominican gave the rein to his eloquence ; but it could not outstrip the course of that hypochondriac malady, which triumphed over all opposition.

It seemed to me there was some deeper cause, which it behooved a sincere friend to fathom. Taking advantage of our being alone together, My lord, said I, in a tone of mingled respect and affection, whence is it that you are no longer so cheerful as heretofore ? Has your philosophy lost ground ? or has the world recovered its allurements ? Surely you would not plunge again into that gulf, where your virtue must inevitably be shipwrecked ! No, heaven be praised ! replied the minister : my part at court has long faded from my memory, and its trappings from my eyes. Indeed ! why then, resumed I, since you have strength enough to banish false regrets, are you so weak as to indulge a melancholy which alarms us all ? What is the matter with you, my dear master ? continued I, falling at his knees : some secret sorrow preys upon you : can you hide it from Santillane, whose zeal, discretion, and fidelity you have so often experienced ? Why am I so unhappy as to have lost your confidence ?

You still possess it, said his lordship: but I must own, it is reluctantly that I shall reveal the subject of my distress: yet the importunities of such a friend are irresistible. To no one else could I impart so singular a confidence. Yes, I am the prey of a morbid melancholy which eats inwardly into my vitals: a spectre haunts me every moment, arrayed in the most terrific form of preternatural horror. In vain have I argued with myself that it is a vision of the brain, an unreal mockery: its continual presentments blast my sight, and unseat my reason. Though my understanding teaches me, that in looking on this spectre I stare at vacancy, my spirits are too weak to derive comfort from the conviction. Thus much have you extorted from me: now judge whether the cause of my melancholy is fit to be divulged.

With equal grief and astonishment did I listen to the strange confession, which implied a total derangement of the nervous system. This, my lord, said I, must proceed from injudicious abstinence. So I thought at first, answered he; and to try the experiment, I have been eating more than usual for some days past; but it is all to no purpose, the phantom takes his stand as usual. It will vanish, said I, if your excellency will only divert your mind by your accustomed relaxations with your household. Company and gentle occupation are the best remedies for these affections of the spirits.

In a short time after this conversation, his lordship became seriously indisposed, and sent for two notaries from Madrid, to make his will. Three capital physicians followed in their track, who had the reputation of curing their patients now and then. As soon as it was noised about the castle that these last undertakers were arrived, the case was given up for lost; weeping and gnashing of teeth took place universally, and the family mourning was ordered. They brought with them their usual understrappers, an apothecary and a surgeon.* The notaries were suffered to earn their fee first, after which death's notaries prepared to take a bond of the patient. They practiced in the school of Sangrado, and from their very first consultation, ordered bleeding so frequently and freely, that in six days they brought his lordship to the point of death, and on the seventh delivered him from the terror of his sprite.

After the minister's decease, a lively and sincere sorrow reigned in the castle of Loeches. The whole household wept betterly. Far from deriving consolation from the certainty of being remembered in his will, there was not a dependant who would not willingly have saved his life by the sacrifice of the legacy. As for me, whom he most delighted in, attached to him as I was from disinterested friendship, my grief was more acute than that of the rest. I question whether Antonia cost me more tears.

---

*   Behind him sneaks
Another mortal, not unlike himself,
Of jargon full, with terms obscure o'ercharged,
Apothecary call'd, whose fœtid hands
With power mechanic, and with charms arcane,
Apollo, god of medicine, has endued.—BRAMSTON,

CHAPTER XII.

THE PROCEEDINGS AT THE CASTLE OF LOECHES AFTER HIS LORD-
SHIP'S DEATH, AND THE COURSE WHICH SANTILLANE
ADOPTED.

THE minister, according to his last injunctions, was buried without pomp and without procession in the convent, with a dirge of
our lamentations.   After the funeral, Madame d'Olivarez called us
together to hear the will read, with which the household had good
reason to be satisfied.   Every one had a legacy proportioned to his
claim, and none less than two thousand crowns: mine was the
largest, amounting to ten thousand pistoles, as a mark of his singular regard.   The hospitals were not forgotten, and provision was
made for an annual commemoration in several convents.

Madame d'Olivarez sent all the household to Madrid to receive
their legacies from Don Raymond Caporis, who had orders to pay
them; but I could not be of the party, in consequence of a violent
fever from distress of mind, which confined me to the castle for more
than a week.   During that time, the reverend Dominican paid me
all possible attention.   He had conceived a friendship for me, which
was not confined to my worldly interests, and was anxious to know
how I meant to dispose of myself on my recovery.   I answered
that I had not yet made up my mind upon the subject: there were
moments when my feelings strongly prompted towards a religious
vow.   Precious moments! exclaimed the Dominican, you will do
well to profit by them.   I advise you as a friend to retire to our
convent at Madrid, for example; there to become a pious benefactor by the free gift of your whole fortune, and to die in the livery
of Saint Dominic.   Many very questionable Christians have made
amends for a life of sin by so holy an end.

In the actual disposition of my mind, this advice was not unpalatable; and I promised to reflect upon it.   But on consulting
Scipio, who came to see me immediately after the monk, he treated
the very notion as the phantom of a distempered brain.   For
shame! said he; does not your estate at Lirias offer a more eligible
seclusion?   If you were delighted with it formerly, the charm will
be increased tenfold, now that the lapse of years has moderated
your sense of pleasure, and softened down your taste to the simple
beauties of nature.

It was no difficult matter to operate a change in my inclinations.
My friend, said I, you carry it decidedly against the advocate of
Saint Dominic.   We will go back to Lirias as soon as I am well
enough to travel.   This happened shortly; for as the fever subsided, I soon felt myself sufficiently strong to put my design in
execution.   We went first to Madrid.   The sight of that city gave
me far other sensations than heretofore.   As I knew that almost
its whole population held in horror the memory of a minister, of

whom I cherished the most affectionate remembrance, I could not feel at my ease within its precincts. My stay was therefore limited to five or six days, while Scipio was making the necessary arrangements for our rustication. In the mean time, I waited on Caporis, and received my legacy in ready money. I likewise made my arrangements with the receivers for the regular remittance of my pensions, and settled all my affairs in due order.

The evening before our departure, I asked the son of Coselina whether he had received his farewell from Don Henry. Yes, answered he, we took leave of each other this morning with mutual civility; he went so far as to express his regret that I should quit him; but however well satisfied he might be with me, I am by no means so with him. Mutual content is like a river, which must have its banks on either side. Besides, Don Henry makes but a pitiful figure at court now; he has fallen into utter contempt; people point at him with their finger in the streets, and call him a Genoese bastard. Judge, then, for yourself, whether it is consistent with my character to keep up the connection.

We left Madrid one morning at sunrise, and went for Cuença. The following was the order of our equipment: we two in a chaise and pair, three mulés, laden with baggage and money, led by two grooms and two stout footmen, well armed, in the rear; the grooms wore sabres, and the postilion had a pair of pistols in his holsters. As we were seven men in all, and six of us determined fellows, I took the road gayly, without trembling for my legacy. In the villages through which we passed our mules chimed their bells merrily, and the peasants ran to their doors to see us pass, supposing it to be at least the parade of some nobleman going to take possession of some viceroyalty.

CHAPTER XIII.

THE RETURN OF GIL BLAS TO HIS SEAT. HIS JOY AT FINDING HIS GOD-DAUGHTER SERAPHINA MARRIAGEABLE: AND HIS OWN SECOND VENTURE IN THE LOTTERY OF LOVE.

WE were a fortnight on our journey to Lirias, having no occasion to make rapid stages. The sight of my own domain brought melancholy thoughts into my mind, with the image of my lost Antonia; but better topics of reflection came to my aid, with a full purpose to look at things on the brighter side, and the lapse of two-and-twenty years, which had gradually impaired the force of tender regret.

As soon as I entered the castle, Beatrice and her daughter greeted me most cordially, while the family scene was interesting in the extreme. When their mutual transports were over, I looked earnestly at my god-daughter, saying: Can this be the Seraphina whom I left in her cradle? how tall and pretty! we must make a good match for her. What! my dear god-father, cried my little girl with an enchanting blush, you have but just seen me, and do you want to get rid of me at once? No, my lovely child, replied I, we hope not to lose you by marriage, but to find a husband for you in the neighborhood.

There is one ready to your hands, said Beatrice. Seraphina made a conquest one day at mass. Her suitor has declared his passion, and asked my consent. I told him that his acceptance depended on her father and her god-father; and here you are to determine for yourselves.

What is the character of this village lordling? said Scipio. Is he not, like his fellows, the little tyrant of the soil, and insolent to those who have no pedigree to boast? The furthest from it in the world, answered Beatrice; the young man is gentle in his temper and polished in his manners; handsome withal, and somewhat under thirty. You paint him in flattering colors, said I to Beatrice; what is his name? Don Juan de Jutella, replied Scipio's wife: it is not long since he came to his inheritance: he lives on his own estate, about a mile off, with a younger sister, of whom he takes care. I once knew something of his family, observed I; it is one of the best in Valencia. I care less for lineage, cried Scipio, than for the qualities of the heart and mind; this Don Juan will exactly suit us, if he is a good sort of man. He is belied else, said Seraphina, with a blushing interest in our conversation; the inhabitants of Lirias, who know him well, say all the good of him you can conceive. I smiled at this; and her father, not less quick-sighted, saw plainly that her heart had a share in the testimony of her tongue.

The gentleman soon heard of our arrival, and paid his respects to us within two days. His address was pleasing and manly, so as to prepossess us in his favor. He affected merely to welcome us home as a neighbor. Our reception was such as not to discourage the repetition of his visit; but not a word of Seraphina! When he was gone, Beatrice asked us how we liked him. We could have no objection to make, and gave it as our opinion that Seraphina could not dispose of herself better.

The next day, Scipio and I returned the visit. We took a guide, and luckily; for otherwise it might have puzzled us to find the place. It was not till our actual arrival that it was visible; for the mansion was situated at the foot of a mountain, in the middle of a wood, whose lofty trees hid it from our view. There was an antique and ruinous appearance about it, which spoke more for the descent than the wealth of its proprietor. On our entrance, however, the elegance of the interior arrangement made amends for the dilapidated grandeur of the outer walls.

Don Juan received us in a handsome room, where he introduced his sister Dorothea, a lady between nineteen and twenty years of age. She was a good deal tricked out, as if she had primed and loaded herself for conquest, in expectation of our visit. Thus presenting all her charms in full force, she did by me much as Antonia had done before; but I managed my raptures so discreetly, that even Scipio had no suspicion. Our conversation turned, as on the preceding day, on the mutual pleasure of good neighborhood. Still he did not open on the subject of Seraphina, nor did we attempt to draw him out. During our interview, I often cast a side glance at Dorothea, though with all the reserve of delicate apprehension; whenever our eyes met, the citadel of my heart was ready to surrender. To describe the object of my love justly, as well as feelingly, her beauty was not of the most perfect kind: her skin was of a dazzling whiteness, and her lips united the color with the fragrance of the rose; but her features were not so regular and well-proportioned as might have been wished: yet, altogether, she won my heart.

In short, I left the mansion of Jutella a different man from what I was on entering it: so that, returning to Lirias with my whole soul absorbed in Dorothea, I saw and spoke only of her. How is this, master? said Scipio with a look of astonishment: you seem to be very much taken with Don Juan's sister! Can you be in love with her? Yes, my friend, answered I : to my shame be it spoken. Since the death of Antonia, how many lovely females have passed in review before me with indifference: and must my passions be irresistibly kindled at this time of life? Indeed, sir, replied the son of Coselina, you may bless your stars, instead of squabbling with yourself: you are not so old as to make your sacrifice at the shrine of love a by-word; and time has not yet ploughed such furrows on your brow, as to render hopeless the desire of pleasing. When you see Don Juan next, ask him boldly for his sister : he cannot refuse her to you ; and besides, if his views in her settlement are ambitious, how can he do better? You have a patent of nobility in your pocket, and upon that your posterity may ride easy ; after five generations, when pedigree herself shall be lost in the confusion of her materials, it may exercise the diligence of learned inquiry, to trace the family of the Santillanes to the beginning of its archives, and consecrate the fame of its founder by the indistinctness of his story.

CHAPTER XIV.

A DOUBLE MARRIAGE, AND THE CONCLUSION OF THE HISTORY,

By this discourse, Scipio encouraged me to declare myself. without considering how he exposed me to the danger of a refusal. My own resolution was taken with fear and trembling. Though I carried my years well, and might have sunk at least ten, it did not seem unlikely that a young beauty might turn up her nose at the disparity. I determined, however, to bolt the question the first time I saw her brother, who was not without his trepidations on the subject of my god-daughter.

He returned my call the next morning, just as I had done dressing. Signor de Santillane, said he, I wish to speak with you on some serious business. I took him into my closet, where entering on the subject at once, I imagine, continued he, that you are not unacquainted with the purpose of my visit: I love Seraphina; you are all in all with her father; I must request you therefore to intercede and procure for me the accomplishment of my heart's desire: then shall I have to thank you for the prime bliss of my existence. Signor Don Juan, answered I, as you come to the point at once, you can have no objection to my following your example. My good offices are fully at your service, and I shall hope for yours with your sister in return.

Don Juan was agreeably surprised. Can it be possible, exclaimed he, that Dorothea should have made a conquest of your heart since yesterday? It is even so, said I, and it would make me the happiest of men, if the proposal should meet with your joint approbation. You may rely on that, replied he; though with some pretensions to family pride, yours is not an alliance to be despised. You flatter me highly, rejoined I; that you are not mealy-mouthed about receiving a commoner into your pedigree, is a mark of good sense; but even if nobility had been a necessary ingredient in your sister's requisites for a husband, we should not have quarreled on that account. I have worked out twenty years in the trammels of office; and the king, as a reward of my long labors, has granted me a patent of nobility. This high-minded gentleman read my credentials over with extreme satisfaction, and returning them, told me that Dorothea was mine. And Seraphina yours, exclaimed I.

Thus were the two marriages agreed on between us. The consent of the intended brides was all that remained; for we neither of us presumed to control the inclinations of our wards. My friend therefore carried home my proposal to his sister, and I called Scipio, Beatrice, and my god-daughter together, for the purpose of laying open a similar project. Beatrice voted loudly for immediate acceptance, and Seraphina silently. The father did not say much against it; but boggled a little at the fortune he must give to a gentleman whose seat required such immediate and extensive repairs. I stopped Scipio's mouth by telling him that was my concern, and that I should contribute four thousand pistoles to the architect's estimate.

In the evening, Don Juan came again. Your business is going swimmingly, said I; pray heaven mine may promise as fairly. Better it cannot, answered he; my influence was quite unnecessary to prevail with Dorothea; your person had made its impression, and your manners pleased her. You were afraid she might not like you; while she, with more reason, having nothing to offer you but her heart and hand . . . . What would she offer more? interrupted I, out of my wits with joy. Since the lovely Dorothea can think of me without repugnance, I ask no more my fortune is ample, and the possession of her is the only dowry I should value.

Don Juan and myself, highly delighted at having brought our

views to bear so soon, were for hastening our nuptials, and cutting off all superfluous ceremonies. I closeted the gentleman with Seraphina's parents; the settlements were soon agreed on, and he took his leave, promising to return next day with Dorothea. My eager desire of appearing agreeable in that lady's eyes, occasioned me to spend three hours at least in adjusting my dress, and communicating the air of a lover to my person; but I could not do it so much to my mind as in my younger days. The preparations for courtship are a pleasure to a young man, but a serious business and hazardous speculation to one who is beginning to be oldish. And yet it turned out better than my hopes or deserts; for Don Juan's sister received me so graciously, as to put me in good humor with myself. I was charmed with the turn of her mind; and foreboded that with discreet management and much deference, I might really get her to like me as well as anybody else. Full of this sweet hope I sent for the lawyers to draw up the two contracts, and for the clergyman of Paterna, to bring us better acquainted with our mistresses.

Thus did I light the torch of Hymen for the second time, and it did not burn blue with the brimstone of repentance. Dorothea, like a virtuous wife, made a pleasure of her duty; in gratitude for the pains I took to anticipate all her wishes, she soon loved me as well as if I had been younger. Don Juan and my god-daughter were most enthusiastic in their mutual ardor; and what was most unprecedented of all, the two sisters-in-law loved one another sincerely. Don Juan was a man in whom all good qualities met: my esteem for him increased daily, and he did not repay it with ingratitude. In short, we were a happy and united family: we could scarcely bear the interval of separation between evening and morning. Our time was divided between Lirias and Jutella: his excellency's pistoles made the old battlements to raise their heads again, and the castle to resume its lordly port.

For these three years, reader, I have led a life of unmixed bliss in this beloved society. To perfect my satisfaction, heaven has deigned to send me two smiling babes, whose education will be the amusement of my declining years; and if ever husband might venture to hazard so bold an hypothesis, I devoutly believe myself their father.

THE END.